A Place To Call Home

A Place To Call Home

A Novel by

Gabriele Wills

MIND SHADOWS

Cover photo by Melanie Wills

National Library of Canada Cataloguing in Publication

Wills, Gabriele, 1951-
A place to call home / Gabriele Wills.

ISBN 0-9732780-0-5

I. Title.

PS8595.I576P53 2003 C813'.6
C2003-901488-6
PR9199.4.W56P53 2003

First edition
Published by Mindshadows
http://www.mindshadows.com
Printed and bound in Canada

Author's Notes

Although rooted in some real historical events, this is a work of fiction. A few historical personages do mingle with the fictitious characters.

Many thanks to Munroe Scott and Dorothy Lumley for their editorial contributions, and Laurie McLean for vetting the legal scenes.

Thanks to the Lindsay Public Library for providing access to archival materials.

Thanks also to Robert Rea of MapleLand Press for so generously sharing his information on publishing.

Without the unflagging love and support of John and Melanie Wills, this book would never have been written or published. Thank you.

This book is dedicated to my parents, Katie and Paul Tavaszi, who were pioneers in their own right. Thank you for choosing Canada!

Book 1

Rowena

Part 1

The Journey

1832

Chapter 1

Rowena felt as though she were struggling up from the suffocating depths of a bog. Yet she was reluctant to surface from the relative peace of semiconsciousness. Her parched throat sharply reminded her of the many bouts of vomiting and retching which had left her weak and trembling.

Far better to keep her eyes shut, and to block out all remembrance and pain.

Strange that she couldn't feel the rolling and pitching of the ship any longer, or hear the ominous creaking of its old, rotting timbers, or the squeaking and scrambling of the rats in the bilge. Perhaps she was dead and had gone to heaven. Perhaps, if she opened her eyes, she would see the Holy Virgin waiting to welcome her as She had Eileen and Seamus....

A sudden chill shook her. Was this what her young brother and sister had felt when their weighted, lifeless bodies had slid overboard, slowly sinking into their unmarked ocean graves? Was this the coldness of death, the icy Atlantic seeping in to paralyze one's very bones?

No! The dead didn't feel pain! Death was supposed to be a blessed relief from life and one's miserable, earthly body. Unless this was Hell.

In a moment of panic she thought it must surely be Satan trying to drag her back down into the darkness. But then she could hear her shipmates groaning and retching -- those telltale sounds to which she had become so accustomed these last weeks.

As she had to the stench of vomit and excrement. And the fear that had been as chokingly thick in the ship's hold as the foetid, stifling air.... The horror as one watched the vile disease torturing its victims with excruciating cramps, turning their bodies blue, eating away at them so that they seemed to shrivel before one's very eyes.... And the eyes -- what terror they expressed as they were sucked into the skull, the soul seeming to scream for release from the pain-wracked shell of flesh that imprisoned it.... The victims struggling for breath... voices no longer capable of moaning... only the rasping breathing of the dying, the weeping of the living.... The final convulsions as though the stricken wrestled with the devil himself.... And not even a priest on board to ease them out of life.... Only the torments of the body and the unshriven soul.

How different this voyage had been at the outset. Her father's excitement had infected them all. Even her mother, reluctant to leave their home in Doneraile to "chase some foolish dream", had smiled when fellow passengers had celebrated the leaving of their troubled land with song and dance as they had sailed out of the Cove of Cork on May 1st, 1832.

Rowena recalled every word of the letter that had arrived a few months earlier from her father's old friend, Liam O'Mara, who had gone to the New World seven years before on a government-sponsored emigration. She could picture the crude lettering, now smudged and stained with constant handling, that traversed the width of the paper and then dizzyingly criss-crossed along its length.

> *To me Dear Friend Patrick O'Shaughnessy and his Family,*
>
> *Me good Neighbour is writing this for me as I be not a Man of Letters meself. Surely, Patrick, this be God's Country. Tis rugged but grand and Bounteous in its Fruits. Wild Berries grow so thick that a Man trods upon them walking to his Byre. The Sky is black with Birds at times, and the Waters so choked with Fish that a Man need only reach in and Pluck them out. And a Man can eat his fill of them, and Venison and other Game, for there be no Lords nor Gamekeepers to Prevent him. I am me own Master now and possess Freehold one hundred Acres of Land, a pair of Oxen, three Cows, Sheep, Pigs, and Fowls. We eat Meat thrice a day and be near Sick with the Abundance of it, when in the Old Country we was Lucky to see it at Christmas. And when I feed Meat to me Dog, I near Bleed for the poor Souls at Home who would envy the Beast his Good Fortune. A Man can make something of hisself in this Country. I need bow to no Man and have Hobnobbed with such as was Gentry at Home. There is more Work than Workers here, Patrick, and a Man with a Trade, such as Yourself, can name his own wage and be Wealthy afore long. And wouldn't it please me Heart to see Yourself again and to share me Good Fortune with you. Yourself and your Kin will always be welcome at Liam O'Mara's Home."*

The letter had gone on to give them rough directions to the O'Mara homestead in Upper Canada. Her father had thought it an answer to his prayers. Hope had restored humour to his eyes that, too often of late, had looked despondent. Her brother, Donal, had shared their father's new-found enthusiasm, eager for an adventure. And a future.

But if times had not been so bad in the Blackwater district of County Cork, her mother, Deirdre, would never have agreed to leave. Once a thriving weaving centre, Doneraile had been having hard times for decades now. Unemployment was high, work scarce, even for a skilled craftsman like her father. Potato crop failures brought starvation to many. It hadn't been unusual these last years to see hungry, half-naked paupers -- sometimes entire families -- wandering the roads, seeking food, shelter, and work.

And although she had hated the ruthless English landlords, Deirdre had hated even more the riots, and the night-time violence carried out by the Whiteboy rebels. These had escalated this past year in protest against the tithes that everyone, even the poorest Catholic, had to pay to the Anglican church. Almost daily there were stories about cattle maimings, about the ransacking or burning of the homes of tithe and rent collectors, landowners and Anglican ministers, and even reports of murders. Rowena herself had seen the glow of distant fires against the night sky, and witnessed neighbours accused of Whiteboy terrorism carted off by the soldiers.

And then the deadly cholera plague had invaded Ireland.

Patrick was taking them away from all that fear and hatred and desperate poverty. Yes, even Deirdre had smiled to feel the clean ocean breeze upon her face as they headed westward to a promised land.

But they were crowded into the hold of the brig, *Devoron*, with two hundred and forty-three other poor and wretched souls, stacked into the rough berths, one atop the other, like so much timber, which was the more profitable return cargo for the ship. Ballast they were.

They'd had to bring their own supply of food, but no one had warned them that the praties would rot quickly in the dank bowels of the ship, or that the rats would share their precious sack of oats. The drinking water was brackish and foul. There was no water for washing; lice had infected them all.

When the storms had hit, after the first calm and sunny week, they had even been denied the deck. The hatches had been battened down, and they'd been left in the stinking, airless darkness. Entombed.

Thundering Atlantic waves had crashed against the small vessel as if determined to shatter it. The brig had pitched so wildly that twelve-year-old Rowena had felt certain sure it would be capsized and swallowed by the wild and merciless ocean. People had wept, wailed, prayed, and cursed during that fearful tempest.

And when it was finally over and they thought that things couldn't get any worse, they found that they hadn't escaped the cholera after all.

Surely Hell couldn't be worse than the next seven weeks had been. Daily, people fell ill. Few recovered. There was no doctor on board -- "not required by the regulations", the captain had told them gruffly. Fearing for the safety of his crew, he'd ordered all passengers to stay below decks, allowing them up on deck only to attend the burials.

Baby Seamus and five-year-old Eileen had been buried on a colourless June day when sky and water merged in a leaden hue so that the vessel seemed to drift in a grey purgatory. Rowena would never forget her mother's heart-rending cries.

More storms had battered them in mid-Atlantic, and the sick, already writhing in pain, were tossed about and often pitched to the floor, if no one lay with them to hold them firm. Rowena was certain that they had somehow earned God's wrath.

Her mother, Deirdre, had done what she could for those who had no families to tend them, but she had brought only a few herbs for aches and fever, and none were effective. She did help a young woman give birth to a healthy boy-child -- an odd little miracle of life among all this death.

Rowena had noticed that Deirdre seemed strangely detached from the horror about her, as if her mind was far away -- in the green hills of Ireland. Or in the deep, cold Atlantic, with the children she had lost.

Rowena, too, had helped to tend the sick, since no one else in her family -- thank the good Lord -- had required her ministrations. She would never forget that pervasive stench of sickness -- as if the diseased bodies were already putrefying before death finally claimed them.

By the time they sighted land -- an eternity later, it seemed -- on June 26th, forty-six of the passengers had perished. Through the billowing mist, Rowena had glimpsed the rugged, desolate shores of Newfoundland. The fog had seemed to seep into her mind, for she remembered little after that -- lying in the filthy, narrow bunk in the darkness of the hold... the intense, crippling cramps... ceaseless vomiting... numbing cold....

It was better to remain in this stuporous state than to face all that again.

A warm hand touched her brow, jerking Rowena into full consciousness. She opened her eyes to discover a bright, blurred white form bending over her. Her eyes focused on the gentle face of what must surely be an angel!

"Ah, you are awake, ma petite. That is good," the vision said to her in a soft, thickly-accented voice.

Rowena gaped uncomprehendingly at this celestial being clothed from head to foot in white. She tried to speak, but her dry throat was constricted, and she managed only a hoarse croak.

"You desire some water, n'est-ce pas?" The being seemed to float away, her robes rustling softly.

Bewildered and more than a little frightened, Rowena tried to sit up, but her head felt heavy and sore. Was she truly dead then?

She glanced about. Her narrow cot was one of seemingly hundreds that lined the walls of a shed. Other angels were tending to the occupants.

"You must not be afraid, ma petite," the kind voice said to her. "You are in the `ospital on Grosse Isle, near the city of Quebec in Lower Canada. I am Sister Terese."

"You're a... nun?" Rowena had never seen one, but had heard of them. With the suppression of the Catholic religion in Ireland, all that Rowena had known were the "hedge" priests who -- not allowed to preach in churches -- held services in fields and barns.

"That is so," Sister Terese said. "Now you must drink this."

She lifted Rowena's head and held the tin cup to her lips. It was surely the sweetest, purest water Rowena had ever tasted. When she had had her fill, she asked urgently, "Please, Sister, where's me Ma and Da?"

Sister Terese smiled reassuringly. "They await your safe recovery nearby. Soon you shall join them. Now I must bring the doctor, and you must be still."

The doctor was a florid, fiery-haired man whose brusque cheerfulness seemed undaunted by the agonized screams of the patients around him. He declared her out of danger, and ordered her to eat well to build up her strength.

Sister Terese seemed always to be at her side, slaking her thirst, feeding her broth and gruel and a sweet herbal tea, and Rowena wondered when the nun slept. Once she herself spent more hours awake, she began to worry about her family, wondering if any more of them had fallen ill -- or died -- during the ten days that she had been sick. Sister Terese told her that no one was allowed to visit the hospital, but that her family would be encamped outside with the hundreds of other quarantined immigrants.

And while she patiently tended to Rowena, still too weak to sit up and feed herself, Sister Terese spoke lovingly about the magnificent city of her birth -- Quebec -- where she now lived in a nunnery. She told Rowena about the war between Britain and France over seventy years before, and a decisive battle on the Plains of Abraham, to the west of the walled city, that had won the French colony for Britain and had cost the lives of both the British commander, General Wolfe, and the French commander, the Marquis de Montcalm. She talked about her ten brothers and sisters, one of whom had become a priest and lived hundreds of miles upriver in Montreal.

And Rowena spoke longingly about her own family -- her mother and father, her older brother Donal, and her younger sisters, Moira, Gwyn, and Alys. Her father was a carpenter, who hoped to make a better life for them in this New World. Her mother had earned a reputation as a healer and midwife back in Doneraile. Surely she could help in this hospital.

The nun had shaken her head. She admitted that they were woefully understaffed, but only the sick were allowed inside the hospital. There were soldiers on guard outside to make sure that the quarantine rules were obeyed.

About Upper Canada the nun could tell her nothing, except that it was beyond Montreal and stretched westward for hundreds of miles -- an unknown wilderness far away in space and time from her own long-established and cultured city.

Rowena admitted she was frightened yet excited by this journey to a strange new life. After describing the horrific two months at sea, she said, "Can there be anything worse ahead? Sure, but I do miss my home!" Those green hills, the patchworks fields enclosed with tumbledown stone walls, the soft weather, even the gentle rain.

"Wait until you see what God has created here," the nun replied.

Rowena was none too sure about God these days. If He hadn't actively been punishing them during the journey, then surely He had forsaken them. Had He been angry at their leaving of Ireland, at their presumption that they would find a better life than He had provided for them there? She dared not ask these questions of Sister Terese, whose faith, she sensed, was profound and unquestioning. She lowered her eyes so that the nun could not read her thoughts. But she was unsure just what powers these kind and formidable women possessed.

As Rowena grew stronger, she chafed at the restrictions that kept her imprisoned. She had been painfully reborn into this marvelous New World, and longed to see the beauties that Sister Terese described. Despite the nun's protestations that she remain in bed, Rowena got up on quivery legs and took her first tentative steps in her new land.

In a few days she was able to walk the length of the rough building that served as a hospital, careful to stay out of the way of harried nuns and attendants. She tried to peer out the small windows but could see only tall bushes and even taller trees.

Now that the icy death-grip of the cholera had left her, she began to feel the heat -- more intense than any she had ever experienced. It drew moisture from every pore, making Rowena feel as if she were stewing in her own sweat.

No one objected when Rowena helped to soothe other patients, to give them water, or to hold the hands of the dying. She remembered only too well the tortures that these unfortunates were suffering, and felt strong and invincible by comparison. And though she thought she'd never get the stench of sickness and death out of her nostrils, she had become inured to the sight of the poisons that the afflicted bodies spewed out.

The doctor chuckled and said, "You're a useful little lass, and I'd like to recruit you. But I've need of your bed, and your family will be anxious to see you. Off you go now, and God bless you. It does my heart good to see some of my patients walk out of here!"

Rowena was alarmed by the dark circles that bruised the pale eyes of Sister Terese, who assured her that she was merely tired, and would soon be sent back to the convent in Quebec to rest. She took Rowena's thin hand, and led her outside.

The July heat seemed even more intense outside, the brilliant, burning sunshine almost blinding after the dimness of the hospital.

The shore of the wooded isle was teeming with people -- so many people that Rowena wondered how she would ever find her family amongst them. Men, women, and children frolicked knee deep in the water -- a cool, inviting blue -- and Rowena longed to hitch up her skirt and join them. Women and girls washed clothes and bedding in tubs or scrubbed them on the rocks at the edge of the river, and hung them over bushes to dry. Tents sprouted about the clearing ahead of her like giant toadstools.

As they walked beyond the line of screening shrubs, Rowena gasped with delight as her eyes drank in the shimmering blue water of the St. Lawrence River, the green of more trees than she had ever seen in her life, the rugged distant coastline of the mainland dotted with clearings and miniature houses, and the misty purple ridge of mountains undulating into infinity. And the smell! The sweet, fresh, delicious fragrance of pine.

Sister Terese smiled. "It is magnifique, n'est ce pas?"

"Oh, yes!" Rowena was overwhelmed by its vastness and beauty. Truly God had created a masterpiece to greet the travel-weary and uncertain immigrants.

Small islands seemed to float upon the broad river, some wooded and wild, others partially tamed with orchards and fields, the whitewashed farmhouses gleaming in the beneficent sunshine. Between them and Grosse Isle more than two dozen ships rode at anchor. Many of these two-masted brigs and three-masted barks were flying yellow flags, proclaiming them to be plague ships. Small boats scuttled from them to the mainland, bringing more immigrants -- the sick as well as the healthy -- ashore.

Following her gaze, the nun said, "Even among all this beauty there is such sorrow. But God has not forsaken us, ma petite. He tests our strength and courage and love. We cannot know His ways or plans. We must accept that He loves us, and pray to Him for guidance. To despair is to deny God. But I think you are strong, and will find your way in this life. Now I must give you into the care of a soldier, who will help you find your family."

Rowena clung to the nun's hand, reluctant to have a stranger guide her through the noisy and boisterous throngs. Then she heard a familiar voice shouting her name, and noticed Donal dodging among the people toward her. She flung herself into his arms.

"Sure, you're a fine sight, scrawny as you are!" Donal exclaimed, hugging her tightly.

Sister Terese smiled. "Good! I leave you in capable hands, I think. May God go with you, my children."

Rowena detained the nun. "Thank you, Sister. I wish I could live in your beautiful city and visit with you every day! Will I ever see you again?"

The nun chuckled. "One day we shall meet again, but not in this great country, I think. One even more beautiful -- the Kingdom of Heaven. Au revoir, ma petite!"

"Come on," Donal said. "Ma's near addled with grieving over you, thinking you're lying dead and buried somewhere and us not knowing. Wouldn't let us near that shack they call a hospital. And there's many that come out of there feet first. I've been looking for you every day since we landed here a fortnight ago."

"How are the others?" she asked, fearing to hear bad news.

"Right enough. Alys doesn't like the mosquitoes -- nasty biting bugs they be -- and Moira's worried sick about you -- you know how she is. Gwyn's always wandering away and getting lost -- no sense of direction that girl."

"And you're as red as the Indians are supposed to be!" Rowena exclaimed, noticing his sunburnt face and bronzed arms.

"Sure, and this is as fine a place as any to spend the time waiting. Have you ever seen the like!" he said with awe and excitement. "They've been giving us fish and fresh-baked bread. Sure you never tasted the like! Some of the other lads and me have been exploring the island, as much of it as the soldiers'll let us see, anyway. It's rocks and trees and hills. There's actually a farm down at one end, and soldiers' barracks..."

"I'll bet you didn't get that far without sneaking past the guards!" Rowena said astutely.

Donal grinned. "At t'other end of the island is a hill with a big signalling tower for sending messages to the mainland, and three cannon to blast the ships that try to go upstream without stopping here -- this being the quarantine station."

"That's never the truth! Have you seen them do it then, fire the cannon?"

"Nay, but that's what the soldiers say. Reckon they might be having us on a bit."

Rowena felt giddy as they zigzagged among the hundreds of encampments. The exertion and excitement made her tremble, but Donal, a strapping lad of thirteen, put his arm about her and practically carried her the rest of the way. "Sure, you don't weigh more than thistledown," he said.

Rowena heard a cry of disbelief, and a moment later was gathered into her mother's warm arms and then lifted into a crushing embrace by her father. Her younger sisters crowded around her, regarding her as one returned from the dead. A moment later they were all talking at once, trying to tell her everything that had happened in the past three weeks.

And it seemed to Rowena as if this were not her family at all, not the same frightened and dispirited, pale and dirty people she had last seen aboard the ship. Their eyes sparkled, their bare arms and faces were sun-kissed and radiant, and they looked healthy and robust. Even her mother had lost that haunted look and seemed content.

She felt a surge of strength with the sudden welling of happiness that threatened to spill over in joyful tears.

"I found some mint in the woods," Deirdre said. "I'll be making you some tea, and then we'd best start fattening you up or you'll be blowing away in the wind!"

"The food's good here," seven-year-old Gwyn told her. "And I found some berries in the woods. Razzyberries, they're called."

"Raspberries," Her mother corrected.

"...And I'll get you some, Rena!" Gwyn continued.

"If you haven't already eaten every last one on the island!" Donal said teasingly.

Gwyn was a chubby little girl who was fond of her food. She had already turned a gypsy brown and, with her chestnut hair and amber eyes, she resembled neither of her parents. "Reminds me of my grandmother," Patrick had said more than once. And they'd all heard the stories of that formidable woman. If it hadn't been for her skill at making the best poteen -- illegal Irish whiskey -- in the district, and her sharp and well-used tongue, the O'Shaughnessys would have perished long ago.

"Sure, I'd love some," Rowena said to her sister. To the rest she said, "You know what I'd like best of all just now? To wash the stink of the ship and the sickness off me in the river. Sure, but it looks inviting!"

The O'Shaughnessys' tent was next to the woods, so it was shaded by trees for a good part of the day. But now the sun beat down on them, and though it felt wonderfully healing, Rowena longed for the cool caress of the cleansing water.

Most of the other immigrants were down at the shore, laughing and shouting, some engaged in playful antics that resulted in people splashing headlong into the water. She could understand their almost frantic abandon. Anyone who had been cooped up in one of those "coffin" ships would be delirious with joy at the fresh, pure air, the stunning vistas, and the feel of a new and exciting land underfoot. And for some -- those who were starting to feel the nausea, and the cramps creeping up from the extremities -- there was the fear that death might claim them too soon.

Donal laughed as he pulled off his shirt. "I'll take you to the water. But you'll freeze. Then you'll be glad of the heat." He turned his face to the sun. "Have you ever felt such a sun? 'Tis so strong and bold. Sure, doesn't it feel like this country is that much closer to God?"

"Don't talk daft, Donal," Deirdre scolded. "God doesn't favour this country any more than Ireland! Nor its people."

Donal and his father exchanged knowing glances, which Rowena could interpret. To them it ***was*** a favoured land, but they wouldn't try to convince Deirdre. She'd come to the realization eventually. Being such sentimental creatures, women couldn't be expected to let go of the Old Country so easily.

"I've washed your clothes," Deirdre said. "So take these clean things along. And this bit of soap. 'Tis all we have left, so be careful with it. I'll have the tea ready for you when you get back. And then you'd best be resting." Deirdre pulled Rowena to her in a quick, fierce hug, as if she needed to reassure herself that her eldest daughter was real.

"I'll come, too," ten-year-old Moira said. "I'll get me feet wet, anyway."

Moira was only nineteen months younger than Rowena, but completely different from her older sister. Rowena had always been tall for her age, and graceful. She (and Donal) had inherited Deirdre's Black Irish beauty -- cool, blue eyes, porcelain-pale skin, and thick, raven-black hair -- a stunning combination. Moira had inherited her father's curly red hair and freckles -- freckles that, for the moment, seemed lost amid Moira's fiery sunburn. Patrick was not a tall man, and like him, Moira was petite. And clumsy, she'd always thought. Donal, with his rugged handsomeness, and Rowena, with her ethereal beauty, had always seemed like the ancient Irish kings and queens to Moira. She was content to be allowed to follow them, even proud to be their shadow.

"Me too," Gwyn said quickly. "I'll come, too."

"I thought you were going to find berries for Rena," Donal said.

"Later. I want to go with you now," Gwyn said.

"Ma," Donal appealed to Deirdre. It was one thing to take Moira, who was always quiet and did as she was told, and quite another to have to take a stubborn seven-year-old who was forever getting into mischief.

"You stay with me, Gwyn," Deirdre said, "and help me make dinner. And you can play with Alys."

Gwyn sulked. "She's just a baby!"

"Am not!" three-year-old Alys replied, stung by the remark. Alys was a pale version of Moira, with red-gold hair and bleached freckles.

"'Tisn't fair!" Gwyn maintained. "I never get to go along. Moira can help you, and I'll go!"

"You don't even like the water," Moira said, feeling herself begin to quiver, as she always did when she had to deal with her quarrelsome younger sister.

"I don't care! I want to watch. I want to be with Rena!"

"Come lass," Patrick said placatingly. "You and me'll go and visit the soldiers, and see if they have a fine fish for us today."

Gwyn's face was still squashed into an angry pout, but the mention of food and the thought of going somewhere completely alone with her father had stayed her tongue. But Gwyn was never one to be grateful for treats -- she figured these were the very least that life owed her.

The three eldest children escaped. Donal led the girls along a woodland path, saying to Rowena, "We found this quiet spot where t'others can't be bothered to go."

"I can see why!" Rowena replied. The dead pine needles were prickly beneath her toughened bare feet. She and Moira stepped gingerly, but Donal seemed to have leather hide on his soles, for he strode cockily onward.

Donal gave her a supporting hand up on a granite rock, blistering hot where the sun touched it. And before them lay a delightful little cove sheltered from the strong sun by the overhanging branches of white birch and towering pines. They sat down on a hump-backed slab of pink and black granite that sank slowly into the water. The rock was rough and warm to the touch, and sparkled in the dappled sunlight.

"'Tis heavenly," Rowena sighed, and Donal seemed pleased.

She wriggled down the rock so that her toes touched the water, and gasped with the icy shock.

Donal rolled up his tattered trousers and jumped in. The water reached almost to his knees. "'Tis a fine, sandy bottom," he said.

The sounds of the encampments were like a far-off buzzing of bees. In the shelter of the trees and rocks, Rowena could imagine that this was their own private paradise. She stripped off her soiled dress and plunged into the water in her cotton shift, feeling the iciness envelope her with breath-snatching force. With knees and hands she touched the gritty bottom, and then flipped onto her back and floated with her face to the heavens.

She drifted on the gentle swells, and felt herself a part of the powerful river. Its life-giving energy seemed to ripple through her as the water washed over her. It was a baptism to complete her rebirth.

Donal said, "A lad from Cork showed me how to swim. Said he fell off a wharf into the ocean when he was but a wee babe, and knew right away what to do. Could swim ever since." He showed her a clumsy breast stroke, and she tried to imitate him. But she was too frail to do more than a few weak attempts.

Moira, her skirts hitched up, waded in the shallows and watched them.

"I'll learn it yet," Rowena promised. "But another time."

Rowena scrubbed herself thoroughly with the bit of lye soap, and lathered her hair. Before getting out of the water, she slipped off her soiled shift and donned her clean one, while Donal kept lookout. Her flesh cold but purified, Rowena stretched out gratefully on the warm rock. Moira and Donal joined her.

Rowena felt that this was one of those moments that would stay with her forever, called up easily in memory and sometimes in dreams, special moments that punctuated life.

Her eyes were drawn to a church spire on the mainland, and the bright tin roof that must surely dazzle the eyes of God Himself. She had become fascinated by Sister Terese and her quiet devotion to God. Rowena thought it must be wonderful to be in such close communion with Him, so reassuring. She could picture the convent the nun had described -- stone-walled to keep the busy city at bay, tranquil gardens for contemplation, contented women doing good deeds and earning favour with God. She even wondered if she could become a nun, and thought how marvellous it would be to be constantly in the company of such kind and devout people as Sister Terese. She really must talk to her again before they left the island.

Distracted from her pleasant thoughts by activity at one of the many ships riding at anchor, Rowena said, "Where are they all coming from?"

Donal replied, "Ireland mostly, like us. Some from England and Scotland -- better ships they be, from the stories we heard. Some bringing ladies and gentleman -- or at least, them as think they are." He snorted. "I reckon it won't take long for them to realize things're different here."

"Do you think they are?"

"Sure."

Rowena couldn't imagine a place where there weren't grand, wealthy lords who owned everything, and the poor who owed their living -- or dying -- to the whims of their masters.

She asked, "When do we leave here? Where will we be going?"

"The *Devoron*'s already left with them as weren't sick, so we'll be having to catch the steamboat to Quebec City -- whenever you're well enough to travel. The boat comes every day with supplies."

But she didn't want to think of leaving now. She lay back on the rock and, a moment later, was asleep.

Rowena awoke to the subdued chatter of her family and the strong smell of fish. The confining walls of the canvas tent startled her for an instant, until she remembered where she must be. She heard the larger sounds of the many people who were forced together temporarily by circumstance. Shrill voices somewhere were cursing and blaspheming. Others laughed and sang. Someone played a clever fiddle. Compelled to see these goings-on, she forced herself to get up off the straw bed.

Her family sat on the warm earth in the golden light of evening finishing their supper. They had saved Rowena some fish and bread, and Deirdre served her the cooled mint tea she had prepared hours earlier.

"How did I get back here?" she asked.

"Donal threw you over his shoulder like a sack of praties and carried you back," her father said. He smiled at her lovingly. "You're looking better already, lass."

Rowena ate with relish as she watched the entertainment.

A young couple in shabby clothes, and barefoot -- as most of the people were -- danced a lively jig.

A leprechaun of a man wearing nothing but ragged trousers capered about bellowing, "Sure, we'll all be gentlemen soon!"

All around them people shared -- sometimes not graciously -- the many small fires for cooking. At one, two women were arguing over whose pot would feel the fire next. Their vigorous shouting gave way to pushing and then to an all-out hair-pulling, face-scratching, shin-kicking fight. A couple of soldiers quickly intervened --one getting kicked for his troubles -- and pulled the women apart.

Deirdre shook her head in disgust and said, "It takes more than freedom from masters to make a man a gentleman and a woman a lady."

"We'll all feel better once we're around our own hearth," Patrick said.

"Wherever that might be," Deirdre muttered.

"Somewhere grand, to be sure! We'll leave as soon as Rowena is strong enough to travel," Patrick assured her.

But with more cholera-ridden ships arriving daily, the authorities were anxious to be rid of those who seemed healthy enough. Passage on the steamer to Quebec was arranged for the O'Shaughnessy family just three days later.

Rowena tried to approach the hospital in the hope of seeing Sister Terese, but the guards wouldn't let her near. She felt saddened to leave this special new friend without another word.

The O'Shaughnessys boarded the steamer with dozens of strangers. The people that they had come to know -- too intimately, perhaps -- on the *Devoron* during the harrowing crossing had dispersed during the last two weeks. More friends they would likely never meet again, Rowena thought.

She was excited at seeing Quebec, which was a mere thirty miles upstream, but curiously sad to leave the island. Every day, she, Donal, and Moira had gone to their special cove to cool off from the sweltering heat. She'd even got the hang of swimming, and exalted in the feeling of freedom -- that strange buoyancy that was as close to the soaring of the birds as humans could ever get. She wondered if the place they were going to could be as beautiful as this.

It didn't strike her as curious at first to see the soldiers bringing the coffin aboard. Daily people died and were buried here. Here, not in Quebec. And suddenly Rowena had a terrible vision of Sister Terese with her tired eyes and wan face. She pushed through the crowd of passengers and approached the soldiers as they boarded.

She trembled with apprehension at addressing the red-coated men, who were so often feared in Ireland. But she had to know.

"Please, Sirs. Who lies in this coffin?" she asked.

"Not one of yours," one of the men replied gruffly.

"Is it someone from the hospital?" she persisted. She dared not voice her own suspicion, lest that somehow make it true.

Aware of her agitation, one of the others said more kindly, "It's one of the nuns. Came down with the cholera. They'll bury her at the convent in Quebec."

Rowena felt her heart plummet. "Which one? Oh, please, Sir, you must tell me!"

The soldier shrugged. "They didn't tell us."

And with the boat about to depart, there was no way she could find out. But Rowena could too easily envision the serene face of Sister Terese, now wasted and blackened from the disease. Cholera was not a gentle death.

The image was like a physical blow. Rowena sank onto the large box that contained the few possessions of the O'Shaughnessy family. She hardly noticed the picturesque scenery on their winding trip up the narrowing river. Perhaps this was a dangerous, deadly land, the beauty deceptive. Perhaps it was less heaven than hell.

To despair is to deny God. She remembered the nun's words. But, by Jesus, God had a lot to answer for! So much death. And so much despair.

And yet.... She had no proof that her friend was dead. Perhaps it was another nun who lay in the pine box. Why despair when there is hope -- that's what Sister Terese would say. And Rowena would cling to that hope.

Her gloomy thoughts were dispelled by her first glimpse of Quebec City. It was perched majestically atop a cliff that rose from the sparkling depths of the river. With a backdrop of ancient polished mountains, and the thundering waters of the Montmorency Falls cascading into the river to the east, it was a truly awe-inspiring sight.

With returning energy, Rowena longed to explore the walled city. And to visit the convent.

But before they landed, the captain warned them that cholera was rampant in the city, having claimed the lives of hundreds of inhabitants as well as immigrants who had hoped to make their homes here. He told of people dropping in the streets to die unattended, since the hospitals were overflowing with victims. He said that businesses were closed, that food was scarce, since farmers refused to bring supplies to the plague-ridden city. He urged the immigrants to hire the few boatmen who were still willing to take them upriver, and tarry not a single day in this city of death.

As they docked at the wharves which lay at the base of the cliff, Rowena could see the tar barrels burning -- as they had in Ireland -- to ward off the cholera. The continuous dirge of church bells lamented the many deaths. The black-clad health officials and customs inspectors who greeted them on the dock gave them but a cursory inspection. This hurried and fearful intercourse was their official welcome to their new land.

Deirdre clutched her children protectively to her. Patrick wasted no time in approaching the boatmen to procure transportation.

Rowena watched two sombre nuns meet the soldiers who carried the coffin from the steamer. She stifled the urge to approach them, not from trepidation, but because she no longer wanted to know. Truth was too final. Unassailable. She preferred to think of Sister Terese still soothing the ill and dying back at Grosse Isle. That was how she would remember her.

As Rowena looked around at the dilapidated buildings that cowered at the base of the cliff, she thought again how deceptive the beauty was here. From a distance it had appeared magnificent. But closer inspection revealed evidence of poverty and squalor, and the inevitable sounds and smells of death.

Was it everywhere thus in this strange new land?

Chapter 2

The O'Shaughnessy family sat huddled together on their trunk, shielded from the stinging downpour of rain by a tarpaulin. Rowena leaned against her father, tired after the three weeks of travelling -- by bateau, on foot, and by steamboat -- which had brought them to this pretty village of Cobourg on the north shore of Lake Ontario.

The bateau, a forty-foot, flat-bottomed barge, had laboured up the St. Lawrence from Quebec City. Rowena had enjoyed the leisurely pace, savoring the scenery -- whitewashed villages dappling the shores, church spires punctuating the landscape, ribbon-like fields stretching back from the mighty river, the fluttering sails of stone windmills. She had liked the hearty French Canadian boatmen who had sung their lilting "chansons" as they had rowed against the strong currents of the river. Even now those songs echoed in her head, though she knew not what the words meant.

A l'ombre d'un bois je m'en vais jouer,
A l'ombre d'un bois je m'en vais danser.

What a merry group those "voyageurs" had been! In the evenings, when a crude camp had been erected along the shore, they had sat around the fire drinking rum and smoking pipes, singing, and occasionally even dancing -- by themselves if none of the female passengers could be prevailed upon to have a whirl.

They had shrugged fatalistically at the cholera threat, saying it was the will of God. But even they had not stopped in Montreal, where reports of deaths were even higher than in Quebec City.

Donal thought there could be no finer life than the freedom and excitement these voyageurs enjoyed upon this unpredictable river. Above Montreal, the bateau had been poled through the rapids, although in shallow stretches all the men had been obliged to jump into the swift waters and pull the barge along. Donal had pulled as hard as the rest. Rowena had never seen him so happy.

Where the current was too strong, the boat had been hauled along the shore by oxen plodding along a towpath, and where the turbulent river was most dangerous, the passengers had walked through the steaming forests and swamps, meeting the bateau at a safe rendezvous upstream. Donal had pleaded to be allowed to go along, but had been denied by both his parents and the boatmen.

It was there, away from the cool river, that the heat had become suffocating. The men had shed all but their trousers, but the women had steamed in the gowns that had served them well in Ireland's temperate climate. The girls had stripped to their cotton shifts, but Rowena had felt that, even naked, the heat would be unbearable. The infernal, blood-sucking mosquitoes had attacked them by the hundreds. Alys had wept frequently with the agony of her bites that swelled abnormally large. Gwyn had whined constantly, and Moira had endured everything in silence.

Rowena, still weak and frail, had wondered why God was sending them such trials to overcome before allowing them to reach their new home. Was this place so wonderful that they had to earn it?

At Prescott, in the province of Upper Canada, they had said goodbye to the boatmen. How Donal had envied them their thrilling whitewater ride back down to Montreal.

The O'Shaughnessys had taken a steamer which had wound its way through the breath-taking Thousand Islands, stopping briefly at the flourishing city of Kingston. Here the seemingly endless expanse of Lake Ontario had opened before them. Surely it must be a sea, Rowena had said. Her father had laughingly remarked, "Everything's done on a grand scale in this country!"

They had disembarked at this harbour town of Cobourg, where they now awaited the stagecoach that would convey them north to Rice Lake.

The rain let up, but instead of having cleared the thick heat, it had increased the humidity. Rowena was grateful for the bit of breeze off the lake.

The "stagecoach" trundled up beside them. It was little more than an ox-drawn cart with two rows of seats covered in buffalo hide, which exuded a damp, musty odour. The only other passengers were a fashionably-dressed, middle-aged English couple who looked askance at the bedraggled family who were to be their companions over the next few miles.

"Are you not aware, my good man," the Englishwoman said to the driver, "that the Irish immigrants are spreading pestilence throughout the country? I refuse to have these people aboard!" She barred Deirdre's way with her umbrella.

"We paid our money, same as you," Patrick said brusquely, pushing the umbrella aside. His green eyes stared defiantly at her.

Rowena quivered inside. At home her father would never had dared to challenge the gentry thus. She wondered what would happen now. Would her father be reported to the authorities?

"What impudence!" the woman said. She turned to her husband. "Charles, you cannot allow this!"

"This is a public stagecoach, m'am," the driver interceded. "This fellow here has the right of it, sure enough," he said as he helped Donal lift the trunk into the back of the cart.

It seemed the Englishman had been about to say something, but changed his mind. He looked away as if trying to dissociate himself from the scene. "Leave it be, Livinia," he cautioned.

As the Englishwoman turned her back on them, Rowena was stunned to realize that her father had won the battle. Deirdre grinned at Patrick, who winked back at her as he handed her up into the cart. It seemed to Rowena that her parents had communicated more in that instant than they had for weeks.

The O'Shaughnessys didn't try pushing their luck by expecting the English couple to share their bench seat, so Rowena and Donal sat on the trunk in the back.

Leaving Cobourg behind them, they drove through cultivated farmlands settled long ago by the United Empire Loyalists. The innkeeper in Cobourg had told them about these refugees of the American Revolutionary War whose loyalty to the Crown had been rewarded with free land in this fledgling colony.

Before long, these vestiges of civilization disappeared, and they were swallowed up by the vast, primeval forest of oaks and maples and pines. The land undulated northward, the forest broken occasionally by a patch of meadow or a small farm with the inevitable zigzag fences of split timbers running rampant over clearings stubbled with truncated trees.

Then the forest again. It was overpowering; dense and lush, with broken boughs and uprooted trees, patches of wildflowers, shrubs heavy with August berries. The woods steamed as streamers of sunlight warmed the wet vegetation. And then of course, there were the mosquitoes -- clouds of them sometimes, buzzing about their heads.

Here there were no lake-cooled winds; the heat was oppressive. The air seemed liquid, too turgid even to breathe. Rowena noticed the rigid back of the Englishwoman sag. Even in her fine silks she must be wilting.

The cart bumped over the rough path that could scarcely be called a road. Sometimes it nearly pitched them out as a wheel sank into a deep pothole. It was a teeth-rattling, spine-jolting ride that took them ever farther from the refreshing breezes and open vistas of the lakeshore, where a body could breathe. Rowena had loved the river and lakeside villages they had passed these last weeks, and would have been happy to stay there, forever in sight of the water.

The trees thinned and finally relinquished their dominance to a high, grassy plain. From here the passengers caught their first glimpse of Rice Lake shimmering in the evening sun. It was a pleasant surprise to see the picturesque stretch of water studded with wooded islands. The driver explained that it was named after the wild rice that grew thickly along the marshy shores of the lake. This rice was harvested by the Indians, who had an encampment on the far shore.

Donal eagerly asked about the Indians - where they truly fierce, half-naked savages?

"Nature's gentlemen, I call them," the driver replied with a laugh. "And if there's anything you care to know about living off the land, ask the Indians. They'll show you how to catch fish with spears, at night. That's a sport! Some nights you'll see dozens of bobbing lights on the lake, as they go out in their canoes with burning pitch pine lighting the way. And they'll show you which plants to use for medicines. They're helpful, right enough, but like to keep themselves to themselves and follow their old ways."

They reached the shore of Rice Lake as a fiery sunset streaked the sky and melted across the water.

The inn -- the only building within view -- was a log cabin like many others they had passed. Chickens wandered in and out the open doorway. Pigs foraged in the yard. Inside was one large room with unhewn log walls, the chinks filled with bits of moss and mud. The dirt floor was packed hard and smooth. A fire blazed in the stone hearth -- despite the blistering heat outdoors -- where pots and kettles simmered.

"You have a bedchamber, I trust?" the Englishman enquired of the innkeeper, who came to greet them.

"That we do, and lucky you are that it's not already been spoken for," the man said jovially. "We do get a crush of folk in here some days." He led the English couple to a door that opened into a tiny chamber just large enough to encompass a crude bed.

"Have you nothing better?" the Englishwoman demanded.

The landlord shrugged. "It's either this or you can sleep alongside the rest of the folk up in the loft. It's cheaper."

She pursed her lips as she flounced into the room and shut the door. Her husband said, "It'll do."

The newcomers were invited to sit down to supper at the rough refectory table with the innkeeper, his wife, their daughter and two grown sons, the stagecoach driver, and two carters who had earlier brought crates of supplies destined for the backwoods. The English couple eventually joined them but took no part in the conversation.

"The bush is wild," the innkeeper replied to Patrick's query about what lay in store for them. "But that's where a man can make good in this country. If you stay down at the "Front" -- that's what we call the older, settled areas along Lake Ontario -- well, most of the good land's taken there, or costs you a packet to buy."

"Sure, we saw great stretches of land that had never seen an axe," Patrick said.

The innkeeper snorted. "Crown land that be, and clergy reserves for the English church."

One of his sons added, "And don't those government bastards in York keep thousands of acres of the best land for themselves, till they can sell it to some poor fool for twice what it's worth."

The others nodded in agreement.

"And in the backwoods you're not as likely to find them as think they're still in the Old Country -- acting the aristocrat when they're just down-at-heels, one-time gentry that didn't lose their bad manners when they lost their land," the innkeeper said pleasantly.

The Englishman bristled but said nothing.

The innkeeper continued, "But there's a group of true gentlemen in and about Peterborough. Educated at Oxford and Cambridge, they come out here for adventure and freedom from all that social nonsense back home. But not a one of 'em gives himself airs, or declines to share our humble meals and conversations on their way to and from the Front."

He went on to tell them about the village of Peterborough -- which the O'Shaughnessys expected to reach tomorrow -- and how it had really started in 1825 with the government-sponsored emigration from Ireland, arranged by Canadian, Peter Robinson -- a "true philanthropist and a gentleman with a fine fellow feeling for the poor, long-suffering immigrants". Most had been granted land in and around Peterborough. So grateful had the immigrants been, that they had named their thriving village after Peter Robinson.

It was the same emigration that had brought the O'Maras. Rowena was surprised to realize that after more than three months of travelling, they were actually nearing the end of their journey.

She attacked her meal of potatoes, pork, and coarse brown bread, but the Englishwoman, who sat across from her, picked distastefully at hers. She kicked at a curious pig that snuffled around her feet.

To the amusement of the company, the innkeeper's son said, "Is it pigskin shoes you have on your feet then? Lady Jane don't like that at all." He shooed "Lady Jane" outside.

The Englishwoman's anger was evident in her glare and her ramrod-stiff back.

Rowena studied her surreptitiously. Despite the rough and dirty journey, the woman looked remarkably neat. She'd obviously made an effort to tidy herself -- to pin up stray locks, and brush mud from her skirts -- not for the assembled company, Rowena was sure, but for her own self esteem. Still, sweat beaded her brow and showed evidence on her bodice and underarms. Rowena couldn't help but admire her fortitude, even if she found the woman unpleasant.

After the meal, the Englishwoman said, "I'd like a bath sent to my chamber."

"No bath's here," the innkeeper's wife said curtly as she began clearing the table. "The lake's warm enough. That's where we bathe in summer."

"And you have the audacity to call this place an inn?"

"So it is, and the only one hereabouts. If it don't suit, you're welcome to leave."

"Outrageous!" the Englishwoman said as she marched out. Her husband followed a moment later.

The innkeeper's wife sniffed and said, "There's some as think their shit don't smell. If she stays in the backwoods, she'll learn soon enough we don't take kindly to such a hoity-toity manner. As if I didn't have enough to do without slaving for the likes of her! And there isn't a bath in the finest castle in England that can beat a dip in our lake."

The O'Shaughnessys stepped out into the twilight. Although still humid, the air outside was cooler and certainly fresher than the stifling air indoors. They strolled down to the water's edge. The western sky was tinged with orange, with purple clouds massing in thunderheads. The lake was so calm it lay like a sheet of glass before them, curiously lighter than the darkening sky. On the far shore, past the humpbacked islands, they could see the fires of the Indian encampment.

Patrick suddenly grabbed his wife and whirled her about in a jig.

"Stop!" she cried, laughing. "Is it daft you are, man?"

"Nay, just happy! We'll be there in a few days, Dre! Just think of it!"

"Aye, well," she said more soberly. "I was beginning to think we'd be wandering forever in this God-forsaken place!" To the children she said, "Come, we'll all have a wash in the lake afore bed."

Rowena stripped down to her shift and waded eagerly into the water. It was remarkably warm -- so unlike the chilly St. Lawrence which brought on numbing cramps -- but nonetheless refreshing. Rowena floated and paddled while the others splashed in the shallows.

Rowena hadn't noticed the English couple standing in the deep shadows of a tree until she heard their voices. They obviously hadn't spotted her as she stood shoulder-deep in the lake. The woman was saying, "You cannot do this to me and the girls, Charles! You cannot be so cruel as to make us live among these savages and upstarts who think to be our equals! I've never been treated with such rudeness and contempt! Having to share a table with foul-smelling peasants, sleep in lice-infested beds..."

"Now, Livinia, one cannot expect the comforts of home in such a young and developing colony," her husband said placatingly.

"Why we had to leave the comforts of home, I shall never understand! You tell me nothing specific of our financial burdens -- merely declare we must sell everything and leave England!"

"I will not distress you with the facts, Livinia. You must accept my decision. I assure you that I have not arrived at it without a great deal of deliberation." In a more cajoling tone, he added, "We've been granted a thousand acres, Livinia, and I've been given a position as land agent to the Canada Company in this district. We must be grateful and make the best of things. The girls are captivated by York. Enjoying themselves immensely there. And they'll adapt to Peterborough as well."

"We'll never find them suitable husbands here!"

"You heard the innkeeper mention the gentlemen from Oxford...."

As if he hadn't spoken, she continued, "And what worse horrors await us in the backwoods? I shall never forgive you for bringing us to this state, Charles! Never! Oh, God, I shall die here!"

Rowena could see a dark shape hurrying away, and another following more slowly.

She hadn't noticed Donal behind her until he said, "Foul-smelling peasants, are we? Maybe in Ireland or England. But not here. She ***does*** have a lot to learn."

"I feel almost sorry for her," Rowena said. "It can't be easy to stop being gentry."

"And do you think ***if*** she gets to heaven that God will treat her special? She might as well learn now that she's no different from the rest of us." After a pause, he said mischievously, "Just think, Rena. They could become our neighbours."

"And we'll be invited to tea!" she said.

"And I'll marry one of their daughters!"

Their laughter echoed far across the night-time water.

Storm clouds rolled in to smother the last light of day. They watched distant, soundless lightning playing in the sky, and by the time they got out of the water, they could hear its first threatening growl. They stayed outdoors to dry off until the heavy raindrops began to fall.

The loft of the log cabin was curtained down the middle into separate areas for women and men. Since there were no other female guests, the O'Shaughnessys were given the women's side as their own. The beds were simply pallets of straw laid upon the wooden floor, but they were drier and more comfortable than the hard ground that had so often been their bed on the journey upriver.

The heat of the day was still trapped under the rafters, but open gable-end windows let in the cooling wind brought by the storm. Despite the crashing of the thunder and the drumming of rain on the roof, they soon slept.

Only Deirdre lay awake. The heat bothered her more than the others.

She felt a sudden stab of homesickness so intense that she nearly cried out in pain. She longed to see again the familiar green hills of home. It was a place where you could feel the reassuring presence of those who had walked those hills and lanes before you. That gave you a sense of yourself and of belonging, and of fitting into some greater scheme.

Here, it was as likely that only wild creatures of the forest had ever travelled this way before.

And of course, memories of home always included Eileen and Seamus -- her two lost children who had not even a grave or a marker to show they had ever existed. She mustn't think of them, couldn't allow grief to overwhelm her. That was a part of herself that must remain locked away, for otherwise she might never stop weeping.

She cursed Liam O'Mara for having sent that damnable letter. Patrick had been starry-eyed ever since receiving it.

Men were such dreamers, Deirdre thought. They did what they wanted with little thought of others. Sure, they could always find a way to justify themselves.

Brian O'Neill had been such a one. What a fine figure of a man he had been! Black Irish, like herself, with his dark hair, fair skin, and blue eyes that seemed to look right into your soul. He'd been every man's envy and every woman's desire. And he had been hers -- for a short while.

What a glorious future she had imagined for them. But it hadn't been enough for Brian. He had claimed the only way to end British tyranny was to fight, and so he'd joined the Whiteboys.

Was it really the noble goal of freeing Ireland that had spurred him on, or was it the danger and excitement, the anonymity of night-time raids?

One of the rebels' forays had gone awry, and a rent collector had been killed.

Deirdre never knew if Brian had been directly responsible for the man's death, but the English had hanged him for the murder a week before their wedding day.

So she had finally settled on Patrick O'Shaughnessy, thinking him a steady, safe man, a hard worker, a man with both feet planted firmly on the ground. And sure, here they were, fourteen years later, in an alien, frightening, wild land, their money almost gone, with no chance of returning to Ireland.

They ***had*** to make a new life for themselves here. There were no other options. She had known that the moment they left Doneraile.

And Deirdre had to admit that she had begun to worry about Donal. He was not afraid to speak his mind, and he craved adventure. How long would it have been before the Whiteboys had recruited him, with their promises of justice and glory?

It was for the children that she had finally agreed to come. They would all be better off in a land where they were not condemned from birth to a hard and desperate life.

And yet.... She feared what awaited them here.

Deirdre felt a sharp kick in her abdomen, and caressed the six-month bulge of her belly. "Don't be in a hurry to be born, me little babe. There's naught but sorrow this side of the womb."

• • •

Peterborough was another delightful surprise. It was situated beside a small lake formed by the widening of the Otonabee River. Rippling around it in all directions were lovely hills and high plains, like natural parklands, dotted with clumps of white birches and pines and oaks. Peterborough was a growing community with stores, mills, inns, and even a log church.

Deirdre felt more hopeful about their future home than she had since leaving Ireland. "We could live here," she said wistfully to Patrick.

They were waiting outside the general store in the hope that they could cadge a ride with some farmer heading westward. After paying passage on the steamer from Rice Lake up the Otonabee River to Peterborough, their meager funds would not stretch to hiring a carter to take them the last twenty miles.

Rowena agreed that it was beautiful spot. The storm two nights before had finally cleared away the humidity, so that even the weather in Peterborough seemed ideal -- sunny and warm, the air light and fresh. The sky was periwinkle blue, so unlike the colourless, soggy sky that had loomed over them these last weeks.

Patrick said, "We'll go to Liam's first -- see what he has to recommend. But we can always come back here if the other doesn't suit."

"There's bound to be work here, Pat. Liam's on a farm, maybe in the middle of some God-forsaken wilderness. Like as not he'll tell us to come back here. I'm bone-weary, and the children too. We could settle here, and let Liam know where we are. Let him come to see us!"

"We're that close now, Dre. Only two more days. Maybe Liam knows of someplace even finer." He patted Deirdre's hand. "You'll have your new home soon, lass."

Deirdre resigned herself to his decision with a sigh. Mostly Patrick was easy-going, and could be persuaded to change his mind. But when he was fully determined upon something, as he was now, he dug in his heels. She won the skirmishes, she thought wryly, while he won the wars.

A Scottish farmer agreed to take the O'Shaughnessys as far as Omemee -- some twelve miles closer to their destination.

The views from the hilltops around Peterborough were stunning, but the travellers were soon engulfed by the forest again. The road, though dry, was badly rutted, and the passengers were bounced about on the rickety vehicle which, Rowena was certain, was about to fall to pieces beneath them. The road became little more than a track after a few miles, with rocks, fallen trees, and branches occasionally barricading even this. But the oxen lumbered over everything, resolutely dragging the cart behind them. The O'Shaughnessys, however, chose to walk rather than suffer the bruising jolts of the wagon, and they had no difficulty keeping pace with the farmer.

Between the hills, they encountered long stretches of swamps and black spruce bogs which were traversed by corduroy roads -- nothing more than logs laid side-by-side which, nonetheless, prevented oxen, wagon, and people from sinking into the black morass. Often logs were missing, having been swallowed by the insatiable bogs.

These swamps were eerie places. Thick green scum floated on the surface of the stagnant waters; soft tussocks of grass and moss looked deceptively solid; grey skeletons of trees in crazy, drunken postures reached broken arms toward the sky; cattails and reeds grew to enormous heights. Birds whistled and cawed, crickets hummed, frogs grumbled. Then, as though aware of the intruders in their domain, they ceased, and the swamp became uncannily still with not even a whisper of wind to disturb the rank miasma. It seemed to Rowena as if the swamp had stopped breathing as it warily watched and waited.

Along one of these stretches, a wheel of the wagon broke as it crashed into a gap in the log road. The farmer was well prepared for such a contingency and, with Patrick's help, the wagon was quickly repaired.

No sooner had they reached dry ground again, than they heard a tremendous thundering of hooves on the corduroy road behind them. They turned to see a young man astride a sleek chestnut stallion galloping toward them. He dodged past them without slowing, stirring up a cloud of gritty dust in his wake. As if mesmerized, all eyes followed his progress. Rowena gasped as the horse stumbled, nearly throwing its rider. The man quickly righted himself and pushed on relentlessly.

"He'll kill himself yet," the Scotsman prophesied, shaking his head. "And that poor horse. Such a fine animal. It's a shame! A pity the lad hasn't as much sense as he has gall."

"Do you know him then?" Patrick asked.

"I've spied him often enough. He's one of the Launston lads, from o'er Launston Mills. No doubt he thinks to be home for his supper tonight," the farmer said as though this possibility were preposterous.

Rowena had been captivated by the beautiful horse and its bold rider, and wondered idly if she'd ever see them again.

• • •

"'Tis never Dennis O'Mara!" Patrick cried with disbelief as he studied the brawny, tanned figure before him.

"That's my name right enough," the man replied, looking puzzled. He wiped his brow with his dirty flannel sleeve and laid down his axe. His eyes narrowed in speculation as he regarded the O'Shaughnessys. "Do I know you?"

"Sure, you'll not have forgotten Patrick O'Shaughnessy?"

Dennis O'Mara's face split into a wide grin. He stretched out a large, blistered paw and vigorously pumped Patrick's hand. "May the Saints preserve us! I never though to see the likes of you here, Patrick!"

"Didn't you get me letter then? It must be five months since I sent it."

"No, but the mail service is a lamentable one to be sure. But now you're here and welcome to you! And it's a fool I am to keep you standing here when you must be dog-tired."

Dennis hoisted the O'Shaughnessys' trunk onto his broad shoulders and led his guests to the log house that squatted amid a field of rotting tree stumps. Patrick and Donal, who had carried the box between them for the last four miles, were grateful for the respite.

The O'Mara's house was finer than some of the log cabins they had seen. The logs had been hewn square and the chinks well plastered inside and out. There was a nine-paned window on either side of the door, and smaller ones in each gable end. The ground floor comprised a combined kitchen and living area, with a stone fireplace and chimney, and two bedrooms. Stairs behind the fireplace led up to a sleeping loft under the roof. The wooden floor of the cabin, slightly warped, was covered in multi-coloured rag rugs. A box bed, a cupboard, a table and chairs, and a rocker furnished the room.

A young woman was seated in the rocking chair by the fire, suckling an infant, while an older child played on the floor beside her. The woman looked startled when the O'Shaughnessys trooped into the room.

"This is my wife, Brenna," Dennis said as he introduced the O'Shaughnessys.

"You're welcome, I'm sure," Brenna said, though Deirdre caught her worried glance at the seven unexpected guests and their luggage.

Deirdre felt a sudden attack of panic. Here they finally were, after nearly four months of travelling, and she realized their journey was far from over. She fought the impulse to drop into a chair and weep. What had she expected, after all? That they would be taken in hand by Liam, be looked after and cossetted, a job and house found for them?

After a momentary awkwardness, Dennis said, "Make yourselves to home," spreading his arms out to indicate his hospitality.

"We'll not impose on you long," Deirdre assured them.

"You'll not be rushing out of Dennis O'Mara's house! There's always room for friends."

"'Tis kind you are, Dennis," Patrick said. "Where's your father then?"

Dennis frowned. "Dead and buried these two months, God rest his soul. It was the ague took him -- swamp fever, it is -- and himself never sick a day in his life afore that."

Deirdre crossed herself. How often had she cursed Liam these last months, and how she wished he were here now. Of all her worries and thoughts about their new land, she had never even considered this possibility.

"'Tis truly grieved I am to hear that," Patrick said. "As I was when I heard about your mother and sister."

Dennis nodded. "Ma had the ship fever. We thought she was better, but the travelling was too much for her. She's buried at Kingston. Our Shioban was took the first summer with the ague. She and Da are buried on this land. You can see their graves, if you've a mind to."

"Surely this isn't consecrated ground?" Deirdre asked, shocked.

"No more it is. But there's no church, nor cemetery, nor clergy hereabouts. 'Tis a common practice in the bush to bury the dead on their own land."

"And your father said this was God's country!"

"'God moves in a mysterious way His wonders to perform'," Brenna quoted.

Dennis offered them some green tea, for which none of them had developed a taste, but which they accepted gratefully.

"And where are your brothers?" Patrick asked Dennis.

"Mike's newly wed and living on the next concession. Dermott never took to farming. He was in York, last we heard, building roads. And our Mary's been wed these last four years to a farmer down the way."

"And you with two children of your own!"

"Aye. We had another, but lost him to the dysentery. 'Tis a hard land, though it's been good to us, I reckon."

"You've done well. 'Tis a fine farm you have here. Tell me, Dennis, have you heard of anyone needing a carpenter, hereabouts or in Peterborough? We're after finding a place to settle afore the winter comes, for we've been told 'tis a fierce time of year."

"To be sure. Well now, I heard tell in the tavern at Launston Mills just last week, that Launston is fixing to build himself a fine mansion. And they say he's planning to build a distillery. And sure, the government surveyors were just there, mapping out a town next to the Mills. There's work enough for you there, Patrick, and 'tis only six miles from here."

"Is it a nice village?" Deirdre asked.

"'Tis hardly what you'd call a village yet, though there's a grist and saw mill, a tavern, a shop, and a smithy. And no more than fifty folk altogether, though a good many farmers go there, myself included. But 'tis growing."

"What's Launston like?" Patrick wanted to know.

"He's English -- a gentleman, I reckon he was, though I heard he fell on hard times in the Old Country. There ain't many as come to this land without needing to. Launston's a shrewd businessman though. Has connections with some high officials in York -- that's how he got his land, I heard tell, and the government contract to build the mills. But they say he's fair, and likeable.

"He has no wife, just two sons -- Jeremy, who's twenty and helps run the businesses, and Adrian who's fourteen. He goes to the college in York most of the year, so we hardly see him. A quiet, sickly kind of lad he is.

"Launston came about four years ago, and built the mills. You shoulda seen when they put up the dam! It took seven months for the millpond to fill, and they do say that thousands of acres of land were flooded. 'Tis why there are so many swamps hereabouts. And Scugog Lake had been but a pond afore, and now, 'tis a large lake. Sure there are some folk that ain't pleased, but we don't complain. Without the mills there, we'd still be hauling our wheat the twenty miles to Peterborough to be ground."

Launston Mills, Dennis explained was situated on the banks of the Scugog River which flowed north from Scugog Lake and emptied into Sturgeon Lake, one of a chain of many lakes to the north. Travelling through these lakes, you could reach to within a few miles of Peterborough. Though somewhat circuitous, this was a safer way of travelling in spring than by attempting the treacherous roads.

Deirdre was not much cheered by these descriptions. She had disliked the unhealthy atmosphere of the swamps, and had found the countryside increasingly hostile these last two days. She asked Dennis about Peterborough.

"Patrick might find work there, to be sure. But there'll be carpenters there already. In Launston Mills there's a chance for him to get in on the building of the town. You'll not regret stopping there," Dennis said confidently.

But Deirdre wondered.

Chapter 3

Rowena was dumbfounded by her first glimpse of Launston Mills. Then angry. For ***this*** they had travelled more than three thousand arduous miles? For this handful of log cabins and a mill that had the audacity to give themselves a name?

Before them lay the Scugog River, a sluggish, meandering, muddy stream. Cedars and pines jostled one another for breathing space along its banks. A few clearings had been hacked out on the other side, where the cabins squatted. Rowena felt stifled by the press of trees that suppressed even the slightest breath of wind. She wanted to weep as the cart clattered across the hundred foot expanse of log bridge, ever closer to their destination.

The O'Shaughnessys had rested for two days at the O'Maras' farm, and had set out early this morning in Dennis's cart. During the six mile journey, the land had become monotonously, depressingly flat. There had been nothing on route -- or here -- to delight the eye.

"Sure, we're not meant to be staying here?" she said. If God truly intended them to live here, then His was a poor jest indeed!

Dennis chuckled and said, "'Tis never so bad. When we first arrived, there was nothing but wilderness everywhere. I reckon there hadn't been a white man set foot in these parts then. Even Peterborough was only one lonely mill and a couple of houses. But look what can be done in a few years. The same'll be true of Launston Mills. You can tell your grandchilder that your Da built the town, and it wouldn't be a word of a lie!"

There'd be no town without people, Rowena wanted to say. And who'd be daft enough to come here when there were so many pretty places elsewhere?

Dennis stopped the ox-drawn cart in front of a tall, clapboard building from which the burr of saws could be heard. The Scugog River -- what an ugly, suitable name, Rowena thought -- was like a giant lazy "S", with the small settlement nestled protectively within the second of these curves. The water churned and foamed through the waterwheel, tumbled down the shallow rapids, and became languorous once more.

"Like as not you'll find Samuel Launston here," Dennis told Patrick, "though he's more a businessman than a miller. He has a Scotsman, Cameron Abernethy, managing the gristmill, and John Blackbourne runs the sawmill. Launston has an office in here, though he's not above working alongside his men on occasion.

Likes to show 'em he can work as hard as them. Sure, and the men like him for that.

"Paxtons' Inn, Lindsays' store, and Calders' smithy are up the road aways, at the edge of the Launston property. That's where the government's laid out the new town."

When Dennis and Patrick had disappeared into the mill, Donal jumped down from the cart and announced, "I'm going for a look round." He seemed to wait for Rowena to join him, as she always did when an adventure was in the offing.

But she stayed in her seat and said, "What's to see? 'Cepting trees!"

Donal shrugged, his enthusiasm undaunted, and took off up the road.

"I'll go, too!" Gwyn said, starting to scramble down.

Deirdre grabbed her. "No you don't, lass! You'll stay here where I can keep an eye on you." To Donal she called, "Don't go far!" She had already heard from Dennis how dangerous the wilderness could be -- that even fully grown men had been known to lose their way and never be seen again.

"But I don't want to stay here!" Gwyn whined.

"You can't go wandering about here. You heard Dennis tell us that there are bears about. Why, they even come into his yard and steal pigs!" And Brenna had told Deirdre that she never left the children alone in the house when she had to go into the fields to help Dennis. Bears had been known to break into cabins.

Rowena said, "Ma, do we have to live here? Can't you talk to Da? Tell him that we hate this place?"

Deirdre shared Rowena's dislike of Launston Mills and hoped that Patrick would not find a job here. Then they could go back to Peterborough or even Cobourg, where there were churches and schools -- and open spaces. At least there you couldn't imagine bears threatening you on your very doorstep, and didn't feel hemmed in by the infernal trees. But she knew that Patrick now had these grand visions of building a town as fine as Peterborough or the others.

Her heart sank as soon as she saw his face when he emerged from the mill.

"I have me a job!" he cried. "Carpenter to the Launstons. And we've an acre of land for to call our own! Launston owns these five hundred acres here, and has sold us a lot on the riverbank, next to them cabins we saw."

"And how are we to be paying for that?" Deirdre asked, incredulous.

"Launston'll be deducting part of me wage regular till it's paid for."

"Sure there's nothing but trees there!" Deirdre protested.

"And isn't the whole country the same? We have to cut them down, and with them trees we'll build us a fine home."

Deirdre was trying to imagine how long it would take them to clear the trees and construct a cabin. When could Patrick possibly do that if he was working at a job every day? They'd never be in their house before winter -- or before the baby came.

But Dennis said, "You'll be calling a raising bee then. Everybody has them. 'Tis a big social occasion as well as a way of getting work done fast. You invite everyone -- let it be known at the tavern that you're having a bee and word will even get to the area farmers. You have to supply lots of food, Deirdre, and whiskey to keep the men happy, Patrick. They'll bring their oxen and their axes and their families. You'll get to know your neighbours, and they'll have the trees cut and the walls up in a day. They'll expect you to do the same for them when they need help haying, or barn-raising, or corn husking. 'Tis how things are done in the backwoods."

Dennis was right. Patrick used some of his last few shillings to buy several gallons of backwoods whiskey, and Deirdre cooked a long-simmering stew in a cauldron over an open fire. All eight Launston Mills families came, as well as people from nearby farms. Rowena was astonished to see so many friendly people suddenly appear to help them.

There were twenty men and more than two dozen strong boys cutting trees and hauling the logs to the building site. Here, the heavy logs were dovetailed, maneuvered into position, and stacked one atop the other. The men grouped themselves into teams, and impromptu contests of skill or speed made sport of the hard work. The woods rang with the thud of axes and the splintering crash of falling trees, with laughter and curses. It did seem like a party, Rowena thought.

The women fortified the men with cups of water and whiskey, and helped Deirdre to serve the food in shifts and wash the dishes.

It was mid-afternoon, while some men were still tucking into platefuls of stew, that Samuel Launston and his two sons came by. Rowena recognized the eldest son, Jeremy, as the reckless rider who had passed them on the way from Peterborough.

She thought his handsomeness somewhat marred by the obvious disdain with which he regarded his neighbours. His arrogant stance and bored glances suggested he was anxious to be off.

She observed Isla Calder, the blacksmith's daughter, smooth rebellious strands of hair under her bonnet as she smiled shyly in Jeremy's direction. He didn't appear to notice, but Colin Abernethy, the gristmill manager's son and Isla's betrothed, did. He scowled in Jeremy's direction.

Samuel Launston was a large, vigorous man, though neither corpulent nor brawny. His dark hair was silvered at the temples, giving him a distinguished rather than aged look. Unlike his son Jeremy, Samuel greeted people heartily.

In contrast to his father's and brother's dark, robust good looks, Adrian Launston was fair and pale and thin. He seemed interested in the proceedings, watching, almost with envy, the boys who were helping the men cut and haul the logs. Rowena thought he didn't look strong enough to pick up an axe, let alone work alongside the men.

"A fine job you men have done," Samuel Launston said. "How good it is to see our little settlement growing!"

There were nods and grunts of agreement. Patrick said, "Would you and your sons like to join us for a bite and a swig, Mr. Launston?"

"Good of you to ask, O'Shaughnessy, but we've just finished our dinner. Thought we'd come by to see if there's anything we can do, but I notice you have sufficient help."

Rowena didn't believe that the Launston had actually come to work. Although casually dressed in breeches and Hessian boots, Jeremy wore a fine white lawn shirt, and Samuel, a waistcoat and redingote as well. Most of the men -- now in their sweat-stained, dirt-encrusted flannels -- owned nothing so elegant even as their Sunday best.

When the Launstons had gone, she heard a young Irishman named Brendan Delaney say, "Thinks he a fine gentleman, that Jeremy. Wouldn't see him dirtying his lily-white hands working in the mills like his father does. And old Sam's not above bending the elbow with the likes of us, but Jeremy hardly comes near the tavern. Goes to fancy balls in Peterborough and York where he courts 'refined' young ladies 'cause our maids aren't good enough for the likes of him."

Brendan, his older brother Sean, and their friend Ewan Monaghan had recently immigrated, and all three worked at the Launston sawmill.

"Maybe they're too good for him," Ewan Monaghan said. The insinuation precipitated laughter and coarse comments.

"No doubt the good Lord will teach the boy humility in His own good time," Prudence Lindsay, the shopkeeper's wife, said in Jeremy's defence. Prudence was a brittle stick of a woman with a surprisingly deep and melodious voice.

Brendan Delaney winked slyly at her. "So he's bewitched you as well as the other lassies, eh?"

Prudence bristled. "Whist! You're the devil's spawn, Brendan Delaney!"

"That I am, m'am, and proud of it," Brendan jested.

Prudence was shocked by this blasphemy, but her reprimand was forestalled by Cameron Abernethy suggesting, "Best we finish before dark".

By dusk the walls of the house were up, and a good part of the acre had been shorn of trees, leaving behind the inevitable stumps. The enormous quantity of food that Deirdre had prepared had been devoured long ago, but suddenly a bushel of Indian corn appeared. The appreciative folk plunged the ripe, golden maize into the fire for roasting.

A hand on Deirdre's arm drew her aside. "I took the liberty of sending me childer home to fetch back some of our corn crop. As a welcoming present for you, Deirdre," Mary Ryan said. The Ryans were the O'Shaughnessys' closest neighbours.

"'Tis kind you are, Mary."

The most remarkable thing about Mary Ryan was her penetrating gaze. One tended not to notice her overlong face and sharp chin, or her slightly beaky nose, for her enormous, dark eyes, fringed with coquettish lashes, commanded attention and mesmerized. In the Old Country, Mary might well have been accused of having the evil eye, Deirdre thought.

"'Tis the least I can do for a new neighbour," Mary replied. She wrapped her arm about Deirdre's and steered her toward the fire. "Now you must try some of our corn. Our first crop it is, for we've been here but a year ourselves."

The roasted corn was delicious -- tender, sweet, and juicy. The bonfire grew bigger as branches of felled trees were heaped upon it. Logs were drawn up about its perimeter, and served as benches. Although the day was still warm, people were drawn to the fire, for there was an intimacy evoked by the glow of the blaze, and the smoke deterred the ubiquitous mosquitoes.

There was a moment of congenial silence as the brilliant, sun-splashed clouds faded to a dull, metallic blue. The hissing and spitting fire provided the only colour in the otherwise dreary grey of evening. Men thoughtfully lit pipes with fiery brands, while children laid their heads upon their mothers' laps. All eyes stared into the fire as though each were seeking his destiny there, Deirdre thought.

She herself felt strangely at ease with these people, who had, during this one long and busy day, become like old friends. And though her soul still cried out for open spaces and distant green hills, she counted herself lucky to have such good people with whom to share this new life.

The whiskey began to flow more freely. When one of the farmers struck up a tune on his fiddle, Hiram Lindsay -- shopkeeper, postmaster, and strict Methodist -- took his family home.

Mary Ryan told Deirdre, "Hiram doesn't approve of the 'devil's instrument' nor of drinking the 'devil's brew'."

"Nor of smiling," Kate Muldoon, another neighbour, added. "Sure, I've never seen so much as a grin on any of their faces. Such a dour, serious lot!"

"Aye," Mary said. "Hiram takes his responsibility for procreation serious enough, though I can hardly imagine him and Prudence coupling. I'll bet there wasn't a sound nor a sigh between them when those poor children were dutifully conceived."

Someone entreated Brendan Delaney to "Give us a song", and the young man was happy to oblige. He had a mellow, evocative tenor voice that swept up the listeners and transported them to another time and place. The haunting, poignant Gaelic ballad wrung many a tear from eyes other than her own, Deirdre noticed.

In a sudden change of mood, Brendan began a lively drinking song which whetted everyone's thirst. Even some of the women partook of a cup of whiskey. When he sang of a young woman being seduced by a stranger in the woods, Deirdre declared it was time for her children to be abed. Only Donal was allowed to stay up, since a boy of thirteen who had done a man's work that day was no longer considered a child.

Rowena protested as Deirdre ushered the girls into the roofless cabin, but her mother would not be gainsaid.

Alys, who had fallen asleep on Patrick's lap, didn't waken as her father settled her upon the straw that would serve as a temporary bed. Gwyn and Moira gratefully joined their sister and were soon fast asleep, while Rowena lay restlessly, straining to hear all that was happening outside.

The fiddler once again scraped out a tune, and Rowena listened enviously to the jovial laughter and hoots, and the scuffle of dancing feet. She crept from under the blanket that covered the four of them, and peered around the gap of the doorway. She glimpsed flashes of red flannel petticoats as the dancers whirled about in the halo of light. The faster the whiskey flowed, the faster the farmer fiddled and the people danced. To Rowena it had all the flavour of some ancient pagan ritual.

The feverish tempo made Rowena's eyelids heavy, but suddenly she was jerked back into wakefulness. In a blur of movement she had noticed Brendan Delaney steer Isla Calder away from the firelight, toward the trees. Now he lay sprawled on the ground, an incensed Colin Abernethy standing over him shouting, "You bloody papist mick! Keep your stinking hands off my girl!"

Brendan rose to his feet, laughing softly. "I'm thinking you're not man enough for her you...."

Colin pounced on Brendan, and both men began smashing one another. But Colin was no match for Brendan, who was a quick, agile, and dirty fighter.

The music ceased abruptly, and everyone watched the tussle.

Brendan was all over Colin, pummelling him with blows that he could not anticipate and had no time to ward off. As Colin fell to the ground, his face bloodied and already swelling, Brendan delivered a swift, subtle kick to his opponent's groin, causing Colin to double up in agony.

Suddenly Brendan was cornered by Isla's three brothers -- powerful young men, half a head taller than the cocky Irishman. Before Brendan could move, one of them had grabbed him from behind, pinning his arms back in a vice-like grip. The others faced him with clenched fists, the muscles of their massive blacksmiths' arms bulging.

"Been near our sister again have you, you whoring bogtrotter? Happen it's time we taught you a lesson you'll not forget!" But as the speaker's fist shot out, Sean Delaney punched the man in the ribs, deflecting the intended blow. While Ewan

Monaghan tackled the other Calder lad, Brendan rounded on his surprised captor. The cracking of fists, the thud of toppled bodies, the grunts and groans mingled with the encouraging advice, the cheers, and the profanities of the spectators.

The fighters were evenly matched, and although they seemed exhausted, neither the Irish nor the Scots would concede while they could still stagger to their feet. Patrick ended the brawl by dumping a bucket of water over the lot of them. The crowd applauded, well satisfied with the night's entertainment, and called for more grog.

Drained by the violence she had just witnessed, Rowena crawled back into bed. How senseless and stupid men were to fight, she thought. She had hoped that things would be different here, that men wouldn't insult each other because their accents were different, or fight because they believed in the same God but in different ways. But it seemed men would use any excuse to point out their differences and give them a reason to fight.

She couldn't imagine ever liking Launston Mills. And despite what her father and brother thought, there were still wealthy people like the Launstons who might not be lords in name, but who had the power and the influence that people like the O'Shaughnessys could never have.

She gazed up at the thousands of twinkling stars. At least the heavens seemed the same as in Ireland. Strange to think that this same moon smiled down on old friends and neighbours in Doneraile -- a world away from here. She tried to stay awake to share her thoughts with Donal, but fell asleep before he stumbled into his bed.

Deirdre tried to stifle yawns, and was glad when the women finally wandered home with the children, although some of the men remained behind until the last of the whiskey had been syphoned from the barrels.

She stood by the moon-silvered river, having just washed her face in the surprisingly soft water. She looked at the half-finished cabin silhouetted against the dying campfire, and felt her spirits lift, despite her weariness.

"What are you thinking, lass?" Patrick asked as he joined her.

"Just that life might be tolerable here after all," she admitted.

He hugged her to him with the exuberance of someone whose happiness is shared and thus, augmented. "It'll be a grand place. A good place to call home!"

Part 2

The Settlement

1837 - 1841

Chapter 4

Rowena awoke early. The March morning was chilly, but not as desperately cold as so many of the winter nights had been. There was no frost on the quilt this morning, nor the creaking and groaning of the timbers that characterized those bone-chilling nights.

Moira, who lay beside her, stirred and then was still again. Gwyn, Alys, and Brigid slept soundly in the bed next to her, and Rowena could hear Donal's steady breathing from the curtained alcove where he slept.

It was comforting to lie wrapped in the snug warmth of her shared bed, listening to the peaceful slumbers of the others. Soon enough the day, with its endless chores, would begin. There was little time then for idle contemplation. Weariness overcame her quickly at night; so she relished the early mornings when she could allow her thoughts to wander where they would.

One day she would recall these moments with nostalgia for the happy, uncomplicated, carefree existence it had been, or sometimes with surprise at how quickly and finally life had changed and her blissful childhood, ended. And she would wonder that there had been no premonition, no inkling of what tragedies there were to come.

As the night paled, the loft took on shape and depth where there had been only blackness. Rowena could discern the sloping rafters of the roof, stuffed with odd bits of rags where gaps invited the biting winter winds to slice through. The two gable-end windows were similarly padded against winter's onslaught. But in the summer she would be glad of what breezes would cool this attic bedroom.

That had been the most difficult thing to which they'd had to accustom themselves -- this intemperate climate. Those scorching, scalding summer days when you seemed to simmer in your own sweat. The winter nights that snatched and crystallized your breath, paining the lungs, freezing the flesh, wringing the very moisture from your eyes. There was little to choose between the insufferable heat rashes of summer and the inevitable chilblains of winter.

And yet, were they not fortunate to have come to this new land, harsh though it was? Had their lives not been better, their bellies fuller every day these past five years than on any single day before?

She needed only to picture her father to answer that. Every morning when he stepped out the door he would pause, take a deep breath, and let his eyes wander with satisfaction over his holdings. ***His*** land.

He and Donal ran their own carpentry business from the workshop in the yard, crafting furniture and coffins, mouldings and gingerbread. They'd built many a fancy veranda for prospering settlers these last years.

Deirdre herself took a fierce kind of pride in her new home, chivvying the girls through their daily cleaning chores lest the new priest or one of the neighbours stopped by in the afternoon. With amusement, Rowena thought of her mother's indignation whenever a fox made off with one of her chickens, or the rare occasions a bear carried off a piglet. When the ripening corn was sampled by flocks of crows, Deirdre would rush into the field shouting, and flapping her apron at the thieves.

Their house little resembled the pile of timber that had been erected that boisterous day of the raising bee nearly five years earlier. The cedar logs had been plastered with clay and lime, and whitewashed. A veranda, or "stoop" as it was generally called, now stretched across the front of the house like a half-closed eyelid winking at passersby. It looked lovely indeed in summer when it was entangled with creeping vines. A shed jutted out at right angles from the back of the house. One day soon, Patrick had promised, they would purchase a cast iron cookstove, and the shed would become the summer kitchen so that the fireplace would not have to be kept burning during those hot months.

But times were bad, for the last two harvests had been wet and much of the crops, ruined. Prices were already five times what they had been two years before, and some things were not to be had, even for cash -- a rare enough commodity in itself.

So the shed was still just a storage place for wood, and served also as a wash house and pantry. In the yard between the house and the river sat a motley collection of outbuildings -- a privy, an ash house, a brick bake oven, a cowshed and pigsty, and Patrick's workshop.

Rowena chuckled to think how she had detested Launston Mills when they had first arrived. She had even considered becoming a nun so that she could escape to the convent in Quebec City. But the thought of being a thousand difficult, forbidding miles from her family had quickly cured her of that impulse.

And she had soon discovered the beauty in what had seemed to her a dreary and unfriendly landscape. The cooling autumn days had brought the most spectacular colours of leaves she had ever seen. The forests around the settlement had been aflame with crimson and orange and gold. The canopy of painted leaves seemed to burn with hoarded summer light, so that even on grey days, the forest glowed. Fall had also brought migrating birds -- tens of thousands of them, so that their passing eclipsed the sun. And after the hard frosts, Indian summer had come, its soft, misty warmth a memory of summer, a last gift before winter. And even winter, harsh and bitter though it was, could be beautiful -- the trees cloaked with soft clouds of new-fallen snow, or glistening with ice, each twig bejeweled.

Rowena, hearing sounds from below, crept quietly from her bed. Her skin prickled with the damp cold. Quickly she drew her flannel petticoat over her shift and pulled on her brown homespun dress, her thick woolen stockings, and the deerskin moccasins that she wore in the house.

She descended the steep stairs that led from the loft into the one-room kitchen and living area, and found her mother already heaping wood onto the enormous backlog that still burned in the hearth. They crouched by the fire, absorbing its warmth until their stiff, chapped fingers regained dexterity, and their shivering subsided. They sipped mugs of steaming tea, which would tide them over until some of the chores had been done and breakfast, prepared.

And it wasn't until breakfast that Rowena remembered the maple sugar bee at the Winslows' that evening. Everyone was invited to attend and bring spoons to sample the thick syrup when it had been boiled down. There would, of course, be a dance in the barn to round off the evening. It was the social event of the season.

"It should be a fine evening for the sugaring," Donal said as he spread a thick layer of molasses on a hunk of cornmeal bread. Donal, at eighteen, was a handsome lad, taller than his father and broad shouldered.

Patrick agreed. "'Tis a grand way to welcome the spring. Me feet are itching for a bit of dancing."

Deirdre said to Rowena, "I'm thinking we'd best make over one of me gowns for you today. That one's uncommon tight on you now." Deirdre looked critically at her daughter's blossoming figure. Rowena would soon be seventeen.

Rowena beamed at the prospect of owning a new dress. "Which one, Ma?"

"The blue, I'm thinking. Aye, it'll do fine."

"But 'tis your next best!"

"I'd rather see it on you than stored in the box from one year to the next, mouldering away. I've got me grey silk for church and weddings and wakes, and need naught else."

Fifteen-year-old Moira looked wistfully down at her plate. With Rowena shining in a new gown, there would be even less chance than usual of Conn Ryan noticing ***her***.

Conn was the fourth born of Mary and Matt Ryan's ten children. The Ryans were the O'Shaughnessys' closest friends; Donal and Conn had long been best of pals. In the spring and summer, Conn worked with his father and older brothers at the Launston sawmill, and this past winter he had joined them at the logging camp on the Launstons' timber limits to the north. Although Rowena might still think of Conn as another brother, Moira suspected that his feelings toward Rowena had matured into something more serious.

Much as Moira loved Rowena, she sometimes raged inwardly at the injustice of having a sister who was so much prettier, so much more vivacious than she herself could ever be. She had tried everything to rid herself of the freckles that bloomed so readily in the summer sun. Vinegar washes, goose grease, strawberry juice -- nothing helped. Boys paid her little attention when Rowena was about. Even her mother.... Didn't Deirdre think that she might like a new dress? One that hadn't been Rowena's, and thus hung loosely on her smaller frame, making her appear that much younger and undeveloped. Sometimes she wondered if anyone even credited her with thoughts and feelings. She couldn't hope to compete with Rowena; so she never tried. Always in the background. Quiet, shy Moira. Meek little mouse.

Deirdre, however, was not insensitive to her daughter's feelings. Hoping to cheer her up, she said to Moira, "When we've cleaned up, I'll be wanting you and Rowena to get a few things from Lindsays'. And you can go to Yardleys' and buy yourselves a bit of ribbon. They still owe us something for the shelves your Da built, but mind you settle on a fair price."

"I want a new dress and ribbon, too!" twelve-year-old Gwyn stated.

"It'll be a while afore you outgrow the one you're wearing, and you had a new ribbon just last fall. And if there's any sulking," Deirdre added sternly, noticing Gwyn's mouth form itself into a characteristic pout, "then you'll not be going to the bee tonight, me lass!"

Rowena rushed the others through the washing up, and by the time she and Moira set out on their shopping expedition, the younger girl had become infected with her sister's lighthearted gaiety.

It was a pleasant, sunny morning with the flavour of spring in the warm, earthy smell of the air. A week of mild weather had begun to melt the snow, and the road was already dissolving into mud. But the girls were wearing their sturdy boots and calf-length skirts, which would not drag in the dirt.

There were several new houses along the riverbank. The girls passed the Launston mills, quiet still, until the winter cutting of timber was floated downstream with the melting ice. A new carding and fulling mill, owned by the Launstons, was situated on the opposite bank of the river. Farther along what was commonly called "Mill Road" was the Launstons' distillery, and beyond that, the Launstons' mansion.

It was an elegant, white frame, Loyalist style house which caught the eye and drew it along its perfectly symmetrical design. Nine tall, multi-paned windows were spaced across it, and an elliptical transom and sidelights framed the door behind the pillared portico.

Rowena knew all about the house -- the lofty, airy rooms, the graceful oak balustrades, the black walnut wainscotting -- though, of course, she had never been inside. But no expense had been spared on the house, her father had told her, and he and Donal had been proud to be a part of its creation. The furnishings, it had been rumored, had been imported all the way from England! She well remembered the flurry of activity on the dock the day those valuable items had arrived by scow. Half the men of Launston Mills had been needed to transport the large crates up to the house.

"Do you suppose Fionna will keep working at the Launstons' once she's wed?" Moira asked. Fionna Ryan, Conn's eldest sister, had recently become engaged to marry Sean Delaney.

"I don't reckon so," Rowena replied, "though I've not asked her. Speaking of weddings, maybe there'll be another afore summer's out. I've heard tell that Ewan Monaghan's sweet on Maureen Darcy."

"She's said naught of it." Moira was surprised. Although Maureen lived on a farm several miles from town, she was a close friend of the O'Shaughnessy girls. On fine winter Sundays, when there was little farm work to be done, Maureen often spent the day with the O'Shaughnessys after attending morning mass, and returned home with her family after the evening service.

"'Twas Fionna told me not two days since. Happen she'd know, Sean and Ewan being such good friends."

"Maybe Maureen knows naught of it yet."

Both girls were amused by that possibility. Rowena said. "Aye, and knowing Ewan, it'll be a month of Sundays afore she hears it from himself."

Large and powerful man though he was, Ewan Monaghan could be painfully awkward around girls to whom he'd taken a fancy, stumbling over words that came to him easily enough with others. The general consensus among the eligible girls was that the sorer your toes were after dancing with Ewan, the better he liked you.

"Will you be telling Maureen then?" Moira asked.

"Sure, if we left it to Ewan to do his own courting, we'd be taking our grandchildren to his wedding! Besides, I'm thinking that Maureen wouldn't say him nay. No harm in her giving him a nudge."

They arrived at Lindsay Street, the boundary line between the Launston property and the new town. "Victoria" the surveyors had named their paper creation. Yet, neither its citizens, nor the older settlers on the Launston tract referred to it as anything but Launston Mills. There were about two hundred residents in the settlement now. Some people had come in the intervening years only to leave again, calling the village an "unhealthy place to live" because of the many swamps in the vicinity that were thought to exude harmful vapours. But among those who had stayed, one could sense a growing pride in their community, and great expectations for its future.

And Dennis O'Mara had been right -- the settlement did grow quickly. Donal and her father had helped to build many of the new homes and shops. Rowena had to laugh at Donal sometimes, for he swaggered proudly about "his" town as if he had built it single-handedly.

The town now had two taverns, three shops, and had recently acquired a school (which served as a Methodist meeting house on Sundays), a physician, Dr. Jason Worthing, and a resident priest, Father Killeny. The Roman Catholic townspeople and area farmers had banded together last autumn to erect a log church. Deirdre had been particularly pleased with the new church, for, previously, an itinerant priest had infrequently passed through the settlement, and makeshift masses had been held in homes or barns. At least now their chances of suffering eternal damnation had been greatly reduced.

Paxtons' Inn stood on this corner of Mill Road and Lindsay Street. Main Street ran west from the tavern's front door. Hiram Lindsay's general store and post office was beside Paxtons', and next to that, the blacksmith's and then the cartwright's.

The new town presented a strange picture. Not all the surveyed, grid-like streets had been chopped out as yet, but the cleared areas were littered with stumps, so that the few shops and houses among them seemed naked. Main Street was unusually broad, and already, because it was so exposed and well travelled, churned into a muddy quagmire that would become increasingly hazardous to pedestrians, vehicles, and animals as the days grew warmer. A favourite joke among the villagers was Josh Paxton's claim that he had run a pole into the mud on Main Street the previous spring, and it had gone over twenty feet without striking solid ground.

"Look!" Moira cried.

The girls stopped, petrified, in front of the tavern. Bounding straight toward them down Main Street was a deer with a pack of wolves nipping at its heels. Moira drew closer to her sister and clutched at her frantically.

Strong arms embraced both girls from behind, startling them. "There's nothing to fear, lassies," Brendan Delaney said. "They'll not be harming you. 'Tis the buck they're after."

Rowena watched in horror as the young deer, bogged down by the rutted mud, stumbled and was pounced upon by the wolves. Its struggles ceased after a short fight, and the snarling beasts tore ravenously at their kill.

Sickened, Rowena turned away, pressing her face against Brendan's shoulder. He laughed softly as his arm tightened about her.

Suddenly a shot rang out, and another. The skittish wolves whined and growled as two of their pack, and then a third, were slain. The rest fled into the bush to the east of Simcoe Street.

"Fine bit of shooting," Brendan called to Ezra Calder, the blacksmith, as the man and his three sons emerged from the smithy.

"A tasty morsel of venison we'll be having on our table!" Ezra replied with a satisfied smile. "And three fine pelts to sell."

Rowena moved away from Brendan, though Moira still clung to him. "'Tain't a pretty sight," Brendan warned.

Rowena watched the four men drag the bleeding carcass toward the smithy. Other people appeared out of the shops and houses, and a lively discussion of the incident ensued. Close though the community was, there was always a special, if temporary, bond forged between those who had shared an extraordinary experience.

"Best we be going now," Rowena said to Moira as she took her sister's hand. She looked up at Brendan, not quite certain what to say to him, though she had been grateful for his reassuring presence. He grinned at her.

"You've grown some since last I saw you," he observed, running his eyes appraisingly over her. "It does me heart good to see two such pretty faces after a long winter in the bush." Both Brendan and his brother, Sean, had been at the lumber camp. "Will you be going to the Winslows' this evening?"

"Aye."

"Then I'll be expecting you to save me a dance." He tipped his hat jauntily at them and walked back into the tavern.

"Do you like Brendan Delaney then?" Moira asked, noticing Rowena's smirk.

"He's a fine looking man, to be sure," Rowena replied, thinking of his bold, admiring glance, and discovering that she was not averse to his attentions. She had always liked Brendan, but now she was seeing him in a new and rather exciting perspective. A girl could do worse than marry Brendan Delaney.

"Aye, but he's a rascal with women."

"And what would you be knowing about that?" Rowena asked as they stepped carefully across the road and onto the plank walk on Main Street.

"'Tis what Ma said. I heard her and Mrs. Ryan talking about him just t'other day. Seems that Shelagh Ryan's taken a fancy to Brendan, and Mrs. Ryan was saying, wouldn't it be a fine thing if they was to wed, seeing as how Fionna's to be marrying Sean. And Ma was saying that Shelagh'd best watch herself with Brendan, him being such a rascal with the girls and as like as not to break poor Shelagh's heart."

"Maybe he'll be thinking of marrying then, himself being four and twenty already. 'Tis nothing to me."

The subject was dropped as they entered Yardleys' Dry Goods shop. Mr. and Mrs. Yardley and several customers were engaged in idle conversation around the cast iron box stove which squatted on curved legs in the centre of the room. Rowena could feel the dry heat of it from the doorway.

The shop was cluttered with merchandise. The shelves along one wall displayed a variety of china and stoneware dishes, glasses, lamps, Britannia and even some silver cutlery. Hats were to be seen behind glass, as were collars, and a few ready-made garments hung in a corner. Boots, brooms, wallpaper, kettles and pans, cooking and gardening implements, box stoves and cooking stoves, and even books and dolls were available here.

"Good morning to you, Mrs. Yardley," Rowena said.

"And a lovely morning it is," the proprietress replied. "Did you see that ghastly incident which took place outside my window not five minutes ago?"

"To be sure, we did."

"The nerve of those beasts to threaten us on our very doorstep! Why, I could hardly believe my eyes! The Calders will be eating their fill of venison, though I'd not care to touch what those filthy, slavering beasts had killed. Why, supposing they had the rabies!" A shudder passed through the room. "They do say that the critters become bold as you please when the sickness lays hold of them. Mind you, it isn't as though the Calders were bitten by them, like poor old Obediah Miller, God rest his soul." She paused to allow the others to recall the unfortunate man's gruesome death. "But I'd not care to take such a chance! Ah, well... What can I do for you, girls?"

"We'd like to buy two lengths of ribbon, one for Moira and one for meself, if you please, Mrs. Yardley."

"Certainly. Now what will you have? Velvet? Satin?" Mrs. Yardley produced large spools in an assortment of colours and fabrics, and the girls deliberated over their choices. Moira finally decided upon a broad moss-green satin, and Rowena, a sky-blue velvet. Mrs. Yardley approved. "They match your eyes exactly, girls. Will you be needing anything else? We've some delightful new materials in the most beautiful colours," she said, with a sweeping gesture in the direction of the bales. "Some muslin for summer, perhaps?"

It was a strong temptation, but Rowena said firmly, "No thank you, Mrs. Yardley. This'll be all for today."

Rowena and the proprietress dickered over the price of the ribbons until both were satisfied. The agreed amount was duly deducted from the O'Shaughnessys' credit.

Business concluded, Mrs. Yardley asked, "And how are your folks?"

"Tolerable well, thank you, though Da's got a touch of the rheumatism in his back."

Mrs. Yardley nodded knowingly. "It's the damp cold that brings it on. Mr. Yardley suffers from the same affliction. What's your father doing for it?"

He's using one of Ma's liniments."

"Tell him to try mustard plasters. There's nothing like mustard for stirring up the blood and drawing out the pain."

"And a hot mustard bath when nowt else works," Mrs. Abernethy chimed in.

Mattie Abernethy, wife of the gristmill manager, was a large freckled woman with frizzy red hair that invariably sprang from its bonds, giving her a frenzied appearance that was totally at odds with her sanguine character. Mattie competed with Deirdre for the status of local midwife and herbalist, although there was no true rivalry between them. The Scots and English consulted Mattie, and the Irish consulted Deirdre, who had been their only medical help until the recent arrival of Dr. Worthing. Many people were still wary of physicians -- the Methodists mistrusted them completely -- so the two women's custom had suffered little as yet. Their advice was respected, for were there not many who could attest to the benefits of their various tisanes, infusions, poultices, and liniments?

"What good are doctors?" Mattie was wont to say when given the opportunity. "They bleed you and fill you with foul concoctions that are as like as not to make your belly rebel, when what you really need is a tonic to strengthen and purify the blood and set your humours to rights. Why, if you've an injured limb they'd as lief relieve you of it as try to mend it." Of course, no one ever reminded Mattie of Archie MacPherson, whose crushed leg, despite her poultices, had become gangrenous and had resulted in his early demise. What Mattie couldn't cure, well... that was the will of God.

The door opened, and the O'Shaughnessy girls were pleasantly surprised to see Maureen Darcy enter the shop. Maureen was a pretty, buxom girl with languid brown cow's eyes, a ruddy complexion, and brown curls as bouncy as her personality. "And what would you be doing in town on a Saturday morning?" Rowena asked her friend.

Maureen grinned. "Ribbons, is it," she said, spying them in Rowena's shopping basket.

"And what would you be getting for the bee tonight?" Rowena said shrewdly.

"A new bonnet!" exclaimed Maureen, laughing at the other girls' raised eyebrows. "Da says I'm to be putting up me hair. So, I'll be needing a new bonnet to fit it, won't I?"

For a girl to put up her hair was a leap into womanhood, and a declaration of her eligibility for marriage. Rowena thought of her own waist-long tresses caught back with the new ribbon with which, until a moment ago, she had been so pleased. Now she would look childish next to Maureen with her adult coif and store-bought bonnet, though the girls were of an age.

Mrs. Yardley, who seemed to have the ability to participate in one conversation and listen to another, joined the girls, saying, "I have just the bonnet for you, Maureen! The latest style, of course."

Maureen produced a basket from beneath her heavy shawl, and set it gently upon the counter. She rummaged through the straw to expose a clutch of eggs, and said, "Da sent these for you. The hens are laying again, now the weather's warming."

Mrs. Yardley wrinkled her brow. Hastily Maureen added, "Da says there'll be butter come Wednesday, and Hugh'll be bringing the eggs in as usual now."

Mrs. Yardley opened a hatbox, and lifted out a creation so stunning that all three girls gasped in awe. It was a wide-brimmed, brown velvet bonnet bedecked with pink satin flowers, and tied with pink ribbons. Maureen picked it up as though it were more fragile than the eggs she had just handled. She set it carefully upon her head, her normally rosy cheeks flushed even more than usual.

Mrs. Yardley tilted the hat so that it perched at a more rakish angle. "It'll be easier to keep it on properly once you've a chignon to secure it to," the proprietress said, setting a small mirror before Maureen. "There now! Didn't I say it would suit you?"

Rowena and Moira were as surprised by the transformation as Maureen. Rowena knew that she could never own anything so exquisite. Sometimes she felt that Maureen, being the only girl in a family of eight, was overly cossetted. And yet, she did not really begrudge her friend these extravagant indulgences.

"Mind you," Mrs. Yardley said, "this one'll cost you a fair bit more. I've others, of course, though none to match this." She laid several more bonnets upon the counter, much plainer and more serviceable that the one that Maureen removed so reluctantly from her head.

"Will you look at that now!" Mattie Abernethy exclaimed. She was staring out the window, and the others crowded about her.

A young woman was stepping gingerly across the road, trying to hold her voluminous skirts out of the mud. It was Colonel Grimsby's daughter, Amelia. The Colonel, a half-pay officer, and his family had moved to Launston Mills the previous summer.

Amelia was having difficulty. It appeared that one of her shoes was stuck fast in the mud.

"Where do you think her ladyship's stepping out to?" Mr. Yardley jested. "You'd think she was meeting the Governor himself, the way she's dressed."

The others agreed. No one in Launston Mills was ever so elaborately embellished as Amelia Grimsby. They watched in amusement as she tried vainly to extricate herself from the tenacious mire.

And then Jeremy Launston appeared on the scene. He strode out to the frustrated young lady, dislodged her shoe, and scooped her into his arms -- much to the amazement and delight of the spectators. They quickly dispersed to the rear of the shop as Jeremy set Amelia down on the Yardleys' doorstep.

The bells jingled as the door opened.

"I shall be only a few minutes," Amelia was saying to her rescuer as they entered. "I do so appreciate your offer to escort me home, Jeremy. I hadn't realized that the roads were in such an appalling state! I've quite ruined my velvet shoes, I'm afraid. Ah, Mrs. Yardley.... I understand that you have received a new shipment of fabrics. Mama would so have liked to come, but she's confined to her bed, poor darling. It's this unhealthy climate, don't you know. Oh, that grey silk is lovely!" She gestured at one of the bales with an elegant sweep of her gloved hand. Mrs. Yardley promptly displayed her most costly materials on the counter, brushing aside the forgotten bonnets. "I'm certain Mama would adore this. Fifteen yards of that should do splendidly, don't you think? As for myself, I'm quite partial to this lavender-sprigged muslin... though this shot silk is quite divine." Amelia laughed. "Perhaps I shall take them both!"

Rowena, Moira, and Maureen watched these proceedings from a corner of the room, staring enviously at Amelia's fur-trimmed pelisse and soft green cashmere gown. Amelia gave the impression of beauty upon first sight, but closer examination revealed that her aristocratic nose was too long, her chin receded, and her colouring was so fair that her eyelids seemed lashless. And yet, her face was usually so animated that one overlooked the flaws. Her smile was contagious; her laughter, a musical trill.

Jeremy Launston stood patiently and somewhat disinterestedly near the door. He was a devilishly handsome man, Rowena thought, with those high, arched eyebrows, sensuously droopy eyelids, and the dark hair that curved provocatively about the nape of his neck. His hazel eyes caught hers, and she looked away in embarrassment.

"What I wouldn't give to have her wardrobe," Maureen whispered on a sigh, watching Amelia.

Rowena said, "Sure, Ewan couldn't afford to keep you then."

"Ewan Monaghan? What is it you're not saying, Rowena?"

"I've heard tell that Ewan's anxious to be dancing with you tonight."

"And are my feet likely to be trod on?" Maureen asked with a grin.

"If I were you I'd be wearing me sturdiest boots, to be sure!"

Maureen's laugh died on a gasp.

Amelia Grimsby was twirling the precious velvet bonnet about with interest. "It's rather attractive, don't you agree, Jeremy?"

The shop's patrons, no longer pretending to converse while covertly watching the proceedings, turned their eyes upon Jeremy to await his judgement.

"Quite suitable, I'm sure," was his noncommittal reply.

"The brown and pink will set off your fair colouring nicely, Miss Grimsby," Mrs. Yardley said.

"Hm. It's not quite ***de rigueur***, is it? Somewhat plain, don't you think? Some ostrich plumes perhaps. Pink, of course. I do believe I have some at home that I could use. Yes, that would make it quite acceptable for everyday. I do tire of bonnets so quickly, don't you know. I'll not bother to try it on now. I'm sure Mr. Launston has more pressing matters to attend to. Just send it with the fabrics and if I find it unsuitable after all, I shall return it myself." Amelia swept from the room. Jeremy nodded to the patrons and followed her.

"How could she!" Maureen said angrily, watching Mrs. Yardley return the prized bonnet to its nest. She marched up to the counter. "Mrs. Yardley, you should have told her the bonnet was spoken for!"

"Now, Maureen, I couldn't be sure, could I? I'm certain it's a trifle more expensive than even your father would allow, though I know how generous he is with you. One of the others will suit even better. You need something to set off your brown hair -- this green felt, I think. And..." She drew out a box from beneath the counter. "...if we attach a silk posy, it'll be just as fetching as the other. At half the cost."

"'Tisn't the same."

Mrs. Yardley tut-tutted as she set about decorating the hat.

Rowena and Moira said their goodbyes and left. Having dawdled longer than they had intended, they rushed over to Lindsays', purchased the few items their mother had requested, and hurried home.

The O'Shaughnessys' midday dinner was enlivened by the girls' detailed account of the morning's diversions. Deirdre and the children were wide-eyed with horror at the tale of the wolves, though Patrick and Donal were amused. They all laughed at the story about Amelia Grimsby.

"Maybe Mr. Jeremy will soon be taking a wife," Deirdre said.

"Aye," Patrick said. "Though I can't see him choosing a flibbertigibbet like that young lady."

"There's no accounting for a young man's fancies. I feel sorry for the maid meself. She's been gently bred and not used to the hard life of the backwoods." Deirdre shook her head. "Walking about in velvet shoes at this time of the year! She's a fish out of water, that one."

"Not like the Colonel. Never seen such a man for hunting and fishing."

"'Tis always harder on the womenfolk."

"Are you speaking from experience then, Dre?"

"Sure, I suppose it grows on you, this wild country," she replied with a grin. She had long since forgiven Patrick for uprooting them from Ireland and transplanting them here. She even had to admit that Liam O'Mara's letter hadn't been the outrageous lies she had initially thought. But best of all was seeing her children happy and well-fed. Even Donal seemed content working with Patrick, and carving his beautiful wooden birds in his spare time. And the way he'd been eyeing Rosemary

Flannery lately, it wasn't likely that he itched to stray far from town. Yes, Deirdre thought, she had a lot to be thankful for.

At the tale of Maureen Darcy's new bonnet, Deirdre commented, "'Tisn't right, that girl having no mother, being the only female out on that farm amongst eight men, and having the burden of them to reckon with."

Patrick said, "She's got the hired girl to help her out."

"I'd not be giving a farthing for that strumpet! She does naught but wriggle her fanny at the men, hoping for to get her claws into one of the Darcy boys, I'll warrant. Where do you suppose Alec found her? Some gutter in York is where!"

"Toronto, it's called now, Ma," Donal interrupted.

But Deirdre continued as though she hadn't heard. "Said he'd had enough of them orphanage girls, the first one up and dying like she did, and the second, running off with a tinker. But the slut he's got working there now isn't fit company for his daughter. Sure, what would Alec Darcy be knowing about raising a girl anyway? He's got no sense when it comes to women. Worked his poor wife into her grave, and now ruins his lass by giving her whate'er she fancies. And there's many a foolish notion that Maureen gets into her head. Comes from those American ladies' magazines Alec buys for her. Sure, she can't even read! He'd do better sending her to school and getting hisself a wife to run his house."

Deirdre was proud that her children possessed at least the rudimentary skills of reading and ciphering. There were many, like Alec Darcy, who didn't hold with book learning, particularly for girls. But Deirdre felt that it must be a great pleasure and comfort to be able to read the Bible, and for this reason alone, had insisted that her children have the opportunity that she herself had never had.

Two years ago, a shabby, eloquent man named Isaac Swindon had wandered into town with a pile of books beneath his arm, and had announced himself to be a teacher. He had taken up temporary residence in an abandoned shanty on the edge of town, where he had accepted pupils for fifty cents a month. Nearly sixty children had come that first week, not only from the town, but from farms as far as five miles away. Rowena, Moira, Gwyn, and Alys had been among the close-pressed bodies squeezed into the tiny room.

The townspeople had known little about the middle-aged schoolmaster, except that he had spent every evening at Paxtons'.

Upon learning this, the Methodists had immediately removed their children from his wicked influence, and had set about procuring a "real" teacher and a proper schoolhouse.

The cold and snows of winter had further depleted the enrollment, and seasonal ailments had kept the class size fluctuating around twenty. It had been a crude school, with snow squeezing through the cracks to form small drifts that never melted in the chill of the cabin. But a school it had been nonetheless, and the children had learned.

But it had been short-lived. On a cold February morning following a fierce blizzard, the faithful had trudged through the deep snow only to discover that Isaac Swindon was not at home, and that there were only dead ashes in the grate. Investigation had revealed that Isaac had, as usual, spent his evening at Paxtons', and had departed after his customary number of whiskeys -- with an extra shot to keep out the chill. So it had generally been assumed that some unknown misfortune had befallen him on his homeward journey, although some had maintained that, shiftless vagabond that he was, Isaac had simply absconded with the money that his students had already paid for the month. (The fact that his valuable books had still been in the shanty had made not a whit of difference to the adherents to this theory.)

There were those who had even gone so far as to suggest that Isaac had been the devil incarnate come to lead the children astray. Had he not come from nowhere and disappeared likewise, during a storm that only hell's fury could have unleashed? If some accident had befallen him, then why had his body not been found? Had not the Winslows' cow's milk curdled in her teats the very day Isaac had arrived in town? Hadn't young Mary Jane Bexley told her father she hadn't known how it was that she came to be increasing, unless it had been the devil who had done it to her? Fool though she was, no one had believed her ignorance, and the poor girl had drowned herself in the river. There had been a thousand and one ailments and accidents that could suddenly be explained.

It was not surprising, perhaps, that during that merciless winter, during those relentless, grey February days, this idea had appealed to the fancy of many -- to the point that even a grown man had been loathe to travel alone on those blustery nights, lest the devil return for one more victim.

But Deirdre would have none of it. Had not Isaac been kind, and patient with the children? Had he not used the Bible to teach them to read?

On a mild day in mid-March the mystery had been solved. The frozen body of Isaac Swindon had been found in a melting snowdrift not more than two hundred yards from his cabin. A mere mortal after all. Drunk, and blinded by the snow, he had lost his bearings and wandered aimlessly until exhaustion had claimed him, and the cold had lulled him into a fatal sleep, to be shrouded by the snow.

Since Father Killeny's arrival, classes for the Catholic children had been held in the new church on Mondays and Fridays, and the O'Shaughnessy girls attended those now.

After the remnants of the dinner had been cleared away, Deirdre set the girls to their tasks Gwyn and Alys to mending, and Moira to teaching four year old Brigid the skill of knitting -- while she and Rowena dealt with the gown. Deirdre fetched the dress from the chest at the foot of her bed. Rowena slipped into it, catching a whiff of the rosemary that Deirdre kept in the box to scent the clothes and deter the moths.

"The top'll do fine," Deirdre said, surprised that the bodice fitted her daughter more snugly than it did herself. "The waist'll have to come in a mite." She pinched a fold between her fingers and pinned it. "And the hem'll have to come up."

Rowena lifted the wide, floor-length skirt and stepped onto a chair. "But not too much, Ma," she said, fearing that Deirdre would insist upon shortening it to the childish mid-calf length. "It'll not look right too short."

"I reckon you're right. You're too old for to be showing your legs, at any rate."

"'Tis a lovely gown," Moira said to Rowena, suppressing her envy. "It looks grand on you."

"I think it's beautiful," eight-year-old Alys exclaimed. "Oh, Rena, you look like a princess!"

Gwyn said, " 'Tisn't fair that Rena's always getting new things, and all I ever get is Moira's hand-me-downs that ***she*** got from Rena."

"The sooner you learn that the world don't turn for you alone, my girl, the better off you'll be," Deirdre said. "Life isn't always 'fair'. It makes you no promises when you're born, 'cepting that one day you'll die. If the good Lord feels you've been hard done by in this life, well then you'll be getting your dues in heaven."

"But I won't be needing a new dress then, will I?" Gwyn mumbled.

The other girls, sensitive to Deirdre's anger, which Gwyn could so easily arouse, looked warningly at their sister. Truly, Rowena thought, Gwyn seemed almost determined sometimes to annoy her mother, and certainly never learned when to keep her thoughts to herself. This time was no exception.

But Deirdre had heard her. "So long as you've food in your belly and clothes on your back, you've no call for to complain! 'Tis more than I had many a day when I was your age."

Gwyn pressed her lips together, and raised her eyes to the ceiling.

"And you can take that look off your face, miss, or I'll be doing it for you -- with the back of me hand! And you mind what I said afore about the bee. If it's not satisfied you are to be going in the clothes you have, then you'll not be needing to go at all. And that's an end to it!"

There was silence. Deirdre tugged hard on the hem of the gown before flipping it under and securing the fold with a pin. Gwyn, her face screwed into a frown, stabbed her needle into the sock she was darning.

Gwyn really was a greedy little brat, Rowena thought, watching her sister. She would eat as though someone were about to steal her plate, as though she could never assuage her hunger. Always wanting more -- be it food, clothes, or attention. As diligent as she was in these pursuits, so was she lazy when it came to chores and lessons and anything for which there was no tangible reward. A queer one, was Gwyn.

"Turn to your right," Deirdre ordered.

Rowena did, and found herself confronted with her own reflection in the small shaving mirror on the mantle. She could see the high neck of the gown, adorned with a white muslin collar, and the shoulders of the slightly puffed sleeves that tapered down to the wrists, ending in tight muslin cuffs. The colour -- the deep blue of a stormy summer sky -- suited her well, she thought, emphasizing the blueness of her eyes, setting off her black hair far better than her old brown Sunday dress did.

On an impulse she twisted her heavy tresses into a rope, and experimentally coiled it into a topknot. She smiled with pleasure at this suddenly older Rowena who grinned back at her.

"If you'll not be keeping still," Deirdre muttered through the pins clamped between her teeth, "then this hem'll be wandering every which way."

"I thought vanity was a sin, Ma," Gwyn said, "and there's Rena, posing and grimacing at herself in the mirror."

Deirdre looked up and frowned. "You needn't go thinking that, 'cause I'm letting you wear your skirts longer, I'll be letting you put up your hair. You'll be growing up fast enough, and there's no call for to rush it. And it makes no never mind to me what Maureen Darcy does, or any of the other girls, come to that."

"Yes, Ma." Rowena released her hold on her hair, watched it tumble down about her shoulders, and combed her fingers through it.

"And you can stop primping before the looking glass. Gwyn's quite right."

"Yes, Ma." How her fingers itched to wipe that smug grin from Gwyn's face.

Although she chafed at the fetters of childhood, the matter of the hair did not truly bother Rowena. It was the dress that was important to her. She looked down at the wide skirt, and thought that she would need to wear extra petticoats to give it the proper fullness.

"That's close enough to even, I reckon," Deirdre said of the hem. "You can step out of it now. Mind the pins."

Rowena delighted in the feel of the fine, soft wool beneath her fingers as she stitched. It was so unlike to coarse homespun to which she was accustomed.

Patrick often received raw wool in payment for his handiwork, and the O'Shaughnessy girls had learned to transform this into yarn through the tedious processes of carding, spinning, and dyeing. The wool was then given to the weaver, Alistair McDougal, from whose loom they would receive the bolt of rough flannel known as homespun. After fulling, this cloth would be carved up with no regard for fashion, and sewn into dresses, trousers, shirts, petticoats, cloaks, and blankets. The heavier skeins of wool were knitted into socks, stockings, shawls, mitts, and scarves.

Only the cambric for summer dresses and undergarments was store-bought. And this imported wool.

"Will you listen to the wind, then," said Deirdre, pausing in her sewing to stretch her back. All the girls stopped working to listen, though they could hear the howling wind readily enough, could feel it tugging at the cabin, could see it, now sucking on the chimney so that the flames grew higher, then blowing down it to send sparks and soot swirling about and smoke filling the room.

"It'll bring snow afore the day's out, I'll warrant. 'Tis getting so's I can smell it coming. Sure, no matter how long the good Lord sees fit to spare me, I'll never get used to these winters. Snow for over half the year!"

"Will it mean we can't go sugaring?" Alys asked.

"Nay, lass. The snow'll make no never mind to the bee. We'll just be dressing warmer is all."

There was a chatter of excited anticipation as the girls dressed in their Sunday best and helped one another with their hair. When all were ready, Deirdre drew Rowena aside and said with a smile, "There now, even Amelia Grimsby doesn't look as grand in all her fine frills."

"'Tis lovely, Ma!" Rowena hugged her mother, and then twirled about happily.

"I dare say you'll be dancing the night away." Deirdre paused, searching for words. "Though you'd best be watching those lads. Don't let them be taking any liberties. 'Specially that Brendan Delaney. Aye, now there's a smooth-talking divil that's turned many a poor girl's head. Just keep your wits about you."

"Yes, Ma."

After a hurried supper, the O'Shaughnessys called upon the Ryans, and the two families, joined by the Delaney brothers and Ewan Monaghan, walked the two miles to the Winslow farm.

The wind had abated, but had brought with it cold Arctic air. The falling snow whitewashed the dirty browness that would soon enough dominate the landscape. Spring was not a pleasant season here, not until much later when mayflowers bloomed and grasses greened and the leaves unfurled to brighten the bleakness.

The men carried lanterns, for the road presented many obstacles to the unwary traveller. The mud, moulded into hills and valleys these past few days, had hardened thus, and lurked deceptively beneath the fresh snow. Rowena walked particularly carefully, mindful of the unaccustomed length of her skirt, so fearful of dirtying the hem. When she slipped on a patch of ice, she would have fallen headlong into the snow had not Brendan Delaney been so quick to grab her.

"Steady on, lass," he said with a chuckle. Rowena hadn't realized how close behind her he had been. "I've a free arm, if you've a mind to take it."

"Get away with you, Brendan!" she said, hoping that her mother hadn't heard his quip. To walk arm in arm with a man was a virtual declaration of courtship.

Though the light from the lanterns was weak, it was reflected by the snow, which extended the dim aura of light. Rowena could see well enough to note Shelagh Ryan staring at her. Shelagh turned away a moment later to talk to her sister Fionna, and Rowena wondered if that look of hatred on Shelagh's face had been only a trick of the light after all.

Rowena had never got on particularly well with Shelagh, although there was only a few months difference in their ages. Shelagh took after her mother in appearance, with her glossy black hair, intense, dark eyes, and elongated face, but she could look quite pretty when she allowed her face to relax into a smile and her eyes to sparkle. She was obsessed with the misconception that everyone else in the world was happier and more fortunate than she, and so focussed her resentment of this on a hated few, like Rowena. She begrudged others their happiness, and belittled their accomplishments. Shelagh could hardly be more unlike her easy-going eldest brother, Fergus, the gentle Conn, or her fun-loving sister, Fionna. Even Owen, cynical though he was, possessed some generosity of spirit. Rowena avoided Shelagh's company whenever possible.

"You're looking grand tonight, Rowena," Conn said, falling into step with her. Hastily he added, "Not that you don't always... look grand, I mean. 'Tis just...."

"I thank you for the compliment, Conn," she replied, suppressing a giggle. "Sure, 'tis good to have you back!"

"'Tis thankful I am to be here," he said seriously.

"How was it at the lumber camp?"

Despite the falling snow, Conn removed his cap, and ran his fingers through his springy red curls. It was a nervous habit of his that Rowena found rather endearing. It made him appear like a bewildered little boy.

"'Tis hard work. And lonesome. Sure, I don't mind telling you, Rena, I've no liking for the lumber camp. 'Tis too long a time for a man to be away from kith and kin."

"Sure, and wasn't your own Da there, and Fergus and Owen, and half your friends besides? I'll wager you had a grand time an' all!"

"Nay." Conn shook his head as he stared down at his feet. "'Tis no life for any man, being stuck out in the bush for nigh on six months, one day no different from the next. Same slops, same company. It can drive a man mad." He paused. "I seen it. He was a new immigrant. Never been in the bush at all. 'Twas after a cold day out logging. The lads were warming themselves with a drop of whiskey -- though the boss, now, he was that strict about us not drinking much. Some were singing, and some even dancing a jig to get the blood flowing again. Then, all of a sudden, this fellow -- who'd took more'n his fair share of the grog -- starts screaming like a banshee. Near turned me blood to ice, I can tell you. Brendan starts shaking him, see. Not rough like, but just trying to snap him out of it. Sure, if the fellow don't stop screaming and plows his fist into Brendan's gut, and himself not expecting it. He fell hard he did, and the madman pounces on him fit to kill. It took six men to drag him off. But he got away from them and started smashing everything that came to hand -- tables, chairs, bunks -- cursing and swearing all the while. The others were as stunned as scared now, see, and none tried to stop him, for there was a wild look in his eye. The next we knew, he burst out the door with naught but the clothes on his back. Sure, we went out after him, followed his tracks as best we could. But the men's footprints were all over the woods, so we never found him. Nor seen him since.

"The worst of it is that I know how he felt." There was an pained look in Conn's eyes. "Many's the time I wanted to do just that. 'Tis frightening, Rena."

Gently she said, "But you didn't do it, Conn. 'Tis a wonder we don't all feel like doing that at times. Sure, that doesn't mean we're all mad. 'Tis just cabin fever -- nothing for you to fret about, Conn. 'Tis over now."

"Aye. Till next winter. I shouldn't have troubled you with me thoughts, Rena. Forgive me."

"Nay, 'tis best to speak them, and not be letting them fester in your brain. There's naught to forgive. 'Tis best to forget it and enjoy yourself."

Conn grinned. "That I will. And will you be saving a dance for me?"

"As many as you please!"

In the forest outside the town the road was more firmly packed with snow, and the walking, easier. They were passed by the Calders in their "jumper", a low, ox-drawn sled, and then by Major Selfridge, the local sheriff, and his three children in their horse-drawn sleigh, the bells jingling gaily as they bounced along.

Suddenly the sleigh hit something, and the pedestrians watched in amazement as it overturned, tossing its occupants into a snowbank. The men hastened to offer assistance, and found the four Selfridges helpless with laughter at their misadventure. None of them was hurt, for the snow had cushioned their landing. The two girls and their young brother were tugging at their father's arms, but the corpulent Major was stuck in the wet snow. The Irishmen soon had him on his feet.

"Much obliged. Much obliged. Damned nuisance, these infernal roads," the Major said good-naturedly.

The men righted the sleigh, which had suffered only superficial damage, and the Selfridges were once again on their way.

The others laughed heartily. "What a spectacle!" Sean Delaney said. "The Major up to his ears in snow!"

"There's many as wouldn't have been amused in his position," said Matt Ryan.

"Aye," agreed Patrick. "He's a likeable man, to be sure."

"I heard tell," Mary Ryan said, "that he's a mite queer in his ways. Hisself and the childer dress special for dinner and drink wine with their meal!"

"He may be a bit eccentric, but he's no prig," Brendan Delaney said.

"I heard tell he's been letting his eldest girl be courted by Farmer Corbin's son, Angus," Fionna informed them. "That'd be like Amelia Grimsby associating with, say, our Fergus."

"Jaysus Christ!" her brother replied. "You'd not be wishing that creature on me!"

"Did you hear what happened outside Yardleys' this morning then?" Donal said.

Rowena was called upon to relate her version of the event, although the story had already made the rounds of the village.

"There's some folk as weren't meant to live in the bush," Matt Ryan stated when Rowena had finished.

"Aye, and them thinking they're still in the Old Country, and that it's their God given right to be ordering others about and be waited on by poorer folk," Ewan Monaghan said heatedly.

"But they learn quick enough that this is a democratic country, and if they forget, we'll just have to be reminding them," Brendan Delaney said.

"We've a long way to go yet afore we have democracy in this country," Matt said. "You've only to go down to Toronto to see that. 'Tis a handful of uppercrust Englishmen that's running this country -- to ruin. They keep the best land for theirselves, and line their pockets with gold."

"You've the truth of it, right enough," Sean Delaney said. "Just look at that jumped-up Anglican preacher, Strachan. Thinks he's Christ Almighty hisself. Runs the damned Council with his disciples -- Anglican Tories, every last one of 'em -- making laws to suit theirselves, and vetoing bills passed by the Assembly that we vote in. And the Governor -- sure, 'tis said he'll not have a shit without asking Strachan first."

The girls tittered at this crude remark, but the women ignored it, well used to the men's obscenities.

Matt said, "But there's many folk that won't stand for it, like Willy Mackenzie. Now there's a man who's not afeard to speak his mind, nor of putting a flea in the ear of the Tories."

"And don't they know it!" Ewan said. "He's put the fear of God into them for sure, or they'd not have been harassing the man as they have. Why, did you know they even tried to assassinate him, not once, but twice? 'Tis his luck he's got so many loyal supporters, for I've heard he's a leprechaun of a fellow hisself, and wouldn't last long when the Tory bullyboys -- Orangemen, every last one! -- come to rough him up."

"But will he be doing anything, or is it no more than Scotch blarney?" Brendan said. "Nothing's ever done by talk -- we know that well enough from the Old Country. 'Tis action that speaks the loudest, and 'tis the only thing the damned English understand."

"May the Saints preserve us!" Deirdre cried. "Didn't we come to this country to get away from the fighting?"

"A man has to stand up for his rights," Brendan countered. "Sure, this country ain't all that different from Ireland, is it? 'Cepting here they'll sell you a bit of land to keep you quiet. Look at the Launstons now. Got their 500 acres free, just for knowing the right people. Then they sell us a bit of it, making a bundle of money for theirselves, keeping us bound to them by a mortgage and feeling beholden for their 'generosity'. There's always them that's ready to take advantage of weaker folk. I reckon the good Lord was a mite confused when he said, 'The meek shall inherit the earth', for 'tis always been the strong that survived."

"That's blasphemous talk, Brendan Delaney, and I'll not have it!" Deirdre said angrily.

Donal said quietly, as if the woods had dangerous ears, "They do say Mackenzie's planning a rebellion. Mike Flannery has it from his uncle, who lives near Toronto. Says Mackenzie's recruiting men."

Deirdre shuddered, as if someone had walked over her grave, and she was seized with fear. She didn't want Donal to think about such things -- even to know about them. Toronto, a hundred miles to the south-west, had seemed impossibly far away. Until now.

Another sleigh skimmed by; its occupants, the Finches, waved gaily at the pedestrians.

"The Finches seem to be settling in alright," Patrick said. Sensing Deirdre's unease, he changed the topic, hoping that her evening wouldn't be ruined by talk of politics and violence. "Sure, I had me doubts when they first come, but they're not too proud to ask other folk for advice, nor of joining in."

"That's as may be," Mary Ryan said, "but I still have me doubts they'll survive here. Sure, ifn't they be the most helpless looking pair I ever clapped me eyes on! Been used to servants, they have." To Mary, that explained everything there was to say about the newest members of their community.

Edward and Margaret Finch - and their two children, Tom and Anne - had bought a farmstead just north of town, last autumn. They had arrived from England in summer, and Edward had spent weeks looking for an established farm to buy, since he'd had no wish to clear land or build a house. But those down at the Front had been too costly, and so he had decided on the old MacPherson place, which the Launstons had bought from the widow a few months earlier.

Deirdre said, "I've heard tell she's managing fine, though he's not particularly handy."

"Aye," Ewan said. "He comes into Paxtons' often enough. Claims he's as helpless as a babe when it comes to farming, but says he's willing to give it a try. Likeable fellow."

Mary said, "Aye, well... If you ask me, ***she's*** a mite uppity. Doesn't like his easy way with folk, neither. They're a mismatched pair if ever I saw one -- her so staid and serious, and him so happy-go-lucky."

"Irresponsible, I'd call him," Deirdre said. "I reckon she's the sensible one in that family."

They passed the Winslows' farmhouse, and followed the trail into the bush from whence they heard the cheerful crackling of the fires, and saw their welcome glow throw fitful light into the surrounding darkness of the woods. There were already a good number of villagers and other farmers gathered about the huge copper kettles that hung over the flames.

A great deal of hard work and time had been expended collecting the sap from the maple trees, hauling it to this central place, and boiling it down to a thin syrup which had then been clarified. But the sugaring-off was the highlight, and children and adults alike watched the bubbling molasses with mouth-watering anticipation.

The crowd grew larger and more boisterous. Even Hiram Lindsay and his family were there, though they would leave as soon as the dancing commenced. Rowena felt truly sorry for the eight Lindsay children, for their stern father frowned at them if they so much as smiled. What a strange God those Methodists believed in if He regarded laughter as sinful!

Rowena watched a cutter draw up, and was surprised to see Jeremy Launston, Amelia Grimsby, and her brother, Malcolm, alight from it. The trio stayed at the fringe of the crowd.

Excitement mounted around the fires as Farmer Winslow declared that the syrup looked ready, and tested it by throwing a ladleful onto the snow. When it hardened, a cheer swelled up from the bystanders. The younger children rushed to take possession of the toffee-like candy, and Farmer Winslow obliged them by tossing out many more spoonsful. The kettles were removed from the fires, and the men helped to pour the contents into moulds. Some of the thick, gooey molasses was kept for sampling, and the people were invited to dip in their spoons and pass judgement. They needed no further encouragement, and words of praise flowed as thick as the sugar, coaxing a smile from Silas Winslow.

The work, however, was not at an end for the farmer and his sons, since the sap still flowed, and the fires had to be kept burning day and night to boil it down. A few men remained to tend to the business -- to be relieved by others, so that all would have a chance for a fling -- and the rest of the people made their way to the barn, where the farmer's wife and daughters had hot tea awaiting them. Because this was not strictly a working bee, as most were, whiskey was not provided. But the men had brought their own supplies, and liberally laced their tea with it.

The barn -- the largest in the county, Farmer Winslow liked to boast -- was a rambling log structure that comprised several additions. This section housed wagons, carts, and sleds, hay in the loft above, the granary, and the large bare threshing floor which provided a more than adequate dance floor.

Farmer Peebles, a clever fiddler, struck up a lively Scottish reel, and the people soon warmed up with the exertion of keeping time to the music. There were jigs and hornpipes and Irish reels, with Farmer Ridley being the caller-off.

Since the men outnumbered the women, the girls had little chance to rest. Rowena was in great demand as a partner. When she danced with Brendan, his blue eyes never left her. She was thrilled by his attentions, and artlessly returned his audacious stare. Her emerging sexuality responded to her virile partner. The strong hand at her waist, which surreptitiously caressed her, sent a shiver through her. These feelings, so new to her, frightened her at the same time as they delighted, as did the fact that it was Brendan who so aroused her. Brendan, of whom her mother had spoken so disparagingly. Were these the feelings that led girls astray?

"You're the loveliest maid here, mavourneen," Brendan whispered.

The softly spoken endearment excited her, but she said lightly, "How am I to believe that, Brendan Delaney? Just look at Miss Amelia."

"Sure, there's not much to see. She's a face on her that looks like she has a mouthful of castor oil."

Rowena laughed at this accurate description of that young lady's petulant expression. Amelia and Jeremy did not dance; they stood together in a secluded corner. How odd, Rowena thought, that they should be here at all. Jeremy Launston did not usually deign to attend these social functions, although his father, Samuel, sometimes put in an appearance. She found Jeremy's presence a disturbing one, recalling how their eyes had met that morning in Yardleys', causing her to blush. There was such an air of indifference about him, as though all this were beneath him and hardly worth his consideration. Just a look from Jeremy could make most people feel inferior. And yet there was something else in his eyes when he looked at her that she couldn't interpret.

When the dance ended Brendan said, "'Tis almighty hot in here. Would you care to join me for a stroll outside?"

"I'd best not. Ma says you're not to be trusted."

Brendan exploded into laughter. "Does she now? And what would you be thinking then?"

She smiled coyly at him. "Sure, I've not made up me mind."

"Then I'd best mind me manners... for the time being."

When Farmer Peebles took a well deserved rest, the barn echoed with a hundred different conversations as friends and neighbours caught up on the latest news. Maureen Darcy came excitedly to Rowena's side.

"Did you dance with Ewan, then?" Rowena asked with a grin.

"Hm? Oh, Ewan. Aye. Nearly broke me toes, he did, the great lout! Did you see me dancing with Malcolm Grimsby then? Sure, but he's a fine gentleman, that one. And the things he said! 'Surely, you don't live in town.'" Maureen mimicked him. "'I'd not have missed noticing a beauty like you.'"

"You're not going soft on Malcolm Grimsby, are you?" Rowena asked.

"And why not?" Maureen said, stung by the implied criticism. "A girl could hardly do better for herself 'round here."

"Give over, Maureen. He was just flirting with you. It means naught when gentlemen talk like that."

"And what would you be knowing about that?"

"I know that you've only to crook your little finger and Ewan would be your slave for life. And I figure that Colonel Grimsby's got other plans for his son, so you'd best not bother setting your cap at him."

"Are you saying Maureen's not good enough for him then?" Shelagh Ryan asked. The other two girls had not noticed her joining them.

Rowena had not missed the hostility in her voice. "You know very well what I'm saying."

"That I don't. I reckon we're as good as any of 'em."

"Aye," Maureen agreed. "And I reckon I could land him, if I set me mind to it."

Rowena was certain that Maureen was already picturing herself in sartorial splendour as "lady of the manor", but wasn't about to pursue the point with her friend. Shelagh's presence had cast a gloom over her. She was glad when, above the din, someone shouted at Brendan, "Give us a song!"

Brendan was always ready to oblige. He hopped onto the straw bale that the fiddler had used as a dais. As usual, he entertained his appreciative audience with a variety of songs.

Rowena, as mesmerized by Brendan's voice as the others, had forgotten about Shelagh until she said, "You like him then. Brendan."

"No more'n you, from what I've heard tell," Rowena replied with annoyance.

"Aye. And you'd best remember that."

Chapter 5

The winter chill pervaded the barn; so people once more took to the dance floor.

"Oh, do let's go home," Amelia Grimsby said peevishly to Jeremy Launston. "We've done our duty, although why we should feel obliged to make an appearance at every bucolic function, I truly cannot understand."

"Because we wish to retain our neighbours' goodwill," Jeremy said. "One of the strange side-effects of immigration appears to be that any man who owns an acre of land considers himself every man's equal. It's called democracy, and it's an American import -- as are all reprehensible things in this country. These people don't take kindly to class distinctions, particularly in the backwoods. So we appease them by showing that we are not above joining their activities."

"Then we are frightful hypocrites since I, for one, feel quite out of place here. Do look at the Selfridges though! They actually seem to be enjoying themselves."

The robust Major cut a rather comical figure as he bounced about with Fionna Ryan. His round face and balding head were flushed red, and beads of perspiration glistened on his brow. But a wide smile touched his muttonchop whiskers.

"The Major is a rather strange old bird anyway," Jeremy said.

"Did you know he's allowing Priscilla to be courted by a farmer's son? It's really quite scandalous. Her late mother was from a well connected family back home, but Mama thinks I should no longer associate with Priscilla now that she intends to marry beneath her. Not that Priscilla and I had much in common to begin with, but truly, there are so few people here that one ***can*** associate with. I had thought the Finches promising, but Mama discovered that Margaret's father was just a country parson, and Edward's father was a solicitor. Papa says Edward will be hopeless at farming, and predicts they'll soon be off to the city. Oh, I shall surely perish from the cold if we don't soon leave! It's quite ridiculous for us to stand about in this draughty, smelly barn! Do see if you can drag Malcolm away, Jeremy. Who is that child he's dancing with?"

"One of Carpenter O'Shaughnessy's daughters, I believe." He recalled those startling blue eyes that had met his in Yardley's that morning. She was becoming quite a beauty, he thought.

"One of those filthy Irish! Do rescue him, Jeremy, before he catches something."

"I quite enjoyed myself," Malcolm said to Jeremy and his sister when they were outside. "And some of those girls are dashed pretty!"

"Those people are so unclean. And louse-ridden too, I've no doubt," Amelia said with a shudder. "Some of them smelled quite repulsive!"

"I didn't notice," said Malcolm.

"I'm not surprised, since you yourself reek of cheap whiskey. It seems to me that you have already adopted some of the more disgusting habits of these people. It turned my stomach to see them all dipping their spoons into the same pot!"

"You're too squeamish by half, Amelia," her brother said. "You can't expect genteel manners here."

"And why not, pray tell? One doesn't have to become as uncivilized as this country. I still cannot understand why Father chose to live in this isolated wilderness. At least Toronto, or even Peterborough, would have provided us with a select society, but apart from dear Jeremy and his family, there is no one of breeding in this village. Mama finds it most distressing indeed, for there is not one woman whom she can call her social equal. She's quite lonely, poor dear -- as I should be if you, dear Jeremy, were not such a frequent visitor at our home." Amelia put her hand affectionately on Jeremy's arm as he tucked the buffalo robe about her. Jeremy smiled at her as he disengaged himself, and stepped onto the cutter.

"If you detest living here so much, Amelia," her brother said mischievously, "then why not persuade Mama to take you to Toronto for a few months, so that you can shop around for a suitable husband."

"I did not say I ***detested*** living here," Amelia said acidly. "I was merely thinking of Mama."

"Ah, yes, the dutiful daughter."

Amelia chose to ignore his sarcasm. The journey back to town was a silent one, save for the muffled clopping of the horse's hooves and the hiss of the snow beneath the runners. The muted orange glow of the constantly burning fires in the houses provided the only light in the dark village streets.

The Grimsbys' house was situated a block north of Main Street on the bank above the curving river. It was a pretty Regency cottage with French windows opening onto a wide veranda.

"Will you come in, Jeremy? Papa would be delighted to see you, I'm sure."

"Thank you, I will, though I'll not stay long."

The Colonel was seated in a comfortable armchair by the fire, reading a newspaper. Mrs. Grimsby was nowhere to be seen. She had undoubtedly taken to her bed again, and was dosing herself with nerve tonic.

"Good to see you, my boy!" the Colonel greeted Jeremy. "Your father has just left. Beat me at chess again. That makes it three in his favour. Join me in a brandy, won't you?"

"Thank you."

"Enjoyed the bee, did you?" the Colonel inquired as he poured the drinks.

"Hardly, Papa. I'm quite frozen," Amelia replied.

He eyed his daughter's taffeta gown. "Not surprising, my dear, if you persist in dressing fashionably rather than sensibly."

"I suppose you'd rather see me in one of those drab homespun rags."

"It's not the wrapping that's important, my dear Amelia," Malcolm said. "It's what is inside that matters."

"You've been saying the most absurd things tonight, Malcolm! I think you've had quite too much to drink."

Malcolm raised his glass of brandy to her in mock salute.

"Do oblige us by giving us a tune on the pianoforte, Amelia," the Colonel said. "I'm certain that Jeremy would like to hear the new piece by that young composer who's so popular in Paris."

"That would be delightful," Jeremy agreed.

"Do you know Chopin's music, Jeremy?" Amelia asked as she sat down at the piano.

"I'm afraid not."

Amelia slipped into a soft Nocturne, and the beautiful music which had graced the fashionable salons of Paris drifted beyond the house to dissipate in the silence of the forest.

Amelia smiled at the well deserved applause she received. When she resumed her seat on the sofa, she picked up her needlepoint and worked half-heartedly at it while the men talked.

"It boils my blood to read these outrageous lies and slanderous statements which that fanatic Scotsman, Mackenzie, prints!" the Colonel said in disgust as he tossed the offensive newspaper into the fire. "I'm just thankful that the constituents of

York County finally came to their senses and didn't re-elect that troublemaker to the House of Assembly."

"I never read *The Constitution* myself," Jeremy said, referring to the newspaper that Mackenzie published. "What's he advocating now?"

"The usual -- down with the British Colonial Government, hooray for the Republican Yankees. Bond Head should ship the little son of a.... Sorry, my dear," he apologized to Amelia. "As I was saying, the Lieutenant-Governor should ship Mackenzie to the States, since he has such a love for their politics, so that the loyal British subjects of this province would be left in peace. Ironic, isn't it? Upper Canada grew out of the American Revolutionary War; it was settled by Loyalists. Along comes this belligerent little Scot who hasn't forgotten Culloden, and who wants these people to fight ***against*** the side they supported the last time. Where's the logic in that, I ask you?"

"I think the government has paid entirely too much attention to Mackenzie," Jeremy said. "They've made a hero of him among the common people by persecuting him as they have. He should be ignored, like the bothersome insect that he is, because when people react violently to the slander he perpetrates, it gives others the impression that there may be a grain of truth in the blackguard's accusations after all. Archdeacon Strachan has the right approach. He refuses to allow Mackenzie to ruffle him, and his rational, calm intelligence contrasts favourably with Mackenzie's hot tempered, emotional displays."

"Well, perhaps things will settle down somewhat, now that Mackenzie's out of politics and we have a Tory majority in the House. Damned clever idea of the Lieutenant-Governor's to dissolve the House and issue a virtual ultimatum to the people. Once they realized the treasonous intentions of the Reformers, they were quick to show where their loyalties lay - with the Throne!"

"True," Malcolm said. "But I doubt we've seen the last of Mackenzie. I've heard he's collaborating with the Reformer, Papineau, in Lower Canada, and I'll wager they're plotting trouble."

"A revolution?" the Colonel asked with amusement. "Who would fight it for them? A handful of malcontents? We'd have them routed in no time, and Mackenzie strung up for his trouble. What do you think, Jeremy? Are any of the men around here discontented and ungrateful enough to join such a rebellion?"

"Father has always treated his workers well, so I can't imagine any of them risking everything to join Mackenzie. But troublemakers like Brendan Delaney are always looking for a fight, and an excuse that seems politically motivated might attract him." More than once, Jeremy had sensed Brendan's hostility. If he weren't such a good worker, Jeremy would have fired him long ago. "I wouldn't be surprised if Delaney had been with one of those rebel groups in Ireland."

The Colonel grunted in agreement and said, "We're talking about treason -- punishable by hanging, all property confiscated so that the grieving family would be left destitute. Tell the rabble that and then see how strongly they feel about their politics!"

Jeremy was thinking about the Grimsbys after he'd taken his leave of them. They were a good family. The Colonel, a veteran of Waterloo, was one of the county magistrates. Mrs. Grimsby boasted of her titled family connections in England. Amelia was well bred, and had been educated as befits a lady.

But she was pretentious, impractical, querulous and was, in short, not suitable as a wife.

It was a pity really, since he liked the Colonel. He would have to visit the Grimsbys less often, lest Amelia misconstrue his presence as being solely for her benefit. He was beginning to dislike her proprietary air, and scenes like today, in Yardleys', were to be avoided at all costs. He did not wish her to announce to the town, no matter how subtly, that she had any claim on him.

It was time he seriously thought of marrying, for he was already twenty-five. He needed a woman of good breeding who could cope with the rigours of backwoods life -- a woman who could bake and cook and clean if necessary, for servants were often difficult to find and never stayed long. Amelia, he was certain, could do none of these things. He wondered what would happen to the Grimsby household should the housekeeper, whom they had brought with them from England, decide to leave her employ.

His thoughts strayed to the women he had met at the balls in Peterborough. There was only one girl who fulfilled his requirements, he decided -- Harriet Neville.

Jeremy drove past Simon Worthing's house, and was glad to see a light still burning.

"I thought we'd see you at the sugaring-off tonight, Simon," he greeted his friend.

"So I would have been. But I've just returned from the Audleys', where all the children are down with influenza. The social life of a doctor is unpredictable, and often nonexistent."

"Is that a complaint?"

"No, just a statement of fact. I only hope that there are no brawls at the bee tonight. -- Will you join me in a brandy? -- It's been a long day, and I've no wish to start patching up people at this time of night." They sat down in armchairs on either side of the crackling fire. "So... how was the bee?"

"Much as any other. We didn't stay long. Amelia could find nothing to amuse her there."

"I'm surprised she even considered attending."

"That was my father's idea. I'm not sure whether he's playing match-maker -- God forbid -- or whether he truly thought that Amelia would be entertained."

"I take it you don't fancy her?"

"Not as a potential wife. I can envision her becoming like her mother over the years -- prone to vapours and headaches and malaise that confines her to her bed as often as not. What exactly ***is*** wrong with Mrs. Grimsby, Simon?"

"You know I'm not allowed to discuss my patients with anyone, Jeremy." He paused. "But I'll tell you this. I've seen many cases of decline in women, but rarely among the working classes.

"We put women on pedestals, and expect them to be beautiful and charming, but not to sully their hands with any task more demanding than flower arranging or needlepoint. But women have brains too -- although, admittedly, not as advanced as ours. Just imagine how stultifying that kind of life must be! We even expect the women we marry to be virtually sexless, and only credit whores with being capable of passion. Yet all women are the same beneath their gowns, whether they be of silk or homespun. We've taken away too many of women's natural functions. Even childrearing is given into the care of others. So what is left to them? I'll tell you, Jeremy, I'm damned glad I wasn't born a woman!"

"So you think women like Mrs. Grimsby would be happier baking bread and scrubbing floors?" Jeremy asked with amusement.

"Yes. If they'd been taught to regard that as socially acceptable behaviour, which it is in the backwoods. Of course, once our community becomes more settled and 'civilized', it will become more stratified, and idle women will become a symbol of prosperity, as elsewhere. I really believe we do our women a disservice by pampering them and expecting nothing productive from them, by expecting them to live in an intellectual vacuum."

"What do you propose we do with them? Surely you're not suggesting that well bred women are superfluous in modern society?"

"Some of them most certainly feel so. I know a girl in England, Jeremy. What ideas she has! She told me that she ***craves*** for some worthwhile occupation, and has a horror of spending her life just frittering away time. Her name is Florence Nightingale."

"Do you think we should educate women then, and let them compete with us in commerce and medicine?"

"Don't be so quick to scoff, Jeremy. Women are instinctive healers. It's part of a woman's nature to be compassionate, and to care for the sick. And if you believe that women are weak, then you should watch one go through labour and deliver a child. Oh no, my friend, women have stamina, and the sight of blood is nothing new to them. No, I'd say if women could truly comprehend and learn all the necessary scientific information, they would make admirable doctors."

"Ah, but you're not convinced that women ***could*** comprehend, is that it?"

"I'm not certain that women are scientifically minded. I...."

He was interrupted by a loud banging at the door.

"A broken head, do you think?" Simon said wryly before going to the door.

Donal O'Shaughnessy stumbled in. "Jaysus Christ, Doctor, come quick! The Finches' sleigh broke through the ice. They'll be drownded for sure!"

"I still have the cutter hitched," Jeremy said.

The men grabbed their greatcoats, and Simon, his doctor's bag, and they hastened out.

"Hop in, lad," Jeremy said to Donal. "Tell us where to go."

"Just below Paxtons'."

It was only a few minutes drive. They could see the many lanterns, and hear the shouting of the crowd that had gathered at the scene, well before they arrived. Simon and Jeremy elbowed their way through the horrified onlookers to the edge of the river. In the dim light cast by the candle lamps, they could just discern the two children clinging to the edge of broken ice in the middle of the river, which was at its widest here. Brendan Delancy, with a rope tied about his waist, was inching toward them on his stomach. Fergus Ryan was making for a prostrate body a few yards from the open water.

"What happened?" Simon asked.

"They passed us at Paxtons'," Patrick O'Shaughnessy said. "Himself, laughing he was, said they were taking the shortcut across the river, so they couldn't be giving us a lift to home. Sure, we warned them not to try it, but himself just waved us off. Wasn't a moment later we heard the ice cracking and the screams. When we arrived we saw the childer flailing in the water, grabbing for the ice. The missus seems to have been thrown clear, though she's not moved a muscle all the while. There was no sign of himself, nor the horse."

The crowd gasped as the rim of ice broke and the girl slipped back into the river. She struggled feebly, frozen as she was by the frigid water, weighed down by her sodden winter clothing. People shouted encouragement; Brendan scrambled faster toward her, heedless now of his own safety. But she sank a moment later, without a cry or protest. There was only that terrible, gentle slosh of the water as it closed over her, as though she had never been, had never disturbed the calm surface of the river.

The boy screamed. He released his tenuous hold on the ice, and swam to the spot where the girl had disappeared. He splashed about, trying to stay afloat, while his hands groped wildly for his sister.

The people on shore waited breathlessly, willing her to resurface, willing him to hang on until Brendan could reach his side. There was a unanimous gasp as the boy, struggling to regain his hold, visibly flagged, his frozen muscles no longer responding to his will.

Brendan grabbed the boy's hair as he began to sink, and hauled him up. He had just hooked the boy about the chest with his arm and was pulling him onto the ice when it gave way beneath them, and they both splashed into the water.

Those manning the lifeline pulled hard, and Brendan, still holding the boy, resurfaced to the cheers of the onlookers. After several abortive attempts to climb onto the ice, which kept breaking away beneath him, he managed to gain purchase and clambered out with the boy. Fergus, meanwhile, had reached the inert body of Margaret Finch. While the two men dragged their burdens toward shore, the thin ice groaned and protested and threatened to break.

Simon said to Josh Paxton, who stood next to him, "Have you any rooms prepared, Josh? I can't risk taking them to the surgery."

"The wife's already looking after that, Doc. And I'll warrant she'll have some hot broth and tea on the boil." The innkeeper shook his head sadly. "Bad night's business, this. Here, I've a pile of blankets ready."

"Good!" Simon sought out Deirdre and said, "I would be grateful for your help, Mrs. Delaney. Oh, and you too, Mrs. Abernethy," he added when that good woman eyed him quizzically.

"I daresay you would," Mattie replied.

A few minutes later the rescuers and the rescued were safely ashore. They were enveloped in blankets and hurried into Paxtons', where the boy, unconscious now, and his mother were carried to second floor bedrooms.

Simon asked Mattie to see to Margaret Finch, while he and Deirdre dealt first with the boy. They stripped the icy garments from him. His skin was deathly pale, with a bluish cast, and was frigid to the touch.

"We've got to get him warm," Simon said. "And quickly." There wasn't much of a pulse.

They bundled him up in blankets that Mrs. Paxton had warmed by the fire, and down comforters. When Simon had done all he could, he left Deirdre with the boy and went to see to Margaret Finch.

Mattie had already dressed her in one of Mrs. Paxton's nightgowns. A petite woman, she seemed lost amid the fluffy pillows and thick duvet of the double bed. With her ash-brown hair spread loosely about her heart-shaped face, so calm in repose, she looked absurdly young and vulnerable. Simon was overwhelmed with pity for her. He dreaded meeting those cool, grey eyes with the news he would have to impart.

He examined her, and told Mattie, "She has a slight concussion, but nothing seems to be broken."

"Aye. I'd already determined that," Mattie replied. "I reckon she'll be coming to her senses soon."

"Yes. You'll have to ensure she remains in bed. Give her some broth or tea, if she'll take it."

"I was doctoring folk before you were born, lad. I reckon I know what to do," Mattie said testily.

"I'm certain you are a most competent nurse, Mrs. Abernethy. I'll look in on her again in a while."

He made a hasty exit before the significance of his words came to her and elicited a vitriolic reply.

He checked again on Tom, who was now shivering uncontrollably beneath the mountain of blankets. Deirdre looked hopefully at Simon when he had examined the boy. "His pulse is stronger," he told her. "It's a good sign. And his body temperature is rising. But you know that the worst is not yet over. He'll undoubtedly come down with brain fever."

"Aye, poor lad."

"And even if he survives that, well... he may never completely recover his mental faculties." Simon felt another rush of sympathy for Margaret Finch. "I'd best see how Brendan is doing."

Brendan, dressed in clothes that were too large -- undoubtedly something of Josh Paxton's -- and huddled inside a blanket, was sipping whiskey by the fire. He was surrounded by his cronies, who were praising his heroics. Fergus, although also a minor hero, had not fallen into the river, and was thus not lauded as highly.

Brendan confirmed Simon's suspicions that he had received only a slight chill, and would suffer no ill effects from his unseasonal dunking.

As Simon entered Margaret's room he heard Mattie say, "...'Twas the will of God."

Margaret's expression changed from shock to rage. "The will of God? If God can so blithely destroy an innocent child then he is despicable, not worthy of veneration. Don't speak to me of God's will!"

Mattie gasped, and was obviously about to splutter some reply, but Simon intervened. Margaret did not need to be lectured about her beliefs -- or lack of them -- just now. He grasped Mattie by the shoulders and steered her toward the door, saying, "I think a hot drink is called for. Please see to it, Mrs. Abernethy. Mrs. Finch is undoubtedly in a state of shock."

"Well, I never!" Mattie said as she was hustled through the doorway. But at a meaningful glance from the doctor, her outrage subsided, and she did as she was bid. Simon closed the door behind her.

Margaret was trying to rise from the bed. Simon rushed to her side, saying, "I cannot allow you to leave your bed as yet, Mrs. Finch."

"I must see to Tom," she said frantically.

"We're doing all we can for him."

"And will that be enough?" she challenged.

"It's too early to tell," Simon said gently, resettling her in the bed. "But you will be of no use to him if you aggravate your condition. You need absolute rest, and I am going to ensure that you get it. And I'll let you know when there's any change in Tom's condition."

But it was several harrowing days before Simon could pronounce Tom out of danger. It was several more days before he could determine that Tom had suffered only mild retardation as a result of the brain fever.

Long before then, the watery hole that was Edward and Anne Finch's grave had quietly frozen over.

Chapter 6

Harriet Neville felt a blush stain her cheeks as she caught Jeremy Launston watching her, and quickly looked away. She knew she did not look her best when blushing; her neck and face would mottle red in a most unbecoming fashion. Indeed, it was most unlike her to blush at all.

Why was he scrutinizing her so, she wondered. Jeremy Launston was easily the most handsome man in the room. He looked splendid tonight in tight, pearl-grey breeches, lavender-striped silk waistcoat and cravat, and cutaway black coat. Just the thought of him set her pulse racing again -- she, who was not prone to such maidenly vapours. Yet she was far from being the prettiest girl here -- her own sister Charlotte quite outshone her, and was always one of the most popular girls at these balls -- so she would not deceive herself into thinking that Jeremy Launston had any particular interest in her.

She returned her attention to her partner, with whom she was dancing a quadrille, but found him less exciting to contemplate than Jeremy. Instead, she watched the people around her.

There was a small, select society in Peterborough and its environs. Many among them were bachelors, highly educated, eager for stimulating company. They had even started, amongst themselves, a lending library. As it was usually one of them who hosted these social gatherings, they had become known as "bachelor balls".

This one was being held in the largest and most magnificent house in the area, which dominated a hilltop at the western edge of town, and boasted a ballroom. It was owned by the Honourable Nigel Melbourne, who claimed that he loved entertaining, and therefore needed lots of room.

The Honourable Nigel never used his courtesy title, although everyone else did. When he had first arrived in Peterborough, Harriet's mother, Livinia, had investigated him through discreet inquiries in letters to friends back home in England. Harriet's father, Charles, had scoffed at the rather shocking reports Livinia had received, declaring that he didn't believe the vile gossip, that it was just a young man's high spirits blown out of proportion. He liked the Honourable Nigel, who was witty and intelligent. And despite her misgivings about Nigel's character, Livinia would never miss one of his elaborate balls.

This would be the last one of the season, since many people would soon be planting their crops, and generally be too busy with farming or business until the harvest had been taken in.

So there was a special gaiety in the air tonight. The women were resplendent in their most prized gowns. Harriet herself was dazzling in her pink silk gauze, her sister Charlotte had told her. But she felt like a confection -- and not entirely comfortable -- in the elaborate gown. It had belonged to her sister Isobel, and had been created for her in London shortly before their departure to Canada. Harriet had cut down the enormous balloon sleeves to more fashionable -- and less awkward -- tapered ones, salvaging enough material to make a small evening cape. The billowing skirt, patterned with white floral stripes, shimmered as she moved.

Harriet much preferred the simple day dresses she wore about the house, which did not require so many stiff petticoats, and, thus, did not so severely hamper movement. It was quite absurd, she thought, to attempt to follow the dictates of European fashion in this colony. For a woman who performed domestic chores, who trudged through the deep snows of winter or the mud of springtime, who wished to be comfortable in the extremes of this climate, it was ludicrous to do so.

But there were many who did not agree with her -- her mother among them. They sought to maintain the status quo they had enjoyed in the Old Country, and clung to their traditions as though they were a lifeline. They made no attempt to adjust to their new environment, instead, they endeavored to transform everything to suit their requirements, only to be frequently disappointed.

Harriet herself had never been happier or more content than during these last five years. At fifteen, she had already begun to feel ennui in her restrictive female role. Education had stressed deportment, music, fancy needlework, dancing, and all else that would produce a socially adept creature who had no purpose but to amuse herself and others. But here, by necessity, she found her life full and useful. She actually enjoyed cooking, and, with the help of Mrs. Beeton and other cookery books, had become laudably proficient at the art.

The quadrille ended, and her partner escorted her back to her chair.

"Oh, I shall be quite inconsolable until the balls resume!" her sister Beatrice said, sitting down beside her. She fanned herself rapidly. "There's such a paucity of social activity here in summer. We really ***must*** try to persuade Papa to allow us to spend a few months in the capital."

"If Papa had wanted us to live in Toronto, my dear Bea, we would undoubtedly have moved there. You seem to forget that we do not have unlimited funds."

"Nonsense! You take everything far too seriously, Ettie. It is not at all ladylike, and does not become you." Beatrice, though a year younger than Harriet, considered herself much more worldly than her older sister. "Papa has done well here. I'm certain he has more than enough money. After all, what else is there to spend it on? And Papa has said that we may attend the Governor's Ball next month. I am ***so*** looking forward to that! So if we.... Oh, look! Here comes Jeremy Launston!"

Harriet could sense her sister primping beside her as he approached. He bowed to them, saying, "Ladies." Then he turned to Harriet and said, "Might I have the pleasure of the next dance, Miss Neville?"

"Certainly, Mr. Launston."

As he took her gloved hand in his, she tried to avoid meeting his gaze, but could not do so for long.

"Forgive my bluntness, Mr. Launston, but you have been regarding me so intently that I cannot help but wonder if my chignon is askew, or whether I have somehow given offence and you cannot take your disbelieving eyes from the malefactor."

Jeremy laughed. "Quite the contrary, my dear Miss Neville. I find you absolutely delightful. And, as usual, you look most fetching."

"Why thank you, sir. Though I fear your flattery is a shade too exuberant to be entirely credible." Despite her words, she ***was*** flattered by his attention. During their previous social encounters he had never taken any particular note of her. She, unlike her sisters, had never mastered -- or cared to, for that matter -- the fine art of coquetry. She feared now that she might make some terrible *faux pas*, and forever discredit herself in Jeremy's eyes.

"You do yourself an injustice, Miss Neville. I have long admired you. Your sensible attitude has not escaped my notice."

She laughed. "I'm not certain that I find being described as ***sensible*** terribly flattering. One usually thinks of maiden aunts and governesses as being 'sensible'." She was amused now, convinced that he was merely engaging in polite flirtation.

"I must protest, Miss Neville. A sensible woman is most praiseworthy. A flighty woman does not survive long in the backwoods."

"I beg to differ, Mr. Launston. Several of my own sisters are quite impractical, but have not as yet perished."

"Ah, but that is because they have you to guide them, Miss Neville."

She laughed again. "I assure you that you are quite mistaken, Mr. Launston. My sisters seek no guidance from me." She was truly enjoying herself this evening. The lighthearted repartee with Jeremy stirred her blood, bringing a rosy glow to her cheeks and a brightness to her eyes. She herself was unaware of it, but Jeremy was not.

She's quite lovely, he thought. Not as pretty as her sisters, but then they were too much like Amelia -- frivolous and empty-headed. Harriet was what one termed a "handsome" woman, who would age gracefully. She possessed a natural charm and an equally artless aristocratic bearing that impressed him. She had an inner strength that he had encountered in few women, and certainly in none so young as she. He was intrigued by her, and more convinced than ever that he was making the right choice.

After the ball that night, he queried his friend and host, Nigel Melbourne, on the subject.

The Honourable Nigel Melbourne was the youngest son of a Viscount. Having had no desire or aptitude to follow the usual paths of younger sons of the nobility -- either the church or the army -- he had spent a profligate youth. After being sent down from Oxford, he had wasted his time -- and a great deal of his father's money -- drinking, gambling, womanizing, and generally creating embarrassment for his family. So he'd been shipped off to "the colonies" with his inheritance in his pocket and the injunction never to set foot in England again.

The latter had been unnecessary. Nigel had become so enthralled with the grandeur of the country that he would never consider returning to what he termed "the crumbling seat of civilization". He had bought a large tract of land, had taken up horse breeding, and felt that he had at last found his metier.

Jeremy stayed with him whenever he came to Peterborough. They were having a brandy in the parlour, their cravats off, their collars unbuttoned, their feet up.

"What do I think of Harriet Neville? I've never given her much thought, to tell you the truth, Jeremy. She seems quite an intelligent young woman. Not my type though. Now her sister Charlotte is another story altogether. Why do you ask?"

"I'm considering marrying her."

"Not seriously!"

"Quite seriously."

"Why? You're not in love with her?"

"Hardly. I think she would make a good wife. It's as simple as that."

"You cold-hearted bastard!" Nigel said with a grin. "You mean she's the best brood mare you've seen -- good stock, good teeth. Have you seen her legs, though? Must inspect them, you know."

"Very droll. And what do you look for in a woman?"

"Ah, women. I idolize them! Particularly those with beauty, charm, wit, gaiety, affability. A luscious body, a promise of good sport in bed. Unfortunately, none of them idolizes me in return." Nigel refilled their glasses, and said more seriously, "So you're actually going to do it?"

"You haven't persuaded me otherwise, my friend."

"Ah, well, with you out of contention, the field will be clear for me," Nigel said. "You know, I'm quite a reformed character. I'm certain my family would be proud of me -- were I to give them the satisfaction of knowing it. I myself have been thinking that a wife would not come amiss."

"Charlotte?"

"I know that she is but seventeen, and I'm nearly twice her age. But, by Jove, she stirs even my jaded senses! It's a damned good thing that you haven't my superior taste in women, Jeremy. At least now we can still be friends."

• • •

Harriet was thinking about Jeremy the next morning as she was making her sister's bed. He had danced with her frequently, and still his interest in her had not waned. How curious. Now, she could almost believe that she had imagined it all.

"I don't know why you bother with the beds, Ettie," Charlotte said to her as she adjusted her cap in front of the mirror. "It ***is*** Lizzie's job to make the beds. You do enough about the house as it is."

"You know how slow Lizzie is at everything. If I leave the beds to her, then the other chores are never completed. And today is bread baking; so we'll be lucky if she manages to do anything else at all."

Charlotte regarded her sister's reflection in the mirror. "You annoy me so when you fuss about. One would think that you were the housekeeper here!"

Harriet laughed. "And so I am! After all, someone has to do it. And you, my dear Lottie, are certainly incapable of it."

"Oh, Ettie, you really put me to shame. You're always so efficient and sensible, and make me feel quite useless and silly."

"Nonsense!" Harriet protested, though she was beginning to dislike being described as "sensible". "Only one woman can rule a roost. I assure you that I would take umbrage at any interference from you. You just continue to be your lovely, charming, vivacious self, Lottie, and we'll soon have you off our hands in any case."

"You're teasing me again!" Charlotte grabbed a pillow and hurled it at Harriet. They both began laughing

Their merriment was cut short by a piercing wail from below. Harriet picked up her skirts and dashed downstairs, with Charlotte close behind.

"What is it, Mama?" Harriet asked anxiously as she burst into the kitchen to find her mother quite distraught.

Livinia Neville had aged ten years during the five years of "exile" from her homeland. She was just forty, but already her hair was streaked with silver. Her skin was lustreless, dry and wrinkling due to the extremes of the Canadian climate.

But mostly she had aged in spirit. The O'Shaughnessys would not have recognized this woman as their disgruntled travelling companion from Cobourg to Peterborough five years before. (As, indeed, she would not have recognized them in their relative prosperity.)

Livinia ran her fingers agitatedly through her hair, dislodging her frilled cap and freeing strands of salt-and-pepper hair from their bonds. For a moment, she appeared to Harriet like some madwoman.

"That damned fool girl has left us!" Livinia lamented.

"What girl?" Charlotte inquired, thinking that perhaps one of her sisters had eloped. Surely nothing short of that could have occasioned such distress.

"Lizzie, of course!" her mother said, vexed.

The girls exchanged glances. Losing their help was not an uncommon occurrence in this house.

"The lazy baggage!" Livinia said. "Slovenly, ungrateful slut! I told her so!"

Harriet sighed inwardly. "Mama, surely you didn't say that to her face? You know how difficult it is to get servants here."

"Servants? There are no proper servants here. Just rude, untrained girls who demand exorbitant wages, and then have the unmitigated gall to be insolent!"

"What happened, Mama?" Harriet asked.

"I asked Lizzie to set a fire in the parlour and she said to me, bold as you please, 'Do it yourself'. I controlled my temper and informed her that it was not ***my*** place to lay a fire but hers, that she had been hired to do the work here, not to insult her betters. She replied that she was too busy with the baking, and that I would either have to freeze, or dirty my hands. I told her that if she weren't such a lazy baggage she could easily do all the work in this house with time to spare. Whereupon she said, 'I come here to help you out, ma'am, not to be insulted, nor to be treated like a slave. I'll go somewhere where I'm appreciated.' and then she just walked out. And here's the bread rising, and I'm sure I don't know what to do with it."

The girls knew only too well what their mother's efforts at baking bread would produce -- either loaves that would serve well as bricks, or flat, burnt shells containing raw dough in the centre.

"Never mind, Mama. I shall see to the bread. And perhaps Lottie will attend to the fire in the parlour," Harriet said. "I shall bring you a pot of tea there in a few minutes."

Livinia gave a startled cry at the loud knock on the front door. "Do see who it is, Charlotte. I'm really not in any condition to see anyone just now. I think I shall lie down for a while. My head is beginning to ache abominably."

As Charlotte went to the front door, Harriet tied on an apron and set about kneading the dough. That was how Jeremy found her a few minutes later, when Charlotte ushered him into the kitchen.

"Mr. Launston is here to see you, Ettie," Charlotte said in consternation. "I asked him if he would wait for you in the parlour, but he insisted that he did not wish to interrupt you at your work."

"I hope you will forgive this intrusion, Miss Neville, but I am obliged to leave for home almost immediately, and I did wish to have a word with you before my departure."

"Certainly, Mr. Launston. You will forgive me, I trust, if I continue. Our maid has just left us, and I'm afraid that the dough will not wait. Charlotte, perhaps you could inform Mama that Mr. Launston has called."

"I understand that your father is not at home," he said when Charlotte had left the room. "I did wish to confer with him; however, I should discuss this with you first, at any rate.... Miss Neville... Harriet, would you do me the honour of becoming my wife?"

Harriet stopped kneading. She gawked at him in disbelief. "Surely I have misheard you, Mr. Launston!"

"I realize that this may seem rather precipitous to you, Harriet. But I assure you that I have given the matter a great deal of thought."

"Then you are not jesting?"

He walked up to her. "Indeed I am not." He lifted her chin and placed a gentle kiss upon her lips.

"Harriet!" her mother shrieked from the door. "What is the meaning of this?"

"Mrs. Neville," Jeremy said, acknowledging her presence. "I have just taken the liberty of proposing to your daughter."

"Heaven forfend!" Livinia placed her hand over her heart and sank onto a chair. "Is this true, Harriet?" She looked accusingly at her daughter.

"Yes, Mama. Mr. Launston has done me that honour," she said pointedly.

"And what have you told him?"

"I have not had the opportunity to say anything as yet. If you will excuse me, I will accompany Mr. Launston to the door. He has a long ride home."

"I must apologize for my mother's incivility, Mr. Launston," Harriet said to him as they walked down the hallway. "She has had a trying morning, and I fear this has come as a shock to her."

"Harriet, do call me Jeremy."

"Very well, Jeremy." She looked into his eyes and couldn't believe that this handsome man had just asked her to marry him. He had not spoken of love, but then they hardly knew one another. She herself was not sure of her feelings toward him. Certainly she was attracted to him, as she had never been to any other man, but whether that would qualify as love was too early to tell.

Did she really want to marry him? A part of her cried, *Yes, you fool! How could you turn down the most eligible bachelor in the district?* Her sensible part said, *Why would he want to marry* **you** *when he could have any woman?* For once she would not be sensible!

"Jeremy, I must admit that this has come as something of a surprise to me as well. I'm certain you will understand that I must consult my father before I can give you a definite answer. However, I shall tentatively say... yes."

Jeremy smiled as he took her hand and kissed it. "Thank you. I wish I could stay longer, Harriet. We have so much to discuss. But I must be home before nightfall. I shall return as soon as possible."

Harriet leaned against the closed door. It all seemed so unreal. She had never imagined that it would happen like that. Like most young women, she had entertained romantic daydreams of a man declaring his undying love and swearing that he could not live without her. Yet she had always known that reality would be different. Her eldest sister, Isobel, had married at their parents' recommendation, and was quite happy with her husband. Of course, Isobel's husband had been a frequent visitor at their home that first winter they had spent here; so they had all known him well, and none had mistaken his interest in Isobel.

What would marriage to Jeremy Launston be like, she wondered. How easily she could imagine herself drifting down the aisle in her silk finery, Jeremy watching her progress with a smile on his face, perhaps even a hint of affection visible in his features. A sumptuous feast, all their friends celebrating with them, dancing.... She could remember the feel of his arms about her and shivered delightedly. And then... the unspeakable.

Twenty-year-old Harriet had not the slightest idea of what went on between a man and a woman in the "marriage bed", nor could she even imagine. She knew only that the subject was taboo, that even Isobel, who had never kept a secret from her, had blushed profusely and said only, "You shall find out in good time," when Harriet had expressed her curiosity on the subject.

"Is it unpleasant?" she had persisted.

"Really, Harriet!" Isobel had been scandalized. "This is not a subject which a married woman can discuss with an unmarried one, even her own sister. Now do desist or I shall become quite annoyed with you!"

This great mystery seemed most fearful to Harriet. She knew that what occurred between married people was for the procreation of children. But if it was pleasurable, why would no one talk about it? So she reasoned that it must be something quite beastly.

Any further conjectures on the mysteries of marriage were cut short as Harriet found herself hurled forward. Her sisters, Beatrice and Susannah, came in the door.

"Wasn't that Jeremy Launston we saw riding away from our house?" Beatrice asked.

"It was indeed," Harriet said, walking toward the kitchen.

"Harriet! What was he doing here? Did he ask about me? I danced with him last night, and it was just ***too*** heavenly!"

"No, he did not ask about you. He asked me to marry him." She walked into the kitchen. There were squeals from the hallway, and then hurried footsteps.

"You ***can't*** be serious!" Beatrice said. "I was ***convinced*** he had his eye on me!"

For once, her sister's haughtiness irked Harriet. "You are not the only eligible girl around here, Bea, despite what you may think."

"Oh, you're hateful! Mama, did you hear what she said?"

"That was uncalled for, Harriet, and unkind," Livinia said. "I have had enough upsets for one day. I presume that you have accepted Mr. Launston?"

"Yes, Mama."

Livinia nodded. "I thought you might. I know your father will approve. He thinks very highly of the Launstons. I shall go up to my room now, and do not wish to be disturbed until your father gets home."

Harriet was disappointed that her mother did not seem pleased for her. "Mama, do you not approve of Jeremy Launston?"

"I admire him for having the good sense to choose ***you***. And he will be a commendable husband, I am sure. I am merely perturbed at the thought of losing you, Harriet. I don't know how we will manage without you here." Livinia regarded her daughter more kindly, and patted her arm before leaving the room.

"Oh, Harriet, I can't believe it!" Charlotte said. "That Jeremy Launston should ask you to marry him!"

"And what is so unbelievable about that?" Harriet demanded.

"I didn't mean it like ***that***. I just meant, well... Jeremy Launston, of all people! Why, you'll be the envy of every girl in the district!"

Harriet felt herself preening, and wondered how she could ever have doubted the wisdom of becoming his wife.

Chapter 7

Jeremy Launston gazed downstream through the dusty windows of the mill office. The river was high and running fast, and it was difficult to believe that only a few weeks ago it had still been ice-bound.

Spring was not a lingering, gentle season here. It was more like winter and summer struggling for dominion. Snowfalls alternated with thundershowers, mellow, promising days with cold snaps, until finally summer won out and burst upon them with a vengeance.

Flocks of migrating birds blackened the sky at times. Gunfire boomed throughout the settlement as men picked off the returning birds from their doorsteps. Bloodsucking mosquitoes and blackflies exploded from the wetlands to wage war on the defenceless population.

For days the river ice could be heard groaning and creaking before it finally cracked into massive floes that shunted about as the spring freshets chased them downstream.

And the river had spewed its gruesome, human flotsam onto the shore several miles downstream. Most of the villagers had attended the internment of Edward and Ann Finch.

Out of that tragedy had come a bit of luck for the Launstons, Jeremy thought, for he had offered the widow, Margaret, the position of cook-housekeeper, and she had gratefully accepted. He had suspected that she had nowhere else to go, and little money to support herself and her son, Tom. Margaret was an excellent cook and organizer. The house had never been so clean and comfortable, nor the meals so much anticipated.

He thought of his own mother for a brief, nostalgic moment, remembering the warm, happy, and efficient home that she had created. It was ten years since she had died -- and his sister, Hillary, who had been three years his junior. Times had been difficult then, for his father's investments had collapsed with the deflated post-war markets. There had been nothing to keep them in England. Here they had been able to start afresh.

Jeremy could see the Grimsbys' house high on a bank above the river where it snaked northward. Otherwise there was little indication of the growing settlement which the river nurtured.

He was proud to think that his father had virtually created this community. Eight years ago, when they had built the dam and gristmill, there had been only a few isolated farmsteads in Ops Township, and the nearest mill had been over twenty miles to the south.

He well remembered that day they had canoed down the Scugog River - a rather shallow, slow stream - to choose a site for the dam. He had been skeptical then; he had understood why the government had not hesitated to grant Samuel land in this wilderness where few would choose to come. But Samuel, typically, had not been discouraged. He had had visions that were daily being realized.

And so Samuel had chosen this site between the only high banks and above the only rapids in the river.

The mill had encouraged new settlers to these remote but fertile lands, and their needs had enticed Josh Paxton, who had built his inn, and Hiram Lindsay, who had provided the essential general store. Others had gradually followed.

Jeremy felt absurdly pleased that the inhabitants of the "new town" persisted in calling it Launston Mills. It was definitely time for him to be married and to make certain that there would always be Launstons here. He and Harriet had set a wedding date in the late autumn, since he simply had no time before then.

With the winter cutting of timber now being floated in, the sawmill employed most of the able-bodied men in town, and would be busy until the river froze up again. The gristmill, quiet now, would be humming with activity come late summer. They certainly didn't lack for work. It was the markets that concerned Jeremy.

He broached the subject with his father at supper that evening. "I don't suppose you've had any more word about the government going ahead with plans for the canal system?" The Scugog River was part of a chain of inland lakes and rivers that meandered across the central region of Upper Canada. For a decade now there had been talk of constructing a canal system to link them for navigational purposes, effectively creating a lifeline from the backwoods to Lake Ontario and the Front. Some visionaries could even foresee a link to Georgian Bay, thus connecting the two Great Lakes. But despite dozens of surveys and plans, nothing more than a few locks had been constructed.

Samuel replied, "Unfortunately not. They were to have built a lock here this year -- they'd already commissioned the lumber for it, as you know -- but it seems that the government doesn't have any money for it just now."

"Nor the competence to properly undertake such a big project as the Kawartha-Trent Canal System," Adrian added. The College in Toronto, where he had just completed his final year, had sent him home early due to ill health. Adrian had always been a sickly child, down with chest colds and bronchitis every winter of his life. He was thin and pale, unlike his robust and athletic father and brother.

"I didn't know you'd been involved in politics in the city," Jeremy mocked.

"Most of the fellows I was at school with have fathers or brothers in government. I've heard enough about what goes on. They make things quite comfortable for themselves, but fail to take the larger concerns of the country into consideration."

"So, is it a political career you're after then?" Samuel asked. He often expressed his concerns about Adrian's future to Jeremy. They knew that the mills didn't interest the nineteen-year-old boy, and felt that he was, in any case, not strong enough to be an active partner there. "After studying the law perhaps?"

Adrian shrugged noncommittally, showing no interest in that idea as he thoughtfully buttered a piece of fresh, warm bread. "You were talking about markets, Jamie. Just think how many more customers you'd have for lumber if the countryside could be opened up. The way things stand, the Clergy Reserves and the Canada Company holdings are so extensive and ***expensive*** that the land sits idle. Those farmers who were granted or bought crown land are effectively isolated, the roads are nearly impassable because there are no settlers to chop them out of the wilderness, and few people are encouraged to move into such a remote and inhospitable environment."

"But the Canada Company is trying to open up the country by marketing their holdings to immigrants," Jeremy said. "As you know, my future father-in-law is an agent for them."

"For the shareholders in England, who have absolutely no interest in our land or the people. They're only concerned with turning a quick profit. Men of vision, like John Galt, who did try to build communities, to bring in settlers, didn't last long with the company."

"You're sounding like a Reformer," Jeremy said suspiciously.

"But the boy has a point," Samuel said. "I've been thinking that we could encourage the growth of the settlement by selling some of our holdings at a reasonable price, and by offering guidance to new settlers. Most of them are completely hopeless in the backwoods when they arrive."

Jeremy agreed. In addition to the five hundred acres that Samuel had been granted, he had bought thousands more, many of them surrounding the town site. If that land were developed, there could soon be a large and thriving community here. Yet, with the influx of farmers, the problem of transporting the grain to distant markets would become even more pressing.

Adrian said, "I'd be happy to administer such a program for you, Father."

"If you can fit it around your law studies at the university, then yes, by all means," Samuel replied with a contented grin.

Adrian seemed about to protest, but then kept silent.

Jeremy said, "If we did go ahead with this, I'd want to keep some control over who we sell the land to. The last thing we need are more destitute Irish coming in, buying the land with their last shillings, and then promptly starving - or becoming a burden to the community. They don't seem to realize that it takes a few years and lots of backbreaking labour to scratch an existence out of the backwoods."

"That's why we need immigrant aid societies," Adrian said.

"That's why we need to encourage gentlemen farmers," Jeremy corrected.

"You mean impoverished gentry who have even less of a grasp of farming, less stamina and resilience than the peasants, and absolutely no real experience of hardship."

"I'm talking about people like Nigel, and others in and around Peterborough, like the Stricklands and the Reids and..."

Adrian interrupted. "Who are all large landowners with profits coming in from mills and other holdings. We'd have too much competition, Jamie, if we encouraged entrepreneurs like them."

Samuel chuckled appreciatively. "He has you there, Jamie."

Jeremy conceded the point, but said, "We could do with fewer troublemakers like Brendan Delaney, though. He's preaching sedition now, inciting the men to back that rabble rouser, Mackenzie."

"Mackenzie has the same concerns we just discussed," Adrian argued. "The whole country is suffering under the stranglehold of a few powerful and often incompetent or corrupt people in Toronto. Britain has its own problems and has pretty well forgotten us. We've got to forge a viable and fair political system that will make this country survive and prosper."

"And it will do neither if Mackenzie gets his way. He wants to annex us to the United States!"

"These sorts of debates are going on everywhere," Samuel interceded. "I've heard the men often enough. Delaney's no more opinionated than the others."

"He's more contentious and provocative," Jamie said. "The others may grumble, but he encourages them to violence."

"It's just his way. He likes to think of himself as a leader. But I guarantee you that the men are too comfortable to actually fight against the established order. Aren't they all better off - every man Jack of them - than they've ever been in their lives?"

"Well I'd like to get rid of him," Jeremy said.

"He's popular, Jamie. It would be a mistake to fire him without good cause," Samuel said. "I have no problems with him at all. Perhaps if you remember your obligations as a gentleman, and don't expect refined manners from the lower orders, you might have less trouble with him."

It was a gentle rebuke, but Jeremy privately disagreed. He could not so easily excuse the brutishness of so many of the men as just the nature of the lower orders. To him, all men should be reasonable and self-controlled. That was why Brendan Delaney was anathema to him.

It was a hot evening, so, after supper, Jeremy and Adrian decided to brave the mosquitoes outside rather than suffer the heat indoors. They ambled along Mill Road toward the town. The days were almost at their longest, and the golden evening sunlight filtered through the trees, dappling the path.

"So what ***are*** you planning to do now?" Jeremy asked Adrian. He was rather disconcerted to realize that he knew very little about his brother. Adrian had spent most of every year away at school. Since summer was always the busiest time at the mills, Jeremy had not spent much time with him during his holidays. "I gather you didn't really like Father's idea of law school."

"I suppose I could become a competent enough lawyer. I might even enjoy fighting for the underdog. But I've got a different dream. I've given it a great deal of thought," Adrian said. "What's the population of the village?"

"About two hundred, I believe."

"And growing all the time. And the township? Several hundred more people. A few thousand altogether in the county."

"Just where is this leading us?"

"To a newspaper!" Adrian cried triumphantly. "I intend to publish a backwoods newspaper!"

Jeremy was astonished. "That sounds ambitious. But what do you intend to print? There are so many newspapers coming to us from the Front that I doubt if people would invest in another. So many of the settlers are illiterate anyway; your estimate of the potential market is highly overstated."

"But many of the children will be reading now that there are schools here. And that's one of the issues I intend to pursue -- more and better schools, funded by the government. I'm not concerned with making the paper a profitable venture. I want to educate people about their rights as individuals, to provide a sounding board for their grievances. I want to make them aware of what's happening in the government, and how the various issues directly affect their lives. And I intend to inform them of the alternatives."

"You intend to preach reform? Republicanism, like Mackenzie?"

"I know that's a dirty word to you, Jamie, but have you ever really thought about the principles of a republican system of government without equating them with the Americans for whom you profess such a dislike? It doesn't make sense that this country continue to be governed by Britain. How can the politicians there possibly know and understand our needs? And the Governors sent out by the Colonial Office know next to nothing about us when they arrive, and then leave again after a few years. Why, do you know that our present Lieutenant-Governor, Francis Bond Head, was sent here by mistake? It was his cousin, a seasoned diplomat, that the Colonial Office had intended to send, but someone made an error and offered the position to that inexperienced bumbler."

"That's just a rumour," Jeremy said.

"I believe it to be the truth, and so do many others. No one in his right mind would have sent that man here to govern. Anyway, he and the others they've shipped here can't possibly have much interest in Canada. Not like those born here, or those of us who have adopted this country as our own."

Jeremy frowned. "So you think the country should be freely governed by the ignorant masses?"

"But they needn't be ignorant! Not if we had an adequate educational system instead of just one for the wealthy who wish to maintain the status quo: they receive the best education, therefore the best jobs in government, and, once in positions of power, they can make certain that the masses stay relatively ignorant and powerless, and therefore offer no threat to them and their cozy elitist establishments."

"Is that what you learned at that 'elitist' grammar school in Toronto?" Jeremy asked with amusement.

"I was taught to think for myself."

"And you think that all men are equal, do you?"

"No, I don't. Nor do I think that all illiterate people are necessarily stupid. What I'm saying is that everyone should have the opportunity to be educated, to have more than a token voice in the governing of his country. It should be every human being's undeniable right!" Adrian began coughing violently.

"Are you alright?" Jeremy asked worriedly. Adrian was pale as he wiped the perspiration from his face. "Perhaps you should see Simon."

"No, I'm fine now. The road's so dusty... my throat's quite dry. Let's go into Paxtons' for an ale."

They were only a few steps from the tavern, so Jeremy agreed. They entered the long barroom of the two storey inn. As usual, the tavern was crowded. There was a pervasive stench of sweat in the stuffy, steaming, smoke-filled room. Tobacco chewers spat on the sawdust-covered floor, though spittoons were spaced about for that purpose.

The Launstons acknowledged greetings, and seated themselves on a bench in a secluded corner. Josh Paxton hurried over to them.

"Good evening, gentlemen," the landlord said. "Lord, but it's a hot one tonight. Good for business, though. What's your pleasure, gentlemen?"

"Two pints of ale, Josh."

"Right away, Mr. Launston."

"I still want to publish a newspaper, Jamie," Adrian said when he had soothed his throat with a few swallows of the brew. "I need your help to convince Father, and it will require capital. With you on my side, he's more likely to agree."

Jeremy lit a cigar. He was in an awkward predicament. He didn't want to discourage his brother, yet he wouldn't support a radical newspaper. "I'll discuss it with Father, but only on the condition that you won't print any reform propaganda, or any anti-British sentiments."

"I don't intend to print ideas that are 'anti' anything. Only 'pro' - people, progress, Canada! You won't regret this, Jamie, I promise!"

"I sincerely hope not," Jeremy replied with a smile. He wouldn't try to disillusion Adrian. The people themselves would do that soon enough, he thought as he glanced at the motley group of men.

Above the din, he heard a man say loudly to his friends, "What a cesspool this town is. Surrounded by bogs. Ain't fit for decent folk, but the papists like it right enough. They're like pigs when it comes to rolling in muck." The speaker and his friends, who were Orangemen from the neighbouring township of Emily, laughed heartily.

An expectant silence quivered in the stifling air.

Brendan Delaney leaned his elbows on the bar and said to his companions, "I thought I smelled some scum from that pisshole, Emily. I reckon an apology's due to all the good citizens of Launston Mills."

As though he hadn't heard, the Orangeman said, "And have you seen their houses? Christ, my pigs live in better shanties than they do! I always said those papists were lazy, stinking bastards."

Brendan tapped the Orangeman on the shoulder. As the man turned about, Brendan flung the contents of his mug into the man's face. Then all hell seemed to break loose. The five Orangemen lunged at Brendan, only to find themselves up against ten opponents -- the Delaney brothers, Ewan Monaghan, Donal O'Shaughnessy, Fergus, Conn, and Owen Ryan, and three of the Darcy boys.

Tables and chairs went flying, and the bystanders quickly moved out of range of the action. The Orangemen took a severe beating, and within a few minutes, were summarily dispatched onto the dusty road outside the inn.

"If you're wanting to eat some more dirt, just come into town again and we'll be glad to oblige you!" Brendan called from the doorway.

"You've not heard the last of this!" one of the Orangemen called. "You'll live to regret this, I swear it!" Then a string of obscenities wafted into the tavern, making the patrons laugh. The young Irishmen soon had the room to rights again, and then bought a round of whiskey for every man present.

"Let's get out of here," Jeremy said to his brother, disgusted by the scene he had just witnessed. He couldn't understand men's proclivity to violence. It never solved anything, just led to retaliation. With their constant brawling, the Irish only confirmed the low opinion Jeremy had of them.

Brendan saw the Launston brothers walk toward the door. "Won't you be toasting our victory with a friendly drink, Mr. Launston?"

"No," Jeremy replied curtly as he continued walking. Despite his father's advice, Jeremy could not accept or condone such savage behaviour. He knew his father would have admonished them good-naturedly, showing his disapproval without giving offence. But at the moment Jeremy found it difficult even to be civil to Delaney.

"Is it that you're too good to drink with us then?" Brendan challenged.

Delaney was already quite drunk, Jeremy noticed as he turned to face the Irishman. His contempt was undisguised as he said, "It's unfortunate that you have more brawn than brain, Delaney." He walked out.

"Bastard!" Brendan hissed between his teeth. He took a step toward the door, but his companions restrained him.

"You'd best not cause trouble with the boss," his brother, Sean, advised.

"I'll take him off his God-Almighty high horse one day! Aye, and that'll be a sorry day for him."

Chapter 8

The O'Shaughnessy girls followed a rough path along the bank of the river, upstream from the mills. They laughed and chatted as they stepped gaily along, swinging their baskets. They were going berrying, and all were glad to be away from household chores for the afternoon. Alys had chosen to stay home, for she had never grown used to the mosquitoes, and always came up in abnormally swollen lumps when she was bitten. The cedars, which grew particularly dense along the water's edge, seemed to be favourite haunts of these vicious insects. The others had doused themselves in the lavender water which Rowena had concocted. Although it seemed a fairly effective repellent, they did not tarry in the woods.

They had hitched up their thin print dresses to allow the breeze to fan their legs, since no one could see them here. Though they usually went barefoot in summer, they now wore their moccasins for protection from prickly weeds and snakes. The venomous rattler had been common enough in this area when the settlement had been young, but the continuous influx of people, the land clearing and brush burning, was driving that viper deeper into the forests. The harmless snakes, however, were still prevalent, and terrifying enough to those who had never encountered these reptiles in their homeland.

The girls reached a soft, grassy beaver meadow ripe with wild strawberries and dotted with daisies and buttercups. Meadowsweet and honeysuckle thickets grew on the riverbank, alongside lilies and cattails.

Moira plucked posies of wildflowers, and decorated her sisters' straw bonnets with the fragile blooms. Gwyn and Brigid set about at once to relieve the strawberry plants of their heavy burdens. The girls worked silently, listening to the drone of the bees and the rustling of the breeze through the grass as it sought and captured Nature's perfumes.

When her basket was half-filled, Rowena rose from her knees to ease her cramped muscles. "You three stay here," she said. "I'm going to walk on a bit."

"You'd best not," Moira said, alarmed. "There's a bog along there."

"Aye, I know."

"You might fall into it!"

"I promise to be careful. Mind that Brigid and Gwyn don't eat too many of the berries or they'll be sick. I'll not be long."

Rowena ran through the field, unavoidably squashing strawberries underfoot, and entered the cool, fragrant forest once again. Birds whistled and trilled their songs; the staccato rapping of woodpeckers echoed through the woods; squirrels scolded the intruder from safe vantage points in the treetops. Broken boughs and flattened ferns and grasses led Rowena to the swamp.

Drowned trees were merely pale ghosts while thirsty plants and shrubs crowded around them. Colourful, exotic wildflowers were temptingly beautiful. There was not even a whisper of wind to disturb the rank miasma.

Rowena ventured closer. A red-winged blackbird shrieked a warning and flapped from its perch on a bulrush to the naked branch of a tree.

"Don't go any farther!" a man's voice called sharply.

Rowena jumped with fright. She looked around and saw, to her surprise, Adrian Launston only a few feet behind her.

"Come back. It's not safe there," he told her.

Rowena understood why. The ground was no longer solid, but like a squishy, sinking sponge. Quickly she retraced her steps.

"I sometimes think of bogs as living things," Adrian said to her when she had reached his side. "If you listen carefully, you can hear it breathe."

Rowena shivered at his words, for she knew what he meant.

"And they lure unsuspecting young girls like you into their traps with their exquisite blooms."

"You're teasing me!" Rowena accused.

He smiled. "Not entirely. You can sense it too, can't you -- the primeval forces of Nature at work here. Can you feel the trees dying as the swamp sucks their life's blood from them to nourish the beautiful flowers you were admiring? Don't look so frightened. I shan't let it get you."

Rowena didn't know what to think of this odd young man and his rather morbid observations. In appearance he resembled an angel she had seen depicted in a religious painting. His hair was golden; his pale, almost translucent complexion made him seem ethereal, though his smile was warm and genuine.

"You're one of Carpenter O'Shaughnessy's daughters, aren't you?"

"Aye, I'm Rowena."

"An enchanting name. So you're the child of the rowan tree. Don't you Irish believe it possesses magical powers?"

"Aye, it keeps the banshees away. But 'tis bad luck to burn the wood."

"I shall remember that. May I call you Rowena?"

"Certainly, Mr. Launston."

"Adrian. There's no need for formality here. Tell me, Rowena, what brings you to this rather forbidding place?"

"'Tis eerie to be sure, but...." She shrugged. "Somehow beautiful."

"I agree. Swamps are fascinating places - life, death, and rebirth all happening simultaneously."

"I can see the life and death, but not t'other."

"Do you see that sphagnum moss growing there? Those deceptive tussocks that you thought were solid ground? The moss will keep spreading, devouring the swamp until there's nothing left of it. In its place will be a meadow where trees will eventually grow again. Thus the cycle is complete," Adrian chuckled. "Though I rather doubt that Nature will be allowed a free hand in the matter. I suspect my brother intends to drain this swamp some day in order to make the land productive. Jamie is ever the practical one."

Responding to his friendly manner, Rowena felt emboldened to ask, "What is it that you're doing here?"

"I have a keen interest in botany -- the study of plants. I make sketches of them."

"May I see?"

He handed her his notebook. She was impressed with how detailed and accurate the drawings were. Written beside each illustration were extensive notations.

Adrian said, "I'm making records for posterity. I rather suspect that with all the land clearing and lumbering going on, we're going to lose some of these species. I correspond with a professor at Edinburgh University, sending him my sketches and specimens of the flora. So far, we've identified a couple of new species."

It all sounded very high-minded to Rowena, although she thought it a rather odd occupation for a man. "Is that what you'll be doing now that you've finished school?"

"Would that I could!" Adrian replied with a laugh. "I'd like nothing better than to immerse myself in the beauties and mysteries of nature. But I feel compelled to take an active political voice just now."

"Will you be taking a government post then?" she asked, well aware of the system of patronage that gave lucrative and influential positions to wealthy, educated Tories like the Launstons. Just the other day Donal had complained about how the College in Toronto was just preparing the sons of the rich and powerful to step into important jobs. Rowena could not really understand why Donal and his friends thought this so corrupt and unfair. After all, the government needed intelligent and educated men. What good would someone like Donal be, whose skills lay in his knowledge and mastery of wood?

"Quite the contrary," he replied without explanation. "Well, would you be interested in having a closer look at the swamp flora?"

"Oh, yes!"

As they skirted the bog, Adrian pointed out jack-in-the-pulpit, and marsh marigolds. When a fallen tree provided them with a bridge across a wet section, Adrian offered to assist Rowena.

She looked shyly at his outstretched hand and then took it. His grasp was warm and gentle and reassuring. It seemed strange to her, how easily they had drifted into such friendly intimacy

"Now look at this beauty -- lady's slipper. It's an orchid."

"She must be a grand lady indeed who owns such fine shoes," Rowena jested.

"I think it belongs to a wood nymph who danced the night away among the stars. She must have been so weary at dawn that she didn't notice she had dropped one of her slippers. No doubt she'll reclaim it for tonight's revelry."

Rowena was delighted with this fanciful description. "Do you believe in the wee folk then, Adrian?"

"I daren't say otherwise," Adrian whispered. "They might hear me."

They both laughed.

Adrian pointed to a plant with large heads of white flowers. "Now here is a *Eupatorium perfoliatum*, better known as ..."

"Boneset," Rowena said.

"Or feverwort," Adrian added.

"Or agueweed."

"Or Indian sage. The Indians use it for fevers."

"And we also use it for colds, influenza, rheumatism, and dropsy." Rowena giggled at Adrian's suprised expression. She explained, "My mother has taught me all about the healing plants. We gather them and dry them, and give them to the sick in infusions, teas, or poultices."

"Of course! Your mother is one of Simon's rivals."

"Nay! Hardly that. Ma gets called out for fevers and aches and suchlike. Folk don't much like being bled, and prefer the old remedies. But I think Dr. Worthing isn't big on bleeding either, not like some doctors."

"He's from a new school of medicine, more scientifically minded," Adrian said. "He's been studying the Indian medicines -- by trying a lot of them out on himself! He claims that some of them are quite efficacious. Like this boneset, for instance. Though he maintains it's still not as effective as quinine for the ague."

"But there are many that swear by it for the influenza," Rowena told him.

"So you help your mother, do you?"

"Sure, I've been interested in her potions ever since I can remember. 'Tis like magic sometimes, watching people get better after she tends to them."

"There must be a lot to learn."

"There is that! And no room for mistakes, either in identifying the plants, nor in the dispensing of them. But 'tis like second nature to me, like knowing how to cook a stew or to bake bread."

"Then you must have a gift for it. Perhaps I should ask you to tell ***me*** something about the plants here."

She blushed. "Nay."

"Perhaps you could tell me of the healing properties of some of the native plants then. The professor would most likely be interested."

"Sure, Dr. Worthing would know more than me! But I'd be happy to."

"Good! What about these highbush cranberries then?"

"They make a delicious jelly," Rowena quipped.

Adrian chuckled. "They do indeed. Well, do you know the pitcher plant? It's that red and green plant with the water in it? It's carnivorous -- it eats insects."

"You're teasing."

"I'm quite serious. It has little hairs inside those pouches which trap an insect careless enough to venture within."

A shudder tingled through her. The bog seemed sinister once again. It would have had her, too, if Adrian hadn't come along.

"I'd best go now," Rowena said reluctantly. "My sisters'll be worried. Thank you for telling me about the flowers, and for warning me."

"My pleasure. I hope I haven't scared you away with all my metaphorical nonsense about this place. I sometimes allow my imagination to get the better of me."

Adrian was walking with her, so she asked, "Do you come here often?"

"When I can tolerate the mosquitoes. I like the atmosphere. It's conducive to thinking."

"What do you think about?"

"Life. And death."

Rowena wondered what there was to consider about these topics, but didn't ask.

"I hope we'll meet again, Rowena," Adrian said when they reached the path.

She smiled. "Goodbye, Adrian."

Her encounter with him lingered in Rowena's mind long after they had parted. She, too, hoped that they would meet again, for she liked that peculiar young man.

But that possibility was greatly diminished when Gwyn burst out at the supper table with, "Rena shouldn't get as many berries as me! She didn't do her share of the picking."

"Gwyn, you little pig," Rowena said. "You ate at least as many strawberries as you put in your basket today. It'll serve you right if you're sick tonight!"

"What do you mean Rowena didn't do her share of the work?" Deirdre asked Gwyn.

"She went to the bog."

"The bog?"

"'Twas just for a little while," Rowena said defensively. She glowered at Gwyn who stuck out her tongue in response. "Just to look. I found some boneset, Ma."

"You weren't to be traipsing about a dangerous bog alone," Deirdre said angrily. "Have you no sense, girl?"

Donal gave Rowena a sympathetic look. He said, "Give over, Ma. Rena wouldn't do anything stupid. She's not careless like some I know." He looked pointedly at Gwyn who stuck out her tongue at him.

"Your Ma's right," Patrick said. "The swamp's no place for a lass to be going on her own. You'll all keep away from there."

Rowena was keenly disappointed. There was little chance she could talk with Adrian again, since she could hardly stop by his house for a chat or even engage him in conversation were she to meet him on the street. It really was too bad having bothersome little sisters!

Rowena was sweeping out the kitchen when the Ryans came by. The young children disappeared outside, Patrick and Matt retired to the stoop to smoke their pipes, and the women and girls gathered about the table and helped Fionna sew squares for a quilt. Donal, Conn, Owen, and Fergus went to help Sean Delaney work on the house he was building for himself and Fionna. Brendan would retain the original log cabin, with half an acre; Sean's new clapboard house was being erected on the other half acre. The Delaney brothers lived just down the road, and the women could hear the rhythmical thudding of the hammers.

"'Tis quite the house Sean's building for you," Deirdre said to Fionna.

"Aye, and he's that anxious to finish it. I reckon Josh Paxton's pockets have been nigh on empty these last weeks." Fionna giggled. "Sean wants to move up the wedding date. Says September's too long a time to wait, and too near the time he'll have to be going off to the lumber camp."

"He's a hard worker, I'll say that for him," Mary Ryan said. "That house'll be the grandest one in town, next to the Launstons'."

"Now, Ma, don't be exaggerating!"

"Aye, well all that frilly bargeboard that Patrick's carving for him. Any road, you're a lucky lass, no mistake."

Shelagh Ryan jabbed her needle angrily into her square of cloth. Her pout was not lost on her mother. Rowena noticed Mary and Deirdre exchange knowing glances, though they said nothing. It was obvious that Shelagh was envious of her sister. With sudden intuition, Rowena realized that Shelagh fancied herself married to Brendan, but he obviously had no such intentions. For a moment she actually felt a stab of pity for Shelagh.

Rowena's needle flew deftly in and out of the cloth. She heard Fionna talking about the wedding preparations, and the men's conversation trickled in from the veranda, but she paid no heed -- until she heard Adrian's name mentioned.

Matt Ryan was saying, "The young Launston lad was in Paxton's earlier this evening. He's been there quite regular of late, though he never has more than a pint of ale. Comes to talk, he does, and that fair surprised me, it did, himself never saying more than a how d'ee do afore this. Ezra Calder was reading us the latest copy of *The Constitution* where Mackenzie was saying there was a possibility of a revolt happening in Lower Canada, and that the people weren't going to stand for irresponsible government no more. Just joshing like, one of the Calder boys asks young Adrian what he thinks, and damn me if the lad's not a reformer! Said he didn't think force was the answer, but that 'tis time all us folk took an interest in what's happening to this country, and put a stop to the Tories afore 'tis too late!"

Patrick whistled. "I wonder what old Sam thinks about that. And Jeremy -- them both being staunch Tories."

"Happen they don't know, I'd say."

But Jeremy did know and was, at that moment, upbraiding Adrian about it.

Adrian stood quietly in the parlour while Jeremy paced about it. Samuel was at Colonel Grimsby's for his weekly chess match.

"That kind of talk is treasonous!" Jeremy said angrily. "Mackenzie's openly advocating rebellion, and you have the.... the ***stupidity*** to agree with him! And in public, no less! You'd better hope that Father hasn't heard of this."

"I didn't condone the use of violence. I just stated that it's time we stood up for our rights."

"And how do you think that people will interpret that remark? Christ!"

"I wish you'd stop treating me like a child!" Adrian said indignantly. "I'm entitled to express my own opinion. Surely one can criticize the government without being accused of sedition!"

They were interrupted by a knock on the front door. Jeremy went to answer it.

"Ah, Jeremy, I'm glad we've found you in," Amelia Grimsby said as she rustled into the vestibule. "I do so need your advice about a horse that Papa is going to buy for me."

Malcolm grinned lopsidedly. He was already well into his cups, but Amelia had dragged him along for the sake of propriety.

Jeremy was annoyed, not only by the Grimsbys' untimely arrival, but by Amelia's persistence. Why couldn't the blasted girl take a hint! He had hoped to discourage her by his infrequent visits -- accepting only supper invitations with his father, since Samuel would not hear of refusing them -- and by his distant manner with her. But Amelia had contrived a variety of excuses to visit him, and appeared undaunted by his coldness. By God, the last thing he wanted was an emotional confrontation with her! Perhaps tonight was as good a time as any to inform her of his engagement, though it wouldn't be official until the ball in Peterborough next week.

"Won't you come in?" Jeremy led them into the drawing room.

"Now do advise me, Jeremy," Amelia said when she had accepted a glass of sherry. "Papa tells me that you have a friend in Peterborough who breeds horses."

"That's right. I'm sure Nigel will have a mount to suit you. He has everything from draught horses to thoroughbreds."

"Do you know, I haven't even been to Peterborough yet? And it's what - twenty five miles? Papa says the road is appalling, all those swamps traversed by corduroy roads with half the logs missing. He says we'll go by boat through the lakes; although it's a longer route by water it's much less uncomfortable. I'm not sure whether seasickness is preferable to being bounced over rough roads. However.... Well, I suppose we can see your friend Nigel about the horse next week when we attend that ball. Do you know, that's the most extraordinary thing! We've been invited to a soiree, and we don't even know the hosts! What is the name? No, it's quite escaped me, I'm afraid."

"Neville," Jeremy said.

"Yes, that's it! Are you acquainted with them?" Her eyes lit up with excitement. "Oh, Jeremy, did you arrange for our invitation? How thoughtful of you!"

Jeremy felt acutely uncomfortable as he said, " Miss Harriet Neville is to be my wife. The ball is in honour of our engagement."

Amelia gaped at him. "Your... wife?" she echoed in a falsetto voice. Quickly she regained control of herself. With a forced smile she said, "Why, Jeremy, I had no idea! You really are too secretive! Do accept my sincerest congratulations."

There was an embarrassing silence.

"Well, we really must be going now," Amelia said. "I promised Mama we'd not be long."

"There now, Amelia," Malcolm said, "you'll have someone to visit with when Jeremy brings his bride home."

"Quite," Amelia replied, turning pale. "Do come along, Malcolm."

"You ***are*** a sly one," Malcolm said to Jeremy as he accompanied the Grimsbys to the door. "When is the wedding to be?"

"October."

"No sense in dragging out the engagement, eh? Winters are mighty cold here," Malcolm said with a suggestive grin.

"Thank you for the wine, Jeremy. Good bye," Amelia said. She held her head high as she walked out the door.

"Malcolm's an insensitive bastard," Jeremy said to Adrian when the two brothers were once more alone. "I wish there'd been an easier way to tell her. God knows, I've tried in a hundred subtle ways to let her know."

Adrian said, "She took it very well. Considering."

"Considering what?"

"That she's in love with you."

Jeremy scoffed at this idea. "Nonsense! Amelia is bored. Certainly she wants a husband, as do all young women her age. And since I was the only eligible bachelor here, she naturally latched onto me. It wouldn't surprise me if, in her girlish romanticizing, she has convinced herself that she has a *tendre* for me, but it's nothing serious. Doubtless she'll forget me quickly enough when she has a chance to meet other suitors. The best thing for her -- indeed for them all -- would be to spend a few months in Toronto. The Colonel's the only one who has adjusted to this life. Malcolm drinks himself senseless, and Mrs. Grimsby constantly takes to her bed with imaginary ailments."

Adrian was not so sanguine about Amelia. "Have you ever been in love, Jamie?"

"No. Nor do I believe in the sort of love that I'm sure you're talking about. All that poetic nonsense! At best it is passion, volatile and expendable; at worst it's an uninhibited wallowing in an emotional morass. Now, what do you say to a game of chess?"

Adrian lay awake for a long while that night, staring at the moon through the fine mesh of the mosquito curtain surrounding his bed. He thought about the girl in the simple print dress, her bonnet sprinkled with daisies and buttercups, a girl with enchanting blue eyes and a heart-wrenching smile. None of the girls that he had met at social occasions in the city had ever affected him as she had. How refreshing was the sincerity, the unabashed naiveté, the earthy wholesomeness of Rowena. She was a wood nymph, a fairy child of the forest. And he had fallen under her spell.

It was something he had never expected to happen to him. Indeed, he did not want it to happen now. But he could as lief have stopped this flood of warmth and joy that rushed through him at the memory of her, as he could have torn out his own heart.

Even as he drifted into sleep with a smile upon his face, he thought how wrong it was to love her.

Chapter 9

It was a pure, sweet summer day. A soft breeze, cedar-scented, wafted across the yard where Deirdre and the girls were busy with the laundry. The girls -- aprons tied over their print dresses, barefoot, their long tresses restrained by caps -- were silent for a moment, each concentrating upon her task. Deirdre rubbed the clothes vigorously on the scrubbing board set in a large wooden tub. Moira boiled the garments in a copper kettle suspended over a fire, stirring them around and around and occasionally lifting one up with her stick, for inspection. It was Gwyn's job to rinse them, and Rowena's to starch them. Then they were given to Alys and Brigid to hang on the line where they fluttered and flapped and would be sun-bleached and wind-scented.

Rowena began to hum a tune. Moira joined in with the words -- partly in Gaelic -- and soon they were all singing a lively song about a goose-stealing fox.

"That's a fine caterwauling!" Patrick teased, sticking his head out the door of the workshop. He grinned broadly. "Never seen such a grand sight, to be sure -- a chorus of angels washing me clothes! Give us another tune then!"

"Caterwauling, is it?" Deirdre said.

"Nay, 'tis honey to me ears."

Conn came running into the yard calling for Patrick.

"Conn, me lad, what's amiss?"

Conn gasped for breath and then blurted out, "Orangemen... a whole army of them... coming to burn down the town... as revenge for us beating up a couple of them a few weeks since!"

"Holy Mother of God!" Deirdre exclaimed in fright.

"What?!" Patrick cried.

"Angus Corbin stopped in Omemee last night," Conn explained. "Heard them talking about it. There's an ungodly number of Orangemen in that area, and seeing as how today's the Twelfth, they was saying it was the best time to show us that they hadn't forgotten, and that, like the Battle of the Boyne, the righteous would be victorious once again."

Donal had overheard the conversation, and emerged from the workshop.

"Donal, you and Conn get whatever weapons you can find!"

"No, Pat!" Deirdre cried, grabbing her husband's arm. "No killing!"

"We'll not stand by and watch them burn us out! Take the girls to the church. You'll not be safe here if they cross that bridge."

Rowena and Moira doused the fire while Patrick rushed into the house for his musket.

"Get on with you!" Patrick called to them as he hurried toward the bridge where other men were already assembling and conferring. It wasn't just the Catholics who came, for the Orangemen had threatened the entire town.

Rowena picked up young Brigid, and the women started up Mill Road toward the town. Mary, Shelagh, and the other Ryan children joined them.

"If them heathens try to get into the church, they'll be having this to answer to!" Mary said, boldly brandishing a pitchfork.

"I never thought to see this happening here," Deirdre said sadly. Was it all going to start again, she wondered -- all that intolerance and violence that should have been left behind in the Old Country? Was it just the nature of men -- of Irishmen particularly -- to find any excuse for a fight? And leave the women to pick up the pieces. She shuddered as if someone had walked over her grave. She had seen the excitement in Donal's eyes, and feared it.

"'Tis the damned Orangemen. Can't leave us in peace! Came to insult us, and then cried foul play when our boys gave 'em what for! May the Good Lord strike 'em dead!" Mary gave Deirdre's arm a reassuring squeeze. "Our menfolk know what they're doing, never you fear."

More armed men passed the women. As they neared the Launstons' house, they saw Samuel, Jeremy, Colonel Grimsby, and Major Selfridge mounting their horses.

Fionna dashed out of the kitchen and intercepted the women. "Have you seen Sean?"

"Aye," Mary replied. "He's down at the bridge with the others." She grabbed her daughter's arm as the girl started to move away. "You'll be coming with us, Fionna. 'Tis not a girl's place to be interfering with men's work."

"But...."

"Aye, I know. Your Da and brothers are there too. Come along."

There were already several women and children in the church when the O'Shaughnessys and Ryans arrived. Father Killeny was trying to console Kate Muldoon, who was weeping distractedly. Mary marched over and took command.

"There now, Kate," Mary said. "There's no reason to be carrying on so."

"Jacob'll be killed! Then what am I to be doing? Me with eight childer!" Kate began wailing once again.

Mary spoke firmly, yet soothingly, and soon had the woman calmed down. She had a knack for taking control in difficult or unpleasant situations, Deirdre thought. Although Mary could sometimes be overbearing, she was a strong shoulder in times of need, and Deirdre was grateful for her friendship.

Deirdre took comfort, too, from the new church. It was little more than a shell as yet, though Patrick and Donal had begun to build pews. Chairs and crates served the congregation at present. The beautifully carved altar was Patrick and Donal's handiwork as well. What pride and joy she felt whenever she saw the beauties that her men had wrought for the glory of God!

Rowena stood at the window and stared out, though she could see only the empty road and the cedar and spruce jungle on the other side of it. She was afraid for Donal. He had taken part in that fight in the tavern. Was there to be retribution now, if not for the whole town, then for the brawlers? If only Donal weren't so ready to throw punches when other men did!

She thought of his strong, yet elegant hands and how they fashioned such beautiful carvings. He would examine a new piece of wood with his eyes and his fingers. He told her how each carving then sprang into his mind, ready made, and all he had to do was free it from the block of wood. His birds were not chunky and heavy, but smooth and graceful, as if they could truly take flight. To think that those clever hands could so easily become weapons appalled and frightened her.

Strangely, she found herself worrying about Adrian, too, wondering where he was, since she had not seen him with his father and brother. He was like one of Donal's birds, beautiful and fragile, and she could not imagine him capable of dealing with the violent brutes that were about to do battle. Although she was two years younger than Adrian, Rowena felt protective of him. Certainly he was much cleverer than she was, but he seemed somehow naive and unprepared for the real world. She fought the urge to run out the door and through the woods to the swamp, to look for him.

There was a tense silence in the church as the group listened for sounds of gunfire. It was, in fact, too unnervingly quiet -- "Like the calm before the storm," Shelagh said, and was promptly chided by her mother for upsetting Kate Muldoon again. Several of the women, including Deirdre, were reciting the rosary.

Father Killeny joined Rowena at the window.

"Why do the Protestants hate us so, Father?" she asked.

"That's a difficult question to answer, child," the priest said. "And hate is an emotion which knows neither reason nor compassion. You have to look far back into Ireland's history to fully understand."

"Aye, I know about the fighting between us and the English, how they came and took our lands and denied us our rights and religion."

"Then you know how the seeds of hate were sown."

"But this isn't Ireland!"

"Aye, but prejudices die hard. We can only pray that time, and God, will temper them."

A single shot rang out.

• • •

Jeremy Launston spurred his horse forward, cursing under his breath. The damned Irish, always causing trouble! Now he and his father, the Colonel and the Major would have to put a stop to this incredible situation before someone was hurt.

Most of the town's able-bodied men and boys were already at the bridge when the four riders arrived. The boys were collecting rocks to use as missiles; Matt Ryan was organizing the "troops", spreading the men with guns along the riverbank while those with axes were being instructed to chop down the bridge -- the only one which gave access to the town from the east.

"Hold on there, men," Colonel Grimsby ordered. "There's no need for that yet."

"And just what is it you're proposing we do?" Brendan Delaney asked sarcastically. "Welcome the bastards with open arms?"

"Haven't you caused enough trouble already, Delaney?" Jeremy said. "You are the man chiefly responsible for this unpleasant business. I suggest you shut up and listen to what the Colonel has to say."

Brendan glared at Jeremy, but said nothing.

Colonel Grimsby addressed the men. "We four propose to ride out and meet the foe with the intention of dissuading them from their present course of action."

"And leave us cowering here like a bunch of old women?" Brendan said. "Not likely! They're coming for a fight and we'll be giving them one they'll not forget!"

Jeremy tried to control his rage. Delaney was insufferable!

Samuel Launston spoke calmly. "Would you risk your lives and your homes instead of allowing us to reason with the invaders? There will be no fighting this day if I can help it!"

"Aye, he's right," several of the men agreed. "We'll not be fighting 'cepting to protect our homes and families."

"If it's a fight you want, Delaney," one of Blacksmith Calder's boys said, "then I'll gladly oblige you myself!"

"It's agreed then," Colonel Grimsby said, pleased. "You, Garth Calder, keep a lookout on the other side of the river. If we should fail in our negotiations and the enemy comes marching down the road, you give the signal to the men to chop down the bridge, and then get the hell out of the way. Matt Ryan and Ezra Calder, I leave these men in your charge."

The delegation rode across the bridge and along the dusty trail. The suspense was as thick in the air as the heat, Jeremy thought, and wondered if the others were as apprehensive as he. None of them carried arms. They had only the weight of their offices behind them -- the Colonel as magistrate, and the Major as sheriff -- and both had had years of military experience, of leading men. Samuel, too, had an easy command of the common man -- a skill that Jeremy admired and suspected that he had yet to develop. It was, after all, expected of a gentleman to be always in control, and not to allow his emotions to sabotage his reason. It was unfortunate that ruffians like Delaney could so easily arouse his ire.

As they crested the hill, less than a mile from the river, they heard the tramp of feet -- a veritable army by the sound of it -- and caught faint snatches of a derogatory song about Catholics and the Pope.

The four men glanced at one another and rode on.

The Orangemen stopped marching and fell silent when they spotted the peacemakers. There were nearly a hundred of them, armed with muskets and carrying unlit torches. A number of these guns were now trained upon the riders.

"Best get out of our way, gentlemen, 'less you want to get shot," the spokesman warned.

"We've come to discuss the situation," Colonel Grimsby said.

"The cowards don't want to fight when they're evenly matched, is that it?" one of the Orangemen yelled.

"I'm certain that none of us wishes to see any blood spilt today," Major Selfridge said.

"You're wrong there! We don't like the way folk treat strangers in your town, and we mean to teach you all a lesson in manners!" This elicited a chortle from the Lodge members.

"The incident in the tavern was unfortunate," Jeremy said. Disgusted as he was by the behaviour of Delaney and his friends, he wasn't about to let these men shirk their responsibility for the fight. "I was a witness to it, and those five of you who were there deliberately provoked trouble." The men didn't like Jeremy's accusation, and several threatening gestures were directed toward him. "Colonel Grimsby is a magistrate. If you wish to press assault charges, he will review your case, and justice will be served."

There was a dissatisfied grumble from the mob.

"I suggest you return to your families," Major Selfridge said. "You are all law-abiding, God-fearing men, and too wise to allow a few hotheads involve you in an act of vengeance which could endanger your lives."

"We'll not turn tail and forget all about it!"

"Aye!"

"This is not the Old Country," Samuel said. "We all came here to make better lives for ourselves and our families, and the sensible men will have left their prejudices behind. Don't jeopardize everything you've come here to achieve. This country is big enough and bountiful enough for us all to live in peace with our neighbours, no matter what their religious beliefs or background may be. If you persist in this illegal course of action, you can be assured that the full force of the law will be brought upon your heads. How long do you think your womenfolk can keep your farms going and your children clothed and fed when the lot of you are in gaol?"

"Just let us get the bloody papists then, those bastards in the tavern. Just so's we can teach them a lesson in fair fighting!"

Samuel was about to speak, but the Colonel forestalled him. "I have a suggestion that I hope you will find satisfactory," he said to the Orangemen, who were becoming impatient with all this talk. "We'll have a competition, a test of strength and skill. You choose your best fighter and he'll box against our best man. We'll hold the match a week Saturday on the town common. Bring your wives and children and we'll show you how hospitable our community really is."

This idea interested the men. After the hot, dry, ten mile walk much of the enthusiasm that had fired the indignant Orangemen had dissipated. Most of them had no personal grudge against the people of Launston Mills, and they realized the truth of Samuel's words. The Colonel's proposal would allow them to save face; so they eagerly discussed it amongst themselves.

"I hope you know what you're doing, Colonel," Samuel whispered. "Tempers will still be running high, and once they get some grog into them, we could have a riot on our hands."

"We'll invite every Scotsman and Englishman in the township to keep an eye on the Irish. At the first sign of trouble from anyone, the Major and I will exercise our legal powers and lock him up in Paxton's cellar. We'll use every cellar in town if need be! And we'll water down the whiskey."

The Orangemen came to a decision. "We agree to your suggestion."

"Excellent! I trust it is understood that there is to be no fighting except between the two contestants?"

"Aye, 'tis agreed. We'll honour our word, never fear. Though if those papists start anything..."

"We shall ensure they don't."

"Next Saturday then."

The Orangemen were less orderly and less vociferous as they, muskets lowered, turned about and began the long trek home.

"That was a stroke of genius, Colonel," Major Selfridge said. "I'd about lost hope of making them see reason."

"But it's not over yet," Jeremy said. "With agitators like Delaney around, there's bound to be trouble next week."

"Then we'll just have to make sure that Delaney hasn't the energy left to incite violence," Colonel Grimsby said shrewdly. "I nominate him as our representative in the match -- and I hope the other fellow beats the daylights out of him!"

They all laughed.

As they rode slowly back to the river, they spied Garth Calder perched high in a tree, and waved him down. He removed his cap and flourished it about joyfully.

The villagers anxiously held their positions. A tense young man accidentally squeezed the trigger of his musket when the four men came into view. The horses shied at the explosion, but the riders quickly regained control of their mounts. Fortunately, the man had not been aiming, and the bullet plunged harmlessly into the river.

"For Christ's sake, hold your fire!" Colonel Grimsby bellowed.

The men lowered their weapons as the horses clattered over the bridge.

"You can all go back to your homes and sleep safely in your beds tonight," the Colonel informed them.

They cheered.

The Colonel raised his hand for silence, and then explained the agreement to them. Brendan Delaney grinned proudly when he learned that he was to be the town's contender in the match.

"You'd best start training then," Fergus Ryan said as he and others crowded about "their man".

"You're a wise man, Colonel," Samuel said. "I think the four of us deserve a drink. What do you say?"

"Best suggestion I've heard all day!"

Chapter 10

The day of the "Great Match", as it came to be known, was cool and grey with rain threatening to disrupt the festivities. But it didn't prevent people from attending, particularly since a holiday had been declared, and the mills and shops were closed.

Rowena thought that Main Street was busier than on the annual June 4th parade day, which was held in celebration of the King's birthday. Oxen and horses, carts and people kicked up the gritty dust as they gravitated toward the common.

Some of the men and boys of the county militia, under Major Selfridge's command, were drilling at the far end of the road. Those who had no guns shouldered brooms, and their uniforms were hardly that since the men were clad in workaday clothes.

"Do you think the Major's expecting trouble?" Patrick said, as the O'Shaughnessys and Ryans ambled up the road.

"Mayhap 'tis a warning to folk," Matt said with a laugh. "Though they're not a fierce looking bunch."

"'Twas a fool notion of the Colonel's, inviting them Orangemen here. What's to stop them from burning us out today then, I'd like to know! Not that pitiful crew, for certain," Mary said, indicating the militia.

"They gave their word there'd be no trouble," Deirdre said half-heartedly.

"I wouldn't give a Hail Mary for the word of an Orangeman! It'll be a donnybrook we'll be having here afore the day's out, you mark me words!"

Deirdre was all too afraid that Mary was right. She didn't trust any of the men not to start a brawl. But she prayed that Pat and Donal would not be involved.

"There'll never be peace among us unless we start trusting folk," Patrick said.

"I'd as soon trust a snake as an Orangeman," Mary replied.

As they neared the common, they noticed a small crowd gathered about one corner of Main Street. In its midst, perched upon a tree stump like a huge crow in a wide-brimmed black hat, was the Methodist circuit rider.

"Repent all ye sinners!" the preacher cried fervently. "Repent! Cast off your wickedness! Purify your souls! Let not your sins condemn you to ***Hell*** on earth and everlasting damnation! Let not the Devil tempt you with his instruments of pleasure, for they are the snakes of Eden! Rise above the lusts of the flesh, for the body is but a shell that withers and dies, whereas the soul lives forever! Embrace not the bottle, but the ***Bible***!" he shouted, holding up his tattered black book.

The congregation cheered.

"I never saw anything so near a smile on Hiram Lindsay's face afore this," Mary commented as they passed this religious assembly.

"You should have seen him at the camp meeting last summer," Donal said.

"You went to a Methodist camp meeting?" Deirdre asked, shocked.

"Just to look, Ma. And an eyeful it was, to be sure! Why, some of the folk were so riled up by the sermons and confessions, 'twas downright indecent," Donal said, suppressing a grin.

Rowena blushed guiltily, as did Conn. She well remembered the evening the three of them had stood in the shadows of the woods, watching the scene by the light of the bonfire. There had been people she knew, like the Lindsays staid, stern people at other times -- transformed into strangers who had revelled in an orgy of self-condemnation and such ecstasy of promised salvation that her cheeks had burned with embarrassment.

"You keep away from them Methodists, Donal," Deirdre ordered. "I've heard what goes on at them camp meetings -- more the divil's work than God's. Sure, 'tis no place for decent, God-fearing Christians to be. You'd best not forget that." Deirdre turned to Rowena. "Nor you, miss."

Rowena and Donal exchanged amused glances.

The common was a cleared block at the surveyed centre of the town. There were, as yet, no houses to the west of it --only a hill rising out of the cedar swamp next to this public square. The men were already jostling one another for ringside places, having relegated their women and children to the perimeter of the field. The two innkeepers, Josh Paxton and Arthur Stirling, were busy dispensing whiskey from the huge barrels -- donated by the Launston distillery -- which had been hauled over that morning. Rowena saw the Launstons talking to the Colonel. Adrian was glancing about casually while his father and brother were nodding in agreement with something the Colonel had said. Adrian's eyes swept past Rowena, but then he looked back at her in recognition and smiled.

His heart lurched. Rowena had been in his thoughts constantly these past weeks, Daily he had returned to the swamp, hoping to see her again; daily he had been disappointed. And he had wondered if perhaps she had been no more than a Galatea of his Pygmalion imagination. But she was all too achingly real. Even amidst this sea of babbling humanity, he could feel her magic reach out and touch him.

Rowena returned his silent greeting, and hastily lowered her eyes as a blush suffused her face. How she wished she could talk with him again!

Nearly every villager and most of the township farmers were present. Their number was almost doubled by the Orangeman, their families, and spectators from neighbouring townships. The two Irish factions eyed one another warily, and avoided each other as much as was possible in that confined square. The Catholics had not forgotten the impassioned plea for peace, tolerance, and brotherhood that had rung out from the pulpit the previous Sunday. Father Killeny had deliberately absented himself this day to avoid arousing the ire of the Orangemen by his reverend person.

The two fighters, stripped to the waist, were finally brought forward. The people cheered wildly as excitement swelled from a ripple to an all-engulfing wave. Colonel Grimsby, who was acting as referee and town spokesman, climbed onto the makeshift dais. He welcomed everyone to the match, and expressed his hope that the visitors were enjoying the hospitality of Launston Mills. Then he introduced the contestants.

"Representing Emily Township is Bruce Macnair."

There was a resounding ovation for this hefty, red-haired brute who was flexing his muscles for the benefit of the audience.

Rowena felt frightened for Brendan, who was physically no match for his opponent. The Orangeman laughed and jeered when Brendan mounted the platform, and comments like, "Bruce'll knock him dead with one blow!" were bandied about. But Brendan seemed unworried. He grinned as he acknowledged the clamourous praise he received from his supporters.

Colonel Grimsby explained the rules. "I insist upon a fair, clean fight. There is to be no gouging, no kicking, no butting, and no hitting below the belt. Contestants, take your places, and may the best man win!"

Rowena and the others around her could see little of the fight. She could only hear the cracks and thuds as bare fists hit their marks, and the exclamations of the audience, whether of approval or dismay. Each snap seemed to reverberate through her own body; each grunt and groan caused her stomach to knot; each cheer screamed in her head like an obscenity. She bobbed up and down, trying to see over the heads of the men, for the anguish of not knowing what was happening was greater even than watching the brutal, bloody fight.

Suddenly there was a unanimous gasp, and then exultant cheers from the townspeople. Brendan Delaney had knocked the tree-trunk of a man cold!

The Colonel gestured for silence, and addressed the crowd. "The winner of today's bout is Brendan Delaney."

There was a shattering round of applause, whistles, and hurrahs.

"Let us also show our appreciation of his worthy opponent." This was done. "The people of Ops Township sincerely hope that today's gathering will be the beginning of friendship between them and their neighbours from Emily, and that any differences which may arise can be settled in as civilized a manner as that of today."

"A return match" someone yelled.

"Aye, we'll have a rematch next year in our township!"

"A rematch," the Colonel echoed. "What say you, citizens of Ops?"

A cheer answered his question.

"So be it!"

Brendan was hoisted upon the shoulders of his jubilant friends, and paraded down Main Street and back. He had a bloody gash above one eye, which was already swelling shut, a couple of loose teeth, bruised ribs, and raw knuckles. But he was ecstatic as he revelled in the adulation of the villagers.

The men's spirits rose as the spirits in the barrels rapidly diminished. A few minor scuffles broke out, but these were quickly dealt with by the Major and the Colonel, and the offenders were left to "cool their heels" in the cellars of the two inns.

Farmer Peebles, never without his fiddle, was called upon for a tune, and gladly obliged. His eldest son accompanied him on a mouth harmonica, and the toe-tapping music soon had people bouncing to its rhythm on the green.

Donal, his eyes bright with the excitement of victory, grabbed his mother's hand and whirled her about. Caught up in his exuberance, Deirdre was soon laughing and feeling a decade younger. Her son was a charmer, she realized, and was not surprised. After all, he was like his father in so many ways.

The dance over, Donal offered her his arm with an exaggerated flourish, and escorted her back to the others. Then he sought out Rosemary Flannery, who was about the only girl in the district who could match his enthusiasm and skill on the dancefloor. She was a tall brunette with luminous green eyes, a beautiful smile, and a pleasing manner.

Deirdre sighed, thinking that Donal would soon be lost to her. There was no mistaking that penetrating look the two young people exchanged as they danced. Deirdre could almost feel the energy that passed between them. And yet, she was glad that Donal had found someone like Rosemary, who was a respectable, hardworking, and fun-loving girl. And she was strong. She could keep Donal out of trouble.

Rowena, too, noticed Donal's intense looks at Rosemary, and she envied them both. She looked about for Adrian, and was disappointed by his absence. But it had been ridiculous for her to hope that he would ask her to dance. Much as she had enjoyed his company and felt comfortable with him, nothing more could ever come of it. He was, after all, a Launston. Not for the likes of her.

She was grabbed by the hand, and turned to see Brendan grinning at her.

She shook her head at him. "Sure, I was that worried about you! I thought you'd be done for."

"Me? It'd take more than a bloody Orangeman to do me in!"

"He was near twice your size!"

"'Tis the technique that's important, mavourneen, not the size of the man," he said with a suggestive grin. "He was a great lumbering ox, to be sure. Come and dance." He pulled her tightly against him for a moment, and kissed her heartily on the lips.

Rowena drew back, shocked by his boldness and the bruising pressure of his mouth on hers.

"There's more where that came from, if you've a mind to sneak away with me," he whispered.

"Get away with you, Brendan Delaney!" she replied laughing, making light of his advances as she attempted to keep a respectable distance from him.

"Sure, but you're a lovely lass, Rowena. I've a mind to make a woman of you."

"If you'll not hush, Brendan, I've a mind to blacken your other eye!"

"You're a darlin', to be sure!"

Rowena was relieved when she was finally able to escape from Brendan. His eyes often strayed to her that evening, and she squirmed under his predatory gaze. She should have been flattered, she thought, for he was a handsome man, and a lively and amusing companion. Sure, she liked him well enough -- as a friend -- but his persistent advances frightened her. She was no longer certain, as she had been several months ago, that she would enjoy being courted by Brendan, though she did not understand this growing reluctance.

Chapter 11

"Patrick won't be having much work this winter if there's another bad harvest," Deirdre said to Mary Ryan over a cup of tea one wet, cold August afternoon. As they often did, they were both sewing as they talked. There were always so many chores to be done, but Deirdre found this the most pleasant of all, since it allowed for companionship and conversation. "Folk won't have enough to spare to be buying fancy pieces of furniture."

"Aye, 'tis right bad," Mary agreed. "And us with two weddings next month! I told Shelagh to wait -- folk might get the wrong impression, since Hugh Darcy's only been courting her this last month. But she's a strong-willed lass, and says she'll not wait."

"No need to wait if she knows her own mind."

"Sure, I'm thinking her heart's still with Brendan, an' all. Seems he's looking elsewhere though." Mary glanced toward Rowena, who, along with her sisters, was making tallow candles by hand-dipping.

"Hugh Darcy's a good man," Deirdre said, not looking up from her mending. "A better man than Brendan could ever be. Shelagh should be counting her blessings."

"Didn't I tell her that meself? 'Shelagh,' says I, 'you'll find no better husband than Hugh.' Sure, he'll be running that big farm one day, and my girl won't be wanting for nothing."

"An honest, God-fearing man he be, too. I couldn't be asking better for me own girls."

"To be sure. But there's that about Brendan, now, that the lassies can't seem to resist."

Deirdre snorted with derision.

"Then again, I don't rightly trust the man meself. You know why it is that Brendan and Sean left Ireland, don't you?" Without waiting for a reply, Mary continued. "They had to, is why. Were with the Whiteboys, and though I'm not rightly sure what it was they done, I did hear tell that the soldiers were after questioning them about a murder. Sean's harmless enough, I reckon, but I wouldn't be putting it past Brendan."

"I hadn't heard that. Mind you, I've never trusted Brendan. And I don't like the way he's filling our Donal's head with all this talk about joining Mackenzie if there's a rebellion."

"Sure, all the men are talking about Mackenzie these days. 'Tis all it is. Just talk."

"Let's hope so."

"Aye, well, 'tis all so far away, isn't it? We wouldn't even hear the half of it if the Flannerys didn't have kin near Toronto. Mike's always over, telling the boys about the news from the city. But if you ask me, neither a tale nor a woman that's been passed about that often is worth having!"

"'Tis lucky you are that your menfolk have jobs at the lumber camp again this winter," Deirdre said.

"We've done well by the Launstons, 'tis true, though I reckon we've helped them build their fortune." Mary chuckled. "You know what I'd like to see afore I die? I'd like to see all these cursed trees cut down. I'd like to see what the land really looks like!"

Neither one of them said aloud what Deirdre was sure they were both thinking -- that it would never look like home, like Ireland.

After a pause, Deirdre asked, "Is Fionna still quitting work at the end of this week?"

"Aye, though the Launstons haven't found anyone to replace her. There's not many a girl that's not betrothed nor wed now, though some that aren't are too proud to do an honest day's work. There now! I've just had a thought. Your Rowena could take Fionna's place at the Launstons'. They always pay cash, and the money'll come in handy this winter -- 'specially seeing as how you're expecting another one," Mary said, referring to the fact that Deirdre was pregnant once again.

Deirdre crinkled her brow. "Rowena? Working at the Launstons'? I don't know about that."

"Sure, she's seventeen. She's not stepping out with a lad, is she?"

"Nay. There's time enough for that."

Rowena, who had overheard the conversation, was considering the idea. It frightened her somewhat, the thought of working in that big house. But she'd see Adrian!

Deirdre raised the subject at supper that evening.

"No daughter of mine'll be working if I can help it," Patrick commented.

"But I want to, Da," Rowena said. "I'll be doing the same as what I do here, and getting paid for it. And Ma has enough help."

"I thought we came to this country so's none of us would have to stoop to cleaning other folks' boots," Donal said.

"There's nothing shameful about doing a day's work and getting paid for it," Rowena retorted. "'Tis no different than if you build them something and they pay you for it."

"The lass is right," Deirdre interceded. "'Tis not like in the Old Country. She could work there a year or two, till she's wed, and have a bit of her own money put by."

"There's sense enough in that, I suppose" Patrick conceded.

"If it doesn't suit me, I'll not stay on," Rowena said.

Patrick shrugged. "If 'tis what you really want."

"Thanks, Da!"

"Brendan won't much like it," Donal said off-handedly as he munched a piece of pie.

"And just what is it to him, I'd like to know?" Deirdre demanded.

"Happen he's taken a fancy to our Rowena."

"Well, he'd best look elsewhere!" Deirdre turned to Rowena. "You've not been encouraging him?"

"Nay!"

"I've not much liking for Brendan. And it worries me to see you so much in his company, Donal. The man's a bad influence."

"Leave the lad be, Dre," Patrick said. "Brendan's a fine man, and a hard worker. If he's serious about our lass...."

"Happen you're addled, Patrick O'Shaughnessy! Brendan's not a marrying man. If he was, there's one or two girls in the township he ***should*** be marrying!"

"Now, Dre, that's just gossip. Sure, I can't make out why you've taken such a strong dislike to the man."

"Because he's dangerous."

When the evening chores had been completed, Rowena dashed over to the Ryans' to talk to Fionna. She cut across the yard and through the head-high stalks of corn still dripping from the afternoon rainstorm. She clambered easily over the snake fence that delineated the boundary between the Ryans' and the O'Shaughnessys' land, and once more plunged into a forest of maize.

Mary greeted her when she entered the hot kitchen. "You've decided then, have you?"

"Aye. Is Fionna here?"

"She stepped out with Sean not five minutes since. Will I tell her you'll be going with her in the morning then?"

"Please."

"She'll be leaving just afore half past six."

"Hello, Rowena," Conn said as he walked in.

"Have you fetched Daisy back then?" Mary asked her son.

"Aye, but the pound keeper says the Launstons'll not let our pigs forage in their woods any longer if they keep going into town and destroying folks' gardens."

"What are we to be doing with the contrary sow then?"

"Keep her fenced in the yard, I reckon."

"She'll find nothing to eat there unless she breaks into our cornfield. Happen we'll slaughter her for the wedding. Will you take a cup of tea, Rowena?"

"I'd best be getting back now."

"I'll walk with you," Conn offered.

Rowena smiled at him. "If you like."

They scattered the protesting geese as they strolled through the yard down to the river. They walked along the shore in silence until they reached the fence. Rowena hopped onto it and sat down on the damp rail.

"Do you like it here?" Conn asked abruptly.

"Aye," she replied with a shrug, not sure what he meant.

"I mean in Launston Mills."

"'Tis as good a place as any other, I reckon, though I hadn't much liking for it when we first arrived. But... 'tis home now. Why are you asking such strange questions?"

Conn plucked the cap from his head, and ran his fingers through his hair. "Owen says the States is the place to be if a man really wants to make something of hisself."

"The States?"

"He's thinking to go there. Says there's not much future here while this country's still under British rule."

"Sure, you'll not be leaving, Conn?"

Conn rumpled his hair again. "I've been giving it some thought."

"Have you not been happy here? Don't you want to be a part of this town as it keeps growing? Have your children grow up here, enjoying all the things we did?"

Conn looked into her eyes. "Aye. I'd like that very much."

Rowena looked away. She gazed at the calm, seemingly sluggish river which belied its underlying strength.

"Rowena...."

She leapt to the ground on the other side of the fence and faced him. She had been foolish not to notice until now that Conn's feelings toward her had changed. Gone was that easy and uncomplicated childhood friendship. In its place was something that threatened their whole relationship.

"It's Brendan, isn't it?" Conn asked.

"Nay! It's me. You've always been a good friend to me, Conn, and as dear to me as me own brother. But I can't ever see it being more than that."

He understood. With a sad smile he said, "I reckon I'll be sticking around, anyway. I've never been much of an adventurer."

She grinned. "It'll be a better place for having you here. Thanks for walking with me."

She hated hurting and disappointing him. She could almost feel his pain as she watched him slowly retrace his steps.

Rowena ambled along the riverbank. The mist that drifted over the calm water was suddenly pierced by the haunting cry of a loon. It was a strange and beautiful bird that could suddenly appear and disappear, because it could swim for great lengths underwater. Its call was eerie, like the lament of some long-lost Celtic soul.

Rowena noticed Donal sitting between the two water willows -- the only trees on their land that had been spared the axe. He was studying the loon carefully, and she knew that he intended to make a carving of it.

Quietly, so as not to disturb the bird which now swam close to the shore, she sat down beside Donal. They both watched the loon, with its black head and beak and its distinctive black and white necklace, until it suddenly dove under the water and disappeared.

"Will you make that one for me?" she asked. "I like loons."

"Sure," he said, starting to whittle at a block of wood.

"I feel terrible," she confided as she rested her head on her drawn-up knees and stared out over the water, idly watching to see if the loon reappeared.

"Because you're going to be a servant to the Launstons?"

"Hired help, not a servant."

"'Tis the same no matter what you call it."

"There's nothing wrong with it, so just don't start lecturing me! And anyway, I'm kind of excited about that -- having me own paid job."

"Alright then. You're unhappy because Ma doesn't like Brendan and you do?" Donal guessed.

"No! I like Brendan well enough, but he sort of frightens me."

Donal looked at her seriously. "Then you'd best watch yourself with him. He's taken a powerful fancy to you, and he's not the kind of man to take rejection easily."

"Sure I've done nothing to encourage him!" Rowena said indignantly, somehow worried by Donal's earnest warning. "'Tisn't fair that I should feel guilty for his feelings, nor for Conn's neither."

"So that's it, is it? You finally realized that Conn's in love with you?"

"How did you know?"

"I've eyes in me head, same as most other folk around here -- except one I could mention."

"And I suppose it's my fault that he loves me?" Rowena snapped, angry still because she did feel culpable.

"I don't reckon you can blame anybody. Conn loves you, just because you are who you are. 'Tisn't his fault either. And Brendan -- well, you're just too beautiful for him to resist."

Rowena was taken aback by his words. She, beautiful? Irresistible?

Donal laughed at her stunned expression. "When you look like that, you don't exactly inspire poets! Sure, life was easier when you were just a bothersome little sister. Now I'll have to defend your honour from every eligible man in the district!"

"I was never bothersome," she replied. "And I have no interest in any men in the district."

"But they're taking notice of you."

"I'm really sorry about Conn. I do like him, you know. I wish men and women could just be friends, and not have to worry about things like love!"

"You are still such a child," Donal said with a grin. "You'd best have a talk with Ma some time. Get her to tell you about marriage and all that."

"But I don't want to get married!" Marriage, from what Rowena could see, was just a life of bondage and hard, endless work for women, with a new baby to care for every year or two.

Of course, she'd seen enough animals copulating to understand the mechanics of sex, though she couldn't see its appeal. It seemed to her a messy, brutal sort of act that just meant another mouth to feed in nine months. And she'd helped her mother often enough with birthings these last couple of years to realize that giving birth was an even more brutal and messy business, and dangerous for both mother and child.

So why were so many girls in such a hurry to get married? She would much rather have an interesting job to do which paid her enough money so that she needn't feel dependent upon a man.

And somewhere in her future would be just the right man for whom she would gladly bear children and enjoy making a home. But not yet.

The lonely cry of the loon echoed down the river.

Chapter 12

Rowena stepped into the damp chill of early morning. A thick grey mist hovered over the river and drifted through the yard. There was a fesh, clean, cedar and damp earth smell about the morning.

"You'd best not be going without your boots," Deirdre called from the doorway.

Rowena gasped and rushed back into the house.

"You're all in a dither this morning." Deirdre took her daughter firmly by the shoulders. "Don't let the Launstons scare you. You're as good as any of them. You'll be doing them a kindness if they take you on."

Rowena straightened her shoulders.

"Aye, that's the spirit."

But Rowena's courage dissipated with each step as she crunched along the quiet road to the Ryans'. She had decided not to cut across the cornfield lest she dirty her freshly-laundered frock. Her stomach was in knots, and her meager breakfast threatened to disgrace her. She swallowed hard as she knocked on the Ryans' door.

"You look like a lamb going to slaughter," Fionna said to her as they walked along.

"What's it like, working there?"

"'There's plenty of work, to be sure, and you'll have to mind you do it proper. Margaret Finch is mighty strict about that. Her son, Tom, does the woodchopping, and looks after the stables, though he'll give you a hand with any of the heavy work you can't manage on your own -- like taking down and cleaning the stovepipes. You know he's a mite simple since the accident, though not so much that you'd really notice. A quiet lad he is. Margaret does the cooking and washing up, and generally runs the household. Mind you don't let her order you about too much. She's not a bad sort, though she gets a mite uppity at times, and likes everything just so." Fionna lowered her voice, although there was no one who could overhear them. "It sets me to wondering if mayhap she's more than a housekeeper to a certain member of the family."

Fionna nodded at Rowena's shocked expression.

"She's not a bad looking widow woman for nine and twenty. Takes particular care of herself, she does. Still has all her teeth, and says it's from brushing them every day. I wonder they don't wear away! And she'll only use this store-bought *Pears* soap that comes all the way from England! And she bathes twice a week, even in winter! Sure, 'tis nothing to me, 'cepting when she expects other folk to do likewise. Didn't I tell her a thing or two!"

A hearty shout shattered the early morning calm and startled Rowena. The girls turned around to find Brendan and Sean running to join them. They were clad in their workaday clothes -- grey flannel shirts and trousers, coarse linen overshirts belted at the waist, peaked caps, and scarves knotted around their necks.

Sean greeted his bride-to-be with a lusty smack on the lips, and a playful tweak of her bottom. He maneuvered her aside, and whispered something to her that evoked giggles.

"Sure, wouldn't I like to be greeting you like that," Brendan said, falling into step with Rowena.

"You'll have to settle for a handshake and a how-d'ee-do."

"You're a hard lass, Rowena." His arm slipped with practiced ease about her waist. He felt her tense, and grasped her tighter before she could slip away from him.

"Leave go! ***Brendan***!"

"Not till you tell me what it is I said or done to be making you so unfriendly."

She stopped wriggling. "You're expecting too much of me, is all. Ma says..."

"So it's your Ma, is it?" He grinned wryly. "Been telling you to stay away from me, has she?" He let her go then. He'd have to tread carefully with Rowena. She wasn't like the other girls, who were only too pleased for a bit of slap and tickle -- if not more besides.

Shelagh Ryan had practically begged him for it. But, he knew what her game was -- to get pregnant so he'd have to marry her. So while he'd fucked her, he'd told her that that was all she was ever going to get from him. She hadn't been so willing to spread herself for him after that. But there were always easy women to be had.

Sure, Rowena wasn't like the other girls at all, constantly creeping into his thoughts, disturbing his peace of mind, and stoking an unquenchable fire in his loins whenever she was near.

"Do you think I'd be doing anything to hurt you, mavourneen?"

She considered this seriously, her brow furrowed, her lower lip caught between her teeth. Christ, he wanted to take her right then and there! Her cool blue eyes looked openly into his own as she said, "Nay, I reckon not. Leastways, not meaning to. But I'm not daft, Brendan. I know what it is you're wanting from me, and you'll not be getting it! So you'd best look elsewhere."

Brendan laughed as she marched on. What a little spitfire she was! There was nothing for it. He had to have her -- even if it meant marrying her. He laughed the louder at that. That wench had him by the balls right enough, to make him consider such a drastic step. He relished his freedom. He never lacked for female company when so inclined, yet had no nagging wife awaiting his arrival at nights, ready to scold him for drinking too much or staying out too long. But with Rowena, now, that was different. He wouldn't tire of having her in his bed night after night. It warranted some thought, that did.

"Will you be getting a move on, Sean! We're already late." Brendan called.

Fionna and Sean exchanged one more brief kiss, and then Fionna hitched up her skirts and ran to catch up with Rowena.

"Sure, you're in the divil of a hurry, Rowena," she said breathlessly.

The wolf whistles from behind caused Fionna to turn around with a laugh. "'Tis daft you are, the pair of you!" she yelled at the men.

Rowena did not look back.

"I think you've the right idea, Rowena," Fionna said. "'Tis best not to be letting a man know how you feel about him too early. Sure, didn't I tell Sholagh that many a time. You play him along, letting him take just so many liberties with you from time to time, so's to keep his blood simmering, and he'll come 'round right enough."

"Fionna! I've no interest in Brendan, if that's what you're thinking."

"Sure, it's not our Conn you're after having, though he's pining for you. And our Shelagh's so jealous that it's you Brendan's after and not her, that she'd as soon spit in your eye as look at you. She's marrying Hugh Darcy out of pique, after Brendan as good as told her that she'd never be wearing his ring. So who is it that you fancy?"

"No one, as yet."

"And I'm the Virgin Mary! Give over Rowena, and tell."

"Truly, Fionna."

They passed the outbuildings -- the stable and driveshed and the Launstons' original log house. Rowena's heart pounded as they crossed the yard toward the rectangular one and half storey kitchen wing at the back of the house.

The kitchen was larger than the entire ground floor of the O'Shaughnessys' house. A massive black cast-iron cookstove squatted near one wall; a built-in cupboard stretched half the length of the room, with plates, jugs, and cooking utensils in neat array upon its shelves. There was even a stone sink with a drainpipe which emptied into the yard! But Rowena had little time to study all this as Fionna introduced her to the housekeeper. Of course, they had seen each other before, but had never formally met.

Margaret Finch was a petite woman with smokey grey eyes and sleek ash brown hair neatly plaited and wound about her head. She was dressed in soft gray with a crisp white apron tied about her slender waist, and exuded an air of fastidiousness.

Rowena would never forget that tragic night of the sugaring-off, but there was no evidence of it in Margaret's face.

"Nice to meet you, Rowena," Margaret said as her eyes swept critically over the girl. To Fionna she said, "They're breakfasting early this morning - Mr. Jeremy is going to Toronto -- so you'd best take her in right away. Oh, and do knock before you enter, Fionna, and leave your friend out in the hall until she is summoned."

"Sure, I wasn't about to barge in on them!" Fionna retorted. She removed her bonnet, donned an apron and mob cap, and then led Rowena through the door into the main part of the house.

"They always breakfast in the parlour," Fionna informed her as they stopped outside the first door. "You wait here." Fionna smoothed her apron, knocked, and entered the parlour.

Rowena clasped her cold hands to keep them from shaking. She had never been inside such a grand house -- it was even bigger than it appeared to be from the outside! She peeked down the hallway to the beautifully carved staircase which curved upstairs.

Rowena jumped when the door opened. Fionna winked reassuringly at her, ushered her into the room, and closed the door behind her.

Rowena stood nervously facing the three men. There was a hint of a smile on Adrian's face, and Rowena was grateful for that gesture of encouragement.

Adrian hid his astonishment at the sight of her. How often he had dwelt on that brief but happy time they had shared, dreaming of what might have been were circumstances different.

But he had convinced himself that to meet her again would be folly. If she worked here, he would not be able to avoid her. What a cruel trick of Fate to cast her constantly in his presence!

"So, you'd like to work for us, Rowena?" Samuel Launston said.

"Yes, sir."

"I can hardly believe you're old enough! Why, it seems like only a short time ago that you and your family arrived here, and you were but a child! I'll never forget that time when you and your brother and his friends borrowed Josh Paxton's canoe and promptly got yourselves lost in the marsh at the mouth of the river! It was lucky for the lot of you that the Indians found you and brought you back."

"Yes, sir." Rowena was somewhat embarrassed to be reminded of that disastrous exploit, but Samuel's casual and friendly manner did put her at ease.

His deep, rumbling laugh was soothing. "It taught Josh a lesson too, I can tell you. He never again loaned out his canoe to the lads as payment for errands they had run. Always paid the boys in cash after that. Ah, well." He turned to Jeremy. "You'll deal with this, eh? You know better than I what Harriet would want." Samuel rose from his chair, and said, "Goodbye, my dear," before leaving the room.

Rowena had a quick glance around the parlour, which was furnished with a round breakfast table and chairs, a plush sofa, an upholstered wing chair, two candlestand tables, elegant Sinumbra lamps, and a rich patterned carpet which felt luxurious underfoot. The most striking feature of the room was its brightness, for it had tall windows and pale yellow walls that reflected even this morning's grey light.

Rowena's delight in the room was suddenly forgotten as she encountered Jeremy's scrutiny. He lounged casually in his chair, one elbow resting carelessly on the back of it.

Another Irish wench, he thought, and wondered if this one would be any better than Fionna, who cleaned only the visible dirt, leaving that under beds and furniture untouched unless Margaret was constantly behind her. Harriet would not tolerate such slovenliness, he was certain. It was unfortunate that one couldn't obtain proper, trained servants.

At least she appeared neat, Jeremy thought as his eyes travelled down her person, lingering for a moment on the taut bodice of her gown. He was surprised, and more than a little vexed to find himself stirred by her womanly figure, so ripe for the plucking, yet with an aura of innocence.

"I don't suppose you've had any experience in this type of work?"

"Only at home... sir."

"I thought as much. Well, we've not much choice, since Fionna must be replaced. We'll give you a try. Fionna will acquaint you with your duties. You will take orders from Mrs. Finch until my wife takes over the running of this house. Your salary will be twelve shillings a month, Halifax currency. You will receive your breakfast and dinner here. We expect our servants...."

"Help, sir," Rowena interrupted, and was appalled by her own boldness. She blushed.

"I beg your pardon?" Jeremy said with annoyance.

"I'm not a servant, sir."

With a grimace he said, "Yes, of course. You're 'hired help'. As I was saying, we expect our ***help*** to be clean and tidy in person. Mrs. Finch will explain more specifically. Have you any questions?"

"No, sir."

"Then tell Mrs. Finch that you have been engaged. She'll take you in hand."

"Thank you, sir." She left the room, quietly shutting the door behind her.

"I wonder how long that one will stay," Jeremy said to Adrian. "With her looks, I expect she'll soon be snapped up, and we'll once again be looking for a maid. Well, I must be off! Are you feeling alright, Adrian? You look a bit off-colour today."

"I'm fine. You needn't worry about me."

"I'll see you in a few days then. Keep an eye on things, won't you? I rather suspect there'll be one or two diasters with the new girl on the job."

"You can rely on me," Adrian replied with a smile.

In the kitchen, Margaret Finch was explaining Rowena's duties to her. "You'll be expected at six thirty every morning. Your first task is to tidy the parlour, since the gentlemen usually spend their evenings there if there are no visitors. You'll bring all the lamps from the parlour, dining room, study, and drawing room -- if that room was used -- into the scullery. You'll find all the equipment necessary to clean and refill the lamps and to trim the wicks, as well as the silver polish, blacking, and so forth in the scullery. After breakfast you'll set the parlour to rights once again. Bedrooms are done next: beds made, chamber pots emptied and washed, washstands tidied, bowls cleaned, slops removed. The feather beds must be properly fluffed; the mattresses are turned weekly; bedding is stripped and washed every fortnight. All carpets are swept weekly; floors are swept daily and scrubbed once a fortnight. All rooms are dusted daily, the wood waxed and polished as necessary. You'll scrub the kitchen floor once a week, when I'm at the shops."

Rowena was overwhelmed by all these chores. Margaret smiled at the girl's bewildered expression. "You'll catch on fast enough. Last thing before you leave each day, you'll fill the water jugs in the bedrooms, and bring the candleholders down and leave them on the hall table by the stairs, making sure to replace the candles each day -- we use the short ends in the kitchen. As for you, you'll be given a supply of aprons and caps which you must launder yourself -- mind they are well starched. You're expected to wear a clean apron daily, and a fresh gown at least once a week. I also trust that you will keep your person clean and free from vermin. I recommend that you bathe at least once a week, even in winter. An unclean person gives offense."

Rowena wondered if winter baths were as bone-chilling an ordeal here, in this kitchen warmed by that monstrous stove, as they were in the O'Shaughnessys' cabin, where water could freeze in a kettle only a few inches from the fireplace.

"Can you manage some breakfast now?"

Rowena was warmed by Margaret's kind smile. "Aye."

After breakfast, Rowena began her apprenticeship with Fionna.

She was awed by the grandeur of the rooms and their sumptuous, expensive furnishings. A rich blue silk Sheraton sofa with matching chairs, a mahogany chiffoniere, small Regency tables, a card table covered in blue baize, a gilt mirror above the mantle, and a colourful Brussels carpet graced the predominantly blue drawing room. The dining room across the hall contained a long walnut table with ten damask-covered chairs set invitingly around it, a marble-topped sideboard with a silk splash curtain on a brass rod, and a cabinet gleaming with silver, cut crystal glasses and decanters, and a fine Sevres china service. Rowena wondered how she would keep all the rooms clean, and their contents polished and sparkling as such exquisite things deserved to be. Fionna, she noticed, did not appear too concerned -- a flick of her feather duster sufficing.

Rowena was disappointed that she rarely saw Adrian during her first few days, and when she did, she received merely a polite 'hello' from him. Despite her brave words that she was no servant, she was all too well aware now of the gulf that existed between them. People like Adrian did not socialize with people like herself. Hadn't she said as much to Maureen, when Maureen had expressed her interest in Malcolm Grimsby? Adrian had simply been kind to her, that day at the swamp. So Rowena couldn't understand why she was dejected.

By Saturday -- Fionna's last day -- Rowena was accustomed to the household routine. The following Monday she approached the house confidently, each room now intimately known to her. Jeremy had returned, Margaret informed her, so there was another bed to make up this morning.

How comfortable and cozy it must be to sleep upon the downy softness of the feather bed, she thought as she was fluffing the tick in Jeremy's room. So different from the lumpy straw mattress that was her bed. Just once she would like to experience such luxury. Why not? It wouldn't do any harm, and no one would know.

She sat down tentatively on the edge of the bed, thrilled with its softness, and then lay back. Surely, it was like sleeping on a cloud!

Suddenly the door opened. Rowena jerked up and froze as she faced Jeremy.

Jeremy's surprise at finding the girl lying upon his bed quickly changed to anger -- due as much to his own reaction to the tantalizing vision before him as to the girl's audacity.

Rowena saw him frown. She jumped off the bed, flustered and mortified. "I'm sorry, sir," she stammered, her face burning.

"I'd advise you to stay out of gentlemen's beds unless you have something other than making the bed in mind," Jeremy said coldly.

"Oh... no!" She was horrified by his implication.

"So this is how you work is it?"

"No, sir. It'll not happen again," she said in a tight voice as she stared down at her boots.

"I sincerely hope not! Such impudence will not be tolerated a second time!" Jeremy noticed a tear escape from beneath her lashes. He was astonished when she dashed past him. Shaking his head in exasperation, he picked up the pocket watch for which he had come.

Rowena, blinded by her tears, collided with Adrian at the foot of the stairs. He grabbed her by the shoulders to steady her.

Her tears melted his resolve. How hard he had tried to avoid her these last few days, only to find her possessing his mind and soul all the more.

"What's wrong, Rowena?"

Jeremy was irritated when he discovered his brother trying to comfort the girl. "You needn't concern yourself with her," he told Adrian. "She's distressed because of her own foolishness!" He strode past them and out the front door.

"You mustn't let Jamie upset you so," Adrian said gently to Rowena as he handed her his handkerchief. "He's a bit curt sometimes, but he's not as fearsome as he may seem."

"I didn't mean no harm," Rowena confessed between sniffles.

"I'm sure you didn't. But just what did you do to put Jamie in such a foul humour?"

"I just wanted to know how it felt to lie on a feather bed...."

"And Jamie discovered you in his bed, is that it?"

Rowena nodded.

Adrian burst into laughter. "Oh, Rowena, you're priceless! I'm not surprised that Jamie was perturbed -- finding a beautiful girl like you in his bed!"

"Don't jest, Adrian."

"I assure you, I'm not." She looked up at him and their eyes held. "I've thought about you often since that day we met at the swamp. I had hoped to see you there again."

"I'm not allowed. Da thinks 'tis dangerous."

"Perhaps he's right. One finds rare and delightful things in swamps." Tenderly he wiped a tear from her cheek. His fingers lingered there for a moment, his touch sending a shiver through her.

"I'd best be getting back to me duties."

"Yes, I suppose you must."

Chapter 13

"That's never the truth!" Rowena said, laughing. She stopped her dusting and turned to face Adrian.

"Every word of it! Then the Master said sternly, 'This is not the time for levity' -- that was one of his favourite expressions."

"What happened then?"

"Sanderson got five whacks of the cane across his palm."

Rowena grimaced. "Does it hurt much, being caned?"

"Like the dickens. But if you turn your hand just so..." Adrian demonstrated, "...as the blow falls, it's not so bad."

"Tell me more about Toronto," Rowena entreated as she recommenced her work.

"We weren't allowed to go into the city on our own, only as a group to attend St. James for church services on Sundays. We'd see the Lieutenant- Governor there and all the big Tories and their fashionably dressed wives and daughters, as well as some of the soldiers from the garrison. It was quite a spectacle. In the winter we often had skating parties on the Bay, and -- can you believe it? -- the Headmaster cut quite the most dashing figure of us all on the ice! There would be as many cutters skimming across the frozen Bay as there were boats sailing it in summer. The ladies would be muffled in furs; the young gentlemen would have impromtu races.

"Sometimes we'd skip out after classes and wander about the city. We'd go down to the market to watch the people and perhaps buy ourselves an ice or a pastry. One of our favourite places was down by the Bay. There is an elderly couple who live in a small cabin by the shore, and they rent boats. Mrs. Myles was always delighted to see us, and she would press tea and cakes on us and chide us if we didn't do justice to the repast. Her husband is quite a character. He has only one arm, but he can handle a boat better than most men with both limbs. He'd been a smuggler once, ferrying tea and such across from the States."

"Did you ever get caught?"

"In the worst way. One day we ran smack into Archdeacon Strachan. Nearly bowled the old fellow over. Well, of course, he knew us by our uniforms, and some of the boys personally. Gave us the worst dressing-down we'd ever had. We were quaking in our boots the rest of that day and all the next, expecting a summons from the Headmaster. It never came. Funny thing. I'd always heard that Strachan had been a strict disciplinarian when he'd been a teacher, so I never expected any lenience from that quarter."

Rowena could picture it all so vividly as he spoke. He was opening up the world to her, describing people, places, events that she could never have imagined. Since she had never ventured more than a few miles from Launston Mills since her arrival five years ago, the town had become her universe. That the sun actually shone and the stars smiled down upon people in other unknown, unseen places was unfathomable at times. Had she given it any conscious thought, she would have believed that even Ireland no longer existed, with so many of its people transplanted here. Now that universe was expanding, encompassing all that she had seen through Adrian's eyes.

How she treasured these times when he would come and talk to her! It required all her willpower to carry on with her tasks while he unravelled his tales. He delighted her with his imitations of characters like that arrogant popinjay, Sir Francis Bond Head, and the Archdeacon, sermonizing from his pulpit in his booming Scots burr.

But it was disturbing as well. She was becoming hopelessly enthralled by Adrian. There could never be more between them than this, however much she might fantasize otherwise, or rail against the seeming injustice of it. And yet, she could be content as long as the days stretched on like this forever.

Adrian sought her out again that afternoon as she was scrubbing the hall floor. He sat on the second to last step. "I was making some notes for my first edition, and I would like your opinion. What do you think of Canada ruling itself without the intervention of the politicians back in London?"

Rowena wondered if he was teasing her, but his eyes held no mockery. How unlike his brother he was! "You'll not be wanting my opinion," she said with a laugh.

"Whyever not?"

"Sure, what would the likes of me be knowing about such things?"

"I imagine you've heard enough talk of politics to have formed an opinion."

Reluctantly she said, "I reckon us Irish have nothing to be grateful to the English for. I didn't... I mean, you're different, Adrian."

He smiled. "I understand. Your people's history has certainly not endeared us English to them."

"Sure, I don't understand it! People fighting and hating each other. It should be different here!" Rowena recalled with a shudder that day the Orangemen had threatened the town.

"It will be, when people can forget that they're Irish or Scotch, French or English, Protestant or Catholic. If they realize that they're all citizens of a new country -- a free, progressive, democratic country, if they choose it to be."

"Will you write about that?"

"Yes."

"Sure, you've not been writing down what I've been saying?" she said, seeing Adrian still applying pencil to paper.

He turned the pad toward her and smiled at the surprised look on her face. She took the paper from him and stared at the clever sketch he had made of her. It was too flattering a portrait, she decided. The girl he had drawn had an endearing naivete about her, a gentle beauty that belonged to a pampered, well-bred lady. "'Tis never me," she said wistfully.

"You've never really looked at yourself before, Rowena, for that is how I see you. You keep it. I've already done a few for myself."

She turned away from him, trembling with inexplicable emotion.

Adrian felt her sadness in the depths of his own soul, and knew well its cause. He should never have allowed this to happen. That he should suffer from unrequited love was one matter; that she should, was more than he could bear.

He rose abruptly and left her without a word.

The sky was leaden, so heavy that it touched the very ground over which he trod. He followed the path through the woods without seeing it. His whole being was back in that hallway. Adrian did not slow his pace -- though his lungs ached with the exertion -- until he had reached the swamp. But even its comforting familiarity was altered by the fog. Distant trees were totally obscured; near ones were no more than ghostly outlines. The swamp sounds came from nowhere and everywhere.

What was he to do? What could he do?

To continue seeing her like this would be increasingly difficult for them both, yet not as painful as never seeing one another again. Could he -- dare he -- carry out the mad, selfish idea that had been fermenting in his brain these last few days? A heady brew indeed! His father and brother would be horrified, but that was not what concerned him the most.

Would it be fair to Rowena?

Had he been totally honest with himself, Adrian would have realized that the right and noble thing to do was to stop his relationship with Rowena before things went any further. But the truth was that it was not only his heart that craved her love, but also his body. He'd had little experience of women; a few clumsy encounters with whores that had left him feeling manipulated and unsatisfied. He wanted to experience real physical love. And he wanted Rowena.

Two days later, as Rowena was tidying the parlour, Adrian joined her. She had seen him only briefly the previous day. He had not stopped to chat with her as usual, but had left the house immediately following breakfast, and again after dinner. She had been confused and hurt, knowing that he was purposely avoiding her, but not why. How fervently she had prayed last night that their friendship had not come to an end!

There was a strange, almost feverish gleam in his eyes this morning. "Come, I want to show you something," he said, taking her by the hand.

"But I've not finished here."

"That can wait."

"Where are you taking me?" she asked as he led her out to the yard.

"To my office."

Adrian opened the door of the old log house. It creaked back on unoiled hinges, and he pulled her into the dim interior. A thick layer of dust shrouded the empty rooms; spiders had industriously spun traps to entangle trespassers, and mice and chipmunks had left evidence of their invasions behind.

"Sure, it wants a good scrubbing!" Rowena said, brushing cobwebs away from her face.

"I'll have Tom do it before the press arrives. It should be here next month. Jamie ordered it from the States." Adrian chuckled. "For all my brother's contentions about disliking Americans, he's only too willing to do business with them."

"I'd be happy to clean this place for you."

"Haven't you enough work already?"

"I wouldn't mind, truly. What will you be doing with all these rooms?" Rowena asked, walking about. It was much larger than the O'Shaughnessy's cabin, having a parlour, kitchen, and two other rooms on this floor.

"I'm certain they'll all be used."

"It must be exciting to print a newspaper! Writing things that other folk'll read and think on! You're clever to be able to do that."

"Thanks for your confidence. Father and Jeremy are indulging me in what they consider to be a whim. Father thinks that once I get all this 'nonsense' out of my system, I'll be ready to settle down to some real work. So I'll just have to prove myself to them."

"You will." Rowena swept her feather duster across the desk, sending up clouds of the fine dirt which seeped into all the houses from the dusty roads.

"I didn't bring you here to work." Adrian put a restraining hand on her wrist; the physical contact was a sharp jolt to his senses. He drew her, unresisting, into his arms. She trembled when his lips touched hers in a gentle kiss, and responded when his mouth became more insistent and demanding. He pressed her closer, moulding his body to hers, and she could feel his throbbing manhood straining against her.

Rowena drew away, shocked and breathless, appalled that she had allowed this to happen. She tried to move away, but he still held her tightly. She could not look at him. Her face burned with embarrassment. Everything had suddenly changed between them, too quickly and drastically for Rowena's liking. His obvious physical desire had put an end to their innocent friendship. Anger was among the many conflicting emotions she experienced at that moment. Adrian was no better than Brendan, perhaps even more devious.

"'Tis wrong. We shouldn't be here at all, alone like this."

"I love you, Rowena."

She looked at him in astonishment. There was a tender, searching look in his eyes.

"You love me too, don't you?"

"Aye." How easy it was to say it. "But...."

"I want to marry you. Don't look so surprised. You captured my heart that first day in the swamp."

Rowena was speechless. Thoughts and emotions spun dizzingly through her mind. It was all too much, this sudden leap from humiliation and hurt to ecstacy. "'Tisn't possible, us getting wed!"

"Don't you want to marry me?"

"Oh, yes!" She leaned her head against his shoulder, forcing back tears of either sadness or joy -- she knew not which. "They'll never allow it, your family."

"You let me worry about that. I thought we could live here. There are plenty of rooms, as you said. It's all we'd need for now." Adrian held her at arm's length and looked into her eyes. "Surely those aren't tears. I couldn't bear to think I'd made you unhappy."

"I can't believe this is true, that I should be so lucky. That you could love me."

He hugged her. "I'll talk to Father and Jamie tonight. Perhaps you should allow me to talk to your parents as well."

She gasped. "They'll never approve, you being Anglican!"

"Then I shall adopt the Catholic religion. It matters not to me, as long as there is nothing to stand between us."

Adrian began coughing -- violent spasms that frightened Rowena. "Are you alright?" she asked anxiously. She laid her hand upon his brow. "You've a fever."

"It's nothing," Adrian assured her when he had regained his breath. He took her hand from his forehead and kissed it. "You're not to worry. We'd better get back to the house before Margaret misses you."

Rowena managed somehow to finish her chores. But her fears were rekindled when she met Adrian in the hall that afternoon. His skin glowed with a yellow pallor; he was shaking and seemed about to collapse.

"Will you help me to my room, Rowena?"

She dropped her broom and offered her shoulder as a crutch. Slowly they climbed the steps. Rowena lowered him onto the edge of his bed.

"The basin!" Adrian cried, trying to raise himself.

Rowena understood and quickly fetched it, holding it for him while he retched over and over again. He finally sank back, exhausted. "Sorry," he croaked.

"Don't fret yourself. I've tended sick folk often enough." She pulled off his boots, and covered him with a blanket. His forehead was hot and dry. "You're burning up!"

"Cold.... So cold."

Adrian still shivered, so Rowena removed several more blankets from the box at the foot of the bed, and wrapped him in them.

He began coughing again. Rowena was terrified when she noticed the blood on his handkerchief.

I'm going for the doctor."

"Stay with me.... Please."

"I'll be back, I promise." She gave him a brief kiss.

With a pounding heart, Rowena flew downstairs and into the kitchen. "It's Adrian," she said to Margaret, who was doing dishes. "He's desperately ill."

"Send Tom for Dr. Worthing. You go and fetch the two men from the mill." Margaret hurried upstairs.

Rowena was not aware of the rain as she ran to the stables to send Tom on his errand, and then raced to the mill. She stumbled in, breathless and drenched.

Rowena had never been inside the gristmill before. It was a noisy, busy scene; the elevators carrying the grain to various floors, the whirring millstones grinding the grain, the hum and throb of the driveshafts in the nether regions. The men looked curiously at Rowena, and then returned to their work. She glanced about frantically, but did not see the Launstons. She noticed a cubicle -- surely the office! -- in the far corner of the room. Carefully she made her way across the room, and knocked on the door.

Jeremy was surprised to see Rowena standing in the doorway, her wet clothes moulded to her, strands of hair which had escaped from beneath her cap, clinging to her cheeks.

"Adrian's terribly sick!" she burst out. "I thought it was the ague, but..."

Jeremy noticed the familiar way she spoke of his brother, but he spared no thought for that now. "What's wrong?"

"He's coughing blood."

Oh, God! He'd been afraid of this. He should have realized earlier. "Has the doctor been summoned?"

"Aye."

Jeremy grabbed his coat, and strode out of the office with Rowena at his heels. She nearly collided with him when he stopped abruptly and addressed one of the men. "Find my father and tell him to go home immediately. Try the sawmill first. Abernethy!"

The miller hurried over at the summons.

"See to things here. I'll not be back today."

Rowena had to run to keep up with Jeremy. The icy rain lashed at her; the wind snatched her breath. She was shaking with cold by the time she reached the house.

"I advise you to change out of those wet clothes," Jeremy said.

"But Adrian...."

"Do as you're told, girl!" he interrupted angrily before bounding up the stairs two at a time.

Rowena was frantic with worry, but she realized that she wouldn't be allowed to see Adrian now. Dejectedly she went to the kitchen, and stood shivering before the stove. Margaret joined her a moment later.

"How is he?"

"The doctor's with him now. Oh, Rowena, you're soaked through! You'll catch your death! Out of those wet clothes right now!" Margaret went to her bedroom in the loft above, and returned with a blanket. "Well, come along."

Rowena peeled off her dress and shift, and snuggled gratefully into the warm, rough blanket. Mary hung her clothes beside the stove, and then poured them both a cup of tea. The rain pattered remorselessly on the windowpanes as they sat waiting.

They were startled by the clanging of the bell. They both jumped up.

"You can hardly go like that," Margaret said. "You stay and warm yourself."

But the heat didn't melt the coldness within her; she remained numb as she listened to the rain and the ticking of the clock.

When Margaret entered Adrian's room, Jeremy said to her, "Stay with him, Margaret. I'll relieve you later."

Simon explained the treatment of medication to her -- repeated doses of calomel, Epsom salts, and quinine tonic -- and the two men left the room.

"It's more than the ague, isn't it?" Jeremy asked his friend.

"I fear so."

"We can talk in the drawing room."

"How long have you suspected, Jeremy?" Simon asked, when he had accepted a snifter of brandy from Jeremy.

"Months," Jeremy answered gravely. "He denied there was anything wrong, but I should have known better! The College wouldn't have dismissed him early if they hadn't considered his condition serious."

"You can't blame yourself. There's little that can be done anyway. He must rest, and a change of air would help. A few months down at the Front might benefit him, once he has recovered from this ague. Of course the best thing for him would be someplace warm for the winter, like the south of France. But I don't suppose that that is feasible now. An ocean voyage at this time of the year might prove even more harmful. But if he's not improved by the spring, you should consider taking him away from here for a year or two. It's the only possible cure."

"My mother and sister died of it. We didn't have the money then for them to go away, though Father had promised he would have some by the spring. They never survived that harsh winter." He paused. "Will Adrian make it through the winter?"

Simon met Jeremy's penetrating gaze, and knew that he couldn't lie to his friend. "I honestly don't know. If he takes great care, there is a chance. But it is impossible for me to predict anything at this point. You know as well as I what a vile disease consumption is."

The two men hadn't been aware of Samuel's presence. From the doorway he said, "It makes the victim appear usually beautiful as it eats him up inside."

Rowena donned her damp dress, tidied her hair, and decided not to spend another idle, agonizing minute in the kitchen.

The door to the drawing room was open, and she saw the solemn expressions on the men's faces. Fear seized her.

Jeremy spotted her before she had a chance to knock. "What do you want?"

"Begging your pardon, sir. I was wondering if there's anything I can do to help?"

"I'm certain that Margaret could use Rowena's help," Simon suggested.

"She's only a child!"

"With her mother's gift for nursing the sick. She's had lots of experience with the ague."

"Alright," Samuel said. "Run along then, girl."

Rowena took a deep, calming breath before entering Adrian's room. He was no longer shaking with the chills, she noticed, but was sweating copiously, and nearly delirious with fever.

"The doctor says I'm to help you, Mrs. Finch."

"You can clean out that bowl and bring a jug of fresh water. Then you can sit with him while I prepare supper."

Rowena sat despondently beside Adrian's bed. She rinsed a cloth in cold water, wiped his face, and then applied the compress to his brow, constantly rewetting it when it had absorbed the heat of his fever.

Adrian opened his eyes once when she was ministering to him, and attempted a smile. "You came back."

"And didn't I promise I would?" She took his hot hand in hers. "How are you feeling then?"

"Better... now that you're here. You know, when I first saw you, you reminded me of one of those fairy people you believe in." He spoke slowly, haltingly. "Sometimes I wonder if you are real."

"Real enough. Now you must be quiet and sleep, Adrian." The chills would begin again soon, Rowena knew -- a violent shaking that rattled and ached the bones.

"She's right," Jeremy said from behind her. He had overheard the last part of the conversation, and had been shocked by the seeming intimacy between his brother and the maid.

"Ah, Jamie... glad you're here... something I must discuss with you."

"Not now," Rowena cautioned, afraid that Adrian would raise the subject of their marriage. "You must get well first."

"Feel so sick, Rowena...!"

She had anticipated his need and had the basin ready for him.

Jeremy watched helplessly as spasms wracked Adrian's frail body. When these had subsided, Rowena made Adrian comfortable, and soothed him with cool hands.

"I'll stay with him now," Jeremy said. "It's time for you to go home."

Rowena knew it was useless to protest, and reluctantly departed.

She slept little that night, though more, it appeared, than the Launston household. Margaret was bleary-eyed and yawning as she prepared breakfast.

"Is he better?" Rowena inquired the moment she arrived.

"Yes, thank heaven! The crisis is over and he's been sleeping peacefully these last few hours. Mr. Sam's with him now."

"Will I be needed in the sick-room?"

"I think not. You have your chores to do, as always, but go about them quietly."

Rowena hid her disappointment, and wondered if she would see Adrian at all that day.

She entered the drawing room to collect the lamps. After opening the drapes, she gathered the empty glasses and set them upon a tray, and then picked up a lamp. She was startled when she noticed the booted feet upon a stool. She looked up and saw Jeremy lounging in a wing chair, a snifter of brandy held carelessly in one hand.

He had been watching her as she had moved about the room.

Jeremy didn't know what to make of this girl. She was beautiful, he admitted grudgingly, but she was Irish and Catholic. Just what was Adrian's interest in her? The young man had repeated her name over and over in his delirium early this morning. Jeremy could understand a man taking his pleasure with a girl like her, but he suspected that his foolish brother had already formed a deeper attachment to the wench.

He had thought of dismissing her, but Margaret couldn't manage on her own. Well, as soon as Adrian had recovered from this ague, Samuel would take him to Toronto for several months. That should end any relationship that was blossoming between Adrian and Rowena.

Jeremy and Rowena stared at each other for a long moment in the early morning gloom. He caught her off guard when he suddenly asked, "What is there between you and my brother?"

"Nothing, sir," she stammered.

He raised an eyebrow in disbelief.

"We're just friends, is all. Mr. Adrian's kind to me."

"Indeed?"

"Yes, sir."

"Adrian is dying."

Rowena gaped at him. Anger, fear, despair choked her. "'Tisn't true!" she cried, sinking onto the sofa opposite Jeremy. But she knew he wasn't lying. She wanted to scream out her pain, but she wouldn't let Jeremy see the depth of her grief, or expose herself to his mockery.

Jeremy saw the anguish in her eyes, and regretted that he had told her so bluntly, so cruelly. Her reaction confirmed his suspicions though.

"Why?" was all Rowena managed to say.

"He has consumption."

It wasn't fair that Adrian should die. Not Adrian! He was so good, so kind, so gentle. God couldn't allow this to happen!

Rowena rose from the sofa with such dignity that Jeremy was surprised. Without saying anything, she picked up a lamp and walked out of the room.

Rowena performed her tasks automatically, taking some measure of comfort in keeping busy, though she was being torn apart inside. Jeremy searched her out that afternoon, and found her polishing silver in the scullery.

Rowena wasn't afraid of him anymore, nor intimidated by him. She was not the same young girl who had run from him in tears only three weeks earlier. She looked at him almost defiantly.

"Adrian is asking for you."

Jeremy accompanied her to his brother's room.

Adrian was looking much improved. Though Rowena knew that he would suffer repeated, although less severe relapses over the next few weeks, she mouthed a silent prayer of thanks that he had survived the worst. Adrian was sitting up, propped against the pillows, and was sipping a cup of tea.

"You must have work to do, Jamie. You can entrust me to Rowena's care."

"It would not be proper for me to leave you two alone here, now that you are better."

"I've hardly recovered enough to be capable of causing a scandal!"

Adrian's laugh became a cough. Jeremy saw Rowena tense, and hoped that she would not lose her composure and upset his brother.

She didn't disappoint him. She walked over to Adrian. "I'm so glad you're better," she said with a smile.

"I should be up and about in a few days. Thanks for your help yesterday. You have the gentle touch of an angel," Adrian said, reaching out and taking her hand. "Not like Jamie. He thinks I'm a sack of potatoes!"

Jeremy was disquieted by the scene. He admired Rowena's sense when she said, "You must take care of yourself, and I'd best be getting back to me work."

Jeremy didn't see the look that passed between them -- a look that said so much more than words ever could.

Chapter 14

It seemed to Rowena as though the fiddler had stretched her nerves taut and was grating his bow across them. The leaping and stomping of the dancers made the floor tremble and her head pound. The odour of close-pressed, sweating bodies mingled nauseatingly with the greasy stench of the many tallow candles which burned fitfully in the wall sconces.

Rowena longed to escape from this wedding feast, but she could not offend the Ryans, who had gone to much trouble and expense to provided the villagers with a memorable celebration. They had rented the ballroom of Paxtons' Tavern -- a long assembly hall which occupied much of the second storey of the inn. It served not only as a meeting place for any type of community gathering -- social, political, or religious -- but it also accommodated travellers, dormitory-style, when the inn's four bedrooms were occupied. Tonight it was festooned with garlands of late summer blooms, sheaves of wheat, and multi-coloured ears of Indian corn. Long tables laden with food -- including the juicy, smoked hams of the unfortunate sow, Daisy -- stretched across one end of the room, and Josh Paxton served liquid refreshments at the other.

Rowena felt suffocated in the hot, fetid, airless room. She observed the festive scene without feeling a part of it.

As with most social events, a general invitation had been issued to the townspeople and area farmers. The Methodists, of course, did not attend, but a good portion of the population had come to have a good time. The women were adorned in their best gowns, many of silk, still smelling slightly of the mothballs in which they were stored year round. The men wore their carefully preserved redingotes; their waistcoats strained over spreading paunches; their stiff collars chafed reddened necks.

Father Killeny moved about the room, engaging everyone in conversation. He was well liked and respected, not only by his congregation, but by most of the settlers, for he was always prepared to give solace or advice indiscriminately. 'One-eyed Jack' Spragg, an old trapper who owned land north of the town, was regaling the young children with tall tales. Alys and Brigid were among his enthralled audience.

Conn and Moira were engrossed in one another, which pleased Rowena. She had never seen Moira so happy. Donal and

Rosemary Flannery, who were a strikingly well-matched couple, dominated the dance floor as usual.

Gwyn was busy sampling the food, and Deirdre and Mary were among a circle of babbling women. Patrick and Matt -- despite their wives' entreaties of "no religion and no politics!" -- had joined the political discussion at the bar. Josh Paxton was generally the best informed villager, since travellers were always eager to divulge the latest news to their host.

Maureen Darcy was flirting with Malcolm Grimsby, much to Ewan Monaghan's obvious disgust. He was pouring beer down his gullet as though it were water. Fionna, every inch the radiant bride, danced and chatted and laughed even more exuberantly than usual. When he wasn't dancing with her, Sean looked proudly and lovingly at his bubbling bride.

Shelagh was sombre and reserved in comparison. Her husband, Hugh Darcy, seemed anxious to please her. Rowena had always liked Hugh, who, though generally a man of few words, was kind, generous, and even-tempered. She thought he deserved a better wife than Shelagh, who even now glanced surreptitiously at Brendan as he conversed with the men at the bar.

Satisfied that no one would miss her, Rowena slipped into the hall and fled quietly downstairs. She had thought the barroom empty until she heard an indiscreet giggle from a dark recess. She suspected that another match was in the making.

Once outside, Rowena breathed deeply of the crisp night air heavy with the musty scent of summer's decay. She drew her shawl about her shoulders, and turned her face to the stars. The curious, greenish glow of the Northern Lights flickered across the sky.

How she envied Fionna her happiness and promising future. Tears of self-pity quivered on her lashes, but she squeezed them back stoically. Adrian would not die! They would marry, just as he had promised!

Adrian had pretty well recovered from the ague now; yet that meant that he would soon be off to Toronto. She could bear the separation if it meant that Adrian would regain his health. But what if.... No! She'd not think of that!

"Sure, 'tis too lovely an evening to be out here alone," Brendan said from behind her.

She spun around. He wore no coat, and had removed his collar and cravat long since; his silk waistcoat was unbuttoned. He was leaning casually against a veranda post, puffing on a cigar.

"What's it like, cleaning the Launstons' dirt?"

Rowena turned away from him without replying, and walked toward the river.

"Have you been learning your manners from them too?" Brendan said as he grabbed her arm.

"Leave me be!" She could smell the whiskey on his breath as he moved closer to her.

"What else do you do for the Launstons besides muck out their byre?" he taunted as his arms imprisoned her. His hand slid up to fondle her breast.

Seething with indignation, Rowena slapped him across the face. Brendan released her in astonishment, but before she could move away from him, he seized her wrists in a crushing, painful grasp.

She froze with fear at the rage in his eyes. For one breathless moment she thought he would strike her.

Brendan chuckled as he loosened his grip. "You'd best not provoke me, mavourneen."

Rowena pulled her hands away, and rubbed her wrists. "And you'd best keep your hands from straying."

"'Twas just a bit of fun. No harm meant; none done."

"Not for want of trying on your part."

"You've the divil of a temper."

"Aye, and you'd best not be forgetting it."

She had changed, he thought. Gone was the bounce from her step, the sparkle from her eyes, the ready smile. It was as though she carried the world's burdens upon her young shoulders. An innocent no more.

It was his speculation as to the cause of this change in her that had aroused his anger a few moments before. Had Jeremy Launston forced himself upon her, seduced her perhaps?

Christ, it galled him to think that Launston might have had what he himself had been craving these last months! He'd kill the bastard if he discovered that Launston had taken advantage of Rowena in some way!

"What's wrong, mavourneen? Sure, I've seen happier faces at a wake."

"I just want to be left alone, is all."

"Nay, you've been brooding enough for one night. Come on," he said, grabbing her by the hand, and leading her back to the inn. "The newlyweds will be leaving shortly, and we'll be chivareeing them."

She held back. "But they've done nothing wrong!" Chivarees were the usual way for people to show their disapproval of a match.

"'Tis just a bit of foolishness for the fun. Not a real chivaree." Brendan dragged her along. "I'll be seeing a smile on that pretty face afore the night's out."

Rowena saw her mother frown when she and Brendan returned to the ballroom. He swung her onto the dance floor before she could protest.

It wasn't long before the newlyweds bade their farewells, leaving the guests to dance and drink until dawn. No doubt there would be many a drawn face and wilted gown at mass the next morning.

Some of the young people accompanied Shelagh and Hugh to the farm, though most of them made the shorter trek with Fionna and Sean. Brendan, Rowena, Moira, Conn, Donal, and Rosemary were among the latter group. It was a merry, noisy parade that joked and clowned its way down Mill Road to the new house that Sean had built. The young people cheered as Sean swept his bride into his arms, and carried her over the threshold. When he had placed Fionna on her feet, he turned to the spectators. "I'd like to thank all of you for your good wishes, and for helping to make this one of the happiest days of me life."

"'Tis all downhill from here, Sean!" one of the young men said.

"You're all welcome to return to the inn and enjoy yourselves," Sean suggested.

"But not like you'll be enjoying yourself, eh Sean?"

Fionna had already disappeared, and someone yelled out, "You'd best get upstairs and warm your bride's bed afore I do it for you!"

More ribald comments bounced back from the closed door. Cheers and applause greeted the faint flickering of a candle in a second floor window. Several more people turned up with a supply of pans, lids, and spoons. As soon as the light was extinguished, these various instruments crashed against one another in deafening discord. Handfuls of coarse sand were flung against the bedroom window.

The window suddenly flew open, and Sean stuck out his head. The sight of his nightdress caused many a maid to twitter. "If you'll not be leaving us in peace," the irate bridegroom said, "then I'll be crowning you with the chamber pot!"

This evoked appreciative laughter, and the revellers agreed that the couple had paid their dues. They retreated, anxious now to return to the dancing and drinking, though some took this opportunity of freedom from parental surveillance to engage in a bit of sparking. Rowena noticed Donal and Rosemary sneak off into the shadows of the trees.

Rowena hung back from the boisterous procession. She had no wish to return to the inn. She paused as they passed the Launstons' darkened house.

"I'm thinking 'tis about time I found meself a wife," Brendan said to her.

"Then I'll be wishing you luck," Rowena replied warily, quickening her pace to catch up with the others.

"Rowena...."

She ran to the tavern.

Chapter 15

On the Monday afternoon following the wedding festivities, Rowena was scrubbing the kitchen floor when Adrian walked in. "Has Margaret gone to the shops?" he asked her

"Aye."

"Good! Then we have a little time to ourselves." He offered his hand, and helped her to her feet.

"But I have to finish the floor before Margaret returns."

"We must talk."

She nodded.

"Let's go to the swamp."

"'Tis too far!"

"Not through the woods."

"You'd best not tire yourself, Adrian."

"You're beginning to sound as bad as the rest of them! I feel perfectly fine, Rowena. As fit as I did before. And I'm tired of being a virtual prisoner in this house. Jamie's had Margaret guarding me like a watchdog."

They went outside and across Mill Road into the crackling autumn forest. Brilliant red and orange and gold leaves fluttered to the ground around them. Somnolent bees bumbled about as if stupefied by the dense, musty smell of fall. The grasses had turned ochre and rust, and the summer flowers had withered, though, for a few, their season of glory had just begun.

"September has always been my favourite month," Adrian said. "There's something poignant about it. Some people think it tragic -- that autumn is like death. But it isn't. It's just the season when Nature goes into hibernation, to emerge, refreshed, in the spring."

They arrived at the swamp, serene and beautiful and much changed since Rowena had last seen it. Cattails and milkweed had burst open, spilling their fluffy down to the winds which carried their seeds aloft. There were no mosquitoes now. Nothing to disturb Adrian and Rowena. They sat down on a dry, sun-warmed bank.

"I feel that this is our place, Rowena. It's our refuge from the world. I believe that nothing bad could ever happen here." Adrian took her hand in his. "You know that they intend to send me into exile for a few months?"

"Aye."

"It's a damnable situation! No one asks my opinion! Simon Worthing tells me that I'll probably die if I stay here.... You do know about that, don't you?"

Rowena looked away. "Aye."

"I thought so. You keep staring at me as though you'll never see me again."

She winced.

"I ***will*** die if they send me away from you!"

"I don't want to talk about it! Please!"

"You have to face the truth. We both do."

Rowena began weeping, and Adrian took her into his arms. "Oh, Rowena, I do love you so. Don't cry, my darling. Be happy while we're together. For my sake."

She pressed her face against his shoulder. She couldn't believe he was dying. He was so vital, so alive!

As if to prove her thoughts true, his lips met hers and his hands began caressing her, gently, leisurely. Not like Brendan's demanding, possessive gropings. Adrian's hands were reverent and soporific. And clever. He had unhooked her bodice and freed her breasts before she realized what had happened. She clasped her hands before her to shield herself from his gaze.

"Oh, Rowena, I would never hurt you. Don't deny me this."

She resisted very little as he pulled her hands away. "You're so beautiful," he said in awe. "With my body, I thee worship." He lowered her onto the grassy bed. She gasped at the pleasure that tingled through her as his mouth came down on her breast. She could no more have stopped their lovemaking then, than she could have stopped loving him. It seemed so natural, so right.

Later, their passion spent, they lay drowsily in each other's arms. Rowena had never felt happier. She felt stronger and more confident in his love, and was sure that, together, they could survive anything. The impending separation no longer held such dread for her.

Adrian said, "I shall talk to Father and Jamie tonight, about our getting married. Everything will be alright, you'll see."

But it wasn't.

They met Jeremy, livid with anger, in the kitchen when they returned.

"Jamie, you're back early."

"Not early enough, I think! Both of you come with me!"

Meekly they followed him to the study.

"Just what the hell do you think you're doing?" Jeremy demanded after slamming the door. "Do you know what people would say if they saw you together?"

"Don't patronize us, Jamie. We're not children."

"That's precisely what worries me!"

"But it needn't! It's alright, don't you see? We're going to be married!"

"You're what?!"

Rowena shrank back under Jeremy's fierce glare. "Leave us!" He ordered.

When she hesitated, Adrian said, "Let me talk to Jamie alone. Don't worry."

"Sit down," Jeremy said to his brother when they were alone. He took a few minutes to compose himself, knowing it would solve nothing if he lost his temper with Adrian. "Just how far has this relationship gone?"

Adrian looked down, and didn't reply.

Christ! That little slut! So that was how she had hooked her claws into Adrian. No doubt she hoped to be a rich Launston widow soon! "So, it's like that, is it?"

"I love her, Jamie, and I want to marry her. Would you deny me happiness?"

Jeremy flinched. He decided to try another tactic. "You're hardly being fair to the girl, under the circumstances."

"Don't you think that I've agonized over that myself? But I feel so much better, and stronger. You'll think me a romantic fool, no doubt, but... she's like the sun to me, Jamie. Her smile warms me and makes me feel good inside. Her love sustains me."

Jeremy couldn't understand this sentimental nonsense. Yet Adrian's words and rapt expression when he spoke of her touched him deeply. No, he could not deny Adrian happiness.

But what about the girl? He was certain that she had no romantic illusions, and was interested only in the Launston name and money. It was even possible that she had another man's bastard in her belly, in which case her objectives were obvious.

Adrian was much too impressionable. He lived in a world of his own making. He had to be protected from the wench, for it would surely destroy the young man to discover her true nature.

"We'll discuss this again when you return from Toronto."

"I'm not going."

"But you must! Simon says you'll recover more quickly away from here."

"I don't believe that."

Jeremy's patience was ebbing. "Surely he knows better than you! If you refuse to go, I'll not give another thought to your marrying that... girl. She'll be sent home in disgrace, and you'll not be allowed near her!" Adrian's disconsolate expression cut him to the quick.

"I don't understand why you dislike her so, Jamie."

"Are you sure you're not deluding yourself about her, Adrian? She's a damned pretty girl, granted. I've come across a few of those myself, and thoroughly enjoyed their company. But I never felt obliged to marry any of them."

"Rowena is no whore," Adrian said coldly. "If you think that all girls of her class are merely to be used for entertainment, that they have no morals, and are not as 'worthy' and respectable as 'ladies', then it is you who are deluding yourself, Jeremy. You think that if I go away I'll forget about her, or she'll forget me. But you've never been in love, have you? You'd understand then, that nothing you could say or do could change what I feel for Rowena. Or perhaps you're expecting that I'll not return."

"That's not true! Look, Adrian, if she's that important to you, you can marry her when you return. I won't stand in your way, and I'll deal with Father -- though God knows how he's going to take this! But I'm truly concerned about your health. I insist you take Simon's advice and get a few months' rest in a healthier atmosphere."

"You won't try to dissuade Rowena in my absence? You won't dismiss her?"

"No, I give you my word. We'll just continue as we have until now. I think it best if we say nothing to anyone as yet, or there will be unnecessary gossip while you're away -- and that could only harm Rowena."

"I suppose you're right."

"I suggest that you and Father leave for Peterborough in a few days, so that you will have a chance to rest up for my wedding. It's less than a fortnight away. You can go to Cobourg from there, and take a steamer to Toronto."

"And be home by Christmas!"

"Yes."

"I'm going to tell Rowena."

Jeremy was relieved that the problem had been shelved. Now he had time to consider a more permanent solution.

He couldn't know then that he would, for the rest of his life, reproach himself for having persuaded Adrian to leave.

Chapter 16

Rowena sniffed appreciatively at the dried catnip. She liked the aromatic mint and could understand why it was such a soothing herb. This catnip would be used for colicky babies, high-strung children, and as a calming tea for fevers and colds. She crumbled the dried leaves into a labelled jar, which would join the others on the shelf where her mother stored her concoctions.

Rowena enjoyed the harvesting and preparation of the many plant medicines that her mother dispensed to the sick. They grew a variety of useful herbs and flowers in the garden, some of which had to be picked by the light of a full moon, when the plants were at their most potent. She enjoyed those evenings, working in the silvered darkness next to her mother. She felt then some eerie sort of connection with the women who had come before her -- her ancestors, whose knowledge and skill had been passed down to her through her mother.

Best of all were the times when she and her mother would go off alone to harvest wild plants from the woods. Moira showed no aptitude for distinguishing between plants, some of which were highly poisonous, Gwyn had no interest in medicines and no patience or compassion for the sick, and Alys and Brigid were too young. So these were special times, when Rowena had her mother all to herself. Deirdre would talk about the different properties of the plants, and how to dispense them and in what quantities. While some plants were relatively harmless even in large doses, Rowena knew how critical was the dosage of others, like the potentially poisonous foxglove.

They had also learned of many useful native plants from the Indians, like the squaw root and the pretty spring-flowering trillium which aided in childbirth.

Rowena recalled her discussion with Adrian about plants, that fateful day they had met at the swamp. But then, he was never far from her thoughts. His presence still lingered in the big house, in the rooms where he had entertained her with stories while she'd worked. She hugged those memories to her and replayed them constantly in her head as she went about her chores. But even here, at home, there were little things that made her soft-eyed with remembering.

She had given him comfrey and lungwort to take with him to Toronto to help ease his cough and prevent lung hemorrhage. There was so little else she could do for him. Except pray.

But she was never sure that God was listening to her or that she understood his methods. She had to admit that He'd been pretty good to them these last five years -- none of her family had been deathly ill, and their luck seemed to have changed for the better. But she was wary. Perhaps He sent trials when people became complacent. Perhaps happiness had to be earned through pain. Like childbirth.

Donal interrupted her gloomy thoughts when he shoved a carved bird beneath her nose and said, "What do you think of that?" It was a swallow in full flight. "It's for Rosemary," Donal explained.

"'Tis lovely. Though not as beautiful as my loon," Rowena said proudly.

He grinned. "Sure, that was a masterpiece!"

"Rosemary will treasure it, for certain sure," Rowena told him.

Donal dropped into a chair at the table next to where Rowena was stripping the leaves from the bunches of dried herbs she had taken down from the ceiling. "I'll give it to her as something to remember me by," he said. "I thought I might go to the lumber camp this winter, seeing as how there's not much work for Da and me around here."

Rowena threw him a sorrowful look. Deirdre, who had overheard, said, "Give it time, lad. Your Da's looking for work, and you may be needed here."

"Sure, I don't mind, Ma. They say the pay is good."

"You'd be wasted there, with your skill. 'Tis a hard and dangerous kind of work, in the camps."

They were interrupted by a knock at the door. It was Kate Muldoon, come to have a consultation with Deirdre. Donal took his cue when Deirdre nodded her head toward the door, and made his escape. The younger girls were over at the Ryans' this evening, and Patrick had gone out earlier.

Kate accepted a cup of tea. Rowena continued working at the table as the two women sat down in front of the fire.

"That's better," Kate said appreciatively. "That November cold has a way of getting into me bones. Sure, and it doesn't take leave of them till May!" She lowered her voice as she said, "Now, Deirdre, I'm needing something for to regulate me courses."

"You're not with child, are you, Kate?" Deirdre asked cautiously.

Rowena knew why. The herbs that Deirdre could give Kate could cause a miscarriage. Abortion was against the laws of God and man. But there were some women -- those with too many children or with no husband -- who thought it no sin to get rid of their mistakes before they quickened, at about four months.

"Nay, nay! I've had twelve childer already, and God's left me with eight to care for. Sure, I wouldn't be foolish enough to be getting any more! Nay, 'tis just these cramps and back-aches, but nothing happening."

Rowena didn't believe her, and was sure that Deirdre didn't either. But her mother said, "Rowena, make up a mixture of squaw root and pennyroyal for Kate."

The woman looked at her gratefully. "'Tis obliged to you, I am! Sure, a woman can't be going to a man doctor and talking about such things. What could men understand about women's ailments anyway, I'm asking? Not that I don't like Dr. Simon, mind. He's such a kind gentleman." Relief made Kate talkative. But after Rowena handed her the packet of herbs and Deirdre had given her strict instructions on how to prepare the infusions, Kate paid them and left.

"She's going right home to try it," Deirdre said to Rowena. "And the sooner the better, if she's with child, as I suspect."

"Then why did you give it to her, Ma?"

"I'm thinking she's paid her dues. Bearing a dozen children is hard work. God gave us these plants to use wisely, lass." She looked at Rowena suspiciously and said, "You're not having trouble with your courses, are you?"

Rowena, her face in the shadows, hoped her mother could not see her hot blush. She had missed her last period, and was beginning to suspect that she was pregnant. But it was too early to be sure. "Nay. Sometimes 'tis not much to speak of, is all," she said. And if that were not all, could she possibly keep it a secret until Adrian returned? It was not easy to hide anything when one lived in such confined quarters with so many others.

She never once considered resorting to the abortion herbs. Adrian would undoubtedly be as delighted to become a father as she was to bear his child. And so long as they married before she gave birth -- which would be next June -- there wouldn't be much of a scandal.

She was saved from further questioning by Patrick, who came in with a big grin on his face. "You don't have to worry now, Dre! We're fixed up for a while. Jeremy Launston's hired Donal and me to make renovations to the mills. Should keep us busy for a month or more, and he's paying well."

"And just in time, too!" Deirdre said with relief. "Donal was thinking to go to the lumber camp."

Rowena wondered if Jeremy had done that to be kind, or whether he really needed work done. She wasn't quite sure about him, and certainly didn't trust his motives.

Margaret Finch had nothing but praise for him, but Rowena wondered if he deserved it. His offer of a job to the new widow may have seemed like kindness to her at the time, but Rowena knew what a jewel Jeremy had found in Margaret.

She and Margaret had become good friends during the last two months. She knew now how desperate Margaret had been after her husband's death. Her own parents were dead, and she'd had no wish to burden her brothers and sisters, who had families and enough responsibilities of their own. Her husband's family in England would have taken her in from duty, but Margaret had had no wish to be beholden to them nor relegated to some role as unpaid companion.

She had enjoyed running the Launston household -- until the new mistress had arrived.

Rowena had been pleasantly surprised by Harriet's unpretentiousness and friendliness. She was not at all the haughty beauty Rowena had expected Jeremy to choose as a wife. Despite her informal manner, however, there was no mistaking her authority.

Margaret had taken umbrage the moment that Harriet had so graciously descended upon the kitchen and snatched the reins from her hands. Harriet often cooked the meals now, delegating more menial chores to Margaret, and had taken over the shopping, depriving Margaret of her enjoyable weekly outings. Harriet had even questioned some past accounts in the household books.

"All that amiable 'Margaret this' and 'Margaret that' won't wash with me," Margaret had complained to Rowena. "It's insincere, and more condescending to my way of thinking than if she kept her distance and called me Mrs. Finch, the way a housekeeper is properly addressed. And I wish she'd leave the running of the house to me. Certainly the gentlemen never had cause for complaint before. I don't know what I am half the time -- housekeeper once minute, skivvy the next, depending upon ***her ladyship's*** mood. Jeremy's a good, kind man, and deserves better than that woman!"

Rowena was beginning to see Margaret's point of view the very next afternoon.

Simon Worthing frequently came to tea in the kitchen with Margaret and her. Rowena could see his deep fondness for Margaret in the way he looked at her -- with joy and admiration. Rowena's presence made his visits seem less like courting than a friendly get-together, but it was obvious to Rowena that both Margaret and Simon took them seriously. She always tried to leave them alone together for a while.

Simon respected Rowena's knowledge of healing plants and often questioned her about various remedies that she and her mother used. He was saying, "I agree that chamomile makes a soothing and harmless tea, but I don't consider it a medicine. Not like willow bark, which alleviates pain, or dogbane, which is a strong heart stimulant like digitalis."

"And I suppose you've tried them both?" Rowena asked, remembering what Adrian had told her.

"I don't give my patients what I wouldn't take myself," Simon confided.

Rowena giggled. "And what do you think about those that hasten childbirth?"

Simon laughed heartily, and Margaret smiled. He said, "Fortunately, they do have other uses, too."

"Oh, Simon, I didn't realize you were here!" Harriet said, coming into the kitchen. She seemed truly surprised, almost insulted, that she hadn't been made of aware of his presence. "Jeremy isn't home yet, but I expect him shortly. Shall we take some refreshment in the parlour?"

"Thank you, Harriet, but I've already had tea. Actually, it's Margaret I came to see."

"Margaret, you're not ill, are you?" Harriet asked with immediate concern.

Simon answered. "Just a social call, Harriet."

"I see," she replied. Rowena didn't miss the chilling look that passed between mistress and housekeeper. Harriet donned an apron and set about preparing the evening meal. "You'll join us for supper, won't you Simon?" It seemed a pointed reminder to the doctor that, as a family friend, his place was in the dining room, not the kitchen.

But Simon, an equable soul, was undisturbed by Harriet's implication. "Thank you, Harriet, but not today. In fact, I must be on my way. I have several more calls to make before evening surgery. Some other time perhaps."

When Simon had gone, Margaret said, "Come, Rowena. We have chores to do elsewhere." She led Rowena into the main house. Once the door to the kitchen had closed, she said between clenched teeth, "How I detest that woman! She's chummy enough with the ***servants*** when it suits her, but let us not make the mistake of thinking ourselves equals. And God forbid that we should have a mutual friend! Let's set the dining room table."

As they spread out the white linen tablecloth, Rowena said, "It doesn't bother Simon, though."

"Nor Jeremy, I think," Margaret said. "Of course, he knows that my family was as good as his, back in the Old Country. Even Harriet's family had declined into genteel poverty before coming here and wrangling important and lucrative positions through their government connections. The Launstons have always behaved as though they're grateful to me for coming here and organizing their household. You wouldn't believe how chaotic things were when I arrived! But Harriet is constantly undermining me, as if we were in some sort of battle for control."

Setting out the expensive china, Rowena said, "Just think, Margaret, when you and Simon marry, you'll be coming here as a guest."

Margaret stopped working and looked at her in astonishment. "Marry?"

"Sure, he's in love with you. 'Tis as plain as day."

Margaret looked perturbed. "It's too early. I'm still in mourning. You shouldn't talk so, Rowena!"

"But it's true, isn't it? And you love him, too, don't you?"

"I don't know." Margaret looked at the shiny silver knife she held in her hand as if trying to see into her soul through her reflection. "I loved my husband once, or so I thought. Then it all went wrong somehow. We weren't suited. We grated on each other. When he died I wasn't surprised nor very sorry. Just terribly sad, as though I'd failed him somehow. Sometimes I even feel that he died because I didn't love him enough. That's a terrible thing to admit. How can I even think about marrying another man so soon?"

"But you and Simon ***are*** suited, Margaret. Surely you can feel it?"

Margaret looked probingly at Rowena. "You're very young to be talking with such confidence about love."

Rowena wished she could tell her about Adrian. How she longed to shout out her happiness, and share her apprehension. But she had promised not to mention their arrangement to anyone.

She said lightly, "Sometimes others can see things about us that we can't. And wouldn't I love to see the mistress's face when she has to entertain you in her drawing room!"

Sure, how would the mistress react when she discovered that Rowena was to be her sister-in-law?

Chapter 17

"I'm that frightened," Deirdre confided to Mary Ryan as she put down her mending. The two women were sitting before a roaring blaze on a wintry, grey afternoon in December. The older girls were at the shops; the younger children were out playing in the powdery, new-fallen snow. "'Tis been a week, and not a word we've had from him. Something's wrong, I can feel it in me bones."

"Don't fret yourself, Deirdre," Mary said. "He told you he was going hunting with Mike."

"Aye, but hunting what? Pat met Seamus Flannery at Paxtons' last evening. Seamus said he hadn't seen hide nor hair of his brother Mike in a week, and never heard tell that Donal was with him. They're up to no good, the pair of them. You know that Mike's a supporter of Mackenzie. He's made no secret of it." And Mackenzie was planning a rebellion -- that was no secret either, though many did not believe it. "And Brendan's been poisoning Donal's mind all summer, with his tales of Irish rebel heroes. No sooner had Brendan gone off to the lumber camp, than Donal and Mike began talking of joining Mackenzie."

"Aye, well, Donal has enough sense to be keeping out of trouble, I'm thinking."

"Nay, he's just like his father!" Deirdre said angrily, but then was appalled at her hasty words. She hoped that Mary would not pick up on them, but in vain.

Mary regarded her slyly. "He's never like Patrick. But, sure, that's not what you were saying, is it? What is it you're not telling me?" But Mary's face lit up a moment later. "Of course! Donal's father was that lad you told me about, the one the British hanged! Sure, I should have guessed then! There's not a bit of Patrick in your Donal. Well, well," Mary said with a self-satisfied air.

"Promise me you'll not be telling anyone, Mary. Swear it!"

"Does Patrick know?"

"Aye. He knew afore he married me that I was carrying Brian's child. I never deceived him, if that's what you're after thinking! But sure he's the only one who knows. And I'll not have word of this getting back to Donal!" Deirdre fixed her friend with a fierce stare. "Swear it, Mary!"

Mary lowered her eyes. "Sure, no one will be hearing it from me lips, Deirdre, never fear."

But Deirdre was not reassured. As close as the two women were, Deirdre had never wholly trusted Mary. Not that she expected Mary to blurt out the secret to the first person that she met. But it was the kind of thing that Mary might let slip, for she had a careless tongue, and did seem to take a self-righteous attitude in exposing the weaknesses and sins of others.

So Deirdre had another burden on her troubled mind. Patrick and Donal had already finished the renovations at the Launstons' mills, and there was no more work to be had. Patrick was spending more and more of his idle hours at Paxtons'. This baby had been troubling her more than the others had. She felt so weary; each day was an ordeal to get through. Moira had been moping about ever since Conn had gone off to the lumber camp, and was even short-tempered at times. And now there was not only Donal to worry about, but Mary's silence as well.

And then there was Rowena. She really would have to confront her daughter tonight. There was no sense in delaying that -- indeed, no time for it.

• • •

Rowena straightened up, her back aching from scrubbing the floor. There seemed to be more work now that Harriet had taken over the household. Certainly there were more visitors; already Mrs. Neville, Beatrice, and Susannah had been to stay, and Nigel and Charlotte Melbourne had just departed, having stopped over for a few days on their way back from Toronto.

Once this job was finished she still had the drawing room furniture to polish -- no easy task since the mistress had littered the rooms with vases and lustres, wax flowers under glass and cluttering bric-a-brac. Dozens of paintings, tilting ominously forward, hung over doorways, and a step ladder was needed to dust them.

The house had altered since Harriet had come to rule it. Her first assault upon it had been to wallpaper all the rooms. Rowena had watched in dismay as the soft blue of the drawing room had succumbed to gilt flowers and curlicues, and the cheerful yellow of the parlour had been suffocated by busy vines and funereal urns of blooms. More furniture had been stuffed into the rooms, destroying their elegant simplicity.

But she wouldn't be doing this scrubbing and polishing much longer, Rowena thought gratefully. Adrian was returning in two weeks! She could hardly wait!

Lately she had been plagued with fears, though Adrian's weekly letters assured her that he was improving. Those were the only times Jeremy ever spoke to her. He never alluded to the fact that she was to be his brother's wife. Was Jeremy contriving some way to keep them apart?

Rowena was jolted from her thoughts as the front door flew open, and Jeremy strode in on a blast of icy air. Rowena watched dirty puddles form on the newly scrubbed floor as Jeremy shook the snow from his boots.

"Has my wife returned from the shops?"

"No, sir."

"Come to my office," Jeremy said, marching down the hallway without a backward glance.

Rowena rose eagerly from her knees. There must be another letter from Adrian!

She dried her hands on her apron, straightened her cap, and followed Jeremy. He was standing at the window with his back to her when she entered the study. "There's a letter for you on the desk."

Her heartbeat quickened when she noticed it lying there, her name written across it in the ornate handwriting she had come to know so well. Adrian always included a separate letter to her in his correspondence with his brother -- much to Jeremy's disapproval, she knew. She well remembered the day that first one had arrived. Wordlessly, angrily he had handed it to her. When she had finished reading it, he had forbidden her to answer it or even to keep it. She had choked back tears as he had snatched the beloved missive from her fingers, and tossed it into the fire. But she had accepted Jeremy's terms, and he had never denied her those few moments of private joy.

Rowena now held the letter to her cheek, postponing the moment of pleasure to savour it all the more. She broke the wax seal, carefully unfolded the paper, and began to read.

My Dearest Rowena,

How I long to be with you again! I count the hours until our departure from this detestable city, and console myself with the thought that, by the time you receive this, there will be less than a fortnight separating us. Father plans to spend no less than five days on our journey home, and will not listen to my entreaties for haste. He feels that a more speedy trip will be detrimental to my health, though he cannot know that you are my best medicine. How often I think and dream of you, my darling, and of the happiness that will soon be ours.

Your potions have also worked wonders for me, and I take them faithfully, as I promised you I would. They are magic medicines wrought by your healing hands. How can I be anything but much improved?

Since I have been stronger, Father has accepted several social engagements for us, at which I have been exposed to some of the nubile young ladies of the city -- a ploy no doubt devised by my cunning brother to test my love for you. But you need not fear, my darling, for those frivolous young women interested me not one whit. I have told Jamie so most strongly in my letter, and hope he feels truly ashamed at perpetrating such a low scheme. I could think only of you and of the warm, loving home we will make of that lonely old cabin. Even as I write these words I can feel strength flowing through my veins. Was there ever a man as fortunate, as happy as I? I think not, for I am certain there can never have been another such as you.

May God protect you, my darling.

Faithfully yours,
Adrian

While Rowena was absorbed in the letter, Jeremy was studying her. She read slowly, often with difficulty -- a fact which emphasized her humble background, and reminded Jeremy once again that she was not a suitable wife for his brother.

He had not been able to discover any evidence to discredit Rowena. Of course, it was possible that she had a 'follower' among the men who spent the winters in the lumber camps, but this he couldn't prove. Once Adrian came home there would be no way of stopping the boy from marrying her.

Jeremy glanced at the chapped, work-roughened hands which held the letter, at the streak of dirt upon her brow. It surprised him to realize that he was moved by those red, painful-looking hands that were, nonetheless, long and slender and even graceful. He looked again at her face, at the alabaster complexion framed so strikingly by her mass of black hair which was never totally tamed by her muslin cap.

As he stared at the long, black lashes that swept over those disturbing, ice-blue eyes, Jeremy wondered what was happening to him. Why was his whole body so aware of her? Why did he suddenly want to possess her with a passion he could barely suppress?

Jeremy poured himself a large brandy.

He did not want to admit, even to himself, that Harriet was a disappointment to him. Before their marriage he had thought her lack of passion a virtue, but he had expected to melt her defences once they were wed. How wrong he had been! Harriet dutifully submitted to him, but she took no pleasure in their sexual union and, thus, dampened his own.

He was certain that Rowena would not be like that, for her very movements were sensual. For one absurd moment he actually envied Adrian this girl.

When Rowena had completed her second perusal of the letter, she raised her eyes and was startled to find Jeremy's intense, dark gaze upon her. She was confused by his look, and the way his eyes held hers. Finally he looked away, and said coldly, "You may leave now."

She rose from the chair by the fire, and placed the letter upon the desk. "Thank you, sir."

Jeremy glowered at the letter for a long time before picking it up and skimming through it. He had never before read Adrian's letters to Rowena, and felt like an intruder. He crumpled the note in self-disgust before tossing it into the fire. The paper burst into flames for a brief moment, and then crumbled into charred ashes.

A few minutes later there was a knock on the door, and Harriet entered. Her cheeks were still mottled pink from the cold. "I've been to see Simon," she said.

Jeremy glanced up sharply. "You're not ill, are you?"

She gave him a tentative smile. "He has confirmed my suspicions. Jeremy, I'm..." She lowered her eyes. "... with child."

Jeremy beamed as he jumped up and went to her side. "I had no idea!"

"It's early yet, and I wanted to be certain before I told you."

He took her in his arms, and kissed her heartily. "This is wonderful news! When is the child to be born?"

"July."

"I'm delighted! Absolutely delighted. And so will Father be. Well, we must toast your health, and that of our son."

Jeremy poured her a sherry and himself, another brandy. While they drank and chatted, Harriet was happier than she had been since her wedding. This was the first time they had been at such ease with one another, the first time she had seen Jeremy so unabashedly happy himself. It should always be like this, she thought. Had she finally discovered a way to please him?

The restraint between them had not begun on their wedding night. Doubtless Jeremy had not expected her to enjoy her deflowering. He had even been considerate, reassuring her that it would be better the next time. But during the following days, she had found it only marginally less painful, and certainly not enjoyable. Still, she had done her duty as a wife, as her mother had warned her she must, but that had not seemed to satisfy Jeremy. He had become increasingly impatient with her, and she had wondered what he expected of her.

"There is something else," Harriet said. "I've asked Margaret to make up the spare bedroom for me. I should be be more comfortable sleeping on my own."

"Surely that isn't necessary yet. Did Simon suggest it?"

"No." Harriet's cheeks were flushed as she said, "But since we have achieved our purpose, there is no longer any reason for us to... share a bed. You do understand, don't you, Jeremy?"

"No, I do not! What you're saying is that you find my attentions distasteful, isn't it?"

"Please, Jeremy! You're making this very difficult for me!"

"And you are being unreasonable, Harriet. Do you expect me to live like a monk until after the baby is born? Have you forgotten your vows -- to love, honour, and obey?"

"Haven't I given you what you want? I'm carrying your child. There's no reason for us to... to...."

"Make love?"

"No!" Harriet said heatedly. "You have my love. What you speak of is a degrading act which a woman bears for one purpose only -- to have children. Any further relations between us at this time can only be construed as sinful!" Harriet walked to the door. "I trust you will repect my wishes in this matter, Jeremy."

When the door had shut, Jeremy hurled his glass against the stone fireplace.

Chapter 18

Patrick was late for his supper. Deirdre and the girls had already starting eating when he burst into the room.

"Mackenzie and his men have taken Toronto!" he shouted. "Aye, 'tis true. Ten thousand strong they were! Marched right into the city not two days since. Had Bond Head's supporters routed in no time. And all the citizens came out on the streets to cheer them on. What a grand sight it must have been!"

Deirdre's blood ran cold. "Holy Mother of God! That's where Donal's been!" Her exclamation was barely a whisper, as though she feared hearing the truth of the words herself.

"If he was, then he'll be a hero," Patrick said.

"Maybe a dead one!" Deirdre said crossly. "Or a traitor, if they lost." Was this her divine punishment, she wondered. Was her son to die a traitor's death, like his father afore him? In sudden panic she said, "You must find out what's happened, Pat!"

"Aye, lass, I'll be going back to Paxtons' soon as I've had a bite of supper. Maybe there'll be more news by then." As he gobbled down his meal, Patrick tried to reassure her. "Sure, I don't see how they could've lost! Didn't Bond Head send all the troops in the province to Lower Canada nigh on two months ago to help the army there fight the French Canadian *Patriotes*? Sure there wasn't more than a handful of soldiers left in Toronto! And how many of the militia do you think would be fighting for the Governor? Not many, I'm thinking. Sure, even the Tories don't like that arrogant bastard!"

"Maybe, but they like Mackenzie even less. They wouldn't be letting himself just walk into Toronto to take over the government, not without a fight. Not without bloodshed."

Patrick kissed her worried brow, and then shrugged into his blanket coat. "I'll be off to see if there's any more news. Don't you be fretting now, lass. Donal knows how to take care of himself."

But Deirdre could turn her thoughts to no other purpose. There had been a reckless streak in her beloved son since he was a child. She had thought it tamed these last years, as Donal had learned Patrick's painstaking craft, and had absorbed some of his equanimity. But she had sensed her son's restlessness.

Donal had always been her favourite child, not only because he had been her firstborn, and only surviving son, but because he was Brian's son. Sure, she had come to love Patrick over the years. That was a quiet, gentle emotion, born of his love for her, nurtured by mutual respect and happy companionship, strengthened by shared joys and sorrows. A more contented and abiding love, she was sure, than she would have had with quixotic Brian. But every once in a while, she would allow herself the luxury of remembering those intensely passionate days that had conceived Donal, as wisdom and responsibility might recall some carefree childhood frolic -- with a smile and a poignant yearning for what could never be again.

But Deirdre had not forgotten the other problem that needed to be dealt with. When the girls went to bed, she detained Rowena. Deirdre, now eight months pregnant, moved about with difficulty because of her large size and swollen limbs. She sat down wearily in the rocking chair by the fire across from Rowena, and carefully watched her daughter as she said, "I noticed you've missed your courses again."

Rowena blanched.

"What have you done, girl?"

"I'll be getting wed."

"Aye, that you will! 'Tisn't Brendan Delaney, is it? You weren't meeting him on the sly?" That was Deirdre's greatest fear concerning Rowena. She herself couldn't understand the antipathy she felt for the man. There were some people that one disliked instantly upon first meeting, and to whom one never warmed. Brendan was such a one for her. His easy charm did not touch her, except with an ***un***easy sense of distrust.

Rowena shook her head. "I'll be marrying Adrian Launston, soon as he returns."

Deirdre was momentarily speechless. "Adrian Launston? Are you daft then, girl? They say he's dying."

"He's better now, Ma."

"Holy Mother of God! What have I done, letting you go to work there?"

"But I'll be getting wed, Ma." Rowena's eyes pleaded with her mother to understand.

"And why have you said naught of this afore?"

"Jeremy thought it best to say nothing till Adrian returns."

"Sure, why do you think that is then? Do you really believe the likes of them will be letting the lad wed you? Lord, but you're a fool, lass! Gentlemen like that take their pleasure with simple girls like you. Aye, but they don't wed them! Like as not they'll have turned the lad against you, if he ever intended to do the honourable thing by you. Or they'll have found him a suitable wife in Toronto, and there'll be naught you can do but hang your head in shame!"

"'Tisn't true! Adrian loves me! He's been writing to me every week. Beautiful letters, Ma. He's a gentle, kind, honest man. He's even willing to become a Catholic."

"A man'll say anything to have his way with a lass!" Deirdre looked sharply at Rowena. "Have you confessed your sin?"

"'Tisn't a sin to love."

"'Tis a sin to fornicate! May the Saints preserve you!"

Despite Deirdre's angry words, she felt sympathy for her naive daughter. Sure, hadn't she been in the same shoes once -- pregnant by a man she could not marry?

What was happening to her family? Her two eldest children seem to have been living secret lives of their own, that she was only just discovering. It was frightening to realize that she no longer had control over their lives. Terrifying to know that they were both in trouble, yet there might be nothing she could do to help them.

Brian O'Neill had been only eighteen why the British had hanged him for treason. And she had been seventeen when she was pregnant with Donal.

The door opened and Patrick walked in, looking glum.

"Something's amiss!" Deirdre said in alarm.

Patrick said, "The latest report is that there were only a few hundred reformers, and disorganized at that. Some of them are in gaol now, and the militia is scouring the countryside for the rest -- especially Mackenzie. There's a price on his head. For treason."

There was an anguished silence in the room. The cold winter air that had rushed in with Patrick's entrance was like the chill of the grave, a portent that Deirdre did not wish to dwell upon. She hugged herself not only for warmth, but to contain the fear that threatened to unbalance her. There was nothing she could do but wait for news of Donal.

Distractedly, she said, "We've another problem, Pat. Rowena's with child."

Patrick stared at Rowena in shocked disbelief that slowly sizzled into anger. He raised his hand as if to strike her.

Rowena didn't move. Her father had never hit her. Nor did he now. He lowered his arm and clenched his fists.

"She says she's to be wed," Deirdre explained. "To Adrian Launston."

"Jaysus Christ!" He dropped into a chair near the fire. After a long silence he said, "I'll be having a talk with Mr. Jeremy tomorrow. And you'll not go near that house again unless it be as a bride!"

"There's nothing to discuss, Da. 'Tis all settled. Adrian will be back afore Christmas, and we'll be wed. And I'll be going to work tomorrow, same as always -- 'less you want people to talk."

"She's right, Pat," Deirdre said, "There's naught we can do until Adrian returns."

And that was sooner than anyone had expected.

"They're back!" Margaret Finch informed Rowena when she arrived at work the next morning.

"Who?"

"Why, Mr. Sam and Adrian, of course. They arrived late last night. They thought it best to get away from Toronto with all the trouble there -- no doubt you've already heard about that...."

Rowena wasn't listening. Adrian was back! She could hardly contain her excitement. "How is he, Margaret? Is he well?"

"Adrian? The journey tired him, naturally, but no doubt he'll be fine after a few days rest." Margaret wrinkled her brow. "You look like the cat that got into the cream. You're not sweet on Adrian, are you, Rowena?"

"Aye."

"Oh, Rowena! You know, I've become very fond of you. I wouldn't want to see you hurt by a childish infatuation that could lead nowhere."

"Sure, don't you see, Margaret, we're in love, and we'll be wed now that he's back. But you're not to say anything yet."

Margaret gaped at her in astonishment. "Who knows about this?"

"Jeremy."

Margaret's incredulity gave way to a smile. "I ***am*** happy for you, Rowena," she said, giving her a hug. Gleefully she said, "Whatever will Harriet say?" They both laughed.

Rowena went eagerly about her chores, though she was impatient to see Adrian. And a little frightened. Perhaps her mother had been right after all. She knew from Adrian himself that Jeremy had been scheming to separate them. Or perhaps Adrian's ardour had cooled.

The parlour door opened. Rowena turned to face him. He was thinner and paler, but there was a bright sparkle in his misty-blue eyes. They stared at one another, each seeking reassurance in the other's face. Then, joyfully, Rowena ran to him and threw herself into his arms.

Jeremy discovered them thus, clinging to one another. He was both embarrassed and touched by the scene. Well, he wouldn't stand in Adrian's way any longer. Let her make the boy's last few months happy ones.

Simon had informed him last night how ill Adrian really was, and that there seemed little hope of his recovering. With luck and proper care, Adrian might see the spring.

The lovers weren't aware of Jeremy's presence.

"You're more beautiful than ever, Rowena," Adrian said, holding her at arm's length and gazing at her with wonder.

"That must be because I am going to have your child," she replied simply.

"Is it true?"

"Aye. It'll be born in June."

Adrian embraced her. "I'll be the proudest father ever!"

Jeremy groaned. Hadn't he expected this?

Rowena spotted him then, and quickly drew away from Adrian. Adrian glanced about. "Ah, Jamie...."

"Yes, I heard. Are you sure that it's your child she's carrying, Adrian?"

Both Rowena and Adrian reddened. "What are you suggesting?"

"Just answer the question."

Adrian's eyes blazed. "I am certain it is my child! I would stake my life upon that. I pity you your suspicious nature, your inability to comprehend and to feel love. Rowena and I are going to be married immediately, with or without ***your*** permission!"

Jeremy was contrite. He hadn't wanted to hurt Adrian, but no doubt he had deserved those icy words. There was nothing he could do but agree. "You needn't elope, if that's what you have in mind." To Rowena he said, "Bring your parents here this evening, and we'll discuss the arrangements."

But events were already underway which would prevent that meeting.

A formidable army of the Peterborough Militia, under Major Tybald, marched into Launston Mills late that afternoon, waving the British flag and firing muskets into the air. They tramped up Mill Road to Main Street, attracting a crowd of curious townspeople in their wake.

Jeremy, too, went to see what the devil was happening.

Major Tybald stood in the middle of Main Street, and addressed the people. "As you've probably heard, the government troops and loyal militia have squashed a rebellion in Toronto. Word has reached us that the rebel leader, William Lyon Mackenzie, is hiding out in this area. There's a one thousand pound reward for any man who'll give us information leading to the arrest of that criminal, Mackenzie. And it'll be the gallows for anyone found harbouring that traitor! I ask you now, loyal citizens, have any of you seen the blackguard?"

The crowd murmured, but no one replied.

"Then you'll not mind if we search your homes!"

Jeremy laughed when he related this scene to the others.

"I hope they don't catch him," Adrian said.

Jeremy frowned. "You'd best keep your own counsel when Tybald comes here, as he undoubtedly will. Though I wonder if he'll have the temerity to pry about our house. I've met him before. In fact, he attended our wedding. He's a bit of a fool, but I suppose we'll have to offer him our hospitality."

"Don't treat this lightly," Samuel cautioned. "The province is in an uproar. The Lieutenant-Governor is no longer amused by the Reformers. Men are being arrested on the slightest suspicion, and we saw the homes of Mackenzie supporters vandalized and burned to the ground. I doubt that Mackenzie is hiding out this far north-east of Toronto. But he'll try to make for the States, and because the border at Niagara will be the most closely watched area, Mackenzie may try to sneak in to Lower Canada and cross there."

It was Rowena who answered the door when Major Tybald and over a dozen of his men arrived. "Fetch your master, girl!"

The others had heard the commotion in the hallway, and came out of the parlour.

"Good to see you again, Major," Jeremy said pleasantly.

"I trust you have no objections to my men searching your house?"

"Certainly not. We ***are*** all on the same side you know, Major."

"Won't you join us for a drink in the drawing room, Major?" Harriet offered.

"No thank you, Mrs. Launston. I regret I'm here on business."

"Well, I expect you'll be needing a place to stay tonight, Major Tybald," Samuel said. "You and your men have had a long journey -- for nothing, I'm afraid. I'm sure we can put you up for the night, and the townspeople will be happy to billet your men."

"Thank you, Mr. Launston, but we expect to reach Omemee tonight."

They stood about expectantly in the hall. Tybald's men returned, shaking their heads. He nodded to them, and then turned to Samuel. "It is my unpleasant duty, sir, to arrest your son, Adrian Launston, on the charge of high treason."

Rowena thought she would faint.

"What?!" both Samuel and Jeremy cried in disbelief.

"I have," the Major said, pulling a document from his breast pocket, "a warrant for his arrest."

"This is absurd!" Jeremy said angrily. "You've made a stupid mistake Major!"

"Indeed I have not. It has been known to us for some time that your brother's sympathies lie with the rebels. We're aware of the fact that he intends to print subversive propaganda. He was overheard, not two weeks ago, making treasonous comments about the government. We've arrested men on less evidence than this."

"My brother is young and impressionable and sometimes indiscreet, I grant you, but you can hardly arrest him for that! Our family has faithfully supported the government and the Crown!"

"We have no doubts about your loyalty, or your father's. However, I submit that the reason your father spirited your brother away from Toronto with such ungodly haste, once it was obvious that the insurrection would fail, was that your brother had been in league with the traitors."

"Then you are an ass, sir! My brother is ill. You can see that for yourself. He can hardly have been involved in the plot!"

"We'll let the judge decide that." Major Tybald signalled to his men, and they moved in on Adrian

It was a nightmare for Rowena. She ran toward Adrian. "No! Leave him be!" The men pushed her away.

"My son is desperately ill, Major Tybald. You cannot arrest him!"

"I'm sorry, Mr. Launston, but I'm only doing my duty. Take him away."

Rowena clawed at Adrian's captors. Jeremy rushed over to rescue his brother, but was quickly restrained by several large men. "By God, I'll have your head for this, Tybald!" Jeremy swore, struggling uselessly as he was dragged back. "I'll go to the Governor himself if need be!"

"You do that, sir. Have you a coat for the boy?"

Margaret produced Adrian's greatcoat, muffler, hat, and gloves.

Rowena was still trying to reach Adrian. One of the men said, "Get this little vixen away from me before I swipe her."

Margaret gently put her arm about Rowena, and drew her away. Rowena looked helplessly, hopelessly at Adrian. There was such sadness and regret in his eyes as he was being led away. She began sobbing, and Margaret held the girl in her arms, tears coursing down her own cheeks.

"What the devil is that stupid girl blubbering about?" Samuel asked irritably when the men had gone.

Jeremy was enraged. "That contemptible swine!... Harriet, pack me a bag! Margaret, take Rowena into the parlour, and then tell Tom to saddle my horse!"

"What are you planning to do, Jeremy?" Harriet asked anxiously.

"I'm going to get Adrian released! The bag please, Harriet."

She hurried upstairs as bid. Jeremy said to his father, "There's something you should know. I had intended to mention it tonight." They walked into the parlour. Jeremy poured three large brandies, and handed one to Rowena. "Here, drink this."

She accepted the glass with trembling fingers. "They'll hang him, won't they?"

"They won't. I promise you that."

She looked into his eyes, and believed him. She took a big gulp of brandy, choking on the fiery tonic.

Jeremy turned to his father. "Rowena is carrying Adrian's child."

Samuel's mouth fell open. He, too, took a large swallow of brandy.

"He wants to marry her."

"This is damnable! The whole situation. You must get him out of gaol, Jamie. He'll die there -- if he even survives the journey."

"I'll not return without him."

All this was his fault, Jeremy thought with remorse. He should have let Adrian stay and marry the girl. Then none of this would have happened. His father was right -- a cold, damp, prison cell would finish Adrian. And Rowena would be left with his bastard.

Chapter 19

Donal O'Shaughnessy had to admit that life in Upper Canada had been pretty good compared to Ireland. Despite the alleged corruption and patronage in the colonial government, he had never felt any particular injustice done to himself or his family.

So it had not really been for noble motives or high principles that Donal had accompanied Mike Flannery on his trek to Toronto to join the reformers. It had been mainly for the excitement.

Well, excitement he'd had aplenty, Donal thought wryly to himself. In fact, now that he was alone, he could admit to himself that he was damned scared. Scared, hungry, exhausted, and cold. So cold. He snuggled deeper into the straw, but couldn't stop his teeth from chattering. He squeezed back childish tears that no man of eighteen should succumb to, no matter how desperate his plight.

If he wasn't caught soon, he'd probably die of exposure. It was because the patrol had been so close that he'd tumbled down the bank without checking what lay below. What a shock it had been to be engulfed by the icy water of a shallow but turbulent stream! His clothes had been frozen on him by the time he had reached this barn, and his stiff, careless fingers had barely been able to shed them. He'd found some old sacking to wear; thin though it was, it was dry. He hadn't dared risk going to the house. Even if the occupants were sympathizers, the patrol would likely be here soon to search the place. He'd certainly given himself away by running.

In a perverse way he hoped they would catch him, for he was tired of running and of the constant fear, to say nothing of the physical discomforts he had endured these last -- how many days? He was no longer sure. In fact, all the recent events were muddled in his mind.

Sure, he remembered the day he and Mike Flannery had arrived at his uncle's house in Newmarket, a few days early they had thought, only to find that confusion among the leaders had started the rebellion prematurely. They had hastened down to Montgomery's Tavern on Yonge Street north of Toronto, arriving late that Monday night. The floor had been carpeted with men trying to sleep amid the hubbub of arriving stragglers wondering what the hell had happened to change the plans for an attack on the 7th, three days hence.

Mackenzie, like a man possessed, had ranted and raved, bounding from one room to the next and in and out the door, tearing off his flaming red wig at times and flourishing it as though it were the Governor's head he held as he shouted that they should attack Toronto now and not await daylight.

The groans they had heard from an adjoining room, they'd been told, had been those of Colonel Moody, a Tory, who had been mortally wounded by the rebel guards when he had not stopped at their command. He had been a long time dying.

They had learned that Captain Anderson, who was to have led them into battle, had himself been killed by a Tory. There had been rumours that shiploads of Orangemen were coming to the defence of Toronto, fully armed, unlike the rebels who had brought only pikes or pitchforks if they hadn't possessed muskets.

If it hadn't been for the dying man and that lunatic gleam in Mackenzie's eyes, Donal would have laughed at the absurdity of the situation. Surely those few hundred ill-equipped men, led by others without military experience who could not even agree amongst themselves, were not going to attempt to take Toronto! Surely the citizens of Toronto couldn't take them seriously!

But it seemed that Toronto -- or more particularly, the Lieutenant-Governor -- had finally taken the threat seriously. Very faintly, the rebels had heard the bells of Toronto ringing out the alarum.

Donal had slept little that night. Mackenzie, Samuel Lount, and the other leaders, arguing throughout the night, had still not reached a decision by morning, but by noon on Tuesday, Mackenzie had taken charge of the attack. The men, about eight hundred strong by then, had started the long march down Yonge Street. It was not without a sense of foreboding that they had ascended Gallows Hill. There they had met a delegation of emissaries who had come to discuss a truce.

"What the divil is ***he*** doing with them?" Mike had said, puzzled.

"Who?"

"Dr. Rolph. He's supposed to be on ***our*** side!"

"Mayhap he's seen the lay of the land, and decided to change allegiance," Donal had said. Though Mike had scoffed, there were others who had been of a similar mind.

Mackenzie and Lount had sent the peacemakers back to the city for a written document of terms, but the rebels, meanwhile, had continued to march south to Bloor Street, just a mile and a quarter from the city. Later, Rolph and the others had returned to tell them that the truce was off.

The men had been confused and demoralized by all the indecision and the delays, and most particularly by Mackenzie's erratic behaviour. He had never stayed still. Muffled in several greatcoats, looking more like a small deranged bear than a rebel leader, he had galloped hither and thither on his pony, disappearing to no one knew where at times. Twice he had broken into the homes of wealthy Tories, threatening and harassing the women and servants, and burning down one of the houses. He had shouted and cursed at his troops for no apparent reason, except to vent his spleen, it seemed. It had been the more rational Samuel Lount who had smoothed things over and kept many a man from abandoning the cause.

But then Mackenzie had received encouraging news from the city, via Rolph, and the eloquence for which he had become famous had rallied the men to march on to certain victory. In the December twilight they had set off down the final stretch of Yonge Street, a motley assembly of potential heroes -- or traitors -- some with rifles, some with pikes, but the majority with only pitchforks or clubs.

Donal had felt the thrill of danger then, as the darkness had closed in on them, as the trees had seemed to press closer to the road, as the dimming silhouettes of the men in front had moved up and down like a wave, the ground beneath their feet shuddering as if in terror.

They had gone about half a mile when there had been a sudden explosion of light and sound. In the darkness, and from their position near the rear of the column, Donal and Mike had seen little of what had happened. But others had seen their front ranks fall, and thinking them dead and an army of Tories awaiting the rest of them, had panicked and run. Donal and Mike had been carried along in the press of retreating men, despite the commands and imprecations shouted at them by Mackenzie. They hadn't stopped running until they'd arrived back at the Bloor Street toll gate. Although no one had been hit by the snipers, the men had refused to attack again in darkness.

And many had deserted that night.

Mackenzie had assured those remaining that reinforcements would arrive, along with Colonel Van Egmond, a veteran of the Napoleonic Wars. But Donal had become increasingly doubtful of Mackenzie's sanity, for that next day Mackenzie and a handful of mounted men had robbed a mail coach, and had attacked other travellers and taken them prisoner.

And Mackenzie had ignored a message from Rolph to disband the rebels.

"Sure, they know we're here," Donal had said to Mike. "Do you think the Tories are just going to be waiting around for us to walk into the city and say, 'We're taking over'? God knows what sort of reception they're planning for us, while we sit around here twiddling our thumbs, with more men leaving than coming to join us! I say we cut out while the going's good."

"I never took you for a coward, Donal. You know there's not a soldier left in the whole province. And how many of the militia do you think the Tories can raise? Sure, most of them are on our side! So if the Tories want to keep power, they'll have to take up arms themselves. I wouldn't miss facing Strachan and that little runt of a Lieutenant-Governor -- if he has the guts to pick up a gun. But if you haven't the stomach for a fight, Donal, then off you go."

"I'm no coward, Mike! But I'm no fool either. How can you trust that man?" he had said, referring to Mackenzie who at that moment had been dumping newspapers from the stolen mailbags out of a second floor window of the tavern, onto the heads of the prisoners below.

"Sure, he's excitable is all, with a fierce temper when things go awry. But I believe in what he's fighting for..." and Mike had gone on once again to try to educate Donal about the aims of the reformers.

Colonel Van Egmond had arrived the following morning, the Thursday originally scheduled for the uprising, but without reinforcements. He had obviously been appalled that the couple of hundred untrained men were the 'army' that he had been expecting to lead.

Donal had become increasingly restless during that idle morning, and it had been almost a relief when a scout had come bursting in with the news that the enemy forces were marching up Gallows Hill toward them. The hundred and fifty of them with weapons had followed their leaders into the fray.

They'd been deployed in a small wood on either side of Yonge Street, half a mile south of Montgomery's Tavern, and had opened fire on the advancing militia. It was then that all hell had broken loose. Gunfire had seemed to come from every direction, for they had suddenly been surrounded by the enemy on three sides. Cannonballs had crashed into the woods, felling branches and small trees, chasing them across a field as they had retreated. Musket shot had caught men on both sides of Donal and Mike.

They had nearly reached Montgomery's when Mackenzie and the other leaders had passed them, heading north at full gallop. The rebellion had been over in only a few minutes.

The boys had headed into the woods to the west, instinctively away from their homeward direction, although they'd had no time as yet to contemplate the implications of their 'treason'. They had run until they had collapsed, breathless, by the edge of a stream. It was only then that Donal had seen the blood streaming from Mike's arm.

"Jaysus Christ! I didn't know you'd been hit!" Donal had said as he'd tried to stop the bleeding. He'd cut a makeshift bandage from his shirt with his pocket knife, and had tied it about the wound.

"It didn't feel like more than a slap at the time," Mike had replied, grimacing in pain. He'd looked deathly pale, and Donal had been afraid he would pass out, or perhaps even die right then and there. "Sure, we can't stay here. We've not much of a lead on them, and they'll be combing the woods here for certain. If you've a mind to leave me and head out on your own, I'll understand, Donal, and think none the worse of you for it. I don't give much for our chances."

"Save your breath. You'll be needing it for our journey."

Thus had started these last harrowing days.

With a strength born of desperation, Donal had dragged his friend across the countryside, avoiding farms and roads, except where the bush had been too thick to penetrate. They had crossed the first stream with the aid of a fallen log, but had been less fortunate when they had come to the wide Humber River. A rainy November had swollen the streams and rivers, and the cold of December had not yet frozen them. Donal had gone ahead to scout out a bridge, but it had been guarded by militia, so they'd had to travel miles northward until they'd found an unguarded footbridge. Though the increasing cold had slowed his bleeding, Mike had been getting weaker by the hour.

Donal remembered how his muscles had protested in agony at the bulky weight of his friend. By the time darkness had fallen he had not only been exhausted, but hopelessly lost in an increasingly dense forest. Mike had been barely conscious. That was probably the first time he'd really felt the fear. Then it hadn't been of capture, merely of survival. But it had given him the impetus to keep going, knowing that if they didn't find shelter, neither of them would be likely to survive the night.

He'd hardly been able to believe his eyes when he'd seen a glimmer of light in the black, moonless night. Unseen branches had clawed at them, but with a final burst of strength he'd managed to carry Mike into a clearing. Then he had run to the farmhouse, not caring whether the Governor himself was there to greet him.

But luck had been with them once again, for the O'Reillys had been Mackenzie supporters. They had welcomed them, fed them, given them beds, and had tended to Mike's wound. The O'Reilly boys had taken turns on lookout that night, and Donal had slept deeply, untroubled by dreams.

Mike had been worse the following day. His wound had become infected and his body, feverish. It had been obvious that he could go no further. The O'Reillys had offered to care for him until he had recovered.

"We'll say he's one of our sons, wounded in a hunting accident, should any of those bloody Tories come snooping around here," Dermott O'Reilly had said. "But where will you be going, lad?"

"To the States, I reckon. Sure, there's nowhere else to go is there?" Donal had replied, realizing for the first time that when he had left Launston Mills so blithely, he hadn't thought he might never return. Nostalgic visions of his home and family had nearly shamed him with tears.

Well provisioned with bread, cheese, whiskey, and a blanket, Donal had been guided by one of the O'Reilly boys to a concession road that would take him westward, and with vague instructions as to when he should head south. His body had ached that day, but the going had been easy. He'd scrambled into the woods for cover whenever he'd heard an approaching vehicle or horse, and the few pedestrians he had encountered had seemed friendly, despite the unusual appearance he'd presented, with his torn clothes and scratched face.

He had eaten all his provisions that day, and drunk the whiskey to warm himself as he'd curled up in the hayloft of a barn. He'd spent most of the next day dodging militia patrols, convinced at least that he was heading in the right direction. He'd had no food that day, and by evening, had known he must appease the aching void in his belly or he'd never have the strength to reach the border. With some trepidation he had approached a relatively isolated farmstead, reckoning that if the inhabitants were hostile, he'd have time to secrete himself in the forest before the authorities could be summoned.

"What do you want?" the old farmer had said gruffly.

"I'd like to buy some food, if you have any to spare." The delicious aroma of a stew had wafted out, making Donal's mouth water with anticipation.

"Oh, aye? You passed an inn not a mile back. You're one of them, ain't you? One of them damned rebels that have put the countryside in such an uproar. Well, I'll not be accused of harbouring a traitor! The militia have been here twice today, searching and threatening us. Get ye gone!"

The door had slammed shut in Donal's face. He'd turned back slowly, disconsolately, into the dark night. Suddenly the door had opened behind him, the cheery warmth of the light spilling from the cabin. Something had been thrown at him, and had landed on the ground at his feet.

The old man had shouted, "I'll not have it said that Asa Miller turns a hungry man from his door!" The door had slammed shut again.

Donal had picked up the stale end of a loaf of bread with gratitude.

Once again he had spent the night in a barn, but, still hungry and never truly warm despite the heavy blanket, he'd slept fitfully, and had set out early in the frosty, snowy dawn.

That day had seemed a repeat of the last, except that it had been colder, and his progress even slower. Hunger and cold had finally driven him to the outskirts of a village, determined to walk casually into the nearest inn. He'd had the blanket over his head against the driving snow, and the snowy roads had muffled the sound of the horses' hooves, so he hadn't been aware of that last patrol until they'd been almost on top of him.

Perhaps if he hadn't run they'd have thought him just a local.

The cold was the worst now. The wind howled around the barn, slicing through the cracks between the boards with shrieking glee. He was certain he'd never be warm again, never feel the heat of the summer sun on his face....

Donal jerked awake at a jab to his ribs. For a moment he was disoriented and couldn't focus his eyes in the dim light. But then fear pounded through his veins. Four men stood over him, their rifles pointed at his heart.

"Who are you?" one of them barked out.

He tried to rise, but a gun barrel jabbed him back. "Donal O'Shaughnessy," he mumbled through frozen lips.

"A bloody papist!" One of the men spat on him. "And what're you doing here, mick? Been screwing the farmer's daughter in the hay, have you?" The Orangemen laughed.

"No, I just..."

The butt of a rifle smashed into Donal's face. He tasted blood. And terror.

"We saw you running, traitor!"

Booted feet kicked him in the ribs, the groin, the back. He cradled his head in his hands, and tried to draw up his knees as protection from the vicious blows. He had not even a layer of clothing to soften the impact. Again and again they kicked, cursing him. He didn't even realize that the animal screams that echoed through the barn were coming from his throat. He knew only that he was done for.

Vaguely he heard someone shout, "Enough!" and thought it had been his mind screaming for release from this torture. He started retching. Vaguely he was aware that the assault had ceased, that more men were standing over him. "Find him some clothes. You'd better hope he doesn't die," someone said.

Another said, " Why? He has nothing to live for, save the gallows."

Chapter 20

Jeremy Launston was exhausted when he finally sighted the lights of Toronto. For an endless night and a day he had driven himself and his horse unmercifully, stopping only long enough to rest and water the gelding. He himself had taken little in the way of sleep or nourishment, having consumed only an unappetizing breakfast at an inn, after an hour's doze by the fireside.

Now he was stiff with fatigue and cold. He could barely feel his limbs. His breath seemed to crystallize in his lungs.

Christ! Another tollgate. Jeremy gauged the height of the gate which blocked the road and urged his horse forward. They cleared it easily, and were well down the road when they heard the tollkeeper's curses and threats shouted after them.

They crossed the icy bridge spanning the Don River, and entered the city at a slow walk. There were no streetlights, and the only illumination was that which spilled from the windows of the homes, to be reflected by the snow.

"Halt! Who goes there?" a voice demanded.

Jeremy patted his nervous horse reassuringly. "Who the devil wants to know?"

"A sentry of the York Militia!" A young man stepped out from the shadows, his gun pointing at Jeremy. "I repeat, identify yourself!"

"I'm not a rebel, if that's what concerns you. Now allow me to pass, for I have pressing business to attend to!"

"I can't do that, sir, unless you give the countersign."

Jeremy was stupefied. "Countersign? Damn it, man, I've just spent thirty hours in the saddle, and now you detain me with this ridiculous blather about countersigns!" He jerked his horse's reins.

"I wouldn't try that if I was you, sir."

Jeremy decided the young fool probably ***would*** shoot him. "If I were a rebel, you would not now be standing there babbling at me, young man! Be so good as to inform me what I must say to gain my freedom."

The sentry scrutinized Jeremy. "State your name and business, sir!"

"Jeremy Launston of Launston Mills in the township of Ops, District of Newcastle. I'm an Anglican and a Tory, and I am here on official business. Should you wish to verify that, you need only ask the Sheriff, the Chief Justice, or the Archdeacon, all of whom are acquainted with me."

"Very well. Then you must reply to a sentry's challenge with, 'A friend', and tonight's countersign is 'Waterloo'."

"Thank you. I take it I am free to pass?"

"Yes, sir."

Jeremy would have laughed at the absurdity of that encounter had not graver thoughts preoccupied him. He rode along Front Street, which followed the shoreline of the bay, to the Ontario House Hotel, located next to the market square.

His knees buckled when he dismounted at the stables behind the hotel. After leaving strict instructions concerning the care of his horse, Jeremy gratefully entered the warm hotel. He ordered a hot bath and a meal to be taken to his room while he downed a drink in the barroom.

Jeremy eased his aching body into the zinc tub. The water tingled his frozen flesh, bringing it painfully back to life. He nearly fell asleep as he soaked in the bath, but managed to dry himself and climb into the warm bed. His last thought was that tomorrow he would secure his brother's freedom, and prayed to God that he wouldn't be too late.

• • •

Three days had passed since Jeremy had arrived in the city.

He was consumed with an impotent rage. The Governor, the Archdeacon, the Chief Justice -- all the high officials -- were inaccessible. They were engaged in urgent matters of state, he had been informed over and over by the minions who had frustrated his efforts to secure an audience with their superiors. Personal business would have to wait. Submit a written petition -- it would be attended to as soon as circumstances allowed.

And Jeremy had composed an eloquent plea which he was certain no one had yet read.

He was desperate. His anxiety for Adrian increased tenfold with each abortive day. He could no longer afford to play this by the rules. If the officials would not grant him a hearing, then he would force one upon them!

It would be useless to approach the Governor. Bond Head was no longer as sanguine about the loyalty of his subjects as he had been before the uprising, and Government House was now heavily guarded. Even if he managed to evade the sentries, Jeremy doubted that His Excellency would exhibit any sympathy for Adrian's plight.

Jeremy had met Sir Francis Bond Head only once, at the Governor's Ball last May. He had seemed a pleasant enough man, socially, though he was autocratic, and more than a little contemptuous of the colony he had been sent to rule. No doubt he considered the insurrection a personal affront and, like an irate father, would not spare the rod with the fledgling colony.

His best chance, Jeremy decided, was to approach the Archdeacon, the Reverend Dr. John Strachan. Several times now he had been denied admittance to Strachan's home by his surly butler. This time he would not ask.

The Archdeacon's palatial brick home was located in the fashionable residential district along Front Street, west of Yonge Street. It was dark when Jeremy walked up the circular drive. There was no door knob on the outside of the front door -- a gentleman with a butler did not require one. Jeremy thudded the heavy brass knocker.

As soon as the door opened a crack, Jeremy seized the advantage. He heaved his full weight against the door, sending the surprised butler on the other side of it flying. Without hesitation, Jeremy strode into the hall and barged into the first room on the left, which he had correctly surmised to be the parlour.

He faced the astonished occupants.

"What the devil!" the Archdeacon said, rising from his chair.

"I most humbly beg your pardon, sir. I would not have presumed to intrude upon you in such an unforgivable manner were not the matter for which I seek your help one of life or death."

Jeremy felt a poke in his back, and craned his head around to see the flustered butler with a loaded musket in his hands.

"Shall I throw the scoundrel out, sir?"

Jeremy took a step forward, but the gun barrel jabbed threateningly into his spine. "I know you to be a just and compassionate man Dr. Strachan. I beg you to hear me out."

The Archdeacon's calm, arrogant face did not relax into a smile, but Jeremy noticed the twinkle in his eyes. "I think we can dispense with the musket, Hopkins. I'll ring when you're needed."

The butler shook his head as he reluctantly left the room.

"Your face is familiar, but I canna recall your name," the Archdeacon said to Jeremy in his thick Scottish burr.

"Jeremy Launston of Launston Mills."

"Och, aye. I had the pleasure of having your father and brother in my congregation these last months."

"It's about my brother that I have come."

"Then let us retire to my study."

Jeremy bowed to Mrs. Strachan and her seventeen year old daughter, who had recovered from their initial fright at his sudden appearance, and followed the Archdeacon.

"My brother is dying of consumption," Jeremy explained when he had taken a seat.

"I'm truly sorry to hear that," Strachan said sincerely. He himself had suffered much personal loss over the years -- most recently with the death of a son about Jeremy's age. "I knew he was ill, of course, but he had been looking better recently."

"The doctor has informed us that with proper care my brother has a few months left to him. But he is presently in gaol, and likely to die there if I cannot secure his release immediately. You see, several days ago he was arrested on the charge of high treason."

Strachan raised an eyebrow.

"My brother is but nineteen. He is idealistic and he has, in the past, criticized the government. But I assure you that he took no part in the rebellion, nor would he ever condone such violence. I beseech you to intercede on his behalf."

The Archdeacon was silent for a moment. Although he was but five and a half feet tall, Strachan was a formidable figure of a man. Jeremy could read nothing in that inscrutable face which had weathered hard work, sorrow, success, and criticism without expression.

"High treason is a very serious matter."

"But surely it is not treason to voice one's opinions? Dare I say that his objectives are not dissimilar to your own -- the good of the country and of its people -- though you and I might not agree with his proposed methods of achieving those goals. My brother may be guilty of naivety, even foolishness, but he is not guilty of treason. Surely justice would not be served by depriving a young man of his few remaining months of life. Surely ***not*** to act would be the same as condemning an untried man to death."

"You have stated your brother's case admirably." Strachan paused. "Since I know him, and can vouch for his character -- my own daughter found him a most agreeable and harmless young man -- I'll do all in my power to obtain a pardon for him. But you understand that the Lieutenant-Governor must approve it?"

"Yes." Jeremy understood also Strachan's implication that Bond Head's behaviour was unpredictable these days, and that he, Strachan, could guarantee nothing.

"Then call here tomorrow evening. I'll tell Hopkins to expect you." Again there was a twinkle of amusement in his eyes.

"I am deeply indebted to you for your help. I apologize again for my ill-mannered intrusion."

"I shall pray for your brother."

• • •

Early Christmas morning, two weeks after his arrest, Adrian Launston was released from Cobourg gaol by order of the Lieutenant-Governor.

Jeremy was appalled when he saw his brother. Adrian's face was hollow and grey; his clothes -- dirty now, and inadequate for the bone-chilling cold of the prison -- hung loosely on his withered frame.

"Jamie...." Adrian began choking on his own blood.

"We'd have released him soon anyway, sir," the official said to Jeremy, "him not being long for this world."

Jeremy glared at the man with cold contempt, and took his brother away. He wondered if Adrian would survive the journey home.

"Perhaps we should stay in Cobourg until you're feeling stronger," Jeremy suggested as he wrapped Adrian in the buffalo skins on the cutter he had hired.

"No, I want to go home, Jamie."

It was a horrifying trip for them both. Adrian constantly coughed blood. The roads, though better in winter when they were snow-packed, bounced them about. The nights they spent in inns, Jeremy lay awake listening to Adrian's painful breathing, dreading even more to hear it not at all. Jeremy could see Adrian growing weaker, but the young man insisted upon continuing the journey.

They arrived in Launston Mills at midnight, three days later. Jeremy carried Adrian to his bed.

Simon Worthing shook his head sadly when he had examined Adrian.

Jeremy gritted his teeth. There was a cold lump inside him.

"Jamie?"

He went to Adrian's side, and took one of his thin, cool hands in his own.

"I'm dying, aren't I? Yes... I know I am. Bring Rowena to me, please. Wait... Jamie, promise me you'll always look after her and my child. Promise me!"

Jeremy swallowed hard. "I promise."

"Thank you. Get her now."

Rowena thought her heart would break when she saw Adrian. He smiled weakly at her as she dropped to her knees by his side. He reached out to her, and she entwined her fingers in his.

"Sorry... to leave you like this, Rowena." His voice was little more than a whisper now. "It'll be hard for you... All my fault."

"No. I'd do the same again. I love you, Adrian." Rowena choked back her tears. "In the sight of God, we're man and wife. He'll understand."

"People won't understand... They'll be cruel to you and... my bastard." His breathing was laboured, rasping.

"Your son will grow up to be a proud man, proud that he is your son, Adrian. I'll see to that."

Margaret began weeping, and Simon, unable to do any more for Adrian, escorted her from the room. Harriet had already left. Only Samuel, Jeremy, and Rowena were with Adrian as his life bubbled out his ruptured lungs.

Samuel, tears blinding him, gripped Jeremy on the shoulder and then left the room.

Rowena wept abandonedly, clinging to Adrian's lifeless body. Jeremy placed his hands gently upon her shoulders and pulled her into his arms. They stood like that for a long time, consoling each other in their shared grief.

Chapter 21

Samuel was reading a magazine and Harriet was embroidering an infant's gown while Jeremy looked on restlessly. The open Franklin stove, set into the fireplace, radiated a mellow warmth throughout the parlour. A beaded face screen on the table next to Harriet protected her complexion from the heat of the flames.

Jeremy studied his wife as she worked. She was dressed in a sober grey wool gown, trimmed with bands of black velvet and a round lace collar. Neat brown ringlets peeked from beneath her frilly, beribboned cap. Her condition was not yet obvious, though she tired easily these days, and had relinquished the running of the household to Margaret once again.

His thoughts turned to Rowena with a twinge of guilt.

Three weeks had passed since Adrian's funeral, and nothing had yet been decided about Rowena's future. Jeremy had not seen her since the night of Adrian's death. But he had heard of her brother's arrest and imprisonment, and was stirred to pity for her.

"I've been giving some thought, Father, as to what should be done about the O'Shaughnessy girl."

Samuel laid down his three-month-old copy of the *Illustrated London News*. "Yes?"

"I think she should live here...."

"Here?" Harriet interjected. "That would be inviting scandal, Jeremy."

"There'll be talk, of course, but that can't be avoided in any case. If we accept her as part of our family, however, it will be less difficult for the girl and her child. The rumours would involve us anyway, so we may as well acknowledge our responsibility, and salvage some of our self-respect by 'doing the right thing' by the girl. After all, her father has legal recourse to compensation from us through the seduction law. I think it would be unwise to allow things to get to that state."

Samuel nodded gravely. "I see your point."

"As do I, Jeremy, but it would hardly be practical. In what capacity would she live here? Much as I like the girl, I can scarcely envision her spending the evenings in the parlour with us," Harriet said. Indeed, she was fond of Rowena, for the girl had been an efficient servant, and always respectful. But she would not accept her as an equal in this house, would not share her home with another woman lest it be as mistress and maid.

And she feared Rowena's beauty and that indefinable quality about her that made men gaze at her with admiration or desire. It must be women like this to whom men turned for the fulfillment of their baser instincts, and she would not allow Jeremy to be constantly in that girl's beguiling presence. "Just imagine how awkward she would feel. I'm afraid it just wouldn't do at all, Jeremy. Why not just settle some money on her? Find a place for her in the city. Or better still, marry her off to some young man -- one of your millworkers, for instance -- who wouldn't be averse to having a pretty young wife with a substantial dowry."

Jeremy was disgusted by Harriet's suggestion, but Samuel said, "By Jove, that might be just the ticket! Let me see now.... there's Monaghan -- or is he already betrothed? One of the Ryan boys, perhaps, or Brendan Delaney -- it's about time he took a wife."

"Delaney's not a man I'd wish on any woman," Jeremy said. "And I think you're both taking too much upon yourselves. It's quite callous to speak of Rowena as though she were a possession one wanted to be rid of."

"She is, damn it!" Samuel exploded. "Harriet is quite right, and arranging a marriage for the girl is the best suggestion I've heard."

"Are you forgetting that she is carrying Adrian's child -- your grandson, Father?"

"I could hardly forget that! Nor do I wish to be constantly reminded of it! Have you not thought that perhaps the girl might ***welcome*** the opportunity of marriage? If some man were to make a decent woman of her, the gossip would die down before the child was born. People might even assume that the man she marries is the father of the child, and thus the reason for the hasty wedding. That sort of thing happens all the time and is more or less accepted. Our name needn't even enter into the affair -- only her family, Margaret, and Simon know the truth. The O'Shaughnessys, I'm certain, would be as happy to keep the truth from becoming common knowledge as we are. It's a perfect solution to this disagreeable situation!"

Jeremy could see the merit of this idea. It would be to everyone's benefit, including Rowena's and the child's. After all, what was there for women but marriage? "I'll discuss it with her tomorrow."

While her future was being planned in the cozy comfort of the Launston's parlour, Rowena was kneeling on the hard wooden floor in the chilly darkness of the church. Moonlight reflected off the snow, illuminating the world outside and creating ghostly shadows within the empty building.

Rowena was praying -- as she often had these last weeks -- for Adrian, for Donal, and for the child that stirred within her. She prayed for wisdom and strength, for forgiveness, for solace for her anguished, tormented soul.

She did not hear the door open, but she saw the growing circle of light, and for a moment sat transfixed. She looked around warily, and said with relief, "Oh, Father, 'tis yourself!"

"Aye. Were you thinking I was a divine spirit perhaps?" the priest asked wryly as he placed his candle lantern upon a chair.

"For a moment."

"So, 'tis you who's been haunting the church every night, is it?"

"Aye. How did you know?"

"I can see the church door from my study window, though I couldn't make out who the troubled soul was. You are troubled, aren't you, child? I can see it in your eyes."

"Aye."

"Then why not tell me about it?" Father Killeny prompted. "They do say that a sorrow shared is a sorrow halved. Or is it God's forgiveness you're after wanting?"

Rowena felt comfortable with Father Killeny, who was a compassionate and thoughtful man. He was tall and thin, ascetic-looking, like a man who spent much time in contemplation and prayer and little on his own needs or comforts. Rowena was certain that he was in close communion with God.

"'Tisn't a sin to love, Father," she said defensively.

"And who ever said it was?"

"Then why is it a sin for a man and a woman to show their love for each other? ...I mean...."

"Aye, I know what you mean." He frowned. "But the physical union of a man and a woman is for procreation, and not to be indulged in until God has sanctified the spiritual union through marriage. Are you in trouble then? Is that what you're trying to tell me?"

"We were to have been wed by now! I loved him, Father, and I grieve sorely for him," she sobbed.

"Who are you talking about?"

"Adrian Launston."

A pained expression crossed the priest's face. "'Tis a fine mess you've gotten yourself into, Rowena. There now, don't weep. I'm not condemning you. The flesh is ever weak and temptation strong. The Lord will forgive you your sins. 'Tis the people who won't forgive easily. You'd best pray for strength for yourself, and understanding for your neighbours." He looked at her sadly. "Come, child," he said, reaching out to her and helping her up. "Go home. I shall pray for you, too."

The priest walked with her as far as the rectory, just north of the church, and watched as Rowena trudged up Lindsay Street in the snow-bright darkness.

Rowena took her time going home. She hardly noticed the biting cold.

The boisterous noises that emanated from Paxtons' Tavern were like physical blows to her, reminding her that life went on even though hers seemed to have ended. Yet, she had not the peace of the grave to envelope and protect her.

She turned down Mill Road where the trees crowded around her, their naked branches creaking to the whistling of the wind. There was a warm aura of light about the Launston house. She paused for a moment and stared at the log cabin which would have been her home if....

Hot tears scalded her frozen cheeks. There was great, gnawing pain inside her that had already devoured her heart and left a gaping emptiness within. Now it threatened to consume her completely.

The mills were silent once again; the river, frozen. She gazed at it for a long time, almost feeling the sting of the icy water in her lungs. Quickly she crossed herself, and asked forgiveness for the wicked thought which had momentarily possessed her. She ran the rest of the way home, for surely the devil himself must be after her!

Rowena was surprised to find Mary Ryan and Mattie Abernethy drinking tea by the fire. She looked questioningly at Mary who said, "Aye, her time's come."

"Where's me Da?"

"No need to disturb his evening at the tavern. There's enough to do at times like this without having the menfolk underfoot. I've sent the young ones to bed," Mary told her.

Rowena shed her heavy wrap, and hurried into her mother's room. Moira, looking pale and frightened, was wiping Deirdre's brow.

"How're you feeling, Ma?" Rowena asked, sitting down on the edge of the bed.

"Tolerable. You been to church then?"

"Aye. I spoke with Father Killeny."

"That pleases me fine."

Deirdre's body arched with pain, and Rowena winced.

Rowena said, "Will I prepare you something, Ma? Trillium and squawroot?"

"Aye. That would be fine."

Rowena prepared an infusion of the powdered roots -- squawroot to stimulate contractions and trillium to ease things and prevent excessive bleeding.

Watching her, Mattie said, "I brought my own concoctions to hasten things along, if need be. But suit yourself, lass.

Though Mattie and Mary did little as yet, the presence of women who had given birth many times themselves, as well as having helped others, was comforting. But after several unproductive hours of hard labour, Rowena became concerned. If this delivery weren't normal, then she did not yet have enough confidence in her midwifery skills to help her mother through it. When she suggested they send for Simon Worthing, the women laughed.

Mattie said, "Birthing's a woman's business, not a man's, even if he be a physician."

It was a long night. Rowena grew faint with fear watching Deirdre's tortures. Her hand ached with the abnormal strength of her mother's grip. Moira had swooned, and had been dispatched to the other room to make tea for Patrick when he had arrived, but Rowena maintained her bedside vigil.

She tried not to dwell on the fact that she, too, would be suffering these agonies in less than five months time. But the horrible reality was never far from her thoughts.

Deirdre spoke to her occasionally. "'Tis Donal worries me the most," she said once. "I should have let him go to the lumber camp. There he would have been safe. It breaks me heart to think of him in a prison cell. At least I know he's alive. The Flannery's have had no word of or from Mike. Is it cold out tonight? Aye, I reckon I can feel it. Do you think he's warm enough? They'll not hang him, will they? Will I ever see him again, my dear lad? I hope this babe's a boy. For Pat."

Mattie began to look worried. Rowena overheard her whisper to Mary, "It shouldna be taking this long, her having birthed ten others afore. There's some'at nae right."

It was nearly morning when Deirdre began to hemorrhage. Patrick went to fetch Simon Worthing, but the doctor had been called out an hour earlier, so he'd left a message with the housekeeper.

"You'd best send for the priest then," Mattie said.

"No! Oh, no!" Rowena cried.

"I canna stop this bleeding. Only a miracle could save your Ma. There's nowt I can do for her now, poor soul."

And for all her own knowledge and skill, Rowena knew that there was no potion she could give her mother now to save her. Women often died in childbirth. It was one of the hazards of pregnancy, of being a woman.

The baby finally came -- a boy -- stillborn. Still Deirdre's blood seeped from her body. She was barely conscious as her family gathered around her. The girls wept, but Rowena knew her mother was counting on her to be strong. She forced back her own grief, though her eyes burned and her throat ached. Patrick, his eyes brimming, gazed at his wife with disbelief.

Father Killeny came and administered the Last Rites. Deirdre, no longer in pain, smiled gratefully and welcomed her release from the burden of life.

Mary Ryan threw open the bedroom window to allow Deirdre's soul to escape. Then she and Mattie began the task of laying out the body.

• • •

Deirdre and the infant were buried in the Catholic cemetery on the Darcy farm, south of the town.

Rowena felt numb. The past two days had seemed unreal to her -- the rituals of death, the obscene, drunken merriment of the wake. She had had no sleep for two nights and was exhausted, emotionally as well as physically. But it would be a while yet before she could allow herself the oblivion of sleep. The family was her responsibility now; supper had to be set before them yet today.

Brigid kept asking for Deirdre; Alys wept; Moira whined, "What'll we do now?"; Gwyn refused to do what Rowena requested; and Patrick stared morosely into the fire as he drank himself into another senseless stupor.

And things seemed to get worse. Rowena burnt the porridge which was their supper, Alys couldn't keep down the gruel she ate, and when Gwyn, on being told to help Moira with the dishes, retorted, "You're not me Ma! You can't tell me what to do!" Rowena slapped Gwyn's face, and then burst into tears. Gwyn was immediately contrite, and Rowena poured herself a large measure of whiskey.

Had God punished her for her sins by taking her mother? Surely she should have been the one to die, not Deirdre. But then, Deirdre was undoubtedly in blissful peace in heaven with God, while she, Rowena, was left here, heartbroken and filled with guilt and remorse.

And yet... she wasn't sorry about the babe, Adrian's child. She was glad she could give him this, even though he didn't live to see his offspring. No, she regretted that her love for Adrian had caused such problems for her family, but was never sorry for having loved him with body and soul.

"To despair is to deny God," the nun had said to her all those years ago at Grosse Isle. But why was God making it so difficult not to despair?

Gradually, as the initial shock of Deirdre's death subsided, the mundane tasks of everyday life once again filled busy days, and Rowena increasingly became the mainstay of her family. It was she who prodded Patrick out of his apathy, she who urged him to accept the temporary carpentry job at the village of Bobcaygeon some twenty miles away. It was she who comforted the girls on the long and lonely nights when the howling of wolves seemed too close by, and the creaking and settling of the house aroused superstitious fancies.

She herself no longer had time to think or feel anything. It was enough just to get through each day. Gwyn was becoming a real problem, often defying Rowena, going into sulks or tantrums, sharpening her tongue on them all.

When Jeremy Launston came to visit one afternoon in late February, he interrupted another of the almost daily squabbles that Gwyn initiated.

"I'll not do it, and you can't make me do it!" Gwyn cried, running around the table to keep it between herself and Rowena.

"Ma would give you such a hiding if she was here," Alys said.

"Well, she ain't here, is she? And she'll never be back! Never! Never! Never! Do you hear me, you stupid idiot!"

Tears coursed down Alys's cheeks.

"Don't you ***dare*** talk to your sister like that!" Rowena said, furious.

"You're bad, Gwyn," Alys said.

"Not as bad as Rowena. She sinned. With a man. Whore!" Gwyn danced around the table. "Whore! Whore! Whore!"

Rowena could hardly contain her fury. Indeed, she was frightened by the murderous rage that Gwyn had evoked. She made a dash for her sister, but Gwyn deftly kept the table between them.

"Grab her!" Rowena said to Moira.

Moira approached Gwyn diffidently, for in truth, she was afraid of her younger sister.

"If you touch me, Moira, I'll scratch your eyes out! Don't let Rena boss you around. We don't have to do everything ***she*** says!"

It was then that Jeremy knocked on the door. Moira was relieved to go and answer it.

Jeremy had heard the shrieks outside the door, and glanced quickly about the room to see what was amiss. He saw the youngest child, Brigid, huddled against the stone chimney, hugging a rag doll to her breast. Alys sat on the floor next to her, wiping her wet cheeks with the back of her hand. Rowena, her apron and cap askew, tendrils of hair hanging about her face, was glaring at Gwyn whose face taunted her in return. Food and dishes lay scattered -- some in fragments -- upon the floor where Gwyn had swept them with her arm when Rowena had asked her to clear the table.

"Mr. Launston's here to see you, Rona," Moira said awkwardly.

As Rowena looked over at Jeremy, Gwyn pushed the table hard, crashing it into Rowena and nearly toppling her.

Jeremy resisted the impulse to reprimand the thoughtless child. It was, after all, none of his affair.

Rowena glowered at Gwyn, whose grinning face dared her to try anything now, in front of Mr. Launston.

Rowena was close to tears. She was truly at her wits' end with Gwyn. It would be at least another week before Patrick returned from Bobcaygeon, and God only knew whether he could, or would even care enough, to tame the little brat. Rowena felt increasingly like that logger that Conn had told her about -- nearly a year ago now -- the one who had gone berserk, smashing everything in sight, and had run, screaming, into the night.

But she brushed back her errant strands of hair, straightened her apron, and faced Jeremy boldly.

He admired her at that moment, knowing it could not be easy for her to have the responsibility of caring for and raising these children, particularly with her father absent and her brother in gaol. And from what he had heard, Patrick was of little use, even when he was home. Since his wife's death, the man seemed to have lost all interest in life. How unfair, how selfish of him to thrust the burden of his family upon his eldest daughter!

Jeremy was more convinced than ever that it would be in Rowena's best interests to accept his offer.

"I was sorry to hear about your mother, Rowena. Please accept my family's sincerest condolences." That sounded so stiff and formal, though he had not intended it so. He had been worried about Rowena when Simon had informed him of her mother's death. Simon had confided his own concern about her health and state of mind. " And God help her if anything should happen to her brother," Simon had said. "We'll just have to ensure that nothing does," Jeremy had replied.

"Thank you, Mr. Launston."

"I have something to discuss with you. In private, if that's possible."

"The workshop's empty." Rowena fetched her wrap, and assured her sisters she'd not be long.

The workshop was cold. It had been many weeks since a fire had burned here. But at least it offered protection from the wind.

Rowena and Jeremy faced one another. She waited for him to speak.

Jeremy suddenly felt uncomfortable with his mission. There was something in her stance and the way she looked at him which warned him that she would be difficult, if not impossible, to convince.

"My father and I feel responsible for you, Rowena. We'd like to help you in whatever way we can."

Here cool blue eyes flashed angrily. "I don't want your charity, Mr. Launston! If that's all you've come to say then you've wasted your time!"

"Please... allow me to finish," Jeremy said, blocking her way as she started for the door. He'd have to be tactful now. "It wasn't charity we had in mind. I know you loved my brother, Rowena, and I know that the proposition I'm about to make may sound heartless at first, but I want you to consider it carefully. It would benefit both you and the child -- as well as the rest of us, I'll not deny that. Have you given any thought to marriage?"

"I don't understand."

"Surely there must be some young man who's had his eye on you? Someone you wouldn't be averse to marrying? It would be expedient for you to have a husband and the child, a father."

"I see." Indeed she did. God, how she hated him! "Sure, and who do think would be wanting to marry me in me present condition?"

"We thought to settle a dowry upon you...."

"You want to buy me a husband? Damn you, Jeremy Launston!"

Jeremy grabbed her arm as she tried to sweep past him. "Mayhap 'tis the way your kind of people do things," she said, "but I won't sell myself."

"Listen to reason, Rowena! It won't be easy for you to live in this town once people become aware of ... your condition. Your child would have a name...."

"He has a name! O'Shaughnessy. 'Tis as good as any! Since he can't have his father's, he'll have no man's. And you can keep your filthy money!"

Rowena stormed out of the building, leaving Jeremy to ponder where he had gone wrong.

Chapter 22

It was only a few days after Jeremy Launston's visit. Patrick had not yet returned, the girls were all at school, and Rowena was savouring a cup of tea and the unaccustomed peace. Suddenly the door burst open and a dozen men filed into the room. She jumped to her feet. "What the divil!"

"Well, well," one of them said, "you must be the traitor's sister." He was a large, brawny brute with an ugly gleam in his eye. "Alone, are you?"

"Not for long," Rowena bluffed, trying to keep the fear from her voice.

He chuckled as if in disbelief as he straddled a chair and rested his arms along the back of it. "Your father's not in town, so we've heard. Children not here? And, of course, we all know where your dear brother is, don't we? Waiting for the hangman. Hanged by the neck , he'll be. Ever seen that, wench? Not a pretty sight for the squeamish."

A few of the men laughed. The others seemed embarrassed by their leader.

Rowena grew angry at his cocksure, bullying arrogance. "Just who the divil are you? What right have you to come barging in like this?"

He laughed. "The loyal militia, my dear little bogtrotter. The heroes who are keeping this country safe from traitors like you. Admit it now, wench, if you'd been a man, you'd have been there alongside your brother, wouldn't you?"

"Get out of my house!"

"Now what kind of welcome is that for government troops who've had a long journey this day and want nothing more than a sit-down by the fire with a bite to eat and a jug of grog for their pains."

"The inn's down the road."

There was no humour in his laugh now. "Sassy little bitch, ain't you?"

He jumped up, knocking over the chair. His sudden movement so startled Rowena that she stepped back. It was the wrong thing to do

He grinned, revelling in his power to frighten her. "You'd better be nice, wench." He brushed a callused hand across her cheek. When she drew away, he grabbed her viciously by the hair and dragged her over to the door. "Come and see what happens to traitors, wench! See the smoke there? That used to be the Flannery's farm."

She stared in horror at the column of smoke rising above the trees. "What did you do to them?" she demanded.

"Just made sure they wouldn't forget whose side to be on next time. Like I said, you'd better be nice." He pulled her head back so hard she was sure her neck would snap. His mouth closed on hers. She thought she would retch as his tongue tried to force its way into her. She flailed out at him, but he only held her tighter. A few of the men shuffled about and cleared their throats, but obviously none was going to jump to her defence.

Just when she thought she would suffocate, he released her. All his movements were violent and unexpected.

"How dare you!" she spat. "Does your noble government give you licence to molest women as well as burn them out of their homes?"

He ignored her, and said to his men, "I'll meet you at the inn. I have some unfinished business here."

One of the young men said, "Now wait just a minute ..."

"Are you going to disobey orders, lad? I'd think twice about siding with traitors, if I was you."

Rowena took advantage of her momentary respite and bounded for the door -- and straight into the arms of Simon Worthing

"Rowena! What's all this? I thought I told you to rest." He looked at the men. "Good day, gentlemen. I trust you haven't been upsetting my patient?"

"Who the hell are you?" the brute asked.

"Dr. Simon Worthing. And you, sir?"

He waved aside the question with a curt, "Militia," as an answer.

"Well, my patient is not to be disturbed by anyone. I trust none of you has been too close to her. Consumption is extremely contagious. And usually fatal, of course, though Rowena's been holding her own. I have every confidence of pulling her through. Now, if you've concluded your business here, I would advise you to leave. Unhealthy atmosphere, you know."

Without another word, but not without a look of fear, the brute turned and marched from the room, with his men close behind. When the door had shut, Rowena started giggling, and then laughing so hard that tears coursed down her cheeks. And finally she wept in Simon's arms. He rocked her like a babe, and comforted her.

"I'm sorry," she said when her tears were spent.

"Don't be. You needed that. I'll wager you haven't had a good cry since your mother died. You can't keep grief bottled up inside, Rowena."

"But your coat...."

"...will dry. Better now?" he asked with an encouraging smile.

"Aye. Thanks. But how did you know... about ***them***?"

"I passed the Flannerys' on my way back to town -- just after those blackguards had left -- and, of course, I saw the fire. The house couldn't be saved, I'm afraid, but the Flannerys did manage to get some things out of it before the fire spread. Little comfort that is, though. They told me what had happened, and that the men had been talking about paying a visit to the family of the other 'traitor', who was already in gaol. Well, I assumed they must have been talking about you. I'd have been here sooner, but I had to patch up one of the boys."

"Are they alright, the Flannerys?"

"Physically, yes. But it's been a blow to them. The Darcys have taken them in, but they won't be staying long. They've decided to join Mike in the States."

Rowena had heard from Rosemary that Mike had managed to escape across the border, and had suggested that his family follow him. Rosemary was worried about Donal, and came by every other day to see if Rowena had news of him. "I don't understand it... all this."

"This 'reign of terror' you mean? Sometimes I think it's just an excuse for the bullyboys to indulge in legalized violence. They're supposed to be rounding up rebels -- can you believe Mackenzie left behind a list of sympathizers? -- but seem to have taken it upon themselves to punish anyone who ever spoke of reform. They go to extremes that the government wouldn't condone, if they knew of it."

"I fear for Donal."

"I know you do. That's why Jeremy's making inquiries to see what can be done for him."

She looked at him in astonishment. "Why?"

"Because he wants to help you and your family. You don't seem pleased."

"I am! Sure, I'm happy about any help that Donal can get. 'Tis just... I don't like feeling beholden to the Launstons, is all."

Quickly she added, "I know Jeremy's your friend, Simon, but somehow we always seem to be at odds. He never wanted me to marry Adrian, and said some unforgivable things."

"And ***you*** have a healthy dose of pride, Rowena O'Shaughnessy, which sometimes needs to be put in your pocket."

"Maybe you're right. In this case, I'd fall on my knees before the Governor himself."

"Well, let's hope it doesn't come to that."

Chapter 23

Donal O'Shaughnessy shuddered in revulsion as the hammering ceased. Peering through the small gaps between the iron bars of his cell, he saw the scaffold silhouetted against the dawn sky. The half dozen other prisoners who shared the tiny cubicle stirred. Though most, like Donal, had not slept. They'd spent the night stretched on their pallets, shivering as always with the cold, but also with apprehension.

"So, it's up is it?" one of the men said.

"Aye," Donal replied.

"It's a crime, hanging Lount and Matthews!" another said. They'd all heard of Samuel Lount's generous nature, how he had helped countless inexperienced settlers survive their first hard years in this country. Some knew him as a friend. He was a man of God and a man of peace. They knew that he must have witnessed a great many injustices for his conscience to have allowed him to take up arms.

"They're only hanging them because they didn't get Mackenzie. Mac's safe in the States, and snubbing his nose at them. It's not justice the government's after. It's making an example of the leaders they managed to catch, to put the fear of God into us Reformers."

It wasn't much later that they heard Lount's voice from the corridor, bidding them farewell. They crowded up to the window. Lount and Matthews appeared with the sheriff, two clergymen, and some of the prison guards, and ascended the scaffold. Lount looked up and bowed to the prisoners whose faces were pressed against every window of the gaol, many with tears in their eyes. The two men knelt on the trapdoor. Nooses were placed about their necks, and hoods pulled over their faces. One of the clergymen intoned a prayer. And the 'drop' fell.

Donal turned away, sickened. No one spoke. They'd used the last of their meager energies to denounce the hangings. Now there was only sadness and despair.

Donal wondered again what would become of him. Neither he nor his cellmates had yet been tried or sentenced. The others' only crimes had been being supporters of Mackenzie's reform politics. Their names had been on a list that Mackenzie had carelessly left behind at Montgomery's Inn.

Donal could barely recall his arrival at the Toronto gaol. He'd suffered so badly from his beating by the Orangemen that he'd been unconscious for most of the journey to the city. He'd regained his senses once to find himself slung across the back of a horse. But the painful jolting of his battered body had quickly sent him into blessed oblivion again.

The next he'd known, he'd been here, in this cell. A doctor had attended to his wounds and had decried the brutal treatment that had caused them. Donal had been long in recovering; for weeks his urine had been red with blood.

The conditions under which they existed hardly ensured their survival. Donal was still clad in the odd assortment of ill-fitting clothes in which he'd arrived. They were grimy now, and louse-ridden. The bedding consisted of straw pallets and a blanket apiece, all verminous, and never changed. In fact, the vermin could plainly be seen crawling about the room. There was no heat, except that generated by close-pressed, emaciated bodies. Their hands and feet were often swollen and painful with frostbite. Water or ice glistened on the stone walls. The pisspot was often not emptied until it had overflowed. The food, what there was of it, was usually unpalatable. Bullock's heads boiled complete with brains, teeth, and thick with hair, and rat droppings more plentiful than the vegetables.

If prison life was toughening him into a man, it was also turning him into a radical. For months now he had listened to the others' tales of corruption within the government, and had finally begun to understand Mike's revolutionary zeal. If he'd been able to fight the battle again, he would have done so with real conviction.

They were all surprised when, less than a week later, they were herded out of their cell and over to the courthouse nextdoor. For most of them it was the first time in nearly four months that they had been outside that stinking, claustrophobic hole. Without fresh air, exercise, or adequate nourishment for so long, they could barely stagger that short distance unaided. They stood like crooked scarecrows before the judge in his crisp robes and curled periwig.

Donal was dizzy from the exertion; old bruises he had thought healed, pained him. At first he could take in very little of what was happening. It appeared that those who had not been directly involved in the uprising would be discharged from custody upon providing adequate bail. Their properties would, of course, remain forfeit.

The judge then turned to him. "Donal O'Shaughnessy of Launston Mills in the District of Newcastle, the Crown has found no witnesses attesting to your complicity in the plot or in the rebellion. Your name has appeared on no lists of supporters. Although your attempt to evade questioning by the arresting officer is highly suspect, the Crown has no evidence to support a conviction. You are pardoned, and are free to go."

The court's clemency was due in large part to the unpopularity of the executions of Lount and Matthews. Several death sentences previously handed down were commuted to transportation. Many other prisoners who, like Donal, had been languishing in gaol, untried and unconvicted, were released that day.

And possibly all of them were as confused by their sudden freedom as Donal. Although he was relieved, he felt no elation as yet. That required energy that he did not possess. He didn't know what to do. He had no money; his few coins had been left behind in his frozen, discarded garments. He needed shelter, food, clothes, for he could not attempt to go home in his present state.

As Donal shuffled out of the dock, a gentleman approached him. "Donal O'Shaughnessy." He pressed an envelope into Donal's hand. "Compliments of Mr. Launston." And was gone before Donal could react.

The envelope contained a ten pound note. Two hundred shillings -- an enormous sum to Donal.

He was furious. Damn their bloody arrogance! All his pent up hatred for the Tory government, for the upper class who ***mis***ruled the country, focussed upon the Launstons. If they had been present, he would have thrown the money back in their faces. He would rather go begging in the streets than accept Launston charity!

He hadn't noticed the letter at first. He drew it out of the envelope and read:

My lawyer has been instructed to deliver this to you upon your release. Since your mother's untimely death, your family has experienced difficulties which you might help to alleviate. Use the enclosed funds to hasten your return.

With the compliments of
Jeremy Launston

Although the patronizing tone of the note irked him, he was far more concerned with the message. He didn't even stop to wonder why the Launstons should bother with his family. He thought only that something must be seriously wrong.

Chapter 24

Prudence Lindsay's normally dour expression hardened into a scowl when Rowena entered her shop one Saturday afternoon in March.

Rowena smiled and greeted the proprietress and the other customers, which included Harriet Launston, Kate Muldoon, Mary Ryan and her married daughters Fionna Delaney and Shelagh Darcy.

Rowena was surprised that none of them acknowledged her, although Fionna gave her a sympathetic smile while Shelagh looked maliciously smug.

"I'm that sorry, Mrs. Launston," Prudence Lindsay said. "There's not a candle to be had, even down at the Front, so I've heard. Times are bad, as you know."

"We shall have to make our own candles then," Harriet replied. "Thank you, Mrs. Lindsay. Good day."

"There goes a good woman," Mary Ryan stated when Harriet had gone.

"Sure, 'tis a saint she be!" Kate Muldoon said. "Not one as deserves such trouble, and her with child and all. 'Tis right wicked some folk are."

"Aye, and it amazes me how the wicked can pretend such innocence, and come to church bold as you please, flaunting their sins and as good as spitting in the face of decent folk!" Shelagh Darcy said.

Rowena began to realize that the conversation was for her benefit, though she didn't understand their references to Harriet Launston. She had been expecting this -- dreading it -- but it still surprised her that these women could direct such venom toward her. Maybe Kate Muldoon needed reminding that killing her unborn child was a worse sin than loving a man out of wedlock. But Rowena could not bring herself to expose Kate's secrets. Like a doctor, Rowena felt that her patients' confidences were never to pass her lips.

And, of course, Shelagh Darcy had always hated her, so her hostility was nothing new.

Although Mary Ryan said nothing, her black eyes bored into Rowena with sanctimonious satisfaction. Since Deirdre's death, Mary had often come to the house to check on the O'Shaughnessys and to offer advice and help. Rowena had been grateful for her concern and the many small gifts of food that Mary had brought. But, although she might not be ready to condemn Rowena publicly to her face, Mary was also not prepared to stand up for her as a friend.

Fionna seemed embarrassed by her sister's harsh words. She gave Rowena a quick wink, which seemed to say, *Take heart. Don't let them browbeat you.*

And for that little sign of support, Rowena was grateful. Stoically, she stood her ground and said, "I'd like a quarter pound of tea, and half of tobacco, if you please, Mrs. Lindsay."

"Would you now?" the pious woman replied, pursing her lips. "Well, you'll get nothing from me but the door in your face if you ever think to sully these premises with your presence again, you little slut!"

The others gasped at Prudence Lindsay's outspokenness, though Kate Muldoon said, "That's telling her!"

Rowena had paled at the scathing words, but she refused to be cowed. "How easy it is to judge and condemn folk when you know naught of the truth," she said with as much dignity as she could muster. "I'll be praying for you, Mrs. Lindsay, for you've not yet learned the meaning of Christian charity, for all your Bible-spouting righteousness."

Prudence Lindsay's mouth was sucked into the toothless void. "Why that brazen hussy!" Shelagh spat, as Rowena marched out of the shop.

Rowena was quivering inside, though no one who saw her would have guessed. She ran into Maureen Darcy, whose normally apple-cheeked complexion turned a fiery red as she said, "Oh, Rowena! I... I'd best be finding Shelagh," and dashed into Lindsays'. So Shelagh had already poisoned the Darcys against her, Rowena thought sadly.

A group of boys was engaged in a snowball fight on the bank of the river at the end of Lindsay Street, just north of the tavern. They stopped as Rowena came near, and began whispering amongst themselves.

One of the older boys, a MacCready, said loudly, "My Ma says to keep away from scarlet women, lest I be tempted to sin."

"My Ma says ***she*** should be tarred and feathered and run out of town, she did," another ventured.

"My Pa says he wouldn't mind having a tumble with ***her*** himself!"

Rowena cringed inside, and tried to shut out the horrible sounds of their taunting laughter. She turned down Mill Road, wishing she could run, but knowing she mustn't succumb to this cowardly impulse. A snowball hit her hard on the shoulder. Shock gave way to fear as a barrage of snowy missiles was launched against her, accompanied by a torrent of obscenities.

Suddenly a man's voice yelled, "Get away with you, you little hooligans, afore I take me belt to you!"

It was Brendan Delaney.

"Rowena, wait!"

She hurried on, not wanting him to see her tears.

"There now," he said, stopping her flight. "There's no harm done."

She wiped her face and replied, "Thank you, Brendan," and resumed walking, hoping he would leave her alone.

But Brendan fell into step with her. He had just this week returned from the lumber camp. All those long, lonely winter nights, with none but men and precious little booze for company, he had thought of her. Every night she had lain naked beside him in his narrow bunk, until he thought he would go mad with his need of her. It was like a maggot, eating away at his innards.

When he had learned that Jeremy Launston had fathered a bastard on her, he'd drunk half a gallon of whiskey and threatened to kill them both.

Sure, there was a lot of speculation about the father of her child. Some had even thought it was him! Yet who could it have been but Jeremy Launston? Samuel and Adrian had been away all autumn, and hadn't Jeremy been seen visiting the O'Shaughnessys' house last month while Patrick had been away?

The others thought it was a great joke that the haughty Mr. Jeremy had gotten himself into such a fix -- ***randy bugger***, they called him almost affectionately. "But sure, that Rowena's an enticing little temptress," one of them had said. "Who can blame Mr. Jeremy for sampling her charms? I'm willing to do it any time!" Brendan had bloodied the man's nose.

What a surprise he'd had when Samuel Launston had visited him the following day with an intriguing proposition.

They were near the Launston house when Brendan said, "I wanted to wed you, Rowena, but your Ma had an unreasonable dislike of me. I'm still willing, if you'll have me."

Rowena stopped, astonished by his sudden proposal. "You'd wed me now? Surely you must know...."

"Aye, I know. Isn't that all the more reason for you to accept me?"

Her eyes narrowed. "How much did Mr. Launston offer you to marry me?"

Brendan hid his surprise with a chuckle. "Fifty pounds."

Rowena assumed it had been Jeremy who had approached Brendan with that offer. Brendan suspected as much, and wasn't about to enlighten her. It suited him that she should despise Jeremy. She glowered at him and turned to go, but he swung her around to face him.

"Fifty pounds isn't to be spit at. We could have a good life, you and me. You need me, Rowena."

"I don't need you, nor anyone! Now leave go of me!"

"You spread your legs quick enough for Launston." His hand bit into her arm. "But you still think yourself too good for me, eh? I've a powerful need of you, Rowena. I'll have you... one way or t'other. So you'd best think on it." He grinned as he released her, tipping his hat in a mocking gesture, and retraced his steps toward town.

In the Launstons' parlour, Harriet was saying to Jeremy, "I've never been so humiliated! You know what they all think! Everywhere I go, people are whispering, and giving me pitying glances."

"I realize it must be difficult for you, my dear, but I regret that there is nothing I can do. We'll just have to ride out the storm," Jeremy replied. Of course he'd been incensed to learn of the rumours going about the village, but he felt powerless to change public opinion.

"And let the whole town mistakenly believe that you fathered the child?"

"If anyone ever confronts me with it, I shall set him straight. Otherwise, I can hardly approach people and declare that it's not mine," Jeremy replied with impatience.

"Sometimes I wonder...," Harriet began, but then hesitated and turned away from him. She fidgeted with her shawl.

Jeremy frowned. "What do you wonder, Harriet?" When she didn't reply he said angrily, "By God! Are you accusing me as well?"

"You do seem to be inordinately concerned about her," she said without looking at him. It was just her condition, she had told herself so often. She'd heard that pregnant women were prone to irrational behaviour and emotions. Yet she couldn't suppress her jealousy.

Jeremy swore softly, and tried to pacify her. "I assure you, Harriet, that I've never touched the girl. I promised my brother I'd look after her, and I shall do what I can to honour that promise." He placed a comforting arm about her shoulders. "You mustn't upset yourself like this, my dear."

Harriet leaned her head against his shoulder. "I'm sorry, Jeremy. This affair has been rather trying for me."

"I know," Jeremy said soothingly. But his thoughts were of Rowena, and the trial she must be enduring. Alone.

• • •

Rowena was surprised to see Fionna at her door later that afternoon. She handed Rowena a package containing tea and tobacco and said, "You forgot your order from Lindsays'." Seeing that Rowena was about to burst into tears of gratitude, Fionna said briskly, "Sure, I know it wasn't an immaculate conception, so tell me what happened."

Over a cup of tea, Rowena told her about Adrian.

"You know everyone thinks it was Jeremy who seduced you?" Fionna said. "I'll bet he's fit to be tied! And they were really going to let you wed Adrian?"

"Aye. I loved him so, Fionna. There's such an aching emptiness inside me."

Fionna patted her arm. "You know that everybody's talking about you? Sure, you've given them the juiciest bit of gossip they've tasted in a long while! It's taken their minds off the rebel hunts, for sure." Ever since the Flannerys had been burnt out, people had been anxious, and careful not to speak of government reform.

Rowena said, "There's already such a sorrow in me that a few spiteful words won't be making any difference."

But despite her words, Rowena was reluctant to venture into town again. Patrick was required to do the shopping, for Moira had not the courage to face the titters and the snubs. Patrick stopped going to Paxtons' every evening. The girls refused to attend classes at the church after the two youngest had come home in tears one day. None of them attended the sugaring bee at the Winslow farm that spring.

Few people stopped in for a visit -- Matt Ryan often had a chat with Patrick in his workshop; Margaret Finch and Fionna occasionally dropped in to see Rowena.

There weren't many requests for her medical help either. A girl was sometimes sent with an order for a liniment or tisane, but no one summoned Rowena to a sickbed. She mentioned as much to Simon Worthing when he came by on one of his regular visits. He chuckled and said that he had noticed his skills had suddenly been more in demand. He also told her that it was better for her own health not to be encumbered with other people's problems and illnesses just now.

Moira spent most evenings at the Ryans. In her eyes Rowena read mute reproach. Patrick said little -- a reproach in itself -- as if, by ignoring her, the problem did not exist. Gwyn disappeared for many hours at a time and refused to tell anyone where she had been. It was Moira who finally discovered that Gwyn was practically living in the noisy and disorganized Muldoon household.

Rowena's guilt at causing her family such distress weighed heavily upon her. She thought of leaving town, but where could she go? What could she do to support herself and the child, who was becoming a reality now that he kicked and squirmed within her? And who was to look after the family, who needed her, even if they resented her damning presence? There was no escape.

Rowena continued to attend early mass on Sundays with her family. Steeling herself to the slights and whispers, she was determined that the people would not drive her from the church -- her only comfort these days. Father Killeny's pointed sermons on charity and forgiveness did not penetrate the barrier that so many people had erected between themselves and Rowena. She was grateful for the priest's efforts on her behalf, but others thought the well-loved Father had gone soft. They expected him to preach on the sin of fornication, and here he was advocating tolerance! Surely the O'Shaughnessy girl must have bewitched the good priest, she could hear them murmur.

As they were leaving the church on Easter Sunday, Rowena -- as she was meant to -- heard Shelagh Darcy say, "Like mother like daughter, like father like son. Whores and traitors."

Usually she ignored the barbs aimed at her, but this was different. She swung around and demanded, "What do you mean by that, Shelagh?"

"Just what I said," Shelagh replied loftily.

"Leave it be," Patrick cautioned Rowena.

"Nay! She'll tell no dirty lies about my Ma!"

"'Tis no lie," Shelagh countered. "Your Ma told mine that Donal was conceived by a traitor. Hanged for murder he was. Sure, isn't it funny how history repeats itself?"

Rowena looked at her father expectantly. Patrick said nothing in defence of his dead wife. Shelagh's husband, Hugh, seemed embarrassed. Others, who had listened avidly, began whispering.

Without a word, Rowena ushered her family away. When they had left the church far behind, she said to her father, "So, it's true."

"Aye." And he went on to tell her the story of Brian O'Neill. She thought it incredible that, as intimately as she had known her mother, she had really known little about her or her life, except that which they had shared. Of what her mother had thought and dreamt and hoped for, she would never be the wiser. It saddened her immeasurably.

Her thoughts were still far away when she walked into the house, so she didn't even see him at first. It was Alys who cried happily, "Donal!" as she ran into his arms.

He hugged the child tightly, and then each of the others in turn as they crowded around him. His eyes widened in astonishment as he realized Rowena's condition. "'Tis a long story," she said, answering the unspoken question. She clung to him as he greeted her, grateful for his strength, and the uncritical love she so badly needed. She prayed that he, at least, would forgive her once he knew the truth.

"You look well enough," she said to him.

Scrubbed and shaved and in a new suit of clothes, he felt quite human again. He had reconsidered the Launstons' 'charity', and had decided that if he was going to fight the Tories, he might as well use their money to do so. He'd spent the week after his release at a good, but inexpensive inn, feeding his undernourished body and regaining his strength. He'd taken in the sights of Toronto on his daily constitutionals, and had decided that he couldn't spend the rest of his life as a carpenter in Launston Mills.

But Jeremy Launston's message had never been far from his thoughts; as soon as he had felt strong enough, he had started for home.

"Where's Da?" he asked.

"In the workshop, talking to Matt, most likely," Rowena replied. Although he hadn't asked, Rowena said, "Hardly anyone comes to the house anymore."

She seemed near to tears, so Donal said, "Look, I've brought you all some presents!"

They gathered around eagerly for this novel event, and tore open the packages that he produced. Brigid and Alys squealed over their dolls; Gwyn and Moira went into raptures about their fine hair brushes; Rowena was delighted with her looking glass. "But Donal, where did you get the money for these?" she asked.

"Strange that. I don't understand it myself. From the Launstons, no less." He told her about his pardon, and the gentleman who had given him the envelope.

They talked for a long time, telling each other their news. He was heartened to hear of Mike's escape, and then upset to learn of the Flannerys' persecution and of Rowena's encounter with the militia, though she made of light of it -- as he did of his own experiences, each hoping to save the other anguish. Finally, diffidently, she told him about herself, shrivelling up inside as she watched his face darken.

Although he tried not to show it, Donal felt that Rowena had somehow betrayed them. Taking up with a Launston!

Sure, he'd quite liked the man, what little he'd seen of him. Adrian had had an easy and pleasant way about him, and seemed sincere when he'd talked about reform at Paxtons'. And sure, he was surprised at Adrian's arrest, and sorry about his death.

But with his prison-forged hatred of the Tories, Donal couldn't quite forget that Adrian really was one of ***them***, no matter how liberal his views. The fact that Jeremy had been able to effect his brother's release from gaol so quickly just proved that there was one law for the rich and another for the poor. He understood now where the money had come from. In his heart, he couldn't quite forgive Rowena.

She sensed it, but she didn't let him see her pain. And then, because he had to know, she told him about the scene outside the church that morning, and the story her father had related. Aye, ***her*** father. Not his.

Patrick walked in. His face lit up with joy when he saw Donal.

Donal, still confused by the shattering information he had just received, said, "Da?"

Patrick embraced him. "'Tis good to have you home, son."

"Oh, Da!" Donal hugged him fiercely.

Patrick said, "You're to pay no mind to what the gossips say. I've never thought of you as anything but me own flesh and blood."

Donal did just that. He did not avoid going to Paxtons'. He called upon old friends as though nothing were amiss, and invited them home. Casually he -- as well as Fionna -- corrected the misapprehension about who had fathered Rowena's child. He never responded to innuendoes or outright slurs upon himself or his sister, and slowly gained the people's respect. And, truth to tell, he was considered something of a hero in the eyes of many, though none was foolish enough to condone his 'traitorous' actions in public.

The O'Shaughnessy household became more lighthearted with Donal's presence, and even happier as old friends once again began to call.

Rowena harboured no grudges, nor dwelt upon the fickleness of her 'friends'. She was content to be no longer an outcast from the community. Patrick was more cheerful, and no longer drank himself to sleep every night. Brigid and Alys returned to school, happy to be among their friends once again. Moira was ecstatic when she became engaged to Conn. Even Gwyn behaved herself.

Only Donal seemed discontented, Rowena thought. Prison had changed him. Although she admired the man he had become, he seemed a stranger to her these days.

"Come down to the river with me," she said to him after supper one balmy evening in May. "I've a mind to stretch me legs."

As they strolled through the newly-planted rows of corn, Rowena said, "You seem restless."

"Aye, well, I'm dying to be off to Paxtons'." Donal kicked at a clod of earth.

"You know what it is I'm saying, Donal! I've seen the look in your eye when you thought no one was watching. 'Tis more than Paxtons' you're pining for."

"Is it that obvious then?"

"Only to me." It was reminder to him of how close they had always been.

"Sure, I can't stay here, Rowena! I reckon I'd made up me mind even afore I left the prison. I found something to believe in, something to fight for." He brushed aside her intended protest. "Maybe Shelagh was right -- like father like son. I'd never felt very strongly about anything before, but I do now. And I can't just bide here. I have to go away, Rena."

They had reached the river. Rowena stared into the murky water that never revealed what lay beneath. "Do you remember when we first came here, and all this was just a tangle of trees. How I hated it! But how excited you were!"

"'Twas a long time ago. We've changed, Rena."

And nothing could ever be the same again, even if Donal were to stay. "Where will you go?"

"To the States. To join the Flannerys. I do miss Rosemary." She had already written to him several times. "And to join the Hunter's Lodge."

"To fight in the border raids?" she asked in alarm. "To get yourself captured again?"

"I'll be more careful this time," he said wryly. "If enough Americans get behind us, we can still free Canada from British rule."

"I don't understand it."

"I reckon you never will."

"And I'm thinking that makes two of us," Rowena said, referring to the fact that he would never comprehend her love for Adrian Launston. She looked at him with tears in her eyes. They embraced, neither truly understanding the other, but loving each other nonetheless.

Chapter 25

Jeremy could hardly wait for the meal to end. Everyone was silent while a servant removed the plates and set dessert before them. But the awkwardness among the diners did not depart with the maid. Charles Neville had run out of things to say about the growing prosperity of Peterborough. Business and politics were unsuitable topics at the dinner table, and Jeremy's own forays into polite chitchat elicited no response from the women, save a frigid glare from his mother-in-law. Livinia seemed determined to make him feel unwelcome. No matter how blameless he himself might be, his family had been involved in scandals that had become public knowledge even in Peterborough, and their good name had been tainted.

Harriet, obviously tired after the journey, said little, and hardly seemed aware of the tension in the room. Jeremy was still annoyed with her for having insisted upon having the child here, at her parents' house, instead of at home. She had been adamant, even knowing that he would have difficulty visiting her -- since Samuel had recently hastened to the bedside of his dying sister in England, and had left Jeremy in charge of the businesses. She had argued that she would receive better care here, since the Nevilles now had proper servants, imported from England.

Margaret Finch had left the Launstons last month to marry Simon Worthing. The only help they had been able to obtain was Constance Trahern, an appalling cook and a slovenly housekeeper. The local girls had not been allowed near the Launston house, no matter what wages Jeremy had been willing to pay. And though Harriet had never said so, Jeremy knew that she blamed him for their domestic difficulties.

Sitting across the table from her, her image distorted in the candle flame that flickered between them, he felt isolated from her, as though they were strangers once more. Since arriving at the house, Harriet had seemed to become more a daughter and less a wife. She allowed her mother to fuss over her and take command of her. When Jeremy had joined them in the parlour, where they had been engaged in a quiet chat, Harriet had looked at him as if surprised at his presence. And he had felt like an intruder.

But his ire had really been aroused when he'd overheard his sister-in-law, Beatrice, berating Harriet. "I warned you, as soon as I saw her, that that girl would be trouble! But did you heed me? No! You always think you know best! Jeremy can say what he likes, but I don't believe for an instant that that effete and sickly boy, Adrian, sired that bastard upon the girl. She's much more Jeremy's style, and you must surely know that men turn to women like that to satisfy their baser needs." Beatrice had sounded so self-righteous, as if she were glad of her sister's humiliation. Harriet, strangely, had said nothing at all.

"Your second mistake was in not sending the girl far away before it became a scandal," Beatrice had continued. "Every whore has her price. I would have packed her off to Toronto or even Montreal! Do you think that Jeremy will stop seeing her, just because she no longer lives under your roof? You are so naive, Ettie!"

Containing his anger as he'd entered the room, Jeremy had said lightly, "You talk as if you have much experience of men and marriage, Beatrice." He had been pleased to see her flush scarlet in consternation. But Harriet had looked at him with hurt and confusion in her eyes. Beatrice's words had obviously echoed her own doubts. Harriet was so determined to think the worst of him, that he would almost have taken pleasure in confirming her suspicions. And, truth to tell, he'd felt a spasm of regret that they weren't just idle speculations.

Jeremy was thankful when his mother-in-law rose from the table and left, with her daughters following her silently from the room. Charles Neville seemed relieved when Jeremy asked if they could forego the male ritual of port and cigars following the meal, pretending he had to see Nigel Melbourne on a matter of business.

"By all means," Charles said. "And I don't blame you for wanting to escape, Jeremy. Livinia is making altogether too much of this nonsense! If every family were held accountable for the indiscretions of its members, there wouldn't be a socially acceptable one anywhere. You run along and enjoy some of that excellent cognac that Nigel keeps in his cellar."

At the Melbourne residence, Nigel and Charlotte greeted Jeremy warmly, though Nigel couldn't resist a friendly dig. "Your reputation precedes you, old chap. We'll harbour no vile seducers under our roof!"

Charlotte giggled and said, "Pay no heed to Nigel. He delights in being wicked. Well, I shall see to some coffee."

"I don't have to inquire what you've been up to," Nigel said with a grin when they were alone.

"Not amusing, Nigel."

"Been rough, has it?"

"I didn't even do anything, and yet suddenly I'm *persona non grata* around here!

"And ***I'm*** supposed to be the profligate son-in-law! You've made me appear almost respectable. I'm indebted to you, Jeremy. Mother-in-law has been quite gracious lately."

"Well, I wish I could treat the matter so lightly. Of course, she ***says*** nothing. She just makes me feel damned uncomfortable."

Nigel shrugged. "It'll blow over. Bad time for Harriet to stay here, though. It makes it seem as though there's something wrong between you. That 'something', of course, being that luscious, raven-haired beauty who so prettily answered your door when we visited. I, for one, wouldn't blame you if it were. Damn me, if I weren't such a devoted husband, I'd have said more than a 'Good day' to that little piece!" Despite his jest, Jeremy knew that Nigel had not once regretted marrying Charlotte. He had indeed become a devoted husband, much to his own delight. "But, of course, I have eyes for no one but my lovely wife," he said as Charlotte returned.

"And if you keep that up, Mama might even approve of you one day!" she replied.

The Melbournes' bantering relaxed Jeremy, and it was with a lighter heart that he returned to the Nevilles'. Nevertheless, when he left for home the following morning, it was with a feeling of relief. And little regret that his wife had stayed behind.

• • •

Jeremy picked disinterestedly at the congealed mess on his plate. He sat alone at the long, gleaming walnut table with only the ticking of the ormolu clock on the mantelpiece for company.

Finally he pushed his plate away with disgust, and poured himself another glass of wine. He was somewhat surprised to realize how much he missed Harriet. They had never enjoyed the easygoing, affectionate relationship that Nigel and Charlotte had. But Jeremy had come to rely upon Harriet's intelligent conversation at the dinner table, and her presence in the parlour every evening. He wondered if her absence wasn't at least partly intended as a punishment, or designed to make him aware of his need for her. Damn women for making life so complicated!

He thought of Rowena. She must be near her time. Damn ***her*** for always arousing such guilt in him! Once he had condemned her interest in his brother as purely mercenary; now he wished it had been. Had she accepted money, his guilt would have been assuaged, not only because he would have considered his promise to Adrian fulfilled, but because he could have continued to think Rowena unworthy of his brother. Knowing that she wasn't the scheming wench from whom he'd been trying to protect Adrian only augmented the burdens of his conscience. It was his fault that she was soon to bear his brother's bastard rather than heir, and he had done nothing to help her. What was he to do?

Perhaps... once the child was born, Rowena would be willing to take over the job of housekeeper. That way he could look after her, and make certain that Adrian's progeny was properly raised and educated, without making it seem like charity. And to hell with the Nevilles' suspicions! It was a perfect solution for his own comfort as well as Rowena's future! He would discuss it with her right away.

Black clouds were massing in the west. The impending storm promised relief from the sweltering heat wave that had been baking the countryside these past two weeks.

Recalling his last encounter with Rowena, Jeremy became apprehensive during the walk to the O'Shaughnessys'. Why did he even concern himself with her when she so obviously wanted nothing from him? Was his interest in her merely for Adrian's sake? He dismissed these disturbing thoughts as he knocked upon the open door.

The heat inside the cabin was almost unbearable. The fire, needed for cooking, made the place feel like an oven. The dusty, sultry breeze that wafted in the open door and windows offered no respite.

"Is Rowena here?" he asked a flustered Moira.

"Nay! And 'tis that worried I am, Mr. Launston, with the weather closing in and her being... well...."

"Do you know where she is?"

"At the bog, most like. She's been going there most days of late -- she never told me, but I followed her once. And she'll not stay away, though I've begged her to. Seems real queer, she does, sometimes."

"Perhaps I had better look for her. Which way did she go?"

"Alongside the river. You pass the meadow...."

"Yes, I know where it is." That had been Adrian's haunt. "Thank you."

Jeremy cursed the eccentricities of expectant mothers as he hurried along the path. A threatening rumble of thunder broke like a wave overhead. The sky was nearly as dark as dusk. It was going to be one hell of a storm!

Rowena stood forlornly at the edge of the swamp. It was a year ago that she had met Adrian here, and it was here that she felt closest to him. How she ached for him now!

She gasped as another pain gripped her. "Your son is eager to be born, Adrian," she whispered to the wind. It was here he had been conceived, and here, it seemed, that he would draw his first breath, for she had not the strength to return home. And here she would die, if God so willed it. All the agonies her mother had suffered came vividly to mind -- as did fear. Rowena fingered Deirdre's rosary beads and prayed.

That was how Jeremy found her -- oblivious to the clouds of mosquitoes and blackflies, to the thunder, the lightning which flashed across the angry sky, and the first drops of rain which pattered about her.

"Rowena?"

"She looked around, startled. It was only Jeremy. For a moment she had thought....

"Come, before the storm worsens."

Rowena watched the rain disturb the calm surface of the pond. Each drop initiated a circle of waves that rippled outward, colliding and mingling with those of other drops.

"This was Adrian's favourite place," she said aloud. "He came here to think of life and death. I didn't know what he meant then. I do now."

Jeremy was alarmed by her impassive, detached manner, and appalled when he saw her clutch at her swollen belly with pain. "Rowena, is it time?"

"Aye, will you take care of him, Jamie, if I should die?"

Jeremy was almost as disconcerted by her use of Adrian's nickname for him as with her words. "You won't die, Rowena. Not if you'll be sensible and let me take you home."

"It would be best for everyone if I did die."

"That's not true!" He lifted her chin so that their eyes met. Despite his impatience, he said gently, "You promised Adrian you would look after his son."

She gazed at him for a long, tense moment, and finally nodded. Together they turned and left the swamp, taking the short-cut through the forest. The rain beat down with vindictive force as the sky split asunder.

Rowena's contractions were frequent as they neared Mill Road. "I can't go on!" she cried.

"You must! It's not much farther."

But she leaned against him, trembling with exhaustion. Jeremy, seeing no alternative, picked her up in his arms. It was too far to the O'Shaughnessys', he decided, so he crossed Mill Road to his own house. Constance Trahern gawked in astonishment as Jeremy walked in the door.

"Fetch the doctor," he ordered. "And then get Patrick O'Shaughnessy. Well, go on woman!"

"I can't go out that storm. I'll be killed for sure!"

"For God's sake, she's in labour! Do as I say, woman!"

Jeremy carried Rowena upstairs, hesitating for only a moment before taking her into Adrian's room. She moaned as he lowered her onto the bed. He divested her of her dripping garments, ignoring her feeble protests.

Rowena cried out and grasped Jeremy's wrist, squeezing it until her body relaxed once again.

"Don't leave me, Jamie," she murmured.

"I won't" he replied, brushing the wet curls from her face. He felt acutely uncomfortable as he watched her writhe, not knowing how to help her, angry with her for subjecting him to this. He prayed that Simon would not be long.

He wasn't. Jeremy was relieved when Simon and Margaret took charge. He disengaged himself from Rowena's tenacious hold.

"Don't leave me, Adrian!" she cried frantically as Jeremy walked to the door.

Her desperate appeal shook him. Noticing that Margaret was soothing the wretched girl, Jeremy quietly slipped from the room.

Patrick O'Shaughnessy, cap in hand, shuffled about uneasily in the hallway. He questioned Jeremy with a worried look.

"Dr. Worthing and his wife are with her. There's nothing for us to do but wait. Come into the parlour, Mr. O'Shaughnessy."

Patrick seemed to have aged a decade in the last few months, Jeremy thought as he poured two large whiskeys. At thirty-eight, the carpenter looked older than Samuel who was twelve years his senior. The crevices in Patrick's face had long not been smoothed by laughter; the merry twinkle in the eyes that had once viewed life so optimistically was now veiled with the dullness of resignation.

It was not uncommon in this harsh country -- people aging prematurely, their spirits broken by the never-ending toil and the tragedies. Early death, insanity, alcoholism were all too prevalent in the backwoods, Jeremy thought.

Patrick swallowed half the whiskey in one gulp. "Will she be alright, do you think?"

"I'm sure of it," Jeremy replied. But how the hell was he supposed to know? He'd had no experience of such matters!

The two men sat in awkward, anxious silence. Jeremy kept filling up their glasses, and alternated between sitting idly and pacing fretfully. One would think that he was the father!

Outside the storm still raged. Thunder followed hard upon the brilliant splinters of lightning, the noise deafening, rattling the very foundations of the house. Wind whipped the trees, bending them as if they were feathers, and drove the rain against the windows in staccato bursts.

The men were disposing of their fifth whiskey when Simon entered the parlour. He grinned. Jeremy relaxed.

"They're both fine, Mr. O'Shaughnessy. You have a handsome grandson -- Keiran Adrian O'Shaughnessy."

Upstairs, Rowena clutched the tiny new bundle of life to her breast. Hot tears rolled down her cheeks as she gazed with pride and wonder and love -- and pain -- at her precious son. To think that she and Adrian had created this perfect little being! If only he were here to share this joy with her! But perhaps he was. She could almost feel his presence beside her, in his old room, and almost expected him to step whole and well from the shadows. Surely if God had any mercy, He would allow Adrian to be with her in spirit right now. It was a comforting thought. Silently, she renewed her vow to him.

But it seemed an awesome responsibility to have been given the care of this helpless little soul. That she could nourish him with her own body was marvellous, but how was she to protect him from the many dangers that lurked and threatened? The world outside this cozy room suddenly seemed too big and dangerous for such an innocent babe. She was seized with a sudden, fierce protectiveness toward her son. As she stroked his silky, black hair, she made a vow to him as well -- to always do what was best for him, sacrificing her own life if necessary. She couldn't know then how difficult that would be.

Chapter 26

Rowena's throat was tight and her eyes burned as she watched the small coffin being lowered into the ground, but she could not weep. Like most, she was in a state of shock.

Alys O'Shaughnessy was not the only one buried that day.

Father Killeny looked as exhausted as the rest of them. Since there were no other clergymen in the area, he had been interring Protestants as well as Catholics, often digging the graves himself when there was no family member well enough to do so. Or none left.

Rowena hugged the tiny bundle of her son closer, as if to protect him.

But there was no protection against the swamp fever. It struck indiscriminately. There was hardly a family in the district untouched by the ravages of the disease. Many remedies were tried -- herbal infusions, whiskey, and diluted sulfuric acid among them -- and when Simon's supply of quinine had been exhausted, these were no less effective than anything that the doctor could prescribe.

Those still able to stand did what they could to help their families and neighbours. At the outbreak of the epidemic, Simon had recruited Mattie and Rowena to help him, but now Mattie lay ill as well.

The brief ceremony was over -- not much time could be spared for the dead when so many of the living needed care. The mourners dispersed silently and quickly, Patrick and Brendan to build more coffins, which were now just simple pine boxes hastily nailed together, Father Killeny on his horse to visit the farms. Moira returned home to tend to Gwyn, who was recovering from the fever.

Rowena, along with Keir and Brigid, went first to see Ewan Monaghan. Maureen Darcy had been nursing him this past week. Simon was just coming from the bedroom when Rowena entered the cabin. Another one, she thought when she noticed the grim expression on his face.

Simon shook his head sadly. "Can you see to him, Maureen? And let Patrick know, and Father Killeny? They'll arrange the burial."

"Aye."

Rowena left with Simon. "Have you been to see Mattie?" she asked him.

"Yes. She's doing well, but I'm worried about her husband. He's losing ground fast."

"Dear God, when is it going to end?" Rowena said. "Do you know what's causing it, Simon? Is it true what people have been saying?" The fever was believed to have been caused by the miasmic gases emanating from the rotting vegetation in the swamps, of which Ops Township had many. For the most part, these swamps had been created by the Launstons ten years earlier, when the dam had backed up the waters of the Scugog River and its tributaries -- small creeks which stretched like tentacles into the neighbouring townships. Over sixty thousand acres had been flooded, and it was these rank, stagnant waters that were said to be poisoning the settlers.

Simon massaged his brow with an irritated gesture. He didn't look well. "About the swamps?" he asked. "I wish I knew, Rowena. I feel so damned ignorant and useless! It's definitely a type of malaria. And yes, it seems to occur primarily in swampy areas. But as to what specifically causes it, I couldn't tell you. All I can say for a certainty is that quinine is the only effective remedy, and while we wait for a new supply to arrive, people are dying." Simon rubbed his brow again, his eyes crinkled as if in pain.

"You're ill!" Rowena said with concern.

"Just this damned headache! I can't seem to shake it."

"And I'll warrant you've a fever, and your bones ache. You ought to be in bed."

"How could I? I can't leave you to manage on your own!" But Simon suddenly dropped his bag and grabbed his head as though he were trying to keep it from splitting asunder. Rowena knew the headaches that accompanied the ague were often blindingly painful. "Some laudanum... my bag," Simon gasped

Rowena passed the baby to Brigid to hold. She fumbled with the clasp of Simon's medical bag, searched for the bottle, and gave it to him. He put a couple of drops of the tincture on his tongue. It took only a few moments for the opiate to work, and Simon breathed more easily.

"I'm taking you home, and making sure that Margaret puts you straight to bed," Rowena said sternly. Dear God, don't let him die, she thought. Simon and Margaret were very dear to her. They were among the few true friends that she had.

Simon did not protest as Rowena led him home. She and Margaret barely got him to his bed before he collapsed. He was burning with fever. Soon he would be vomiting -- endless, gut-twisting retching -- and the high fevers would alternate with fits of teeth-chattering chills. And although some recovered quickly, with few ill effects, others were debilitated for months, their muscles weak, their limbs shaky, their bodies prone to cold sweats, their minds depressed. If they recovered at all. One in every two was dying.

Rowena saw the fear in Margaret's eyes, and wished she could reassure her friend. "Will you be needing help?" she asked. "You're not to be staying up with him day and night, or you'll be sick as well."

Margaret shook her head. "Tom will spell me. Now don't you worry about me!" Once again she became the strong, efficient woman Rowena had first known. "With more than half the people ill, and you now the only medical help, I'm concerned about ***you***, Rowena. Don't be as stubborn as Simon. There's only so much that anyone can be expected to do."

"Aye. Well... I'll leave you some boneset and willow bark. Make an infusion of a teaspoonful to a cup of boiling water."

They hugged impulsively, as if giving each other strength, and Rowena left.

She made the rounds of the village with her son tucked into the crook of her arm, and five year old Brigid walking alongside, toting the basket of herbs.

It was early evening by the time she arrived at Fionna's bedside. Fionna's father, Matt Ryan, and one of her brothers had died the previous week; her nephew, Shelagh's infant, had succumbed the week before. Fionna, herself pregnant, tossed fitfully in her bed, considerably weakened since Rowena had last seen her.

"She's worse," Sean Delaney said anxiously. "Is there naught you can do for her, Rowena?"

How often had she heard that cry from the heart?

"Get as much of that sweet tea into her as you can, Sean. Make her drink it, whether she wants it or no!" Fionna had taken no nourishment in days. And the recurring, violent bouts of vomiting and profuse sweating quickly depleted the bodily fluids.

"She can't keep anything down now, not even water. She's going to die. I know it." He buried his face in his hands.

Rowena placed a comforting hand on his shoulder. "You have to be strong, for ***her*** sake. If she thinks you've given up on her, she'll not fight. You've got to give her hope and strength to pull her through." And how often had she uttered those words, knowing them to be empty? She suspected that Fionna would not last the night. "I'll make some tansy tea afore I go. Get her to drink it, Sean." She had already tried feverwort, chamomile, dogbane, catnip, horehound, sage, and willow bark. Some patients seemed to respond to one or the other; some never did.

As she put the kettle over the fire, she railed at God for deserting them. All this suffering, this despair, this sorrow! How could she cope with any more? How much compassion could one person be expected to feel?

She looked about the kitchen of this lovely house that Sean had built for Fionna -- could it truly have been only a year ago? Was it just a year ago that Rowena's own world had been happy and carefree and... whole? She knew she mustn't think like that, or her hard won composure would crack. She felt that if ever she began to weep, she would never be able to stop.

Yet she couldn't turn her mind to better purposes. Unwanted memories lingered in everything her eyes encountered. She remembered Fionna lightheartedly sewing those frilly curtains, recalled her friend's excitement at buying the china displayed on the shelves, saw once again the radiant bride that Sean had scooped into his arms and carried over the threshold.

And she couldn't stop the tears. But she had to gain control of herself before Sean discovered her sobbing. Yet there were so many dead and dying to mourn. And there was the constant fear that her own helpless babe might be stricken by this powerful and ruthless foe.

When the door to the kitchen opened a moment later, Rowena stiffened. She wiped her face in her apron, trying, unsuccessfully, to stem the flow of tears.

Brendan asked, "Rowena? It's not Fionna, is it?"

She shook her head, not trusting herself to speak. She didn't move when he put an arm about her and said, "I'm sorry about Alys."

She nodded in acknowledgment, struggling to gain control of herself. Alys -- that gentle, undemanding child.... Brendan's grip tightened.

She hadn't spoken to him alone since that March day when he had rescued her from the taunting boys. And had offered to marry her.

Brendan hadn't forgotten her curt refusal either, but whenever he saw her, especially vulnerable like this, he was ready to forgive her anything. He put his other arm about her and drew her close.

She rested her head upon his shoulder, grateful for the reassuring strength and the concern of another human being. It was some time before she was able to compose herself and move away from him.

She removed the kettle from the fire, and poured the boiling water over the dried herb. "You'll have heard about Ewan," she said.

"Aye... And Fionna's dying too, isn't she?" He didn't have to see the resignation in her eyes to know that. "God-damned Launstons!"

She almost scalded herself with the water. "What is it you're saying, Brendan?"

"What everyone knows! That the Launstons are responsible for this. And where the hell are ***they***, I'm asking? Samuel's conveniently in England, and Jeremy's in Peterborough, hiding behind his wife's skirts!"

Jeremy had gone to Peterborough to see his newborn son; the ague was not prevalent there. The mills here had been closed long ago, for there had been no one to work them. Until the news of his son's birth had arrived, Jeremy had helped by organizing supplies and delivering them to the stricken families in the outlying areas.

"He did his share while he was here," Rowena retorted, and wondered why Brendan could so easily make her feel defensive on the Launstons' behalf.

"I didn't think there would be any love lost between you and bloody Jeremy Launston," Brendan said with feigned indifference.

"Nor is there! Now leave me be. I've work to do, even if you haven't." She pushed past him and left the room.

Fionna died that night. Cameron Abernethy and Hiram Lindsay were among the dozen that died that week.

Mrs. Grimsby had died early on in the epidemic. Now both Amelia and the Colonel were ill.

A haggard Malcolm greeted Rowena. "Father's better," he told her, "but Amelia's feverish again." He poured himself a tumblerfull of whiskey, and managed a tired grin as he said, "My preventative medicine."

"What you need is a few hours of sleep," she told him.

"Sage advice, 'Doctor' Rowena, which you would do well to take yourself."

"I manage." With a kiss and a silent prayer she settled Keir on the sofa in the parlour, leaving Brigid to supervise him.

The Colonel was sleeping. Rowena noticed that the bedding had recently been changed, and all the slops had been removed. Malcolm had been doing his duties well.

Amelia was indeed hot. Rowena had thought her to be recovering, but Amelia was evidently suffering a relapse. Rowena bathed her face and arms with cool water, and tried to get her to drink.

Rowena sweated too. It was unbearably hot, the air stagnant and saturated with moisture, unrelieved by a breath of wind. It was the height of summer, and Rowena pitied those who burned with fever as well, and marvelled at those who shook with the chills under piles of blankets.

Amelia smiled strangely at her, and said, "I'm not afraid of you anymore."

"Sure, whatever would make you afraid of ***me***?" Rowena asked in astonishment.

As though she hadn't heard, Amelia said, "After I met Harriet, I realized that I hadn't necessarily lost Jeremy for good. She's not the kind of woman a man would mourn very long.... It was awfully brave of me to attend their wedding, don't you think?" She shivered as if the memory were unbearable. Bitterly she said, "Mama insisted, of course. She would never pass up such a social opportunity." She paused, and then with a quirk of a smile said, "I was hoping Harriet would die in childbirth. Do you think that terribly wicked of me?" She looked at Rowena, who was too surprised to answer, and said, "I'm not going to die, you know. I'm going to outlive her. And you're not going to have him either. You're just a common girl, after all. Jeremy would never demean himself with you."

Rowena was not too perturbed by Amelia's ramblings; she knew that fevered minds produced strange fantasies. But she did find it disquieting to have her name linked like that with Jeremy's.

Rowena had not spoken more than a few words with him since the night Keir had been born, although their paths had often crossed these last weeks. Soothingly she said, "Of course you won't be dying, Miss Grimsby! There now, you rest."

"Yes. I shall need to look my best when Jeremy returns. Do you think they have the ague in Peterborough?" she asked hopefully.

Malcolm came to relieve Rowena, telling her that the baby was demanding to be fed, and she was thankful to leave.

She went from one house to the next, dispensing her decoctions, cooling fevers, arranging for a neighbour to stay if an entire household was abed, and doing whatever else she could to help. Sometimes it was no more than laying out the dead.

She was glad to see that Mattie Abernethy was improving, but it meant that Mattie was now aware of her husband's death. Her daughter Enid said Mattie had not spoken a word since she'd heard. She'd just lain in her bed, dry-eyed, staring at nothing at all.

Rowena looked in on her. "I'm that worried," Enid whispered to Rowena.

"Ye'll nae have to whisper around me, my girl!" Mattie suddenly said. "I've all the senses God gave me, and my good sense has nae deserted me. I'm gathering my strength. And you'll be no help to anyone at all, fashing about like that! Get me a cup of tea!"

Rowena put a hand on Mattie's brow. The older woman jerked away impatiently. "I've no fever. I'm over the worst. There'll be others needing your help."

"Aye. Well, Enid's done well by you. I'm sorry... about...."

"I know. I wasn't much help to him, for all my skills, was I?"

"You know as well as I do...." Rowena began to protest, but was interrupted.

"...that we can do nothing at all against this plague. You know what's brought it on, don't you? I told Cameron the day we came here that those swamps would be unhealthy. I was all for leaving again, but he'd not hear a word said against the place. Thought the world of the Launstons too, he did. And isn't it their fault that he's dead now?"

Rowena felt a tingle of fear. She was glad that Jeremy and his family were well away from Launston Mills just now.

One of the Lindsay children came in frantic search of Rowena. Hiram Lindsay had not accepted her help, and Rowena doubted that Prudence would allow her into the sickroom, but went anyway.

The room was stifling -- the window shut, the curtains drawn -- and stank of vomit. Prudence's face was dripping with perspiration. Her unbound hair lay in wet strands about her. The sheets were damp with sweat.

As Rowena approached, Prudence's eyes flew open. She stared so wildly that Rowena thought at first she must be wandering in her mind. In a hoarse whisper she said, "Get that creature out of my house! I'll not have her near me!"

"But, Mama, you need help!" her daughter protested.

"I need nothing from ***her***!" she spat. "Wicked, scarlet woman that she is! I'll leave myself in God's hands. It's His will if I live or die." She began mumbling a prayer.

Rowena left the room, but gave the Lindsay girl a packet of herbs and some nursing instructions before leaving the house. Her help had been rejected before, although never so rudely.

The place looked like a ghost town, she thought as she walked up Main Street. There were no shoppers, no carts come in from the country, no one walking. No outward signs of life. Only the hordes of mosquitoes. They were exceptionally bad this summer.

The sky itself was like a grey shroud over the town. It had been like that for days, unmoving, unchanging -- a monotonous, uniform dinginess unrelieved by a patch of blue. It seemed to press ever closer, trapping the hot, sticky air beneath, so that everything was bedewed with moisture. It was enervating, depressing weather that would remain until another fierce storm temporarily cleared the air. The whole summer had been like that.

Rowena stopped in at the Worthings'.

"You look done in," Margaret said. "You're just in time to join me for supper -- and I'll not listen to a word of protest. If you don't take care of yourself, you'll be of little use to anyone. And that little fellow won't be getting any nourishment if ***you*** don't."

"You're probably right." Rowena looked lovingly at her son. At six weeks she could see no resemblance to either herself or Adrian in him. He whimpered now for his own supper, so Rowena put him to her breast. "How's Simon today?"

"Better, thank God, though he had a bad night. He's sleeping now, but I'm going to need a sledgehammer to keep him in bed. He's more concerned about his patients than himself. I don't know whether he thinks himself indispensable or invincible!" Margaret paused, and then asked, "How many today?"

"Two so far. And Amelia Grimsby is getting weaker."

Keir had fallen asleep, so Rowena laid him on the sofa beside her. She did indeed feel done in, and wondered how much longer she could go on like this.

"Come, let's eat," Margaret said, "before my headstrong patient wakes and insists upon joining us!"

After the meal, Margaret insisted that Rowena take a cup of tea in the parlour. Brigid was soon fast asleep next to Keir.

"They're good children," Margaret said. "And Brigid is such a steadfast little soul."

"Aye. She's taken to Keir as if she were his mother, and her but five years old! Sure, it breaks me heart, having to drag her along with me, but she'd not stay home in any case."

"She doesn't talk much, does she?"

"Not since Ma died, and even afore that she was never one with words. She just watches. Sure, it can make you feel right queer sometimes. As though she's sitting in judgement."

A knock on the door interrupted them. Rowena began to gather her things together in anticipation, as Margaret went to answer it. It was Father Killeny, looking for Rowena.

"Thank God I found you! Can you come out to the Hegarty place with me? I hadn't been there for a few days, and now they're all sick." He shook his head. "It's bad. Who's free to come and look after them?"

Rowena thought quickly. There were so few who weren't needed at home! "Jean Calder might come, or Maureen Darcy."

"Leave the children with me," Margaret said. "Keir won't need feeding for a few hours yet. And by all means make use of our pony and trap, Father Killeny. I just heard Tom come in with it." Tom had taken over Jeremy Launston's deliveries.

"That's most kind of you, Mrs. Worthing. We'll try Maureen, shall we, Rowena? We need her brothers' help as well."

They went to see Patrick first, for two coffins, then on to the Darcys'.

Two of the Darcy boys lay ill, but Shelagh was there, so Maureen agreed to come. Her brothers, Brian and Dennis, came as well.

A nauseous stench greeted them as soon as they entered the Hegarty cabin. "Holy Mother of God!" Rowena exclaimed. Three children lay on pallets on the floor, squirming in their own vomit and excrement, crying out for water. Another no longer moved. She went quickly into the bedroom. The scene before her was no better. Mrs. Hegarty, with the grey pallor of death upon her, cradled a dead infant in her stiff arms. Mr. Hegarty lay beside them, delirious with fever, covered in filth.

Rowena swallowed hard to keep her supper down. Wordlessly, she and Maureen set to work. They cleaned up the children first -- washing them, changing their clothes, discarding the soiled pallets and arranging makeshift beds from fresh straw. Rowena coaxed them into drinking catmint tea, after which they settled more comfortably in their new beds. The men hauled in ample supplies of firewood and water, and then removed the corpses for a quick burial.

By the time Father Killeny returned from the internments, the place looked habitable once again. It was nearly midnight when he and Rowena left for home.

She was too weary even to talk, but there was something she had to know. "Father, I reckon this'll sound like a blasphemy, but, sure, how can you keep from losing your faith when you see all this misery and death?"

The priest took no offence. "You're not the first to ask. God sends us trials to test our faith, and to test ourselves, to see how we measure up as Christians. He hasn't forsaken us, child. But if ever we needed to pray, 'tis now."

• • •

By mid-August nearly one third of the population of the township lay buried.

Once the lethargy had left the bodies of the convalescents, and the numbness of shock had left the minds of all, people began to congregate again. And to talk.

Sean and Brendan Delaney were among the idle men gathered at Paxtons' one afternoon. Brendan had been putting Sean to bed dead drunk every night these past few weeks. "I don't want to be sleeping with any ghosts," Sean had said.

They missed their friend Ewan Monaghan too. There were, in fact, too many familiar faces that would never again be seen.

"Did you hear Launston was back?" someone said.

"Came slinking home now that it's safe, did he?" Brendan said. "Sure, and where was he when the rest of us were dropping like flies?"

"He made sure his own family was well away," Sean said. "And don't we know it was the fuckin' Launstons as caused this! But do you suppose they're going to be held accountable for it? Do you reckon some govermint official's going to come along and say, 'Well now, Mr. Launston, your dam's a mite high. You've been flooding too much land -- that don't belong to you, by the by -- and you're causing your neighbours some distress. We think you'd best do something about it.'?"

There were a few wry chuckles.

"All Launston's worried about is how much money he's lost, and when he can open the mills again," Owen Ryan said. "Wouldn't I like a few minutes alone with that cold-hearted bastard!"

"You and half the county," Brendan said. "I've heard tell some of the farmers are so mad they're planning to take things into their own hands."

"And what can they do? March to Toronto and protest to the Governor?" Owen asked. "Most are still too weak to stand. You know as well as I do there's nothing the little people like us can do!"

"We could tear down the dam," a voice said with quiet conviction. The words left an ominous silence in their wake. All eyes turned expectantly to the speaker, a grizzled old man, bent by hard years, but broken by recent tragedy. "Three fine sons, I had. Now they're feeding the worms, and I'm left with nothing but womenfolk and children, and a farm that's half flooded. It's a festering sore that needs to be drained. We've done with trying to talk to the Launstons."

Every man there had been touched by this tragedy, and Brendan could feel their seething, impotent anger, their need to blame someone, other than God, for this catastrophe. With a thrill of triumph he felt that he could stoke this smouldering hatred and turn it against the Launstons. "Sure, he's right! We could chop down that God-cursed dam, and get the Launstons where it really hurts -- in their pocketbooks!"

Normally, Josh Paxton would have put a stop to talk like this, but the innkeeper had been morose since he'd buried his wife and a daughter. It was Conn Ryan who said, "And where would that leave those of us who earn our living from the mills?"

"There are other jobs," Brendan replied. "Other towns even, if need be. Places not ruled by one family, like it's their own private kingdom. Sure, we know our own worth, don't we, lads? 'Tis the Launstons need us, not us them!"

A lot of the men agreed with him, though a few shook their heads. Conn said, "And do you think the law would let you get away with it? Do you think there wouldn't be retribution?"

"Isn't it justice that we're seeking?" Brendan demanded of the patrons. "If we leave it up to the bloody govermint to get off its ass and do something, we'll all be poisoned by those swamps! 'Tis up to us to act, lads, to protect our families."

Jeremy Launston, newly returned from Peterborough, was ignorant of how drastically this old grievance by the farmers had escalated into vindictive hostility. Those living near the flooded lands had been the hardest hit by the pestilence -- proof to most that the Launstons were ultimately to blame.

Jeremy was working alone in his mill office the following day, unaware of the swelling tide of angry settlers inundating the town, gathering momentum from among its bereaved citizens.

Now that the epidemic appeared to have subsided, Jeremy wondered how soon he could reopen the mills and distillery -- and how he would manage without so many of his men, like the miller, Cameron Abernethy, and Matt Ryan, and Ewan Monaghan. He spared a thought, too, for Amelia Grimsby, and for Major Selfridge, who had returned from his border patrol with the provincial militia only to be felled by this unseen foe.

Jeremy was now thankful for Harriet's insistence upon staying with her parents during her confinement. She and the baby would remain in Peterborough until the fall, when all danger of the ague would be past.

Lost in his thoughts, Jeremy had not been conscious of the noise, like that of a swarm of bees and... a dull thumping sound. He glanced out the window, but could see nothing amiss. Wait... what was that tumbling down the river? Wood?

Christ! The dam!

Jeremy ran from his office to a north window overlooking the dam. He was momentarily stunned by the scene of destruction. Dozens of men were hacking away at the structure with axes. Part of it suddenly gave way with a splintering crash, and water and wood cascaded downstream.

The bloody lunatics! What in hell were they doing?

There was a shattering of glass behind him as rocks were hurled through the windows on the opposite side of the building, facing the road.

Those blasted farmers wouldn't get away with this! He'd call out the militia and have the lot of them arrested!

When Jeremy turned from the window, he was surprised to see the Delaney brothers and Owen Ryan standing before him.

"I'm glad you're here," he said to them. "I need your help to stop those vandals from completely demolishing the dam."

"Is that a fact then?" Brendan said mockingly as he stepped forward. "It just so happens that we were looking for you, Launston. There's some mighty upset folk as have a word or two to say to you." Brendan gestured to the others, who began closing in on Jeremy.

Delaney's insolence, and the smell of whiskey that wafted from him, had already put Jeremy on guard. As the three men cut off all escape routes, he knew that his only chance was to reach the desk in his office, in which he kept a hand gun. It wasn't loaded, but they wouldn't know that. Casually he said, "The people are welcome to say as much as they like -- as soon as they stop this senseless destruction."

Jeremy turned and bolted for the office, but Brendan lunged for him and they both crashed to the floor. The others pulled Jeremy up and held him while Brendan belted him in the stomach, knocking the breath out of him. Another punch cracked on his jaw.

"I owed you that," Brendan said with a sardonic grin, as Jeremy dangled between the two strong men who pinned his arms painfully behind him. Blood oozed from the corner of his mouth. He looked at Brendan with hatred.

"I wouldn't mind finishing you off meself, but we'll let the others decide what's to be done with the high and mighty Jeremy Launston."

Jeremy stumbled between his captors as they dragged him outside. He was astonished by the size of the crowd gathered there. Words of abuse and profanities, jeers, and hisses greeted him. With disbelief he scanned the faces: Ezekial Yardley, Josh Paxton, Prudence Lindsay; Darcys, Calders, Ryans, Winslows, Abernethys, O'Shaughnessys. His eyes met Rowena's. She alone looked horrified. It was as though some madness had possessed these people, Jeremy thought, too astounded even to be afraid.

The rhythmic clopping of axes could be heard, as men continued to chop away the dam.

Rowena watched with mounting terror as the mob voiced its cry for vengeance. She, as so many others, had followed the farmers out of curiosity, and few blamed them for wanting to drain the flooded, poisoned lands that bordered their own. But things had gotten out of hand. She was glad that Keir and Brigid were safely home with Moira and Gwyn.

There were no religious or ethnic barriers between the people now. They were united by grief, by an unshakable single-mindedness that made the ordinary God-fearing man -- and woman -- a dangerous foe, an anonymous cog in a potentially violent machine.

Rowena's heart pounded in her throat as Brendan, standing on the top step as though it were a podium, addressed the angry settlers.

"Here's the man you all want!" Brendan shouted.

They raised their voices in a cheer as Jeremy was hauled to the front of the broad step.

"'Tis because of him and his kind that decent Christians like us have been dying!"

The mob acknowledged the truth of Brendan's words. Those who did not wish a personal vendetta against Jeremy were afraid to speak in his defence lest they, too, be persecuted.

Brendan knew he had control of the people. How long he had waited for this moment! "So what will we do?"

Several comments were yelled out, but Brendan, like a priest blessing his flock, stretched out his hands for silence. "I'll tell you what we'll be doing! 'Tis the dam and the mill and the greed of the Launstons that's caused this plague!"

"Aye"!

"So we'll burn the mill!"

Cheers.

"But what are we to be doing with Mr. Jeremy Launston?"

"Throw him into the mill race!"

"Drowning's too good for him," another voice cried. "Ain't he from a family of traitors? I say hang him!"

Rowena could stand no more of this insanity. She fought her way through the people and leapt onto the step next to Brendan before anyone could stop her.

"Is it ***daft*** you all are?"

"This is men's work, Rowena. Stay out of it," Brendan warned her quietly.

She resisted his effort to push her aside. "Men's work, is it?" she asked loudly, her hands on her hips in a defiant pose. "There's not a man among you will have work if you burn down the mill! You, Jacob Muldoon... where is it you'd be without your wage from the mill? How will you be feeding your six childer? You, Zeke Yardley, will you be giving away your goods then, to them as can't afford to pay? And you, Enoch Ridley, where will you be taking your wheat to be ground? And you, Alec Darcy? And you, Silas Winslow?"

The men shifted uncomfortably. They were subdued now, for being thus singled out made them feel vulnerable and guilty. Others, too, recognized the sense she spoke, and Brendan could feel the tide ebbing, slipping away from him. There were mutters of confusion among the crowd, a glimmer of sanity.

"Launston whore!" a voice rang out. Rowena recognized it as Shelagh's.

In that moment of stunned silence, Brendan seized the advantage. He wasn't about to relinquish control of the people, not now when he could taste revenge. By Jaysus, but it was sweet! Shelagh was right -- Rowena had been Jeremy's whore. The way she had leapt to the man's defence vexed him, and convinced him that it had been Jeremy and not Adrian who'd sired her bastard. He grabbed Rowena by the arm and cried, "Aye, that's right! Who is ***she*** to preach to us? Will you be listening to this sinner?"

Brendan held her at arm's length in front of him as though offering tempting bait to a starving wolf pack.

"Jezebel!" Prudence Lindsay cried.

"Strumpet!"

"Harlot!"

The words screamed in Rowena's ears. The surge of hatred directed toward her was an almost tangible entity, and she froze with horror. A stone struck her on the forehead. She was shocked, dizzy. Blood trickled down her face. She noticed her father being restrained by the men around him. Conn Ryan looked, shamefaced, down at his feet. Hugh Darcy seemed sympathetic but impotent. Shelagh positively gloated with satisfaction. People she had nursed so faithfully refused to meet her eyes, although some stared at her accusingly. There were those, she realized, who had resented feeling grateful to someone they had so recently spurned.

The mob pressed closer, outraged righteousness and contempt naked in the eyes that glared at her. Rowena thought she would faint, but Brendan's grip tightened, preventing her from collapsing. Would he just stand by and watch them tear her apart?

Jeremy struggled ineffectually against the two brawny men who held him. That maniac, Delaney!

Another stone struck Rowena hard on the shoulder.

A voice boomed, "Jesus said, 'He that is without sin among you, let him first cast a stone at her'."

A momentary hush fell upon the mob. The people turned toward the speaker, Father Killeny, who had ridden up, unnoticed.

"Are you without sin then, Shelagh Darcy?" he asked.

"This don't concern you, priest!" someone yelled out.

"Aye! It's justice we're after! We'll never get it if we listen to the likes of him!"

Some were willing to hear what the priest had to say, wanting some divine rationale for the recent tragedy. Others resented the papist's interference. They began to argue amongst themselves.

The sound of chopping continued. The crack of splintering wood and the whoosh of undammed water were occasionally heard, although no one paid any heed.

Father Killeny addressed the crowd from his saddle, projecting his voice above the hubbub. "'Let all bitterness, and wrath, and anger, and clamour, and evil speaking, be put away from you, with all malice: And be ye kind one to another, tenderhearted, forgiving one another, even as God for Christ's sake hath forgiven you.' Go home, good Christians. There's been enough mischief and wickedness wrought this day. 'Vengeance is mine, sayeth the Lord.' May God forgive you all!"

"We ain't the ones needing forgiveness!" someone said. "Jesus Christ, some of us haven't any families left! And who's to blame? The God-damned Launstons, is who!"

Voices were raised in agreement.

Father Killeny turned his gaze on Brendan. There were children in the parish who were convinced that God must resemble their priest, for when the good Father looked you in the eye, you felt certain he could read your thoughts. One of those looks was often enough to make you repent your sins.

But Brendan was not so easily cowed. He stared back defiantly. People sensed the power struggle going on between the two men, and fell silent.

A scream shattered the tension. It took a moment for people to realize that it had come from the direction of the dam, but then all eyes turned toward the river. Amongst the timbers tumbling downstream in the turbulent gush of water, a man could be seen, struggling to stay afloat. A massive beam of the ruined dam bounced and bobbed beside him, as though it were partnering him in some macabre dance. A moment later it struck him a deadly blow on the head. He disappeared beneath the churning water.

The crowd was stunned.

Those who feared they had recognized the victim hastened to the water's edge. Others, shocked and ashamed, followed more slowly.

Brendan pushed Rowena away from him with such fury that she would have fallen down the steps had not Jeremy, who had just been released, caught her.

"Are you alright?" he asked anxiously.

"Aye."

But she swayed, and Jeremy lowered her onto the step, where she sat with her head cradled upon her knees until the dizziness passed. Jeremy pressed his handkerchief against the seeping wound on her forehead.

What a touching scene, Brendan thought sarcastically, and wanted to strangle them both. With clenched fists he stalked away, shrugging off Father Killeny when the priest attempted to confront him.

"Are you alright, the pair of you?" the priest asked Jeremy and Rowena.

"Yes. More shaken than anything," Jeremy replied. "Thank you for your timely intervention."

The priest ran his fingers through his hair. "I was almost too late. I was visiting the O'Mara farm, and the good woman informed me that her husband had joined the march on the mill. I thank God that He directed me here with such haste."

"You're looking ill yourself, Father," Rowena said.

"Nothing that a few extra hours of sleep wouldn't cure, as you well know."

"All the same, I'll drop off some herbs for you."

"Aye. Well, if you'll not be needing me, it appears I have another family to console."

Fergus Ryan approached the priest and said, "It was Brian Darcy, Father. The timber he was standing on broke away, and he was washed over the dam. There's no sign of him as yet. Some of the lads'll be going out in a boat, in case he's come ashore downstream. But it's not looking good." Fergus didn't need to say what they all thought -- that Brian could not possibly have survived. They had all heard that skull-breaking crunch of wood meeting bone.

Before he left with Fergus, Father Killeny said to Rowena and Jeremy, "Remember that these unfortunate souls, crazed with grief -- and too much drink, in a good many cases -- now have need of your forgiveness."

When the priest had gone, Jeremy turned to Rowena. "I'm in your debt, Rowena. But why did you interfere?"

"They would have killed you," she replied simply. "I just wanted to make them see reason. I hadn't thought...." She shuddered, remembering her suffocating terror when the crowd's vindictiveness had been directed toward her. She rose from the step.

"Rowena, I had intended to discuss this with you earlier, but I haven't had the opportunity. We have need of a housekeeper. You and your son could have a home with us, if you want the job."

Her cool, blue eyes were inscrutable as she said, "We have a home."

"Then let me help you in some way. I...."

"I don't want anything from you," she said proudly. "Neither for meself nor me son. Your family owes us nothing, so I'll thank you to stay out of our lives." She turned and left.

Jeremy could not understand this strange young woman who one moment risked her life for him and the next, seemed almost to dislike him. But his own feelings toward her were even more puzzling.

He wanted her near him. Not that he loved her, or even that he particularly desired her, he told himself. He just wanted her to be a part of his life. He thought of her often, wondering what she was doing and thinking, and felt almost jealous at being excluded from her daily existence. These feelings troubled him.

She was right. He would have to stay out of her life

Chapter 27

Some of the men who had aided in the destruction of the dam were engaged in its reconstruction.

Jeremy, despite the priest's plea, had sought retribution, only to be informed by the government that the settlers' grievances were legitimate. He had been advised to lower the head of water from twelve feet to ten, to appease the populace, and that, should the government decide to carry out its plans for a navigational lock at the town, a new dam would most likely be built anyway.

Jeremy fumed for a while, disgusted that such lawlessness was condoned, but soon realized there was nothing he could do but repair the dam as quickly as possible so that the mills would not stand unprofitably idle too long.

And he fired the Delaney brothers and Owen Ryan.

Owen went to the States, as he had long threatened he would. Brendan and Sean went to the Lathrop Foundry, where they were immediately hired, since labour was now scarce in the village.

With nearly every family in mourning, there were no celebrations that autumn and winter, which suited Rowena. The dark and dismal winter reflected the bleakness in her sorrowing soul. Only the warm and cuddly presence of her son kept her from despair. She marvelled at how alert and curious and happy he was. Truly he was a God-given gift!

Mary Ryan and her two daughters, Catriona and Noreen, spent many a long winter evening with the O'Shaughnessys. Mary and Patrick took solace in each other's company. Rowena was not particularly surprised, therefore, when one spring day Patrick hemmed and hawed and finally spat out the news.

"I loved you Ma dearly," he said to his children. "Aye, and I miss her sorely. But a man needs a woman's comfort. You've all known Mary a long time. She was your Ma's best friend, and she's always been a good neighbour..." Patrick did not notice Rowena's skeptical look. "... and like a mother to you since.... Well, with Fergus soon to be wed, and Mary with the two young ones still, needing a man's influence, we thought... well, that we'd be... wed."

The girls exchanged glances.

Rowena dreaded the thought of Mary Ryan -- she would never think of her as anything else -- invading their home and taking command.

Keir began wailing. Rowena picked up her son from the crib which stood in the kitchen. She sat down in the rocking chair and bounced him on her knees, much to his delight. He was eleven months old now. A handsome child, but with no resemblance to his father.

Rowena became wistful as she thought of Adrian. She quickly pushed aside the realization that she could no longer conjure up his image in her mind. She had a sense of him -- a gentle, intelligent, caring man -- that comforted her. How unfair that her son should never know him! Nor have a man to call "father".

An idea that she had once so vehemently rejected now asserted itself in her thoughts. Already she could envision the years of loneliness that stretched like a deserted road before her. And she only just nineteen! She wondered if she could ever love again, no longer denying it outright as she had the previous year. But one could marry without such a deep attachment. One had to be practical -- she could not be dependent upon her father forever, particularly now that the 'family' was about to double in size. And she couldn't imagine living under Mary Ryan's rule very long. But how could she support herself and her son? Where would they live? Always those problems.

She thought of the offer that Jeremy had made her last summer, and wondered if she had been too hasty in rejecting it. She suspected that it would not be repeated, and she was too proud to ask Jeremy to take her in. Besides, she was confused about her emotions regarding him. He was arrogant and unfeeling and she should hate him! But she didn't. And that bothered her.

Much as she might try to deny it, she was attracted to him as fatally as a moth to a candle. No matter how much she might wish otherwise, she could not stop the fluttering of her pulse or the catch in her breath whenever she saw him. And it was wrong. It was a betrayal of her love for Adrian. No, she couldn't possibly live with the Launstons.

So what was she to do? Marriage seemed the only solution to her dilemma. But who would have her? She could have been happy with Conn -- she might even have grown to love him -- but she had thrown away her chances with him long ago. He and Moira had finally married at Easter and he seemed to be a good husband to her. Rowena was truly happy for her sister, despite the fact that she envied her.

Rowena grew more restless as the weeks passed. The family that she had so desperately tried to hold together after her mother's death had disintegrated. With Donal and Moira gone, Alys dead, Gwyn rarely in the house, and Patrick infatuated, it hardly seemed like a home anymore.

When Patrick and Mary were married, things became even worse than Rowena had imagined. Mary descended upon them like a battleship in full sail. She turned the house inside out and scrubbed it as though she were trying to remove every trace of Deirdre from within its walls.

Home was no longer that to Rowena. It was merely a place to exist. The house was crowded. There was no privacy, and no sense of belonging which made the lack of privacy tolerable. And Rowena had to admit that it vexed her to see Mary taking Deirdre's place, to witness the loving attention that Patrick bestowed upon his new wife.

Although their obvious delight in one another sharpened Rowena's loneliness, evenings with Moira and Conn were preferable to staying home.

Until that came to an abrupt end one August night.

Conn had bought the house that Sean had built for Fionna. Sean had recently married the widow Flynn -- and her farm -- and had no longer needed his house.

Rowena and Moira sat around the fire in the parlour, for there was an autumn nip in the air. Rowena was sewing clothes for Keir. The child played quietly at her feet with a wooden toy that Patrick had made for him. Conn had gone to Paxtons' for a drink shortly after Rowena had arrived. Moira sat opposite her sister, half-heartedly knitting a muffler for Conn.

"Have you something on your mind then, Moira?" Rowena asked. "You've been fidgeting this last hour or more."

"Aye, I've something on me mind, alright." She rose abruptly, and Rowena looked curiously at her. "Sure, it don't come easy for me to say this to you, Rena, but I'll keep me peace no longer."

Rowena put down her sewing. "Out with it then."

Moira reddened. She opened he mouth to speak and then clamped it shut again. Rowena watched in amazement as Moira paced back and forth, varying emotions chasing each other across her face. Finally she said, "'Tisn't that we don't like having you come for to visit us."

There was a lump in the pit of Rowena's stomach.

Moira's words gushed out in an unstoppable flood. "But 'tis too much for you to be coming here every evening. Conn's at work all day, and the evening's the only time we have together. And it'll not be long afore he goes to the lumber camp for the winter. Sure, don't you think we're wanting some time to ourselves?"

In truth, this was not the only reason for Moira's impassioned speech. It annoyed her to see Conn's face light with a smile whenever Rowena appeared. It galled her to watch him dote upon the child with an almost fatherly concern. Moira would never forget that Rowena had been Conn's first choice.

But Rowena did not know that her sister harboured these jealousies, that Moira felt, as yet, insecure in her marriage. She knew only that she was suddenly unwelcome in her sister's house, and this rejection hurt her deeply.

She swallowed the lump that had risen to her throat, and attempted a smile. "Sure, 'tis thoughtless I've been!" Rowena gathered up her things.

Despite her relief, Moira was contrite. She had not wanted to hurt Rowena, whom she had always admired and loved. "Rena, I didn't mean...."

"Nay. You're quite right! 'Tis selfish I've been to be seeking your company so much! Keir and I'll not be troubling you anymore."

"You'll still be coming for to visit now and then?"

Rowena smiled sadly at Moira, who was so obviously flustered, and anxious now to please. "Aye. We'll be waiting for an invitation, is all."

When Rowena had gone, Moira burst into tears, overcome with guilt. It had been selfish of her to exclude Rowena from a share of her own happiness, when her sister had so little for herself. But then, Moira's own happiness was diminished by Rowena's presence. What should she have done?

Rowena hugged Keir close to her breast as she walked through the twilight. She had never felt so alone, so unwanted. The child, whom she loved with abandon, was all that anchored her to this pointless life, of that she was certain.

It was with dread that she entered her home.

Mary looked up with a scowl. "Have you seen Gwyn then?"

Rowena placed Keir on the floor and removed her bonnet wearily.

"Nay."

Mary turned her dark eyes upon Patrick, who was filling his pipe by the fire and looking as though he wanted to be anywhere but here at this moment. "Patrick O'Shaughnessy, 'tis time you did something about that girl of yours! 'Tain't right that she should be gallivanting around all hours of the day and night! She'll be coming to a bad end, you mark me words! There's some folk as think I'm running an inn here." She looked pointedly at Rowena. "Think they can come here for to eat, and never having to lift a finger to help. Sure, I'll not be standing any more of it! That girl of yours needs a good hiding! Spare the rod and spoil the child, I say. You're too soft, Patrick, and you'll be ruing that some day. So if you'll not be doing it, I will. I've had enough of her sassing and laziness, do you understand me? She's naught but trouble, that one. She needs the divil whipped out of her!"

Patrick did not reply. He sucked on his pipe, to make sure it would draw properly, and then lit it with a burning spill.

"As for you." Mary now turned her ire upon Rowena. "If you're to be living in this house, you could at least be doing your share of the work, instead of bothering Conn and Moira every evening!"

Rowena had felt her gorge rise since the moment she had set foot in the room. She could contain her anger no longer. "I do enough of the work here! But I'm not your maid! I ran this house well enough afore you set foot in it!"

Patrick looked at his daughter, his eyes pleading for peace.

"And a fine job you did of it, and all!" Mary said. "'Twas a pigsty! And 'tis cause of you that Gwyn's become such a hoyden."

"I'll be going to look for her, soon as I've put Keir to bed!"

Rowena picked up her son, and held her hand out to Brigid, who sat in her usual corner by the fireplace with only her rag doll for comfort. She grabbed Rowena's hand gratefully, her eyes still wide with the terror that these confrontations always aroused in her.

Rowena's heart went out to her little sister. She ***had*** been selfish, she thought, spending hitherto pleasant evenings at Moira's while Brigid had to endure lonely evenings here. It wasn't right that Brigid should grow up in such a home, that she should have none of the happiness and security that Rowena herself had known!

Rowena took the children up to the loft. She changed Keir and tucked him up in her bed. Then she helped Brigid out of her pinafore and dress.

"Can I sleep with Keir? Gwyn's not here, and it'll be ever so long afore you come to bed."

Rowena smiled. She pulled the child into her arms and hugged her tightly. "Sure." She tucked Brigid in beside Keir, who was already asleep. What a good child he was!

"Rena, will Ma beat Gwyn when she comes home?"

It irked Rowena to hear Brigid refer to Mary as "Ma", which Mary insisted upon. She could not bring herself to use that form of address, so she usually said nothing at all. That slight had not been lost upon Mary.

"You won't let her beat Gwyn, will you, Rena?"

Rowena had already made up her mind about that. "Nay. Everything will be alright, so you're not to be worrying. Go to sleep now."

Rowena took her shawl, and another for Gwyn, and went downstairs. She did not stop, but went right out the door without a word.

She took a deep breath of the fresh night air, feeling it cool her blood and slow her hammering heart. She was certain that she had never hated anyone as much as she did Mary Ryan. It became daily more difficult even to be civil toward that woman. Mary had been nice enough to Patrick's children at first. She had perhaps even tried to treat them as her own. Now there was no more pretense. And Patrick had not the courage to gainsay her

Rowena strolled along Mill Road toward the Muldoons', who lived nearer the mills. She knew that Gwyn was often in the company of that ragamuffin horde of children. She savoured these few moments of peace. She could even understand why Gwyn was so reluctant to go home.

As she neared the bridge, she glanced at the river and saw, in the moonlight, a small figure sitting on the bank next to the abutments.

She stepped quietly across the dewy grass, and sat down beside Gwyn after draping a shawl across the girl's shoulders. Gwyn did not stir, but sat with her chin resting upon her drawn-up knees, staring at the river. As Rowena watched the moonlight skim across the calm water, she felt closer to Gwyn than she ever had.

She had been too quick to scold Gwyn in the past, Rowena thought, never taking the time to speculate why Gwyn had done whatever she had. Though Gwyn and Deirdre had often been at odds, Rowena was certain that it was Gwyn who, of them all, missed her mother the most.

Rowena slipped off her moccasins and dangled her feet in the warm water.

"Aren't you afeard the snapping turtles'll bite off your toes?" Gwyn asked.

"Nay! Sure, they're all abed."

Gwyn giggled.

"Is that why you never like to bathe in the river? 'Cause of the snapping turtles?"

Gwyn shrugged and became sullen once more.

"I reckon you've come to fetch me back," Gwyn said after a long while.

"You'll be having to come home sometime."

"Home! 'Tain't home no more!"

"Aye, I know what you mean."

Gwyn looked at her sister. "You do?"

"Sure! Do you think you're the only who feels it then? Do you think Brigid and I like it any better than you?"

"Why did she have to die, Rena? Why?"

"I reckon the Good Lord thought it was time Ma joined Him. Maybe He thought 'twas time we learned to take care of ourselves."

"I don't believe in Him! He can't be good if He took Ma away. We needed her more'n He did. I hate Him, and I'm not afeard of Him! Just let Him strike me dead, if He's really up there listening!"

"Whist, Gwyn! Ma would be ever so angry if she heard what you said!"

"'Twas so different when Ma was alive. Do you remember how it used to be?"

"Of course I do!" Too painfully. "But nothing ever stays the same. Remember what Ma said? 'Life makes you no promises.' 'Tis time you learned to accept that, Gwyn."

Gwyn thought her sister foolish. Did Rowena really believe that rubbish about not expecting much from life, and being grateful for the few crumbs of happiness that might be thrown in your direction? There was no way that she, Gwyn, was going to sit around meekly and wait for the supposedly 'good' Lord to dish out whatever meager fare he intended for her. If you wanted to get ahead in this world you had to seize opportunity and mould it to your own purpose. And you had to stop playing by the rules.

"Are you ready to go home now?" Rowena asked.

"I reckon there's no place else to go."

Rowena held out her hand and, after a moment's hesitation, Gwyn took it.

"Let me handle Mary," Rowena said when they reached the house. "She's like to be in a foul temper."

"Where have you been?" Mary demanded of Gwyn as the girls entered.

"Out."

"I'll take no cheek from you, miss! Do you think you can come and go as you please, leaving Catriona and Noreen to do your share of the work? Worrying your Da and me sick? Well, you've another think coming!" Mary snatched up Patrick's strop from the table where it had lain in readiness. "Out to the shed with you!"

"No," Rowena said.

Mary's eyebrows drew together into a solid black line. "I wasn't talking to you."

"But I answered you. And I'll be telling you again. You'll not be punishing Gwyn."

The eyebrows sprang apart. "How dare you tell me what it is I'll be doing or no! Maybe you need a strapping yourself!"

"I'll not let you lay one finger on me, Mary Ryan, nor on me sisters, so you'd best think on it afore you make any more wild threats."

Rowena ushered the astonished Gwyn to the foot of the box stairs -- the girl needed no further prompting to rush up to her bed -- while the even more surprised Mary was gasping for breath.

"Patrick O'Shaughnessy, did you hear what your daughter just said to me? Did you hear how she talks to me? After all I've done for her and that bastard of hers!"

All Rowena's pent-up anger and frustration exploded from her. "You've done nothing for us! You've done nothing but try to tear this family apart. Aye, and to turn even our Da against us! You want nothing here to remind you of Deirdre, not even us! Cause you know you'll never be as good a woman as she, despite the little digs you're constantly making, trying to poison Da's mind against her memory. You know you could never take her place, and that vexes you something fierce, doesn't it, Mary Ryan? Just don't you forget that this was our home afore it was ever yours!"

Mary reached Rowena in two angry strides, and slapped her hard across the face. Then she marched into her bedroom and slammed the door.

"'Tis wicked you are!" Catriona Ryan burst out. "Wicked! Do you think 'tis been easy for us since Da died and Owen left, and with Fergus and Conn more interested in their new wives than us? You've not made us feel welcome here. You've been fighting Ma ever since we came here. You've never even given her a chance!" Catriona and her younger sister, Noreen, followed their mother into the bedroom.

Patrick looked up at Rowena. There was no anger in his eyes, only a profound sadness. "You'd no call to talk to Mary like that," he said at last. "I reckon you owe her an apology."

"Nay, Da, I'll not apologize to her."

"Rena, do it for ***my*** sake. I'm only asking for some peace in this house. 'Tisn't too much for a man to want." He emptied the ashes from his pipe, and began filling the bowl with fresh tobacco.

Rowena did not know him anymore, this man who was her father.

"I'm sorry, Da, but if I was to apologize to Mary, 'twould be admitting that I was wrong. And I'm not. Don't you see what she's doing to you, to us all? Don't you care?"

"She's trying to make a home for us, lass. But you're not making things easy for her. I know she's a might high-handed, but 'tis just her way, don't you see? She's not your Ma, but she is me wife, and for that alone you owe her obedience."

"Is there naught owed to us then? Loyalty from our Da, maybe?"

"'Tisn't a question of loyalty. Sure, lass, you know I'd not allow anything as would harm you. But Mary has raised enough young ones of her own to be knowing what's good for you. I'll be expecting you all to be doing what she says, and I'll not have you gainsay her. There's only one woman can rule a roost at a time."

Rowena was speechless. She could not believe that Patrick had just sided with Mary against his own children -- at least, that was how she interpreted his remarks.

She said not a word as she left him there, chewing on the end of his pipe, and stormed up to bed. She could not tell him how much his words had hurt, or how much respect they had cost him. He had disillusioned her to the point where she could never forgive him or truly trust him again. Patrick had cut that last tenuous bond with her childhood -- the unquestioning love of a child for a parent.

• • •

Brendan Delaney sat alone at a table in Paxtons' downing his fifth whiskey. There were others in the bar, of course, but none of his close friends. Sean no longer had time to come into town for a drink, and the eldest Darcy boys, all married now, made the two mile trip to Paxtons' only once or twice a week.

It was the damned women, he thought sourly. You could almost see the leashes tied about the men's necks. Even when he did come in, Hugh Darcy was loathe to incur Shelagh's wrath by staying too long, or having more than a couple of drinks. Jaysus, but that woman had a sharp tongue! To see his friend cower under the assault of that weapon, formidable though it was, made him want to puke. He'd not be letting any woman dictate to him!

Women were the bane of men's lives. You couldn't live with them, nor yet without them.

The thought of marriage had been on his mind more and more of late. Dammit, if there wasn't but one woman in this town who could keep his interest for more than a few weeks, and that bitch wouldn't give him the time of day!

Leaving this dunghill of a town was an increasingly appealing idea. What was there for him here? The winter nights would become even lonelier, once his friends were at the lumber camp. Jaysus, but he missed those times! He liked the hard, physical, outdoor work, the easy company of the men -- with no women about to make trouble. But that bastard, Launston, had deprived him of that.

So leaving was perhaps the best idea. He'd heard that lumbering was big business in the Ottawa Valley. He'd have no trouble getting a job there, and there'd be a new crop of fillies to pluck when he got to Bytown. Sure, that called for another drink!

Fergus Ryan walked in as Brendan went to the bar. "Ah, Fergus, me lad, you're just in time to help me celebrate!"

Fergus joined his friend and ordered a whiskey. "And what would you be celebrating?"

"The leaving of this stinking town!"

Fergus's surprise gave way to a frown. "You're joshing me."

Brendan put his right hand mockingly over his heart. "'Tis the God-cursed truth! That foundry sticks in me craw, the Launstons are a pain in me ass, and the women -- piss on 'em all!"

Fergus was thoughtful as he walked with Brendan to a table. "Sure, I thought you'd be getting a wife sooner or later, settling down, like the rest of us."

"And who'd I be marrying? One of them pious Lindsay girls? The women in this town that ain't wed, ain't worth marrying, nor even bedding."

"What about Rowena? I thought you fancied her."

"You know she's not said a civil word to me this past year, ever since that day outside the mill. Damned if I'm going near that bitch again."

"She's mettlesome, right enough. But I've always had a fondness for the lass. There's not many as can look into those blue eyes of hers and not be affected. She needs taming is all. And you'd be just the man to do it, Brendan."

"She'd as soon spit in me face as wed me."

"I'd not be too sure of that now. Things ain't what they were. Ma says she's like a cat in heat. Happen she'll take the first man as comes along. Ma was saying just yesterday that Alec Darcy has his eye on Rowena."

"That old codger?"

"Reckon it's been a powerful long time since he had a woman. A man his age often gets a fancy for the lassies, you know. Though I can't imagine what Hugh and the others would say about having a stepmama younger than theirselves! I reckon she'd be wasted on the old man."

"She's not like to wed him!"

"And I'm saying she's not got much choice. Ma's that set on getting her out of the house. What's the girl to be doing? Sure, there's a few lads with an eye on her, but their folks would never be letting their boys marry her. Besides, she needs a man, not a raw lad. I reckon, if you've a mind to have her, there's naught to stop you. She's only a woman, after all, and I never seen any woman get the better of you yet."

Having accomplished his mission, Fergus drank up and said, "I'll be on me way. Think on it, Brendan."

He did, though not for long. He gulped down his whiskey, and left the inn.

Brendan paused outside the O'Shaughnessy house. So Mary was finding Rowena a handful, was she? He chuckled. No doubt the old witch had sent Fergus to tempt him with the prospect of having Rowena. If the old besom was right about the girl, then he'd be grateful for her scheming.

He caught a movement out of the corner of his eye. Surely that was Rowena, strolling along the riverbank! Luck was with him tonight!

Rowena was pondering her future. She could not stay in her father's house much longer, much as she would hate to leave Brigid and Gwyn to Mary's mercy. Indeed, the girls might be better off without her, for was it not her presence that usually provoked the strife in the household? Was it not she whom Mary was determined to be rid of?

Rowena had been astounded when Mary had informed them at supper of Alec Darcy's interest in her.

Patrick had said, "Alec's a fine man and all, but he's too old for the lass."

"Sure, there's no such thing as a man being too old!" Mary had said. "Alec has need of a wife. Mind, she'd not be getting the farm when he's gone -- that goes to Hugh and Shelagh, and the other boys -- but she'd have a good life till then. He's a generous man, is Alec Darcy."

"How dare you try to arrange a match for me!" Rowena had cried.

"If you can't manage it on your own, then 'tis left to me to do it for you. Or are you expecting to burden your Da and me with your keep for the rest of your born days? A girl your age should be managing a house of her own. If a fledgling don't leave the nest on its own, then it's got to be pushed out. And since there's not much chance of a lad wanting a girl like you to take to wife, you should be thanking the Lord that a decent, respected man like Alec Darcy's even willing to consider you!"

Despite the cruelty of these words, Rowena knew that there was a measure of truth in them. But marriage was not her only alternative. She would seek a job. She would ask Margaret and Simon Worthing, or Father Killeny for help, for surely they would know of someone in need of live-in help.

And if all else failed, she would swallow her damned pride and go to Jeremy Launston!

The dewy grass muffled Brendan's step. Rowena was startled when strong hands bracketed her shoulders.

"You gave me a fright!" she said, turning to face him.

"You shouldn't be out here alone, mavourneen."

"Sure, why not? I was safer alone than I am now."

Brendan chuckled. "You're a darlin', Rowena!"

"We've naught to say to one another, Brendan, so leave me in peace."

"You're wrong there." They could see one another quite clearly in the moonlight. "I want you to marry me."

Rowena was dumbfounded. She moved away from him angrily. "Then 'tis truly daft you are!"

"Maybe, but I still want you."

"And do you think I'd wed you after...?"

"Didn't I already explain that to you?" He moved toward her. "I'd not have let them harm you, Rowena."

"They did! And you encouraged them!" Rowena kept backing away from him until she stood on the edge of the bank.

"I admit I was a mite mad. It was the jealousy... seeing you jump up in front of the lot of them, defending your... your lover!" He spat out the final word as though it had burned his tongue.

"My what? You mean you still believe that Jeremy Launston... and I...?"

"You'll not be denying it!"

"Aye! Adrian Launston's the father of my child, whether you choose to believe that or no."

"Is that the truth, Rowena?" He took her by the shoulders as though he would shake the words from her.

She just glared at him.

And he was relieved. It was a dead man he had to contend with, the shadow of that sickly boy. He wanted to laugh aloud. He'd soon have Adrian routed from her mind! "I'm sorry, Rowena... about everything. A man sometimes does unforgivable things to the woman he loves." He spoke quietly, ruefully.

Rowena was disconcerted by this suddenly serious confession. She wanted to get away, but Brendan stopped her. "You'll be falling into the river if you step back any more. Am I so fearsome then?"

"Nay."

"Rowena... you and me, we're both needing someone. I've me own house, but 'tis a lonesome, empty place. Sometimes, of an evening when I'm sitting by the fire, I think of you sharing it with me. Will you?"

He was seductively gentle now, and Rowena was tempted. "I... What about me son?"

"I'd treat him like me own."

"I... don't know."

"Is it persuading you need?" The jesting lightness was back in his voice. He took her into his arms and kissed her.

Rowena was surprised by her response to him. It felt good to be wanted, to be embraced, to feel her senses come alive again.

Brendan laughed softly. "I was right about you, mavourneen. You're a passionate woman, and 'twould be a pity for you to wither away in your father's house. A woman like you was made to be loved."

"But it wouldn't be right, Brendan." She drew away from him. "I don't love you. Nor could I promise that I ever would."

The regret in her voice encouraged him. "Sure, we could be happy anyway! We've nothing to lose, you and I, but everything to gain. Don't turn me away again, Rowena. We'll be good for each other." He pulled her into his arms again. Tenderly he held her, stroking her back until he felt her relax against him. "I need you, Rowena. Let me love you."

God knows, she wanted to be loved, to feel needed! And though she knew him to be temperamental, unpredictable even, she thought that perhaps they could be happy together. After all, could her life be any worse than it was now?

Chapter 28

Rowena's wedding day dawned bright and misty and exceptionally warm for late October. Mary made the usual superstitious comment about it being a good omen, but Rowena was not convinced. To her it was autumn masquerading as summer -- a day of unfulfilled hopes and false promises. And so it proved to be, for by the time she was ready to leave for the church, grey clouds were congregating overhead, obscuring the sun, and a chilling wind was chasing the last of the leaves before it.

Rowena quivered with apprehension as Moira fussed about her, babbling excitedly. She had vacillated between happiness and fear, certainty and doubt, ever since she had accepted Brendan's proposal. Now that the moment to speak her vows was almost upon her, she was convinced she was doing the wrong thing. It was as if she had just awakened from a disturbing dream to find it was too horrifyingly real after all. She tried to quell the panic rising within her.

What had possessed her to agree to this lunacy? How could she marry a man she did not love? All her doubts returned, and Rowena sank onto the edge of the bed, stunned by the onslaught. "I can't do it," she whispered.

Moira, who still chatted though no one listened, did not hear her. "Oh, Rena, do stand up. You don't want to crumple that beautiful dress." Moira looked enviously at Rowena's blue silk gown with its trim of beading, and thought her sister a lucky woman indeed to have landed Brendan. Not that she, Moira, would have wed him! Brendan frightened her with his intensity, his air of animal vitality, so unlike her easygoing, gentle Conn. But just look at what Brendan had already done for Rowena's sake. He had increased the mortgage on his property with Mr. Sam, so that he could buy new furnishings -- a big, sturdy bed among them, the men had jested -- as well as a trousseau for his bride that was coveted by nearly every woman in Launston Mills.

Rowena rose from the bed and began pacing about the tiny room that was her father's -- and Mary's -- bedchamber. She pressed her hands together as if in prayer, and held them to her lips. "I can't do it," she repeated, loud enough for Moira to hear her this time.

Moira looked shocked. "What is it you're saying, Rena?"

"I can't marry him, Moira," Rowena said with desperation. "I don't love him. Sure, I don't even like him sometimes! Holy Mother of God, what could I have been thinking of?"

"Sure, 'tis just wedding nerves," Moira tried to reassure her. Suddenly, she wanted more than anything for Rowena to be married. Moira thought her sister would be less of a threat to her own marriage if she were safely wed to another. And then she and Rowena could once again be friends and companions.

Rowena was shaking her head to deny Moira's words. "Sure, Brendan must love you, Rena. He's been treating you like royalty these last weeks."

"But the point is that I don't love him, and I can't see spending the rest of me life with him." She shuddered as if someone had walked over her grave.

"Sure you can't stop it all now! Not after all the trouble everyone's taken! Not with folk awaiting you in the church this very minute!" Moira was growing angry. How typical of Rowena to cause problems, to dramatize everything, to think only of herself! Shelagh Darcy was so right about her sister.

There was a knock on the door, and Patrick called, "We ought to be setting out for the church, Rena."

"She'll be ready in a minute, Da," Moira answered.

There was a scared-rabbit look in Rowena's eyes as she mutely appealed to Moira to understand and help.

Almost coldly, Moira said. "Sure, what choice do you have, Rena? Do you think you'll be welcome ***here*** forever? Do you think you'll ever be able to hold your head up in this town again if you leave Brendan standing like a fool at the altar?"

Rowena's shoulders sagged as if she could not bear the weight of that truth, or the defeat that it engendered. But, of course, Moira was right. It was too late to stop that inexorable machine that she had set in motion weeks ago with those few simple words that Brendan had coaxed from her. As Mary would say, she had made her bed and now she must lie in it.

She took a deep breath to steady her pounding heart, straightened her shoulders, and stepped into the outer room.

"You look beautiful, lass," Patrick said with pride, and more than a little awe. With her flushed cheeks and that soulful look in her eyes, she was indeed ravishing.

Rowena glanced once more about the home she was leaving behind her, though she had left it long ago in spirit. She answered her father's broad grin with a tentative smile, and took his outstretched arm. In silence they drove to the church in the carriage that Brendan had hired from the livery stable.

Trance-like she drifted up the aisle, aware of the many eyes staring at her, though it was Brendan's riveting gaze that drew her forward. How handsome he looked today in his new suit, his clean-shaven face glowing with triumph and excitement. And then she was beside him, smiling hopefully at him, thinking that perhaps everything would work out after all. Father Killeny's eyes seemed to question her and allow her this one last chance to change her mind. But she had not the courage. The voice that promised to love, honour, and obey seemed not her own.

Her inner turmoil was not evident to the audience, however. To them she was the epitome of the radiant bride. To Shelagh Darcy she was the luckiest woman in the world.

Shelagh said as much to her sister-in-law, Moira, at the reception in Paxtons' ballroom. Brendan was bubbling over with goodwill, dancing exuberantly with all the ladies, matching the men in their drinks to his health, throwing his head back in full-throated laughter at the slightest joke.

"Sure, at least ***he***'s pleased with the match," Moira replied. "I wonder if Rowena is any easier about it, now 'tis done."

"Sure, you're not saying she thought to jilt him?"

"As near as," Moira said, glad to be able to talk to someone about it. She did not consider herself disloyal discussing Rowena with Shelagh, since Shelagh was 'family' and the two girls got on rather well. And truth to tell, Moira enjoyed a sympathetic ear on the subject of her eldest sister. Being able to deride Rowena gave Moira a sense of moral superiority and some badly needed self-confidence.

"She has a nerve!" Shelagh said angrily. "Does she think herself too good for the likes of him them?"

"I reckon she doesn't know when she's well off. There aren't many men who would marry a woman with a... a..."

"Aye, a bastard he is, though you're too polite to spit it out, Moira."

"He's still me nephew, and she's me sister for all that," Moira said hastily, guilt creeping in to temper her tongue.

They were distracted by the tardy arrival of two guests. There was a momentary hush as Malcolm Grimsby and his wife entered the room.

Shelagh gazed at her other sister-in-law, Maureen Grimsby, and snorted. "Now there's one who really has got too big for her boots! Even Hugh finds her a pain in the arse, and, believe me, it takes a lot to rile him up!"

Maureen Darcy had captured Malcolm's heart the previous summer, when she had nursed him back to health during the ague epidemic. She had been his angel of mercy -- a strong, buxom, good looking girl who could dispense with the household chores with ease and still look lovely and fresh enough to tempt a man to keep to his bed... and invite her to share it with him. She had been more than willing.

Maureen Grimsby was dressed in the most exquisite gown that Moira had ever seen. Even Harriet Launston did not deck herself out so ostentatiously. Maureen and Malcolm went often to the city, and she was always full of stories about lavish living, describing in boring detail the expensive hotels, the various entertainments to which they were invited, and the latest fashions as exhibited by the upper classes.

"'Tisn't right, her showing up dressed like that!" Moira said indignantly. "Stealing the thunder from the bride, that is, and unworthy of her. Sure, weren't she and Rowena the best of friends once?" Moira was not aware of her own inconsistency toward her sister -- condemning her one minute, and defending her the next.

Rowena, however, did not mind Maureen's attempt to outshine her. She wanted only for this day to end. Her earlier tension had sapped her strength. Now that the actual ceremony was over and she was no longer Rowena O'Shaughnessy, but Mrs. Brendan Delaney, she felt curiously detached from herself and all this merriment surrounding her. She wanted only to seek her bed. But the realization that she would certainly not be left in peace then brought the colour flooding to her cheeks. She was an innocent in the matters of the flesh, a virtual virgin, for her one sexual encounter, though it had given her Keir, had not given her much experience of physical love. The thought that Brendan would do what Adrian had so gently and lovingly done suddenly frightened her. She stepped a bit more gaily with her partner, smiled more sincerely, and was determined to stay here as long as possible.

Gwyn, realizing that all the members of her family were preoccupied, took the opportunity to slip from the room. She knew that Cormac Muldoon had seen her and would follow momentarily, and once again she experienced that new-found thrill of power.

Gwyn spent a lot of time at the Muldoons, in whose large, disorderly household she felt at ease. She had become aware that sixteen year old Cormac's eyes were often upon her. Her body had been reshaping itself into a womanly form so that she looked older than her fourteen years, and she had seen Cormac's eyes straying often to her bosom. He had practically licked his lips in anticipation. So she had let him brush against her breasts, and had allowed his hand to rest a trifle too long upon her buttocks. And she had felt heady with the realization that she could arouse him at her whim.

She laughed when Cormac joined her outside the inn a few moments later. "Sure, are you following me, Cormac Muldoon?" she said coquettishly. Giggling, she turned and ran toward the riverbank. Cormac caught her just as they reached the trees near the edge of the embankment. He spun her around and pulled her roughly into his arms. She could smell the whiskey on his breath when his wet lips came down on hers. Clumsily he fumbled at her dress and finally managed to free her breasts. His groan of pleasure as he greedily sucked her nipples made her chuckle. But when Cormac's big, callused hand began fumbling under her skirts, she decided she had allowed him enough liberties. She tried to push him away, but he gripped her tighter, and the groping hand became more insistent.

"Cormac! Stop it!" she said, struggling to get out of his bone-crushing hold.

He threw her to the ground, momentarily winding her. Then his six foot bulk came down heavily on top of her. She tried to scream, but a grubby hand covered her mouth and nose so firmly that she felt she was suffocating, and a moment later his engorged manhood ripped into her. A primitive, guttural cry issued from him as his seed pumped into her.

"Jaysus!" he said, rolling off her, shocked by what he had done. "Sweet Jaysus, Gwyn, I never meant to do that." Realizing the enormity of his act, he became frightened. Rape was punishable by hanging. "Don't tell, Gwyn. Swear you won't tell anyone!"

Who was there to tell, Gwyn wondered as she cleaned herself up and straightened her dress. She had never felt particularly close to her father, and since his marriage to Mary he seemed even more inaccessible. Mary would just say she'd got what she'd asked for, and probably punish her as well. Rowena could do nothing. Moira would not want to know. She wouldn't tell Father Killeny. She figured the church had no business prying into people's private affairs, forever condemning them for their inherent human frailty. And she was too ashamed to tell the good doctor.

Though she was aching from the assault of Cormac's unbridled passion, she suddenly realized that she could take advantage of that potent instinct. After all, men were going to stick it into you whether you wanted it or not. You might as well gain something from it. And she swore to herself that no man would ever have her again without a price.

She knew how to prevent herself from getting pregnant, for she had overheard her mother and Rowena discuss those potent herbs often enough. Sure, they'd thought she took no interest, nor ever listened to their talk, but she'd always taken note -- and remembered those things that were important to her.

When she had finished brushing the leaves from her skirt, she turned to the flustered lad beside her and fixed him with a cold stare. "You don't touch me again, Cormac Muldoon. Not until I see your money."

She marched back to the inn, leaving Cormac totally bewildered.

Gwyn returned to the noisy assembly; it seemed that no one had missed her. Brendan grabbed her for a dance, and discreetly pulled a weed stem from her curls. "And what have you been up to -- or down to -- miss?" he asked wryly.

"Sure, wouldn't you like to be knowing!" She favoured him with one of her come-hither smiles.

"You'd best watch yourself, brat, or you'll be getting more than you bargained for."

"Oh, I'm not so sure about that," she countered brazenly.

By Jaysus, the little red-haired minx was trying her wiles on him! He only just became aware of how much she had developed lately. Gwyn, having lost her baby fat, was turning into quite a looker. There was a sensual plumpness about her -- no sharp angles, no jutting bones at the wrists or knuckles or shoulders, just a soft, smooth, dimpled roundness. His smile belied his words as he said in a low voice, "If ever I catch you playing the whore again, me girl, I'll tan your backside!"

Gwyn laughed slyly. "Aye. And then what'll you do?" She slipped away from him before he could reply.

Though he'd never admit it, Brendan felt his blood stirred, and decided it was time to take his new wife home. Besides, he was disturbed by what Shelagh Darcy had told him when he'd danced with her a few minutes earlier. Though he knew her to be a jealous bitch, he had sensed the truth of her words. She had been so confident. So disdainful. Brendan had jumped to Rowena's defence.

But when they were finally alone in their bedchamber some time later, he confronted her with it. "I heard you nearly didn't make it to the church today," he said as he climbed into bed beside her.

Rowena, who had been nervously dreading what was to come, was taken aback by this question. "Who told you that?"

"'Tisn't important. I just want to know whether 'tis true." He pulled her close and began placing gentle kisses upon her face. "Hm?"

She knew that her answer might be critical in establishing their relationship, and that it was too late to tell the truth. "Sure 'twas just nerves. 'Tis...." He stopped her words with a lingering kiss.

"No regrets then?" he asked as his lips travelled down her throat.

"Nay," she whispered, feeling herself to be a terrible liar. But Brendan seemed determined to make her admit... what? Her gratitude? Her happiness?

He laughed aloud. "By Jaysus, but I've waited a long time to hear you say that!"

He had intended to take her slowly, arousing her to his own fevered pitch, and then showing her how a man pleased a woman. But he had been anticipating this for years, and could not delay his need of her. Afterwards he quickly fell into an exhausted sleep.

Rowena lay awake for a long time, listening to the icy wind howling about the cabin. She felt curiously disappointed that Brendan slept, and pleased that the time for doubt and decision was passed. Intimacy with Brendan was not repugnant to her as she had feared it would be. In fact she had begun to enjoy it, when it had ended too abruptly. For the first time she felt cautiously optimistic about this marriage. She snuggled closer to Brendan, and he automatically encircled her with his arm.

Chapter 29

"You really oughtn't to be going, Rena," Moira said worriedly.

"I can take care of meself. Sure, I don't know what all the fuss is about! You'd think wild animals were roaming the streets, the way people talk."

"If you listened to what Conn's had to say, you might be thinking so yourself. Drunk and brawling in the streets, they are. I've been keeping me doors locked day and night. You know that Mary found four of them sleeping in the byre this morning....."

"And a fierce lot they were, to be sure!" Rowena said with a grin, for Mary had easily driven off the trespassers with a few swipes of her broom and a tongue-lashing. "Where do you think all those men can be finding beds? The inns are overflowing, and there's few folk who will open their doors to the fellows for fear of being robbed or murdered. But don't you reckon they're just ordinary men with families of their own, with nary a horn nor a forked tail among them?"

This past week had certainly been an unusual one in Launston Mills, for it was the first time an election had been held in the town. Previously, the men of Ops had had to travel up to thirty miles to vote. This time the town played host to the hundreds of eligible voters in the district. Since the voting was a week-long event, many had come and gone unobtrusively. But a large number had stayed to await the outcome of this crucial election -- to be announced later that day.

The Rebellions of 1837 -- led by Mackenzie in Upper Canada and Papineau in Lower Canada -- had not been complete failures, Rowena thought. Although they had not succeeded in their immediate aims, these uprisings had alerted the British government to the need for more responsible government in the colony. Upper Canada was now known as Canada West, and politically united with Quebec, now Canada East. Toronto was no longer the seat of government; so the power and influence of the hated Family Compact was curbed.

Rowena wondered what Donal would make of it all, although she suspected that even these measures would not satisfy him. Of course, he had long since given up the Hunter's Lodge and its futile raids on the Canadian border towns. He and Rosemary Flannery had married and settled outside of Boston. Donal confided, in infrequent letters, that he sometimes longed to go west, away from the old established areas with their entrenched ideas and structured society. He wrote of freedom and opportunity, and how any ambitious and clever man could become wealthy, no matter how humble his beginnings. She suspected that Donal was still restless, still searching, although Rosemary and his young son would undoubtedly keep a rein on his impulsiveness. Still, Donal would have found all this activity and political fervour in Launston Mills stimulating.

This was the first election for the new parliament. The Tory candidate, a wealthy Torontonian related to the Family Compact, had represented the district for the past fifteen years. Apparently, he was resorting to his usual tactics -- free whiskey for all who supported him, and a cracked skull for those who didn't. The Tories maintained that the Reform candidate was a blackguard of the worst kind, who had threatened to sue all the small landowners in his debt, if they and their friends did not vote for him. He, too, had barrels of free whiskey for his supporters, and was rumored to be buying votes outright at a dollar apiece.

"Brendan will be none too pleased when he finds out you disobeyed him," Moira said as Rowena tied on her bonnet.

"Aye, but he'll be having a lot more to say if there's no sugar for his tea tomorrow."

"I'll lend you some!"

"I've been stuck in the house for a week now, and I've a mind to stroll into town."

Moira looked suspiciously at her sister, "You're not thinking to go up to the green?"

"Seeing as how I'll be close by, I might just take a wee gander at what's happening. I've never seen an election before. Don't look so afeard, Moira. 'Tis only teasing I am!"

Keir was playing with his cousin, Tim, who had just turned a year old. Rowena kissed her son and ordered him to behave while she was gone.

Spring was upon them again, and Rowena squelched along the muddy road, skirting the puddles where possible, and carefully wading through those that were unavoidable. These last few warm days and nights had caused rapid melting of the snow and ice. The river was already spilling over its banks, though the dam was wide open, and many a riverside dweller watched anxiously as floodwaters crept daily, sometimes hourly, nearer their homes. The bridge was in imminent danger of being swept away along with the other flotsam which the waters had garnered on their downward journey. It was only ever in spring that the river displayed such energy, and then its power was awesome. Massive ice flows carried along by the swift, swirling water careened into the opposite bank where the river curved sharply, snapping small trees and low-hanging branches. Sometimes whole trees were uprooted and tossed like twigs upon the water.

Rowena felt great sympathy for the many men who had long and treacherous journeys before them yet this day and the morrow. April was undeniably the worst month for travelling, as roads became bogs, or disappeared entirely, and shallow creeks became raging torrents.

As she had expected, Rowena met not one stranger on her way into town. Main Street, however, presented quite a different picture. It was packed with men, some in various stages of inebriation. There were scuffles in progress -- shoving matches, name-calling, fisticuffs, and the like -- near the common, where the large voting platform was situated. Those who voted were obliged to mount this podium, state their names and the candidate whom they supported, to the jeers or cheers of the attendant crowd. There was understandably a great reluctance to do so, for many felt the disapproval of whichever faction had not won their votes. Thus, men banded together for their own protection, each voting in turn, defying the bullyboys and overly zealous partisans who would be loathe to tackle twenty or more men at a time.

There was a slow migration to the common now, since the results were soon to be announced. There was not much work being done this day, for the men took their politics seriously, and even the foundry had closed for the afternoon, the owner as anxious as his workers to witness the outcome of this close race.

Despite her assurance to Moira, Rowena had been tempted to wander discreetly over to the polling area. But no longer. She could sense the tension in the air, could feel the belligerence of the whiskey-fueled men. She would be surprised if there was not some violence done, no matter the outcome of the election. And she was suddenly afraid for Brendan, who could never keep clear of a scrap.

She intended to go into Lindsays', purchase the few items she required, and hurry home. But just then she saw something that both angered and upset her.

There was Gwyn, walking bold-as-you-please like some cheap tart, arm in arm with a stranger. Without hesitation, Rowena hitched her skirts higher and attempted to run after them. Gwyn and her escort were a block ahead of her, and though they made slow progress, Rowena discovered that she could not go much faster herself. The mud was like molasses underfoot, and Rowena nearly toppled into it twice before resigning herself to a walk.

She stepped onto the plank sidewalks and shop-front stoops wherever she could, but men sprawled or loitered everywhere, and impeded her progress nearly as effectively as the mud had. She jostled them aside with little ceremony, until one young man -- a well-to-do bloke by the cut of his clothes -- grabbed her as she attempted to push past him, and said with a laugh, "Why such haste, my pretty? If it's a companion you seek, you need look no further. I am at your service!"

His friends laughed appreciatively at this ribald insinuation. They were all a bit the worse for drink.

Rowena ignored the remark and tried to press on, but the young man had a firm grip on her arm, and continued to bait her for the amusement of his friends. "I've a cozy room at the inn here. You'll find no better bed, nor companion with whom to share it, I guarantee it."

"I'll thank you to unhand me, sir," Rowena said with icy calm.

The men's laughter attracted the attention of Jeremy Launston, who was riding by on his way to the common. He quickly grasped the situation, and felt anger rise within him. What in God's name was that fool girl doing out on the street today? He edged his horse through the crowd toward the sidewalk.

Rowena was becoming increasingly annoyed with the persistent young jester. She was certain he meant her no harm, that he was merely having a bit of sport with her, but she had no time for this buffoonery. She had already lost sight of Gwyn, and her anxiety was mounting. Well, there was only one way to shake off this pup without creating a scene that would draw even more attention to herself.

She smiled and looked coyly at the young dandy. "I know just what it is you're needing."

"Indeed?" he said, his eyes lighting with interest.

She drew him to the edge of the plank walk, as though wanting to impart her information in private. Before he knew what had happened, she had given him a hefty shove that had sent him flying backwards into a conveniently large puddle on the road.

Jeremy smiled, amused by the way Rowena had so deftly extricated herself from that situation. But she should not be out here at all, exposing herself not only to similar indignities, but to potential danger.

Tempers had been running high all week. Simon Worthing had had a steady stream of patients requiring stitching, bandaging, and the setting of broken bones. Numerous assault charges had been laid. But Jeremy suspected that the worst was yet to come. He had to warn Rowena, even if she did not welcome his advice.

Damn it! He was losing her! She had nearly reached the common, and he could not spur his horse forward in this press of bodies.

Rowena spotted Gwyn no more than ten yards ahead of her. She forged a way through the crowd, her mind already teeming with the angry words she had to say to her sister.

She saw Brendan at the same moment that he noticed her. His face darkened, and she was thankful that he was too far away to admonish her. She had no intention of leaving without Gwyn. As she fought her way through the noisy crowd, she paid no attention to what was happening around her. She was surprised when the men suddenly fell silent. Faintly she heard the announcement that the Reform candidate had won. Then there was only a roar. And a sudden heaving and swaying of the mob like some great, swelling breaker racing to dash itself upon the rocks.

A moment later she no longer knew where Gwyn or Brendan was. She was wedged so tightly in the crowd that she could hardly breathe. The mud tugged at her feet, reluctant to release her, yet the mob kept pressing, pushing her onward, forcing her first this way and then that. Suddenly there was a rift beside her, with no one to brace her. She screamed then, certain that she would be pushed to the ground and trampled. So great was her terror, that she was not even aware that the force of the crowd had lessened, or that she was clinging for dear life to the man next to her, until he shook her off.

Strong arms grabbed her and pulled her from the melee that erupted all around. She gazed up at Jeremy Launston for a moment without recognition. She did not even protest as he lifted her and set her upon his horse, and then swung up behind her.

She stared with an almost detached indifference at the scene of violence spread before her. It was not until Jeremy had urged his horse away from the fighting that her senses returned to her.

"My sister! Gwyn, she's back there!"

"Then let us hope that she had enough sense to get clear of the brawl."

"Let me down! I must go back!" She tried to slide off the horse, but Jeremy held her firmly within the circle of his arms.

"It's too dangerous for us to return there, Rowena. Be sensible, woman! You cannot help your sister now."

She went limp in his arms. Her fright of only a few minutes before had drained her. Jeremy was right, and, in truth, she had no desire to return. They were heading down a sideroad, which ran parallel to Main Street, and though the fighting was a block away, she could hear it all too well. How incongruous those destructive noises were with the deserted silence of this road. She thought fleetingly of Brendan, hoping that he would not be hurt, and suspected that Gwyn's 'escort' would see to her well-being.

Yet none of that seemed real to her at that moment. Only she and Jeremy, the horse beneath them, this empty street existed. And for an insane moment, it was all she desired. She turned to look at Jeremy, and saw in his eyes what must have been in her own. His arms tightened about her. She closed her eyes as his parted lips met hers.

The very core of her being seemed to melt. Had they been anywhere but on a horse in the middle of a public street, Rowena could not say what might have happened then.

The barking of a dog nearby brought her rudely to her senses. She drew away from Jeremy with a start, and stared at him, incredulous. She turned her head to hide the blush of shame that burnt her cheeks

"I... I'm sorry, Rowena." Jeremy was as appalled at what had just occurred, as he was with himself for wishing it had never ended. What was it about this girl that could so inflame him, and make him behave like some callow youth?

But Rowena's response to his embrace had not been that of a demure, happily married woman. It had surprised and disturbed him more than a little when he had learned of her marriage to Brendan. Delaney was the last man he would have wished upon her. He had persuaded himself, however, that it was none of his concern. Yet, suddenly, it was very important to him.

"Rowena, are you happy with Brendan?"

"He's been good to me," she replied, and before he could say anything else, she added, "I can walk from here."

They had arrived at Lindsay Street. "I'll see you safely across Main Street," Jeremy said, as they rounded the corner by the Catholic church.

The skirmish was moving down Main Street. Men battered one another with fists, bludgeons, and whatever came to hand.

Store windows were shattered as stray projectiles, and sometimes even a man, crashed through them. It was nothing short of a riot. The sheriff and his two constables were powerless to stop it. Since many of the local militia were among the rioters, there was absolutely nothing that could be done.

Jeremy stopped his horse in front of Paxtons'. Rowena slid off before he could dismount to help her alight. Still she could not face him. "Thank you for... helping me."

"I trust you will have enough sense to keep away from men's affairs in future," Jeremy replied somewhat coldly.

She nodded and hastened away.

Rowena did not stop at Moira's. Briefly she told her sister of the riot as she dressed Keir, and then went home, leaving Moira bewildered by her abrupt manner and departure.

Rowena's thoughts and emotions were in a turmoil as she prepared supper. She fed Keir and put him to bed early. She paced and fretted as she awaited Brendan.

What had happened to her this afternoon to make her behave with such impropriety? She had invited that kiss like some... Oh, God! Was she addled?

She had been contented enough caring for Brendan, even looked forward to his coming home in the evenings, when he would entertain her with amusing gossip. There had been happy times during the eighteen months of their marriage. Evenings when Conn and Moira, Fergus and his wife, and sometimes Sean and his family had joined them, and they'd talked and laughed, even danced. Brendan's ballads were always popular, and it was at those times, when his lilting voice touched her soul, that she thought she could love him.

In bed he took his pleasure of her, and though his lovemaking aroused her, it did not fulfill her. But she had thought that unimportant. After all, lust was one of the seven deadly sins.

Yet was that not what she had felt in Jeremy's arms?

Thou shalt not commit adultery: But I say unto you, That whosoever looketh on a woman to lust after her hath committed adultery with her already in his heart.

She jumped guiltily when the door opened, but her apprehensions at facing Brendan disappeared when she saw him. His face was bloodied, his clothes torn. She rushed to his side. "Are you alright?""

He waved her away, and sat down heavily in the chair by the fire. Rowena rinsed a cloth in water and began cleansing his cuts.

Brendan said nothing as she ministered to him, but his eyes never left her. She could feel them burrowing into her, trying to violate her deepest thoughts. Her initial concern for him receded now that she realized he was not seriously injured, and the guilt seeped back.

"What were you doing there when I told you to keep to the house?" Brendan demanded. He wondered if she had any idea of how he had worried about her safety when the fighting had started. Until he had seen her ride off with Launston. By Jaysus, but then his rage had returned tenfold! The poor bugger whose face he had smashed would never know that he had Jeremy Launston to blame for his pains. His fists bunched when he saw the colour rise in her cheeks.

"I know now I shouldn't have gone into town." She spoke quickly, breathlessly. "'Twas only a bit of sugar I was after getting. Sure, I'd never have gone near the common if it hadn't been for Gwyn."

"Gwyn? And what's she got to do with your disobeying me? Leave that be!" he ordered, pushing her hand away from his face. "And look at me when I'm talking to you!"

She put the cloth down. "I saw Gwyn walking with a man. A stranger."

"Not for the first time."

She was puzzled. "What is it you're saying?"

"That your little sister's got herself quite the reputation for being obliging to men."

"'Tis never the truth! She's only sixteen! She's...."

"'Tis true, lass," Brendan said quietly. "I'd never be saying it if I didn't know it for a fact."

"Maybe I did wrong by her after Ma died," Rowena said sorrowfully.

It wasn't right, Brendan thought, that Rowena should feel such anguish over that worthless little chit. He wanted to assure her of that. Yet he still raged within at the memory of Rowena with Jeremy Launston, and his desire to hurt her had not abated.

"I reckon you weren't the best example for Gwyn." The shaft struck home, but gave him no pleasure. Nor did it alleviate his own anguish. He wanted to strike at her still, with blows as well as words, though each would wound him as much as her. Yet would that pain not be preferable to this jealousy that consumed him?

He grabbed her arm and pulled her closer to him. "Were you any better than your sister today, going off with Jeremy Launston like that?"

That caused her to wince. What right had she to judge and condemn Gwyn when she had committed the even greater sin of adultery -- no matter if only in her heart?

"Jeremy was only helping me get away...."

"***Jeremy***, is it?" He pushed her away from him. She should have been indignant, as she always was when she felt she had been wronged. But her pleading manner convinced him that she had something to hide, and suddenly he wanted to know no more. Perhaps he already suspected that he had lost her. He had been so certain that, given time, she would come to love him, as he did her.

"Brendan, I...."

He rose abruptly. "I'm going out for a drink."

"Your dinner...."

"I'll not be wanting anything."

She was disturbed by his sudden departure, and no less by his melancholic demeanor. She had wounded him somehow. Could he possibly have guessed the treachery of her heart?

She wanted to go after him, to somehow make amends, ease his pain, assure him.... Of what? that she loved him as a wife ought, as he deserved? Had she not already practiced enough deceit?

She should never have married him. She had used him selfishly to assuage her loneliness. Her very vows before God had been a mockery -- promising that she would love when her heart had been empty.

She had much to answer for in this life.

Brendan had not yet returned when she went to bed, and she tossed restlessly, her mind troubled, her spirits low. She missed Brendan's comforting presence.

Rowena was asleep when Brendan staggered in. Her slumber was one of exhaustion, and she did not awaken. The candle still burned on the stand next to the bed. He stared at her for a long time in the dim light. How virtuous she looked in her sleep, her pale brow as untroubled as a child's.

He did not know what there had been between Rowena and Jeremy, but he swore that no man would ever cuckold him! She was still his.

• • •

"Have you seen the mess downtown then?" Mary asked Rowena the following morning as she stopped by. "A right shambles it is!" She removed the shawl from her head before sinking into a kitchen chair.

That meant she wasn't planning to stay long, Rowena thought. Otherwise Mary would have taken the rocker by the fire. Ever since Rowena had married and moved out of her father's house, Mary had reverted to her old relationship with her -- casual and friendly, yet never hesitating to criticize or to offer advice, even when none was sought. It was as if all those harsh words had never been spoken between them.

"Now, Rowena, have you seen Gwyn?" Mary asked with a worried frown.

Rowena's heart lurched. "Not since yesterday. I..." But she couldn't tell Mary that she had seen her sister with a strange man.

Mary shook her head. "I did try with her, Rowena. Sure, didn't I tell her, just as I did me own girls, that a woman oughtn't to be too free with her favours? But would she listen?"

Rowena felt anger igniting within her. No matter how true Mary's words might be -- for hadn't Brendan told her as much yesterday -- hearing it from Mary's smug lips was hard to bear.

"She never came home yesterday," Mary said. "Hugh told Fergus he'd seen Gwyn going off with a stranger."

"What? You mean she's run away?"

"'Tis what we're after thinking, your father and me."

And that pleases you just fine, Rowena thought. She could imagine how Mary would spread the news through the town. *Sure, didn't I warn him? Didn't I try my best with her?*

"Is Da going to look for her?"

"Ah sure, what's the point? They'll be long gone now."

"But something's got to be done! We'll tell the sheriff. What if something's happened to her? She's only sixteen."

"And more worldly-wise than the pair of us! Aye, and you needn't look at me like that, Miss! Sure I know it galls you that I was right about her, but don't be so stupid that you won't hear the truth! It was Fergus and Conn told me that Gwyn's gotten herself a reputation. And you take my meaning -- or do I have to spell it out for you?" Mary said with asperity. "There's only so much a parent can do for a child. Sure, you'll be finding that out some day! Gwyn's old enough to make her own decisions. If she chooses to make bad ones, then on her head be it. The rest of us are not to blame!"

You could have been kinder, more understanding, Rowena wanted to say, but knew that those words applied as much to her as to Mary. Gwyn had always been a difficult child, even with Deirdre. So could Rowena really blame Mary for Gwyn's rebelliousness?

Seeing her consternation, Mary said, "And don't you go blaming yourself, neither. You didn't have it easy after your ma died. 'Tis Gwyn's nature. Look at Brigid then -- a better behaved, more pious child I've never had the pleasure of knowing! Maybe you can take some of the credit for that, but mostly 'tis the way God made her."

Mary's solicitous attitude doused Rowena's ire. Mary was right, of course. Rowena said, "I'm worried about Gwyn."

"Sure, she won't be wasting any thoughts on us! She's strong, Rowena. And she knows her own mind."

"Do you think she'll come back?"

"I reckon she's got too much pride to do that, no matter what happens."

When Mary had gone, Rowena sat in sad contemplation by the fire. Had she been so wrapped up in herself that she had seen none of the signs of Gwyn's waywardness? She ***had*** noticed that some of her herbs were missing, particularly the abortifacients, and had thought she'd merely been forgetful. That had been soon after Gwyn had stayed to look after Keir one evening. But how did Gwyn know about those medicines?

That Gwyn might have been absorbing all she'd heard Rowena and Deirdre discuss suddenly seemed all too plausible to Rowena. Gwyn had always been an opportunist. And she'd always demanded good, tangible, earthly rewards. She'd only scoffed at promises of heavenly dues or threats of hellish punishments. Truth to tell, Rowena couldn't imagine her dissatisfied, greedy sister settling down complacently to a life as wife and mother unless she had a houseful of servants to command.

If Gwyn had been a boy, she might very well have gone out into the world and done something significant, even great. But what could she do as a woman?

Chapter 30

Gwyn O'Shaughnessy stared with envy at the fashionably dressed ladies and gentlemen who paraded about the racecourse. She took every opportunity to study the speech and mannerisms of the ladies, which she would imitate and practice in the privacy of her tiny room. Every nuance of inflection, every careless hand gesture was memorized with more zeal than Gwyn had ever shown for anything in her young life, for she was determined to become a lady. Or, at the very least, a highly paid courtesan.

She didn't feel too shabby in her second-hand green silk gown, and although her bonnet was not as fancy as she would have liked, it was flattering. Sometimes she was grateful for all those boring tasks her mother had set her. Though she had been a lazy seamstress as a child, she had learned the skill, and had plied her needle with enthusiasm as she had made over the cast-off dress and embellished the cheap bonnet.

Thoughts of home brought no remorse. She despised Launston Mills and would never set foot there again. Here she was in her element, strolling among the gentry, attracting the attentions of young gentlemen and dashing soldiers. She hoped she would make a good catch today, for not only was it a long walk back to her lodgings on March Street, but she was becoming increasingly impatient with her circumstances.

Her first disappointment had been James Porter, the man with whom she had left Launston Mills. What grand tales he'd told her about his land and holdings! She'd expected, at the very least, a substantial farmhouse, acres of cleared pasture land, a hundred head of cattle, and hired help. They had travelled for three days, mostly on foot, since the horse had not been sure-footed in the deep mud. Tired and begrimed, they had arrived at a small log cabin in an isolated clearing, with no neighbours for miles in any direction.

"Why are we stopping here?" she had asked.

"This is it!" he had replied proudly. "I know it's not much yet, but we're going to turn it into one hell of a farm!"

"We?"

"You and me."

"Sure, I don't recall you asking me to marry you." Although it had been exactly what she had been hoping for when she had thought him a relatively wealthy man.

"Didn't, did I? Let's just see how it goes, eh?"

She'd fumed at his cocksure presumption. "So you brought me here to be your skivvy!"

"A bit more than that," he had replied with a grin. "If we get on alright, I'll marry you." He had said that as though he would be doing her a great favour.

Because she'd had no other plan than to escape from Launston Mills, entrusting her future to this man, and because she had not known where else to go and had been too afraid to set out alone on unfamiliar roads, she had stayed. And it had been even worse than being at home. Not only had he expected her to cook and clean and wash, but also to help him with the plowing and planting. And to warm his bed every night.

He had taught her tricks in bed that she would never have imagined. At first she had been indignant that he was using her as a sexual plaything -- until she had realized that that was precisely what she was. Anyway, it had been the only entertainment there had been in their otherwise dreary weeks together. But she had not been prepared to become bound to him for life, perpetually his servant to do with as he pleased. As far as she was concerned, marriage was just a legal enslavement of women, and, unless she found a truly rich man to wed, she would never give herself into bondage. So she had decided to try her luck in Toronto. And when the pedlar had come by just a few weeks later, she had persuaded him to take her along.

She had spent two days -- and nights -- with the pedlar. He was an American, a cheerful, blunt-spoken, big-mouthed, large-hearted man, and Gwyn had enjoyed his undemanding company and his easy-going way of life. He had told her she was welcome to stay with him, and though the carefree life he had painted for her had been appealing, she had been determined to obtain the security and freedom that only wealth could ensure.

He had dropped her off on the Kingston to Toronto road which skirted the north shore of Lake Ontario. With miles of water stretching to the horizon on one side of her, and the open fields of long-settled farms on the other, Gwyn had already begun to feel free. Launston Mills had stifled her -- the ubiquitous forest had loomed about her, hemmed her in like the narrow-mindedness of the people themselves. With a few of the precious coins that she had earned from a number of Launston Mills males, she had bought a passage on a stagecoach to Toronto. Having been so close, she had not been able to delay her arrival in the city that would make her fortune.

That had been four months ago, Gwyn thought wryly, and she was no nearer her goal.

She had been entranced by the city, as wide-eyed as any country girl when she had spied the many different shops, the brick mansions that some called home, the handsome carriages whisking ladies in frothy gowns and gentlemen in stovepipe hats to some undoubtedly elegant gathering. She had marvelled at the macadamized roads, the gas lighting on the downtown streets, and the grand hotels. And she had basked in the anonymity of being one of fifteen thousand nameless faces. It mattered not what she did here; few would know, fewer still would care, and if any pointed a damning finger at her, she would not be forever branded in the eyes of others.

She had taken the cheapest room she could find, at an inn in what she soon came to realize was the least savory part of the city, not far from where she now lodged, among the streets whose very names bespoke degradation -- Deadbeat Lane, Grog Lane, Whiskey Alley.

Her biggest disappointment had been not finding a job in the establishments where she had hoped to meet eligible men. She had tried the large hotels first, only to be told that inexperienced Irish girls could be had for a 'dime a dozen', as the Americans said. The big houses had turned her away, saying they would consider only trained English servants for their staffs. The shopkeepers had taken one look at her shapeless homespun dress and work-roughened hands and declared that they hired only educated, well-spoken young women to serve their customers, although one dressmaker had offered to apprentice her as a seamstress. And her coins had been gone before the week was out. The landlord had threatened to throw her out into the gutter, but had taken her on as a serving maid in the barroom instead. The buxom, red-haired wench with the sassy tongue had increased his custom when it had become known that she could be very obliging -- for a consideration.

But the men who patronized the Butcher's Arms were rough and coarse and stingy with their brass. Gwyn had started loitering on the waterfront near the hotels, and after lightening the purses of a few gentlemen, she had been able to outfit herself more suitably. Soon she had been able to leave the Butcher's Arms, and devote herself fully to attracting the wandering eyes of bored husbands, lonely travellers, and young rakes.

It had come as a surprise -- and a shocking reminder that Launston Mills was not so very far from Toronto after all -- when she had noticed Jeremy Launston leaving the Ontario House Hotel one evening in August. She had not been tempted to approach him for fear that he would recognize her and perhaps even put the law upon her, since she was still legally under her father's guardianship. She recalled the disdainful look Jeremy had once given her when he had come to their house to talk to Rowena. She could imagine what sort of gossip had flowed in the town regarding her mysterious departure, and was certain that Jeremy Launston would have heard of it. But she had been curious, and had followed him at a safe distance. With vast amusement, she had watched him enter the classiest brothel in the city.

So Gwyn was not particularly surprised when she spotted Malcolm Grimsby and his wife at the racecourse that day. Maureen Grimsby was certainly decked out in her finery today, but you wouldn't mistake her for gentry, despite her expensive plumage. She laughed too loudly, gesticulated too wildly, walked as though she were tramping across a muddy barnyard.

Gwyn had never liked Maureen, thinking her unjustifiably proud, and a braggart. Now she thought Maureen pathetic, and stupid as well. She seemed to be doing nothing to curb Malcolm's extravagant betting, nor obviously his over-imbibing, for he nipped constantly from his hip flask which he replenished from a bottle in the hired carriage. Sure, if he were ***her*** husband, Gwyn thought, he'd not be throwing away those pound notes so easily!

Gwyn had heard that the Colonel had had to sell some of his land to keep his son in pocket money. And when that was gone, what would there be for Maureen Grimsby to hang her arrogance upon?

Gwyn enjoyed watching those she knew, who thought themselves unobserved. But she had yet to find a suitable escort home -- and more than that, she hoped, for she would not be able to hide her burgeoning belly under tight corsets for many more months. If only she'd thought to take more of Rowena's special herbs with her, which had worked once before to purge her womb! She had tried soaking her body in hot water and her insides in gin. She had tried violent exercise, and had even thrown herself down a flight of stairs one day. Nothing had worked; this babe was determined to be born. If she did not find a husband or protector soon, then she would have to eke out an existence on her savings during the latter months of her pregnancy, for none would be likely to want her then.

She snared a young Lieutenant with whom she spent the rest of that afternoon -- not unpleasantly, she thought, regretting that he had not the means to qualify as a patron. That evening she took her usual walk along Front Street. When she saw Malcolm Grimsby emerge alone from the American House -- the most expensive hostelry in the city, of course -- she did not hesitate to accost him, since she had no reason to believe he would recognize her. He was too drunk to notice, in any case.

"You seem like a gentleman, sir," she said to him. "Would you be kind enough to escort me home? It seems I've wandered longer than I had intended, and now that darkness has fallen, I dare not risk the journey alone." Her eyes told him that he would be amply rewarded.

"Certainly, my dear," he replied, taking her arm in his. "Lead the way." As they ambled through the gloaming, he said, "What's your name?"

"You can call me Maureen," she replied wickedly. When he stiffened, she pressed herself closer to him and said, "Where do you live, sir?"

"You wouldn't know of it -- a village called Launston Mills."

"Oh, but I ***have*** heard of it. Why, I met a gentleman from there not a month ago! Now what was his name? Handsome fellow. Jeremy something-or-other." Gwyn was enjoying herself immensely.

She used all her whore's tricks to please him -- and God knows, she needed them to bring his whiskey-soaked body to a climax. And she charged him three times her usual rate, which he paid gladly.

When Malcolm had left her rumpled bed, she stretched like a contented cat. "I'm one up on you, Maureen Darcy, though you may never know it," she whispered to herself. And she felt that, in a small way, she had gotten a bit of her own back on Launston Mills.

Chapter 31

"What game is it that Brendan's playing?" Conn said with a frown.

The harvest dance was being held, as usual, in the ballroom of Paxtons' Inn. The room bulged with people; the floor shuddered and groaned under the assault of restless feet.

Moira had every reason to be happy as she danced with Conn. She was pregnant again, but not enough months gone for it to show, and thus prevent her from attending this last fling of the season. The winter socializing was mainly confined to churchgoing and informal visits with neighbours, which she would not need to miss until much later.

Even above the whine of the fiddles and the stomping of the feet, she could hear the soft swish of her silk gown as it swept around her. The sound sent a sharp thrill of pleasure through her as it announced to any who cared to listen that this was no longer young Moira O'Shaughnessy in the cast off dresses of her elder sister, but Moira Ryan, respectable wife and mother -- a woman grown. Even the touch of the fabric, light and smooth upon her skin, almost sensual, made her feel different -- elegant, poised. The earth-brown of the gown was shot with russet threads and trimmed with green ribbons, and she knew that whenever she moved the silk shimmered like flickering flames of fire. She had to resist the impulse to gaze down at it in admiration.

And how could she not be happy in Conn's arms?

Soon many of the men would be going to the lumber camp for the winter. But not Conn, and for that Moira was thankful. She would never forget the misery and horror of that long separation the first year of their marriage. The winter nights had never seemed so endless or so fraught with eerie noises. Even the crash of a crumbling log in the grate had evoked startled cries from her. She had thought sometimes she would go crazy with the loneliness and constant fear. Conn's sister, Catriona, had come to stay with her, but even her company had given Moira little comfort. Catriona had merely scoffed at her fears. The tensions of that winter had brought on the premature birth of her son, Tim, so it had taken little to persuade Conn never to return to the lumber camp. Now, when the sawmill closed for the winter, Conn would do odd jobs around the town, helping Patrick with carpentry work as often as not.

So why was it that she felt her joy dampened as Conn said to her, "Maybe I should have a word with Brendan."

"Like as not he'll tell you to mind your own business, Conn, and so you aught. 'Tis none of our concern."

"Don't you see what it's doing to Rowena?"

Moira felt that familiar resentment rise within her. What was it about her sister that could so easily arouse the sympathy of men? They saw her only as a victim, never ascribing any guilt to her. Sure, Brendan was behaving scandalously, flirting outrageously with that Nan Murphy, and her husband, God rest his soul, in his grave only these four months. But Moira knew that all had not been well between Rowena and Brendan recently, and, though she knew not the cause, she suspected that Rowena was as much to blame as Brendan.

"Best you keep out of it, Conn. You know what Brendan's like when he's been at the drink."

Although Conn agreed, Moira sensed her husband's concern for the woman he had once loved, and that irked her more than a little. She glanced briefly at Rowena, standing alone by an open window, as she and Conn spun past. Rowena was dressed in her favourite blue -- a simple gown adorned only with a white lawn collar and cuffs. Her black hair was sculpted into a tidy, glossy knot atop her head, with a few wispy tendrils softening the hairline.

Moira knew in her heart that Rowena would always outshine her. Her own fussy gown felt suddenly too tight across her expanding middle. The many stiff petticoats which gave the skirt such fashionable girth dragged her down. The ringlets that she had so meticulously trained stuck limply to her flushed cheeks.

She became aware of the pungent odours of sweating bodies, cheap tobacco, and cheaper whiskey that permeated the room. She could feel the dampness of her armpits, the rawness of moist flesh beneath the scraping corset. The sounds of music and chatter and laughter became a cacophony of noise in her ears. The undulations of the floor became a ship's deck on high seas. Her stomach churned.

"Moira?" Conn said as he noticed the blood drain from her face.

"I'm going to be sick!"

Rowena did not notice Moira dashing out. She felt miserable. Humiliated. There wasn't a person in the room who hadn't by now noticed Brendan's preoccupation with Nan Murphy.

She had enjoyed the dancing for a while, until Mickey Kelleher had partnered her and suggested, "While Brendan's busy, you and me could be slipping out for a breath of air."

"He's watching you this very minute, and I'm thinking that if he could read your lips, they'd not be much use to you for at least a week," she had replied flippantly. She had watched him crimson and gawp. He had trod on her toes, and fallen over his own, as though his haste could bring the dance to an early finish. Poor lad.

Lad? Mickey Kelleher was twenty-two -- a year older than herself, though Rowena felt the elder by a decade.

She was so weary of it all. God knows she had tried to right things with Brendan after that election day riot in the spring.

Those few moments when she had abandoned herself to Jeremy had become no more than a dream -- one that had no place in the mundane reality of everyday life. That there could never be anything between her and Jeremy, she had not the slightest doubt.

Although she had tried hard to banish him from her thoughts, it was at night that he would sometimes embrace her once more.

Brendan's lovemaking had become more brutal and demanding these last months, as though he were trying to possess her totally by the very violence of their physical union. Yet that only frightened her, leaving her sometimes bruised and sore, and she withdrew further from him. As he lay snoring afterwards, enveloped in whiskey fumes, she would lie tensely beside him until the memory of Jeremy's tender, searching kiss burned upon her lips once more, and made the ache in her loins an almost pleasurable pain.

Then she would clasp her hands fiercely and recite Hail Marys until she fell into a troubled sleep.

She knew where her duty lay. Had she not freely chosen to marry Brendan? Whether that had been right or wise was beyond question now. She was determined to make the best of it, to be all that a wife should be. She might even find happiness in that again.

But Brendan seemed bent on thwarting her efforts.

It had been his wont, upon arriving home in the evenings, to lift her in an exuberant embrace, and place a smacking kiss upon her lips. Now there was not even an answering smile to her welcome. No longer did he playfully fondle or tease her, or pull her down upon his lap to share a quiet moment before the fire. Indeed, he spent few evenings with her now, going almost nightly to Paxtons'. His smile never lighted upon her; his eyes watched her suspiciously. Gone was all that had been good between them -- the easy companionship, the shared laughter -- and she knew not how to revive it.

Rowena absently fingered the bunches of herbs that decorated the wall beside her, bruising the leaves to release the distinct and pleasing aromas of sage and basil, marjoram and mint, rosemary and thyme.

Rosemary. A whiff undammed a flood of memories. Sprigs of the herb had reposed in her mother's drawers and chests. That blue gown that Deirdre had altered for her -- so may years ago, it seemed -- had been redolent with it.

"Rosemary for remembrance" was the saying.

She remembered the first time she had worn that rosemary-scented gown -- the night of the sugaring bee at the Winslow farm. The night she had so brazenly countered Brendan's flirtations, and had relished his admiration. A night when her world had still been simple and happy. And hadn't her mother warned her of Brendan even then?

She could stay here no longer!

Rowena wended her way through the dancers to one of the doors leading to the hallway. She sought feverishly for her wrap among the many shawls and cloaks dangling from the pegs, frantic to be quit of this place now that she had made up her mind to leave. She threw the woolen wrap about her shoulders, and started for the bedroom where Keir slept beside the other infants and small children.

A startled gasp escaped her when she was roughly grabbed from behind, and spun about.

"And where is it you're going?" Brendan asked, the very softness of his voice menacing.

His lips were curved into a sneer; his whiskey-glazed eyes challenged her. She noticed the powerful muscles of his arms flexing beneath his shirt, and knew that she should fear him. But she was too angry to be afraid.

He could see that anger in her eyes as she unflinchingly returned his stare, and was elated by it. Her defiance always excited him -- but only when he could bend her to his will in the end. Women like Nan Murphy -- who was so eager to please him that she would have spread her legs for him then and there had he asked -- held no lasting appeal for him. It angered him more than a little to realize how strong was his need of Rowena. But if she could not love him, let her hate him. It was better than indifference, and there was pleasure in making her submit to him.

"I'm going home," Rowena stated.

"Is it jealous you are?"

She looked at him sadly. "Is that what you want, Brendan?"

He emitted a mirthless chuckle. "I reckon 'tis too much to be asking of an unloving wife."

She could feel the sorrow behind those bitter words, and a rush of sympathy swept through her. "Brendan, I...."

He didn't want her pity. By Jaysus, but that was an insult, that she should pity him for the love she could not return! "You'll stay till I'm ready to leave."

"You please yourself, Brendan. I'm leaving now."

A callused hand shackled her arm before she had moved a step. "Is it deaf you are, woman? I said you'll be leaving when I've a mind to go."

She should have backed down then, she was to think later, when she blamed herself for what was to happen. But at that moment she could only envision the further humiliations to which Brendan would surely subject her, and she could endure no more. So she stood her ground, her anger rekindled, matching his.

"You've already set the tongues wagging this night, and made a fool of yourself and me! I'm not staying to watch any more, and there's naught you can do to make me!"

"Is that a fact then?" His mocking words little revealed the depth of his rage. It was such an intense, overwhelming emotion that his body went rigid, blood hammered in his ears. He could see the very redness of it as it pounded through his eyeballs. It was so all-consuming that he was sure nothing short of murder would release him from its grip.

Rowena winced as Brendan's hand crushed her arm, but a moment later she cried out in pain as, with a lightning-swift movement, he wrenched at her chignon, ripping out the pins that secured the heavy mass, and wound the rope of hair tightly about his hand. He dragged her toward the ballroom, saying through clenched teeth, "You'll be doing as I say, woman, or by Jaysus, you'll not be living to see the morrow!"

Rowena could neither protest nor resist as he jerked her along. Her scalp stung with a thousand sharp pinpricks, the skin of her face was stretched taut, her eyes felt as though they were bulging out of her head.

The dancers stumbled to a halt. Conversations ceased in mid-sentence. The fiddles screeched to a discordant stop. For a moment the silence was so thick that Rowena thought she would choke on it. And for that moment the scene before her was like some grotesque tableau. Patrick, his hand frozen halfway to his lips, his mouth gaping in anticipation of the whiskey that never reached it, a trickle of saliva slithering like a slug from the corner of his mouth. Mary, speechless for once, her black eyes fixed upon Rowena, not even blinking lest she miss anything. Moira, being supported by a concerned Conn, her sickly pallor blanching even more. All the faces, curious, aghast, some even amused. Rowena saw it all in that second that she was dangled before them like a fisherman's catch.

Then Brendan hurled her to the floor. The sudden release made her dizzy, and she barely had the wits to break her fall with outstretched hands.

"You'll be staying!" Brendan said.

It was Alec Darcy's misfortune that Rowena had landed at his feet, although another might not have acted as he did. He bent down and helped Rowena onto shaky legs. In an effort to dispel the tension, he said lightly, "Come along, Rowena. We've not had a dance yet this night."

Brendan, still fuming, still taut with anger, remembered that Alec Darcy had once considered marrying Rowena. "Take your hands off me wife," he growled.

Alec Darcy threw Brendan a scornful look, and led the trembling girl to the middle of the dancefloor.

A moment later the place was in an uproar. Brendan, his blood boiling, charged at Alec like a mad bull. The unanimous gasp from the crowd warned Alec, but too late. He had time only to release his hold on Rowena before the first blow felled him. He landed heavily on the floor, winded, dazed. Brendan pounced on him, and began smashing his fists into the old man's face.

Sean Delaney, Hugh and the other Darcy boys reacted quickly after their initial shock. They dragged Brendan off Alec. Hugh, a brawny giant of a man, tossed Brendan across the room.

Hugh clenched his fists. The huge muscles of his arms and shoulders bunched. "You bastard!" Hugh hissed, as Brendan staggered to his feet. "Let's see how well you do in a fair fight."

Brendan, his anger somewhat abated, began to realize the enormity of his actions. He saw the Darcy boys help a bleeding Alec to his feet. The old man, breathing heavily, was lowered onto a chair and given a dram of whiskey.

Brendan faced Hugh. There was no mistaking the hatred in the latter's eyes. Brendan had no wish to fight his erstwhile friend, but fight he would if the alternative was to be labelled a coward.

"There'll be no more rowdiness in this establishment!" Josh Paxton said. "You can go out in the street and beat yourselves senseless if you want, but the next man who starts anything in here can take his custom elsewhere in future." The warning delivered, Josh signalled the fiddlers to resume playing.

They did so warily, eyeing the two men for signs of further trouble. The revelers, too, watched in anticipation, whispering among themselves.

Rowena overheard some of the comments from the women behind her. Shelagh Darcy said, "'Tis all her fault, that bitch!"

"Aye, brings nowt but trouble, that one."

God knows, they were right, she thought. This was yet another cross to bear. She wanted to go to Alec to apologize for Brendan's behaviour, to take the blame for his actions upon herself. But she feared angering Brendan further; so she stayed where she was.

She was surprised to find Mary at her side, offering a strong arm for physical support, and moral support by her very presence. Rowena had grown cynical enough to wonder whether Mary was there to make a favourable impression on others, or because she felt guilty for pushing Rowena into marriage with Brendan. Nonetheless, Rowena was grateful for the proffered sympathy. Quietly Mary said, "Sure, Brendan's always had a fierce temper. And when the drink's in him, he no longer has the sense the good Lord gave him."

Brendan and Hugh still stood squared off, each waiting for the other to make a move, Josh's warning ignored.

"Hugh!" Alec's voice boomed out. "Leave it be. We've no wish to ruin the evening for these good folk here."

Although a scrap was a common enough diversion at any gathering -- and heartily enjoyed by all, as often as not -- there was a general sense of relief in the room as Hugh reluctantly turned away from Brendan.

Sean went to his brother's side. "You're daft! Attacking Alec Darcy! Christ! Do you know what you've done, man?"

Brendan furrowed his brow. "Aye. Sure, I don't know what came over me."

"You'd best leave, the pair of you, afore any more harm's done."

"Aye." Brendan motioned to Rowena to join him. Without a word, she followed him from the room. Silently they walked home, side by side, but alone in their individual misery.

• • •

"Brendan Delaney," the magistrate intoned, "you have been charged with unprovoked assault on Alec Darcy on the night of September 26, in this very room in which the court now presides. I have before me the testimonies of a dozen eye-witnesses... And I understand that half the village could bear witness as well... How do you plead?"

Colonel Grimsby looked suitably dour, as though he had donned a judicial persona along with his magistrate's robes. He sat at a table at one end of Paxtons' ballroom -- devoid now of its festive decor -- facing the accused and the many spectators that filled the 'courtroom'. He was surprised at the large turnout, since it was a working day. But then most of them had been at the ball, and this was the true finale to that episode of two days ago.

"I was drunk, your Honour, and I didn't rightly know what I was doing."

"Guilty or not guilty, Mr. Delaney?" the Colonel asked somewhat impatiently.

"Sure, if that's the only choice I have to make, then I reckon it'll have to be 'guilty', your Honour. Far be it from me to call all them witnesses liars."

There were chuckles from the crowd. Brendan -- sober -- could still charm a smile from most with his cockiness. The tension, which seemed to have lingered within these walls along with the stale odours of tobacco and ale, was suddenly dispelled. There was a sound of rustling, as those fortunate enough to be seated settled themselves more comfortably in their chairs. There were whispers and coughs and the shuffling of feet.

The Darcys, however, were not amused. Alec's jaw was swollen and discoloured, and his ribs pained him whenever he took a breath. Hugh, who had been adamant about pressing charges, sat tight-lipped, while Shelagh, beside him, smiled slyly.

Colonel Grimsby had already deliberated over this case. The news, of course, had been all over the village by the following morning, and he'd had no doubt of Delaney's guilt. It was the punishment of which he was uncertain. The man was undeniably a troublemaker, and deserved to spend at least three months in gaol.

But Archibald Lathrop, the owner of the foundry, had had a word with the Colonel that morning. Lathrop had told him what a valuable employee Delaney was, and that he could ill-afford to lose his services at the moment, with business being so brisk. He had offered to stand as a character witness for the accused.

"I find you guilty as charged." The Colonel cleared his throat. "I have before me a letter from your employer, Mr. Delaney, attesting to your excellent work record. It is my opinion that the interests of this community might ***not*** best be served by allowing you to sit idly in Cobourg gaol. However, it is my intention to impress upon you the seriousness of your crime. This community will not tolerate such lawlessness from its citizens. And I warn you, Mr. Delaney, that the next time you are brought before me on such a charge, I shall ensure that we will not be troubled by you for a long time. You are fined five pounds. If the funds are not forthcoming by Friday next, you will spend three months in gaol."

There were many gasps from the audience, for it was a stiff fine. Brendan earned five dollars a week -- a little more than a pound sterling -- so it was a month's wage. Garth Caldor had been fined only one dollar for his part in a fracas during election week.

Brendan was incensed by the excessive penalty. Sure, hadn't he always known the local 'gentry' had it in for him! The Colonel was a good friend of the Launstons, after all. He turned his glare on Hugh Darcy, in whose face he could read no remorse, or forgiveness. Self-righteous prig! He was becoming more and more like his wife. Alec Darcy refused to meet Brendan's eyes.

Brendan grabbed Rowena's arm and urged her through the throng of people. He was impatient to get to work, to burn off some of his anger in the sweaty, blistering heat of that hell-hole. Rowena practically had to run to keep pace with him.

"What are we to do?" she asked him. Rowena had nearly five pounds put by, but two pounds of that was to have been used for the quarterly mortgage payment, due two days hence.

"Pay the fine, and to hell with the mortgage! I could have bought me a hundred acres in the bush for what Launston charged us for an acre! And how generous we thought old Sam, when he gave us the money to set ourselves up, and us never thinking how long we'd be paying him back, and him making more money with the interest. Sure, haven't we repaid the original amount by now? Fuck the bloody mortgage! Let him sue us! I'm sick to death of toadying to the likes of them!" He stopped so abruptly that she nearly collided with him. He stared at her accusingly. "There was a time when Launston offered me money to wed you. I kept my part of the bargain. Maybe I should insist he keep his." He turned and strode away.

Rowena no longer bothered to keep up with him. By the time she reached home, Brendan had already changed into his work clothes, and was coming out the door. He passed her without a word or a look, as if she no longer existed for him.

Rowena went inside, and sat down at the table without removing her Sunday bonnet. She'd have to go and see the Launstons, she thought, and ask for more time to pay. She did not want Brendan to get into even more trouble with the law. So, she might as well go now and get it over with.

It was with great trepidation that she stepped onto the Launstons' portico and rang the doorbell. She had resolved to talk only to Samuel. She could not face Jeremy, not when the memory of their last encounter could still ignite such fire in her veins.

But the maid who answered the door informed her, "Mr. Samuel's in Montreal. He's not expected back for at least a fortnight. Mr. Jeremy's in his office, if you'd like to see him."

Rowena hesitated, but knew she had no choice. She could not await Samuel's return. "Aye," she said to the maid. "Tell him Mrs. Delaney would like to speak to him on a matter of business." She stepped into the foyer while the maid went down the hall to the study.

Rowena tried to breathe slowly to calm her pounding heart and to keep the blood from rushing guiltily to her cheeks. How would Jeremy react when he saw her? Would he be embarrassed to be reminded of his foolishness? Would he even recall that startling kiss that had so insidiously changed her life with Brendan? Or would his eyes once more express the tenderness that had caused her treachery? How could she face him? She would have turned and fled, had not the maid returned just then to tell her that Jeremy would see her.

With a quaking heart she walked down the familiar hall, knocked on the door, and entered. Jeremy was standing by the window, as he had so often done when she had been in this room with him. What she saw in his eyes was pity. And her fear succumbed to indignation.

"You know," she accused in surprise, although she should have realized that he would have heard of her public humiliation.

"Yes, I heard." And he would have locked the bastard up, just to keep him away from Rowena. He came closer to her. "Does Brendan often treat you like that?"

"I didn't come here to discuss Brendan. 'Tis about the fine. I've no doubt you know about that as well. If we're to be paying it, there'll not be enough to be paying you the mortgage this quarter. I came to ask -- would you be willing to give us more time?"

Jeremy went to his desk, rifled through some papers, and drew out a document. "There are only six months left on your mortgage," he said. Then he tore the paper into pieces.

Rowena gasped. "You shouldn't have done that!" She looked at him in exasperation. "Don't you realize that will only make things worse, if Brendan knows about it? He already thinks...." But she bit off the rest of her words, and spun around to head for the door.

Jeremy was faster than she, and stopped her flight. "Rowena, why can I never do anything to please you?" he asked, puzzled. "Why do you always fight me?"

"Let go of me, please!" She struggled to free herself, but he pulled her closer.

"Is it me you're afraid of, or yourself?" he asked softly.

If he kissed her again, she would be lost, she knew. Already she was weakening, anticipating his embrace as his touch sent shivers through her. "What is it you want from me, Jeremy?" she asked in desperation.

His hands dropped from her arms. It was a question he couldn't answer himself. This time he turned away from her.

"Goodbye... Mr. Launston."

Part 3

The Village

1848 - 1849

Chapter 32

Keir O'Shaughnessy had always hated his father. Of course, Brendan wasn't his real father -- the village children had made sure he understood that years ago.

Bastard, they called him, in such a jeering and derogatory manner that he knew he was somehow tainted.

It had hurt him at first, being treated as though he were different, crippled in some way -- like little Jillian Launston, but without the pity with which she was regarded.

Since he was six he had been attending the Catholic school. Classes were held in the church from Mondays to Fridays, taught by Mr. Fitzgerald. The other children had delighted in tormenting him, and he had gone home with many a black eye and bloody nose. Now, even bigger boys wouldn't dare taunt him, for his reputation as a fighter had earned him respect, if not friends or acceptance.

Strangely, it was Brendan who had taught him to fight. Whenever Keir arrived home wearing the evidence of a brawl, Brendan would chuckle and pat him on the back saying, "I hope you whooped 'em!"

Keir had long ago ceased caring what others thought of him. He carried his illegitimacy proudly -- his father had been a Launston, after all! -- much to the disgust of many a sanctimonious citizen. He was not unaware of the disapproving looks, the head shaking, the damning prophecies that he left in his wake. He took pleasure in being different, particularly from people like that.

Keir paused outside his grandfather's house, tempted to step into the workshop and visit the old man. He liked his grandfather, and Patrick was always glad to see him -- a fact which, Keir realized with perspicacity, made his step-grandmother, Mary, like him even less. She was one of those whose eyes tried to brand "sinner" onto his forehead.

Mary irritated him with her constant comparisons between himself and his cousins in which he, of course, was invariably in the wrong or in some way inferior. Whenever he and his cousins were together and some mischief was perpetrated, he was always the one who was blamed. When Uncle Conn was present, it was he who would volunteer to administer the punishment. The two of them would walk sedately to the woodshed where a hickory switch hung for the edification of young boys. When the prying eyes had been shut out, Conn would ask, "Did you do it?" Keir never lied to him, so when he was innocent the switch would land on Conn's jacket, laid over the woodpile, while Keir emitted a couple of convincing howls to satisfy Mary. But even when Keir was guilty, Conn never hit him hard.

Not like Brendan, who whipped him as though he would kill him.

Keir truly loved Conn, but he could not say the same about his Aunt Moira. In her, he sensed some resentment toward himself, although he couldn't understand why. Outwardly she was all smiles and kindness and concern. But there was something in her eyes that made him distrust her. She was the kind of person who condemned you to others behind your back. More than once he had interrupted Moira and Shelagh Darcy gossiping, and Moira had blushed guiltily. Keir preferred his "Aunt" Shelagh's open hostility to Moira's secretive one.

He really should say goodbye to Brigid, he thought. She had always been like an older sister, that gentle and caring soul, and he loved her dearly. A convent had been established in Toronto the previous year, and Father Killeny was arranging for her to enter it as a novice nun. Perhaps they could meet in the city!

But it was best if he said nothing to anyone, not even Brigid, for he wanted nothing to thwart his escape this time.

Keir had run away -- or tried to -- once before. He had taken Gypsy Lane, the road which followed the east side of the river, not really certain where it would lead him, knowing only that Toronto was down there somewhere and that he was determined to reach it. But night had trapped him miles from anywhere. How dark and sinister the woods and swamps were at night! He hadn't even seen the lights of a farmhouse -- just those of the multitudinous stars. The sky in its infinite enormity had frightened him more, making him feel so much smaller than the crowding trees already had. Nighttime marauders had rustled through the undergrowth, their eyes glowing eerily. The trees had swayed in the shushing wind as if shifting from one foot to the other, creeping ever closer. The rusks that he had pocketed had disappeared earlier, and hunger and fear had gnawed at his innards.

Horror upon horrors! A small, flickering, dancing light, like a firefly, had grown larger and larger before his eyes. He had thought for certain it was the fairies or the demons come to get him!

Tears of relief had blinded him when he had recognized Conn's voice and finally spotted him as the ghostly lantern-bearer. He had gone back with Conn gratefully. Even the beating that Brendan had given him had not made him any the less glad that he was safely home.

Keir chuckled to himself. He was ten now, and not afraid of invisible creatures or the "walking dead" which, he strongly suspected, inhabited only the minds of the older folk. This time he would not fail. He had been planning this carefully for weeks, but last night's fiasco had provided the impetus.

Keir had a momentary qualm about leaving his mother at the mercy of that lunatic, but there was really nothing ***he*** could do to help her. Besides, wasn't he usually the cause of arguments between Brendan and Rowena?

Brendan seemed to blame ***him*** for his lack of offspring. "'Tis ***him*** who's cursed us, the little bastard!" Brendan, drunk as usual, had once shouted. "Or is it that you're taking those God-cursed herbs to kill my babes? You've no love for anyone but your Launston bastard!"

And though Rowena had denied it, Brendan had not listened. He never did. Once he'd made up his mind that something was true, that was how it was. The alternative -- that he could not prove his manhood -- was intolerable. Of course it was Rowena's fault.

Keir's feelings toward his mother were ambiguous. He loved her... and yet.... It was her sin that had created him and which had made his short life already such a miserable one. If he was a Launston, why didn't she ensure that he enjoyed some of the benefits of being one? Why couldn't he attend the best school in the province, like his cousin, Richard Launston? He had a keen, inquisitive mind. He had so easily and greedily absorbed all Mr. Fitzgerald's teachings, but he longed to know more, to have his endless questions answered.

Whenever he asked his mother why they never visited his Launston relatives, why the Launstons never acknowledged him, why he couldn't live in a big, splendid house as they did, she merely replied that she wished to have nothing to do with them. How Rowena infuriated him at times like that! She had painted such a marvellous picture of his father -- the kind of father any boy would want -- but then she denied Keir any tangible link with him.

Keir had a vivid mental image of his father -- an idealized portrait that strongly resembled Jeremy Launston. Keir idolized his uncle and wanted desperately to be like him. But how impossible that seemed! He would never have the breeding, the education which set Jeremy apart from other men. And he was a bastard -- a socially unacceptable creature.

Keir arrived at the westward bend in the river where the old dam and mills had been. There were houses along here now, for the mills and the dam had been torn down four years ago when the government lock and dam had been completed farther downstream, nearly at the foot of Lindsay Street. The Launstons had built fine stone mills at the new site. The gristmill had seven run of stones, and the sawmill had four upright and eight circular saws! And these mills were not powered by waterwheels, but by turbines -- a new invention of whose use very few mills in all of North America could boast!

With a population of over 800, the town was spreading over the originally surveyed land, all of it chopped out now -- a flat square pimpled with tree stumps, and houses like huge boils erupting all over it. Only one block of swampy land, just west of the common, remained in its pristine state -- a giant tuft of hair on the face of the town. A dozen shops with stoops and boardwalks lined Main Street. Among the new citizens were a Methodist minister and a Presbyterian preacher, a barrister, a druggist, a tinsmith, a barber, a baker, a butcher, a gunsmith, two saddlers, two shoemakers, two schoolteachers, several tailors and dressmakers, carpenters, bricklayers, stonemasons, painters, and blacksmiths. There was even an impressive bank, constructed of stone, and two new inns calling themselves "Hotels".

Keir paused at the Launstons' house. Two men, perched on tall ladders, were giving the house a new coat of glistening white paint. Keir leaned idly against the white wooden fence, and let his eyes be enticed along the graceful lines of the house.

"Why are you staring like that, boy?" a small voice inquired, with curiosity rather than reproof.

Surprised from his reverie, Keir glanced about and spied the girl sitting on the grass only a few feet from him. She was partly screened by the rows of rose bushes which paralleled the fence. She rose -- with difficulty, Keir noticed -- and with the aid of a crutch, hobbled toward him, dragging her withered right leg. It was Jillian Launston.

"I've seen you go by here before," she said, "but I don't know who you are. Do you know me? I bet you do. Everyone does." She didn't say this with conceit, but almost with sadness. Of course everyone knew of her "affliction".

"Aye, I know who you are."

"You're Irish."

"My mother is, but my father... he was English, same as your folks. I was born here, same as you." Neither of them realized that he spoke the literal truth.

"I like the way you talk. It sounds like music. I love music. Do you?"

Keir shrugged. "I suppose."

Eight year old Jillian was a pretty child with dark curls and large, soft brown eyes. A real beauty she'd be, people said of her, but what a tragedy she was crippled.

"Are you going into town?" she asked.

"Aye."

"I wish ***I*** could," she said wistfully.

"What's to stop you then?"

"I'm not allowed to go anywhere by myself. This fence is my cage. Not like a bird cage so that everyone can stare at me, but so they can't."

Keir was disturbed by her words.

"Father would take me if he were here. I wish I could have gone to Toronto with him! I do so hope he comes home today."

The mention of Toronto reminded Keir of his own plans. He'd best hurry or he'd miss the boat. "I have to be going now."

"Will you talk to me again sometime?" she asked hopefully.

"Aye," Keir lied, and wondered why he hadn't wanted to disappoint her. Perhaps because he sensed in her a kindred loneliness. Besides, she ***was*** his cousin. He could hardly credit it!

Keir glanced back once and saw the pink-clad figure waving to him. He raised his hand, and then turned and ran the rest of the way up Mill Road.

Lindsay Street now extended north to the river where a new swing bridge spanned the water below the locks. At least he wasn't too late -- the steamer was just loading. Keir sauntered across the bridge, his stomach tightening into a knot, his palms sweating, wishing he could run, but not wanting to draw attention to himself. He had that superstitious fear of the unseasoned traveller, that something would prevent his departure at the last moment. He forced himself to stop and look at the yellowish foam that spewed out from the bowels of the mill through three stone arches. The water was generally shallow there, and on a hot summer's day many a boy -- Keir included -- had enjoyed cooling combat with the churning water. But that exhilarating game had been forbidden by parents since the tragedy the previous year.

Young Abe MacCready had been swept into the main current of the river and drowned.

A blast of the steamer's whistle jolted Keir into action. Afraid that he had tarried too long, he dashed past the lock keeper's house and on to the wharf above the locks.

There were only a few passengers boarding from Launston Mills, and fortunately, none of them was acquainted with Keir. He tried to remain calm as he paid his fare -- with the few pence he had stolen from his mother.

This was the steamer *Firefly*'s first summer on the lakes and rivers. She was a lovely ship, a hundred foot side-wheeler with two decks. Daily she sailed from Launston Mills -- where passengers transferred from the steamers that plied the lakes to the north -- south to Port Perry at the head of Scugog Lake. The Launstons had a substantial share in the *Firefly*, as well as owning numerous scows and barges for the transport of their lumber. Today the *Firefly* was towing a load of grain destined for the Front.

Keir mingled with the people on deck, and gradually edged his way into an inconspicuous corner. He breathed a sigh of relief when he felt the engines rumble beneath him, and the steamer glide away from the dock.

Keir thought he should hide himself lest someone -- his mother even! -- notice him aboard the vessel. Yet... it would be a long time, if ever, before he saw his home again, and a pang of regret and longing assailed him. No, he would not deny himself this last glimpse of home.

On the south bank the Launston mansion sparkled in the sunlight. The early autumn golds and reds of the woods surrounding it provided a gilt frame for its beauty. There were several other grand houses in town, up on the rise at the west end, but they jutted out starkly in a barren landscape with which they seemed to co-exist in a state of constant tension. The forest had been the settler's enemy, and every last soldier of this formidable army had been annihilated. But on the Launston tract only the road and the individual lots had been carved from the woods.

The boat swept around the bend to the south. Keir spotted his grandfather's house with its jumble of outbuildings. Equally chaotic -- though how beautiful they suddenly seemed to Keir -- were the flowers and shrubs. Towering sunflowers leaned bright yellow heads against the grey weathered logs of the house; a parade of colourful hollyhocks marched along the fences which had disappeared beneath a tangle of wild cucumber vines, already turning a rusty scarlet; Virgin's bower smothered the workshop, while morning glories claimed the privy, and trumpet vines, the woodshed. The creepers had taken possession of the stoop as well, and Keir could almost feel the dark, leafy coolness of the veranda where he liked to sit with his grandfather and inhale the aromatic smoke of the old man's pipe while listening to his stories of times long passed.

Keir's breath caught painfully in his throat when he realized that he might never know such pleasant, contented evenings again.

The old corduroy bridge had been removed when the locks had been completed, but the abutments were still visible. Along the west bank here, next to his grandfather's house were Conn and Moira's and then his own home. Keir tried to flatten himself into the woodwork when he spied his mother cutting herbs in the kitchen garden. She didn't glance up, though Keir almost wished she had seen him. He stared, as if trying to burn that picture of her into his mind, until he could see her no more. A lump in his throat choked him.

Two more houses and then the forest. Launston Mills was behind them.

The muddy ochre river -- known as the "Styx" to its navigators -- like the path of a drunken man, wandered hither and thither were it would. Drowned trees delineated its original banks, before the dam had raised the water level, and weeds and rushes warned of dangerously shallow water.

It was twenty-two miles from Launston Mills to Port Perry, eight miles along the river and the rest, across Lake Scugog. Stretches of marsh lined its shores, for the lake had grown from a pond with the building of the first dam. The wild rice which grew in its waters was harvested still by the Indians who lived in the vicinity.

Because of several refueling stops -- piles of cordwood were stacked at strategic points along the route -- and the difficulty of navigating the treacherous waters, it was nearly four hours before Port Perry came into view.

Keir quivered with apprehension. He was reluctant to admit to himself his fears of venturing to a strange city about which he knew practically nothing, except that it had a population of over twenty thousand. Twenty thousand! He couldn't even imagine that many people, especially not in one place. But at least no one would be able to find him there. Although she was rarely mentioned, Keir had discovered that he had an aunt, Gwyn, who had run away years ago, and he wondered if she, too, had gone to Toronto. Should he try to find her? How would he do that?

His first concern, however, was to reach Toronto. He had spent his few pence for the ticket. Already his stomach was protesting the fact that he had missed his noonday dinner.

An idea tempted him.

Standing a few feet from him was a well-dressed gentleman. Keir had earlier seen him stuff a few pound bank notes into an outer pocket of his redingote. A corner of these bills peaked temptingly from their sanctuary.

Keir knew that stealing was a sin, but he had stolen some coins from his mother and God had not yet struck him dead or otherwise demonstrated His disapproval. It should be a sin for some folk to have so much and others to have nothing! Surely -- if he pleaded his case well -- God would forgive him if he were to take just a little from someone who would hardly miss it.

Still, he had reservations. He could almost feel the flames of hell licking at his bare feet. Besides, how did one go about stealing from someone's pocket without being caught?

Keir pondered this problem as the steamer drew up to the dock at Port Perry. His heart pounded at the mere thought of doing such a wicked and daring deed. But he couldn't go back home! Not after what had happened last night! His back still stung from the cuts of the switch. If his mother hadn't threatened Brendan with a carving knife, that lunatic might have killed them both.

Keir remembered the fierce look in his mother's eyes as she, knife in hand, had backed away from her husband and hissed, "If ever you lay your hands on me or my son again, I swear to God I'll kill you!"

Brendan had gurgled drunkenly and replied, "I'll see you both in hell first!"

Rowena had shielded Keir, and they had inched out the door and run to Conn's. Keir hadn't seen Brendan since. Nor did he ever wish to again.

Perhaps... if he was to bump into that gentleman and let his fingers fasten onto those protruding corners of the bills.... Yes. He'd wait until they had disembarked, in the confusion on the dock, before he made his move, for he'd have to disappear pretty smartly once he had the money.

The wharf was crowded with boxes and crates -- supplies from the Front destined for the backwoods. Dozens of people milled about, loading and unloading, waiting to board, or just idly watching all this activity. Keir finally saw his chance and took it. Lightly he fell against the man... felt the notes in his hand... begged the man's pardon... surreptitiously conveyed the bills toward his own pocket....

A strong hand gripped Keir's wrist. His heart stopped beating.

Warily he glanced over his shoulder to find... Jeremy Launston!

"Pardon me, sir!" Jeremy called to the man Keir had just robbed.

Keir wished the earth would open up beneath his feet and swallow him. Even the flames of hell seemed more inviting than facing his uncle. He tried to pull away, but Jeremy held him by the shoulders, digging his fingers into Keir's collarbone.

The gentleman looked around.

"This young man," Jeremy said, "found these notes on the ground. Would they happen to belong to you?"

The man reached into his pockets. "Indeed they would!" he replied, frowning as he eyed Keir.

Keir guiltily handed the money back. There was no escape now.

"I do not understand how those notes could have fallen from my pocket." The man appraised Jeremy, and seemed satisfied that he was dealing with a gentleman. "Do you know this boy? Can you vouch for his honesty or should I summon a magistrate?"

"I am a magistrate. And this young man is my nephew. I trust you are not insinuating, sir, that my nephew is a thief!"

"Not at all," the man blubbered. He glanced uncomfortably about at the amused spectators. "Thank you, boy," he said to Keir before hastening away in embarrassment.

Keir was too flabbergasted to do anything but gape at Jeremy. He had expected to be hauled before the authorities.... He hadn't even realized that Jeremy knew him!

Jeremy had been surprised when he had noticed Keir among the disembarking passengers, and astonished to see the boy picking someone's pocket! Jeremy had been keeping an eye on his nephew over the years, though he had thought it best not to interfere in the boy's life. Not unless necessary.

He studied Keir. He was a tall, strong boy for his age, with the look of Rowena in those arresting blue eyes and narrow face framed with black hair. There was little of Adrian evident in the boy -- the set of the mouth perhaps, the lean frame.

Keir had recovered himself, and suddenly made a dash past his uncle. But Jeremy had anticipated it, and pulled the boy up short.

"Just where do you think you're going?" Jeremy demanded, holding Keir by the collar.

"'Tis naught to do with you!"

"You think not? Having just prevaricated on your behalf and saved you from being sent to gaol, I think I am entitled to an explanation."

Keir returned Jeremy's stare with defiance, but finally looked away, ashamed.

"What are you doing here, Keir?" When the boy didn't answer, Jeremy said, "Running away from home perhaps?"

Keir looked at him in surprise.

"I thought as much. You're coming back with me."

Alarm registered on Keir's face. "I'll not go back! Never!"

Jeremy was dismayed by Keir's vehemence and his renewed struggles to escape. "Tell me why!"

"Because I hate him!"

Keir's loud declaration drew the attention of the crowd once again, and Jeremy thought it prudent to discuss the situation more privately. "Come. We've twenty minutes before the boat leaves. Convince me if you can why I shouldn't take you home. Then I will decide what should be done with you." He gripped Keir by the arm, and led him along the shore of the lake, away from the village. "I'll release you if you give me your word you'll not try to run away. I trust I can rely upon your honour. You are, after all, a Launston."

"I promise," Keir said resignedly. He stopped walking and faced Jeremy. "But why do you admit that now when you never have before?"

"What? The fact that you're a Launston?"

"Aye."

"I've never denied it."

"But you've never even spoken to me before!"

"Is that a reproach?"

"No, sir."

"I'm still waiting for an explanation."

Keir hesitated at first, but then the words tumbled out, tripping over one another in their haste. Jeremy became grave at the boy's words and at the anger, the hate, the pain which accompanied them. He was disturbed by the injustice Keir had suffered, not only at the hands of Brendan Delaney, but by virtue of the boy's very existence -- a bastard.

And if the boy was telling the truth, then things were much worse between Brendan and Rowena than even rumour suggested. Jeremy had managed to allay his own feelings of guilt these last few years by deceiving himself into believing that Rowena and Keir no longer bore the stigma of the shame that he had brought upon them. Now it returned to him, magnified tenfold. He had wronged his brother, Rowena, and their son, and he could never rectify that. But he could and would do all in his power to make life easier for Rowena and Keir. That would only begin to repay the debt he owed them, though his own conscience would never be appeased. He prayed that God would forgive him, for he could never forgive himself.

The steamer shrilly announced its imminent departure.

"You're coming with me," Jeremy said to Keir.

"But you said...."

"I'm not taking you back to your home, but to mine."

Keir's eyes widened.

"Come, or we'll miss the boat."

Keir just stood and stared.

"Don't you trust me?"

"You mean... I can live with you?"

"Yes. It's where you rightly belong." Jeremy held out his hand.

Keir took it. He could hardly believe this sudden acceptance. But what would his mother say? Once they were aboard the boat, Keir put this question to his uncle.

"I shall just have to convince her that it would be in your best interests," Jeremy replied, wondering how he would achieve that impossible task. "Tell me, Keir, what would you most like to do? Have you any ambitions?"

"I'd like to go to a proper school, like... like my cousin Richard," Keir answered promptly.

Jeremy was impressed. He knew the boy was intelligent, for he had discreetly questioned the Catholic schoolmaster concerning Keir's abilities. Mr. Fitzgerald had praised the boy's aptitude, but condemned his behaviour. No doubt Keir needed more challenging schooling which would leave him little opportunity for misbehaviour.

"So be it then! The term has only just begun, so there shouldn't be any difficulty enrolling you at the College. It's much different from the kind of schooling you've had thus far. You'll have to apply yourself faithfully to your studies, and to behave in every respect like a gentleman so as not to bring disgrace upon yourself or me. If you're willing to comply with those terms then I shall gladly finance your education."

"Yes, sir!" Keir's eyes glowed.

Jeremy smiled at his nephew's delight. It made him feel good to do something for this poor boy who deserved better than what life had dealt him until now.

He wished... yes, he would admit that he wished his own son were more like Keir. Ten-year-old Richard was already something of a prig, and Jeremy often despaired of his son becoming the kind of man of whom he could be proud. Richard had always had everything, and that was undoubtedly the reason he expected no less, and accepted everything as though it were his God-given right rather than something for which he should be grateful. Perhaps Keir would be a good influence upon Richard.

The return journey passed quickly and pleasantly for them both, as Keir ceaselessly questioned Jeremy about Toronto. By the time they reached Launston Mills they felt quite at ease in one another's company. Jeremy had even granted Keir permission to address him as "Uncle".

With a fluttering heart, Keir followed Jeremy into the magnificent hallway of the mansion he had so often admired from afar. He gazed about with awe.

Harriet emerged from the parlour. "Ah, Jeremy, we were hoping you would..." She faltered when she noticed Keir. "... return home today."

"Hello, Harriet." Jeremy dutifully brushed her cheek with his lips. "This is Keir O'Shaughnessy," he said, putting his arm about the boy's shoulders and urging him forward.

Keir snatched the cap from his head and crumpled it in both hands. "How do you do, Aunt... Mrs. Launston," he added quickly when he saw Harriet press her lips together in a gesture of rebuke.

Harriet regarded her husband with a querying, disapproving look. Jeremy's explanation was forestalled by Jillian. "Papa! Oh, I knew you'd come home today!"

A smile lit Jeremy's face. He hurried over to his daughter, and picked her up in an exuberant embrace. She giggled delightedly.

"How's my little angel?"

"I missed you so!" she replied, hugging him.

"And I missed you, sweetheart. Come, there's someone I want you to meet."

"I know him! He's the boy I talked to in the garden today."

"Well, Jilly, he's your cousin, Keir O'Shaughnessy."

"Really, Jeremy!" Harriet protested.

"My cousin?" Jillian echoed, puzzled.

"I shall explain it to you later, sweetheart. Keir and I have some business to attend to just now." Jeremy set her down. To Harriet he said, "Keir will be staying with us. See that a room is prepared for him."

"Not until you and I have discussed this, Jeremy!" Harriet said firmly.

"Later, Harriet." Jeremy's tone was equally firm. They stared at one another, Harriet defiantly, Jeremy with that look that bespoke male authority. His command, "Please do as I ask", could not have been misinterpreted as a request. Harriet still hesitated, but finally looked away in defeat. Without another word she walked into the drawing room.

So, it would start again, she thought miserably, Jeremy's interest in that Irish wench. Harriet dropped onto the sofa with a feeling of profound weariness.

There had, of course, been other women. Oh, she was well aware of that. Indeed, it was apparently necessary for Jeremy's well-being, since she herself had denied him her bed since the difficult birth of Jillian. Harriet had wanted no more children -- had not the courage, she sometimes taunted herself, to undergo the unpleasant pregnancies and painful births. And she still could not bear for Jeremy to touch her in that disgustingly intimate way. So, of course, she knew that other women provided her husband with whatever sexual gratification he needed. But Jeremy had been discreet, as befitted a gentleman, and, she suspected, confined his affairs to the city.

Although Harriet had sometimes speculated about the women who shared her husband's bed, she had never been too concerned about that side of their married life. She was content to be his companion -- or a glorified housekeeper, perhaps, as her sister Beatrice had once mocked. And although she would have preferred Jeremy to be celibate, the whores in Toronto posed no threat to her. But Rowena would.

Keir and Jeremy walked pensively down Mill Road. Keir thought it fortunate that he would be away at school and didn't have to live with the Launstons. He had sensed, in Harriet's antagonism toward him, more than the usual righteous disapproval with which others regarded him.

Jeremy too thought about Harriet. He hoped she would not prove difficult in this matter. She had to obey his wishes, of course, but she could make life unpleasant for them all. And now there was Rowena to contend with.

Jeremy felt uneasy about the meeting. During the past seven years he and Rowena had never exchanged more than a polite greeting. They had shared too much to behave as casual strangers, yet he was never quite prepared for the emotional tension that seemed to exist between them. It was his own guilty conscience, he reasoned.

Jeremy was momentarily speechless when Rowena answered his knock. Keir had told him about the previous night, but Jeremy hadn't expected this -- her blackened, swollen eye, and the bruises which disfigured her beautiful face. This was outrageous!

Rowena was astonished to see Jeremy with Keir, and appalled that Jeremy should see her in her present state. She turned away quickly, trying to hide her face in the shadows. "Keir, where've you been? You had me worried!"

"I found him in Port Perry," Jeremy explained. "Running away."

Rowena was shocked.

"May I come in?"

Rowena stepped back reluctantly and allowed Jeremy to enter. She didn't look at him. Shame overwhelmed her.

Jeremy sensed this and confronted her. Gently he lifted her chin until their eyes met. He could read everything there -- the suffering, the hopelessness, the guilt which was not hers but Brendan's -- and it was as though he could feel her pain just through this visual contact. Deep within him there was a spark of tenderness toward her that burst into flame. He had to restrain himself from taking her protectively into his arms.

Rowena could see the empathy in his eyes, could feel it in the fingers that lightly brushed her cheek. She thought she would weep. It had been a long time since a man had touched her with compassion rather than hatred.

"How could he do this to you?" Jeremy asked quietly. "How could you stay with a man like that?"

Rowena moved away from him then. "And what is it I'm to be doing? I recall that you were only too willing to sell me to Brendan once," she said bitterly.

"I? What are you talking about?"

They had both forgotten Keir's presence. He was intrigued by this exchange.

"Brendan told me that you had offered him money if he would marry me. 'Twas after I'd told you I'd have no part of your schemes!"

"I never approached Brendan with such an offer!" Jeremy considered for a moment, and then said, "It must have been my father's idea. I'm sorry, Rowena. But that's long past. I came here to discuss Keir's future."

Rowena faced him warily. She was afraid now.

"I promised my brother on his deathbed that I would take care of you and Keir. I've been neglecting that duty."

Rowena felt strangely disappointed by this confession. So his concern for them was only from obligation. "I remember telling you once before that we didn't need or want your help."

Keir clutched the edge of his chair in frustration. Why was his mother so stubborn?

"Pride is a commendable attribute, but not in excess."

"I'll not accept your charity!"

"It's hardly charity, Rowena. Your son is a Launston. It's only right that I do something for him."

"He's had no need of you these last ten years, nor has he now!"

"You think not? Perhaps you should ask him what he wants before you speak for him. Keir and I have already discussed the matter. He wishes to attend the College in Toronto, and I've agreed to send him."

"No! You'll not take my son away from me!"

"Rowena, listen to reason! What kind of life is this for the boy? Can you really believe he's happy when he tried to run away today? I have so much to offer him. Will you deny him the education he desires, and a chance to make something of his life?"

Rowena knew she had lost. How could she compete with Jeremy? He ***did*** have so much more to offer Keir. And he was right. Brendan abused the boy; Keir would run away again. Either way she would lose him. And hadn't she once made a vow to always do what was best for her son?

She tried to swallow the lump growing in her throat. "Is it what you really want?" she asked Keir, her eyes pleading with him to deny Jeremy's words.

Keir looked down. "Aye."

"Then I reckon I've nothing more to say." She sank into a chair, defeated. What would her life be like without Keir? She wouldn't cry. Not yet.

Jeremy took her hand in his. "You won't regret this, Rowena. You have a fine son. He'll be a credit to you and his father, God rest his soul."

The door flew open with a crash, startling the three occupants. Brendan staggered in. "Well, well, and what have we here? Come to visit me wife, the whore, have you Launston? She been obliging you in me absence, has she?" It was all going wrong again, Brendan thought. He had come home, contrite, just slightly liquored so that it wouldn't be so hard to apologize to her, and then here she was, entertaining Launston. And his blood was up.

Keir cringed. Brendan, he knew, was in his most dangerous mood. His tauntings and insults were always a prelude to his outbursts of violence.

"Or is it your bastard you've come to see? I always reckoned he was yours, though she had me convinced otherwise for a while. Sure, you've only to look at the bastard to see who sired him!"

"Keir is my nephew," Jeremy responded coldly. "I'm making arrangements with his mother to send him to school."

"Is that a fact then? Sure, I don't recall you asking my permission to take me boyo."

"Since he's not your son, I don't see how that concerns you."

"Don't you now? Then I'll be telling you. 'Tis me that's been clothing and feeding the little bastard these nine years, and I'll be wanting some return on me investment, as you might say. His mother and me was discussing that just last night." He grinned lopsidedly at Rowena. He knew he was taking the wrong approach again, that he was only aggravating the situation, and alienating Rowena even more. But he never could think or act rationally with her. Anger bubbled through his veins, and there was that familiar need to strike back at her, to get some sort of emotional response even if it was fear or hate. "Looks like I ain't convinced her yet that the bastard's old enough to work in the foundry."

Jeremy suppressed his own anger. "I would have thought you'd be only too pleased to relinquish your responsibility. You obviously have no affection for the boy, mistreating him as you do."

"Right you are. But you see, it pleases me to have him here. Getting a bit of me own back on the Launstons is how I look at it. And seeing him don't let me forget what his mother is. I might be tempted to otherwise, for she's as cold as a nun's tits in me bed."

Rowena, seething with indignation, jumped to her feet. "Have you no decency?"

She had unwittingly put herself in dangerous proximity to Brendan. He struck out at her, but Jeremy was faster. He pulled Rowena back, and moved in front of her. He was incensed by Brendan's coarseness and brutality. "Let's see if you can beat a man as easily as women and children."

Brendan chuckled, and rolled up his sleeves. "I've been waiting a long time for this."

"No, Jeremy!" Rowena cried frantically. "He'll kill you!"

Brendan winced inwardly. Of course she was on Jeremy's side. He clenched his fists harder. He ***was*** going to kill Launston, and by God no one would stop him this time! "And when I'm done with him, it'll be your turn, you fucking bitch!"

"Get out of here, both of you," Jeremy ordered, but neither Rowena nor Keir moved.

Brendan lunged for Jeremy, who dodged and landed a fist in Brendan's stomach and another on his chin, sending him reeling backwards. Brendan grinned at his opponent as he dabbed the back of his hand to his bloody mouth. Jeremy parried the next blow, but Brendan sneaked in a vicious left that cracked two of Jeremy's ribs. A hammer-like fist ploughed painfully into his face. Jeremy managed to twist aside to avoid the knee that aimed for his groin, the fingers that groped for his eyes. This was no gentleman's fight. The taste of blood in his mouth infused him with a primitive rage. He had never been inclined toward violence, but now he felt that he could easily kill Brendan.

It was too difficult for the spectators to tell who had the advantage. Both men fought with deadly intent. Rowena squeezed into a corner, clutching Keir to her, praying for divine intervention. Fearing for Jeremy's life.

Suddenly Brendan fell backwards over an upturned chair. His head struck the stone hearth. He lay still. Cautiously Jeremy bent over him.

"Is he dead?" Keir asked.

"No. Just out cold." Jeremy leaned heavily against the table. Each gasping breath sent a knife-thrust of pain through his ribs. Rowena produced a damp cloth, and wiped the blood and sweat from his face.

"Pack your things, Keir. Just as much as you can carry, and quickly. You too, Rowena. You're coming with us."

"I can't," she stated flatly. "He's still my husband."

"You're not safe here. You'll bear the brunt of his anger when he comes round, and I'll warrant he'll be in a dangerous mood. I won't leave you here with this madman."

"He'll just come for us."

"Let him try."

"And put him in a worse temper? Nay, I've caused you enough trouble this day."

Jeremy grabbed her hand which was gently dabbing at his face. "I'm not leaving without you," he said, staring into her eyes. "If he tries anything, I'll have him arrested. For God's sake, Rowena!"

She nodded. Before she left the house, she slipped a pillow beneath Brendan's head and covered him with a blanket, but otherwise left him where he had fallen.

Fortunately, they met no one on the road at that supper hour, though it was possible that someone in the half dozen houses they passed noticed the strange procession. Harriet greeted them in the hallway as soon as they entered the house. "What is the meaning of this, Jeremy? Good Lord... whatever happened to you?"

"If you would show Keir to his room, and then join us in the drawing room, I shall explain everything, Harriet," Jeremy said wearily.

"Very well. I've had one of the rooms above the kitchen prepared for the boy. It hasn't been used for some time, but I'm certain it will prove adequate. Come this way," she said to Keir.

Jeremy ushered Rowena into the drawing room, bid her take a seat, and poured them each a glass of brandy before dropping into a chair himself.

Rowena tried not to think of the last time she had been in this room. She tried to occupy her mind with details: the new wallpaper -- dusky roses climbing up grey trellises; an equally sombre carpet; heavy crimson drapes with gilt fringes and tassels; a print of Victoria and Albert; a daguerreotype portrait of Harriet and the children.

Rowena felt acutely uncomfortable. She didn't belong here. How could she possibly stay? "Jeremy, I...," she began.

Samuel walked in. "Thought I heard you come in, Jamie. Oh... how do you do?" he greeted Rowena. He squinted and then said, "It's not the O'Shaughnessy girl, is it? Damn me, but what happened to the both of you? Been in a brawl, have you?"

Harriet joined them. "Just what I was about to ask."

"Where's Jilly?" Jeremy inquired.

"I've sent her to her room."

Jeremy explained the situation in a few carefully chosen, words, exposing no more than necessary of Rowena's private life to avoid humiliating her.

Samuel was silent, but not so Harriet. "I trust I may speak freely without giving offense," she said. "I cannot see that any good will come of this arrangement, Jeremy. Send the boy to school, if you feel it your duty. I shall even consent to his presence here during the holidays, since I suppose we do owe it to your brother to ensure that his offspring is properly cared for. But having Mrs. Delaney in my home is another matter entirely. I'm certain she would feel as uncomfortable as I. It was a gallant gesture on your part, Jeremy, to assist her like this, and, of course, she's welcome to stay the night now that she is here. But surely she has her own family to rely upon and to provide her with refuge."

Despite Jeremy's tact, Rowena had felt ashamed and degraded as fragments of her life had been revealed to this company. She rose with dignity. "I never intended to impose on your hospitality, Mrs. Launston."

"Would you take the job of housekeeper?" Jeremy asked her. "You needn't feel obliged to anyone then."

"But, Jeremy, we've managed quite well without a housekeeper," Harriet interrupted. She tried to subdue the panic rising within her. She doubted that Jeremy realized how much this confrontation hurt her. That it was even necessary to defend her home against this woman was proof of his indifference toward her. Would he ever know how much she loved him, even if she didn't desire him in a physical way? All she wanted from him was some caring and consideration. But he seemed to think her devoid of feelings, impervious to emotional pain. And without a thought of how it might affect her, Jeremy had just offered what was essentially ***her*** job to another woman.

Jeremy flashed her an angry look. To Rowena he said, "Think about it. You'll stay here as our guest until you've decided what you wish to do."

"If you'll excuse me, I'll go and see to my son."

"Yes, of course," Harriet said. "I'm afraid there isn't a room prepared for you; however, you may use the one next to the boy's. I'm sure you wouldn't mind seeing to it yourself. There's linen in the chest at the foot of the bed... But then, of course, you are familiar with the running of this household."

"Thank you, Mrs. Launston."

When Rowena had gone, Jeremy said, "Well, Harriet, I've never before known you to be rude to a guest in our home!"

"A guest! You thrust a former servant upon me without warning and expect me to receive her as a guest?" She knew her voice was too harsh, her tone too shrewish, but she was on the verge of losing her self-control.

"If you two will excuse me," Samuel interposed, "I'm getting too old for this sort of thing. Settle it between you, by all means, but don't be too long about it for I'm damned hungry." He too left the room.

"You're being unreasonable about this, Harriet. What possible objections could you have to Rowena's staying on as housekeeper?"

"We do not need another servant, and I do not want that woman living in my house and interfering in our lives!"

"There's no need for hysterics, Harriet. I wouldn't expect you to entertain Rowena in the drawing room every evening. She'd have the kitchen quarters to herself."

"That arrangement would be very convenient for you, wouldn't it?" she said bitterly.

"Whatever are you talking about?"

She hadn't wanted to confront him with it now, but the angry words spilled from her. "I'm not unaware that you have been seeing other women. But I refuse to harbour your doxy under my roof!

"Of course you will deny it. But I saw the way you looked at that woman." Like you have never looked at me, she wanted to scream. "You cannot convince me that there is nothing between you! I've always suspected it. Do you expect me to believe that her husband hit her, and you, without just cause?"

"You're a fool, Harriet. And you've tried my patience too far! Rowena will stay. There's nothing further to discuss. Kindly see to supper now. I want nothing."

Harriet drew herself up regally and swept from the room.

Sanctimonious prude, Jeremy thought. He should have asserted his marital rights long ago, and taught his wife a little humility. But then he would be no better than Brendan Delaney.

God, what an unsavoury mess this was!

Despite his assurances to Rowena, Jeremy knew he had no legal weapons with which to save her from Delaney. She was Brendan's wife. It was within his rights to demand that his wife return to him. The law allowed him to beat her, rape her, abuse her in any way save to kill her. It was damnable! At least Delaney had no power over Keir, since the man had never formally adopted the boy, but what could be done to help Rowena?

He could try bluffing Delaney, who probably didn't know the extent of his legal rights. But that he, a magistrate, should indulge in such deceit....

He poured himself another drink.

Rowena declined supper, and Keir ate his in the kitchen -- at Harriet's suggestion. Among the three diners in the dining room, only Samuel did justice to the meal. Harriet pleaded a headache and excused herself, not having touched her food. Jillian, sensing the tension, and unhappy that her father wasn't present, just toyed with her supper. She finally left the table, and went to seek him out.

"Hello, sweetheart," Jeremy said absently when Jillian joined him in the drawing room.

"Why is everyone so upset?" she asked as she crawled onto his lap. "Mama's gone to bed, Grandfather just kept shaking his head at supper, and I've not seen that boy at all! He's not really my cousin, is he? He's not like my cousins in Peterborough."

"Keir is your Uncle Adrian's son."

"But why hasn't he been here before? Why...?"

Jeremy silenced her. "It's a long story. You'll understand when you're older."

Jillian grimaced at this typical adult response, but said nothing. She snuggled up to her father, and was contentedly quiet for a while.

"Are you thinking about the trains, Papa? Will we have trains, like you said?"

Jeremy had almost forgotten about this -- one of the reasons for his prolonged stay in Toronto. A charter had been granted several years ago for a railroad to be built from Launston Mills to Port Hope, on the shore of Lake Ontario. What a boost that would be to the community! A fast, direct route to the Front, and from there to the American markets. And what a saving it would be to the Launston enterprises.

But the repeal of the Corn Law in Britain two years ago had hurt the Canadian economy; Britain no longer gave preference to Canadian timber, and the markets were saturated. Thus, Canada had been sucked into the whirlpool of worldwide depression. No one was willing to invest money in railroads now.

"We'll have trains rumbling through Launston Mills one day," Jeremy said. "But not yet. And now I think it's time for you to be in bed, young lady."

Jeremy spent the rest of the evening discussing business with his father. When Samuel retired, Jeremy returned to the drawing room, and poured himself another drink.

Rowena sat in the dark bedroom above the kitchen. She had made up the bed, intending to spend this one night here in peace. She knew now that she couldn't, that there was no peace for her here. She had resolved not to accept Jeremy's offer -- tempting though it was -- for she could not live in a place where she was so obviously not welcome by its mistress. She must leave tonight, for Jeremy would surely try to dissuade her if he were aware of her intentions. She knew she would weaken under his intense gaze. She admitted to herself that she wanted him to stop her.

Rowena bundled her few possessions into her shawl. Quietly she crept from the room, pausing a moment outside Keir's bedroom. She restrained herself from looking in on him, and dejectedly descended the stairs. It was a dark, moonless night, and the kitchen was a yawning black hole. Rowena groped her way across the room toward the door.

A scraping sound, a hiss, and then a bright flash of light somewhere behind Rowena startled her. She swung about. By the light of the lucifer he held in his fingers, she saw Jeremy sitting in a chair. He lit a candle with the match, and said, "Where are you going?"

"To my sister's. For tonight." Though, God knows, Moira would not appreciate her request for sanctuary again so soon. Of course, Moira never refused to help her, though she did have a way of making people feel guilty for requiring her to do her Christian duty. It was the kind of help that Rowena would gladly have forgone if at all possible.

"I thought you would do something like this. Harriet left you little choice."

"'Tisn't just that. Don't you see, Jeremy, I don't belong here!" She moved away from the door, toward the light. "Nor anywhere else. You see this?" She held up the bundle. "'Tis all I own in the world, all I have, except for my son. I've no place to call home. My father's house, where I was happy as a child, belongs to another woman now. There's no joy for me in my husband's house, no sustenance for my soul, now that you have taken my son away from me. I'd perish there.

"'Twasn't always so, but 'tis the drink that's corrupted Brendan. He's tortured by his own weaknesses, and tries to confirm his manhood with his fists. And still I pity him, and feel in many ways responsible, for I've only added to his soul's burdens. But I can't return to him.

"So I must find a place for myself. A place where I belong -- even if it be no more than a grave!"

She burst into tears, and made a dash for the door. Jeremy intercepted her, and caught her in his arms. Touching was like a physical jolt to them both.

"God!" Jeremy groaned.

Their lips met. The passion which overwhelmed them was almost frightening in its intensity.

Jeremy held her tightly. "I thought I was destined never to know a woman's love."

"Oh, Jamie, how could I stay now?"

"How could you leave, Rowena? "

"Don't tempt me into committing a greater sin that I already have," she pleaded. "We're neither of us free to love. We would only hurt others by our selfishness. Think of our children."

His hand dropped reluctantly from her shoulders. "You're right, of course. Forgive me. This won't happen again," he said sadly. "But you must stay. Please."

Awkwardly they faced one another, afraid to touch lest they rekindle the passion for which they both longed.

Rowena took a step toward him, but then turned and fled upstairs.

She slept little that night, and when she did it was to dream of Brendan, of Keir, of Adrian. They were the ones who stood between her and Jeremy. Her husband, who owned her as one might own a cow, to whom she was irrevocably chained until death. Her son, who had suffered enough through her sins. Even Adrian, dead these eleven years, interposed himself and made her love for his brother seem vulgar and immoral.

She must be cursed! It was iniquitous to feel such desire for a man! Rowena got out of bed, and picked up her rosary beads. She knelt on the floor, and commenced the long recitation after imploring the Virgin Mary to purge her of her sinful weakness.

Jeremy didn't seek his bed that night. He paced the drawing room, drinking too much, tormented by his own demons. Guilt was the most persistent. That he should covet that which he had denied his brother was the ultimate irony: that Rowena should be inaccessible to him, the ultimate punishment.

The soft September dawn was shattered by an insistent pounding upon the front door. Jeremy, who had dozed off in a chair, woke with a start. He felt wretched. His mouth was pickled in brandy, his tongue, tobacco-smoked. His sore jaw reminded him of yesterday's encounter with Delaney's fists, as did his ribs when he rose stiffly from the chair. He shook his head, fuzzy from too much alcohol and too little sleep, and ran his fingers through his hair. Who the hell was calling at this time of the morning?

Jeremy nearly collided with Rowena in the hall. She had been up long ago. Until this moment she had deceived herself into thinking that her prayers had been answered. Now that she saw him -- weary, dishevelled, bearing the scars of his fight with Brendan -- she wanted only to take him into her arms.

The renewed thundering on the door broke the spell that had held them motionless.

"I'll answer it," Jeremy said.

"It'll be Brendan. I have to face him."

Jeremy nodded reluctantly. "Wait in the drawing room." As Rowena started toward it, Jeremy reached out and detained her. "Don't go back to him, no matter what he says." It was as much an appeal as an order.

Rowena didn't reply.

Jeremy unbolted the front door. Brendan shoved his way impatiently into the foyer, and demanded. "Where's me wife?"

Brendan, though sober, still bore the evidence of the previous evening's dissipation, as well as the marks of Jeremy's fists. His lower lip was swollen, one of his eyes was puffed up and discoloured, Jeremy noticed with distinct satisfaction. He regarded Brendan with contempt.

"She has nothing to say to you, though I have. Rowena has accepted the position of housekeeper here. She won't be going back with you."

"The divil she won't!" Brendan attempted to push past Jeremy, but his way was blocked.

"If you go near her again I'll have you arrested for assault. And this time you won't get off as lightly as you did in the Colonel's day."

Brendan smirked. "'Tain't a crime to teach me wife a lesson."

"Attempted murder is. Yesterday you threatened to kill her. I was a witness. If you so much as touch her again, I'll see that you're locked up."

Brendan's confidence wavered, but then he said defiantly, "And stealing a man's wife is a crime! I'll be talking to her afore I leave this house!"

Rowena, who had listened anxiously from just inside the drawing room, now stepped into the hallway. Brendan seemed embarrassed when he saw her. It was usually like that in the sober light of dawn, after one of his violent fits.

"I've come to take you home, mavourneen." He hadn't used that endearment in years. "Launston can keep the boy. The bastard's always been the cause of trouble between us. Maybe things'll be different now."

She looked into his bloodshot eyes. Often in the past she had been softened by his remorseful pleas for forgiveness, and had believed his promises of reform. "I'm not going with you," she replied quietly. She saw the muscles in his jaw twitch as he clenched his teeth, and was afraid.

"Your place is with me! Have you forgotten your vows, woman? 'Tis your duty to obey me."

Rowena shook her head. "'Tis no use, Brendan. You destroyed everything good between us long ago. Leave me in peace, I beg of you."

"The divil I will!" He took a step toward her, but Jeremy grabbed his arm.

"Get out of my house, Delaney, or I'll throw you out."

Brendan suddenly laughed -- a wry chuckle that Rowena well knew was a danger signal.

"A man don't take kindly to being played the fool. You'll be regretting this, the pair of you," Brendan swore, his voice low, but full of menace. He laughed again. "When the time's right, you'll be paying for this. That'll give you something to think on." He spat contemptuously on the floor, and walked out.

Rowena shivered as she said, "He means that. He'll do something dreadful, I know it! I must go with him, Jamie. I'd never forgive myself if...."

"Do you think I'd let you go back to that lunatic? He was bluffing. He wouldn't dare try anything. You'll be safe here, I promise you."

"But will you be?" she asked in a taut voice.

"You let me worry about that."

Keir was already in the kitchen when Rowena returned to it. He was standing at the east window, looking out over the lawn to the stables. "I saw Da... ***him*** here. It's alright, isn't it? He can't make us go back, can he?"

"No. But if ever you see him again, you stay clear of him, do you understand?"

Keir was startled by her vehemence. "Aye."

They prepared breakfast together in silence. Having thought all their troubles were over now, Keir was disappointed to see his mother looking so grim, even afraid at times.

The two daily girls arrived, and were clearly astonished to find Rowena and Keir in the kitchen. Rowena briefly explained her position, and then sent the girls about their chores.

Keir breakfasted in the kitchen with Rowena, the two maids, and Tom Finch, who still worked for the Launstons. Tom was a lanky young man of one and twenty, and a bachelor still. The girls often eyed him during the meal and giggled, but Tom was as quiet and apparently unconcerned as he had been as a boy. His real love was horses, and only on that topic did he ever discourse at length. Tom had moved out of his step-father's house four years ago when Simon and Margaret's third child had been born. He had made a home out of the Launstons' old log cabin, and seemed content.

Keir helped his mother with the dishes, and then wandered aimlessly around the room. He longed to explore the rest of this magnificent house, but he had not the courage to do so uninvited. He had not yet met his grandfather, and the thought of running into that formidable old man kept him from venturing into the main part of the house.

When Rowena asked him to fetch some water, he gladly complied. The stone well was not far from the kitchen. Keir released the latch on the windlass, and the bucket plummetted down the dark tunnel, splashing into the water far below. He turned the crank, and the bucket creaked and groaned its way back to daylight. Keir hoisted it onto the stone wall, and then poured it into the container he had brought. He used his cupped hands as a dipper, and drank greedily of the refreshing, sweet water. He almost choked on it when a deep, gruff voice startled him.

"So... you're Keir."

Keir faced his grandfather. The old man's hair was a silvery gray; his face, somewhat flabby and lined; his teeth, rather sparse; but otherwise he did not look his sixty years. He walked tall and erect, a slight paunch distorting his otherwise athletic physique. His brown eyes critically appraised his grandson. Keir gulped.

"There's not much of your father in you."

Keir said nothing. He just stood and gawked, forgetting even to breathe.

"A pity you're not more like him," Samuel said, the relief in his voice belying his words. He seemed to imply that the physical dissimilarity somehow lessened Keir's relationship to the Launstons.

Samuel turned to go, but Keir managed to say, "I'm like him, though. At least I want to be. Uncle Jeremy said I could go to school. I'll be a credit to my father, you'll see!"

Samuel's bristly white brows were drawn together as he looked back at Keir. "You've your mother's spunk, I'll say that for you. But don't make any claims on me, boy. You may be a Launston by accident of birth, but not in name. Don't forget that."

Keir swallowed these harsh words though they stuck in his throat and caused his eyes to burn. He'd show the old man one day! He'd show them all what he could do, that he was a good as any of them!

Keir spent the rest of the morning rambling about the gardens and outbuildings. He visited Tom in the stables, and was introduced to the horses. He wished he could ride one of these splendid creatures.

"That's my pony - Sugarplum," Jillian said, joining him.

Keir must have betrayed some surprise at her words for she said fiercely, "I ***can*** ride, you know. Better than you, I bet!" She set her curls bouncing with a haughty toss of her head, and hobbled over to Sugarplum. She slipped him an apple, and patted his nose. When the horse had devoured the treat, she threw her arms possessively about his neck, and laid her cheek against him. "Papa gave him to me for my birthday. He comes from Uncle Nigel's stables." Jillian stared past Keir with a puzzled look upon her face. "There's that man again," she said. "Watching us. That one who made such a fuss and commotion in the house this morning. I saw him leave, from my window," she added by way of explanation.

By the time Keir had turned around, Brendan had vanished. His covert action, combined with Rowena's near terror this morning, sent a tingle of unease up Keir's spine.

Jillian turned on him petulantly. "I don't like you anymore, boy! Go away! Nothing's been the same since you came here!"

Keir was taken aback by this sudden change in her. "I live here now," he countered.

"Well nobody wants you! You don't belong here. You can't be Uncle Adrian's son because he's dead!"

"He ***was*** my father, and I've as much right to be here as you!"

The two children glared resentfully at one another. Jillian would have run, had she been able, but still she managed to move swiftly out of the stable. In her haste she caught her lame foot, and shrieked as she tumbled awkwardly to the ground. She lay on the grass and pummelled it peevishly with both fists while she sobbed in frustration.

Keir was beside her in a moment. He picked her up, though she squirmed and struggled like a hooked fish in his hands. "Are you hurt?" he asked, handing her the crutch.

She regarded him strangely, the tantrum having abruptly ceased, and said smugly, "Richard will hate you." Then she limped back to the house, leaving Keir totally bewildered by her erratic behaviour.

He didn't see her again, or his grandfather or Harriet, for the following morning he and Jeremy left for Toronto.

Chapter 33

Jeremy watched his awe-struck nephew with amusement as the stagecoach trundled across the bridge that spanned the swampy Don River valley, and entered the city. The boy had exclaimed with unabashed delight at his first glimpse of Lake Ontario stretching unbroken to the distant horizon. He had plagued Jeremy with questions. Was the United States really on the other side of this *ocean*? Could one ever see that country from here? How long would it take to sail across the lake?

The three other passengers in the stage had exchanged the knowing smiles of the well-travelled, yet some of Keir's excitement seemed to infect them. When Jeremy pointed out the new gaol -- a stern grey fortress frowning over the Toronto harbour -- the passengers glanced out the window as though they, too, were seeing it for the first time.

Keir sat on the edge of the straw-padded leather seat, and craned his neck about so that he would be certain not to miss a single thing. But there was so much to tantalize and divert the eye! As they trotted along Front Street he could see the westward curving arm of the sandy peninsula which widened into a treed hand seeming to offer the harbour and city protection from the vast lake and all that lay beyond. Streets ran northward from the lakefront to be crisscrossed with military precision by roads running east and west. Houses, shops, hotels, and taverns elbowed one another, while pedestrians, horses, oxen, carts, wagons, and fashionable carriages vied for road space. Dogs, cats, and pigs ferretted around the streets, adding to the confusion.

The stage proceeded at a funereal pace through the throng of people and vehicles crowded about the quadrangular red brick market building which, Jeremy informed Keir, reached north to King Street, Toronto's main thoroughfare. Farmers came from miles around to sell their produce here, Keir learned. His mouth watered as he glimpsed stall upon stall of ripe fruits and vegetables and great carcasses of animals suspended from gigantic meat hooks.

Jeremy related a gruesome accident that had occurred here fourteen years earlier. An enthusiastic mob of people had crowded the wooden gallery, which girded the building, to listen to Sheriff Jarvis denounce the mayor of Toronto, William Lyon Mackenzie. His speech had evoked appreciative cheers and such a stamping of feet that the gallery had collapsed, impaling several unfortunate persons upon the deadly meat hooks below.

Keir shuddered. His vivid imagination easily conjured up this scene of horror; the splintering sound of wood, the terrified screams, the tangled mass of broken and bleeding bodies....

"I recall that," the elderly lady passenger informed them. "And I heard that the disaster met with applause from Mackenzie's supporters, since most of the dead and injured were Tories. I never could abide that villain, Mackenzie! Too bad he was never caught and hanged as a traitor, as he deserved!"

They passed the fish market on the beach to their left. Maidservants and housewives with straw baskets upon their arms haggled with Indians and fishermen over the prices of freshly caught eels, whitefish, salmon, pickerel, perch, sturgeon, masquelonge, herring, and bass. The pungent smell of fish wafted into the coach, causing the elderly lady to press a lavender-scented handkerchief to her face. Schooners, steamers, canoes, and skiffs lined the many wharves which stretched into the placid bay.

Ahead of them squatted an unusual wedge-shaped building constructed at an acute angle where Front Street and Market Street converged. This was popularly and descriptively known as the 'Coffin Block', Jeremy told Keir, and it was here that the stagecoach stopped.

Keir eagerly alighted from the cramped vehicle, and took a deep breath of Toronto. It was not an altogether pleasant smell, for the stench of animal and human ordure was unmitigated by the pervasive fragrance of cedar and pine as it was at home. Yet there was a fresh breeze blowing off the lake -- clean, unscented, light -- so different from the close muskiness of the backwoods.

"Come," Jeremy said. "I've hired a carriage. We'll dine first, for I've no doubt the journey has given you an appetite, and I myself am parched from the dusty ride. Then we'll pay a visit to my tailor. That suit seems ready to split at the seams."

Keir looked down at his travel-stained, Sunday-best outfit, the only suit he owned. It had been clean two days ago, at the outset of this trip. Despite the careful mending and letting-out his mother had done, it was shabby. His trousers barely reached the tops of his ankle-high boots, and the sleeves of his too-tight jacket ended well above the wrists. He was embarrassed at the thought of arriving at the school in such garb, and was grateful for the offer of new clothes.

The carriage took them two blocks farther along Front Street to Yonge Street, where it halted before a long, white, pillared hotel with three tiers of galleries stretching across its facade. It was the grandest hotel Keir had ever seen. It was here, at the American House Hotel, that the famous British novelist, Charles Dickens, had stayed during his brief visit six years ago. Keir had never heard of that literary personage, but he was determined to acquaint himself with that writer's works.

Keir walked shyly beside his uncle as they entered the dim lobby lit with flickering gas sconces. Large, dark, overstuffed furniture, gilt-edged mirrors, patterned carpets, marble-topped tables, heavy velvet draperies over frilly lace curtains, and tall, potted palms decorated the cavernous, high-ceilinged room.

The dining room was equally large and ornate. A soft murmur of voices was accompanied by the gentle strains of music from a quartet tucked unobtrusively in one corner. The fashionable ladies and gentlemen made Keir acutely self-conscious in his ill-fitting, rustic garb. He felt very young, very awkward, very ignorant as he faced his unperturbed uncle across the table.

"Good afternoon, Mr. Launston. A pleasure to see you again so soon, sir," the waiter said as he handed them menus.

"Thank you, James."

Keir glanced at the card with a fluttering stomach, wondering what was expected of him.

"Shall I order for you?" Jeremy asked, noticing the boy's panic-stricken face.

"Yes please, Uncle."

"Good. We'll have the oysters on half shell, consommé, pheasant pie, roast of beef; an ice, I think for dessert, and a bottle of the usual."

While Jeremy was ordering, Keir looked down at the array of silver cutlery which shone on the crisp white linen before him. Whyever were there so many different sizes and shapes of forks, knives, spoons, and a variety of crystal goblets? Surely he wouldn't require all these to eat his meal!

Keir glanced surreptitiously about the room, and wondered if he would ever be as self-assured in such sophisticated and intimidating surroundings as his uncle appeared to be.

Keir watched closely as the waiter returned with a bottle of wine, uncorked it, passed the cork to Jeremy, and then poured only a mouthful of the deep red liquid into Jeremy's glass. Jeremy rolled the cork between his fingers, sniffed it, and laid it aside. He picked up the glass, held it up to the light, passed it beneath his nose, and finally took a sip, retaining it speculatively in his mouth a moment before swallowing. He smiled and nodded to James, who then poured them each a full glass. Keir was fascinated by this incomprehensible and somewhat dramatic ritual.

"Shall we drink a toast to your first visit to Toronto?" Jeremy suggested, raising his glass.

Keir lifted his glass and grinned at his uncle. "I've never had wine before," he admitted in a hushed voice, and then wondered why he had whispered.

"Go easy on it," Jeremy advised. "Wine is meant to be savoured, not gulped."

Keir's tongue recoiled with shock as the dry burgundy assaulted it. The pungent fumes wrinkled his nose. He swallowed quickly, grimacing inwardly. He had expected nectar and had tasted instead, a bitter potion little better than his mother's herbal concoctions.

Yet... it had a heady after-taste. Keir tried another sip, and this time his tongue didn't curl up. By the time he reached the bottom of the glass, he was beginning to think that a person could quite easily become accustomed to this unusual beverage.

Meanwhile he had wallowed in other new taste sensations, always carefully watching how Jeremy approached his food, and then following his uncle's example. The mystery of the silverware was thus revealed to a rather incredulous boy who pitied the person responsible for washing up.

Jeremy watched his nephew with pride. He had been pleased to see that Keir, though hungry, had not attacked his meal like a foraging hog -- as, unfortunately, too many people did these days -- but had, by discreet observation, discovered the proper order and use of the implements, and had eaten with commendable grace.

Keir definitely had potential, Jeremy thought. The boy was bright, spirited, and there was a blithe charm about him which hardship had not been able to destroy. Yet the boy would not have it easy at school. Jeremy knew it was essential to disclose the truth about Keir's parentage to Richard, before his son imagined a more scandalous relationship between himself and his cousin. If the other boys discovered the truth they would be more subtly cruel to Keir than the children of Launston Mills had been.

Even without the stigma of bastardy, Keir would be ridiculed. His lilting Irish accent, although not as pronounced as Rowena's, was unmistakable. The Irish were generally not highly regarded, particularly since so many destitute refugees of the potato famine had swamped the city these last two years. Keir would probably be the only Catholic, which presented a different type of problem.

"How do you feel about your religion, Keir?"

Keir was puzzled. "I go to church every Sunday, if that's what you mean, Uncle."

"I'm afraid you may have difficulty attending church here," Jeremy said frankly. "Most of the boys are of the Anglican faith, and thus the boarders attend St. James. Since you are not allowed into the city on your own, you probably won't be able to attend mass regularly."

"Then I'll go to St. James with the others."

Jeremy raised an eyebrow.

"'Tis the same God, isn't it? I'd not be a sinner if I prayed to Him different, would I?"

Jeremy smiled. "I should think that God would understand, though I'm not so sure your mother or Father Killeny would."

"Then we'd best not tell them."

They grinned at one another. "Well, if you've had enough to eat, we should be going," Jeremy said.

"Yes, thank you, Uncle Jeremy. That was the most delicious food I've ever tasted -- but you'd best not tell Ma that either!"

The carriage took them up to King Street, the fashionable and social thoroughfare of Toronto. What a variety of shops -- new brick ones dwarfing the older wooden ones - -and what tempting displays in the windows! There was a store that sold only tobacco, and one, only books, while another proclaimed a selection of confectionery ices. The road was macadamized, and lined with board sidewalks, with gas lamps marching along one side. And the people! All shapes and classes in a variety of costumes. Several scarlet-coated soldiers caught Keir's attention until it was jolted away by the sight of a huge black man. Keir had never before seen a Negro. And there was St. James Cathedral, the bastion of the Church of England, its spire piercing the skyline.

At the tailor's Keir was measured, and the materials were selected for several school outfits and a new Sunday-best suit. His boots were still adequate since he had just grown into them, and had worn them only on Sundays.

In less than an hour they were driving along the waterfront once again, as Jeremy took Keir on a brief tour of the city. They passed Bishop Strachan's home -- known as the 'Palace' since his ecclesiastical promotion -- and the House of Assembly in the next block, which had been the seat of Upper Canada's government until the union of the Canadas in 1841. They continued west through the fashionable residential district, toward Fort York, and returned eastward via King Street. They drove quickly past the cholera hospital, packed with Irish immigrants who had come to Canada to escape the devastating famine which had been ravaging their country, taking its toll in millions.

The carriage turned north onto a gravelled drive lined with young chestnut trees. Sunny green fields spread out on either side of them, and Keir glimpsed, with a racing heart, a crowd of boys watching teams of white-clad youths engaged in a game he did not recognize.

"That's cricket," Jeremy answered Keir's query. "A very popular game. I'm certain you'll catch on to it quickly."

Keir felt his courage ebb. His hands grew damp with nervousness; his throat was tight and dry. The delightful lightheadedness induced by the wine was replaced by nausea.

The school, Keir knew, was the finest in Canada West, and he surmised that only the sons of the wealthy could afford to attend it. His brief association with Jeremy had already shown Keir how little he knew of the ways of such people, and he feared he would fit in like a common ox among thoroughbred horses.

Perhaps it was not yet too late to change his mind.

But Jeremy would be contemptuous of such cowardice, Keir thought, and he would lose his own self-respect. Besides, he was determined to succeed in this world to which he so desperately wanted to belong. He gritted his teeth and straightened his shoulders.

Jeremy sensed Keir's inner turmoil, and felt sympathetic. "Although physical and athletic competence are respected," he said, "you'll find that intellectual prowess is even more esteemed."

Keir did not fail to grasp the full import of Jeremy's words. He needed more than the language of his fists to defend himself here. But then, when had an O'Shaughnessy ever been at a loss for words?

Straight ahead of them was a porticoed square brick building of two tall stories. Smaller four-chimneyed blocks surrounded the main building. These, Jeremy explained, were the residences.

Keir waited in the cool dimness of the hall while his uncle conferred with the headmaster in the office. He wriggled on the hard wooden bench, twirling his cap nervously in his fingers.

He jumped when the door opened and Jeremy, with an encouraging smile, bid him enter. Keir swallowed hard as he stepped into the room and faced the man in clerical vestments who sat behind the desk.

"This is the principal, Keir," Jeremy said. "The Reverend Mr. Sutton."

"How do you do, sir?"

"Now, if you'll excuse me, I shall look for my son."

"Certainly," the principal said.

Keir felt his excellent meal curdle in his stomach at his uncle's desertion. As soon as the door closed behind Jeremy the headmaster said, "Your uncle has informed me that you are willing to attend our Anglican church. You realize that, since there are now separate schools in Toronto for those of the Roman Catholic persuasion, we no longer receive requests for admission from people of your faith. We have, therefore, made no provision for attendance at Catholic services."

"Yes, sir."

The principal watched Keir carefully as he said, "Do you fully understand the implications of such a rash decision, young man?" He elaborated. "Your church would not look kindly upon one who abandonned his faith."

"I've not said I'll give up my faith, sir. I can't see what harm it would do anyone if I learned about yours though."

"This is a serious matter. One cannot change one's religion at will to suit one's purposes. Such a man has no true faith -- a very contemptible and dangerous position."

Keir could see the doors of this venerable institution closing in his face as he replied humbly, "Yes, sir."

"However... since your father was an Anglican there's no reason why you shouldn't adopt his religion -- if you so choose. Your father, by the way, was an excellent student. I was the classical master at the time. Let us hope that you will emulate him."

Keir noticed a hint of a smile in the headmaster's eyes. He forgot all his earlier doubts when he realized that he had been accepted.

"Your uncle and I agreed that it would be prudent not to mention to anyone your relationship to the Launstons. Such an unnecessary disclosure would cause us all problems. I'm certain you understand."

"Yes, sir."

"Good. Now, as to your educational background.... Have you studied any of the Classics - Latin, Greek?"

"No, sir."

"Then you will have to work very hard indeed."

"Yes, sir," Keir replied eagerly.

While this conversation was taking place, Jeremy was walking across the playing field in search of his son. He found him among other boys his age, engrossed in the cricket match. Jeremy laid his hand upon Richard's shoulder, and the boy looked around in surprise.

"Father! What are you doing here?"

Richard was a rather insipid looking boy, neither handsome nor plain, but rather nondescript, like his mother. But this vapidness did not extend to his character. He would become the kind of man one might disregard at first glance, but never at a second.

"I'd like to speak to you, Richard. Perhaps you would accompany me to the headmaster's office."

"Is something wrong?"

"No. Just a matter that you and I must discuss in private." When they had left the crowd behind them Jeremy said, "It's a family concern, and one, which I think you will agree, should go no further than this conversation between us."

Richard frowned and looked wistfully back at the game as a cheer shattered the air.

Jeremy continued. "You never knew my brother, Adrian, or much about him, though I would have revealed these facts to you once you were older." Jeremy was finding this difficult. How would Richard react? How to be tactful, yet truthful? He plunged in. "My brother was to have been married, but was prevented from this by his arrest -- you already know about that and his subsequent death. However... he fathered a son."

Richard stopped walking. "A son? A bastard?"

Jeremy frowned at Richard's bluntness. "Yes. Your cousin's name is Keir O'Shaughnessy. That's why I'm here today. Keir will be attending school with you."

Richard shot his father an outraged look. "You brought him here? Why here?"

"Because he's my responsibility now," Jeremy said, placing his hand affectionately on his son's shoulder. "Life has not been easy for him. A good education will give him a better chance."

Richard jerked away angrily from his father's friendly grasp. "He'll ruin us! They'll all laugh at me! How could you, Father?"

Jeremy glowered at his son. "I'll not tolerate histrionics, Richard. No one need know the circumstances of Keir's birth."

"But I'll know! And I'll be ashamed to be seen with him!"

"That's enough!" Jeremy ordered, angry at his son's arrogant display of temper. "Keir is your cousin. Nothing will ever change that. You will be civil toward him, and you will keep your own counsel with regard to his background!"

Richard pressed his lips together and tilted his nose skyward. How like his mother he looked when he struck that righteous pose, Jeremy thought with distaste. This was not the first time that Jeremy had despaired of reaching his son. Richard was too much Harriet's child. He had imbibed, with his mother's milk, her ability to shut out all appeals to reason once her attitude toward something had crystallized.

Keir, having undergone a brief oral examination in various subjects, welcomed the arrival of Jeremy and Richard. The boys scrutinized one another warily, and took an instant dislike to each another -- Keir, because of Richard's condescending attitude, and Richard, because he saw Keir as a threat to his good name, and perhaps, not quite consciously, a threat to Richard's already shaky relationship with his father.

"Well, Richard," the Reverend Mr. Sutton said, "your cousin will be quartered in your dormitory, so I expect you to initiate him into the school routine. I'm certain I can rely upon you to set a good example for Keir in all matters. I shall leave him in your capable charge then. You are both dismissed."

Richard showed no reaction to this tacit bid for peace. "Yes, sir," he said. Without looking at either his father or Keir, he turned and walked from the room.

"Thank you, sir," Keir said to the headmaster before following his cousin.

Jeremy shook hands with the principal. Both were aware of the delicate, perhaps explosive, situation that Jeremy had precipitated. "You'll keep me informed?"

"You can rely upon that, Mr. Launston."

Keir had just fetched his carpetbag from the carriage when Jeremy joined the boys. "I'll see you at Christmas vacation," he said to them.

"Goodbye, Father," Richard said stiffly.

"Goodbye, Uncle Jeremy, and thanks!"

Chapter 34

In another part of the city a woman lay dying.

This was not a district that Keir would have believed could exist, nor one that Jeremy was familiar with. Many of the dwellings were mere one room hovels that often housed pigs as well as a dozen people. Crude, dilapidated taverns teemed with drunken, rowdy, cussing men and women. Cheap whores, some little more than children, loitered in the alleys.

In a boxy room in one of the squalid tenements, Gwyn O'Shaughnessy was slowly bleeding to death. She was still lucid enough to appreciate the irony of this -- it was God thumbing his nose at her, she was sure. She had sought an abortion not only because she could not provide for another child, but because she had been so terrified of dying in childbirth, leaving her darling Gavin an orphan.

She recalled only too well the horror of Gavin's birth, nearly seven years earlier. It had been as she had suspected -- once her condition had become obvious, she had been unable to procure customers. The bit of money she had managed to save had dwindled alarmingly quickly to cover the costs of a room, food, and wood for heating. The latter she had often done without, particularly during the last weeks of her pregnancy, although it had been a frigid January. When the baby had started to come, she had not even known what to expect, had not arranged for a midwife to attend her, had not even had a friend to summon for help.

The pains she had at first mistaken for indigestion, for she had eaten only sporadically the previous few days, and not well. But then they had become stronger and more insistent, and finally she had thought the devil himself was tearing at her insides. Her screams had eventually brought an irate neighbour to her door. Although that woman had been gruff and hard, she had stayed to see the babe born.

Gwyn hugged Gavin to her now, as she had then -- protectively, lovingly. Then, she had sworn to him that she would do whatever she could to make life better for him than it had been for her.

And for a while, life ***had*** been better, for she had found herself a 'patron'. Joseph had not minded the child, so long as he had been out of the way. Fortunately, Gavin had been an easy, co-operative baby, who had slept most of the time. They had been able to move to a suite of rooms in a better part of the city. For the first half of his young life Gavin had been warm, comfortable, and well fed. And Gwyn had acted the lady, spending all her earnings on expensive clothes and rich foods, and living a dream fulfilled.

If she ever thought about her home and family it was to picture herself strolling the streets of Launston Mills in her exquisite gowns, flaunting her cleverness, for surely she had earned this wealth for herself. And she'd pitied her stupid sisters who lived squalid, dreary lives with no beautiful things around them, dependent upon stupid, grimy men who knew nothing about the art of lovemaking.

She had a talent for pleasing men, she'd thought, and she took great care to keep herself beautiful and desirable. She had the wit of one twice her age and no one could tell from her sultry voice and careful pronunciations that she was anything but a well-bred lady. She'd kept up on the latest gossip and society news to entertain her companion with witticisms as well as with her body. She'd felt irresistible and powerful.

Then Joseph had stopped visiting, and the takings from casual encounters had not sustained them in that extravagant lifestyle. But so convinced had she been that another man would soon succumb to her spell, that she had not at first stopped her lavish spending. But no one had come to rescue her this time.

Gradually during the past three years she and Gavin had moved to cheaper and cheaper rooms. And as her "fortune" had depleted, she had sold most of her elaborate gowns and all the trinkets and baubles on which she had wasted her money.

And as the quality of her wardrobe had diminished, so had the calibre of her clientele. She had been caught in a whirlpool of poverty, spiralling ever downward with no chance of escape. Lately, she had not even had the courage to look at herself in a mirror. She felt old beyond her twenty-three years, contaminated by filth, diseased by the dirty men who pawed her. More and more often of late, she and Gavin had resorted to theft in order to keep from starving.

"Well, now, my little man," she said to the child. "I've a job for you to do. And it might be the hardest thing you'll ever have to do in this life. I have to be leaving you... Through no wish of my own, my lamb!" She gripped him fiercely when he started to protest. "You listen to me, and do just as I say! You go to the priest down at the big church, and you tell him your ma's gone and you want to get to your Grandda's in Launston Mills. God knows if he's still alive, but there'll be some kin of yours there -- Rowena or Moira or Brigid. One of them will take you in." How she hated the thought of sending him to her family, but what alternative was there? The orphanage? At least her family would look after him.

"No! I'm not going to leave you, Ma! I'm not going to ***them***!" Gwyn had not neglected to tell him of her family in the backwoods, and the picture she had painted of them gave him no desire to know them. Narrow-minded, censorious, snooty bunch! His mother couldn't tolerate living with them; how could she send him there?

Gwyn seemed to divine his thoughts. "If I could arrange it any other way, lamb, I would. Just don't you believe the lies you'll be hearing about me in that town. You know your ma well enough. And you know there's not another being on this earth that'll love you as I do. Don't you ever forget that." Panic overwhelmed her as her limbs tingled into numbness and her vision darkened. She couldn't see him properly anymore. God damn it, she didn't want to die! And she didn't want Gavin to watch her. "Go now, my lamb. Go! And don't come back!"

The frightened child was tempted to ignore her command. Somehow he felt that if he stayed with her she wouldn't die. She couldn't. Mothers didn't just desert you like that! But if he turned his back on her she might just slip away from his grasp.

He was still child enough to obey her orders, and yet worldly enough to know that his own childish logic was unsound. He'd seen enough deserted children. Enough hunger and destitution and even death to have few illusions about life. He was as hardened and cynical as the other street arabs that foraged an existence in the gutters of this city.

Gwyn felt herself beginning to float. For an instant she was held back by a desperate embrace from her son. When he released her she felt once again that feathery lightness that made her suddenly laugh to think she must be drifting heavenward. And far away, at the end of a nearly endless corridor, she heard the door slam behind Gavin.

Chapter 35

"Well, I must say that you don't look well, Harriet," her mother said, almost accusingly. "You've been crying again. I do wish you would tell me what is wrong! You arrived here three days ago in such a state, and haven't even had the courtesy to speak to me about it! You just mope about."

Harriet was staring into the fire and half-heartedly sipping her tea. Livinia had arranged for Beatrice to escort Jillian to a neighbour's, where the child might enjoy the less gloomy company of someone her own age.

"I assume your husband has done something to upset you. You really mustn't be too proud to tell me, you know. I ***am*** your mother, and I do have some experience of marriage!"

"Oh, Mama, really!"

"Is it another woman?" Livinia asked bluntly.

"I've told you that I will not discuss it, Mama! I wish you would refrain from speculating! I know you have never been particularly fond of Jeremy, but you will remember that he is my husband, and I will not have him denigrated by anyone! Do you understand?" Harriet rose angrily from the couch. "Now, if you will excuse me, I am in need of a breath of air. You're all stifling me here!" She rushed from the room, practically in tears, leaving an astonished Livinia in her wake.

Harriet grabbed her wrap and stormed from the house. She didn't slow down until she had reached the river, several blocks away. There she had to stop to catch her breath and ease the stitch in her side, although she almost welcomed the pain. For days now she had felt as though she existed in a dream. She wasn't even quite sure how she had come to be here, in Peterborough, with Jillian. At the time she had felt only a desperate urgency to get away from Launston Mills, from her home, from Rowena. And from Jeremy.

She sauntered alongside the river, grateful that so few people knew her in this burgeoning community. She felt a bit freer in this relative anonymity. Now perhaps she could sort things out in her own mind.

She had wanted to unburden herself, but to whom? Her mother was already too biased against Jeremy. Her father, though he had been especially solicitous these last three days, was really quite useless about this sort of thing. It would only embarrass him, and he'd bluster something about that being the way things were done in society. Bea had been trying even harder than Livinia to wheedle information out of her, but she would use it to preach and gloat, and not to sympathize. Bea was unmarried and likely to remain so, and that state had done nothing to improve her temperament. The men she had considered eligible had found her too opinionated and overbearing, and those who had asked for her hand in marriage, she had considered boorish backwoods oafs. Isobel was almost like a stranger to Harriet these days, for she and her family had moved to Cobourg, and the sisters rarely saw one another now. Practically the same was true of Susannah, who had married Mortimer Locke, a lawyer, and lived in Toronto. Charlotte had never been the type of person that others felt they could burden with their troubles. And Harriet had no close female friends to confide in.

Though Harriet wandered about for hours, she was no nearer a solution. It was obvious that she could not long remain under her parents' roof. But the thought of returning to Jeremy sent a knife-thrust of pain through her heart.

"Your mother is wondering whether you are lost, whether you have fallen into the river and drowned, or whether some Indian brave has made off with you."

Harriet looked with surprise at the rider that she had not noticed draw up beside her. "Nigel!" she said.

"At your service, milady." He gave her a mock bow, and then dismounted from his horse. "Well, at least you haven't yet told me to get lost. By all accounts I expected to find you either extremely unwelcoming, or floating peacefully downstream like the fair Ophelia."

She couldn't help but laugh at his flippant tone. "You would have made a wonderful court jester."

"I do what I can to please. Now tell me what Jeremy has done to catapult you so precipitously into our midst?"

She found it difficult to take offence at his query, but she did say, "So Mama has sent you to conduct the inquisition."

He held up his hand as if taking an oath. "I must admit to having become somewhat fond of my mother-in-law over the years, but my loyalty does not run to being a spy for the dear lady. The question was prompted by concern for you and my dear friend, Jeremy. I am inordinately fond of you both, and would do whatever I could to see you happily reunited." In an uncharacteristically serious tone, he added, "I really do want to help, Harriet. You have my word of honour that anything you tell me will go no farther. I shall not even tell Charlotte, if you so wish it."

But how could she tell Nigel what she had seen in the kitchen that night, and what she had heard her husband say to another woman?

Harriet had lain in her bed that evening that Rowena had reappeared in their lives. Tormented by jealousy and anger, she had been unable to rest. But, as usual, she had tried to find some justification for Jeremy's actions so that she could forgive him. And she had recalled how bruised his poor face had been, and had realized that she had not even enquired how badly he had been injured. Guiltily, she had risen from bed and gone in search of him, for she had wanted to be reconciled with him. But he had not yet been to his bedchamber, nor had she found him in the drawing room or the office. It hadn't been until that moment that Harriet had suspected the worst. She had opened the baize door to the kitchen just a crack, and had almost cried out in anguish when she had witnessed that passionate scene between her husband and Rowena. But what had devastated her had been Jeremy's comment to Rowena that he had never known a woman's love. That he had not acknowledged her own love and devotion to him these past eleven years, even if he could not return it, had wounded her deeply.

How could she tell this to Nigel? How could she possibly explain that she felt shattered, betrayed, worthless?

"No one can help me with this, Nigel. It is something I must decide for myself.... Although there are not many alternatives. But I do thank you for your offer."

"I have every faith in your making the right decision, Harriet. Do remember one thing -- Jeremy does need you. He just hasn't realized it yet himself.

"Come. Charlotte has insisted I bring you back to our house. I'll send word to your mother that you are alive and well, and that you'll be dining with us."

They had a pleasant stroll to the house. Nigel was so easy to talk to, and his witty rejoinders made her laugh.

The Melbourne's house was a magnificent two and a half storey brick building of Neo-Classic influence, with two enormous wings -- one housing a billiard and smoking room, and the library, and the other, a ballroom and conservatory.

With a chuckle, Harriet said, "Does your family know how well you have done in 'exile'?"

"Good Lord, I hope not! Or the next thing I know, I'll be playing host to any number of beastly young nephews sent out to the 'colonies' to give them backbone. I can visualize it all now. The family saying, 'Just look at what Canada has done for Nigel. A miraculous transformation of character! Let's send all the little blighters out for reformation.' No thank you. I shall remain the black sheep of the family gladly. Though I fear I have enemies. Just last week I received a letter from my eldest brother, the heir apparent, after... how many years has it been? A dozen or more? He heard, through an acquaintance who had visited our poor little colony, that I had become quite respectable. So he wrote to find out if it was true. I am sorely tempted to disillusion him."

Despite his words, Harriet sensed that he was pleased by this first step toward reconciliation with his family.

Supper was relaxing and enjoyable in the Melbournes' company. They never lacked for conversation, discussing everything from politics to horses to local gossip with equal avidness. Their deep affection for one another was evident in the little looks they occasionally exchanged and those meaningful glances that bespoke intimacy and mutual devotion. It made Harriet's own marriage seem a pitiful, empty thing. What was there left to save, anyway? She and Jeremy had co-existed like polite strangers in the same household these past few years. They shared so little. But Harriet had been grateful for even that.

After dinner, Nigel excused himself, pleading work, leaving the two sisters sipping coffee in the drawing room.

"I shall not press you for details of what has happened between you and Jeremy," Charlotte said, "although I'm willing to listen, if you care to tell me. But I do have some advice for you that I hope you will consider seriously. Ettie, it's time to stop this nonsense of separate bedrooms, if you expect to have a marriage at all."

Harriet was surprised, and somewhat embarrassed. But Charlotte forestalled any protests. "I'm sure you don't want to discuss this, and no doubt you will say that it is none of my business, but I shall have my say, nonetheless. A marriage cannot remain viable if you discard an essential part of it. Physical intimacy is an expression of love; it's an emotional anchor. You have cast your marriage adrift, and it appears to be heading for the rocks."

"Don't be ridiculous, Lottie!" Harriet said, her face burning. "This is not a proper subject for discussion!"

"Pooh! Don't be so stuffy, Ettie. Love is beautiful and not something to be ashamed of. It's that kind of priggish attitude that degrades sexual intimacy into something vile and improper and fit only for whores and men."

"Really, Charlotte!"

But Charlotte ignored her, and continued, "And if you insist upon driving Jeremy to seek physical love with another woman, then you have no cause to complain if he should become emotionally involved with her as well. And all I can say is that you are a fool, Harriet!"

Instead of the outraged reply Charlotte had expected of her, Harriet burst into tears. "You're probably right," she sobbed. "But I cannot abide his touching me... like that. It's all so humiliating!"

"But it isn't! You mustn't think of it like that. Do you remember the marriage vows? 'With my body I thee worship'? It's a way to express your love. It's not a time for self-consciousness or false modesty. If you love Jeremy you would give yourself wholly to him, body and soul, without shame or guilt or regret. Perhaps you would even enjoy it, if you allowed yourself to."

Harriet could never imagine that possibility, but she could sense the wisdom of her sister's advice. In any case, was there any other way to salvage her marriage?

Chapter 36

Jeremy felt impatient with the slowness of the steamer as it churned through the murky water of the Scugog River. This restlessness, which had been nagging him since he had left home nearly a week ago, intensified as he neared Launston Mills. He had a sense of impending disaster that he just couldn't shake.

Rowena, looking sombre, greeted him at the door. His smile faded as he said, "What's happened? Where is everyone?"

Rowena lowered her eyes. She had been dreading this moment. "Your father's still at the mill. Mrs. Launston and Jillian... left for Peterborough on Saturday."

"Did they indeed? But that's not all you have to tell me, is it?"

"Mrs. Launston said to tell you that neither she nor your daughter would return here until I had left."

"The devil she did! We'll see about that. And I know what you're thinking. You can forget it!"

"Nay. I'll not come between you and your family."

Rowena felt his anger as he gripped her arm and pulled her into the drawing room. "It's enough that I have one difficult female on my hands without having your stubbornness to contend with! Sit down!" He poured himself a drink, and then stood with his back to her at the window.

Rowena sat demurely in the chair, her fingers tightly entwined. She had been agonizing over her decision since Harriet had delivered her ultimatum. She knew she should have left while Jeremy was away, but she had so longed to see him again. Her conscience had not been made easier by Moira's visit yesterday. It was wrong of her to stay, Moira had said. Harriet's hasty departure had already generated rumours. Must she always cause trouble for their family, Moira had asked, and then had urged her to return to Brendan, even though Moira knew better than anyone what indignities Rowena had suffered at her husband's hands.

She had been plagued with fears of Brendan's reprisals. Brendan had disappeared, Moira had informed her. He hadn't been to work, nor to Paxtons', nor been seen by anyone in town for days. Rowena had feared that Brendan might have followed Jeremy and Keir to the city, or Harriet and Jillian to Peterborough. But she sensed that he was not far away, and she was left to wonder how and when he would exact his revenge. He had even invaded her dreams, terrorizing her, never allowing her a moment's peace. The dark shadows and nighttime creakings of this large, virtually empty house, had sent shivers of apprehension through her.

But perhaps it would be one of the others who would suffer at his hands. Rowena could not bear that responsibility. It was better to face him than to wait for him to make his move. Jeremy would not understand this. He would scoff at her fears.

Jeremy was contrite over his abruptness with Rowena. He went to her, and took one of her cool hands in his. "Forgive me."

His touch was comforting. Too long she had been alone, relying upon herself. "Oh, Jamie...."

He kissed her fingers. "I missed you, Rowena."

"And I, you."

His hands tightened on hers. "There's nothing for you to worry about. I shall go to Peterborough tomorrow to fetch Harriet back. She has no choice but to accompany me."

Rowena drew her hands away at this pompous declaration, wondering if Jeremy realized the irony of his words.

He did, and he also sensed her disapproval. As he left her side, the door opened and Samuel walked in.

"Glad you're back Jamie. You and I must have a talk. If you'll excuse us, Mrs. Delaney?"

When she had left the room, Samuel said, "Well, you've landed us in a fine mess, my boy. Just what is your intention in installing that woman in this house? I'm an old man, Jamie." He paused to take a pinch of snuff. "Too old for these domestic disruptions -- your wife running home to her parents with my granddaughter, saying she'll not live in the same house with your mistress. Is Rowena your mistress? None of my business, of course, but you've already stirred up a wasp's nest of gossip about town. Damned inconsiderate of you. A man of your age should know better! If you must carry on with the girl, be discreet about it!"

"I'm not 'carrying on' with her! Harriet is being unreasonable about this entire situation...."

"I think Harriet is right!" Samuel interrupted. "You've succeeded in reviving old scandal which took us long enough to live down the first time, and I, for one, am damned displeased about it! That woman will have to go! Your responsibility is to your wife and family. You have no choice."

"I don't agree...."

"I don't give a damn! You'll see that that woman is out of ***my*** house by morning!"

Jeremy fumed as the door slammed shut behind his father.

Supper was an uncomfortably silent meal. Samuel spent the evening in the study while Jeremy pondered his problems alone in the parlour.

He would leave for Peterborough first thing in the morning, he decided, and persuade Harriet to return. And Rowena?

Samuel would certainly demand her departure tomorrow. He must do something to help her, for he could not allow her to return to Brendan. The thought of that animal laying his hands on her filled him with rage.

An exciting idea asserted itself. He would find her a place to live in Toronto. He could visit her there, far from the prying eyes of this gossipy, censorious village. They could be free there. No one need know. No one would be hurt. Rowena would be safe. And she would be his.

But would she consent to such an arrangement?

Jeremy extinguished the lamps in the parlour, and stepped into the hallway. The house was shrouded in the deep stillness of midnight. The single lamp on the hall table cast a meager, eerie light.

Impulsively Jeremy picked up the lamp, and strode into the kitchen. It was in darkness, as he had suspected, yet his disappointment was keen. He lingered for a moment at the foot of the stairs which led to Rowena's room, but there was only silence. He turned away.

Rowena had retired early, but it was a long time before she slept. Yet there was no respite, for her frightened mind gave substance to her tormenting thoughts, and created a nightmarish reality. She saw herself lying in her bed, a crack of moonlight splitting the darkness of the room. Brendan, with that dangerous grin contorting his face, advanced slowly toward her. She was unable to move; the bedclothes weighed her down, trapping her. Fear choked her, and though she screamed inside, no sound left her parted lips. Still he came closer.... His fingers brushed her cheek.... She tried to pull away.... His hands closed about her throat like an iron band.... He laughed as she struggled in vain.... The band tightened.... She gasped for breath....

Rowena woke to the sound of her own scream. She was sitting up in bed, panting, her whole body shaking to the rapid pounding of her heart.

Suddenly the door opened. Rowena gasped.

"Rowena?"

"Jamie! Oh, Jamie!"

He hurried to her side, and she threw herself into his arms. He held her shivering body tightly to his own. "Are you alright? I heard you scream."

"'Twas a dream. Brendan.... 'Twas horrible!" She clung to him, taking solace and strength from his vital presence.

Jeremy's fingers wove through the rich, soft mass of curls which hung loose about her shoulders. His hand moved down her back in a gentle, seductive caress. He pressed her closer, feeling her warm nakedness through the thin nightgown. He had never before desired a woman with such intensity, with every fibre of his being. He heard her moan as his lips moved down her smooth, ivory neck.

Suddenly he released her, and moved away. It was wrong of him to take advantage of this situation. He had given her his word.

"Don't leave me, Jamie," she whispered. She could not bear to be alone now. She needed him; nothing and no one else mattered at this moment. Reason and guilt were creatures of the day, and had no tangible reality in these vulnerable, lonely hours of night.

Her lips met his as though she drew life and breath from him. A passion such as neither had ever known possessed them. They revelled in it, and it was like a celebration of life.

"I love you, Rowena," Jeremy whispered as she lay in his arms afterwards. "God, how I love you!"

She winced at these words she had so longed to hear, and snuggled closer to him.

He ran his fingers lightly across her breasts, marvelling at her beauty. He had never seen Harriet naked.

"Do you remember that day I found you lying in my bed?" he asked with amusement.

"Aye. You terrified me."

"Was I such a monster then?"

"In some ways," she replied with a grin.

"I suppose I was rather an arrogant young fool. I see in my son much of myself as a boy, and I despair. But perhaps he'll find a girl like you who'll teach him a little humility. If only things could be different for us, Rowena. If only...."

She pressed her finger to his lips, silencing him. "You mustn't talk thus. I don't want to think of anything but this moment. 'Tis all we have. Tomorrow will come too soon."

"But it needn't end here. Do you think I could let you go now?"

"You must."

"No! I have an idea. I'll find a place for us in Toronto. You'll have your own home, and I'll be with you whenever I can."

Rowena was stunned by this proposal. The thought of spending endless nights like this one with Jeremy was a tempting one, but she wanted to share more than his bed, and that was impossible. And what of the days they were apart? How could she bear the waiting, alone in a strange city, far from her family and friends and the only way of life she knew? Like an outcast.

"'Twould never work," she said sadly. Once again she would become a man's chattel. She would be as much a prisoner of his love as she was of the holy vows she had spoken with Brendan. "'Twould be wrong."

"Not for us, Rowena."

"We're not alone." What would happen to her if he tired of her five or ten years hence when her beauty began to fade and familiarity staled their relationship? What of the children she would surely bear him? Bastards, all of them.

"Must we always think of others before ourselves?" Jeremy said bitterly. "Is ***our*** happiness not important?"

"Could we truly be happy, thinking of no one but ourselves?" she rolled onto her back, and stared at the ceiling. "Once I thought that God's punishment came quickly, like a lightning bolt. But 'tis much slower and more painful than that. "Tis in a look in my son's eyes that makes me feel guilty and ashamed. 'Tis the pain I feel watching him suffer for my sins. 'Twill be with me till I die."

Guilt. More soul destroying than the eternal fires of hell. Yes, Jeremy understood that well.

They lay side by side without touching or speaking. There was nothing left to say.

An intense stab of loneliness wrenched a muffled sob from Rowena as Jeremy left her bed. She turned her face to the window to hide her tears.

She noticed it at first without awareness, without curiosity or surprise. A flickering glow that paled the moonlight. And then the sounds penetrated her consciousness -- the frantic neighing of horses, and sinister crackling hiss.

"Listen!" she cried, jumping out of bed.

Jeremy heard it too. Fire.

Quickly Rowena pulled on her dress, her fingers fumbling with the buttons. Jeremy opened the door. A wisp of smoke curled into the bedroom. He grabbed Rowena's hand and pulled her into the hallway. Smoke was billowing up the stairwell as though it were a chimney. They plunged down the steep stairs into the thickening, blinding, choking smoke. Rowena stumbled, but Jeremy's firm hold broke her fall.

The kitchen seemed to be engulfed in flames on all sides. Coughing, their eyes burning, they stumbled into the scullery next to the stairs. Jeremy groped for the window and threw it open. Outside, they sank to their knees, gasping for breath.

The calm night was violated by the chaotic sounds of burning wood and the screams of the terrified horses. Rowena and Jeremy glanced about in horror. The forest which surrounded the house on three sides was ablaze. Parched by the hot, dry summer, the trees burned fiercely.

And the house....

"Holy Mother of God!" Rowena cried.

The ground floor was an inferno, flames licked voraciously higher.

Jeremy's face was ashen. "Father!" He ran to the front of the house. Rowena was right behind him. Vaguely she was aware of a bell clanging urgently far away, barely discernible above the roar of the fire.

Rowena clutched Jeremy's arm as he started toward the steps. "You can't go in there!"

He pushed her away. "I must! Get Tom. Release the horses. Go!"

Breathlessly she watched him leap up the steps and fling open the door. He disappeared as though into the jaws of hell itself.

Rowena ran blindly toward the stables, hot ashes falling about her. She spotted Tom lying face down in the yard. Blood matted the hair on the back of his head. Was he dead? "Tom?" She shook him. "Tom!"

He opened his eyes and winced. He looked puzzled as he raised a hand to his wounded head. He noticed the fire, and forced himself to his knees. "God Almighty!"

"Are you alright? You must help me, Tom! Jeremy's gone after his father."

Tom staggered to his feet. The horses were in a panic, battering their hooves against the stable door, which shook and cracked under the assault. "Get back!" Tom ordered as he lurched toward the stable. He unlatched the doors, and flattened himself against the wall as the terrified beasts galloped out in confusion. They careened about, heading first in one direction, then pulling up short and swinging about. The trees formed a fiery arch over the road, blocking all escape routes. Finally, they plunged into the river.

Rowena rushed back toward the front of the house, though the heat from the burning trees nearby was blistering. Her heart pounded when she noticed the leaping flames devouring the interior. Even the portico was ablaze now. There was no sign of Jeremy.

Tom held her back. "No!" she shouted, trying to struggle out of his grasp. "Jamie's in there! I must find him!"

"I'll go. Stay back."

She saw Tom silhouetted against the melting interior, and then he too was gone.

Why did no one come? Were the townspeople not aware of the fire? But she remembered having heard the fire bell.

Every citizen had been summoned by that alarm, but the burning trees flanking Mill Road prevented them from even getting close to the house. Bucket brigades manned by men, women, and children stretched in lines down to the river. The filled buckets passing hand to hand among them were used to douse the shower of sparks which threatened to ignite not only the buildings at the edge of the burning forest, but also those along the path of the wind which the fire had created to nurture itself. Similarly, the inhabitants of the houses along the river to the east -- the O'Shaughnessys, Ryans, and others -- were protecting their homes from the encroaching flames.

Rowena was aware of none of this as she waited anxiously for Jeremy and Tom to reappear. She heard a loud crash, as though the ceilings had collapsed, and pressed a fist to her mouth to stifle a scream. She must not become hysterical. Jeremy needed her. She clenched her hands and prayed.

Although it had seemed to Rowena an impossibly long time since Tom had entered the house, it was in fact only a few minutes later that he reappeared, carrying Jeremy over his shoulder. Wordlessly, Rowena helped Tom to the riverbank, where he laid Jeremy down on the grass. Rowena dropped to her knees beside him.

Jeremy didn't move. Tears coursed down her soot-blackened face as she noticed his burnt hands. He was barely breathing.

"I found him at the bottom of the stairs. Looked like he'd fallen down them. Overcome by smoke, I reckon," Tom said, when he'd regained his breath. "He never reached Mr. Sam."

Her eyes never left Jeremy's face. She willed him to live. She entreated God to spare him, promising Him that she would never again sin if He allowed Jeremy to live. She would have sold her soul to the devil, had he offered her a deal.

It seemed an eternity before Jeremy coughed and struggled painfully for breath. Rowena wept with relief when his eyelids fluttered. He groaned as he tried to move his hands.

"Lie still," she urged gently.

"Father...?" It was a rasping whisper.

"I'm sorry, Jamie. So sorry. There's nothing we can do for him. You tried."

He pressed his eyes shut. "Oh, God!"

There was a thundering, sizzling crash as part of the roof collapsed, sending up scintillating embers like a fireworks display, which rained about them.

"We can't stay here," Tom said. "The canoe's our only escape."

The canoe, covered in ashes, lay on its side a few feet from them. Tom quickly righted it, and slid it into the water. Rowena steadied the craft as Tom lifted Jeremy into it, and then scrambled in. She grabbed a paddle, and helped Tom steer the canoe away from shore.

It was a frightful sight, that conflagration. The orange glow of the sky was reflected in the water so that even it appeared to be aflame. The house was a mere skeleton, crumbling under its own weight. The stables and the outbuildings were burning. The fire raged through the hundreds of acres of woods to the south. Black smoke drifted like a pall over the town.

Jeremy was barely conscious when they reached the wharf near the locks. Tom once more hoisted Jeremy over his broad shoulder, and they started across the bridge.

They heard a unanimous gasp from the townspeople as a burning branch landed on the roof of Paxtons' Inn, but it was quickly extinguished with a bucket of water by one of the men on a ladder. A cry went up as the weary trio was spotted on the bridge. Several strong men relieved Tom of his burden.

"Take him to my house," a voice ordered. A comforting arm slid about Rowena's shoulders. She walked without feeling her legs; the noise and confusion barely penetrated her numbed senses.

Simon Worthing coaxed her into an armchair. Margaret pressed a glass of brandy into her hands. Rowena stared at nothing, though she could see it all still, smell the stench of it on her clothes, feel the horror of it suffocating her. "We couldn't reach him," she mumbled. "Oh, God, we couldn't get him out!"

"Samuel?" Margaret inquired softly.

"Jamie tried. He'll be alright, won't he?" Her eyes were wide with fear. "I must go to him!"

Margaret urged her back into the chair. "Simon will see to him. Now drink up."

The brandy burned its way down her raw throat. Her nerves tingled back to life. Slowly she became aware of her surroundings; the impeccable parlour; Margaret, with uncharacteristic smudges of soot on her face and clothing; Margaret's children sitting obediently upon the sofa, watching Rowena curiously until Margaret shooed them back to bed; the dying embers of a fire in the hearth -- a cheerful warmth to take the September chill out of one's bones... nothing frightening or threatening about it... but how absurd it seemed while that bonfire raged outside, roasting the town. She wanted to laugh, yet the normality of this cozy, domestic scene calmed her shattered being. There was an insistent throbbing in the ankle which she didn't realize she had sprained on her flight down those precipitous stairs.

Tom dropped into a chair, exhausted. Rowena suddenly remembered the wound on his head. "Margaret, you'd best be seeing to Tom." She turned to the young man. "How came you to be lying before the stable with that nasty gash on the back of your head?"

"I heard the horses, you see. So I went out to check. I saw the fires then, just taking hold about the house. And something hit me. Next thing I knew, you were bending over me."

"What on earth could have hit you?" Margaret asked as she dabbed at her son's head with a wet cloth. "It was a fierce blow."

"Or who," Rowena said, her face reflecting a horrifying thought. "Brendan!"

It was barely a whisper, but the other two had heard. They stared at her, shocked. "What are you saying, Rowena?" Margaret demanded.

Rowena didn't hear her. Brendan had set that fire. She knew that without a doubt. It had happened because of her. She had caused Samuel Launston's death as surely as had Brendan.

"Oh, no!" she screamed. "Holy Mother of God, save me! I can't bear it!" She sobbed uncontrollably.

Margaret was alarmed by this hysterical outburst. She tried to calm Rowena, but the younger woman pulled away from her, shouting, "What have I done? 'Tis all my fault! God forgive me, 'tis all my fault."

Simon came into the room. "What's wrong?" He looked at his wife.

"She thinks Brendan set the fire."

"Has she any reason for assuming that?"

"Someone bashed me on the head," Tom said. "But I saw them first, small fires everywhere about the house and the woods. They didn't start by accident, I'll swear to that."

Simon went to Rowena, and took her firmly by the shoulders.

"'Tis all my fault."

"No!" he said, staring hard at her. "You can't blame yourself."

"I should have been the one to die, not Samuel!"

Simon shook her. "Stop this, Rowena! Do you want Jeremy to hear you? He's been through enough tonight."

As though he had slapped her, she suddenly went limp. "How is he?"

"His hands are badly burned, but he'll recover. He's sleeping now. I've given him a draught to ease the pain."

Simon fetched a glass of water, added a couple of drops of laudanum to it, and handed it to Rowena. "Drink this. It will relax you." When she had finished it he said, "Now go with Margaret. She'll show you to bed."

"No, I couldn't sleep."

"That's precisely what you need."

"I don't deserve all this kindness. Don't you understand...?"

"Nonsense!" Simon interrupted. Gently he said, "You have no proof that Brendan started that fire. He hasn't been seen around town for a week. Even if it is true, you can't blame yourself."

She looked at his kind, plain face, into his compassionate eyes. "I should have gone with him. Then none of this would have happened."

"No one thinks harshly of you for leaving Brendan. We all... well, it was common knowledge that he beat you. Rowena, you can only accept a limited responsibility for another person's actions."

If only she could believe that. But she was too tired to argue. So drowsy. The room seemed to recede....

Rowena woke in the late afternoon. Her mind was fuzzy, and she was grateful just to lie there absorbing the soft comfort of the bed, idly gazing at the beam of sunlight that squeezed through the curtains. Gradually the tragedy of the previous night seeped back into her consciousness.

Jamie! She must see him!

She was surprised to find herself clad in a nightdress with her own gown nowhere in sight. Her ankle was bound in bandages, and when she put her weight upon it, a tingling, pricking pain shot through it. Stoically she ignored the discomfort.

A jug of fresh water stood beside the china basin, and Rowena quickly washed, noticing that the soot had already been sponged from her face. She grabbed the woolen shawl which was draped across the back of a chair, and, wrapping it about her shoulders, hurried from the room.

She found Margaret in the kitchen, setting a pot of tea to steep. "You're just in time. Did you sleep well?"

"I did, thanks. How's Jeremy?"

"As well as can be expected. Simon is with him now."

"You look tired, Margaret. Have you not had any sleep yourself?"

"There's hardly been time. Simon's had to treat a few minor burns, and Garth Calder toppled from a ladder and broke his leg. It's been a busy night. Things have only just begun to settle down." Without looking at Rowena she added, "Tom left for Peterborough this morning, to inform Harriet. No doubt she and Jillian will return with him."

"Thank God they weren't here!" Rowena said. "I keep thinking about that poor crippled child. How would she have managed to escape from the fire when her grandfather couldn't?" She shivered. "Let me look after Jeremy while you and Simon rest."

Margaret sighed. "There's little enough to do for him. Simon is keeping him drugged. But you can sit with him. I'll find you a dress. I'm afraid yours was ruined."

"You're too kind, Margaret."

"Nonsense!"

A little while later Rowena was sitting next to Jeremy's bed, watching him with inexpressible sadness. He slept feverishly, despite the laudanum. His hands were encased in thick paddings of bandages. He didn't regain consciousness once during her vigil. Though Simon urged her to get some sleep, she stayed with Jeremy during the long night, suffering with him.

Only when Simon insisted she leave the room so that he could tend to Jeremy did she go. But she didn't wish to sleep. She stepped into the early morning drizzle. How good it felt, that cool, soothing, life-giving rain. She turned her face to the grey sky and let her tears mingle with the rain.

The town was quiet still, though she sensed the bustle of preparation which was beginning behind closed doors and curtained windows. She wandered down Lindsay Street. The tavern and shops had been saved, though the ravaged forest behind them still smouldered as the rain quenched the last of the fire. The acrid smell of smoke, of destruction, was everywhere.

The entire stretch of forest on the Launston tract, from the river to the north and east, to Lindsay street in the west, and to the Darcy farm to the south, had been destroyed.

The church had not suffered, Rowena was glad to notice. She went inside, surprised at first to see the neat rows of long tables set against the walls. Of course. It was Friday -- a schoolday. An ordinary morning for most people.

The altar had been moved to make way for the teacher's desk. Rowena knelt before the crucifix. She prayed a long time.

When she returned to the house, she was anxious to be at Jeremy's side. He was worse. The burns had become infected. He was delirious with fever. Rowena applied cold compresses to his brow, and spoke softly to him, though she knew he was not aware of her.

The minutes ticked painfully by, yet too swiftly for Rowena. Harriet would arrive this evening, she was certain. Her own presence would no longer be required.

"Rowena?"

"I'm here," she replied, her heart pounding.

Jeremy opened his eyes. They were foggy with pain. "Is it over? The fire?"

"Aye."

"Water," he croaked, trying to raise himself. He groaned and fell back onto the pillow. Rowena lifted his head and held a glass to his lips. Jeremy drained it and lay back.

It was then that Rowena heard Harriet's voice in the next room. She smoothed back a damp curl from Jeremy's brow, and said, "I must be going now. Harriet is here. She'll be looking after you."

"Stay." It was a plea.

"I cannot. Oh, Jamie... I love you," she whispered brokenly. Swiftly she touched her lips to his.

The door opened, and Harriet swept into the room. She didn't even glance at Rowena as she hastened to Jeremy's side. "I came as soon as I heard. Nigel is bringing Jillian. Oh, Jeremy, I'm so sorry... about everything." Tears misted her eyes, and Rowena saw the depth of Harriet's love. And she knew how impossible her own love for Jeremy was. She had no place in his life.

Discreetly she left the room.

"Take care of him, Simon," she said. "And thank you both for everything you've done for me."

"But, where are you going, Rowena?" Margaret asked.

"Home. Where I belong."

"To Brendan?" Simon inquired with a frown.

"I doubt he'll be back, though I'm not afraid of him anymore. You're not to be worrying about me."

The day went out as it had come in -- grey and wet. Rowena trudged wearily along Mill Road, her heart saddened by the bizarre, blackened landscape -- the magnificent trees now charcoal stumps. The house.... She didn't want to look at it but her eyes were drawn to it. All that remained were the crumbling stone chimneys.

She passed her father's house, happy to see it had survived, and continued on to her own. It hadn't changed. Some of the apple trees had been slightly singed by the heat of the fire. The garden needed weeding; the huge orange pumpkins were nearly ready for plucking. Otherwise it was the same.

Rowena's breath caught in her throat as she entered the house. Here it seemed as though she had never left. The chairs that had been overturned during Jeremy's fight with Brendan still lay where they had fallen. The meal she had been preparing, dried and mouldy now, was in the pot suspended over the dead ashes. The cloth she had used to wipe the blood from Jeremy's face lay crumpled upon the table, rusty with dried blood.

It was almost impossible to believe that her whole life had changed since she had last been here, only a week ago.

But she would not allow despondency to overcome her. She changed into one of her calico dresses, tied on an apron, and set to work.

Chapter 37

Because of Gavin O'Shaughnessy's penchant for courting trouble, his arrival in Launston Mills was to be forever associated with the fire. In fact, he arrived at least a week thereafter.

Although the O'Shaughnessys had been forewarned of his arrival by Father Killeny, in the upheaval caused by the disaster they were not prepared for him. It was just one of the many things he would hold against them.

With the cunning of a street-wise city child, he was quick to assess the reactions of these strangers. Moira seemed to regard him suspiciously, as though she expected him suddenly to do something outrageous. She hesitated a moment too long before giving him a dutiful hug and reticent smile. It was evident that she mistrusted him and resented his coming into their lives. Rowena's welcome was more sincere, but she seemed wrapped in some private misery, and not fully receptive to those about her. It made him feel that he was a rather inconsequential part of her life. His step-grandmother, Mary, he disregarded after the first glance, deciding his mother's wicked description of her had been apt. She obviously disliked his coming, and he hadn't expected anything else. But he was most disappointed in his grandfather. The old man seemed to regard Gavin's very existence a nuisance, and his presence here, an unwelcome burden.

And the boy wasn't far wrong in any of his assessments, although the adults would have been surprised and embarrassed by his perspicacity. After Father Killeny had informed them of Gavin's impending arrival, they had discussed amongst themselves what should be done with him. Mary had refused to have anything to do with Gwyn's by-blow. Hadn't Gwyn caused them enough trouble already? Patrick had not wanted a child in the house, particularly one that was bound to cause trouble between him and Mary. Jaysus, he was getting to be an old man; didn't he deserve some peace and quiet? Moira had argued that she had six of her own children to care for, and not room for another. And when they had all looked so hopefully at Rowena to do the proper thing by taking the boy in, she had replied simply, "I have to fend for meself now. I got me a job at the Lathrops. I'll be working from morn to night six days a week, so I've no time to be caring for a child." And so it had been left to Patrick to offer his grandson a home.

It came as a bit of a shock to Patrick, as he surveyed the lad, to see the O'Shaughnessy traits in him -- the rusty hair and green eyes. For a moment it was a resentful Gwyn that stared at him through those eyes.

All this Gavin sensed. Not one of them had expressed any regrets about his mother's death -- he didn't know that they had agreed it best not to remind him of it -- and he would never forgive them for that either. Sure, he'd bide with these people who would have preferred never to know him, or even of him, because he had little choice. But he decided that he would make no effort to endear himself to them. They had treated his mother unfairly, and if they didn't like him as he was, well then... fuck the bleedin' lot of 'em!

Chapter 38

It was many weeks before Jeremy fully recovered, and he had not proven an easy patient. Once the infection and fever had left him he had become restless, impatient with himself and everyone about him.

And he was bitter. Bitter about his father's death, the loss of his home, and the loss of Rowena.

How cruel of Fate to tantalize him with a taste of love and then to deny him its nourishment! He had been certain that, given time, he could have brought Rowena around to his way of thinking. But tragedy had intervened. And then Harriet had descended upon him, solicitous, affectionate, flirtatious even. She was so obviously trying to win him away from Rowena, and although he knew she would never totally succeed, he was human -- and vain -- enough to enjoy her efforts to do so.

Jeremy stared numbly at the charred rubble that had once been his home, until vivid memories of his father and brother filled him with remorse. In a way he had been responsible for both their deaths. He clenched his fists and welcomed the pain that shot through his healing hands.

It hadn't taken Jeremy long to learn the villagers' conjectures concerning the cause of the fire. Damn Brendan Delaney to hell! If ever he got hold of that Irish bastard again he'd slowly squeeze the life out of him!

Jeremy looked ruefully at the purple contorted flesh of his hands, which seemed as though they were not a part of him. Only the pain was real.

Delaney was hardly likely to return if he was guilty and, although the law wanted him for questioning, there was no concrete evidence against the man.

The November air knifed through him, but Jeremy noticed it not. He walked around what had once been the garden. A part of him had been destroyed with this place. His soul, like his hands, was permanently scarred.

He would not stay, he suddenly decided. There were too many painful memories here. He would sell the mills, move to the city, start afresh on some new enterprise far from this grubby little place!

Yet, even as these thoughts formed in his mind, he knew he would never leave. He could not abandon all his father had worked to achieve. This town was his heritage.

Jeremy had still been bed-ridden when Samuel's remains had been interred, but he had heard that every villager and every farmer in the district had come to the funeral. Samuel had been eulogized as the town's founder, and the mourners had wept in agreement. The people were determined to ensure that "Launston Mills" became the community's official name. Samuel needed a no more fitting epitaph than this.

Samuel would scoff at his son's cowardice if he were here now, Jeremy thought. The old man would draw his bushy brows together as he contemplated what must be done first. Jeremy could almost picture him striding about, his hands clasped behind his back, as he pondered.

Jeremy kicked viciously at a scorched beam. He would not rebuild here! He would sell this wasteland as town lots. The settlement needed room to expand, and he had no wish to remain in the centre of it.

One-eyed Jack Spragg had recently sold his two hundred acre tract north of the town to the Launston Land Company -- in which Jeremy had a controlling interest. The old trapper had been infected with gold rush fever and had gone to California to make his fortune. That parcel of virgin land would provide a secluded site for a new house.

The snow, which had threatened all day, began to fall. Soon it would whitewash this blackened landscape, mercifully shrouding it like bandages nursing a wound. Nature would heal itself. Life would flourish here again. The lovely pink fireweed, nurtured by destruction, would be the harbinger of this rebirth.

Jeremy walked away. He had much to occupy his thoughts as he ambled back to the Launston Hotel on Main Street where he had rented a suite of rooms.

"Jeremy, I've been worried about you! It's such a cold day. And you've not worn any gloves," Harriet said when he entered their sitting room.

"Don't fuss, Harriet! The gloves pain me more than the cold. I'm neither a child nor an invalid that you need constantly nag at me!"

Jeremy regretted his unkind words when he saw her wounded expression. Harriet had been invaluable to him during his convalescence. She had made certain that the work at the mills had continued as usual; she had struggled through the account books with little help from him. She still acted as his hands, for his own could not yet hold a pen. But her mothering stifled him.

"I'm sorry," he said.

Harriet had become used to his bad temper these last weeks, and forgave him instantly. She knew that his physical dependency upon her was one the things that annoyed him, that being reminded of his disability irked him.

So long as that was all that had caused his outburst. How she feared Rowena, feared that Jeremy might be obsessed by her and do something irrational. Every time he left their rooms, she imagined him going to see Rowena, and fantasized foolish but frightening scenarios, like their running off together. A more realistic and devastating image of them in bed together she refused to dwell upon, although it frequently attempted to intrude upon her thoughts. Her own relationship with Jeremy was still a precarious one; she had yet to re-establish their intimacy. But she was determined to do it.

"You've been to the house," she said with sudden conviction.

"Yes." He looked at her in surprise. And for a moment she seemed a stranger to him. What he saw was a handsome woman, self-assured, with shrewd eyes, a mouth that could easily press into a disapproving line, but that now smiled gently at him. It was a warm smile that seemed to reach out to him, requesting a response in kind.

And he gave it. It made him feel generous and good about himself, almost noble. "Let's have some tea, and I'll tell you what I've decided about our new home."

Harriet's tension dissipated on an imperceptible sigh.

Chapter 39

Rowena plodded homeward in the twilight. She was thankful for the lengthening spring days, for she was weary of going to and from work in the darkness of winter mornings and evenings.

Still, she was fortunate to have obtained domestic work at the Lathrops -- the money she had managed to save from Brendan's wages had disappeared with him. The Lathrops, who owned the foundry where Brendan had worked, lived in a handsome brick house on Bond's Rise, that fashionable new residential district on the hill at the northwest end of town. It was a long walk to her own home, but Rowena didn't mind. It was revitalizing after a hard day's work, and she had no need to hurry home. Only an empty house awaited her.

She forced back self-pitying thoughts. She had her independence, friends and family around her, her faith to sustain her, and her son for company during his holidays. She needed no more, she told herself firmly.

Rowena passed the common and stepped out of the ankle-high mud onto the plank sidewalk. She didn't glance at the brightly lit Launston Hotel on her left. Although she dreaded meeting Jeremy every time she passed, she had not yet encountered him. Since the fire she had seen him only briefly when he had brought Keir home for Christmas vacation.

How often she had lain in that large, cold bed at night and wished that Jamie were beside her! How often she had relived in her mind that one night of ecstasy. God forgive the wicked weakness of her flesh! She knew she would do the same thing again, if she had the opportunity.

She passed the newer, gaily painted frame stores and artisans' shops. Next to them Yardleys', Paxtons', Lindsays' were dingy old relics. Yet a sense of comfortable familiarity emanated from them. Paxtons' could not compare with the rather ostentatious Launston Hotel, but the old log inn was still the most frequented one in town.

Rowena turned down Mill Road. The twinge of pain that had at first accompanied her along this now-desolate street had diminished over the months, although she felt it would never completely disappear.

A figure suddenly lurched toward her from the shadows of Paxtons' outbuildings. She froze. Brendan, she thought with horror.

The man groaned and then stumbled, falling full length into the mud.

Rowena's first reaction was to run. But she could not leave the poor devil lying there with the chill of night closing in. Carefully she approached the prostrate figure. She was almost afraid to look at his face lest it be Brendan. She rolled him over warily, expecting Brendan suddenly to laugh and grasp her wrist, or leap up and close his hands about her throat. There had not been a journey through these dark streets that she had not feared Brendan's sudden appearance. And his reprisals. In her mind she had already died a thousand different and horrible deaths.

But it was only Malcolm Grimsby. Drunk as usual.

Rowena shook him. He flailed his arms ineffectually, as though he were batting a bothersome fly.

She wondered what to do. She could not leave him here, possibly to die of exposure. He had few friends, and certainly none who would look for him.

"Come along, Malcolm. I'll be taking you home," Rowena said. She squatted down beside him and lifted his head.

"Lea' me 'lone."

"Don't be daft, man! You're not a dog to be lying in the gutter! Get to your feet!" She tried to drag him up, but he was dead weight. He whimpered when she released him, and curled up, shivering. He was worse than a dog, she thought with disgust.

Rowena marched to the stables. She found a bucket and plunged it into the horse trough. She doused Malcolm with the icy water.

He coughed and spluttered. "Wha' th' hell!"

Rowena urged him to his feet. She braced her shoulder under his armpit and led him away.

"Wha' th' hell's goin' on?" Malcolm shook his head in confusion.

"I'm taking you home."

"Don' wanna go home... Lesh have 'nother!"

"Shut up and walk."

He leaned heavily upon her, and Rowena winced under the burden.

"Who th' hell 're you? My guardian angel?" He laughed helplessly and tripped, nearly toppling them both.

Rowena avoided Main Street, preferring the dark but shorter path that wound along the riverbank behind the shops in the first block of Main Street. They proceeded painfully slowly; Rowena carefully steered Malcolm away from the edge of the steep bank. Malcolm stumbled often. Rowena's muscles ached as he relied more and more upon her for support. She was ready to collapse herself when they finally reached the house.

Maureen and Rowena dragged Malcolm into a bedroom, and lowered him onto the unmade bed. Silently they stripped off his wet clothes. By the dim, flickering light of the one candle, Rowena noticed the week's growth of stubble on Malcolm's once-handsome face, which was now puffy and flabby. His clothes, torn and rudely patched, bore more stains than those of the mud from which Rowena had rescued him.

Maureen looked at Rowena in embarrassment. "Thank you for seeing him home."

"I couldn't leave him... where he was."

A baby started to wail. The two women left the bedroom, where Malcolm was already snoring.

"Sit yourself down, Rowena. Will you take a cup of tea?"

"I'd be grateful to sit for a minute, but I'll not trouble you for tea."

Rowena looked about her as Maureen tended to the infant in the cradle near the fire. Large clods of dried mud lay about the kitchen floor; cobwebs curtained the corners; the stench of tallow candles could not disguise the odours of filth and neglect. Rowena strongly suspected that the dirt-encrusted dishes which were scattered about had been accumulating for several days.

Nothing had been the same here since the Colonel had died. That had been five years ago. The Colonel had gone ice fishing -- a skill he had learned from the Indians -- in early spring, and had never returned.

Maureen sat down opposite Rowena. She unbuttoned the bodice of her dress and offered a breast to the hungry infant.

Rowena was overwhelmed with pity for this woman who was no older than she. Lines and shadows and an angular thinness had robbed Maureen of the voluptuous charm of her youth. The lack of several teeth -- one for each babe, according to popular belief -- emphasized the gauntness of her pale features. Strands of greasy hair hung limply about her face and neck. Her nails were ragged and dirty; some of her fingers were deeply, painfully cracked with the constant exposure to cold. But most distressing was the look of despair in Maureen's eyes.

"I don't know what to do anymore," Maureen suddenly confided, as if she had read Rowena's thoughts. "I can't keep him from the bottle. 'Tis like a sickness with him. And there's no more money. 'Tis gone. All of it." She spoke in clipped sentences with long, bitter pauses between. She did not look at Rowena or at the baby sucking greedily at her breast.

"He's drunk and gambled it all away. The last few years I've had to sell the silver, and then the parlour and dining room furniture. Nice pieces they were. The rooms are empty now. Closed up. We can't even heat them. He doesn't realize. Doesn't think about where the money comes from. Doesn't care. Them as never worked for it don't know the value of money. He laughed when I said he had to get a job. Said he was a gentleman. Gentlemen don't do manual labour. And what could he do? Himself never having worked a day in his life, never even chopping the wood. 'Tis why I've had to go to work, scrubbing floors at the hotel. Me, that once had maids of me own! And himself taking the money without a thought spared for his children! They'd be starving if it weren't for the scraps I bring home from the hotel kitchen."

Tears glistened in Maureen's eyes. Rowena was at a loss. What words of comfort could she offer? What words could salve shattered hopes and dreams, and fill empty bellies?

She walked home with a heavy heart. Drunkenness was common in this hard country, and not limited solely to men. Countless families suffered because of it. Surely something could be done to stop it! Maureen was right. It was a sickness, perhaps the most vile of all, for it claimed a man gradually, wearing away his strength, his character, his humanity, bit by bit, year by year. And it eroded the happiness and security in family relationships. She couldn't help but think of Brendan. Whatever had been wrong between them had been exacerbated by his drinking. He had never hurt her when he'd been sober.

A sudden rage seized her as she passed the Launston distillery. Did Jeremy ever think about the children who went hungry while he profited from their parents' folly? She was certain he never had.

Rowena entered her cabin. She was removing her bonnet when she saw him sitting in a chair by the fire. She stared in surprise.

"The door was open," Jeremy said. "I didn't think you'd mind if I waited in here."

"I've no reason to lock the door. There's nothing here anyone would want." He had changed, she noticed. His sorrows had aged him. And his hands.... Sharp memories of that tragedy -- and the events preceding it -- flooded through her, destroying the defences she had so carefully erected during the past months. Why had he come?

Fear suddenly gripped her. She rushed toward him. "'Tisn't Keir? There's nothing wrong with him, is there?"

"No, he's fine."

"Thank God!"

She turned away from him as she unclasped her cloak with trembling fingers.

Jeremy noticed her agitation. He wanted to reach out to her, to offer his love and protection. But so much had changed since that fateful night in September. It was as if their passion had ignited the conflagration, and all that devastation now lay between them. And he feared she would rebuff him once again.

He was wrong. If he had taken her into his arms then, she would easily have set aside her Catholic conscience and taken him to her bed and into her lonely, empty life. Her back was still turned to him; her body quivered in anticipation of his hands upon her shoulders, his lips upon her neck....

He didn't move from the chair.

She almost wept when she realized he would not come to her. Undoubtedly he had perceived the folly of their passion. He was the richest man in the district, and she, but a servant. By seeing her, Jeremy would risk not only his marriage, but his reputation. She had already turned down his offer to set her up secretly as his mistress in Toronto. So what was left for them? Their love had always been doomed. Straightening her shoulders, she turned to face him.

"I have news of Brendan," he said.

Rowena stiffened.

"He's dead."

She stared numbly at him as she slowly crossed herself.

"He was working at a lumber camp in the Ottawa Valley during the winter. He was killed in a drunken brawl in Bytown a few weeks ago."

She thought of Brendan, not as she had last seen him, but as the man he had once been -- charming, vital, amusing. A man with a zest for living. She remembered a young man with merry, teasing eyes and a voice that could make the angels weep. It was for that lost soul that she grieved.

Jeremy could read nothing in her eyes. Her silent detachment made him uncomfortable. He rose. "If there's anything I can do...?"

"You could close the distillery," she said fiercely. She was suddenly, uncontrollably, illogically angry at Jeremy.

"What?"

"It was the whiskey that turned Brendan into an animal. And there's others like him. I found Malcolm lying in the mud tonight, dead drunk. Have you seen him and his family of late? Your whiskey's destroying them all."

Jeremy was taken aback by the accusation, and her anger. He could not know that she was lashing out at him because she desired him and railed at the unfairness of it all. So he responded in kind, his tone that of the arrogant man she had disliked. "Do you hold me responsible for their drunkenness? Do you think that if I stop making whiskey, men will stop drinking it? They'll get it anyway. It's not the availability of liquor that makes men drink. It's a weakness in their characters. There's nothing I can do about that."

"Don't you feel guilty, making money from others' weaknesses?"

"There's no place for sentimentality in business."

"I see," she said coldly.

"Do you, Rowena?" He walked out.

She leaned heavily against the closed door. Was there never to be any peace between them? Were they always to clash in some violent emotion -- anger as easily as love?

She looked about the room by the glow from the blaze in the hearth. Jeremy must have stoked and fed the fire, for usually it was barely smouldering by the time she arrived home from work. As she bolted the door, she thought how this sad and lonely cabin was like her heart, filled with memories, but empty now and locked against the world.

At twenty-nine, she was a widow -- twice over, she thought, for she had always considered Adrian her husband in the sight of God. She might as well be a nun, like her sister Brigid, for she could no longer endure the anguish that earthly love inflicted.

The man that she loved with a frightening passion could never be hers, apart from that one brief, tantalizing moment.

She buried her face in her hands and wept.

Book 2

Keir

Part 4

The City

1856 - 1859

Chapter 40

The summer day was so hot that the earth sizzled. But it was only the shrill hum of the grasshoppers and the buzzsaw scrapings of the cicadas that created the illusion. The air seemed liquid as the sun sucked moisture from all it touched. In the dingy workshop the atmosphere was unbearable.

Keir paused in his work to wipe the dripping sweat from his forehead. He combed back his damp black hair with his fingers, and swiped at the horseflies that whizzed about his head. He was already stripped to the waist, though it was barely mid-morning. Sawdust was glued to the firm muscles of his arms and chest, except where rivulets of perspiration continually washed it away.

Keir glanced at his grandfather who was bent over his own work, not merely because of his concentration on the task, but because rheumatism would not allow him to straighten his back. Keir wondered how the old man could tolerate the heat with his flannel shirt still buttoned at the neck and wrists.

Keir resumed his work in silence. Not the companionable silence that he and his grandfather had so often shared in the past, but a silence born of awkwardness between people who had little in common but the ties of blood.

As always, his thoughts turned to Toronto.

During the last eight years he had come to know the city well, had shared in its frivolities as well as its disasters. He and the other boys had attended musical evenings at the new St. Lawrence Hall -- including the magnificent performance by the 'Swedish Nightingale', Jenny Lind -- and the many parades and public holiday celebrations. He had seen 'P.T. Barnum's Grand Colossal Museum and Menagerie', and the Agricultural Exhibition of '52, which had drawn thousands of people. He had lived through the dreaded cholera epidemics that had raged through the city in '49 and again in '54. He had witnessed the 'Great' fire of `49 which had destroyed more than fifteen acres of the downtown section of Toronto, and had claimed St. James Cathedral as one of its victims. He and his schoolmates had closely followed the events of the Crimean War, and had celebrated the fall of Sebastopol last year as heartily as the citizens of Toronto.

Keir felt an affinity with that city. He belonged there as he never had in Launston Mills. Next year he would be nineteen and independent, with all the rich and varied pleasures of city life to taste and savour!

This was his last summer at home. Only a few more weeks of helping his grandfather, and controlling his temper with his mother....

They'd had another argument last night. She had upbraided him for spending so much of his time at the Launstons' when his grandfather needed his help. She had accused him of disloyalty to his kin, of unwarranted arrogance, and even of greed. It was always the same, but once she would push him too far, and he would say unforgivable things that should never be voiced.

It had developed slowly, his intellectual rejection of his mother's family. Their thick, rustic speech, mutilated by grammatical errors, had begun to jar on his sensitized brain. His philosophical questions had been answered thoughtlessly by religious rote, and glaring logical fallacies had been accepted with indifferent shrugs. It was the indifference that irritated him the most.

His family trod the narrow path of ignorance, content just to look down at the familiar motions of their feet, never lifting their eyes to the riches around them. Their lives were simple, physical, uncomplicated by deep thought. They accepted the Catholic credo with blind, unquestioning faith. And Keir was ashamed of them.

"Sure, 'tis a blistering day," Patrick said, interrupting Keir's musings. "Hot as Hades." He laid down his chisel and tried to ease his aching back. "`Tisn't me best work, this." He indicated the carving on a cabinet. "Me eyes ain't what they used to be, though me hands are steady enough, eh?" He held them out for Keir's inspection.

Keir felt a twinge of sadness and guilt as he gazed at the thick, callused fingers splayed out before him, at the purple ridges of veins and gnarled tendons jutting out on the backs of the old hands. "Why not take a break, Grandda?" It had been a long time since he had used that childish form of address, preferring the more dignified "Grandfather".

Patrick had noticed, and seemed pleased. "Aye. 'Tis the heat, you see. Wears a man down, though they say 'tis good for the rheumatics." Patrick rose painfully from his chair. "Will you join me outside for a smoke, lad?"

"If you like."

Keir headed for the veranda, but Patrick stopped him with the words, "Nay, we'll not be going to the stoop. Mary'd have a word or two to say about that, and I've no mind to listen to her bickering."

As he followed his grandfather to a bench behind the ash house, Keir could not suppress the momentary scorn he felt for the old man's cowardice.

"You think careful afore you choose a wife, me boy. I reckon women are like cats -- all gentle and purring one minute, and spitting and hissing the next, and a man maybe never knowing what it was he done amiss. Even me Deirdre had the divil of a temper at times. Nay, a man never knows a woman till he's wed her and bed her."

It was the first time Keir had heard the old man criticize, albeit obliquely, his shrewish wife.

"Have one of my cigars," Keir offered as Patrick was searching the depths of his trouser pockets for his pipe.

"Don't mind if I do." Patrick chuckled as he sniffed and examined the cigar. "'Tis an age since I had anything this good. You can afford these on your allowance, eh?"

"Uncle Jeremy is very generous."

"Sure, you done well for yourself, lad, getting in good with the Launstons." Patrick raised a hand to stave off Keir's anger. "I mean nothing by it. I reckon as how they owe it to you." He paused. "I'm right proud of you, Keir. So's your ma, though like as not she's not said as much to you. She tells me of the prizes and the praise you won for yourself. Says you got the gift of the silver tongue when it comes to debating, and that you can play that English game -- cricket, is it? -- as good as any Englishman.

"Aye, you done well, and I'm thinking you've a promising future. Better'n any O'Shaughnessy afore you. Sure, I'm wishing I could be around to see it all."

"Of course you'll be around."

"Nay, lad. Me time's near. I seen me Deirdre more and more of late. Comes to me in me dreams, she does, as young and handsome as the day I wed her. I'm wishing you could have known her, Keir. Sure, there wasn't a girl in all County Cork as could compare with her. 'Tis a lucky man I've been. Had a good life, I reckon. I'm ready to meet me Maker."

Resignation to death. It angered Keir, that religious belief that life was less important than some amorphous existence after death. It made life a fearful slave to death.

Keir couldn't understand Patrick's attitude, because he himself believed that death was the end. There was no God, no heaven, no hell. Only the immediate, sentient present.

That was another subject about which he and his mother so bitterly disagreed. The church was an important part of Rowena's life, but Keir had rejected both the Catholic and Anglican teachings. Religion existed through bigotry and hypocrisy. Churches manipulated and subjugated the people in their struggles for power. Keir knew well the lessons of history; he'd learned of the bloody wars, the atrocities that had been committed in the name of God.

Such a God he could not worship.

"I'll just be closing me eyes for a bit," Patrick said, leaning his grey head against the rough, weathered wood. "Maybe you could recite me a passage from the Good Book, or something you learned at school."

It came easily to mind. How often he had been required to write it out as punishment for some misdemeanor. A lesson in humility, the Masters had called it.

Keir began reciting Gray's "Elegy Written in a Country Churchyard".

The curfew tolls the knell of parting day,

The lowing herd wind slowly o'er the lea....

Patrick sighed and let the pastoral essence of the words wash over him.

Keir's voice droned on rhythmically, automatically, as he gazed, unseeing, at the sluggish river before him. He faltered when the poem's message intruded upon his consciousness.

Let not Ambition mock their useful toil,
Their homely joys, and destiny obscure;
Nor Grandeur hear with a disdainful smile
The short and simple annals of the poor.
The boast of heraldry, the pomp of power,
And all that beauty, all that wealth e're gave,
Awaits alike the inevitable hour.
The paths of glory lead but to the grave.

"A fine sight this!" Mary said, coming upon them suddenly. "Have you nothing better to do than to sit about dreaming?"

She turned her piercing black eyes on Keir. "As for you, I'll thank you to put on your shirt. 'Tain't decent for a man to be seen in the altogether."

"It's how God made me." The thoughtless reply was tinged with sarcasm.

Ugly red splotches mottled Mary's thin, sharp-featured face. "You dare to speak His name? You, as hasn't darkened the inside of the church these three years? You, that's sold his soul to the divil himself?"

"Leave the boy be, Mary," Patrick interceded wearily.

"Like as not he's been filling your foolish old head with his heathenish notions!"

"Nay, Mary. He was reciting me some fine poetry."

"A boy his age should be doing a decent day's work, not spouting poetry! Just look at John and Tim -- younger'n him and doing men's work alongside their fathers," she said, referring to Fergus and Conn's eldest boys. "Yet 'tis him that's after thinking he be too good for his own kinfolk! 'Tis an iniquitous world when the wicked get rewarded for their sins. But God'll get His vengeance yet, you mark me words, boy!"

Keir concealed his anger as he rose. His Irish self wanted to fling her spiteful words back into her face, but his well-bred English self warned him that dignified restraint would be more effective. Ignoring Mary he said, "I'll return tomorrow, Grandfather. I suggest you rest for the remainder of the day. It's too hot for you to be working."

Mary's toothless mouth flapped like a fish's. "Will you listen to that now! He 'suggests'. And who's to be doing the work, I'd like to know?" she shouted at Keir's retreating back. "We're not all of us living off Launston charity!"

"Bitch!" Keir muttered under his breath. "Bitch! Bitch! Bitch!"

By the time he reached home his temper had cooled. It was senseless to let people like Mary irritate him. Her opinions were of no consequence.

Keir filled two buckets from the rain barrel. In the sheltered yard he stripped naked and doused himself with the tepid, stagnant water. As he scrubbed himself with harsh lye soap, his thoughts turned with pleasant anticipation to the afternoon. His daily visits to the Launstons' home, 'Thistledown', were his salvation during the holidays.

Keir laughed when he recalled that his first friend at the college had been one of the Irish maids, Molly Hogan. She had stopped him on the stairs one day soon after his arrival with the words, "Sure, I've seen happier faces in a coffin! You've not had bad news from home?"

Ten year old Keir had responded instinctively to the kind concern in her voice. "I don't belong here!" he'd burst out, uncomfortably close to tears.

"Whyever not, I'd like to know?"

"I'm not like them."

"Then you should be thanking the Lord! Ain't there a few of the little divils I'd like to swipe with me broom!"

"You don't understand."

"Don't I now? Happen I know that nothing ever comes easy to us Irish. But here you be, with a chance to make something of yourself. Wouldn't I like to trade places with yourself!"

"You?"

Molly had placed her hands defiantly upon her hips. "Aye! And what's wrong with a girl wanting to have some book learning?"

"I can't imagine the Masters telling you what to do, Molly," Keir had replied with a grin.

"Get away with you!" she'd said, and they had both dissolved into laughter.

He had often conversed with her after that. She had entertained him with descriptions of city life, acquainting him also with the seamier sections of Toronto where so many of the destitute Irish immigrants tried to eke out an existence. She had talked of Ireland, her eyes suddenly old and filled with sorrow as she'd relived the horrors of the famine that had driven her away. She and a brother had been the only ones of a family of ten to have survived the hunger, the voyage, the diseases.

But Molly, ever a practical girl, had never dwelt long on the hardships of her life. "If we brood o'er the bad things in life, there'd be no time to enjoy the good," she had often said. Her optimism had been infectious, and had inspired Keir to work all the harder.

He had been grateful for Molly's friendship then, but later it had become an embarrassment to him, exposing him to ridicule, and he'd been thankful when she had quit service to marry the Irish tavern keeper she had so frequently mentioned.

Keir had no lack of friends at the college now. One of them was Richard Launston. That friendship had developed unexpectedly.

It had become almost a custom for the boarders to raid the orchard of a cantankerous old sea captain who lived across the street from the college. One September night of Keir's fourth year at the school, both he and Richard had been among those chosen for the annual foray. They had been lowered out the second storey windows of the dormitory on bedsheet 'ropes', and had climbed first the cast iron schoolyard fence and then the six foot high wooden one across the street. While they had been stuffing their pillowcases with apples and pears, they'd heard the dogs barking -- large, vicious boxers which had nipped more than one daring thief in the past.

Keir had already been atop the fence when he'd seen Richard lose his grip and fall back down. Without thinking, Keir had tossed his plunder to one of the boys in the street, and had jumped down to help his cousin. With cupped hands he had boosted Richard up, and had barely had time to escape the snarling dogs himself.

Keir had been hailed as a hero. Richard had graciously shaken his hand. That following summer was the first time Keir had been asked to Thistledown. Now it seemed more his home than this place.

Keir towelled himself vigorously, slipped on his white lawn shirt and riding breeches, and pulled on his boots. Already sweat was beading on his brow. He decided it was too hot to reheat the food his mother had left for him. He would dine at Paxtons', which still served the best and cheapest meals in town.

There was little trace now of the conflagration that had desolated this landscape eight years before. The network of streets that had replaced the forest was lined with matchstick homes, rented, for the most part, to those refugees of the Irish potato famine who had sought new lives in this thriving town.

The older settlement along the river -- which included Keir's home -- had been dubbed 'Punkin Hollow' because every home boasted a pumpkin patch. This newer settlement adjacent to it had earned the epithet of 'Shantytown', though coarser labels were often applied to it.

It was the closest Launston Mills had to a slum.

This was not, Keir knew, what Jeremy had envisioned when he had sold the land to an entrepreneur from the city. The ill-built homes, huddled close together, had already fallen into a state of disrepair. Doors hung drunkenly from broken hinges; there were gaps between planks where the unseasoned wood had warped; shingles had blown away during storms. Although the agent who collected the exorbitant rents made eloquent promises of improvements, none were ever forthcoming. Those tenants who had made their own repairs had had their rents raised -- because their houses were now more desirable and more easily rentable. The angry tenants' complaints of the inadequate water supply -- there was only one well to service the entire area -- fell on deaf ears. The stench from the privies, located side-by-side on the narrow lots, fouled the air. The pigs, geese, and dogs that foraged freely here only added to the atmosphere of filth and disorder.

Shantytown was a festering sore that most people tried to ignore. Those who complained of it blamed the predominantly Irish tenants, and cited it as another example of the inherent laziness and degeneracy of the Catholics.

Keir kept to Mill Road, skirting Shantytown. Even before he reached the mills he could hear the whine of the saws and smell the sweet fragrance of sawdust. Men shouted and cursed as they loaded scows with lumber, planks, and railway ties.

Lumbering was big business, not only for the Launstons, but for the town. The expanded sawmill, with the aid of steam power, worked year round and employed hundreds in its many facets.

An economic boom, abetted by the Crimean War and the reciprocity treaty with the United States, had followed the depression of the late '40s. The Launstons were rapidly becoming extremely wealthy and powerful. Jeremy was constantly expanding his business interests.

His latest venture was in railroads. He had invested in various companies, but his largest share was in the railroad that was being built from Port Hope to Launston Mills. The faster, more efficient rail transport would further stimulate the lumbering business, to say nothing of the general economy of the community. Already Jeremy and several other influential citizens had applied to the government to have Launston Mills incorporated as a town.

Launston Mills could conceivably mushroom into the most important centre north of the Front. It was ideally located on a chain of lakes and rivers that stretched into the virgin wilderness. With the railroad link to the Front, Launston Mills could become the funnel for the natural wealth of the north. The town's only serious rival for this enviable position was Peterborough, which possessed equal advantages.

Across the river a gang of men wielding picks and shovels were cutting back the bank to prepare the railbed. Carters were busy too, hauling away the rock and soil, while further downstream at the wharf, rail yards and sheds, a station, and a grain elevator were under construction.

There could be a profitable future for him here, Keir thought as he continued on to Paxtons'. He suspected that Jeremy would offer him a position of some sort when he graduated next summer. But Keir knew he could never live in this small-minded town. Nor did he want it said that he owed his success solely to the generosity of the Launstons.

Keir decided to have an ale before going into the dining room for a hot meal. Paxtons' barroom was already busy as men filed in during their dinner break. Keir sat down at a table near the open door, taking advantage of the bit of fresh air that squeezed into the stuffy room. He noticed Malcolm Grimsby seated, as usual, in a dark corner.

Those who had known Malcolm only in his youth would not recognize him now. Neither his hair nor his beard had been trimmed -- or washed, it seemed -- for months. His clothes, filthy and malodorous rags, hung loosely on his emaciated frame. His skin glowed with a sickly yellow pallor.

Malcolm stared morosely into his half-empty glass, unaware of the activity about him. He muttered something to himself and then drained his glass, refilling it with shaking hands from the bottle that stood before him.

He wouldn't be long for this world, people predicted. Nor was there much to keep him here now. He had become melancholic since his wife's death, over a year ago. And her drowning hadn't been an accident, it was rumoured. Maureen had gone slightly mad after two of her children had succumbed to diphtheria and the infant -- her eighth-born -- to dysentery. Yet no one begrudged Maureen her resting place in the Catholic cemetery.

One of Maureen's brothers had taken in the five other children. Malcolm had been forced to sell the house to settle debts, and now drank away what little money remained. Josh Paxton allowed him to sleep in a room above the stables.

"What'll you have, sir?" a serving girl asked Keir.

"A pint of ale, please."

"Make that two more, Betty," a familiar voice said from behind Keir. He turned around as a hand clapped him on the shoulder. "You'll not mind if we join you?" Conn Ryan asked.

"Not at all."

"'Tis been an age since we had a drink together, eh?" Conn said as he and his eldest son, Tim, seated themselves. "Our womenfolk have gone to the farm to visit Shelagh and Hugh so we though to take our dinner here. You've not eaten yet?"

"No, I...."

"Then I'll be ordering something for you as well. What do you say to a pasty? They make 'em real good here."

"Maybe Keir was thinking to dine formal in the dining room," Tim said. He was a youthful reflection of his father, right down to the springy red curls.

Conn queried Keir with a look.

"I'd be happy to join you."

"Good! And we'll have three pasties, Betty," Conn said to the girl when she placed brimming mugs of ale before them.

"Your not working at Grandda's today?" Tim asked Keir.

"I did."

"You'll be off to Thistledown then."

"That's right." Keir did not fail to notice his cousin's sneer.

Nor did Conn. "Slainte!" he said, raising his mug. He took a satisfying gulp. "Sure there's nothing like a fine brew for washing the dust from a man's gullet. Well, Keir, you'll be off to school again soon."

"Yes."

"And what'll you be doing when you're finished next year?"

"I've no definite plans as yet."

"Like as not, Mr. Jeremy'll have a job for you, eh? The men were saying as much just t'other week when you were touring the sawmill with Mr. Jeremy and Mr. Kayne."

Geoffrey Kayne was the general manager of the Launston mills. Jeremy was rarely involved with the direct supervision of things these days.

Conn lowered his voice as he continued. "They was saying as how you might be working with Mr. Kayne."

"Uncle Jeremy hasn't mentioned anything to me."

"Like as not, he will afore long. And there's many that's hoping you'll take it -- you being one of us, in a manner of speaking."

Keir was surprised by this, but noticing the scowl on Tim's face he realized that many would not welcome him in such a position of authority.

"Things aren't what they used to be," Conn said after a few mouthfuls of the meat pie. "Not like in Mr. Sam's day. Hardly a day passed that we didn't see himself. He'd ask after our families and suchlike. Worked side by side with us as often as not. I'll wager Mr. Kayne's never run a saw in his life! But he's a sharp one to be sure. Never misses a trick. But he never talks to a man personal like. The men haven't much liking for him, I'll tell you that."

"I'm sure he has much to occupy him, as does Uncle Jeremy," Keir said, feeling it necessary to defend Jeremy against Conn's implied criticism.

"That's as may be, but there's some things old Sam wouldn't have done if he was here today. Why just t'other day Paddy O'Brien lost an arm to a saw -- and not a drop of whiskey in him, though Mr. Kayne claimed he was drunk. 'Tis the machinery that's not safe, though nothing's been done about that. Now Paddy's got no job, and a wife and nine children to feed. In Mr. Sam's day, when a man was disabled working at the mills, himself would give him an easy job he could do -- sweeping floors and suchlike -- and not much cut in his wages if he was a family man. Now a man gets showed the door without so much as a thank 'ee. There was a time when Mr. Jeremy would have done things different."

"Perhaps Uncle Jeremy isn't aware of this," Keir said uncomfortably.

"Sure, that's why we need someone like you there!"

"Nothing would change," Tim said. "What does ***he*** care about the likes of us? He's one of them. He takes Launston money without thinking that it's our sweat that's earned it for him." Tim left the table, and joined friends gathered about the bar.

Conn ran his fingers nervously through his hair. "Don't pay no mind to Tim. He envies you, Keir, having a good education and the chance to be doing whate'er you want in life. The lad's a hard worker, but I'm thinking his heart's not really in the job. You'll not hold his words against him?"

Even as children, Keir and Tim had not been close friends. During the past eight years they had seen very little of one another, and it was during this time that animosity seemed to have grown between them. Keir was angry at Tim's accusation, but the pleading look in Conn's eyes prompted him to say, "No."

Conn smiled gratefully. "I'm thinking if you two was ever to really know each other, you'd be friends."

Keir doubted that, but said nothing. He noticed Gavin wander in and order an ale. The boy was tall for his fourteen years, and though he was broad in the shoulders, he needed fleshing out. Still, he could easily be mistaken for a man of eighteen. He, too, worked at the sawmill.

Gavin's presence always made his relatives uneasy. It was his unpredictability that they feared -- or perhaps it was the ease, and apparent unconcern, with which he got himself into trouble.

He had already seen the inside of Launston Mills' new jailhouse -- once for petty theft and twice for drunken brawling. He had annoyed, and even alienated, a good many people, speaking his mind without temper, but also without tempering his thoughts, even when these were insulting or abusive. It was that casual, unemotional disrespect that irritated Mary the most. Her own vituperative comments seemed to slide right past him, and even made him laugh. How she hated him! She had made certain that he had been sent to work as soon as he had been old enough.

Gavin was a steady worker who never shirked a job when it was set him, but who also never took the initiative. He had not shown any ambition, other than a self-indulgent hedonism -- reminiscent of his mother. He had formed no close relationships with anyone, although he could be pleasant and agreeable when he chose. He gave Keir and Conn a nod, but did not bother to go over and talk to them.

"I'd best be getting back now," Conn said to Keir.

"Thank you for the dinner, Uncle Conn."

"Sure, 'twas me pleasure, lad."

Several of the workers were shuffling out. One of the crowd of young men to whom Tim had been talking said loudly, "Sure, some of us has to be getting back to work now. Not like certain lucky bastards in here."

The speaker was Charles "Chunky" Muldoon, a hefty lad slightly older than Keir, and one whose meaty fists Keir had encountered often as a child. Chunky's remark was for his benefit, Keir knew, but he chose to ignore it. He would not give Chunky, or the spectators, the enjoyment of a fight, either verbal or physical. That would only lower him to their level. Keir drained his mug and rose.

Chunky chose that moment to leave as well. As he passed Keir, he fell hard against him, jolting Keir into the table.

"Mind where you're going, bastard! You don't own this town yet."

There was laughter. All eyes were on the two young men.

"Kindly allow me to pass," Keir said coldly to Chunky who still blocked his way.

"Will you listen to that then? Ain't we got fancy manners! You want me to move? Then make me... if you can." Chunky grinned stupidly at Keir.

There was an amused, expectant silence in the room.

"Give over, Chunky," Tim said as he headed for the door. "You can't provoke Keir into a fight. They've made a coward of him."

Chunky guffawed loudly. "You go run to your ma's skirts then, kid!"

Keir brushed off the hand that patted him on the head, and walked away.

"Tain't his ma's skirts he's interested in," someone yelled out. "'Tis that Launston vixen's!"

Keir's clenched fists itched to release the rage that boiled within him. The men's laughter followed him up the street. He was more incensed by his cousin's scathing condemnation than by Chunky Muldoon's bullying. He wished that he had ploughed his fist into that beefy lout's ugly face, just to prove his cousin wrong.

Keir had not forgotten how to fight. Despite Jeremy's belief to the contrary, the college boys often settled disputes with their fists. This was done in a formal and ritualized manner, much like the old duels, with each contender having his 'second', and a referee to ensure that the rules were strictly enforced. Keir's early training in the art had stood him in good stead on several occasions.

Keir reached the gates of Thistledown. The house was not visible from the road. All that curious passersby could see were a high stone wall and an impressive wrought iron gate with a large flowing *L* inscribed in the decorative arch above it. Keir proceeded up the long, winding drive.

Most of the mature hardwoods had been left standing, although the saplings and underbrush had been cleared to give the property a park-like spaciousness. Eventually, these trees gave way to great stretches of carefully tended lawns and formal gardens.

The house was a pleasing eclectic mixture of architectural styles. Basically it was a larger brick version of its predecessor, with two recessed wings flanking it -- the library on the west and a conservatory on the east side. The Doric-columned portico, the Palladian window above, the belvedere on the roof, the french windows opening onto the terrace and gardens added a touch of whimsy to its stately beauty.

It was a marvellous house inside as well. The marble fireplaces were for decor rather than necessity, since the building was heated by a monstrous furnace in the basement, which forced hot air through ducts into all the rooms. There was a cistern in the attic, from which water was pumped not only into the kitchen quarters, but into 'bath' rooms where fixed tubs -- large enough to stretch out in! -- could easily be filled by turning a gilt tap. There were also indoor water closets that utilized the flow of water under pressure to keep them sanitary. It was truly amazing what luxuries modern technology could supply!

Keir dined often at Thistledown. Long gone were the days when he had felt insecure and uncomfortable in such formal situations. The social graces were second nature to him now. Even Harriet Launston accepted him -- to a certain degree.

Keir passed the sunken garden on his way to the brick outbuildings situated a good distance behind the house. Jillian, dressed in a green riding habit, was already at the stables. Her chestnut curls hung freely to her waist, and the hat which her mother insisted she wear had, as usual, been discarded. Keir could detect, among the hay and manure smells of the stable, the lavender fragrance that Jillian invariably wore, claiming it an effective mosquito repellent.

"Richard's gone for the day," she told Keir.

"Where did he go?"

"With Papa to Omemee to see how the railroad construction is progressing. They did think of asking you along, but Richard said you were obliged to work for your grandfather in the mornings. Still, there's no reason why you and I shouldn't go for our usual ride. You could look more pleased, Keir!"

Keir hid his disappointment as he gallantly said, "I can't think of anyone with whom I'd rather spend the afternoon."

"Well you don't have to dissemble with me. I'm rather insulted that I wasn't asked along as well. Do they think that I'm not interested in the trains? You know, more and more I've been thinking of the injustices I suffer because I was born a woman. Richard's going to get all this," she said with a sweep of her hand, "and I'm going to packed off to become the wife of some 'suitable' man. Do you think that's fair? Oh, do hurry up with the horses, Tom! And don't bother saddling one for yourself. I don't care what Mama said, I'll not be followed about like some helpless child!"

"But it's not proper for a young lady to be riding out unchaperoned," Tom Finch replied.

"Faith! Surely Keir is capable of looking after me!"

"But that's just the point, Miss Jilly...."

Keir recalled the ridiculous but ugly insinuation that had been hurled at him at Paxtons' not long ago. Yes, people talked. And they were always prepared to believe the worst.

"Don't be silly, Tom! Keir is my cousin. He can be trusted."

"But the Missus...."

"Damn it, Tom! You're not coming, and there's an end to it!"

Tom shook his head as he led the two horses into the yard. "It'll be my hide if the Missus finds out."

"She won't. Unless you tell her." Jillian threw her arms about him impulsively. "Thanks, Tom!"

He lifted her into the saddle and said with a grin, "You'd best watch that cussing tongue of yours. I'll not be held responsible for that as well."

She laughed delightedly as she spurred her horse forward. She took the wooden gate at a gallop, not waiting for Tom to amble down and open it. She saw him shake his head as she looked back to wave. The bubbles of her laughter burst about his ears.

Keir was riding his own mare, 'Banshee', which Jeremy had given him for his sixteenth birthday. What a delightful surprise that had been! Banshee was a powerful young horse, but Keir had to push her now to keep up with Jillian. His cousin rode with all the vitality and zest that she couldn't manage on her own feet. Many thought her reckless, but Keir knew she was always in perfect control of her mount, even though some of her stunts might be unwise or even dangerous.

Jillian plunged through the forest along the well-worn path that led to the river. Not once did she glance back to see if Keir followed. Where the trail forked, she reined in sharply and waited for Keir to reach her. Her face was flushed with the heat and that wild, wide-eyed exhilaration that she felt whenever she was in the saddle.

"I've changed my mind," she said. "I want to take Gypsy Lane out to the lake."

"Which means we have to go through town. Your mother would certainly find out...."

"Oh bother! I despise all those stuffy old rules! Proper ladies don't do this or that," she mimicked. "You're not a coward, are you, Keir?"

For the second time that day that reprehensible word 'coward' struck a discordant note within Keir, but Jillian cantered off toward town before he could reply. He had no choice but to follow her. She slowed to a walk as she reached the populated streets, allowing Keir to catch up with her. She proceeded deliberately slowly, inviting attention.

As they turned down Main Street, Keir said, "We'll be all day getting there at this pace."

She smiled sweetly at him, but did not quicken her pace. Keir squirmed as curious eyes followed their progress. Paxton's door, directly in front of them at the end of the street, was still open, and Keir could feel the stares emanating from the dim interior. The tavern was never without customers.

Just before they reached the junction at Lindsay Street, Jillian slapped her horse's flank with her riding crop and shot forward, leaving Keir in her dusty wake. He was sure he could hear men's laughter as he rounded the corner in front of the tavern.

Jillian did not slacken her speed as she crossed the bridge. The lone pedestrian, warned by the clatter of hooves, jumped aside as she thundered past. It was Keir who heard the muttered oaths and who felt embarrassed for his cousin's rudeness. He knew better than to admonish her, however. Only Richard and Jeremy could do that with any success.

He soon forgot the incident as the peace of the countryside enveloped him. Gypsy Lane meandered through fertile farmland, most of it already shorn of trees, and sprouting fields of golden grain or acres of Indian corn which stood six feet tall in the August sunshine. Split rail fences lined the road while rows of upturned tree stumps divided the fields. Masses of goldenrod and Queen Anne's lace claimed any waste or fallow land. Here and there herds of freckled cows and clouds of sheep grazed complacently. Crows and blackbirds flapped out of the way of the riders; a hawk circled lazily overhead, dipping and soaring on the almost visible heat waves. Jillian caught her breath as a great blue heron maneuvered its large, unwieldy body into graceful flight from the swampy reaches of the lake.

They left the dusty, rutted road and descended to the water's edge through a cool, sweet pine forest. Beneath the cloudless sky, the mud-bottomed lake shimmered a deceptive sapphire blue.

Jillian started to slide from the saddle before Keir had reached her. He ran over and grabbed her before she fell.

"You should have waited until I was here!" he scolded as he set her carefully on the ground.

"Oh, I knew you'd be there to catch me," she replied airily. He could not hear the rapid pounding of her own frightened heart.

"And what if I hadn't been?"

"You sound like Mama! If, if, if! If I weren't lame I wouldn't be needing your help at all!"

Keir looked down with compassion at the bent head that barely reached his shoulder. He knew how she despised pity, and that self-pity was as detestable to her.

Jillian looked up at him brightly. "Well, sir, I am at your mercy. What do you intend to do with me?" Her large brown eyes teased him.

Keir offered his arm for support, since she did not have her walking stick. "Whereto, milady?"

They sat down beneath the towering pines. A refreshing breeze skimmed over the lake. From the direction of the Falls, a steamer towing cribs of logs was chugging toward the mouth of the Scugog River. The stark white canvas of a sailboat was visible near the distant north shore.

"I'm glad Papa didn't cut down all the trees on the lake," Jillian said, gazing at the desolate western shoreline. "But I suppose he would have if this land hadn't already belonged to others. It's so ugly when all the trees are gone. Like the town. Papa says that citizens should plant shade trees along the streets, but most people just laugh at the idea. When the town is incorporated, I think Papa should become Mayor." This thought seemed to appeal to her. "He'd do great things! He has such visions of what Launston Mills could become! I'm sure he'd clean out Shantytown for a start -- get rid of those decrepit shacks and dirty people. Do you remember how it used to be, before the fire?"

"It wouldn't be quite so simple. Those people need somewhere to live. You can't just turn them out and demolish the buildings."

"Why not? No one wants them anyway. Filthy Irish!"

Keir frowned but said nothing. Despite her keen and usually logical mind, Jillian could be infuriatingly, unreasonably childish at times. Keir knew that her contempt of the Irish stemmed from Brendan Delaney's 'murder' of her grandfather.

"Did I mention that Papa wants to talk to you when he returns? He's going to offer you a position when you graduate next year. Did you know?"

"No."

"I heard him discussing it with Geoffrey and Richard. He wants you to become Geoffrey's assistant. I think he'd like you to take over Geoffrey's job some day -- which is hardly fair in my opinion. Will you accept the position?"

"I think not. I have no wish to live in this town."

"Whyever not?"

"People have long memories."

"Ah, you're afraid."

"I am not!"

"Methinks the gentleman doth protest too much."

"I don't want to fight for acceptance all my life! It's different in Toronto."

"Only until someone discovers the truth. You can't run away from it, you know. It's like the sword of Damocles poised over your head, held by a fragile strand that could break in an instant."

"I'll take my chances." Keir was annoyed by the truth of her words. The fear of discovery constantly gnawed at him.

"Richard did say you wouldn't accept. He doesn't want you to, of course."

"Why?"

"Because you're a threat to him." To Keir's dumbfounded expression she replied, "You should hardly be so surprised, with Papa taking such an interest in you and planning to place you into an influential position in the family business -- which will one day be Richard's. Why, you get along better with Papa than Richard does! He's always been jealous of you."

"But we're friends!"

"You really don't know him very well, do you? Richard's philosophy is 'know thine enemy'. Papa is delighted with your and Richard's friendship. Consequently their own relationship has improved. Richard doesn't have to compete with you quite so openly now."

"I don't believe it!"

"You're too trusting, Keir. Oh, Richard does admire you, and I'm sure he'd like you a great deal if you stayed in Toronto. He's afraid you'd be successful in the business and that Papa will bequeath you a substantial share of it. He will be pleased if you turn down Papa's offer. And although I love you dearly, for Geoffrey's sake I'm also glad that you won't accept."

"Why?" He had already guessed the answer, but hoped he was mistaken.

"Because he is eminently 'suitable', of course," she said with a grin.

"You can't be serious! He's nearly twice your age!"

"I prefer men to boys," Jillian said loftily, stung by Keir's reaction. "Geoffrey is charming and kind, and he treats me like a woman. And I don't want to discuss him with you! Help me to my horse, please."

He did as she asked, but could not refrain from inquiring, "Has he mentioned marriage to you?"

"We have an understanding -- not that's it's any of ***your*** business. We'll wait a couple of years, until I'm eighteen."

Keir lifted her into the saddle and handed her the reins. "I don't trust that man, Jilly. I wouldn't want to see you hurt."

"Don't be absurd! Geoffrey wouldn't hurt me."

"Are you sure it's you he's interested in and not your father's money?"

She blanched as though he had struck her a cruel blow, and Keir regretted his words.

"How dare you! Oh, you're hateful!"

Keir grabbed hold of the reins before she could escape from him. The horse pranced about skittishly as they both fought for control.

"Jilly wait, I didn't mean...."

"Let go!" She struck out at Keir with her riding crop, slicing it across the back of his hand. She seemed shocked as she gazed at the blood she had drawn, but rode off without a word as Keir released his hold.

Tom was already rubbing down her mare when Keir arrived at Thistledown. "Miss Jilly's changing for tea," Tom informed him. "Said she'd meet you on the lawn."

Ten minutes later Jillian greeted him with her usual effervescence, as though nothing untoward had occurred between them. She never held grudges; she herself expected forgiveness without asking for it. She waved aside his attempted apology as she unceremoniously plopped herself down beside him on the cool grass beneath the sprawling branches of an ancient oak.

"Won't you miss times like this when you're in Toronto?" she asked. Keir was used to her capriciousness and her quicksilver changes of moods, and wouldn't have been surprised if she were about to try to convince him to stay in Launston Mills. But Harriet Launston and Geoffrey Kayne were strolling toward them, and Jillian fell silent.

"Mr. Kayne's waiting for your father," Harriet said to Jillian. "I suggested he might like to take tea with you and Keir."

"You don't mind if I join you?" Geoffrey inquired affably.

"We'd be delighted," Jillian said.

"Do come and join us ladies if the children become tiresome, Mr. Kayne. You really wouldn't be disturbing our meeting. We'd welcome your advice."

"Thank you, Mrs. Launston."

Both Geoffrey and Keir hastened to assist Jillian as she struggled to her feet. "Allow me," Geoffrey said, leading Jillian to one of the garden chairs encircling the white wrought iron table.

Keir noticed a becoming, though uncharacteristic, blush on his cousin's cheeks as she accepted Geoffrey's escort. She really was enamoured of the man, he thought, appalled.

Keir studied Geoffrey more closely. He was undeniably intelligent, a shrewd businessman. He was tall and slim with a rather prominent nose and a handsome smile that never quite reached his grey eyes. His dandified dress gave him an aura of self-assurance, almost arrogance, yet he seemed an amiable fellow. His manners were highly polished, his words, smooth and correct.

Too correct, Keir thought. Geoffrey Kayne was a charlatan. He was ambitious, and his every action was calculated. Geoffrey had already made himself indispensable to Jeremy. If he married Jillian, his future with the flourishing Launston empire would be secure.

"I understand your mother and several other good ladies are drawing up a petition to send to the Bishop," Geoffrey said as he seated himself next to Jillian.

"Yes. Mama feels quite strongly about having a church established in town, with a resident minister. She says the visits from the clergy of other parishes are too infrequent to be of much good."

"There are now enough families of the Anglican persuasion here to profitably establish a church, I'm certain."

"Mama is quite irate at the church's seeming indifference to some of its flock. There is a church of practically every denomination in town, save ours."

"Quite so. The Catholics are planning to build an impressive new edifice, so I've heard. The new priest has ambitious schemes."

"Having a church doesn't appear to have changed the Catholics much. What I mean to say is, Mama thinks that a church will help to cure, or at least curb, the 'moral corruption', as she terms it, that has seeped into town. Yet, as far as I can see, it's the Irish who are the cause of it, with their constant drunkenness and brawling, and they haven't even the excuse of a lack of moral guidance."

"I think you do the Irish and injustice, Jillian. It's true that they are hard-drinking men, but -- despite what's been said of them -- they ***are*** hard workers. Our lumber camps would be practically empty if it were not for the Irish."

Geoffrey's patronizing defence of the Irish irked Keir even more than Jillian's outspoken disdain.

"Why, just look at Keir," Geoffrey continued. "You could hardly accuse him of such dissipation as you mentioned."

Jillian giggled. "I never think of Keir as being Irish. But then, he is also my cousin; so one would hardly expect him to be conventional."

Geoffrey smiled. "I do concede that point"

A liveried footman deposited a silver tea tray on the table before Jillian. Keir said little during the tea time conversation. Geoffrey had the ability to make him feel extremely young and relatively ignorant. He listened half-heartedly to them, and wondered whether he would always be relegated to a kind of social limbo -- to the Irish he was too English, to the English, too Irish. But once again thoughts of Toronto cheered him.

Jeremy and Richard joined them as they were finishing the tea and cakes.

"The work is progressing on schedule," Jeremy informed them. "Trains should be rolling into Omemee by the end of September, and into Launston Mills by Christmas! By God, but we've waited a long time for this! I want you to start planning the official opening ceremonies right away, Geoffrey. Make certain you get the Lieutenant-Governor and as many dignitaries as possible to attend. It's time we made the rest of the province aware of our existence, and our potential as the economic capital of the north!"

Jeremy sat down. "I'm damned if I want tea on a day such as this." He rang the silver hand bell on the tray, and a moment later, as though he had been waiting unseen for just such a summons, a footman appeared. Jeremy ordered a drinks tray, and then said to Keir, "Well, it's about time we discussed your future, don't you think?"

"Could we discuss it in private, Uncle Jeremy?"

"No need. Everyone here knows what my proposition will be -- even Jilly, if I know my daughter -- and I'm sure they're as anxious to hear you accept as I am."

Keir dreaded this, but he knew that if he didn't make his stand now he would drift into a life he didn't want and couldn't tolerate. "Uncle Jeremy, I must tell you that I intend to remain in the city when I've finished my studies. I have a friend at the college whose father owns the *DAILY CHRONICLE*. He knows of my interest in journalism, and has guaranteed me a job upon graduation. I've decided to accept his offer."

"The *DAILY CHRONICLE*," Jeremy said scornfully. "You intend to work for that reformist rag? I must admit I expected better of you, Keir. I thought you had ambitions that would do justice to your talents. It seems I was mistaken." His voice was cold, his manner, brusque. He was damned disappointed in the boy, whom he had begun to think of as a second son -- a son that he and Rowena shared. How pleased he had been of the friendship that had developed between Keir and Richard. Already he had envisioned them all working harmoniously together, one big, happy family and he, its patriarch. Dammit, he liked the boy! Richard tended to sullenness at times, but not when Keir was present. A bit of rivalry was healthy, and kept his son in line. Keir had succeeded at school even beyond Jeremy's expectations. He was proud of the boy. And he would miss him.

"I'm sorry to disappoint you, Uncle Jeremy." And grateful that Jeremy hadn't reminded him of all that he owed the Launstons.

"You have a year yet. Should you change your mind, there will be a job for you here. If not... I'll see that you have an adequate allowance."

"I couldn't accept."

"Nonsense! There's no reason for you to wallow in poverty for the sake of false pride," Jeremy said irascibly. Keir knew his uncle was thinking of Rowena. "I set up a trust for you many years ago. The interest should allow you to live comfortably, as befits a gentleman, until you reach the age of majority. You can do what you like with the capital then. Consider it your inheritance from your father."

"Thank you."

Geoffrey Kayne's face was, as usual, indecipherable; Jillian smiled sympathetically at Keir. Richard regarded his cousin wryly, thinking him a fool to throw away such a future, but so grateful and delighted that he wondered if he could keep his face from splitting into a grin. Since he had just won a major victory over his cousin -- who had made his life uneasy these past eight years -- he could afford to be generous to him. With enthusiasm he queried Keir on his plans, and revealed his own intentions to study at the university.

Hard as it had been for Keir to disillusion Jeremy, the worst was yet to come. Rowena had to be told as well.

"You'll not be coming back then," she said when Keir had explained his plans that evening. She did not look up from her spinning, but the set of her shoulders and the increasing fervour with which she worked betrayed her trepidation.

"I'll be home for visits. It will be only a day's travel to Toronto once the trains are running."

The spinning wheel flew.

"I can't stay in this town, Ma."

"Sure, and whyever not? 'Tis where you were born. 'Tis where your kin are. I knew no good would come of your having too much learning. You should be working alongside your grandda and be content -- you've got his skill with the wood. But you're a misfit, that's the trouble. You don't belong with the gentry neither, much as you like to think you do."

"There is no 'gentry' such as you speak of," Keir said in exasperation. "The only difference between us and the Launstons is education and money. I have the knowledge -- that will help me earn the money. My peers accept and respect me. I ***am*** one of them."

"It matters not what I think then. You'll do what you like in the end."

"I just want you to understand."

Rowena looked at her son without revealing her anguish. Could she really blame him for wanting to leave? What was there for him here, after all? He could never work with Patrick because Mary would be forever sharpening her tongue on him.

Patrick and Mary had both been disappointed by their marriage, Rowena thought wryly. Neither one could measure up to the other's dead spouse -- the kind and gentle Deirdre, and the strong and resolute Matt. So Mary often vented her frustration with bitter words, and Patrick grew more resigned, always seeking an easy peace.

In any case, Keir was intimidatingly intelligent and knowledgeable, and not content to work merely with his hands. He had Jeremy's drive and ambition, and needed something challenging. It frightened her sometimes, for he seemed more Jeremy's child than hers. So, in a way, she was glad that Keir was not going to work for his uncle.

And if Keir did accept Jeremy's offer of a supervisory job at the mill, his relationship with his cousins would become even more strained, Rowena thought. They resented him, and truth to tell, the boys were worlds apart. Keir was right to think that he didn't fit in, and she knew it was not merely his education that set him apart.

"I know 'tis not been easy for you, bearing the shame of me guilt. Maybe I don't blame you for leaving."

"Ma...."

They were interrupted by an agitated knocking at the door. Keir walked over, thankful for the intrusion, and opened it. A shabbily dressed young girl practically tumbled into the room.

"Mrs. Delaney, beggin' your pardon, me Ma says could you come quick for to look at me sister, she being real poorly an' all."

It was one of the O'Donovan children from Shantytown.

"What ails her then?"

"Sure, she's been fevered and shakin' like the divil himself be rattling her bones and nothin'll bide in her stomach."

Rowena shoved a variety of herbs into a bag, lit a candle lantern, and left with the child. Keir watched the bobbing light proceed up the road when he went out to the stoop and lit a cigar. It was a sultry night; the air was thick, oppressive. Quilted clouds obscured the moon, portending rain.

Keir paced about restlessly. It was too hot to go indoors and settle down with a book. He had no wish to go to Paxtons' or any of the other taverns frequented by clods like Chunky Muldoon.

He felt a keen longing for Toronto, for the nighttime bustle of its gas-lit streets. He wondered why anyone would choose to stagnate in this backwater when the city could offer such variety and excitement. He would never feel lonely there.

Keir sauntered down to the river, stripped off his sticky garments, and plunged into the cool water. The only light in the dark night was that which spilled feebly from the homes along the riverbank. Eruptions of raucous laughter echoed through the stillness; the gentle strains of a lullaby emanated softly from some cabin in 'Frenchtown', the area on the other side of the river inhabited mostly by the families of French-Canadian lumberjacks. The bang of a door, an infant's wails, screamed recriminations all mingled with the quivering melody of the crickets' lament.

Keir swam out to the middle of the river, easily resisting the tug of the current as the water impatiently swept around the bend on its way to the millrace.

Chapter 41

Keir walked jauntily down the gas-lit street swinging his silver-topped cane, oblivious to the fierce buffeting of the wind and the ominous rumble of thunder.

He had just completed his first assignment as a full-fledged staff reporter for the *DAILY CHRONICLE*. After more than eight months of learning the more menial chores of newspaper publishing, he was understandably elated with his new position -- no matter that he was as yet limited solely to the coverage of social events. He would soon prove himself worthy of bigger and better things!

Besides, the annual bazaar to raise funds for the Orphans' Asylum had not been such a dull affair as he had feared. The nubile young ladies who had presided over the various booths had subtly vied with one another for the attentions of the gentlemen.

Keir smiled as he drew an embroidered handkerchief from his breast pocket. It was infused with the expensive French scent of the enchantress from whom he had purchased it. He would never forget those unusual violet eyes that had so frankly returned his stare. She had seemed almost angelic with her ivory complexion and moon-silvered hair, but her seductive smile had dispelled that illusion of untouchable innocence. She was undeniably the most beautiful woman Keir had ever seen.

He wished he'd had a chance to talk with her, to discover her name, but she had been surrounded by many other admiring males, some of whom she appeared to know well. Yet her eyes had strayed often to his, flirtatiously inviting his attention, although never allowing her gaze to linger overlong on his. When he had approached her on the pretext of purchasing something, she had pretended disinterest and had turned from him to chat with one of the scarlet-coated officers from the garrison.

Keir was determined to see her again.

He paused for a moment outside the 'Shamrock Tavern', and listened to the muffled hum of conversation, punctuated by bursts of laughter. He thought of stopping in to see Molly Hogan -- or rather, O'Day, as she was now -- for it had been a while since he had visited her. Wouldn't she be surprised to see him in his fine new suit of clothes: black frock coat, ash-grey trousers with broad black stripes running down the sides, pale yellow silk waistcoat, gold watch chain, pearl studs, black silk cravat, grey kid gloves, and tall black tophat. He knew he cut a dashing figure, and was once again grateful for Jeremy's generosity. He could never have afforded to dress and live so extravagantly on his salary.

But he would have to see Molly another time. His friends were awaiting him at the Rossin House Hotel and he was eager to reach them. It had occurred to him that one of them must surely know the mysterious beauty with the violet eyes.

He quickened his step as he turned down Deadbeat Lane. Although he was not unduly worried, he knew it was best not to tarry on these unlit alleyways which provided him with a shortcut. Dressed as he was, he would attract the attention of the beggars, the prostitutes, and the rogues who infested these dark streets like vermin.

He did not glance at the miserable little hovels that lined these narrow lanes, though he was careful not to stumble over the rubbish strewn about. He could not, however, ignore the foetid stench of excrement and rotting refuse. This was much worse than Launston Mills's Shantytown.

Keir gripped his cane tighter as a drunk staggered toward him. The man stopped to relieve himself on the street and then continued. Keir passed him warily. He was momentarily startled as something shot past his leg, and then noticed a skinny cat pounce upon another mangy creature that was tearing at a dead rat. They screeched and growled as they fought over the meal.

Keir turned with relief down the wider Whiskey Alley. At least here he did not feel hemmed in by the shadowy darkness. Here the lights from the nearby main streets reached tentatively down the road. There were several run-down taverns along here, and the boisterous noises were somehow reassuring.

A young girl in a ragged, filthy dress, which she had long since outgrown, stopped him. "Please, sir, can you spare a copper?"

Large eyes appealed to him from a dirt-smeared face. Her legs were bare, and she shivered beneath the thin shawl that she clutched with reddened fingers. The icy rain that had begun to fall seemed to slice through her.

Keir felt compassion for the child, so inadequately dressed against the wet chill of the April night. As he handed her a twenty-five cent piece, he wondered whether she would benefit from it or whether her parents would spend it on drink. That sort of thing happened all too often. But that wasn't his concern.

The girl stared open-mouthed at the silver coin in her grubby palm. "Thank you, sir! God bless you!" she called after him in her Irish brogue.

"Hey, mister, you looking for a woman?"

Keir hadn't noticed the speaker approaching. She sidled provocatively up to him from an alleyway. Her pelisse gaped open to allow him a glimpse of ample breasts above a low-cut gown.

"Blimey, but you're a good looker." She tried to entwine her arm in his. "I got a place you can stay till the rain lets up."

Keir shrugged her off. Beneath the cheap perfume he could detect the nauseating smell of her unwashed body. Her cheeks and lips were heavily rouged, her eyes outlined with kohl. Even in the dim light he could see the hard lines of her aging face. Probably has the pox as well, he thought.

"Hey, don't you want a good time?" She gripped his arm tenaciously, and tried to steer him toward the narrow alley from which she had emerged. "I don't come cheap, but I'm worth it." She laughed huskily. "Bet I could even teach you a thing or two."

Keir felt an insistent tug at his other arm. It was the beggar girl. "Get away quick!" she urged.

Before Keir realized what was happening, the woman had struck the child a vicious back-hand blow across the face, which sent the girl sprawling to the ground. As Keir jerked the woman away to prevent her from attacking again, the child screamed, "Behind you!"

Keir spun about to find two hefty men lunging at him from the alley. He swung the heavy metal end of his stick, catching the assailant armed with a club on the side of the head. The thug crumpled to the ground with a stunned grunt of pain. Before Keir could strike out again, the other man was upon him. He just had time to dodge the full impact of iron fists, though the glancing blow sent him reeling backwards. The walking stick fell from his hand.

Keir parried the next jab and cracked his fist into the man's already-broken face. Again and again he smashed at the brute, taking care to avoid the crippling groin kicks and the hands that groped for his hair and gouged at his eyes. With his concentration focussed upon his attacker, Keir was only vaguely aware of the screeching -- like that of the two cats earlier -- behind him.

The woman had tried to retrieve the club, but the beggar girl had jumped her. They tusselled on the ground, scratching, biting, kicking, ripping at each other's hair. The woman, though stronger, was hampered by her massive skirts and restraining corset, and the child was quick-witted and agile. She squirmed out of the woman's grasp, seized the bludgeon as she sprang to her feet, and whacked Keir's assailant across the back. Keir saw the man's look of surprise before he crumpled, breathless, to his knees.

The woman shrieked abuse as she hurled herself like a wildcat at the child, but Keir pulled the girl behind him, and roughly pushed the whore away. He heard the two men groaning as they slowly regained their senses. He grabbed the child's hand and hurried her away.

"I'll kill you if ever I get my hands on you again, you little bitch!" the woman screamed after the girl. "I'll tear out your guts with my bare hands and feed 'em to the dogs!"

Keir did not slow down until they reached a well-lit thoroughfare. He was dismayed to see the numerous scratches on the girl's face and bare arms. She had lost her shawl. The rain was pounding down unmercifully now, whipped by a gale-force wind; the sky crackled and exploded. Keir removed his frock coat and draped it about the girl's slender shoulders. It reached almost to her ankles; she seemed lost and pitiful beneath its folds.

She looked at him in astonishment, but snuggled gratefully into the warmth of the wool jacket.

"I don't know how to thank you for your help," Keir said awkwardly. "Allow me to walk you home."

"'Tain't necessary." She removed the coat reluctantly and held it out to him. "I'll be going now."

"Whereto?"

She gazed at him with enormous green eyes, and shrugged. Then she walked away, hugging her bare arms about her for warmth.

Keir almost let her go, not wishing to become involved with her life. But he knew that if she hadn't intervened, he would be lying in the alley now with his head laid open.

He gathered her up in his coat, and turned her to face him. "Have you a home?"

She shook her head.

"No family?"

"Nay."

"Where have you been sleeping?"

"In stables mostly, since me sister died and the landlady threw me out."

Keir knew what he would do. "You're coming with me."

She pulled back from him, her eyes wide with fright. "Nay!" she cried, and would have fled from him if he not had her firmly by the arm.

"Come. I'll not harm you."

"I'll not go back there! You can't make me go back! I'll run away again!"

Keir shook her to stop her hysterics. "What are you talking about?"

"You'll not turn me over to a constable or take me to the orphanage?"

"No. You'll come with me -- quietly -- to meet a friend of mine. She's a nice woman. You'll like her."

But the girl did not budge. "Does she run a brothel, this 'friend' of yours?"

"Of course not!"

His astonishment must have convinced her, for she relented. She trudged docilely beside him.

"What's your name?"

"Megan Maguire."

"Do you know those men and that woman, Megan? The ones in the alley?"

"Nay, though I seen them work before. She 'tices men down a dark alley or into a doorway, and then the others bash him senseless and steal his money and boots and whate'er else they fancy. You'd've been a right good catch for them -- I reckon they wouldn't of left a stitch on you. Mostly they roll the drunks after payday. You was asking for trouble, walking through there alone at night. We don't get many toffs strolling about there."

Keir smiled wryly as he rubbed his sore jaw. "I'll remember that."

Megan swayed beneath his arm and would have fallen had he not held her up. "Are you alright?"

"Aye," she replied uncertainly.

"When was the last time you had something to eat?"

She thought for a moment. "Yesterday morning."

They continued on in silence.

Keir did not want to cause a disturbance by ushering Megan through the front door of the Shamrock Tavern, so he steered her down the arched driveway that led to the stables at the back of the inn. He felt her resist.

"We ain't going to the inn?" she croaked.

"Indeed we are."

He pushed her forward. He was beginning to lose his patience, for he was wet through to his skin, and cold through to his bones. She strained against him as he shoved her into the kitchen. The startled occupants -- a cook and two kitchen maids -- voiced their protests at this transgression.

"'Ere! That's the little guttersnipe wot stole one of me pork pies last week!" the cook accused, advancing toward Megan with a long-handled spoon poised menacingly in the air.

Keir glanced with amusement at Megan, who had shrunk against him in fear.

"I... I come to pay," Megan said swiftly, drawing the money Keir had given her from its hiding place inside the bodice of her dress. She held up the glittering coin that was payment enough for a dozen pies.

The cook sniffed and said, "Well, that's some'at, I reckon, though you oughtn't to be stealin' in the first place." She looked sharply at Keir.

He addressed one of the maids. "Inform Mrs. O'Day that Keir Shaughnessy wishes to see her."

The girl looked at the cook for approval, and then disappeared through the door to the barroom.

"Something smells delicious." Keir walked up to the warmth of the cooking stove. "Do you suppose we could have some supper? I'll pay for it, as well as the pie." Megan still held the coin in her outstretched hand, and Keir pushed it away.

"Just one plate. For the child," Keir said when the woman hesitated. "See to it, will you?" The authority in his voice prompted her to obey. He might not look like a gentleman just at the moment, but his manner was unmistakable.

"Keir O'Shaughnessy! I didn't believe Peggy when she told me. What in heaven or hell happened to you?"

Keir laughed. "I did so want to impress you too, Molly. It's good to see you again."

She grinned. "Sure it does me heart good to have you here. Though I should be scolding you for not visiting more often. And Peggy," she turned to the maid, "it's Mr. ***O***'Shaughnessy to you next time."

"Peggy was quite right, Molly. I dropped the 'O' -- it simplifies things."

"You're still Irish for all that, Keir," she said shrewdly. "With or without the 'O'. But please yourself. Come, we'll go to me parlour."

Molly looked quizzically at him as he drew Megan forward, but said nothing. When they were ensconced in the privacy of the parlour, Keir said, "Molly, this is Megan Maguire. If it weren't for Megan, I'd look an even sorrier sight." He accepted a glass of brandy as he related the story. Megan sat with stooped shoulders before the open fireplace, and stared into the flames. Keir noticed her skinny body shudder as the warmth melted the ice in her bones.

The maid Peggy deposited a tray of food on the small table next to Megan. The girl approached the meal diffidently at first, but after several bites, she attacked it ravenously.

Keir watched in amusement as she held a chop in her fingers and ripped the meat from it with her teeth. In the brightness of the room he could see her clearly for the first time. Beneath the dirt and the superficial wounds he noticed that she had a pert little face. Her hair, though tangled and dirty, was a light auburn that would probably shine beautifully red when clean.

"How old are you Megan?"

The second porkchop was poised halfway to her lips. She returned it to the plate before answering. "I'll be fourteen soon."

"What happened to your family?" Molly asked gently.

"Megan wiped the back of her hand across her greasy mouth. She looked down at the nearly empty plate as if with distaste. Finally she said, almost inaudibly, "Me folks died of the ship fever -- me Ma, afore we reached Canada; me Da, only a few days after we got to Toronto, though he'd been ailing a long while. They put us in the Orphans' Asylum, me sister, me two brothers, and meself. That was three years since. The boys were sent to work on farms not long after; me sister and I got sent to work as kitchen maids in different houses." Megan frowned. Without looking at Keir or Molly she continued. "The cook, she beat me and locked me in the cellar when I did something wrong... Sure, I never could do right by her! So I ran away, but I didn't have nowhere to go and a constable caught me stealing an apple at the market and he took me to gaol." She shivered. "I was there a few days..." Along with the lunatics and prostitutes and murderers, she could have added, but didn't. "...till I got took before a magistrate. He said I'd done a wicked thing, running away from the kind folk as took me in. Said I was ind... indentured, meaning I had to stay in that house till I was eighteen. Said if I ran away again, I'd be kept in gaol. The cook gave me a right good walloping when I got back.

"She used to take me to the market with her, to carry the baskets. 'Tis there I saw me sister one day, looking poorly she was. She told me she'd run away too, after the master of the house had tried to have his way with her. She had lodgings not far from here, and 'tis where she brought me when I ran away that same night.

We took in sewing -- we're both real handy with a needle -- and we worked day and night at it, it seemed, but we made barely enough money to keep us in food and lodgings. Then me sister took ill. There was no money for a doctor, and she said she'd not got to the hospital. Said it was where folk went to die. But she died anyway."

The child's face could have been carved from stone, Keir thought, but the slight trembling of her hands revealed her emotions. To Molly he said, "Have you an extra bed? I'll pay for Megan's keep until she can fend for herself."

"That'll not be necessary," Molly stated decisively. "She can help about the place. There's more than enough work to be done, and if she's a good worker, she'll get a wage besides."

"You realize you'll be breaking the law by taking her in?"

"That makes no never-mind to me! What kind of justice is it that sells children into slavery? She'll stay if she likes, and that's a fact. What do you say, Megan?"

Megan stared first at Molly and then at Keir. "I can stay?"

"So it seems," Keir replied.

Megan gazed at her hands. A smile lifted the corners of her mouth. Keir was startled by the transformation when she raised her head. She looked childishly young and happy.

Peggy appeared in response to Molly's ring, and was told to set up a bath -- with carbolic -- in the scullery. Molly took Keir's coat from Megan and handed it to the maid with instructions to dry it and brush it. "The shoulders are torn," Molly said. "And a new coat too, by the looks of it."

"I can mend it!" Megan said.

Molly looked at Keir and shrugged.

"Why not let her try," he said.

Molly provided needle and thread, and watched with surprise as Megan swiftly repaired the shoulder seams, retaining the fullness of the sleeves without kinking them into folds. "Where did you learn to sew like that?"

"Ma taught me. Grandda was a tailor."

"Sure, ain't I lucky to find a clever girl like you? Come along now. I'll wager 'tis an age since you seen soap and water."

Megan rose reluctantly from her chair by the fire. She glanced shyly at Keir as she said, "Thank you, sir."

"I'm sure you and Molly will get on just fine," Keir replied with a smile -- not realizing the devastating effect it would have on a young girl already infatuated with her handsome rescuer, who seemed every inch a fairytale prince. "I must be going now, Molly, but I'll return soon."

"You do that!"

Megan strained about for one last glimpse of Keir as she was ushered into the kitchen wing. While Peggy was filling the zinc tub, Molly attacked Megan's tangle of hair with a stiff brush. The girl sat quietly under the painful tuggings. She stepped into the steaming tub without protest, and let Molly scrub her.

Dressed in one of Molly's too large shifts, Megan sat in front of the parlour fire sipping a hot rum toddy while her hair dried. She answered Molly's questions politely, but without enthusiasm, and was grateful when Molly showed her to a tiny bedroom in the attic.

When she was alone, Megan opened her palm and stared at the silver coin shimmering in the candlelight. She held the talisman to her lips, and smiled before extinguishing the candle and snuggling into the clean, warm bed.

The storm raging outside was destined to enter the annals of the city's history, for its violence and power sliced a channel through the sandy peninsula, creating the Toronto Islands. But Megan Maguire was aware of none of this. She fell into a sound sleep with the coin clutched tightly in her hand.

Chapter 42

Keir watched the assembling congregation with growing anticipation.

This was the first time he had attended church since he had finished school, nearly a year ago. As he observed the fashionable crowd he thought that perhaps his motives for attending this service were not dissimilar to those of the people around him -- to see and be seen.

He nodded to various acquaintances -- old school chums mostly -- and then scanned the faces again for those violet eyes that had haunted him these past few days. He had no reason to suspect that she attended this church, but the most prominent Toronto families did patronize St. James (which had been rebuilt after the fire). Besides, Richard was probably right in advising that if a man wanted to retain his good name in society, he had to be seen at church.

Keir had almost begun to despair of seeing her when she walked in.

Many an eye turned to observe her progress up the long aisle. The elegant simplicity of her mauve silk gown enhanced her beauty and set her apart from the overly-embellished ladies lost beneath the frills and furbelows of their stylish attire. There was open admiration on the faces of young gentlemen, while ladies inclined their heads toward one another in whispered conversation. But the object of this varied attention seemed oblivious to it all.

She was with Richard's Aunt Susannah and her husband. Harriet's youngest sister had married Mortimer Locke, who was now a judge. Puzzled, Keir turned to his cousin and said, "I thought you didn't know any violet-eyed beauties."

"I didn't realize you were talking about Rebecca," Richard said. As if reluctant to explain, he added, "Rebecca Melbourne is the niece of my Uncle Nigel. Her father thought she might benefit from a year or two in the colonies, rather than a finishing school on the continent. She spent most of the winter in Peterborough, so Aunt Charlotte took pity on her and sent her to stay with Aunt Susannah who, as you know, has a busy social schedule -- more suited to a young girl's fancy than dull days in the backwoods."

"So you've known her for six months or more and never mentioned her?" Keir said. "I'm surprised."

"Are you?"

Keir noticed a flicker of -- what? annoyance? -- on Richard's brow, but it passed so quickly that he could not interpret his cousin's thoughts. It made him wonder again about the accusation that Jillian had once made about her brother. If Richard felt any hostility toward him, Keir had never been aware of it. Richard frequently invited Keir to join him and his friends for an evening on the town. They laughed together, drank together, gambled together, and had even visited a few brothels together.

Yet, Keir realized, his cousin had never invited him to the more refined gatherings that he regularly attended. Keir had never met Richard's friends in their respectable drawing rooms, but always in taverns, and disreputable ones at that. The young blades considered it something of a lark to frequent 'dens of iniquity' like the 'Wigwam', which was reputed to be run by a notorious gang of criminals, and it was to places like this that Keir accompanied them.

"Perhaps you could introduce me to her after the service?" Keir suggested.

"Certainly. And I'm sure my aunt and uncle will be pleased to meet you again."

The words seemed almost a veiled threat, since Keir suspected that the Lockes knew all about him. The last thing he wanted was for Rebecca Melbourne to know the truth about him. But Keir could read nothing in Richard's expression.

His thoughts galloped ahead to the forthcoming meeting. He heard not a word of the sermon; his eyes never once reached the pulpit. Although he was impatient for the service to be over, he relished the opportunity to study Miss Melbourne at his leisure, and was grateful for the fashion of shallow-brimmed bonnets which allowed him to capture her face in profile. She appeared to be totally absorbed in the reverend minister's pontifications, and Keir was again struck by the ethereal beauty of her flawless face. For such a divine vision he would attend church regularly!

The congregation dispersed into the warm April sunshine, lingering, as was the custom, to socialize and to make arrangements for afternoon visiting. Richard and Keir jostled their way into the crowd of friends chatting to the Lockes and their guest.

When Keir was introduced, he noticed no reaction of horror -- or even recognition of his name -- from the Lockes, and breathed more easily. But only until those violet eyes looked into his.

Abruptly she turned away from him and said, "We haven't seen much of you lately, Richard. Have you been studying frightfully hard? Surely you have this afternoon free? It's too lovely a day to devote to stuffy old law books. We are 'at home' today."

"Stuffy old law books, eh?" the Judge cut in. "No doubt you expect the boys to learn law by imbibing a cup of tea at the Judge's, eh?" Everyone laughed politely at this drollery, but none so heartily as the jester himself.

"Rebecca is right, Richard," his aunt said. "You ***have*** been neglecting us. We all admire studiousness, but you mustn't overdo it. We'll be expecting you -- and your friend -- for tea at four."

"Of course, Aunt Susannah. We'd be delighted," Richard replied.

As though the invitation were somehow distasteful to him, Keir thought in amazement. He himself rejoiced at this unexpected opportunity. Was it possible that Richard disliked Rebecca Melbourne? If so, he need fear no rivalry from his cousin.

Keir hardly tasted the excellent dinner he and Richard had at the Rossin House Hotel. As they strolled to the Lockes' house on Jarvis Street, Keir had to restrain himself from striding leagues ahead of Richard in his eagerness to get there.

But once there, he was just another of the many bodies in the drawing room, just another of the many admirers who hovered around Rebecca and clamoured for her attention. Only Richard was not among them. With an ironical smile on his lips, he watched her from afar.

She was a practiced flirt, a tease. She could easily bring colour to a young man's cheeks, or cause even a practiced tongue to trip over itself. And she seemed to relish the unease she created in her admirers as much as she did their flatteries.

"Do you attend the university as well, Mr. Shaughnessy?" she asked him after she could no longer ignore his presence without seeming rude.

"No. I'm a reporter with the *DAILY CHRONICLE*."

She arched a pretty eyebrow at this. "Indeed? Then you'd best beware the Judge. He has nothing but contempt for journalists, particularly those who subscribe to liberal ideologies. I wouldn't have thought you a Grit, Mr. Shaughnessy." Her eyes mocked him.

"I'm not involved with the political opinions espoused by the paper. Not yet."

"I see. Then what is it you do?"

"I cover social events at present."

"Ah. So you are here to glean the latest gossip from us."

The others laughed. Keir bristled.

"Now you gentlemen must excuse me," Rebecca said. "I really must go and talk to my cousin Richard. He's not really my cousin, of course, although we do share an aunt and uncle."

Rebecca glided away from them, knowing full well that her disappointed admirers were watching her every move. Much as she enjoyed their adoration and attention, they often bored her -- so many were witless in her presence, and she despised those she could so easily intimidate. Few spoke to her as an intelligent person, as though her beauty precluded that possibility. Sometimes she considered that beauty a curse. But only sometimes.

"Have you not forgiven me?" she asked Richard when she had reached his side. She kept her voice low, though there was no one close by.

"I didn't realize you had requested it," he replied stiffly.

"Oh dear, I can see I am not to be easily forgiven. It meant nothing, you know. It's unlikely to change the course of history. It was a lark, a bit of excitement in an otherwise dreary existence. It was a mere fling! You've had lots of those, I'm sure."

"I'm a man!"

"And I should have been born a man! Instead I am but a stupid female, the weaker sex, expected to be chaste and good and willingly dominated by the superior sex. But that is something I shall never be, Richard -- not for you or anyone. If you want me, you'll have to take me as I am. I know you have no illusions about me." She smiled wryly. "But while you are deliberating, I may very well change my mind about our 'understanding' -- which you quite shamelessly extracted from me before I left Peterborough." When she had been nearly mad with boredom! There had been no chance of any dalliances there, under her uncle's watchful eye. He remembered his own dissolute youth only too well.

"Beware of my cousin, Rebecca," Richard said. "He might prove more than you can deal with."

"Ah, yes, the bastard." Her eyes met Keir's across the room, and her interest was piqued. He certainly was handsome. And it would annoy Richard tremendously if she were to play up to Keir Shaughnessy. "I doubt that, Richard. He is just a man after all." She left Richard's side, content that she had vexed him. At least he still cared.

Rebecca couldn't understand why she cared about Richard. Perhaps it was the ruthlessness she sensed beneath his calm, polite exterior. Even his rage, when he had found her in a compromising position with that soldier, had been icily controlled. She felt he was destined for greatness, and that excited her. As the wife of such a man, she too could have great influence. Power. It was a heady feeling to be able to manipulate people, but how much more power men were able to wield! With the right husband, she could share that.

She had already decided she would never return to England -- which would delight her family. They had not yet lived down her 'scandalous' behaviour with the head groom. It was that which was responsible for her banishment to the colonies. At least here she enjoyed somewhat more freedom than she had at home, where even her books had been censored lest she read something 'inappropriate'.

But even though her Canadian aunts were more liberal, Rebecca still felt stifled by restrictions. When all the guests had departed she would have liked nothing more than a bruising gallop in the park to rid herself of her restlessness. Instead, she had to change her frock once again, and attend the evening church service. Afterwards they would return to a light supper, a quiet hour in the drawing room where the Judge would read and Susannah would work on her endless embroideries, and then bed. Alone.

The days were often no more exciting -- a sedate ride in Queen's Park next to Aunt Susannah's carriage; teas and committees and 'good works'. Generally, Rebecca found the company of other women dull. Few were interested in or knowledgeable about anything outside their households and social sphere. None that she had met had aspirations beyond becoming or being a wife and mother. Rebecca longed to emulate Anna Jamieson, that strong-minded, independent woman who had fearlessly jaunted about the country, and whose book of her Canadian travels Rebecca had read even before leaving England. She craved adventure, excitement, even danger.

Fortunately the evenings were often spent at concerts, musicales, plays, balls, and soirees, which gave her the opportunity of male company. She saw Richard and Keir often during the following weeks. There was no challenge in enticing the Irishman, who was so obviously infatuated with her. It was Richard's reaction she liked to see whenever she flirted with Keir. It was Richard's assessing gaze that sent shivers down her spine, though she would not be averse to having a 'fling' with the virile Irishman either. An affair, particularly with someone unsuitable, was risky and therefore highly stimulating.

Sometimes her body ached for the touch of a man. Yes, Keir would do very well. For the time being.

Chapter 43

It was more than two months after his encounter with Megan Maguire that Keir finally kept his promise to return to the Shamrock -- although it was a nuisance for him to go out of his way this evening to see the girl.

Keir did not recognize Megan immediately, for she no longer resembled the bedraggled waif he had plucked from the gutter. Dressed in a print frock protected by a large white apron, her rich red hair tumbling from beneath a muslin cap, she no longer looked so young or helpless. But Keir had not expected to find her in the taproom, dancing about between the tables, juggling frothy mugs of ale. When her green eyes met his, her pretty face brightened with a smile.

Keir frowned and strode up to the bar where Molly and her husband, Mike, were dispensing drinks and chatting with the customers standing about the long polished counter.

"So, you've come back after all," Molly said to him.

"I'd like to speak with you. Privately."

Molly shrugged. "Sure."

Keir followed her to the parlour.

"You're looking quite the dandy this evening," Molly said when she had closed the door. "Quite the toff."

Keir sensed disapproval in her observation, but ignored it. "What do you mean by allowing Megan to serve that riffraff out there?" he demanded.

Molly cocked an eyebrow. "Riffraff, is it?"

"I'm surprised, Molly, that you would allow a child to be exposed to the drunken attentions of your clients."

"Megan can take care of herself. She's seen and heard worse, and the customers are pretty harmless. She knows how to handle them, and Mike and me wouldn't let no harm come to the girl," Molly replied indignantly.

"I brought her here so that she would have the opportunity to grow up in a decent environment."

"You'll find nothing indecent happening under this roof, Keir O'Shaughnessy! 'Tis a respectable establishment that we run here. And who are you to come strutting in here like a bleedin' lord, telling me what it is I should or shouldn't be doing in me own house! Don't you try your highfalutin airs on me, boyo! I know you for what you are, not for what you like folk to think you be. I'll thank you to leave now."

Molly's amber eyes glowered at him as dangerously as any feline's. Keir left the room without another word.

Megan waylaid him in the barroom. "Hello, Mr. Shaughnessy! Do you like me new dress?" She twirled about happily before him. "Molly bought me the material, and I made it me... myself. And I'm going to school now -- days -- so's I can learn me... my letters, and how to talk proper like. Molly says even girls have to have some book learning, though me Da never held with it. He used to say that edication gave folk notions above their stations, and made 'em unhappy in the end, but Molly says there's more harm in being ignorant than not, so long as I don't think me... myself better'n other folk that be'nt as lucky as me." Megan finally stopped for a breath.

Keir glanced ruefully at Molly, who was watching them from behind the bar, and tipped his tophat to her. He bade an abrupt farewell to Megan and walked out.

Megan stared after him, disappointed that this longed-for encounter had been so brief. And not promising, judging by the expressions on the faces of the two people she loved most in this world -- Molly and Keir.

Megan had settled quickly into life at the Shamrock. She enjoyed the bustle of the place; the regulars were like a community of friends. Molly was like an older sister and best friend, and Mike, like a kindly uncle. Sometimes -- for no apparent reason even -- she would feel happiness welling up inside her, threatening to explode in a shout of pure joy. She even enjoyed school, once she had become used to the idea of spending time away from her beloved new home. But she was determined to become an educated lady, so that Keir could be proud of her. For Megan had made up her mind that one day she would marry him.

Chapter 44

The train to Launston Mills followed the east shore of the Scugog River for the last few miles. There were a few isolated cabins along the opposite bank, but it was the new Catholic church that caught the eye -- a red brick building of cathedral-like proportions with buttresses and a soaring steeple. How incongruous that imposing edifice seemed next to the squalor of Shantytown which sprawled in its shadows.

The sight of his mother's house revived painful memories that Keir fought to subdue. It had been a year since he had been home. And he wouldn't have come now -- not even for Jillian's wedding -- if Rebecca Melbourne weren't here.

His grandfather's house, old and grey, sagged on its wooden foundations. Patrick had been dead nearly two years now, but Keir could almost imagine him rocking on the overgrown stoop, smoking his corncob pipe.

Punkin Hollow passed out of view as the train chugged around the bend. It hooted once more as it approached the station, and hissed and squealed to a stop.

The incorporated town of Launston Mills was rapidly growing and changing. Smokestacks pinpointed the various manufactories that had sprung up in the last few years: a boot and shoe factory, another tannery, a furniture factory, an agricultural implements factory, and another foundry.

Launston Mills had also acquired the unpleasant aspects of a 'boomtown'. Stores and businesses had been haphazardly constructed without regard for architectural beauty or durability, and were too often squeezed unceremoniously between the older shops on Main Street. Homes had been as quickly and carelessly erected, and some of the factory owners had built cheap row housing to accommodate their employees. Amid all this there was not one tree to soften the harsh skyline of roofs and smokestacks, or to hide the ugliness, the ramshackle disorderliness that assaulted the eyes -- despite Jillian's assurance of aesthetic improvements once her father became mayor.

There were different kinds of people in town as well. Along with the older settlers, the craftsmen, artisans, merchants, and labourers, there were now to be found architects, surveyors, and engineers; several barristers and solicitors; insurance agents, real estate agents, and money lenders; a growing class of clerical workers; and even some who were listed simply as "gentlemen" in the town's first 'Directory'. More unsavoury characters were attracted to the town as well -- con men and prostitutes among them.

Yet this period of frenzied expansion precipitated by the railroad had come to an abrupt halt with the depression that threatened to bankrupt many investors and businessmen. Several unfinished and vacant manufactories attested to that.

Keir alighted from the train, and collected his bags. He was surprised to find Tom Finch awaiting him with one of the Launston carriages.

"It's good to see you again, Keir!" Tom said with a wide grin as he grasped Keir's hand in a warm greeting. "I've been reading your columns for the *CHRONICLE*. What a time you must be having in the city! Not to my liking though, except the races now. I'd like to see a steeplechase sometime. We've a new mare in the stables, which you can ride while you're here. Not as spirited as Banshee, but she'll do. How's the old girl doing, anyway? I suppose you don't get much time to ride her in the city?"

"Not as much as I'd like, Tom." When they had stowed his luggage aboard the carriage, Keir said, "You go ahead. I'm going to visit my mother before I come up to the house."

"Sure thing. You give her my best, eh?"

It was with trepidation that Keir trod the familiar path along Mill Road. His mother should be home from work by now. He hadn't informed her that he was coming.

The door stood open to the warm summer evening, and Keir saw her preparing a simple supper. Rowena turned at the sound of his footsteps. Her blue eyes, so like his own, lighted at the sight of him. She took an eager step toward him and stopped, not certain that this fine young man in his expensive togs would welcome her embrace. He didn't move.

"I was wondering if you'd be coming... for the wedding."

"It was rather a last minute decision.... I've been so busy."

"Aye. I reckoned you must be.... It's been a while since you answered my letters.... I've been reading your columns.... The Lathrops get the *CHRONICLE*, you see. Seems there's lots to keep a young man busy in the city."

Rowena, at thirty-eight, had retained much of the beauty of her youth -- unlike so many of her contemporaries upon whose countenances the inevitable hardships and sorrows of life were deeply, indelibly engraved. Like letters upon tombstones.

"Have you taken your supper?"

"I... won't be staying, Mother.... The Launstons invited me to Thistledown."

"I see. You're shamed to stay here."

"Mother, please let's not argue."

Her eyes flashed. "You come into this house like a stranger, with never a hug nor a kiss, calling me 'Mother' as if I wasn't your own ma, and you're after thinking I should be grateful you come to see me at all! Well, I don't need you, not if you come here figuring 'tis your duty to visit me, hoping to ease your conscience. You needn't bother yourself to come again, 'less it be like a true son." She turned her back on him so that he wouldn't see her anguish, and resumed her work.

Keir stood awkwardly watching her, surprised and hurt by the caustic words that he realized were true enough. And yet, he was strangely relieved, as though she had suddenly given him that long-desired freedom from his past.

"I'm sorry it has turned out like this, Mother. Goodbye."

Rowena almost called him back, tempted to break through that brittle upper-class shell that Keir had encased himself in, tempted to crush this arrogant young man into a fierce, motherly embrace and remind him of who he really was. But she feared that that might alienate him even more.

Best to leave him to find his own way for a while, for he seemed to have only contempt for her opinions, her way of life. But she feared that he might never reconcile himself with his past. She feared that he, too, might forever desert her, as had the other men she had loved.

She couldn't help the bitterness that welled up inside her at the thought of them. Her father, who had given his loyalty to another when she herself had most needed his help. Her adored brother, the best friend of her childhood, who had forsaken them all to pursue his own selfish dreams. He had dragged his family to California during the goldrush a decade ago, and although he'd made no fortune, he wrote that the beautiful land with its pleasant weather was itself the greatest prize. But being more than three thousand treacherous miles away from here, Rowena knew she would never see him again this side of the grave. She had only that beautifully carved loon to remind her of Donal.

Her other prized possession was a fading sketch of the lovely young girl that Adrian had loved. It was not really her, she still thought, and wondered if Adrian would have been disappointed in her, in the real woman, had he lived and they, married. That had been twenty-one years ago -- more than half her lifetime. And surely she was a different person from that naive girl who had thought nothing could stand in the way of love, and even that she could become a Launston!

She had loved Adrian with a tender adoration that bore little resemblance to the fierce passion she felt for his brother. It was Jeremy who had truly lodged in her heart, and for whom she ached. Would he have come to her even once this past decade had he known that she would have taken him gladly and without regret to her bed? Could he ever sense the longing that emanated from her lonely room, reaching out to him across the nighttime silence? Did he even think of her at all?

She saw him rarely, and never alone for more than a moment. Worst of all was when she opened the Lathrops' door to find Jeremy standing there, and sometimes Harriet as well. She couldn't meet his eyes, afraid that she would see only indifference or even pity there. Afraid that there was no spark of love or concern for her left in him.

And so she felt that Jeremy, too, had abandonned her. And now her precious son, Jeremy's protégé. The one person she loved more than life itself. And surely Jeremy was partly to blame for that.

Keir walked pensively to Thistledown. What guilt he felt over the rift with his mother he managed to rationalize.

Thistledown was already ablaze with light, rivalling the spectacular sunset in beauty. Keir was thankful that only the butler greeted him at the door. The family and guests were dressing for supper, Keir was informed. He was shown to his room, where he quickly washed and changed. For a brief moment he thought of the difference between this large, elegant chamber with its luxurious carpet and comfortable four-poster bed, and the spartan attic and hard cot that would have welcomed him at his mother's house.

The others were already in the drawing room when he entered. Harriet's sisters and their families, as well as her parents, were the other guests that were staying. Richard, Rebecca, and the Lockes had been here a week already.

They greeted him pleasantly enough, although he sensed disapproval from Livinia Neville. A shiver of dread crept up his spine. Surely everyone here knew who he was -- even Rebecca by now. But her smile revealed nothing other than pleasure at seeing him again.

Then she resumed her conversation with Richard, and Keir watched them jealously. If he had ever truly thought Richard impervious to Rebecca's charm, he thought so no longer. His cousin was unabashedly enjoying her company.

"You're looking well, Keir," Jeremy said when he had completed the introductions.

"Thank you, sir. May I say the same about you?"

"Ha! Would that you could! Well, it's good to have you here again. Glad you could make it."

"So am I, sir." Keir accepted a glass of sherry from one of the footmen. He had been apprehensive about this, his first meeting with his uncle since he had refused Jeremy's generous offer of employment two years ago. Keir loved and respected his uncle as much as he ever had as a child. He sensed that their past differences had been, if not forgotten, at least forgiven.

"I've been reading your columns. Quite good, as far as they go. You have an ascerbic sense of humour. I think your talent is wasted on such frivolous stuff."

"I hope to graduate to more serious reporting soon. The editor was particularly pleased with my article on the Orange Day Parade riot last month."

"Appalling, that growing violence between the two Irish factions! One man dead in the fracas, and the streets looking like a battleground." Jeremy shook his head. "They shouldn't bring old grievances to a new country. That's something my brother felt very strongly about -- hoped to educate the masses and make them proud to be Canadian. I say this whole country needs unifying. We're getting too big to be a colony. I'm all for this 'Confederation' idea that the Conservatives are advocating."

The butler announced supper, and the double doors to the hallway were opened by the footmen. Keir saw Rebecca accept Richard's arm, so he went to Jillian's side. She greeted him joyfully.

The company ambled across the hall to the dining room and took their allotted places. Keir found himself between Charlotte Melbourne, whom he liked, and her niece, whom he didn't know. He couldn't keep his eyes off Rebecca, who was seated well down the opposite end of the table from him, next to Richard. In her glittering watered-silk gown she exuded a sensuality that was irresistible.

The supper was hardly a simple affair. A delectable assortment of dishes was paraded out by the footmen, but Keir paid little attention to it. He found the evening a strain. He worried that someone might blurt out his secret. He envied Richard his proximity to Rebecca, and tortured himself with wild conjectures as to their relationship.

Keir hardly listened to the conversation, which ranged from the upcoming wedding to Harriet's latest 'cause'."

"Well, Jeremy, what do you think of your wife's new committee?" Nigel Melbourne asked with amusement.

"A lot of nonsense," Jeremy said. "Here we have a group of ladies who have nothing better to do than to tell men not to drink alcohol -- and they themselves do not decline a glass of sherry, or wine with dinner. It defies logic!"

"It does nothing of the sort!" Harriet retorted. "When the average yearly consumption of whiskey is 10 gallons per capita -- that is, for every man, woman, and child in this country! -- and about ***three times*** that number in Toronto, then it is definitely time for action. And since it is mostly men who over imbibe, it is left to us women to do something!"

"Now you've got her going, Nigel, we'll never hear the end of it until she has converted us all!" Jeremy said.

"Well, it wouldn't hurt you to moderate your consumption of port and brandy, Jeremy," Harriet replied. "All we are advocating is moderation, not abstinence. We're urging men to reduce their daily intake of hard liquor to a pint. I don't think that is unreasonable. We're not even concerning ourselves with ale or cider or wine."

"How have the ladies' activities affected the profits of the distillery?" Nigel asked.

"Not at all, I'm glad to say. Though Harriet has been urging me to sell it. I may just do that in order to restore domestic harmony," Jeremy said with a grin. "I have a frightful vision of Harriet leading a march on the distillery, the ladies all waving their Temperance banners and chanting 'Down with purveyors of vice and poverty and broken homes!'"

"You may be able to jest, Jeremy," Harriet said. "But you'd better take a closer look at your town first. I detest going there now. Even at mid-day there are drunks staggering about. And in the spring, when the loggers come in from the camps, a decent woman can't walk down the street without being accosted by drunks. It's disgraceful!"

"It's just the men letting loose after a hard -- and dry -- winter in the bush. You know we don't allow alcohol at the logging camps anymore, Harriet."

"Yes, well, you had too many men chopping off their legs or dropping trees on themselves. That was bad for business."

When the meal was finally at an end, the ladies withdrew to the drawing room and the gentlemen to the smoking room for port and cigars. Here the conversation revolved about the economic state of the country, with the Judge advocating higher tariffs to protect the struggling new home industries -- and to fill the depleted government coffers -- and Jeremy maintaining that northward and westward expansion was the solution to the current depression.

Richard and his cousins were engaged in a game of billiards, but Keir declined. He slipped out one of the french windows to the flagstone terrace.

He almost wished he hadn't come to Thistledown. What hope had he of becoming better acquainted with Rebecca now that Richard had designs on her -- and would contrive to keep them apart?

He heard the swish of a gown, and turned. Rebecca's fair hair and pale complexion made her appear ghostly in the moonlight. The silver threads of her gown shimmered sinuously as she approached him.

"What a lovely evening! Drawing rooms can become such stuffy places, don't you agree, Mr. Shaughnessy?" She walked to the low balustrade that edged the terrace, and turned her face to the stars.

Keir joined her. "Need there be such formality between us? My name is Keir."

"Keir Shaughnessy," she said, as though tasting the words. "You're Irish, I take it?"

"My father was English. He died tragically young and my mother married an Irishman a few years later."

"I see. Curious that you should adopt his name."

"He was the only father I ever knew." How he hated these lies and equivocal half-truths!

"Why is it that you are not staying with your family now, Mr.... Keir? Launston Mills is your home, is it not?"

"I have no close family left." Keir was becoming impatient with her probing questions. He placed his hands on her soft, bare shoulder. She shivered.

"You're cold."

"No, I...."

He pulled her into his arms. Her mouth met his with an eagerness that surprised him. A breathless moment later, she drew away from him with a chuckle. "You are presumptuous, Mr. Shaughnessy. I haven't even allowed you the liberty of using my Christian name."

"I apologize if I have offended you, Miss Melbourne," Keir replied, playing along with her.

"I shall forgive you this time." After a pause she said, "Lovely as this place is, I look forward to returning to the city. I've become quite enamoured of the Don Valley on my daily rides. There are delightful, cool glades there. And few prying eyes."

The french window to the drawing room opened, and Harriet said, "Ah, there you are, Rebecca. Isn't there a chill in the air tonight?"

Rebecca took her cue and went in, as she was expected to. Keir stayed on the terrace a while longer, savouring the solitude. Reliving that kiss, feeling once again the softness of her lips, the sweet taste of her mouth. And he nearly shouted out in triumph at the invitation she had extended him. The Don Valley would indeed make an interesting place for a rendezvous.

When the men joined the ladies in the drawing room, games of whist, backgammon, and chess were organized. People retired early that evening and rose late, resting in preparation for the wedding celebrations the following day. But Keir had never been one to waste such fine mornings abed. He was down at the stables by seven and, after an invigorating ride, was still the first one in the breakfast room. Jillian and Jeremy joined him as he was helping himself from the covered silver dishes, warmed by spirit lamps, that stood on the sideboard.

The three of them chatted congenially over an unhurried breakfast, and Keir felt pleasantly relaxed for the first time since arriving at Thistledown. The breakfast room was adjacent to the conservatory and accessible to it by a french door. Two walls of windows invited the morning sun to stream in.

Jillian spoke excitedly of her honeymoon trip to Europe, frequently glancing at Jeremy who stared dully into his coffee cup.

"Oh, Papa, I shall be home before you miss me! And we will visit often when we return." To Keir she said, "You must see the house Geoffrey built for us. It's up on Bond's Rise. Have you seen the gazebo that Papa had built last summer? Mama calls it a folly, since she can see no practical use for it. But I adore it, and Papa and I often take our tea there."

"I haven't seen it."

"Then I shall show it to you. Will you excuse us, Papa?"

He waved them away.

Rebecca and Richard entered the room just then, and Keir followed Jillian somewhat reluctantly through the conservatory and out onto the lawn.

"I'm so happy you came!" Jillian said as they strolled arm-in-arm across the dewy grass.

"Did you think I wouldn't?"

"I'm beginning to think that you came only to feast your eyes upon Rebecca Melbourne."

"You know that's not true."

"I know nothing of the sort. Don't tell me you'd rather be with me than with Rebecca, for I wouldn't believe you."

"Jillian...."

"Never mind. I know I'm being childish and silly. She's beautiful and witty and charming -- and rather worldly -- and I shouldn't blame you for preferring her company."

"Do I detect a note of jealousy in that remark?" Keir teased.

"Geoffrey's hardly taken his eyes from her since she arrived."

"I'm sure you're imagining things."

"Perhaps. Oh, Keir, that's one of the reasons I wanted to talk to you. You understand what it's like, being different. I'm afraid."

"Of what?" Keir asked.

They had reached the octagonal lattice-work gazebo, and stepped inside. Jillian sank onto one of the cushioned garden chairs. "Marrying Geoffrey. What I mean is, I'm worried that he might... find me repulsive. He's never seen my leg." She looked unhappily at her tightly-entwined fingers.

Keir said gently, "No man could find you repulsive, Jilly."

"You're just being kind."

"Do you believe that Geoffrey is so shallow that he won't overlook such a trivial affliction?"

"He's not shallow!" Sadly she added, "And it's not trivial. I know how much Geoffrey admires beauty. My leg is hideous. And Geoffrey enjoys dancing. How envious I am when I watch him waltz with other women."

"But he's marrying you. Surely he loves you."

"Of course he does! Are you implying that he's marrying me for some other reason?"

"I thought you were the one with doubts."

"No!... Yes... Oh, I don't know what to think anymore! If only Rebecca weren't here!"

"Jilly, if you're not certain about Geoffrey, then don't marry him. It's not yet too late."

"You've never liked Geoffrey, have you?" she accused.

"You're sometimes impossible to talk to, Jilly! What do you ***want*** me to tell you?"

"That I'm doing the right thing." Her eyes pleaded with him.

"You know I can't do that. You're the only one who can judge."

"I do love him."

"Then I hope with all my heart that you'll be happy."

Jillian threw herself into his arms. "Promise me you'll always be my friend, Keir."

"I promise."

The day was a languorous one for the guests. There were idle games of croquet on the lawn, a sumptuous dinner, strolls in the garden, a lavish tea on the terrace, a late supper.

Keir had no private conference with Rebecca that night; Richard never left her side.

Keir had no more opportunity to talk with Jillian either. Just as well, he thought, since he was tempted to dissuade her from marrying Geoffrey. Her own doubts seemed to have vanished, however, for she was every inch the radiant bride when she appeared at the new Anglican church for the wedding ceremony the following morning. She leaned heavily upon Jeremy's arm, so that her progress up the short aisle was not too ungainly.

Harriet Launston bit back tears as she watched her daughter being given legally into the care of another man. Snatches of her own wedding flitted through her mind. Her last minute doubts, echoed this morning by her daughter, came readily to mind, as did memories of her wedding night. And so many nights thereafter. Suddenly she wanted to snatch her daughter back, to keep her innocent and protected, hidden away at Thistledown. Where she would grow old and crusty like Bea?

So of course she did nothing.

But how she would miss Jillian! Her days were so empty now that she had a houseful of servants. Jeremy would not hear of his wife demeaning herself with cooking when he had obtained the best chef in Canada West. Jeremy would never understand that when he had given her leisure from household chores, he had deprived her of what she enjoyed most in life. So she had started clubs and committees and charities to occupy herself -- all acceptable ways of idling away her time. She sighed. Perhaps grandchildren would soon give her a new interest in life.

She wondered -- and worried -- about Richard and Rebecca. She recalled what Nigel had once told her about fearing his brothers would send him their reprobate sons. But he'd never expected their daughters. Somehow she would have to prevent Richard from making a disastrous mistake.

Chapter 45

The 'Palace of Industry' was a monument to the growing industrialism of the country. Constructed in less than three months, this cast iron and glass cruciform-shaped hall had already been dubbed the 'Crystal Palace'. Although it was not as opulent as its namesake in England, the citizens of Toronto took great pride in it.

This was where the Agricultural Exhibition of 1858 was held, drawing people from all over the province, and even from the States. Fine art and the latest advances in technology were among the many exhibits. Encircling the fountain in the centre was a fragrant and colourful floral display arranged by the Toronto Horticultural Society.

There were to be horse races and yacht races, a bazaar, and a fireman's procession during the festive week. Tonight there was a torchlight parade and an 'illumination' -- for which all citizens were urged to place candles or lamps in their windows -- with a climax of fireworks on the lakeside exhibition grounds.

The city was indeed resplendent this night. Wrapped in a gauze of gold with the Palace like a sparkling diadem upon her head, Toronto mocked the disparaging soubriquet of 'Hogtown'.

Such were Keir's thoughts as he roamed about the grounds. He jotted down descriptions that he would later weave into an article.

Would he see Rebecca tonight, he wondered. She hadn't returned to Toronto with the Lockes after the wedding; so he assumed she must have been in exile in Peterborough these past weeks. All his glorious plans of meeting her on her daily rides had evaporated. But surely the Melbournes would be in town for this Exhibition. Richard had told him that he would be here tonight with a party of friends, but Keir hadn't asked if Rebecca would be among them. And how would he find them in this crowd? It seemed as if every citizen were out this night.

Keir meandered his way past hoop-skirted women -- whose steel cage crinolines presented formidable obstacles -- avoided the children darting to the street vendors for their penny's worth of hot roasted chestnuts or bull's eye candies, and reached the hall once again. He lingered by the fountain, hoping to spot Richard's party when they entered the building, but the heady perfume of the flowers soon became nauseating. Like a greenhouse, the building had retained the day's heat, and the humidity of the densely packed hall became unbearable. Keir moved on to make brief notes about the art exhibit.

A gentle touch on his arm caused him to look about. He stared into violet eyes.

"All alone, Mr. Shaughnessy? What a pity."

Keir saw that the Lockes and Melbournes were engrossed in the paintings. Only Richard had observed Rebecca's overture.

"Why not join us, Mr. Shaughnessy? Don't you agree, Uncle?"

It was the Judge who replied, "Eh? Ah, hello, Shaughnessy."

"I was suggesting that Mr. Shaughnessy join us, since he appears to be here alone."

"Quite right. Not a good idea to be alone in such crowds. Have to watch out for the rogues and pickpockets, don't you know? They want to make sure I'm kept busy in the courts," he laughed.

The Judge moved on to view the next painting, and Rebecca joined him and the others, leaving Keir perplexed by her sudden desertion.

Richard fell into step with him. "You don't understand her, do you?"

"Do you?"

"How like an Irishman never to give a straightforward answer to a simple question. But yes, I believe I do understand her."

"Are you going to impart this revelation to me?"

"I doubt that you would like what I have to disclose," Richard said.

"Are you implying that there is something discreditable in the lady's character?"

"I'm merely stating that she is not what you envision."

"I was not aware that you had mastered the art of mind-reading."

Richard laughed. "It requires no sorcery to divine your thoughts, my friend. You possess an expressive face."

"What is the point of this conversation, Richard? Are you attempting to warn me away from Rebecca?"

"I wouldn't presume to do such a thing. I just don't like to see you wasting you time -- and your affection -- on a lost cause, that's all."

Keir laughed. "You're an arrogant bastard, Richard!"

"It is not I who is the bastard, Keir."

Keir's anger lasted only an instant. "I suppose you've told her about me."

"Don't flatter yourself that your name has ever come up in our conversations. But as your friend, Keir, I advise you to stop living a lie."

"Don't be offended if I don't take your ***friendly*** advice, Richard," Keir said sarcastically.

Richard shrugged. "I meant well."

They were outside now, amid the swelling crowds awaiting the fireworks display. It was as Richard and Keir hurried to catch up with the others that Keir heard his name called.

He glanced about and saw, to his chagrin, Megan Maguire scampering toward him. Following her more sedately were Molly and the maid Peggy.

"Oh, Mr. Shaughnessy, ain't it exciting? I never seen fireworks before and I'm all atwitter! Did you see the parade? Molly and me put candles in all the windows at the Shamrock and didn't it look grand!"

Keir didn't know what to say, how to extricate himself from this mortifying situation.

Molly rescued him, "Good evening, Mr. Shaughnessy," she said as she took the girl by the shoulders.

Before Molly could steer her away, Megan said, "Will you be coming to visit us again, Mr. Shaughnessy? It's been an age since you last come."

"Of course."

Megan gave him a winsome smile, and then went obediently with Molly.

"Friends of yours, Mr. Shaughnessy?" Rebecca asked.

"Acquaintances."

"If I'm not mistaken," Richard said, "that was Molly Hogan. She was a chamber maid at the college years ago. I didn't realize that you'd kept up your friendship with her, Keir."

Keir shot his cousin a chilling look.

The first explosions of fireworks and the exclamations of the spectators prevented further conversation.

Chapter 46

Rebecca, Rebecca, Rebecca.

Keir was obsessed by her. Helplessly, hopelessly. He was in torment. She teased and tempted, provoked and promised -- enough to keep his blood boiling and his rage at bay.

Had he been less enamoured of her, this latent anger would have railed against her humiliating treatment of him. But he refused to believe it was merely a game. Like the other infatuated swains, Keir had accepted Rebecca's challenge with the conviction that he would be triumphant. How sweet would be that victory!

That winter was a long one, but there were many diversions to entertain Toronto's society and to keep Keir's columns filled -- the inevitable balls and soirees, dramatic and musical evenings, sleighing parties, carriole ice races and skating on the Bay. Christmas witnessed the second Toronto performance of Handel's *Messiah* at the St. Lawrence Hall.

The winter would have seemed even longer had Rebecca not been rescued from Peterborough by Susannah Locke just before Christmas. Susannah had taken pity on the girl, whom she liked to have around -- having no children of her own. So she had persuaded Nigel and Charlotte to let Rebecca return to the city. Nigel had relented, grateful to be rid of his sullen niece, whom he had unwillingly kept in Peterborough at Harriet's request.

Though Keir saw Rebecca frequently, he made little progress in his courtship. His only consolation was that her other suitors -- Richard included -- seemed to have no more success than he.

With spring, the flowers of Toronto's society were once again in full bloom upon its streets. 'Doing King' -- and outdoing one another in fashions -- was the chief preoccupation of the elite between the hours of three and six. Parading along a quarter mile stretch of King Street, young ladies, under the watchful eyes of their mamas, and gentlemen would meet and talk, and many a prelude to matrimony took place here. It was known as the 'Social Exchange' to some; others referred to it as a 'Vanity Fair'.

Rebecca referred to it scathingly as a cattle market, although she was required to accompany Susannah there on occasion. She relayed all the latest gossip to Keir when she met him for their frequent rides in the Don Valley. It mattered not to

Keir that a Melbourne groom was never far behind them. He had Rebecca to himself.

One June day, as they skirted the Don River, Rebecca lost her hat. She reined in her horse, and looked about with annoyance at the bonnet floating downstream. "Fetch my hat, Jenkins," she said to the groom. "Perhaps it can be salvaged."

A hint of a smile curved her lips as she watched Jenkins ride back. He dismounted, and searched about for a long stick with which to fish out his mistress's hat.

"Do hurry, Jenkins," Rebecca called irritably, "before it is swept away! Are you afraid to get your feet wet?"

The groom hesitated for a moment, thinking, no doubt, of his shiny leather boots, which would surely be ruined by such foolhardy gallantry. Hastily, and with some embarrassment, he pulled them off and waded into the river.

With a laugh of pure delight, Rebecca spurred her horse into a gallop and disappeared into the woods. Keir followed. He did not look back to see how Jenkins reacted to this trickery.

Laughter still sparkled in her eyes when she finally stopped and turned to face Keir.

"You planned that!" he accused.

"Clever, wasn't it?"

"Yes, but what will happen when Jenkins reports your escapade to the Lockes?"

"He won't. He is no longer a young man. It wouldn't be easy for him to find another situation -- without a reference. The Lockes would not be pleased, and it would take little to convince them that Jenkins is past his usefulness. I shall make that perfectly clear to him."

Keir felt sorry for the hapless Jenkins.

"Don't waste your pity on ***him***," Rebecca said, as if divining his thoughts. "Sometimes I could scream for want of privacy! Oh, Keir, you don't know how long I've wanted to be alone with you."

He could hardly believe her words! He dismounted, walked over to her, and held out his hands. She slid from the saddle into his arms, and clung to him, trembling, as he covered her face with kisses.

"A married woman is not so restricted," Keir whispered.

She pushed him away peevishly. "What is marriage but a change of gaoler? From parent to husband!"

"Rebecca, I love you. I would do anything to make you happy, if you will let me."

She wrapped her arms about him, moulding her body against his, and responded avidly to his kiss.

Keir thought nothing of taking a willing woman, but Rebecca Melbourne was no whore. He could not violate her. She would despise him for taking advantage of her.

Such were his few rational thoughts. But he could not stop himself. She made no protest as his hands explored her perfect body. Indeed, she strained against the confines of her garments as though she could not wait for his hands to touch her naked flesh.

He lowered her onto the grass with the vague thought that at last he had power over her, that surely she would consent to marry him after this. Then he could think no more, only feel the ecstasy of claiming her. He heard her moans, felt her answering shudder, and rejoiced with insane happiness.

This was victory. He was sure of it.

Tenderly he kissed her flushed cheeks, her closed eyes. "Marry me, my darling."

She wriggled out of his grasp and sat up hastily, rearranging her clothes.

"Rebecca...."

"I will not discuss marriage!" She didn't look at him.

"As you wish."

They rode back through the woods in silence. Keir was miserable. He was certain that she despised him for seducing her. But hadn't she enjoyed their lovemaking? She needed time. That was all.

Jenkins was sitting beneath a tree, smoking a pipe and drying his socks. He jumped to his feet and pulled on his boots when he saw the two riders approaching.

Rebecca glanced disdainfully at the waterlogged bonnet that lay on the ground beside the groom, and said, "Dispose of that thing, will you? It was never one of my favourites."

• • •

Keir spent a wretched night worrying. The morning was damp and grey, but he waited for hours by the Don bridge for Rebecca to appear. She didn't.

Anxiety replaced disappointment. If the Lockes learned of what had happened, there would surely be dire consequences for both himself and Rebecca. And what if she accused him of rape? He could swing for that.

These nagging doubts were dispelled when he saw her at the ball that evening.

She was breathtaking in a dusky rose silk gown that fitted her closely to her tiny waist, and then cascaded to the floor in scalloped tiers edged with silver thread. It was daringly décolleté, with narrow, off-the-shoulder straps. A diamond-studded comb fastened a festoon of silk roses to one side of her chignon.

Keir had expected her to look somehow different, to bear witness of his possession of her. Yet it might never have been. Her attitude toward him was no different than on the many previous social occasions at which they had met.

With searing jealousy he watched her coquettish dalliance with other men. There was one in particular -- an officer from the garrison -- who was receiving the full benefit of those violet eyes.

Rebecca granted Keir one dance, a waltz. As he took her into his arms, he could think only of how her body had felt beneath his without the unyielding corset and stiff crinoline.

"You look exquisite," he told her.

"Did you think I wouldn't? What do you suppose a ravished virgin should look like?"

The flippant remark stung. "I'm sorry, Rebecca."

"Do spare me the tiresome apologies! If you do something, at least have the courage not to regret it afterwards. Conscience-stricken people are such a bore! Do you really think I would have allowed it to happen if I hadn't wanted it to?"

She laughed at his surprise. "You are a darling fool, Keir! I'll be there tomorrow, as usual."

Keir wondered that he could remember enough of the decor, the supper menu, and the list of prestigious guests to write up his article that night. He was exonerated. Could any man be as happy as he?

Keir was at the rendezvous well before the appointed hour. Rebecca arrived late, with Jenkins in tow. They rode in single file along the paths through the thickly wooded and sometimes swampy valley. Turtles and snakes, sunning themselves on rocks near the water's edge, darted into the thickets of willow and alder or splashed into the water at the sound of the horses' hooves.

When they were well north of the city limits, Rebecca ordered Jenkins to remain behind while she and Keir rode on. The groom grimaced in disapproval, but did as he was bid. Keir wondered what Rebecca had said to ensure his silence.

As soon as they were out of sight of the groom, she became carefree. Their lovemaking was sweeter than before.

They met often like this, for over a month. Keir was deliriously happy, and though he wondered why she would not discuss marriage, he did not press her. He began making his own plans.

Keir was twenty-one now, and in possession of the money that Jeremy had given him. Already he was searching for a suitable house. Already he envisioned Rebecca as its mistress.

Once again he broached the subject with her.

It was July. One of those hot, sultry, oppressive days when the very air seems too turgid and dense to breathe. No mitigating breeze fanned the city. They had made love slowly, languidly, and now lay naked in one another's arms.

"I must dress," Rebecca said, kissing him briefly before leaving his side. "I'm afraid Susannah is becoming suspicious."

"If you married me we wouldn't have to go on with this deception."

As he watched her pull on her lawn shift, chamois trousers, quilted petticoat, linen shirt, and grey broadcloth skirt, he wanted to rip those ridiculous garments from her and possess her once more.

"Didn't I tell you? I'm going to marry Richard."

The words screamed in his brain. Surely she was jesting!

She buttoned her short, tight jacket. "I accepted him a fortnight ago. Our engagement will soon be announced."

Keir jumped up. He spun her around roughly to face him, digging his fingers into her shoulders. "You're lying!"

"Am I?" Her violet eyes mocked him. She shrugged him off. "Anyway, it makes no difference to us. After a few months in Launston Mills, I'll persuade Richard that we should have a house in Toronto -- where I intend to spend most of my time. Then you can come to me there."

Keir couldn't believe he had heard her correctly. "You're already planning to deceive Richard, and you're not even married to him yet?"

She laughed. "Don't be so stuffy, Keir! In English society it is common practice for married women to take lovers. Just as their husbands keep a mistress."

"This is crazy! It's some stupid joke, isn't it? For God's sake, Rebecca, I love you!"

"You Irish are romantics. That's why you're forever doomed to disappointment. Richard and I have much in common. We're both ambitious." She regarded him as she loosely bound up her hair. "What you have to offer, I can get from any number of men -- and have. Did you really think that I would marry a bastard?"

He thought he could kill her then.

"You're a ruthless bitch!"

"You ***are*** common. Too bad you've had to spoil it all, Keir. I've rather enjoyed these little trysts. Come and see me again when you've grown up."

"I doubt that you'll be so smug when your indiscretions are exposed."

"Blackmail, Keir? And who will believe you when your secret is disclosed? You'll never be anything but an Irish bastard playing at being a gentleman. Goodbye, Keir."

Keir felt as though his dignity, his very manhood, had been stripped from him. He seethed with such savage fury that it truly frightened him. He wanted to wound, to destroy -- anything! -- to relieve himself of this volcanic wrath.

When he had dressed, he rode like a demon out of the valley. He spared no thought for his beloved mare, nor for himself. Not until the lathered, exhausted horse stumbled and nearly unseated him did he slow his suicidal pace. He stopped at the nearest inn.

Several hours later Keir staggered into the Shamrock Tavern. He hadn't been there since his clash with Molly more than a year ago.

"Molly, me darlin', give us a large whiskey," he muttered in a thick brogue.

Molly eyed him with concern. "'Tain't whiskey you're needing, Keir."

"If you'll not serve me, then I'll be going elsewhere!"

Molly glanced about anxiously as this loud declaration attracted the attention of the other customers. "I'll give you a glass, but you'll be taking it in me parlour."

"Whate'er you say, Molly."

Megan Maguire watched Keir follow Molly -- none too steadily -- into the back room.

"You'd best tell me what's troubling you, Keir," Molly said when she had handed him his drink.

He laughed bitterly. "Sure, I came here so's you could gloat, Molly. Seems you were right after all. Folk'll never accept me for what I am."

Molly regarded him sadly. "Your friends know, do they?"

"***Friends***! I have no friends, Molly."

"Sure, you got us! Why not tell me what happened?"

Keir stared dejectedly into the empty grate of the fireplace.

"Was it a woman? One of them high-class ladies?"

"High-class tart, you mean." He scowled. "She's going to marry my cousin. I wasn't good enough for her."

"That purple-eyed one? The one as was with you at the exhibition last fall?"

"You're very perceptive, Molly. Fill up my glass, there's a darlin'!"

"I reckon you've had more than enough to swim home with."

"Not yet."

When Keir stepped into the hall he saw Megan tiptoeing away. She had been listening at the door.

"Well, if it isn't little Megan Maguire!"

She turned to him with a warm smile. "Hello, Mr. Shaughnessy."

"You're looking quite grown up. Old enough and pretty enough to warm a man's bed."

"Keir Shaughnessy!" Molly said furiously. "How could you say such a thing to the child?"

"Come now, Molly. All women are whores at heart. They need only the opportunity to show it."

"If you weren't so crocked, me lad, you'd be feeling me boot!"

• • •

Three weeks later Molly went to Keir's lodgings.

Keir was sprawled across his bed, partially dressed. Several empty whiskey bottles littered the floor next to him.

The unremitting pounding on the door resonated painfully in his head. "Go away, whoever the hell you are!"

"'Tis Molly. I want to talk to you."

"Go away!"

"I'll not be leaving till you hear me out!"

Keir swore as he sat up. His head ached unmercifully. When the room stopped spinning, he staggered across to the door and unlatched it.

Molly was shocked by his appearance. His face was pale and haggard; his eyes, blurry and bloodshot.

"I feel worse than I look. What do you want, Molly?"

She pushed past him into the room, and seated herself in an armchair. "I noticed you've not been writing for the paper."

"I've been fired."

"Drunk on the job? Or didn't you trouble yourself to go to work?"

"If you've come here to reproach me, you can damn well leave!"

"I come 'cause I was worried about you. With good reason, seems to me." She glanced about the room with a frown.

"You disapprove of what you find? Sure, Molly, I'm just playing the role I was born to -- the debauched, dissipated, reprobate Irishman."

"You're a fool, Keir, letting one woman wreck your life. You were always willing to fight for to make a good life for yourself, and then the first woman that spurns you turns you into a coward. Seems to me she weren't good enough for you anyhow. Having rich folk and fancy manners ain't what a man should look for in a woman. I'm thinking maybe it weren't just her you were after, but the kind of life she represents."

Keir sat down on the edge of the rumpled bed, and rubbed a hand across his brow. "My head's splitting open. Can't you leave me in peace, Molly? I'm in no mood to listen to your ludicrous suppositions and moralizing platitudes. What did you hope to accomplish by coming here?"

"I was hoping to keep you from destroying yourself with self-pity! So your pride's been hurt. 'Twasn't the first time, and it'll not be the last. Keir, you'll never be happy or at peace till you accept yourself for what you are, and stop trying to be what you're not. If you can't accept the fact that you're a bastard, how can you expect other folk to? A man's strength comes from knowing his own worth, and being true to hisself."

Keir made no reply.

"Well, 'tis what I came to say. And if you have any decency, you'll apologize to young Megan for what you said t'other night! That girl thinks the world of you."

"More fool her.... Yes, you're right. Tell her I'm sorry."

"Tell her yourself!"

As Molly rose from the chair she noticed two telegrams lying on the table beside her. One was unopened, but the other had been read and carelessly tossed aside. Molly glanced at it without compunction. It read, "You Ma has typhoid. Come as soon as possible. Conn."

"How long have you had this?" Molly demanded.

Keir glanced up. "A day or two."

You've not opened t'other one. When did it come?"

"This morning."

"Well? Ain't you going to read it?"

"Be my guest."

Molly ripped open the envelope. "'Your Ma is worse'," she read aloud. "'Is asking for you. Please come.'... And why are you still here?"

"I'm not going home."

"Your ma might be dying. Does that mean nothing to you?"

"Mind your own damn business, Molly! For Christ's sake, just leave me alone!"

"Ain't it about time you stopped thinking about nobody but yourself? You think your ma's had it easy? If you desert her now, when she has need of you, then you can go to the divil where you belong!"

Molly slammed the door behind her.

Keir sat motionless for a long time. The murderous rage he had felt at Rebecca's treachery had long since left him. She had warped his love for her into hatred, but even that had burnt itself out. With her had gone all his dreams. He felt empty inside.

As he reached for a new bottle of whiskey, he caught a glimpse of himself in the mirror. He stared without recognition at the kind of man he had always despised.

He hurled the unopened bottle at the mirror. Both shattered upon impact, showering splinters of glass and amber liquid about the dressing table and rug.

Damn Molly for being right!

Carefully he scooped up the fragments of his destruction.

Chapter 47

Keir quickened his pace as he neared home. He was filled with a sudden dread that perhaps he would be too late. His heart pounded as he entered the cabin.

"Simon?" Margaret Worthing appeared from the bedroom. "Keir! Thank God you've come!"

"How is she?"

"Her fever's broken, but she hasn't responded for nearly two days. It... doesn't bode well."

Keir walked into his mother's bedroom. He was shocked by the sight of her lying so deathly still in the large bed, her skin a sickly grey, and flaccid about her emaciated frame.

He took one long, slender, cool hand in his. "Ma? I've come home."

Her face was curiously devoid of expression, as though she were already at peace.

"Don't die," he whispered. "Please don't die." He squeezed her hand tightly as tears formed in his eyes. He sat like that for a long time, staring at her, waiting for some flicker of life.

"How did this happen?" Keir asked Margaret when she brought him a cup of tea.

"There's an epidemic of typhoid in Shantytown. Simon says it's because of the unsanitary conditions there. You know how your mother is. She never refuses to help anyone. She was spending every night nursing the sick, as well as working at the Lathrops' twelve hours a day. Then she collapsed at work one day. Simon is at Thistledown. Harriet Launston was visiting the sick in Shantytown, and now she's down with the fever as well."

"Thank you for your help, Mrs. Worthing. I'll stay with her now."

"Be sure to send for me if you need me... or Simon. Otherwise he'll be back to see her tomorrow. I'm glad you were able to come, Keir. It'll do your mother no end of good to have you here."

The silence of the sickroom was unnerving -- at times, unbearable. Keir talked to his mother, hoping for a response. But there was none. She seemed hardly to be breathing.

He had much time for reflection as he sat there, hour after hour.

The old log house, so little changed over the years, evoked powerful memories of childhood. Happy, loving times when there had been no dissension between him and his mother. Times when he had not been ashamed of what he was, not contemptuous of his family. How inexcusably selfish and arrogant he had been these last years! A bastard in more than one sense of the word.

How ironic if Rowena were to die now when there was so much left unsaid between them.

Moira and Conn were pleasantly surprised by his presence when they came over that evening.

"We told your ma you'd come, soon as you could get away," Conn said. "Come and have supper, lad. And you look like you could do with a sleep. Moira's been staying with your ma nights. She'll let us know if there's any change."

"Thank you, Uncle Conn, but I'd like to stay with her. I appreciate all you've done."

"Think no more on it! What are kin for if not to help in times of trouble? Rowena's done more'n her share of that."

It was a long night. The deep stillness was broken only occasionally by the shrieking of a nighthawk or the barking of a dog somewhere in Shantytown. Keir wasn't sure when he drifted off to sleep, but he was suddenly roused. The candle on the table next to him spluttered. He quickly extinguished the flame, recalling the old superstition that it was bad luck to allow a candle to go out on its own. Outside the night was paling. What had awakened him?

Rowena stirred.

"Ma?"

Her breathing was audible now, almost a sigh as she raised a frail hand to her brow. Her eyes opened. She gazed at him uncomprehendingly.

"Ma...." His voice broke. He clutched one of her hands tightly.

Rowena smiled weakly. "You came home."

"Yes. I've come home. To stay."

There was an answering pressure from the hand he held.

"Is there anything I can get for you, Ma?"

"You've already given me what I wanted most." She smiled again. "But I wouldn't say no to a cup of tea."

Keir leaned over and kissed her on the cheek before going into the kitchen. "You'll be fine now, Ma."

"Aye."

Keir felt lighthearted as he stoked the dying fire, and set the water to boil. When he returned to the bedroom with the tea, he saw that she had fallen asleep again, but this time into a healthy, normal sleep.

Keir took the cup and went out to the stoop. He sat down on the rough step and sipped the hot, sweet liquid thoughtfully. A gossamer mist drifted up from the river; dew hung heavy on the vines that curtained the veranda.

Had he really meant what he had said to her?

A few candles burned in the windows of Shantytown. Yawning men and women emerged from the shacks into the tiny yards to wash. Keir noticed a couple of children dragging buckets to the well. He wondered how many children in Launston Mills went to school -- the town now had a grammar school as well as two elementary schools -- and how many worked twelve hour shifts in factories alongside their parents, or even longer hours in the retail stores.

The blast of a factory whistle, and then another nearby, summoned the workers from their beds.

The town already had one paper -- a Conservative one. Perhaps it was time a Reform voice was heard here. The idea of publishing his own newspaper suddenly appealed to Keir.

Yet to come back to this town with its petty prejudices.... To live in this place to which Richard would bring his bride....

Conn came from his house next door, carrying a plate covered with a cloth. He looked anxiously at Keir as he approached.

"Ma woke up a short while ago. She's going to be alright, Uncle Conn."

Conn grinned broadly. "Thank the good Lord!" He handed Keir the plate and said, "Here's some breakfast for you, lad." He turned to Tim, who had just come over. "Run home and tell your ma that Aunt Rowena'll be needing her broth."

Tim gave a hoot of delight as he hurried away.

"Uncle Conn, I want you to know that I'm going to be staying here, in Launston Mills. I'm going to start a newspaper."

"Is that what you really want, Keir? There's many a young man hankering to go to the city, and some as do. Not many that come back."

"It is what I want."

"Sure, then we've been twice blessed this day! You eat up now afore it gets cold. And I'd best be on me way. 'Tis near starting time."

There was a great deal of activity about the place that morning. Moira and her daughters came and fussed over Rowena; the Worthings arrived, and Simon proclaimed Rowena out of danger.

When the others had gone, Keir took Rowena another cup of Moira's chicken broth.

"I meant what I said, Ma, about staying."

She smiled at him. "Not on my account, Keir. 'Tis enough to see you here... like this. You've given me such joy by coming home. But truly, I want what's best for you. If you've made a life for yourself in the city, then I'm the first to wish you well there."

"No. That was an illusion, a dream I had that went awry. I'm tired of living a lie. I think I've finally come to terms with who I am. And I've realized that there's important work to do here. I want to do something that's going to make a difference, not just report on social events and society gossip!"

Rowena greeted his plans with enthusiasm. "Sure, your father'd be happy if he knew. 'Tis what he wanted to do."

"I wish I'd known him. I wish...."

Rowena put her hand on his arm. "You can be proud to be his son. Don't listen to others."

"Suddenly I feel very unworthy of him. And of you. Ma...."

"I know what you're wanting to say, but there's no need. We both said hurtful things we didn't really mean. The past is best forgotten."

They spoke of the newspaper, and Keir soon had her laughing when he described how he would redecorate the house. He insisted she not return to the Lathrops', and Rowena complied. She made no mention of the Launston money that would finance all this. She had come to realize that the Launstons did owe her son something. His father would have wanted it that way.

"As soon as you're well again, I'll settle my affairs in the city. I want you to come with me. You've never been to Toronto."

"Sure, what would I be doing in such a grand place?"

"I want you to meet some friends of mine. You'll like Molly O'Day."

• • •

Harriet Launston died of typhoid fever that day.

She never had a chance to stop Richard's marriage to Rebecca. She never saw her first grandchild, who was born to Jillian just a week after the funeral.

Fortunately, she never knew of the tragedies that both would precipitate.

Part 5

The Town

1862 - 1864

Chapter 48

Rowena breathed deeply of the night air. She had just spent a strenuous twelve hours delivering a young woman of her firstborn child, and though Rowena was weary, she was also exhilarated by the miracle of birth.

Spring, too, made her feel like that. The air was balmy, and smelled of new life sprouting from the earth, of apple blossoms and lilacs. With each successive year she welcomed spring more avidly; yet each year seemed to pass more quickly. Her father had been dead six years now, her mother, for twenty-four! She herself would soon be two-and-forty

She could hardly credit that, for she felt no different from the woman she had been at twenty or thirty. Would she remain eternally young in spirit as she watched her body shrivel into old age? Would the passage of years continue to accelerate, and speed her into oblivion?

She shook her head as if to clear away these dreary thoughts, and walked briskly toward Main Street. If Keir was still in his office, as she suspected, they could go home together.

As she passed the edge of Shantytown, she glanced at the second house from the corner and noticed dim candlelight through the windows. Gavin must be home. Rowena thought that perhaps she should stop in for a brief visit, since she had not spoken to him in many months, but she was loathe to do so. Not even her guilty conscience could persuade her otherwise.

And why should she feel guilty, she wondered. Because she found it difficult to like her twenty-year-old nephew? Sure, she had tried to establish a rapport with him over the years, to make allowances for his difficult childhood, but he had never responded to her overtures. He seemed to care for no one, not even the girl he had living with him at the moment -- and without the benefit of clergy, at that.

Sure, morals seemed to be looser these days, but no one could condone such sinfulness. Yet, strangely, people were not unduly shocked by Gavin's domestic arrangements. He had earned the reputation of being an amoral scoundrel, so they expected little else of him. And Gavin cared nothing for the opinion of others.

He had not lasted long in his grandfather's house after the old man's death. Rowena had offered him a bed, but he had declined, and had found himself a room in a boarding house. And then another, and another. For the past eight months he had been living here, in Shantytown, and already he had had a run-in with the agent who collected the rents.

Gavin had not been satisfied with the customary response to complaints, and had ended up in police court charged with assault. Having inflicted little real damage to the agent, Gavin had only been fined and warned. Thereafter he had abused the man verbally with such a spate of filthy words and nasty threats that Gavin had become quite notorious. In fact, the monthly rent collection had become something of a sideshow in Shantytown. And now Gavin was two months behind with his rent. Rowena wondered whether he didn't have the money -- for the boy was improvident, spending freely on anything that gave him pleasure -- or whether he was withholding it in protest. She didn't even dare to speculate what would happen next, although images of brutal evictions witnessed in her childhood came to mind.

As Rowena continued toward Main Street, she was startled to see a mob suddenly round the corner. There were nearly a hundred of them, all carrying torches. The silent determination with which they marched toward her made her skin crawl.

So this was the Vigilance Committee that had set the town on its ear these past two weeks! She could see the leader clearly now -- Ephraim Lindsay, son of Hiram and Prudence, and fanatic Methodist. Ephraim was tall and thin and carried himself proudly. With his black clothes, cadaverous complexion, and dark eyes that burned with religious zeal, he was a frightening vision. Rowena was glad that she was not the object of his scorn, although she knew very well that he considered her a fallen woman. Like an avenging angel he descended upon a house close to where the old Catholic church had been.

This self-appointed morality squad of respectable, law-abiding citizens had stunned the rest of the community with its first attempt at routing out the vice that had become more prevalent and flagrant over the years. With the influx in early spring of the men who spent sober and celibate months at the lumber camps, the town resembled a biblical Sodom. Whores strutted about the streets on the arms of drunks, and had even been seen copulating in alleyways. Now that most of these men had gone home, the prostitutes worked more discreetly in brothels. The vigilantes had burned down the most disreputable of these.

Despite this drastic act, the community had sympathized with the aims of the vigilantes. When the Chief Constable had been seen rushing from a burning bordello with his shirt and trousers unbuttoned, the righteous wrath of the townspeople had been unleashed upon him. Little wonder immorality had become rampant in Launston Mills! When it was discovered that not only had the Chief Constable been a patron of the whorehouses, but also a protector, the vigilantes had been seen as an instrument of God Himself. There was then no thought of curtailing their activities -- illegal and dangerous though these might be.

Rowena watched as Ephraim pounded on the door, and in a booming voice, worthy of any preacher, called, "Come out, ye sinners, or we'll burn you out!"

A few moments later a middle-aged woman peeked out the door. "Get you gone from here! You've no right to pester decent folk!" She spoke boldly, but there was fear in her voice.

"You lie, Jezebel! Take your harlots from this den of iniquity. Get out of our town! We know what to do with whores if they show themselves here." On one of their previous forays, they had seized a woman and put her in the pillory on Main Street. She had been a pretty redhead, Rowena recalled. Watching Ephraim lick his thin lips, Rowena suddenly wondered if his fanaticism was not fueled by more than religious fervour. That was a decidedly lecherous look on his face. And when he had spoken those words -- whore, harlot, and the like -- his tongue had lingered overlong on them as if he enjoyed the taste of them. As if they stimulated him.

He said, "We'll not tolerate you here, lewd fornicators! We'll not allow you to pollute our town with your lust and your shamelessness. Only fire can cleanse the blight you have brought to our town, as hellfire will cleanse your souls!" Still the door did not open. Ephraim deployed others to encircle the house, torches at the ready.

"They're getting out the back way!" someone yelled.

The crowd, buzzing now like swarming bees, made for the rear of the house. There were screams from the departing women when they saw the vigilantes, but no one made any attempt to detain them. They, and the few men who had been with them, were treated only to sharp tongue lashings. Carrying what few possessions they could, they headed toward Main Street.

Rowena wondered what they would do for the night, since there were no trains leaving until morning. They would probably find rooms at one of the many hotels -- and perhaps even ply their trade while there. She herself left the scene, not quite sure what her reaction was to what she had just witnessed.

Sure, it had bothered her to see the streetwalkers, some heavily painted and scantily dressed. But not more than the drunks, who stumbled about the streets every day of the week. And to threaten violence and destruction wasn't right. Ephraim Lindsay, and those like him, made her blood run cold. She sensed his hypocrisy, and thought him more vile and despicable a creature than either the whores or the drunkards.

Rowena hadn't gone more than a few steps up Main Street when a man accosted her. "Hope you're not goin' to dis'ppear quick as t'other ones did! Christ, you'd'a thought they was going to a fire, the way they run past me." He gripped her arm, and tried to pull her toward the Launston Hotel. "I got me a room here. C'mon."

"Leave go of me, you fool!" Rowena said, as she tried to squirm out of his grasp.

"Ah, no, I'll not let you get away from me, too!"

"Do as the lady says," a familiar voice said from behind her. It still had the power to make her tremble. "You've made a dreadful mistake, sir, and owe this lady an apology."

"Huh?" the man squinted drunkenly at Rowena. "I thought she was with t'others. Them whores as went by. Lady, you say? Beggin' your pardon, m'am, I'm sure." He walked away -- none too steadily.

Rowena burst into laughter. "I don't know whether to be flattered or insulted," she said, turning to Jeremy. "Not half an hour ago, I was bemoaning my age, and here's a comely young man wants to take me to his bed. Maybe he was more drunk than I thought!"

Jeremy smiled. "To me you look as beautiful as ever. And that young jackanapes was lucky I let him off so lightly."

They stood for a moment in awkward silence, the amusement gone. Jeremy said, "It's been a long time, Rowena."

"Aye." And it seemed as though she had loved him forever. Their lives were inextricably entwined, yet they could not even publicly acknowledge a friendship between themselves.

Jeremy sensed her thoughts. He knew only too well the irony of their relationship. But, damn it, he was getting too old to be so circumspect! "Come, we're going to have a few drinks together and discuss old times. I'm beginning to realize that we're a dying breed."

Jeremy led her into the Simpson Hotel, where he requested a private sitting room. When they were ensconced in one, Rowena said, "If this gets out, there'll be talk."

"There always is, no matter what one does. We've weathered worse storms than this could stir up, haven't we? Will you have a sherry?"

"Cider, if you please."

Jeremy ordered it, and brandy for himself.

He'd put on weight, Rowena thought as she studied him, and his colour was not good. The overwhelming conviction that he was seriously ill sent a chill through her.

Rowena said, "I never had the opportunity to tell you how sorry I was about Harriet."

"Yes. I miss her." More than he thought possible. She had become a close companion. She had encouraged him to share his thoughts and wishes and dreams with her. She had been intelligent enough to listen to his schemes and to criticize or offer new ideas or a different perspective. It wasn't until she was gone that he'd realized how much he had loved her.

But in a way so different from what he felt for this woman, sitting opposite him. With Rowena, it was some irresistible physical attraction that even now was a powerful magnet. The realization that they were both free to marry suddenly hit him. But it was too late. Jeremy was only too well aware of how drastically the social gap between them had widened. He could never marry her; he could not envision her as mistress of Thistledown. His friends would rebuff him, his children would despise him, and he and Rowena would probably end up hating one another. And he was sure that she would never consent to being his mistress, although, by God, she still stirred his blood!

Seeing the regret in his eyes, Rowena said, "I hadn't meant to remind you of your sorrow.... Jeremy! What is it?"

He was clutching his chest, his face crumpled in pain. His right hand struggled to reach the pocket inside his jacket. "My pills!"

Rowena found the bottle, extracted a pill, and placed it in his mouth. Within a couple of minutes Jeremy began to breathe more easily. Quivering with fear, Rowena had taken one of his hands in a fierce grip which she now relaxed. "What is it?"

He gave her a tired grin. "Heart trouble, so Simon tells me."

"And is it foxglove he's given you in those pills?"

"Digitalis, he said, which comes from the foxglove plant, I believe. You would have made a good doctor, Rowena."

She shook her head. Then, raising his hand to her cheek, she said, "You've not been following Simon's orders, have you? Take better care of yourself. Please."

Jeremy put his other arm around her and drew her close. They stayed like that for a long time, wrapped in an affectionate embrace. It was nearly as sweet as their lovemaking had been, for it was an affirmation of a love more deep and abiding than physical lust. It was an acknowledgement of the bond between them, a promise of friendship and support.

When Jeremy released her he said, "I wish things could have been different between us, Rowena." He allowed himself to dwell on the possibilities, but only for a moment. "By God, I'm getting old! You know I'm a grandfather now, twice over?"

He paused, and then, shaking his head, said, "I worry about them, Jilly and Richard. I'm beginning to think they've both made disastrous marriages. But of course, they won't confide in me, and wouldn't take my advice if I offered it. And aside from securing my grandchildren's inheritance, I don't know what else I can do to protect ***them*** either. The only one I have no misgivings about is your son. Keir seems to be the most level-headed one of all. He's a damned fine journalist. Although I mightn't agree with his liberal views, I can still appreciate his talent. His little newspaper is doing well, so I hear."

"Aye, that it is. And I don't think he's once regretted coming home."

The noise had been there for the past few minutes, trying to intrude upon their intimacy, but only now they became aware of it. "Is that the fire bell?" Rowena asked.

"We'd better find out."

They went outside, where they were immediately assailed by the smell of smoke. The Simpson Hotel occupied the first quarter of the block at the southeast end of Main Street, right across from Lindsays' General Store. Rowena and Jeremy looked down Lindsay Street, and saw a fire raging on the fringes of Shantytown.

"The vigilantes must have burned that house down after all," Rowena said, telling Jeremy what she had witnessed.

"Damn them, I knew this would happen if they weren't stopped! It's been such a dry spring, and there's a strong wind now. Those shacks sitting cheek by jowl won't stand a chance. The whole area'll go up in flames!"

Even as he spoke they could see flames leaping from one house to the next. The dry wood crackled; the fire roared as the southerly wind fanned it. From every quarter of the town, people were appearing, summoned by the bell. But the few buckets of water that they threw onto the flames made no difference. The fire was moving inexorably toward Main Street as well as eastward through Shantytown.

Jeremy said, "With this damned wind, there's nothing to stop the fire from reaching right to the river. I'd better go and arrange some sort of protection for the mills. Is there something about us, Rowena, that precipitates disasters?" He squeezed her hand, and then went off.

Knowing that it was the civic duty of every man, woman, and child to render assistance during a fire, Rowena headed down Lindsay Street. The smoke was thick and laden with burning cinders that were already landing on buildings a block and more from the edge of the fire. And setting them alight. Rowena joined the others in helping to drag furniture from the homes in the fire's path, but it did little good, for they had no time to cart it away before the fire consumed it as well.

The dense smoke drove people back. Rowena was in front of the Simpson Hotel when she met Keir. The roar of the fire was terrifying. The sky glowed red. The air was hot and choking as the fire sucked oxygen from it and spewed back roiling clouds of smoke. People a dozen and more miles away saw it as a giant bonfire on the horizon. The townspeople scattered to their homes in panic -- those who still had homes left -- to save what they could of their own possessions. It was obvious now that the entire town might go up in flames.

Rowena said to Keir, "I suppose there's not much point in us trying to get home."

"I think we'd be too late, Ma. It looks as if all of Shantytown is already gone."

"I hope to God folk have had the sense to get away!" she said, thinking of Moira and her family. "So what can we do? I see the Paxtons are dousing the inn with water, but that'll not save it this time, I'm thinking." And Jeremy was at the mills. Rowena wondered what he was doing there, and wished he hadn't gone. The buildings being of stone and the roofs clad with tin, they were at least less inflammable than the old log and rickety clapboard dwellings.

They could see houses igniting spontaneously from the intense heat generated by the conflagration. Burning embers landed on the roof of Lindsays' and set it ablaze. Keir and Rowena retreated up Main Street. Shocked and mesmerized, they and the people around them -- the homeless and the curious -- watched Lindsays' and Paxtons' fall. In a moment, both sides of Main Street were ablaze, and the fire crept ever westward. It jumped the river, too, by way of the bridge, and before long they could see fire to the north.

"Holy Mother of God!" Rowena said. "'Tis like a vision of hell!"

Jillian Kayne had a similar thought as she watched the inferno from the veranda of her house on Bond's Rise. From her vantage point she could more readily see the extent of the fire -- could see it spreading eastward, northward, westward... With a surge of panic, she wondered if it could actually reach her house. In that illogical moment of fear, she had already imagined the scenario: she, struggling to get her son, and the servants, to safety. Geoffrey was never around when he was needed, she thought bitterly.

She didn't know where he had been this evening, for she no longer believed his excuses of working late at the mills, but he would undoubtedly be downtown now, doing something heroic. For a moment she allowed herself the luxury of contemplating her widowhood. But Geoffrey would do nothing dangerous, of course, only something impressive that would earn him the approbation of others.

Keir had been so right about him. These past four years had been filled with disillusionment and misery. Once Geoffrey had secured her as a possession, all pretense had ceased. Not that he mistreated her in any way. He was just cold and indifferent -- except in public, where illusions of a good marriage had to be maintained. And because she could do nothing to remedy her mistake and did not wish to burden her father, she maintained the farce. Just as Geoffrey knew she would.

As soon as Geoffrey had learned of her pregnancy, he had moved into his own bedchamber. She had known from the first that he had found intimacy with her repulsive -- that look of revulsion when he had seen her withered leg was burned into her memory. And because the babe was an heir, he hadn't touched her since.

And though she had begun to hate him, it galled her to think of Geoffrey seeking his sexual favours elsewhere. As to who was obliging him, she had a terrible conviction that she hardly dared to admit, even to herself. It was all too sordid. And if Richard ever found out....

Jillian shivered, and hugged her arms about herself as her eyes once more focussed on the scene before her. She prayed that her father and brother and Keir and all the other people she cared about would be safe. But she could do without Geoffrey.

Rebecca Launston watched the conflagration from the belvedere on the roof of Thistledown. She felt like celebrating -- ordering champagne and drinking it while the town burned -- but knew the servants would think that decidedly odd and probably report it to Jeremy. And she really didn't want Jeremy to know how much she hated this place and longed to escape. If the mills burned down, perhaps she could persuade Richard to move to the city and invest his money there.

But she knew it was a vain hope. The Launstons would stay in this pathetic little community they had founded.

What a fool she had been to choose Richard! She had envisioned being back in the Toronto by now, mistress of a suitable townhouse -- and a suitable male. But this was not England, and people were not civilized!

Richard had already begun to play the dictatorial husband on their honeymoon trip to New York, never letting her out of his sight, admonishing her for flirting too freely with one man or another. He had kept that up, even here, in Launston Mills. It was only since the birth of their son that he had begun to relax his vigilance.

And Rebecca had felt able to breathe once more. Yet, Richard's eyes were forever trying to ferret out her thoughts. Whenever they were together, she could feel his assessing gaze upon her and sense his suspicion. It rather amused her to think that she was a constant torment to him, for he would never trust her.

Not that she could be trusted, of course. But he had known that before he'd married her. And with so little freedom and privacy, it was damned difficult to be anything but saintly in this town!

Of course, that was part of the thrill of it, too, arranging a suitable rendezvous -- dangerous at the best of times -- and outsmarting Richard.

As she watched the frenzied flames devouring the town, Rebecca's own restlessness grew. She did not fear that the fire would reach as far as Thistledown. Baby Stephen would be looked after by the nanny in any case, and there was no reason for

Rebecca to stay here when all the excitement was downtown. She sent word to have her horse saddled, and appeared at the stables a few minutes later dressed in her riding habit. Tom, already used to his new mistress's ways -- and temperament -- did not even try to dissuade her from venturing into town.

With the sky nearly as bright as day, and the road therefore well lit, Rebecca galloped into town as if she were the fire bent on consuming all in its path. She felt strangely exhilarated.

She pulled her horse up short as she rounded the corner from Cambridge Street onto Main Street. Most of the townspeople stood before her, gazing eastward. They faced the rivers of fire that flowed toward them as if they could stop them by sheer force of will. But in the face of such a destructive force, they had never been more impotent.

Keir stood outside his office with a bundle of documents under his arm, regretting that he could save no more, thankful that he, unlike so many others, did have insurance. When he saw Rebecca, he felt a flutter of longing for her. Wild and dishevelled, exuding an aura of sensuality like a cat in heat, she was utterly desirable.

She saw his look, and gave him one of her seductive smiles in return. If only she could get Keir back, life here would be much less dull. She found the maturing, cynical man much more enticing than the infatuated, idealistic boy he had been three years ago. She found his ambivalent feelings toward her not only thrilling, but challenging. She could make him desire her again. And she would. Planning his seduction would give her something to wile away the long and useless hours that filled her days.

Soot-blackened and weary, the people around her looked at Rebecca who was as yet untouched by the fallout from the fire. And they all hated her just a little, she sensed.

Stunned and disbelieving, the townspeople watched the first block of buildings fall and then the second, but here the fire finally began to flag. The wind had died down, so now there was only the windstorm that the fire itself created. It was not strong enough to propel the flames across William Street, and so the westward advance was halted. Similarly the fire was contained within the first block to the north and to the south of Main Street.

By three o'clock in the morning the fire had burned itself out. Those who had homes, went to them. Those who didn't, bedded down on the common. Rowena and Keir went to his office, where a cot and an armchair sufficed as beds. It wasn't until then that Rowena even thought of the loss of her own home. And she was worried about Moira, but Keir assured her that the Ryans had undoubtedly escaped by following the river southward, and were now comfortably ensconced at the Darcy farm.

Neither of them slept long. When they emerged from the office at daybreak, the scene before them was surrealistic in its strangeness. The original settlement, the town that Rowena had known for thirty years, was nothing but a smouldering ruin. She could see where Punkin Hollow and her own home had once been, half a mile away, across an expanse of smoking cinders. Across the river to the north, the railway station and a nearby hotel, the carding mill, a factory, and blocks of homes had disappeared. Altogether five hotels, two mills, the distillery, and ninety-six other buildings lay in ruins. Looking eastward, all that Rowena could see were the new Catholic church and the other buildings that had been south of the fire's origins, and most of the Launstons' stone mills. The outbuildings and fences had gone, but the grist and saw mills seemed to be intact.

It inspired Rowena with optimism. "I reckon everyone'll be rebuilding soon. But right now we have to do something about ourselves and the hundreds that are homeless. And hungry."

By noon, cartloads of food and some clothing were arriving from the district farmers. Hugh Darcy came by in the afternoon to inform Rowena that the Ryans were safe, and invited her and Keir to stay at the farm until they could make other arrangements. She thanked him, but declined, for she knew she would never be truly welcome under Shelagh's roof. She had already decided to accept the Worthings' offer of accommodation at their new and spacious home on Cambridge Street.

She and Keir were enjoying supper with Margaret and Simon and two of their children that evening, and discussing the catastrophe. Rowena recited her account of the vigilantes' activities, and concluded by saying, "I didn't really think they would burn the house down."

"They didn't," Simon said, "Or so Ephraim claims."

Rowena saw Margaret flash Simon a meaningful look. "Then how did the fire start? Does anyone know?" she asked.

Simon shovelled a forkful of potatoes into his mouth, and tried to ignore her question. Margaret would not meet her eyes.

"What's wrong?" Rowena asked. "You two are behaving most peculiar. Is it something I'm not allowed to know?"

Simon looked at Margaret with resignation, and then said to Rowena, "You'll hear it anyway. Rumour has it that Gavin started that fire. To get even with the landlord."

After a moment's stunned silence, Rowena said, "Is it true?"

Simon shrugged. "The general consensus is that the fire started at his house. Gavin claims he was out, and left some candles burning, since he'd expected to be home soon. Whether he did it purposely or through negligence, only he knows, but it seems he was in some way responsible."

"The idiot!" Rowena said crossly. "There are times when I wish he'd never been born!"

Chapter 49

Keir stepped out of the office of the *LAUNSTON MILLS OBSERVER*. He lit a cigar, and surveyed with pride and satisfaction the flurry of construction across the street. By midsummer the "Shaughnessy Block" should be completed.

The fire that had rampaged through town a year ago had, in many respects, been a boon to the town. A quick glance along Main Street attested to that. Solid, flat-roofed, three-storey brick commercial blocks were arising from the ashes of the wooden shops. Many housed two or even three shops on the ground floor, and offices or living quarters in the stories above. Although they harmonized with their neighbours, the buildings achieved individuality through the ornamental cornices, friezes, window labels, pilasters, and crowning pediments or parapets. Because of the unusual width of Main Street, the tall blocks did not face one another like threatening armies, glowering, poised to strike. Instead, they sat back complacently with ample breathing space.

The old shops along the western half of Main Street, untouched by the flames, looked like ragged beggars in comparison. Some people facetiously suggested that the fire could have done a more thorough job.

Although the formidable task of rebuilding their lives and their town had not daunted the majority of people, a few had not had the heart to begin anew. Josh Paxton, an old man now, had sold his land to Ephraim Lindsay, and had moved to his son-in-law's farm. The "Lindsay Block" was now squarely situated at the eastern end of Main Street, where Paxtons' popular tavern and the Lindsays' original store had once been landmarks.

The Launstons had not rebuilt the distillery, but a stone woolen mill had gone up farther downstream, and the "Launston Savings and Loan Company" had been established to help finance the reconstruction of the town.

In the aftermath of its devastation, Launston Mills had finally acquired a fire engine, and the town council had passed a by-law prohibiting the erection of wooden structures in the business section. The notorious Shantytown landlord had sold his holdings to the Launston Land Company. Jeremy had ensured that the old Launston tract was re-surveyed and was now selling in reasonably-priced half acre lots.

Shantytown was no more.

The poorer families had dispersed to the southern and eastern fringes of town where most rented and a few had built cabins on cheaper land. It was not uncommon for these "Shantytowners" to lease the old homes of the prospering middle class who, in turn, had constructed fine brick houses on the ruins of Shantytown.

The residents of Punkin Hollow had, with a few exceptions, been quick to rebuild on their original sites -- some, like Fergus Ryan, on land that their fathers had purchased over thirty years before. Perhaps that was why the name "Punkin Hollow" was not only to endure, but eventually to encompass all that had been the Launstons' original land grant.

Mary Ryan O'Shaughnessy, now a brittle old woman, had sold the remains of the O'Shaughnessy homestead, and had moved in with Fergus. Keir had persuaded Rowena to sell the Delaney land, and to share his new home.

Rowena, however, had protested his selection of a site on Bond's Rise, where affluent merchants, bankers, and factory owners like the Lathrops resided. She had finally approved of a five acre "park" lot on Cambridge Street, close to the Worthings'.

Keir glanced west to the intersection of Main and Cambridge, where a red brick town hall-and-market building was under construction. Four blocks north of this his own house was nearing completion.

Keir returned the greetings of passersby. He was surprisingly contented here. His newspaper and printing shop were a success. His powerful editorials on such issues as working conditions, free schools at all levels, and extending the franchise by eliminating property restrictions earned him the support and respect of many.

"Mornin', Keir. A grand mornin' it is, an' all."

"Good morning, Eamon."

Eamon Devlin seated himself on the bench and began to fill his pipe. He was a regular visitor on fine days. He had been a lumberjack until a few years ago when one of his legs had been crushed by a log and had required amputation after gangrene had set in. There wasn't much for him to do now, except to depend upon his six grown sons for support. So Eamon spent his days doing his "rounds" -- going from one shop to the next to "chew the fat".

"Do 'ee think it like to happen then, that them Yanks'll turn on us next? There's them as say for a certainty that when this here Civil War's over them soldiers'll be marchin' right up to our very doorsteps."

"There are those who fear such an invasion is imminent." And Donal O'Shaughnessy had hinted as much to his sisters in his brief and infrequent letters. He was fighting the Confederates at the moment, as a true American, and was prepared to fight the British -- in Canada -- as a true Fenian. "We are in a rather precarious situation at the moment, with our government in such a state of confusion and virtual stalemate."

"Aye. Do 'ee favour this idea of Macdonald's then?"

"Confederation? Wholeheartedly! I believe that if we are to survive, we must consolidate and become a nation. As a colony we've become more of a headache to Britain than an asset. We're floundering right now, and I doubt that Britain is all that concerned with saving us this time. If we don't help ourselves then it will be left to the Americans to do so. We could be annexed to the States without even a struggle."

"I can see the truth of that right enough. I'm wonderin' if 'tis such a bad idea an' all."

They spent some time debating this issue, and Eamon left, satisfied. Keir was just about to return to his office when he noticed the Launston carriage coming up the street.

It was Jeremy -- His Worship, the mayor. Keir had been expecting him.

The brougham drew up to the stoop. Jeremy's face was stern when he alighted from the vehicle.

"Good morning, Uncle Jeremy."

"I'd like to speak with you."

"Certainly."

Keir led the way through the front office, past the press room, and into his private office at the rear. The room was equipped with a desk, a safe, an easy chair, and a bed and washstand -- Keir had been sleeping here since the fire.

As soon as the door was shut, Jeremy slapped the newspaper that he had drawn from his pocket onto the desk. "How dare you impugn me like this!"

"I had hoped that you wouldn't take this personally, Uncle Jeremy."

"Damn it! How else am I supposed to interpret this?" Jeremy picked up the newspaper and quoted:

> *...What is questionable, however, is the wisdom of our ambitious municipal officers in augmenting the community's present debt by some $85000 to secure this*

northern rail line. Not only will this forestall imperative civic improvements, but it will once again necessitate an increase in taxes for which the citizens are promised only a general increase in prosperity at some future time. Some might dispute whether these nebulous benefits will indeed justify their dipping deeper into their already-strained pockets for many years to come. Others might wonder when our hazardous roads will be improved and lighted, and whether ditches will ever be excavated to drain the swampy areas of town. It would be prudent for our officials to re-examine their priorities before committing the town to such rash and grandiose schemes.

The newspaper was smacked onto the table once again.

"It's libelous, by God! Implying that I granted that railway bonus, not for the benefit of the town, but to further my own interests. You have done me a grievous wrong."

"You must admit that this does involve you in a conflict of interest -- you are the major shareholder of that railway company, and your lumbering concerns will derive immediate benefit from a line to the north. However, I never suggested that this was the reason for your decision. Perhaps you are not aware of the financial straits that most people are in because of the fire. It is for these citizens that I appeal to you to reconsider." Keir looked ruefully at his uncle. "I do know what you envision for this town, Uncle Jeremy, but I think you are striving for too much, too quickly."

"I see. I never thought that you would turn against me, Keir. That you could malign me thus, after all I've done for you, wounds me deeply.... Isn't it ironic that my money financed this rag?" Then he was gone.

Keir was left with grave thoughts. Bit by bit over the last few years he had come to realize just how powerful the Launstons were. Keir was not unduly worried that Jeremy would consciously abuse that power; he was a man of integrity. But Keir was not at all certain that Richard would be as scrupulous once he was in control of the Launston empire.

Keir scanned the latest edition of the *LAUNSTON EXPOSITOR* that afternoon. He grinned wryly when he read the editorial:

Our illustrious confrere has once again demonstrated his narrow-minded, parochial views in his latest attack upon His Worship, Mr. Jeremy Launston, and the councillors for their decision to aid in the building of a railway to the northern counties. The editor of the OBSERVER would have us believe that prosperity can be measured only in the number of street lamps and macadamized roadways of which a town can boast. The sagacious reader will immediately recognize this as hogwash. Such short-sighted attitudes are for the craven, the hidebound who cannot see beyond their front doors, who are incapable of profound visions. What sane man would choose a shanty now when he could have a mansion in the near future? Our confrere would have us believe that the citizens of Launston Mills would prefer the shanty, so long as the street in front of it were paved. Such an assumption is an insult to the intelligent man....

This diatribe continued at some length. It did not surprise Keir. Jeremy owned the *EXPOSITOR*.

Keir's thoughts were still on the issue when he walked up Cambridge Street that evening. The spring mire had dried, leaving the roads deeply rutted and mined with axle-breaking potholes.

The fire had not reached up Cambridge Street. The houses lining the first few blocks, though mostly pleasant clapboard dwellings, were surrounded by rickety board fences whose occasional broken or missing members allowed glimpses of rubbish-strewn yards and the hodgepodge of tumbledown outbuildings. Farther along, on the gentle rise of land, were newer brick homes -- like the Worthings' -- on larger lots. Then Keir's house, close to the northern boundary of the town.

He came almost daily to check on the progress, anxious now to move in. Only some of the interior fittings remained to be done.

Keir was proud of his Italianate "villa". A square Tuscan tower, reaching a storey higher than the rest of the house, was embraced by the crook of the "L" shaped building. The two tower balconies, the heavy paired brackets under the wide eaves, the window trim and shutters, and the veranda across the long arm of the "L" were a rich forest green against the blonde brick. It was a truly imposing structure. Keir had named it "The Brambles".

The front entrance was set into the bottom of the tower. Keir unlocked the door and walked in. He wandered through the large, empty, echoing rooms, mentally furnishing them. The ground floor of the forward-jutting wing comprised the double drawing rooms. The front one, facing east, was in shadow, but warm evening sunlight streamed in through the french windows of the other, spotlighting the dancing dust motes. This would be his favourite room, Keir decided. Here he would spend evenings alone with his mother, or with close friends; the other drawing room would be used only for formal entertaining. The french windows overlooking the garden would remain uncurtained; Keir detested the modern penchant for shrouding rooms in heavy, sombre draperies.

He stood at the window and gazed out. The vegetation on these five acres had been mostly scrub. Keir had had most of it cleared out, except for a few pines along the boundary of the property. He had planted, instead, maples and oaks and an apple orchard amid the sprouting grass which had been seeded in early spring. A garden had been laid out, and Rowena had already planted herbs and flowers.

Keir was about to turn away when he saw a figure emerge from behind the carriage house. A woman.

For a moment he feared it was Rebecca. Lately, she had taken to riding by at about the time he usually came to the house. They never talked, beyond greeting each other with a polite "good evening", but her eyes tempted and taunted him. He'd been stunned at first to realize that she was pursuing him. Did she really think he would forgive her treachery, her arrogant, devastating rejection of his love? Did she think he had so little pride? Yet he couldn't help feeling somewhat triumphant over Richard, whose wife preferred her ex-lover after all. But he pitied his cousin as well. Shrewd, selfish, and ruthless, Rebecca couldn't be an easy person to live with.

But he was relieved to realize it wasn't Rebecca. Her back was to him, and her hat concealed her hair, but she didn't move with the seductive grace that was Rebecca's. So who the devil was she? Keir unlatched one of the french windows and strode out to confront the trespasser.

She turned at the sound of his footsteps on the gravel path. There was something strangely familiar about her smile, but her identity still baffled him. Stunning green eyes. Auburn hair.

"Hello, Mr. Shaughnessy."

"Megan?"

"You've not forgotten me." She was amused by his surprise. She had been preparing herself for this encounter for days, hoping to make a favourable impression. If the truth be told, she had been preparing herself for this encounter for four years -- when Keir had left the city there had been no doubt in her mind that she would one day follow him here. But she had also been determined to come to him as an educated and independent woman. He would never know how hard she had worked to achieve that goal. And he'd never know how wildly her heart pounded as she stood before him.

"Megan Maguire! I hardly recognized you." Indeed. She was a woman now, and a handsome one at that. She regarded him frankly, with an air of self-assurance that seemed unusual in a nineteen year old. He had noticed that her speech was more refined, though there was still a pleasant lilt in her voice.

"It's been four years," she said.

"I suppose it has.... But what on earth are you doing here?"

"I had an interview for a teaching position in town today."

"So you're a qualified teacher now. I do remember Molly mentioning in one of her letters to Ma that you were attending the Normal School." Keir had taken Rowena to Toronto after she had recovered from the typhoid fever. During that brief visit she and Molly had become fast friends, and they corresponded regularly. "And you've applied for a position here?"

"They advertised for a teacher, so I applied, and was asked to come for an interview." She laughed. "They, too, wondered why I would choose to work in Launston Mills. Wouldn't I miss the city, they asked me. But I assured them that I had friends here, and I was tired of city life."

As they ambled toward the house, Keir said, "And how did the interview go?"

"I think I have the job," Megan replied with a grin. "Though I'm to wait for a letter, as official confirmation."

"You must have impressed the board."

"I come well qualified," she stated simply, but without conceit. She knew her strengths and never wasted words minimizing her abilities, not after working so damnably hard to get where she was. She had gone into the interview determined not to show how desperately she wanted the job, knowing that they were lucky to get her. "I graduated at the top of my class."

She saw the flicker of surprise on his face, and was satisfied at his reaction. She would make him forget the dirty, hungry urchin he remembered her being. She would make him see her as the woman she now was. And she would make him fall in love with her. To her it was as inevitable as her next breath. It was simply a matter of making him see how well suited they were, and how much she loved him.

Megan felt joy welling up inside her, threatening to erupt in a burst of uninhibited laughter. It was difficult to contain her happiness. She wanted to throw her arms about him, and open her heart to him. Instead, she took Keir's arm and said, "When I inquired about you, I was told you were building this mansion, so I thought I'd surprise you here. Will you show me the house?"

"Of course." Keir had been taken aback by her intimate gesture, not certain whether it was intended to be merely friendly, or whether she still harboured her childish infatuation for him. He dreaded the latter, wanting no complications in his life now that it was on an even keel. It was enough that he had to contend with Rebecca's games. But as Megan chatted on, he began to relax, and even to enjoy her company. She spoke to him unselfconsciously, like an old friend -- and unlike a lovesick girl.

But he didn't know what an effort it was for her to keep the adoration from her eyes and a nervous tremor from her hands.

Megan exclaimed with delight as he conducted her about the house. They climbed the tower, and stepped onto the uppermost balcony which faced the river to the east. The Launstons' extensive properties were to the north, but Thistledown was not visible from here.

The town lay in a saucer-like depression before them. The sinking sun gilded the multitude of rooftops that rippled away to the south and east, and glinted off the tin roofs of the mills and factories. Miniature farm buildings dotted the sun-warmed hillside far across the river.

"It's a lovely town," Megan said almost reverently. "It seems so peaceful."

"You may think it too peaceful after a while."

"It's just what I've been looking for. I've had enough of cities. I was born in Belfast. Did you know that Toronto is becoming known as the Belfast of Canada? Just last month I went with Molly and Mike on a moonlight cruise on the lake in one of the big steamers. It was mostly Catholics on the excursion. There was a welcoming committee on the docks when we got back -- a bunch of young Orange hooligans throwing rocks at us and shouting curses that would curl your ears! I've heard the Catholic boys treat the Orange outings to the same sort of shenanigans."

"You'll find that kind of prejudice wherever you go, Megan."

"I know. Maybe I'm just a romantic, thinking small-town life is gentler and more easy-going than city life. Well, I suppose I should get back to the hotel for supper."

"You must come and dine with us, Megan. Ma would never forgive me if I didn't bring you back for a visit, and there's always more than enough food on the table. Ma's staying with my aunt Moira until this house is finished, but if you're not intimidated by the thought of meeting half a dozen of my cousins, you're very welcome to join us."

"If you're sure I'd not be intruding...."

"Not at all!"

By the time they reached the Ryans', Keir had already acquainted Megan with the cousins she would meet tonight -- Tim, Mary, Deedee, Eileen, Kate, Patrick, and Daniel. Megan was warmly welcomed by the family. With artless ease she endeared herself to them all. When Moira, somewhat flustered -- and resentful -- at the presence of a supper guest ordered her daughters to set the parlour table, Megan assured her that she wanted no such formality on her account, stressing that she liked the cheery kitchen which overlooked the river. Conn was won when Megan praised the house that he and his sons had built. The older girls became her lifelong friends when she promised to help them sew gowns that any fashionable Toronto lady would envy for Mary's forthcoming wedding. Everyone was enchanted with her lively anecdotes about city life. When she described the Prince of Wales's visit to the city three years ago, they could almost hear the fanfare of trumpets and see the procession along the flower-strewn streets lined with cheering crowds.

Keir noticed that Tim rarely took his eyes off Megan the entire evening. She had made another conquest, it seemed. It was nothing to him. In fact, Keir wished Tim well. Megan would undoubtedly make a good wife. Since he himself was not interested in her in that way, he was only too glad to think that she might yet be related to him. He liked her open, honest, unpretentious nature. She was a good person, and he wished her well.

When Keir and Megan departed, she left a rosy glow in her wake, as if she had brought them each some good news to gladden the soul. Conn said, "Sure, she's a bonny lass. A real treasure."

"Aye, that she is, " Moira agreed, envious of the girl's admirable character. She couldn't imagine Megan ever feeling the jealousies, the anguish over real or imagined slights, the pettiness and meanness of spirit that had been hers at that age.

When she gazed at Conn with his graying hair and thickening waist, she marvelled at the intense and selfish love she had once felt for him. But she'd been idealistic then -- a romantic. Life had browbeaten her these past twenty-odd years. And she knew Conn for what he was -- a very mortal man with faults and mannerisms that annoyed her beyond endurance at times. She even thought him stupid on occasion, and things he said frequently grated on her nerves, bringing her close to screaming. More often than not she had to stop her tongue from criticizing him -- not often enough, according to Rowena, but then what did she know? She was free. Only Shelagh understood and sympathized with her. Women like themselves were martyrs to their families.

To Rowena she said, "Do you think she's the girl for Keir? Sure, they make a handsome couple, and 'tis time he took a wife. That big house of his will be a right lonely place for just the two of you. Now with Megan about...."

"You're a born matchmaker," Conn said with a grin. "I can see you'll not be resting till you've had your cry at their wedding."

"You'd best leave them be," Rowena cautioned her sister. "Keir'd not take kindly to our interfering. He's not ready for marriage."

"He's five and twenty!"

"'Tis what every mother says of her sons, no matter how old they be," Conn teased.

"Now you're talking in your boots, Conn Ryan," Moira said heatedly. "'Twould please me just fine if Tim was to take a wife. That might take his mind off all this union nonsense."

"The 'Sawyers' and Millworkers' Benevolent Society', Ma," Tim corrected her.

"'Tis a union all the same, no matter what fancy name you put to it. And it'll land you in heap of trouble, you mark my words." And even as she spoke them she felt a shiver of fear for her eldest. "A girl like Megan would straighten you out soon enough."

Rowena, too, had seen Tim's interest in Megan. But Megan was in love with Keir -- she would have known that even if Molly hadn't written to tell her. But was Megan's love strong enough and patient enough to wait for Keir's wounds to heal?

Rowena cursed Rebecca Launston.

Chapter 50

Richard Launston was cursing Rebecca as well.

God knows, he'd had to put up with a lot these past four years, but she was going beyond forgiveness -- and decorum -- these days. No one had seen her since tea time; she'd gone without leaving a message. And they had been expected at the Lathrops for dinner an hour ago. She knew how he hated being late for engagements, even social ones. And how he detested scandal.

Angrily, he sloshed some more whiskey into a crystal glass, and downed the drink in one gulp. He wanted to hurl the empty glass to the floor, but his sense of propriety had not yet deserted him. Instead he slammed the glass onto the tray and refilled it.

Bitterly he wondered where Keir was tonight. Or was it Geoffrey that Rebecca was with? He had no proof, of course, only his own keen observation of his wife in the company of other men. And he hadn't failed to notice how resentfully Jillian regarded her sister-in-law, or the shared anguish she tried to communicate, and which he rejected.

He had tried to avoid thinking of Rebecca at all, knowing he could not fail to find her at fault. He had important business to occupy his thoughts. He had no time to worry about a wayward wife. Let her amuse herself as she would, he had sometimes convinced himself. After all, she was a spoilt, self-indulgent child at heart.

Selfish, heartless bitch!

She was a trollop at heart. When she had tried her whores tricks on him she had merely repulsed him, making him realize how many others she had pleasured before him. And she seemed to delight in tormenting him with her past indiscretions. They had yet to broach the subject of her current ones.

But she seemed to be precipitating a confrontation. How dare she do this to him! She owed him some loyalty and obedience, even if not in bed! He'd not let her get away with this!

Rebecca walked in, dressed in her riding habit, and greeted Richard with a curt "Hello". She poured herself a sherry and slid into an armchair. "I've just had the most marvellous gallop up to the Falls and back! Have I missed dinner?" She shrugged at his silence. "I'll have something brought on a tray. I just adore these long days when twilight lasts until ten. I hate being cooped up indoors while the day lingers." There was a note of resentment in her voice. Not that she was justifying herself. She never did that.

"What's the matter, Richard? Have I spoilt some plan of yours?" she asked with sarcasm rather than concern.

"We were expected for dinner at the Lathrops an hour ago," Richard said through clenched teeth. He could barely trust himself to speak. He was so close to losing the self-control upon which he prided himself.

She gave a pretty shrug of her shoulders. "I find them a bore. I trust you sent our regrets -- pressing business, unavoidable delays -- the usual. You're so good at that Richard. I don't suppose I've ever known a more preoccupied man."

She watched him to see if the barb struck home. And then she seemed to lose interest. Carelessly she pulled some pins from her hair so that the silvery mass tumbled about her face and shoulders. She shook her head and combed her fingers through her hair. When she had poured herself another sherry and resumed her seat, she looked at his white, angry face in surprise and said, "Surely, you're not going to make a scene about this, Richard. Over a dinner with the Lathrops?"

"Who were you with?"

"No one, of course," she replied, but her eyes taunted him. "Who in this God-forsaken village would I possibly care to spend my time with? My horse is better company than the locals."

"You can spare me your backwoods wit. It may suffice to entertain your city friends, but does not amuse me."

"But then there is so little that does, my dear Richard. I am hardly to blame for your dour personality."

She tossed off that remark as easily as her drink. But when she rose to get another, Richard blocked her way.

"I asked you who you were with."

"What business is it of yours? I told you before we married that I would never allow you to treat me as a possession. If you are disappointed in our arrangement, then I can tell you that I am doubly so! I expected to be the wife of an influential and powerful man. I did not expect to be buried alive in this intellectual and social wasteland!"

She winced as he grabbed her arm in a painful grip. "Well, you haven't been out discussing philosophy with someone! I can smell him on you. Is it Keir? Or Geoffrey?"

Her anger gave way once more to amusement. "Really, Richard! Don't be vulgar."

He released her then, knowing there was no way he could impose his will upon her. She was too strong and too cold-blooded.

"You don't really want to know the answer anyway," she said as she poured herself a brandy this time. "You've never been one to upset the emotional apple cart, have you, Richard?"

A strange noise made her stop suddenly. A choking, gasping, pain-filled noise. She and Richard both turned toward the door, which they hadn't heard open, and saw Jeremy there, clawing at his chest, his face a horrible mask of disbelief and pain. A moment later he collapsed.

As Richard rushed to his father's side, Rebecca summoned the servants, and sent a messenger for Simon Worthing.

Simon arrived a scant ten minutes later. But too late to help his friend. Jeremy had died in his son's arms, unable to voice the questions he so desperately wanted answered. Surely not Keir? And not Jilly's husband!

What sort of curse had Richard brought upon the family....?

• • •

The town went into mourning. Black wreaths or strips of black crepe hung on the doors of the closed shops on the day of the funeral. Main Street was crowded with people dressed in their best mourning, watching the sombre cortege pass. Many wept openly.

When the earth had closed about Jeremy, the people shed their sadness with their black garments, and resumed their everyday lives, knowing things would never be quite the same now.

Rowena had not lingered by the grave with the family, as had Keir, for she knew she would not have been welcome. So she returned that evening for her own private farewell to her love.

The Protestant cemetery was a good two miles south of the town. It was situated on the banks of the Scugog River, and separated from the new Catholic cemetery by a small tributary stream. It was a truly tranquil place, never more than now, in the golden light of a midsummer evening.

Every step of the way was a heartache for Rowena. Although she had been worried about his health, his death had still come as a shock to her. In his arrogance he had seemed invincible.

Vividly she recalled the reckless young man she had first seen driving his horse relentlessly along the dusty trail to Launston Mills. There, in that strange and menacing wilderness of thirty-odd years ago, she'd had no inkling of how their lives would be linked. And when their eyes had first locked in mutual appraisal that spring day in Yardleys', she could never have guessed that that spark of attraction would one day ignite an all-consuming love. Still sweet upon her lips was the taste of that first guilt-ridden kiss, when she had been wrapped protectively in his arms, the two of them lost in some private heaven while just a block away all hell had broken loose. Most blissful and painful of all was the memory of that one bittersweet night when they had consummated their passion in forbidden ecstacy.

The wildflowers she had picked en route trembled in her hands as she approached the fresh mound of dirt next to the grassy graves of Harriet and Samuel and Adrian. She placed the flowers upon his grave and murmured a prayer for him.

Goodbye, my love, she whispered.

Before leaving, she paused by Adrian's tombstone. Nearly twenty-six years he had been dead. She could hardly recall him now.

How little we leave behind to mark our existence! A stone slab engraved with a name and a life span. Nothing to say what kind of man lay beneath it. No words of praise, or condemnation. Only the fickle memories of the living. With their passing there would be nothing to distinguish him from any other but a name.

For the first time, Rowena thought of Brendan, lying forgotten in a pauper's grave in Ottawa. No man deserved such an ignominious end.

Chapter 51

Jillian Kayne missed her father more than she ever thought possible. With him she had felt safe and loved and worthy of being loved. Without him she felt frighteningly alone and abandonned. If it weren't for Alexander and his childish devotion to her, she would feel totally lost.

Geoffrey cared nothing for her. Richard seemed little interested in her life, and refused to listen to her whenever she tried to talk seriously to him about her troubled marriage. Her sister-in-law treated her with scorn and amusement. Rebecca was certainly not one with whom to share a confidence. And Jillian would have nothing to confide to her anyway, since she strongly suspected that it was Rebecca with whom Geoffrey was having an affair. Jillian had no close friends, no one with whom to discuss personal matters, no one to offer advice or encouragement or emotional support.

Keir would, but he seemed lost to her as well. Geoffrey disliked him, and strongly disapproved of him. Jillian had rarely seen him so angry as the time she had casually suggested that they invite Keir to dinner one evening.

How dare she consider inviting that bastard into their respectable household! Her father might think him socially acceptable, even acknowledge him as his nephew, but they -- the Kaynes -- never would, and she'd best remember that! Such things might have been done in the old days, but in modern, civilized circles it was scandalous even to consider it! And moreover, he didn't approve of the man's politics. What in God's name did Jillian imagine they would have to say to one another?

How unfair of Geoffrey to deprive her of her one true friend! She had never been afraid to speak her mind to Keir; he had been more of a brother to her than Richard. Richard had always been so secretive, sly even. He had never shared his feelings, she was sure, for he trusted no one. She would have pitied him, had she not felt such misery for herself.

Jillian hugged four year old Alexander, who had crawled onto to her lap for his bedtime story. She often marvelled at the perfection that was her son, that wonderful little being that God had given to her to safeguard. From the moment that she had felt his first kicks in her womb, she had begun to love him with an intensity that sometimes frightened even her. If ever she should lose him....

She could never think beyond that point, for there lay madness.

Jillian often spent the best part of her days with Alexander. Sandy was an extremely bright child, and a happy, easygoing one. If he had a fault -- and Jillian did not consider it so -- it was that he clung to his mother. His dependence on her irritated Geoffrey. They'd had many quarrels about it. Jillian had not even wanted a nanny, but Geoffrey had been outraged at the idea that his wife demean herself with nursery chores. He had hired the first without Jillian's approval. That woman had resented Jillian's "interference" in the nursery, and had not lasted long. Since then there had been a succession of women, each willing and ready to take charge, but finding herself thwarted by the mistress. Few were prepared to stay in such a powerless situation. Geoffrey's latest find had just arrived from Glasgow, and a more dour Scotswoman Jillian had yet to see. A gaoler she might have been.

This power struggle with Geoffrey was really getting out of hand. She would have to confront him yet again. Did he think that this woman would intimidate her as well as her son?

Geoffrey was using the boy. Why did he resent Sandy's love for her? Was it because the boy did not show much affection for his father? But how could he when his father was always so stern and critical, and rejected any physical overtures of affection, such as hugs.

When Jillian had finished the story, the nanny said, "Come along now, Alexander. Time for bed."

Sandy ignored her. He turned a sad face to his mother, and said, "Will you stay with me? Until I go to sleep? Please, Mama. I don't want to be alone."

He looked truly frightened, and she could understand his reluctance at being left with Nanny Robertson. Jillian was always ready to give him everything that it was within her power to give -- and that she thought would be to his benefit. "I'll stay with you for a while, darling. You climb into bed now."

"That's most irregular, ma'm. Now you must heed me in this. I've raised half a dozen children, and as this be your first, you'd be wise to take my advice. It'll do nobody any good, your giving in to the lad. 'Tis what I say that goes in the nursery, Ma'm. I was told that most particular by Mr. Kayne. You're a soft-hearted woman, ma'm, and not the best judge as to what's good for the lad."

"How dare you, Miss Roberston!" Jillian said. "I am the boy's mother! I do know my son -- much better than you ever will, I daresay -- and I do know what is best for him. And it is I who will decide what is to be done, when, and by whom. Do you understand me?"

"My wife is, as I warned you, Miss Robertson, strong willed and misguided," Geoffrey said, entering the room. "I've set you a difficult task, I'm afraid, getting this situation in hand, but I'm sure you'll find it a challenge worthy of your talents." He smiled at the woman, and she muttered a respectful "Yes, sir" in response. Then he turned to Jillian. His eyes were cold, although his lips formed themselves into a pleasant grin for the benefit of the nanny. "Come, Jillian. You seem to have forgotten that we have a dinner engagement at your brother's house. And you're not even dressed." His voice sounded as if he were gently chiding a thoughtless child.

She knew that he hated to make a scene before servants, so she said, "Indeed I have not forgotten, Geoffrey. But since Nanny Robertson is so newly arrived -- and tired from her journey, I daresay -- I thought it best if we stayed at home this evening. Richard will not mind our cancelling. He always claims he has so much to occupy him, and so little time for socializing. Send the groom with a note, would you?" Her eyes challenged his, but how she hated these confrontations! Marriage for her was a constant battle, a struggle to gain some power, and to keep her self-respect.

"That would cause a great deal of inconvenience to two households, and I am not prepared to upset the servants just to satisfy your whim. We are expected at eight. Say goodnight to your mother, Alexander. Come, Jillian."

She could feel his anger. He was breaking his own rule about not arguing in front of the servants. Jillian felt a trickle of fear down her spine. For the first time in her life she wondered if she would be strong enough to withstand him. "I really do not feel well enough to go, Geoffrey," she said apologetically. "But I wouldn't want your evening to be spoilt. You go, by all means, and take my regards."

"There's absolutely nothing wrong with you, madam, and we all know it. Miss Robertson has been hired to look after Alexander. She is eminently qualified, and receives excellent remuneration for her services. There is nothing for you to do here. You will leave this room now, or I will drag you from it. I trust you will be sensible and spare us that embarrassment."

Jillian felt the blood drain from her face. For one horrible moment she thought she would faint. But she gathered her strength, and rose from the edge of Sandy's bed. She channeled it all into her next words, which she spoke calmly and with the wry amusement with which one regards the statement of a fool. "Don't be melodramatic, Geoffrey. You'll frighten Sandy ***and*** Miss Robertson. If this dinner is that important to you, then of course we shall go. What a lot of fuss to make about an evening with my rather boring brother!"

She bent down and kissed Sandy goodnight, making light of the entire scene through her nonchalance. She felt like a traitor to her son -- how she longed to stay and comfort him, poor wretched child in the care of that woman -- but she knew she had lost this skirmish. It was best for Sandy and for herself to acknowledge defeat and retire with dignity.

The child's cries of "Mama! Don't go! MAMA!" that turned into screams as she left the room, tore at her heart. She felt his anguish in herself, but she knew there was nothing she could do. Not at the moment. Damn Geoffrey! He wouldn't dare have treated her -- or Sandy -- like this if Jeremy were alive. Damn Geoffrey to hell for his cruelty! If she had had a knife in her hand at that moment, she would gladly have plunged it into his unfeeling heart.

When she was safely in her own room, she sat on the edge of the bed and inhaled deeply, trying to quell the murderous rage that threatened to choke her. After a few moments the blood stopped pounding in her head, and her muscles began to relax. As she lay back on her bed, regaining control of herself, she thought of how much she hated Geoffrey. The intensity of that feeling startled her.

So he had finally declared war. Well, she was ready for a full-scale assault. She had come to realize with terrible clarity that she had no rights and no power, except that which Geoffrey so "generously" allowed her. The substantial dowry that she had brought into the marriage had become his by law, as had she. She was a possession, a chattel. If she were to leave him, or if he could prove infidelity, he could throw her out onto the street, penniless, and deny her access to her son. She was a mere woman with no legal rights, even with regard to her son. She had to tread very carefully indeed.

A few minutes later she rose, and quickly dressed herself in one of her finest gowns. That was not only to give her courage, but to annoy Geoffrey by giving this dinner an exaggerated importance. All the while she strained to hear sounds from the nursery, and tried not think of Sandy's screams as she had left him. She would win in the long run, she was certain; somehow she would free Sandy -- and herself -- from Geoffrey's tyranny.

When she appeared in the drawing room half an hour later, she didn't miss Geoffrey's initial reaction of surprise. When he realized the implications, he frowned and said caustically, "There was no need to dress for a ball, Jillian. You'll look ridiculous."

"But you gave me to believe this was an important evening, Geoffrey. And I sincerely hope I shan't look ridiculous! This gown was ruinously expensive." She smiled at him. "Since you insisted upon going, don't you think we should leave? You know how my brother hates guests to be late."

As she sat beside him in the carriage for the short ride to Thistledown, she felt nervous. Never before had she been so uncomfortable in Geoffrey's presence -- as though he were a threatening stranger. She really knew very little about him, aside from what she could surmise from his behaviour. Never had he spoken to her on intimate terms, revealing anything about himself.

But she didn't want to know him, she realized. There was nothing in him that she admired. The man she had fallen in love with had been a sham. How often she had seen Geoffrey turn on that easy charm with attractive women. And whenever she saw them captivated by it, she saw herself and how foolish she must have looked to people like Keir, who had tried to warn her.

They arrived at Thistledown too quickly for Jillian. Already she was finding the evening an ordeal.

What a farce, she thought, as she entered the drawing room and greeted her brother with a perfunctory kiss, and likewise her sister-in-law. They all knew -- surely even Richard couldn't pretend blindness any longer -- of the illicit relationship. Yet how easily they all chose to ignore it, even deny its existence. How frightfully civilized they all were!

Well perhaps she would stir things up a little.

Rebecca, as usual, was stunning in a sapphire blue gown that was also a shade too formal for a family dinner in Launston Mills. Jillian said, "Richard, you really must take Rebecca to the city soon. She seems to be in desperate need of a new wardrobe. I see she's wearing one of her better gowns this evening, probably for lack of a more suitable one for such an insignificant dinner -- since there's no one to impress but us. Geoffrey was positively livid to see me in this thing, but since he rarely takes me to the city with him these days, there's little opportunity for me to wear it." She gave a little laugh, hoping it didn't sound as false to them as it did to her. "It'll be hopelessly outmoded before long, so why not wear it, I thought."

There was an embarrassed silence in the room. Geoffrey tried to ignore her, as though she didn't exist and hadn't spoken. Richard gave her one of those big-brother frowns that meant "Stop making a fool of yourself". Rebecca, surprisingly, blushed, although Jillian didn't think her sister-in-law would be mortified by anyone's behaviour, no matter how outrageous.

Rebecca sensed in Jillian a recklessness she was unfamiliar with, but which she instantly admired. She hadn't known Jillian in her youth. Since her marriage to Geoffrey, she had been rather subdued, almost meek. Until tonight. In her present mood, Jillian was capable of anything, Rebecca thought. And although Richard -- and presumably Jillian -- knew about her and Geoffrey, to actually have the relationship acknowledged in public would be too déclassé.

Not that she particularly cared about its demise. Geoffrey was beginning to bore her, and she had designs on more interesting prey. But there would be a scene, and that she could well do without. Family squabbles were really too revolting. Well, she would just have to distract Jillian. Or play along with her.

"You're absolutely right, Jilly," she said. "How clever of you to realize! Men are such insensitive creatures, are they not? And unobservant, don't you find? Isn't it fortunate we women are more astute?" Rebecca bestowed one of her brilliant smiles upon her sister-in-law, but there was a hint of female conspiracy about it.

Jillian saw through Rebecca's words, and suddenly realized that she didn't hate her. Perhaps they were both victims of loveless marriages. Rebecca couldn't have an easy life with Jillian's staid, unemotional brother, not when she herself was so much his opposite. And perhaps Rebecca didn't like Geoffrey much either. Perhaps Jillian was even grateful to Rebecca for showing her what sort of man Geoffrey was, and freeing her from his attentions.

Jillian didn't think that she would ever really like Rebecca, but she felt a curious bond with her, a tenuous link that might be broken in an instant, but that for a moment, at least, made them understand and sympathize with one another.

"It is indeed," Jillian replied, gaining confidence. "Although I fear it makes our husbands wary of us. They do not like to be bested by what they consider -- so mistakenly, of course -- to be our inferior intellects."

"I'm afraid Jillian has been badly misled by articles by those radical American women who claim to be fighting for women's rights," Geoffrey scoffed. Now that the conversation had resumed a general tone, he resumed his usual pompous demeanor. "The fact that you can believe those pithy arguments proposed by those females, just proves to me that women ***are*** possessed of inferior intellects."

"That fact that we put up with you men at all must prove that point, Geoffrey," Rebecca said lightly. He frowned, but before he could make a suitable rejoinder, she said, "Do let us go in to dinner."

When she had the opportunity at the dinner table, Jillian introduced another topic that she knew would annoy both her husband and her brother. "Have you spoken with Keir lately, Richard? I haven't seen him for so long, and I do miss his company. Why, we practically grew up together! Do you ever have him to dinner? I thought I'd stop in at his office one day to see how he's getting on."

Richard broke the momentary silence that greeted those words. "Keir and I were never close friends, Jillian. We have so little in common. And I'm sure you're not unaware of the attacks he has been making on us in his newspaper."

"By 'us' I presume you mean yourself and Geoffrey, and your running of the mills. His editorials seem perfectly justified to me, Richard." She gave him a hard, accusing stare. "Father would never have let things get out of hand. Not only was he much admired by the people, as you know, but he was also an astute -- and successful -- businessman."

"You would do well to keep silent about things you know nothing of," Geoffrey said coldly.

"I know more than you realize. I never went away to school as Richard did. I was educated at home, where Father was invariably conducting business, and trying out his ideas on Mother and me. I do know how Father ran the businesses, and even helped him to keep the books at times." Seeing the shocked expressions on both men's faces, Jillian said, "Father never underestimated the intelligence and resourcefulness of women."

Geoffrey regarded her curiously, as though the creature he had been carefully moulding these past five years had suddenly run amok. She smiled sweetly at him, although it was an effort to keep the smile from turning into a grimace.

Rebecca became infected with Jillian's devil-may-care attitude. Usually these evenings were incredibly tedious, but for once she wasn't bored. Perhaps she and Jillian were more alike than either realized. Like a good hostess lightening the conversation, she said, "Keir has built himself a rather charming place on Cambridge Street. Haven't you been to visit him there, Jillian?"

Jillian nearly burst into laughter at this unexpected support from Rebecca. "I thought I should leave my card, but that seemed much too formal for a childhood friend, so I've done nothing as yet, I regret to say." She could see Geoffrey's mounting anger, and rejoiced that she could get some reaction from him. She didn't expect jealousy -- or even want it -- but anything was better than indifference.

"It would hardly be prudent for you to do so," Geoffrey said.

"What? To visit my cousin?"

"An unfortunate relationship, and one that no one would expect you to honour."

"Oh, but I do, Geoffrey. My loyalty to friends is not such a paltry thing that it can be dispensed with at a whim -- or a command."

"You owe that man nothing, Jillian! He is doing his damnedest at the moment to disgrace your family's name in this town."

"I rather doubt that, Geoffrey. You and Richard seem to be accomplishing that all by yourselves."

Rebecca smothered a laugh in her napkin. Geoffrey, truly livid by now, said, "I fear you've been imbibing too much wine, Jillian...."

"Don't be so stuffy, Geoffrey," Rebecca said. "You know she's right."

Geoffrey regarded his mistress with surprise. What the bloody hell was the matter with the women tonight?

As if reading his thoughts, Richard said, "I fear our wives are overwhelming us with their wit tonight, Geoffrey. But since you and I do have serious business to discuss, perhaps we could ask them to withdraw now."

"Do you see the men's ploy when they are losing arguments?" Rebecca asked Jillian as they rose. "They think they can win merely by dismissing us." But when the two women were alone in the drawing room, the lighthearted comraderie they had shared suddenly vanished. Instead of revealing their innermost thoughts, they talked of safe, superficial things, in which neither was particularly interested, and which soon became a chore for them both. The silences became increasingly longer.

When she and Geoffrey drove home some time later, Jillian found it necessary to marshal her defences once more.

"I can't understand what got into you tonight, Jillian," he said as soon as they were seated in the carriage.

"I'm sure I don't know what you're talking about."

"You can play the stupid female admirably when it suits you, can't you?" She didn't dignify that remark with a reply, so he said, "Your behaviour was atrocious!"

She knew she had to remain calm and in control of herself. To lose her temper now would be to give him the upper hand. "Oh come now, Geoffrey. It's unlike you to exaggerate. That is not to say that I'm not ***capable*** of atrocious behaviour -- I seem to recall more than a few instances of it in my youth -- but since I've been married, I've been the soul of discretion. Don't you agree?"

Her flippancy aggravated his anger so much that he hardly knew what to say. How dare she mock him! But he was also worried. She was no longer the obedient, complacent, manageable wife he knew.

Well, he would squash this rebellion soon enough. He would not tolerate insubordination from his wife like that fool, Richard. There was only one master is his household. He would be only too glad to remind Jillian of that if ever she challenged him like this again.

Chapter 52

Megan Maguire settled quickly into life in Launston Mills. Although her teaching job didn't begin until September, she had chosen not to spend the summer sweltering in Toronto. She had found herself adequate lodgings at the Widow Flynn's, and was accepting all invitations from the Ryans, and Keir and Rowena, and so far there had been plenty to keep her entertained. She'd been in town only a week when she accompanied the others to the annual games between Ops and Emily townships. There were contests of skill and speed and strength for young and old alike, and the day was rounded out by a dance on the green. Megan was fascinated to discover that this enjoyable, friendly gathering had actually come into existence through a grudge match some twenty-six years earlier, at which Brendan Delaney had been the town's hero.

Helping to prepare for Mary Ryan's wedding kept Megan busy throughout July. She spent most of her days at the Ryans', designing and sewing the gowns with much-admired skill. Consequently, she was often in Tim's company, and it took him little time to become beguiled by her. Her inveterate cheerfulness buoyed the spirits of those about her. With her dry Irish wit and guileless observations she made them all laugh. Even his mother was a happier person in Megan's company, and without Moira's incessant complaints and criticisms ringing in their ears, the Ryan family itself was more lighthearted. It was as though Megan had cast a spell upon them all.

Megan was unaware of the effect she had on others. Being herself obsessed with Keir, she didn't notice that Tim was falling in love with her.

Moira said to him one evening after Megan had gone home, "Why don't you court her, Tim? She's not Keir's property. There's no reason why he should have everything."

"She has eyes for no one but him, Ma, and well you know it," Tim said dismissively. It was an automatic reaction to deny whatever his mother suggested. But the more he thought about it, the more he realized how right Moira was. There was no reason why he should step aside and wait for Keir to come to his senses.

But Tim's attempts to win Megan's affections proved as futile as he had initially feared. Nothing he did seemed to change her attitude toward him. Tim, ever an impatient man, finally came right out and asked her to marry him, the day of the Regatta.

Megan, the Ryans, Keir, and Rowena all took the steamer to Sturgeon Point that perfect August day. The steamy days of summer were over; the sky was a crisp, clean blue; there was a nip of fall in the air. But it was pleasantly warm while the sun shone. Under the cloudless sky, the lake stretched before them to distant shores, a deep, shimmering, sapphire blue.

They had brought a substantial picnic with them, and ate it while they watched the canoe and sailboat races. Keir admired the steam yachts that were docked there. The Launstons had the biggest one, of course. It gleamed with mahogany and brass. But there were many other respectable launches, and Keir said that he hoped to acquire one some day. Boating was becoming popular, and a few wealthy people had already built summer houses on the lake.

Tim said all he could ever manage was a canoe, and asked Megan if she would care to go for a paddle in one, since there were some for hire.

She didn't really want to leave Keir's side, but was reluctant to refuse such an enjoyable adventure. She had always wanted to try canoeing, and didn't for a moment suspect that Tim had an ulterior motive

He showed her how to hold and maneuver the paddles, and once they were securely aboard -- not without a near mishap -- he reassured her that they would stay close to shore.

"I'm glad to hear that, because I can't swim," she said, becoming slightly apprehensive now that she was so close to the water.

"Don't worry. I wouldn't let anything happen to you," Tim replied.

Her paddling was awkward and ineffective at first -- though it caused them both some merriment -- but she soon had the technique. It was an exhilarating feeling, skimming so easily and silently through the water. They rounded the point, toward Fenelon Falls, and were out of sight and hearing of the crowd. Here there was only the gentle wind, the rustling trees, the dip of their paddles. It was tranquil and beautiful, and Megan wished only that Keir were here to share it with her.

From behind her, Tim said, "Let's pull over here for a moment," and steered them toward shore.

"Let's not stop yet," Megan said. "I'm having a wonderful time!"

"Are you?"

"Of course I am."

Tim grabbed onto an overhanging branch of a tree, and said. "Hold onto this and carefully turn around. There's something I want to say to you."

Megan clung to the branch and stood up. The canoe wobbled dangerously beneath her, and she was glad that it was shallow here. "This had better be important," she teased.

"It is. Will you marry me?"

She had not yet sat down, and almost toppled into the water in surprise. Tim jumped up to steady her, but his abrupt movement started the canoe rocking violently. Megan clung to the branch, but Tim missed it and splashed headlong into the water.

Megan was so helpless with laughter that she could hardly hold on. It was all too ridiculous. When the canoe finally stopped rocking, she sat down and looked at Tim who stood beside her in the waist-deep water, dripping wet. He wasn't laughing. "I meant it," he told her, somewhat piqued by her mirth. He bent over and gave her a swift, hard kiss on the mouth.

That stopped her laughter. "Don't, Tim. Don't spoil everything."

"Spoil what? For God's sake, Megan, I'm asking you to marry me. I'm trying to tell you that I love you."

"I wish you wouldn't. I can't return your love, Tim. I'm sorry. Truly."

"Keir's not the only man in this world. If you gave me a chance...."

"He's the only man for me. Now stop it, Tim. I don't want to hurt you. I like you as a friend. You remind me of my brother Sean."

"And what if Keir doesn't want you?" He couldn't help showing his bitterness, though he instantly regretted the harshness of his words.

Megan shrugged, and said, "I have a career that I've worked very hard for. When I marry, I'll have to give it up, because you know that married women are not allowed to continue teaching. It's not something I'll give up lightly."

"And is there nothing I can say to make you change your mind?"

She shook her head. "Just be my friend."

Tim ran his fingers through his wet hair in a gesture of frustration. "If it's either that or nothing, I reckon you've a friend for life. But I'm warning you now, Megan Maguire, that you haven't heard the last of this."

• • •

Once or twice a week Megan would meet Keir at his office, and walk to The Brambles with him where she would stay to supper. The *LAUNSTON MILLS OBSERVER* had moved into its new premises in the Shaughnessy Block. The weekly newspaper had a staff of four -- a master printer, a compositor, and two apprentices -- with Keir as publisher, writer, and editor. As well as the newspaper, posters and leaflets for various organizations were printed, and the contract to publish the town's directory had been secured. Books were sold here as well.

Keir was just about to close the shop one such evening in late August when Rebecca walked in.

He wasn't really surprised. Their "accidental" encounters had been like foreplay. And although he had anticipated a confrontation, he hadn't prepared himself for it. His first thought was that Megan was due to arrive at any moment, and he did not want her to witness any embarrassing scenes.

"Mrs. Launston. What can I do for you?"

"What an irresistible question! How shall I answer that?" When he didn't respond to her quip, she said, "You seem preoccupied, Mr. Shaughnessy."

"I have an engagement. Is it a book you want?"

"Let's stop this ridiculous charade, Keir! You know damn well why I'm here. Do you want me to abase myself completely by spelling it out?"

"There was a time when I would gladly have seen you as humiliated as you left me. But I no longer care, Rebecca. Do you understand that?"

She didn't let him see her disappointment. In her fantasies she had already made love to him in a dozen different places -- those secret, special places by the lake, where she sought privacy. She had never taken Geoffrey there. Or Richard. "One doesn't have to be in love to enjoy one another's company. You can't deny that you find me attractive still." She placed her hand upon his arm, and ran her fingers lightly up his sleeve to his shoulder. "We had wonderful times, Keir. Remember? I didn't want it to end as it did. But you expected too much from me. And perhaps I did make a mistake in marrying Richard. He's not half the man you are."

Her fingers had travelled up to his face, and she had moved so close to him that their bodies lightly touched. Her voice was mesmerizing, her eyes languid. He smelled her familiar perfume that brought back images of those heady times.

Keir took her hand away from his face. "It's no good, Rebecca. You ***are*** a beautiful and desirable woman, but you're also my cousin's wife."

She moved away from him angrily. "Richard doesn't care about me, except as a possession. If I were made of porcelain he would like me better, but I serve the same purpose."

"It may not matter to you that you are his wife, but it does to me."

"Ah, ever the man of conscience." She gave a wry chuckle. "I've never been rebuffed before. It's a novel experience, but not one I expect to repeat. Goodbye, Keir."

Rebecca nearly collided with Megan, who had watched part of the encounter through the glass door. Fascinated and appalled, she had stood rooted to the spot, with barely enough sense to move out of the way when Rebecca swept through the door.

The two women eyed one another assessingly for a brief moment, and then Rebecca mounted her horse and galloped away. She needed to get to the lake to pull herself together, to plan new stratagems to alleviate the tedium of her useless, empty existence. Although she was bitterly disappointed in Keir, she was never one to waste time on regrets.

Megan, too, was bitterly disappointed. Of course she recognized Rebecca Launston as the beauty Keir had been with at the Exhibition all those years ago, and Molly had told her of Keir's affair. Keir saw her standing outside the door; so she went in, although she hardly knew what to say.

Keir said, "I suppose you couldn't avoid seeing that little scene just now. It was extremely indiscreet of Rebecca. But I'd appreciate it if you mentioned it to no one."

"Of course.... Are you still in love with her?" She hadn't meant to ask, but she felt suddenly insecure and desperate. Her dreams and plans had been shattered. How utterly naive she had been to think only of her own needs and desires, and ignore Keir's.

The query quivered in the air between them. Megan thought he would admonish her for her impertinence, but he said, "The woman I loved never really existed, except in my own romantic imaginings. That won't happen a second time."

The words should have reassured her, but they didn't. They seemed to be warning her against making a similar mistake.

Was he telling her that he couldn't live up to the image she had of him?

Keir wasn't free of Rebecca's influence, Megan thought. She had made him wary of love, and that distrust was a more formidable foe than Rebecca herself.

Chapter 53

"I can't agree to help," Keir said to Megan. They were sitting in the parlour at The Brambles. Rowena had gone up to bed early, as she often did when Megan came to dinner. Megan was grateful for the opportunity to be alone with Keir, but it seemed to make no difference to their relationship.

"If the workers are unionized," Keir continued, "there's bound to be trouble before long. They'd agitate for higher wages and shorter hours. There would be strikes and lockouts which would undoubtedly lead to violence."

"But you agree with what they want -- a nine hour day, improved working conditions, restrictions on child labour, and disability compensation for those maimed on the job."

"Indeed I do. I've expounded on those topics often enough."

"Then why won't you support Tim and the others who are trying to organize the Benevolent Society for those purposes?"

"Because I believe that changes must be made by the management, not forced upon them by the workers through a type of blackmail. That would only lead to serious confrontations that would benefit no one."

"And you think the mill and factory owners will do this willingly?"

"Most are not unreasonable men. If they're made to see the wisdom of these measures, they'll eventually institute them."

"Is it reasonable for Richard Launston to cut back on the overtime pay that his father had granted the workers? Is it reasonable of him to fire experienced men and hire instead, young boys at a meager wage? Your cousin has threatened to dismiss any man who so much as mentions the word 'union'. Even so, nearly eighty percent of the millworkers have secretly pledged to join, and they've agreed to walk off the job if anyone is fired for this reason."

"And how many of them will actually do so when the time comes? After a few whiskeys they're all ready to throw down the gauntlet."

"What choice have they? If they don't fight for changes, they'll never get them."

Megan's passionate defence of the union bothered Keir more than he cared to admit. "You've been well tutored by Tim. Did he send you here to plead his case?"

His arrogance angered her. "Tim doesn't want your help. I happen to believe in this cause, and I have faith in Tim! It's easy for you to write idealistic editorials that offend no one and accomplish nothing. You write of reforms, yet you won't support an organization that could effect these, because you don't want to antagonize your Launston cousin. You can't be on both sides this time, Keir. You have to make a choice." Megan stopped, fearing she had said too much. "I'd best go."

Megan couldn't look at him as she prepared to leave. She'd spoiled everything, she was sure. They'd had a precarious friendship, but it had been better than nothing at all. Or had it? She no longer knew. Perhaps she should opt for Tim. Keir obviously did not care about her. And, if truth be told, he was not the paragon that she had fallen in love with. There were aspects of his character that she would have changed -- his damned, know-it-all arrogance for one!

"I'll walk you home."

"No... I'd rather be alone."

"Megan, I don't think you should become involved in this. If there is trouble...."

"I can take care of myself. You may not have noticed, but I'm no longer a child!"

Keir returned to the parlour after Megan had left, pondering her accusation. She was mistaken in thinking his reluctance to support the union had anything to do with Richard. In fact, Keir held Richard responsible for the current unrest at the mills.

If Jeremy were alive, he would have this situation under control. He would, as he had before, summon the spokesmen to his office, overwhelm them with rhetoric and a few promises, and the men would return to their jobs well satisfied. But Richard was answering the workers with threats rather than conciliation. He would see the mills closed -- thereby losing vast profits -- before he would buckle to any of their demands.

Keir was right. Two days later, Tim and eight other men were fired for 'seditious conspiracy', and blacklisted. If this gesture was an attempt to intimidate the other employees, it failed. The majority of them, true to their word, walked off the job. Those who refused to do so were treated to rough persuasions by their comrades, and a few were bodily carried from the sawmills.

Keir rushed over to the mills as soon as he heard the news. A crowd of several hundred was already gathered outside. There was obvious dissension among the people. Wives berated husbands for bringing 'ruination' upon their families. Scuffles broke out when some men attempted to return to the mills.

A hush fell over the people as they watched nervous clerks scurry out of the offices, and nail posters along the wooden fence. The gate was shut; there was an ominous silence as the rumble of the turbines and steam engines ceased. The last plume of smoke belched out of the stacks, and dissipated in the chill October air.

Then there was pandemonium as men hastened to read the posters which confirmed their fears.

The mills would be closed until further notice. Any man wishing to return to work should go to the offices of Crowley and McMillan, Solicitors, where he would be required to sign a contract to that effect. There would be a probationary period of six months, during which he would be docked ten percent of his present salary for the inconvenience he had caused his employer. The employees would be given two days to accept these terms -- there would be no negotiations -- and then the management would begin hiring workers from outside the town.

Richard had been well prepared for this contingency. These proclamations had been printed days ago.

Tim and his eight compatriots climbed aboard a dogcart. Tim called for silence. It was granted grudgingly. The crowd was in an ugly mood.

"Friends, I know what you're feeling now...."

"***You*** ain't got a wife and children to feed!" Someone yelled.

"We're either gonna starve, or we'll be worse off than afore, iffen we go back to work!" another added.

Tim waited for the shouts of agreement and the curses to subside. "We'll never get anywhere if we don't stick together now! Don't you see that's what Launston's hoping for? Solidarity is our only strength, our only hope! We have two choices. Either we go back to work under Launston's terms, or we stand firm together -- every man of us -- and wait for him to accept ***our*** terms! He can't run the mills without us, and if he tries to bring in scabs then we'll send them back with a few pains for their trouble!"

"We'll starve before Launston does!" one of the women shouted.

"No one will starve. We'll help each other. I'm not saying it'll be easy, but it'll be worth it in the end. We ***will*** win if we stick together! And we need to show Launston that we mean business. Those of you who haven't signed up for membership in the Sawyers' and Millworkers' Benevolent Society, do it now, before you go home. We'll take this list to Launston tomorrow, and tell him that we'll return to work as a fully organized union of men, without a cut in pay, and with the same benefits as we had when his father was in charge. That'll be a start, and we'll not settle for less!"

Keir glanced at the cheering crowd in the gathering darkness. Among the grumbling objectors were faces he didn't recognize. Hard, tough men. He didn't know everyone in town, but these shady characters aroused his suspicions. One way to ensure strife was to introduce a few vociferous and pugnacious rabble-rousers among the workers. Keir had no doubt that this was what Richard -- or Geoffrey -- had done.

Keir could see further implications in the hiring of roughnecks. If there were any damage done to the mill property, Richard could have the leaders of this disturbance arrested. Without them the men would become disorganized, and their resistance would fizzle out.

As Keir made his way toward Tim, he noticed Megan standing with Conn and Fergus. The sight of her in this potentially dangerous situation angered him.

"You shouldn't be here, Megan," he said when he reached her side. "Go home."

"I'll go when I please!"

He grabbed her by the arm, and pulled her along. "Come and listen to what I have to tell Tim. That might put some sense into that stubborn little skull of yours!"

Her own pique vanished when she listened to Keir's suspicions.

"I'd advise you to keep men on guard throughout the night, " Keir concluded, "and for God's sake don't let any of your men become incited to destruction."

"I thought you were against us," Tim said.

"I don't approve of your methods, but I approve even less of Richard's. For what it's worth..." He looked wryly at Megan. "... you have my support."

Tim didn't like feeling grateful to Keir. Keir was everything he himself wanted to be -- handsome, educated, to some degree both rich and powerful, and the possessor of Megan's heart. And while Tim had a grudging admiration for his cousin, he wanted to hate him. Instead he held out his hand. Keir took it.

"Perhaps you can talk this recalcitrant young woman into going home," Keir said to his cousin. "I'm sure you have the powers of persuasion that I seem to lack."

"I'll walk Meg home myself, soon as I get some men organized. If you're right about those thugs then I don't want her to be on the streets alone."

"They're not here to molest women. But suit yourself."

Megan watched Keir walk away without another glance at her.

"Settle for second best?" Tim asked.

Tim wouldn't listen to her protests that she could safely make her way home.

"They'll not miss me for the ten minutes it'll take to put my mind at ease," he said as he marched her away.

There was only a sliver of moon tonight to light the way. They took the shorter route to Megan's lodgings on Peel Street by going along the riverbank near the alleyway that serviced the commercial blocks on Main Street.

"I'll not rest easy, knowing the danger you'll be in tonight," Megan said.

"I didn't think you cared."

She couldn't see his grin in the darkness, but she sensed it. "You're being daft, Tim Ryan, and you know it yourself! You're a dear friend, and I'd not like to see you hurt."

"'A dear friend'. Nothing more?" He wasn't smiling now. "Haven't you given up on Keir yet? Would it be foolish to ask you again if you'd marry me?"

"Oh, Tim, I...."

Suddenly she was grabbed from behind. Her startled scream was stifled by a large paw that clamped tightly over her mouth as she was dragged backwards. "Keep still and you'll not be hurt," a gruff voice whispered in her ear.

Terror and revulsion seized Megan when she realized what was happening. She could barely discern the struggling forms, but she heard the sickening thuds and cracks, and Tim's cries of pain as three other brutes set upon him.

Holy Mother of God, they were killing him!

Her captor gripped her tighter as she squirmed in his arms. Megan fastened her teeth viciously onto the filthy palm over her mouth, at the same time stomping the heel of one boot onto his foot. The man loosened his hold in that moment of pained surprise, and she tore away from him with an ear-shattering scream that she hoped would rouse the town.

She ran, but she hadn't expected to get far. She crashed to the ground, crushed under the weight of the ruffian who had tackled her.

"You'll pay for that, bitch!"

She knew what he intended to do, but she couldn't move. Her face was pressed into the dirt. She could taste the grit of it on her lips, and blood -- she didn't know if it was his or her own. She couldn't even scream, for her very breath was being squeezed from her lungs.

There was silence behind them, and then one of the others called, "Let's go. We're finished here."

"I ain't finished with her yet. The bitch nearly bit clean through me hand!"

"Someone's coming! Let's get the hell outa here!"

Megan could breathe again as his weight lifted from her, but only for a moment. He kicked her savagely in the ribs.

They were gone as quickly and as stealthily as they had appeared.

Megan could see the blur of approaching lights as she struggled to her knees. Her breath came in painful gasps. She clutched at her side, and gagged on the bile in her throat.

She heard the running footsteps, and then felt an arm encircle her shoulders. She recognized Keir's voice saying her name.

He held her as she retched. She leaned against him, and let the tears come.

Then she became aware of the others about them, of their shocked exclamations and subdued talk. She saw the half-dozen men by the light of the torches they carried. Conn and Fergus were among them, bent over Tim, their faces pale and frightened.

"Holy Mother of God, is he dead?" she asked, trying to stand up.

Keir gently restrained her. "Don't look."

"He's not dead," Fergus said, but his tone did little to reassure her.

A cart, which someone had been sent to fetch, trundled up the alley.

"You'd better not move him until Dr. Worthing arrives," Keir advised. "I'll return as soon as I've taken Megan to my house."

Keir helped Megan to her feet. He couldn't prevent her from looking at Tim. Someone had placed a jacket over him, but she could still see the mangled body that lay there. His face was covered in blood; it was swollen beyond recognition. His legs were crumpled into unnatural, grotesque positions.

She stared, horror-struck.

Keir caught her when she fainted. He climbed onto the cart, and ordered the driver to make haste. Keir himself was still numbed by the brutality of the attack upon his cousin. He had not suspected even Richard capable of such an atrocity.

Keir's outrage intensified when he wondered what they had done to Megan. Her clothes were torn, her face was bloodied.... It didn't bear conjecture. She would tell him soon enough.

Keir had heard her scream, as had those around him. She and Tim had been less than two blocks away. That blood-curdling cry had wrenched at his innards. He had never felt such dread, such desperation, as he had in those few minutes it had taken to find her.

He gazed down at the girl cradled in his arms. Was it love, this gentle, yet intense affection he felt for her?

When they arrived at The Brambles, Keir sent the driver back with the cart. Briefly he related the events to Rowena as he carried Megan to one of the spare rooms. Leaving Rowena to look after the girl, he saddled his horse and returned to the others.

Simon Worthing had arrived, and was setting Tim's legs in splints. The Chief Constable was at the scene as well. "It's monstrous," he said. "We'll find the men responsible for this!"

Keir said, "I think the assailants are long gone, and unlikely to return to Launston Mills. And I'm certain you'll find it nearly impossible to pin this on the man who's really responsible."

"You're talking in riddles, Keir. What do you know about this?"

"Nothing that would stand up in court."

Chief Duncan grunted. "Well, I'll have to question the young lady. Maybe she can identify them."

"I doubt it, Chief. Those men weren't locals," Keir said.

The men carefully placed the unconscious victim onto the cart. Conn clambered in, and sat protectively next to his son. Keir had never seen him look so grim. "Someone'll pay for this," Conn swore, almost inaudibly.

Keir tied his horse behind Simon Worthing's rig, and rode with the doctor.

"I heard what you said to Duncan," Simon said. "But just what were you implying?"

"Tell me about Tim first. Will he recover?"

"Probably, yes, as long as we can stop infection from setting in. It looks worse than it is. He has fractured limbs, and contusions and lacerations about the face. He'll be in pain, and certainly immobilized for some time, but I don't think there's any internal or permanent damage. They're not the kind of indiscriminate injuries one finds in most beatings."

"What are you saying?"

"I'm not really sure. It appears to have been a... calculated attack. The assailants knew what they were doing. They inflicted painful and messy injuries, but nothing serious enough to kill." Simon glanced at Keir. "Tell me your suspicions."

Simon was silent for a long time after Keir had finished. "I can't believe Richard capable of such barbarity. I've known the boy all his life. It's incredible!"

"Richard didn't do it. I'm sure he didn't hire those thugs, or even know anything about them. He may simply have told Geoffrey Kayne to 'deal' with the union spokesman, and left him with the details. Richard's responsible for this nonetheless." They had reached the Ryans'. "Will you go to The Brambles and examine Megan when you're finished here?"

"Of course. Are you going back there now?"

"As soon as I've seen my aunt I shall pay Richard a visit."

"Keir, don't do anything rash."

"I must try to make Richard aware of what he's done. At least I can prick his conscience -- if he has one."

Surprisingly, it was Moira who took command in the Ryan household. Conn seemed devastated. He poured himself a tumblerful of whiskey, and sat down at the kitchen table, his head in his hands.

But Conn wasn't in the kitchen when Keir returned after helping Simon restrain the patient while he set the bones. "Where's your father?" Keir asked Deedee.

"He went out," she sobbed. "I heard the door shut a while back."

A terrible thought crossed Keir's mind. "Where's his gun?"

"He keeps it over...." She gasped. "It's gone! What's he going to do, Keir? Holy Mary, Mother of God, what's happening?"

"I'll bring him back, don't worry. And don't say anything to anyone!"

Keir knew where Conn had gone. He prayed he would be in time to stop him.

The gate to the grounds of Thistledown stood open. Keir galloped up the drive, apprehension tingling up his spine.

He saw a lonely figure silhouetted against the light that spilled from the windows. Conn's head was bent; he held the old flintlock carelessly in one hand. He was walking away from the house.

Keir dismounted, and approached his uncle with trepidation.

"I couldn't do it," Conn said, weeping. "I couldn't kill the God damned son-of-a-bitch, not even for what he did to me son! I'm a coward. Always have been."

"No, Uncle Conn. You're a wise man, not a cowardly one. Come, I'll take you home."

"Nay, lad. I'll go alone. I'll not do anything foolish, never fear." He patted Keir's arm and trudged away.

Keir strode up the steps and pounded on the front door. He pushed his way into the hall when the butler answered. "Where's Richard?"

"Just a minute, Mr. Shaughnessy! You can't just barge in here like this!"

"It's urgent! Where is he?"

"I shall see if Mr. Launston is in. If you'll kindly wait here?"

But Keir followed the servant to the study, pushed past the man, and burst into the room.

Clarence Gifford, the editor of the *LAUNSTON MILLS EXPOSITOR*, was in conference with Richard. He was startled and flustered by the intrusion -- guiltily so, Keir thought. But not Richard. Calmly he said, "I think we've covered everything, Mr. Gifford. I'll bid you goodnight now. It would seem that Mr. Shaughnessy is anxious for an interview as well."

When the door had closed behind Clarence Gifford, Richard said, "It's been a long time since we've had the pleasure of your company in this house. Brandy?"

"This isn't a social visit."

Richard decanted a glass for himself. "I didn't imagine it was at this late hour. I was about to retire. Well?" He seated himself in the leather armchair behind the desk, and confidently challenged Keir with a look.

"What you did today was spiteful and self-defeating. You should have paid more attention to your father's methods, and absorbed his business acumen rather than Geoffrey's. But what you did tonight was despicable, villainous."

"I don't know what you're talking about."

"So, you don't know what crimes are being committed in your name? Perhaps you should ask Geoffrey, or one of your other henchmen."

A slight frown creased Richard's brow. "Explain yourself."

Keir did, sparing Richard none of the gory details. "I see that even you blanch at such cruelty."

"You can't seriously believe that I had anything to do with this?"

"I may never be able to prove you culpable in this, but I can damn well impeach you in the eyes of this town."

"If you print any of this, I'll sue you for libel. And I'll win."

"I wouldn't give you the satisfaction of that. You can rely upon my subtlety."

Richard's normal sangfroid deserted him. "Let's not be so hasty, Keir. I assure you, I am innocent in this matter. You intend to act as judge and jury, and to crucify me without a fair trial. That's hardly sporting of you."

"Was it sporting to break a man's legs?"

"Broken bones will heal. A damaged reputation will not. Is what you intend to do to me any less despicable? If I find that one of my men is responsible, I'll see that he answers for it. Will that satisfy you?"

"No. You should have considered the consequences before giving that man carte blanche instructions to do your dirty work." Keir walked to the door. He stopped and said, "Don't try any of your underhanded tricks on me, Richard. You'll not get off so lightly a second time."

The cousins glared at one another. Keir turned and walked out.

Simon Worthing was just leaving The Brambles when Keir arrived. "How's Megan?"

"Still in shock. She's bruised and has two broken ribs. I've given her a sedative, and I've sent Chief Duncan away. He can question her tomorrow."

"She wasn't...."

"Raped? No. But from what she tells me, she might have been if you and the others hadn't arrived at the scene so quickly."

Keir looked in on Megan, but she was already asleep. Rowena had tea ready for him in the parlour, but he declined it and poured himself a brandy.

The troubled look on her son's face prompted Rowena to say, "You look weary. Why not go to bed?"

"I have work to do yet. There'll be a special edition of the *OBSERVER* out tomorrow. I rather suspect that the *EXPOSITOR* is planning something similar, and I intend to anticipate Clarence Gifford's lies."

Keir went to his study. He lit the kerosene lamps, sat down at his desk, and drew a sheaf of papers before him. He stared at the unsoiled, inviting surface, thinking of what Megan had once said -- that his writing had no real influence. How wrong she was. His scratchings would do more than mutilate the pristine whiteness of the paper before him.

He dipped his pen into the inkwell, and began to write.

The words gushed out like the waters of a burst dam, carrying with them all the flotsam of emotion that had stirred him. When Keir finally laid down his pen five hours later, he felt less than pleased with himself.

Richard had been right. Keir was not proud of being his executioner. But what choice had he? Justice could not be served by the law alone in this case, for there would be no evidence to implicate Richard. If Keir did not expose him, then Richard would go unpunished.

What vagaries of Fate had cast him in this damnable role?

Keir flexed his cramped fingers, and leaned back in his chair, glancing out the window. It was dawn. He wondered if Richard had spent a peaceful night in slumber.

Keir climbed the tower, and watched the sunrise from the upper balcony.

"How serene the town seems in the sunlight," Megan said from behind him. She was wrapped in a blanket. A large bruise on one cheek was starkly outlined against her pale face.

"You should be in bed, Megan."

"You look as though you've not been to bed at all."

"I spent the night writing that article you've been pestering me about, supporting the union and condemning Richard. That should please you."

"But not you?"

"I was keen enough at the outset. But now... I pity Richard. He too is a victim, as much by his own hand as any other, perhaps. Who can pinpoint all that makes a man what he is, or what influences him to act as he does? But I know what power the written word has. Once I've finished with him...."

"You won't destroy him, Keir. You may besmirch his image a bit -- maybe he'll never be elected mayor of this town, but that would be all to the good. I'm sure you're doing the right thing."

"I wish I were as certain." Looking at Megan, he thought how comforting she was to be with. And how beautiful she was. Not classically beautiful, like Rebecca, but with a spiritual beauty that illuminated her pert features.

She, mesmerized by his intense stare, and anticipating a kiss as he moved closer to her and put his hands upon her shoulders, felt a tremor of excitement.

"You're shivering!" Keir said, breaking the spell. "How thoughtless of me to keep you standing here!"

He wouldn't listen to her protests as he ushered her back downstairs. She was disappointed when he left her, his manner once more that of an older brother. For a moment, on the balcony, she had thought that her soul had finally touched his. And he had drawn back as if burned.

Keir gulped down some breakfast, and hurried to his office. He didn't come for dinner, and when he arrived home in the evening he was exhausted. And angry.

"It was all for nothing," he told Megan and Rowena. "Richard has won. After what happened to Tim last night, the other organizers got scared. The article in the *EXPOSITOR* has convinced the men to return to their jobs, and now there's no one to dissuade them."

Keir sank onto a chair. "Listen to this." He opened a copy of the *EXPOSITOR* and read:

> *... Mr. Launston, ever a generous man, has decided not to punish those men who walked off the job yesterday, despite the losses in production that this irresponsible act has caused him. Every man who, by midnight tonight, agrees to return to work will be fully reinstated at his former wage. Such magnanimity is laudable.*

"They swallowed that, the poor sods. You should see them all lined up outside Richard's solicitors' office. They act like condemned men who've been given a reprieve. Most have forgotten why they walked off the job in the first place."

Keir read on:

> *It has just come to our attention that a heinous deed was committed last night. Timothy Ryan, the union spokesman and one of those responsible for inciting yesterday's walkout and the subsequent riot outside the mill, was severely beaten. Chief Constable Duncan has*

discovered no clues as to the identity of the attackers. We know that there are many good and honest men, not carried away by Ryan's socialist rhetoric, who were nonetheless physically forced by his supporters to leave their jobs. We know that their appeals to reason were met with violence from Ryan's mob. We can therefore surmise that one or two of these souls, with misguided heroics, took it upon themselves to put a stop to Ryan's insidious influence. We cannot condone the actions of these few well-meaning men, but we can understand that they, fighting for their livelihood, for their families' very existence, might in desperation resort to the same tactics that had been used on them earlier.

"Surely no one can believe those lies!" Megan said indignantly.

"People are confused. Some do believe it. Some would rather believe that than the alternative I've implied. God knows if my article achieved anything."

Rowena said, "If you hadn't told Richard you were going to write it, I doubt if he would have been so 'generous' to his employees. Weren't they to get a ten percent cut in wages originally?"

"Yes."

"You'll get no thanks for it, but you've done the millworkers a good turn then," Rowena said. She was saddened to think of how things had turned out -- the two cousins pitted against each other. Jeremy would be livid with them both -- with Richard, for his lack of business sense, and with Keir, his lack of family loyalty. But if Jeremy were here, none of this would even have happened.

"And there'll be more subtle repercussions," Megan said. "Perhaps Richard will get rid of Geoffrey, and reinstate some of his father's methods."

Richard might be morally responsible, Keir thought, but Geoffrey had been the actual villain. Keir had always thought that a ruthless and vicious soul lurked beneath Geoffrey's cultured veneer. Until that moment, he had never really considered what Jillian's life must be like under the rule of that son-of-a-bitch. It was not a pleasant thought.

Chapter 54

It was All Hallows Eve, a little more than a week after the aborted strike at the mills. Gavin O'Shaughnessy was hurrying along the woodland path through the early twilight. It wasn't that he was afraid of the spirits that were said to walk the earth on this day, just that he was in a hurry to return to his lodgings to dress for the Halloween dance. He'd been out to the Moore farm, where the widow was only too glad of male company. And he always made sure he was well paid for his pains -- if she'd ever noticed a few coins missing after his visits, she'd never mentioned it.

He took a few more than usual today, for he needed something to tide him over until his new job started. He snorted. That son-of-a-bitch, Geoffrey Kayne, had refused to keep any of Tim Ryan's kin in his employ when he'd heard that the Ryans were starting up their own sawmill. That had been Keir's idea, and his money was going to finance it.

Gavin thought it daft to try competing with the Launstons, but Keir had suggested they concentrate on the local market, and Conn was particularly enthusiastic about the idea. He, Fergus, and their sons were experienced millworkers, and they were well-liked in town.

Which was all very well for them, Gavin thought, but he'd never cared to be thought of as a member of that family -- or any family. He was a man unto himself, a man without ties, chains, or a yoke. And he resented being lumped in with them. When the foreman had told him he was fired, Gavin had stormed into Geoffrey Kayne's office and confronted him about it.

"You fuckin' son-of-a-bitch!" Gavin had shouted at Geoffrey when the man had explained. "What have they got to do with me?"

"They are your family," Geoffrey had replied calmly. "One usually feels a certain loyalty to one's family."

"You're full of shit! Do you think they give one fuckin' damn about me? You think I'm gonna sabotage the mill, or somethin'? For them? Christ, they can go to hell for all I care. And so can you, you fuckin' bastard!"

And before he had sauntered out of Geoffrey's office, he had said, in a menacing voice, "Maybe we'll meet again, ***Mr.*** Kayne, on some dark street, some time when you least expect to see me."

"Are you threatening me?" Geoffrey had demanded.

Gavin had just laughed, and walked out. Of course it had been an idle threat, just to worry that bastard a bit. And by the look on Geoffrey's face, Gavin was certain he'd put the wind up him.

A sudden noise wiped the grin from Gavin's face. He had never been fanciful, but night was closing in, and an atavistic fear crept up his spine. The naked branches swayed and creaked in the wind; against the twilight glow on the horizon, they looked liked bony fingers clawing at the wintry sky. The wind itself moaned like a lost soul.

Gavin stopped to listen, hearing at first only his own thumping heartbeat. Then he heard it again. The snort of a horse.

As he cautiously moved toward the sound, he could hear muffled voices. And then he saw them. Geoffrey Kayne and Rebecca Launston. She was just mounting her horse, but Gavin could guess what this secretive encounter must mean. A moment later, Rebecca rode off.

"Well, well," Gavin said, startling Geoffrey. As the man was recovering his composure, Gavin moved to stand between Geoffrey and his horse. "Been screwing the boss's wife, eh?"

"You're an offensive brute, O'Shaughnessy. You don't know what you're talking about." He didn't know what Gavin had overheard, but there had been little for him to see. It had been too damned cold for them to do more than make plans.

"I wonder if Launston will think that when I tell him."

Remembering their last encounter, Geoffrey was apprehensive, being alone with that ruffian in these lonely woods, miles from town. Almost with relief he said, "Blackmail, is it?"

"Call it what you like."

Disdainfully, Geoffrey threw a bank note onto the ground in front of Gavin. "There's a dollar."

Gavin laughed. "I can be bought, but not that cheap."

"It's all I have." Geoffrey countered coolly, trying not to let Gavin see his fear.

"Best you check again. Or would you like me to do it for you?" Gavin stepped closer to him, and fingered the lapels of Geoffrey's jacket. "Don't know what your wife would say to the state of this fine coat when you got home. And how would you explain the bruises?"

Geoffrey pushed Gavin's hand away, and pulled out two five dollar bills. "That's all you'll get from me, you little bastard. Don't come near me again, or I'll deal with you the way I dealt with your cousin."

"That can work both ways, ***Mr***. Kayne. Best not forget that."

Geoffrey hurriedly mounted his horse, and galloped off toward town.

Gavin chuckled as he pocketed the money. Sure, this must be his lucky day! Even the three mile walk back to town no longer seemed so forbidding.

Geoffrey was fuming. Angry with himself for having allowed that scum to intimidate him, he was planning what to do with the bastard if ever Gavin should threaten him again. Perhaps it was a good idea of Richard's, sending Geoffrey to England for the winter to conduct some business for him there. Geoffrey had begun to feel uncomfortable, not only at the mills, but also around town. There was more than one disgruntled employee who would be only too happy to stick a knife in his back. A few months away from here, and things would settle down. People would forget.

If only he could take Rebecca with him! Then he wouldn't care if he ever returned to this place. But she had only laughed at his suggestion that she journey to England to visit her family. He knew that her interest in him had cooled while his own passion burned hotter than ever.

So when Geoffrey arrived home he was in a foul temper. When he couldn't find a servant to stable his horse or take his coat, he became livid. He burst into the parlour, where Jillian was playing with Sandy, and demanded, "Where the hell is everyone?"

Jillian said, "I allowed the staff to go to the Halloween dance. There's a cold dinner laid out for you in the dining room. I've already eaten."

"How dare you dismiss the servants while I still require their services!"

"Had you been on time, Geoffrey, there wouldn't have been a problem. Since I had no idea where you were or when you would return, I thought it unnecessary to detain them any longer."

Grumbling, Geoffrey said, "Take Alexander up to the nursery and then join me in the dining room, Jillian."

"I've given Miss Robertson the evening off so that she could go to the dance with the others." Jillian stared at him defiantly, anticipating an explosion of wrath.

Instead, Geoffrey smiled, a nasty, vindictive smile. "You're always trying to best me, aren't you, Jillian? Don't you know that you haven't a hope in hell of winning? I've just made a decision. I am going to take Alexander and Miss Robertson to England with me. Perhaps by the time we return next summer, you'll think differently about defying me."

"You can't be serious, Geoffrey?" Her shocked voice was barely more than a whisper.

"You'd better start packing the boy's things. We'll be leaving in a few days." Geoffrey started to walk out of the room.

"I won't let you take him!" Jillian cried desperately.

Coldly, Geoffrey said. "You have no choice. Even a court of law can't stop me from doing what I wish with my son. You'd better take heed, madam, or I might decide it would be in the boy's best interests to leave him in England with my sister. You're turning him into a milksop. Look at how he cowers behind your skirts. It sickens me." With that look of disgust that Jillian knew only too well, Geoffrey turned and walked from the room.

"Mama! What did he mean? I'm not going anywhere without you!" Sandy threw himself against her and clung to her as if he were in immediate danger of being torn from her arms.

Jillian drew her son into a reassuring hug. "You know Mama wouldn't let anything like that happen, don't you, my darling? Come... quickly now."

Jillian knew there was only one thing that they could do -- run away. Their best bet was to go to Charlotte and Nigel's in Peterborough. Geoffrey would never dislodge them from the Melbournes, and within a week he would have to be away if he was to sail before winter. And then she and Sandy would be free of him for six glorious months. Beyond that, she dared not think.

Nor could she confront the fear that loomed in the back of her mind. A monstrous, horrifying, paralyzing fear.

Jillian glanced into the dining room as they passed, and was pleased to see that Geoffrey was imbibing freely of the wine. She was tempted to lace his whiskey with laudanum, but couldn't risk it. With no supper companion, Geoffrey would soon be finished his meal. Noisily, they ascended the stairs, but once in the nursery, Jillian whispered, "We have to be quiet now. You do just as Mama says. No questions just now. You know how important this is, don't you?"

She thrust a few of his clothes into a bag, and grabbed his warmest overcoat, hat, and mitts. Then she went to her own room for her fur-lined cloak, and the few jewels and coins that she possessed.

Quietly, tensely she waited to hear Geoffrey walk from the dining room to his study. When she had heard the click of the study door, she forced herself to wait five minutes more, though each moment was an agony. Now that she had decided to escape, she could hardly wait to get away. She would not breathe easily until they were well on their way to Peterborough. Even the prospect of driving through near pitch blackness, on bad roads, through swamps and deep forests did not daunt her -- or frighten her as much as another encounter with Geoffrey.

But she did one more thing before leaving. She went to Geoffrey's bedchamber. From the drawer of his bedside table she took his pistol. She would feel safer with that as a travelling companion.

"Now, my darling, we are going to have an adventure, just you and I. But you must be brave and good, and as quiet as a mouse until we're well away. Do you understand me, Sandy?"

The child sensed her desperation. He nodded.

They started down the back stairs -- narrow, steep stairs that creaked, but that were farther from the study than the main staircase. It was not an easy journey for Jillian, and she almost wept with frustration at her slow progress. She felt like one in a nightmare who is pursued, but finds herself trying to run in quicksand. At any moment she expected to see Geoffrey's face suddenly peer up the stairwell at her, or hear his angry voice slice through her.

When they reached the kitchen, Jillian thanked God that she had given all the servants the night off. Although they preferred her to Geoffrey, their presence would have made it difficult to escape. And if Nanny Robertson were here, it would have been impossible.

It took them but a moment to leave the house, but once in the carriage house, the delay in preparing the horse and buggy preyed upon her taut nerves. She jumped at every noise, and was certain that every movement she made must surely be heard by Geoffrey. It was impossible to muffle the horse's clops and the clatter of the wheels as she led the beast onto the drive. She and Sandy clambered aboard, and slowly she urged the horse forward, praying that their luck would hold.

Once they were on the street, she whipped the horse into a gallop. She took the shortest route through the town, not caring now who spotted them. Once they reached the outskirts, she stopped to light the lantern, without which they could not travel on such a dark night. Although her sense of urgency had not left her, she took the time to prepare a bed of blankets for Sandy, who was already nodding off. She settled him with a hug and a kiss, urged him to sleep, for it would be a long journey, and promised him that everything would be alright.

She didn't know that Geoffrey had seen them leave and was already on their trail. He did not think Jillian foolish enough to head for Toronto -- after all, she had no money. He knew of only one place where she could be assured asylum -- Peterborough.

Jillian had almost begun to relax when she heard the pounding of hooves on the road behind her. *Oh, God, don't let it be him*, she prayed. *Don't desert me now. Don't let me have come so far only to strike me down. What have I done to deserve Your contempt?*

She knew she could not outrun the rider, so she pulled to a stop and waited. She never once feared the supernatural, even on this Halloween night. The spectre of Geoffrey was much more frightening than any devil or headless horseman of the imagination.

She quivered with anticipation. And when she saw her worst fear realized, when she saw Geoffrey's triumphant sneer, she felt that God had truly deserted her. There was no one to help her fight this monster. Only herself.

She fingered the pistol in the pocket of her cloak. Before leaving the house, she had made sure that it was loaded.

"You pathetic creature! Did you really think you could get away from me? Did you think you could steal my son? Did you...."

Jillian drew out the pistol and fired. She was a good shot; her father had taught her well.

Geoffrey lay on the ground, blood oozing from his chest, his face frozen into a mask of astonishment. Jillian looked at him in horror. "Dear God! What have you made me do, Geoffrey?" she whispered to the wind. She looked at the pistol as if it had fired the shot of its own volition; with fear and revulsion she threw it away. And although she hated to go near him, her own survival was uppermost in her thoughts. It must look like robbery, she realized. She nearly retched as she bent over the body. Quickly she turned out his pockets and took his billfold and pocket watch.

When she climbed back into the buggy, she was surprised -- and thankful -- to see that Sandy still slept. Without even thinking, she turned the horse around and headed for home. The servants had not yet returned, so she took care to erase the evidence of her departure. She woke Sandy, and told him that they would not be going away after all. She would make everything right with papa. Did he have a lovely sleep? And lovely dreams?

There was no need to tell anyone about the adventure they'd almost had. It might get them both into trouble. It would be their secret. Could he keep a secret? For mama?

She hated to lie to him, but the truth was too horrendous. Even Jillian was unable to face it as yet. When she had Sandy tucked up in bed, and his clothes carefully returned to their cupboards and drawers, she went to her own room with a large glass of brandy. It wasn't until then that she began to shake. Or that the enormity of what she had done began to sank in.

To avoid confronting the truth, she mentally retraced her steps, wondering if she had thought of everything. After removing the contents, she had disposed of Geoffrey's billfold by tossing it and the watch into the river -- not a wise move perhaps, but what else could she have done? Tossed them into the woods, where they might still be found? Buried them somewhere? Where? How? Perhaps she should have left the billfold at the scene. But a thief would never have left such a valuable item behind.

The scene. It flashed into her head. A nightmare memory. Geoffrey's ugly, arrogant grimace. The sound of the explosion. Geoffrey falling....

Oh, God, she'd murdered him!

Had she replaced Sandy's clothes in the proper drawers? Miss Robertson was sure to notice if anything was amiss. Had any of the neighbours seen or heard their hasty departure? Should she say she had taken Sandy for a drive? So late? On such a blustery night? But if anyone in town had seen her, and she were to say -- if questioned -- that she and Sandy had spent a quiet evening at home, the authorities would wonder why she had lied. But she had been well muffled against the wind. Would anyone have been able to recognize her? Oh, God, what was she to do? How could she carry on a pretense of ignorance and innocence? Perhaps she should confess now. But murderers were hanged, even women. The shame that that would bring her son, the stigma that he would bear were unendurable to contemplate.

There was no time for remorse or conscience now. She had committed a vile deed in order to save her son from his sadistic father. To give in now would mean that Geoffrey had won after all, and that his death had been for naught. She would need all her courage and fortitude to see this through. For her son's sake.

Chapter 55

When the news of Geoffrey Kayne's murder swept through town the next day, no one was particularly surprised. Or sorry. A few speculated on who would have been brave and foolish enough to do such a thing, but the general consensus was that a stranger had done it. After all, most of the townspeople had been at the Halloween dance.

Rebecca Launston eyed her husband suspiciously throughout dinner, but he gave no sign of a guilty conscience. That Richard had killed Geoffrey in a fit of jealous rage was an exciting thought, but highly unlikely. It was too bad about Geoffrey, but it certainly solved her problem. He had become impossibly possessive lately. Still, it was unfortunate.

Richard, meanwhile, wondered if Rebecca and Geoffrey had had an argument during which she had shot him, perhaps inadvertently. He knew Rebecca to be capable of outrageous acts, and he feared that her recklessness would yet destroy them both. But he did not ask her where she had been last night while he had worked late at the mill.

Rowena and Moira were both thankful that their menfolk had been at the dance, and were thus above suspicion. Tim was recovering, albeit slowly, but no one had a better motive for murdering Geoffrey Kayne than the Ryans. Moira thought it was God's vengeance -- whatever misguided soul had done it, he had been merely the instrument of God.

So it came as a surprise to everyone when, a few days later, Chief Constable Duncan arrested Gavin O'Shaughnessy on suspicion of murder.

Jillian went to see Keir that evening, requesting a private interview.

Keir could sense her agitation, but only because he knew her so well. When he showed her into his study, she seemed a fraction calmer, and took time to admire the room. "Strange to think that you have been living here more than a year already, and I've never been to visit you. I would never have thought that you and I could drift so far apart."

"Well, our lives are different now. Things have changed since...."

"Since I got married. If only you knew! Can we be heard? Could you lock the door?"

"Jillian what is it?"

"I don't know what to do, Keir! I couldn't think of anyone else to help me. Oh, I could never go to Richard!"

"I'll do whatever I can for you, you know that, Jilly."

"First you must promise me that you will never, ***never*** tell anyone what I'm about to tell you. Promise me!"

He smiled at her vehemence, which reminded him of the mercurial girl she had been, but gave his word.

"There are times when I envy the Catholics their secret confessional!" She looked him straight in the eye and said, "I killed Geoffrey."

"***What***?"

Quickly she explained, her voice breathless, like someone running. "...And so I pulled out the gun and... and...." She buried her face in her hands. "God, how often I have relived that horror! Geoffrey comes to me in my dreams and taunts me." She glanced up at Keir with a tear-streaked face. "I could probably learn to live with that -- my conscience -- but I cannot let an innocent man be hanged. Is the court likely to find him guilty?"

Keir was momentarily at a loss as he tried to assimilate what she had just told him. His silence unnerved her, but his first words were comforting. "My poor, Jilly. How you must have suffered with that man."

She almost broke down at his gentle concern, but she was afraid that she would never be able to stop the flood of tears that threatened.

Keir poured them each a drink, and then said, "I'm afraid that Duncan's got some pretty damning evidence against Gavin. Duncan's not like the last Chief -- the one that was run out of town for his involvement with brothels and corruption. He's thorough and honest -- perhaps a bit overly zealous. There are three things that convinced him it was Gavin: Gavin came to the dance later than anyone else, he was suddenly in possession of a great deal of money, and he'd been heard to threaten Geoffrey when Geoffrey fired him. Whether that will stand up in court or not, I couldn't say. But you're not thinking of going to Duncan with your story, Jilly?"

"That poor man is already in gaol, and he'll be there until the next Assizes. I can't let someone else be blamed for something that I did!"

"'Poor man', indeed! Gavin's a scoundrel! I'd like to know where he ***did*** get that money from. I doubt that it was obtained honestly. Let him stew in gaol for a few months. It won't do him any harm." Keir thought, but didn't add, *Let him hang, if need be.*

Rather him than you. He'll never be more than a scoundrel, a wastrel, a curse to the O'Shaughnessys. "There may not be enough evidence for a conviction. Wait to see what happens at the trial. If things go badly...."

"I can always confess. Yes. Perhaps you're right." The anguish in her eyes when she looked at him cut him to the heart. "I never meant to... If only he hadn't....!"

Keir poured her another drink. Then he sat beside her and took one of her hands in his. "You know I'll always do what I can to help you, Jilly. You need only ask. I wish there were more I could do now."

She squeezed his hand in a gesture of thanks. "I feel as if I've lost complete control of my life. With... Geoffrey, I had already lost much of it. Now he has stolen all of it from me. I feel like this is all a nightmare. But I'll never wake up, will I?"

Chapter 56

Jillian spent the next few months in purgatory. She slept badly -- her dreams too often invaded by Geoffrey -- ate little, since her stomach seemed constantly knotted, and so, grew thin and wan. She was sometimes short-tempered with the servants, though they forgave her instantly -- poor widow woman. Only with Sandy did she smile. With him she behaved as though they had little time left together. For that was indeed how she felt.

God would punish her. He had singled her out for his disfavour even before she was born. Why else had he crippled her? He had given her the wits of a man, but in a frail woman's body. He had given her the most precious gift in the world -- her son -- but soon He would snatch the child from her... Even more than execution, she feared lifelong imprisonment.

Damn it, Geoffrey should be found guilty of his own death!

Keir, meanwhile, had not been idle. He had procured the best criminal defence attorney in Canada West, Marcus Edgerton, for it was crucial that Gavin not be found guilty. Some of the other family members raised eyebrows at what they considered an extravagance. Surely one of the local lawyers would have sufficed? Who was going to pay this fancy fellow from the city? He was living so lavishly at the new Launston Hotel that Keir would be broke before the trial even started.

But Keir dismissed the complaints, and said he'd do the same for any of them. Did they think Gavin unworthy of the best defence?

Tim, bored and restless as he lay bedridden, had much time for thought. And one particular thought occurred to him. Had Keir murdered Geoffrey? Was that why he was so anxious to see that Gavin was not convicted? Sure, he knew that Keir had been at the dance with Megan, but maybe he'd encountered the man later. Who knew exactly when Geoffrey had died? The doctor had said between nine and midnight, but how accurate was that? An hour or two either way could implicate many more people. And would the police use the same sort of reasoning to implicate his father, should Gavin go free? Could Conn prove that he had come home with the rest of the family that night, and not gone out again?

Tim broached the subject with Megan. She visited him frequently, and though he appreciated her concern for him, it rankled that her concern was not deeper. Perhaps that was why he blurted out his suspicions to her so bluntly, even though he knew it would only alienate her more from himself, rather than from Keir.

"Keir? Murdered Geoffrey?" she demanded. "Why would he have done that? All this lying about is addling your wits! You know very well he was with me at the dance!"

"Why are you so fierce?" Tim asked her. "Have you maybe had your own doubts?"

"Don't be daft, Tim Ryan!" But she was shocked at his words. A glimmer of doubt ***had*** formed in the darkest corner of her mind, and nagged her in the small hours of the night. Then, all manner of unwelcome thoughts invaded her mind and disrupted her equanimity. Keir had seen much of Jillian Kayne lately. Moira had told her that Keir and Jillian had been very close once. And Keir had seemed distracted lately.

And now that Jillian was free to remarry....

"If you'll not stop making these outrageous comments, Tim Ryan, then you'll have to do without my company!"

He grinned. "You'd think I'd know better than to attack your hero by now, wouldn't you? But then, I thought maybe he was getting a bit tarnished, and that you weren't being so blinded by the halo of light reflecting off him."

She laughed then. "You ***are*** daft!"

"And you're so beautiful, especially when you laugh," Tim said wistfully. "Megan...."

"Don't, Tim!"

"Not to worry. I don't dare ask you to marry me again! Seems every time I do, something bad happens to me," he said with a laugh. Then, more seriously, he added, "I just want you to know that I'll always be here for you, if ever you need me. Like if that damn cousin of mine ever falls off his pedestal!"

Richard Launston began to worry as the trial drew near. How much of Geoffrey's life would be made public during the trial? Did someone know of Geoffrey's affair with Rebecca? If so, it would impute a strong motive for Geoffrey's murder to himself, to say nothing of the scandal that that information would cause.

By the time the trial began, there was a great deal of excitement in town. For one thing, it was the first time such an important trial had been held in the new courthouse, and those who could, flocked in to watch the proceedings. For another thing, it involved the murder of one of the local elite, by one of the local ne'er-do-wells.

That was certainly one of the points brought out by the Crown attorney -- Gavin's record of violent behaviour, his disrespect of person and property. It was even implied that he had deliberately burned down his house in Shantytown after a quarrel with the landlord's agent, thus causing the "great" fire. But the most damning evidence had yet to be introduced.

"Mr. Shier, you were in the outer office, going about your clerical duties, on the day that the accused was fired from his job, is that correct?" the prosecuting attorney asked the witness.

"Yes, sir, I was," the clerk replied.

"Will you tell the court what you heard."

"Yes. Well, O'Shaughnessy was yelling at Mr. Kayne, using the most foul language that I couldn't repeat here, sir. But the last thing he said to Mr. Kayne was, 'You'll see me again, Mr. Kayne' -- emphasizing the 'Mr.', disrespectfully, if you take my meaning -- 'on some dark night when you won't be expecting me.' Mr. Kayne asked, was that a threat, but O'Shaughnessy just laughed."

"Are you sure of the accused's words? You couldn't have misheard them?"

"No doubt about it, sir. O'Shaughnessy had already opened the door to Mr. Kayne's office, and was standing practically next to me when he said that. I remember thinking I was glad it wasn't me that he was talking to in that fashion, or I wouldn't have felt safe walking the streets at night."

"Objection, m'lord," the defence attorney said casually. "It is my understanding that those words were not addressed to the witness. Therefore his feelings and speculations are immaterial to this case."

The judge said, "Please confine yourself to answering the questions, Mr. Shier."

"I have no further questions, your honour," the Crown attorney said.

The defence attorney rose. He seemed to have an immense skeletal structure clad with just enough flesh to hold it all together. So his hands were enormous, yet his fingers were slender, even graceful. He had a huge head, on which his powdered wig seemed doll-sized, but it was perfectly proportioned to his body. He was an imposing figure, and used his massive size to advantage. He movements and words tended to be slow, deliberate, carefully measured, so that the audience would anticipate each word as if waiting for some profound revelation. But he could suddenly turn and hurl a question at a witness as if throwing him a burning brick. His technique had everyone mesmerized.

"Mr. Shier, you spoke of foul language used by the accused. Were these words ones that you are not accustomed to hearing in the mills?"

"Well, sir, the men do tend to cuss a lot, with no womenfolk around."

"So these words were not unknown to you, nor even uncommon in your environment?"

"That's right, sir. But we don't often hear them in the office!"

Marcus Edgerton raised a quizzical eyebrow. "Indeed? Have you never had occasion to use those words yourself?"

"Well... on occasion."

"Such as when you're upset perhaps?"

"Pretty upset, yes."

"If you lost your job, for instance, your livelihood, would that be an appropriate occasion for such language?"

"Objection, m'lord," the Crown attorney said. "As our learned friend himself pointed out, the witness's speculations are not relevant to this case."

"M'lord, I am trying to establish the fact that the defendant behaved no differently from most men in his position," Edgerton said.

"Objection overruled. Answer the question, Mr. Shier."

"Yes, I might. But not to the boss's face."

"No, that takes a great deal of courage. Did you like your boss, Mr. Shier?"

The witness looked flustered. "Well, he wasn't always an easy man to work for."

"Perhaps you could elaborate on that for us. In what way was Mr. Kayne a difficult boss?"

"He was an impatient man, and when things weren't done fast enough or to his liking, he'd tear a strip off you, so to speak. I reckon the thing that was resented most was that he was unreasonable about his expectations sometimes."

Edgerton seemed to be collecting his thoughts, but the silence was well calculated. "So, getting back to my original question, Mr. Shier, did you like Mr. Kayne? A simple yes or no answer will suffice."

"No, I didn't. But I didn't bear him any grudges, either."

"Ah, so you're implying that others did?"

"Well, there might have been one or two."

"Or more? Come now, Mr. Shier, surely Gavin O'Shaughnessy was not the only disgruntled employee?"

"No."

"In fact, Mr. Kayne was generally not well liked by any of the mills' employees, is that not so?"

"Well, most of us remember better days, sir, when Mr. Jeremy ran things." The man looked apologetically in Richard's direction, no doubt thinking that he was putting his job in jeopardy by speaking so frankly. "Mr. Kayne became more demanding after Mr. Jeremy's death. We weren't treated as fairly anymore."

"Hence the walkout at the mills last fall. Thank you, Mr. Shier." Edgerton turned abruptly and sat down.

The witness seemed confused to be suddenly released from cross-examination. The judge said, "Thank you, Mr. Shier, you may step down."

The Crown's next witness was Katie Muldoon, Cormac Muldoon's eldest daughter. She was a black-haired, sloe-eyed beauty, but of slatternly habits, like the rest of her family. She was evidently nervous as she took her place in the witness box. The entire Muldoon clan -- a formidable crowd -- seemed to be there, and a couple of them yelled out words of encouragement.

"Silence in the court!" the judge demanded. And he got it. No one wanted to miss a word.

"Miss Muldoon," the prosecutor said, "you are a friend of the accused."

"Was," she replied sullenly. "Ain't seen him these last months, have I?"

There was laughter, but it was quickly silenced.

"You were a friend of the accused on the night of the Halloween dance, is that not so?"

"Sure."

"And did you have an understanding to meet at the dance?"

"We did, but the bugger didn't show up till past nine."

"So he was late?"

"That he was, and didn't I give him a piece of me mind!"

"Did he give you any explanation for being late?"

"Said he'd been doing a little business."

"Did he tell you what?"

"I asked him, but he just laughed and bought me a drink. And damn me if he didn't pay for it with a fiver! I ain't never seen so much money as he took outa his pocket that night."

"Did you ask him where he got the money from?"

"Damn right I did. Said it was business, but none of mine. Said there'd be more where that came from. Looked right pleased with himself, he did."

"Had you ever known him to have so much money before?"

"Christ! You gotta be joking! Gavin?"

"Just give us a yes or no answer, please, young woman," the judge said.

"No, sir... m'lord. I ain't never seen him with so much money before."

"Thank you, Miss Muldoon. Your witness," the prosecuting attorney said to Marcus Edgerton.

No one in the room except Cormac himself knew of the relationship he'd had with Gavin's mother. Only Gwyn would have appreciated the irony of the situation.

"Miss Muldoon, you said that the accused stated, 'There would be more where that came from' when you questioned him about the money." Edgerton said.

"That's right."

"Did you think then that he might have murdered someone?"

"Course not!"

"What ***did*** you think about where the money might have come from?"

She shrugged. "Reckon I thought he might have put the touch on someone, like his rich relatives."

"Someone who would keep supplying him with money, which is how most of us would interpret that statement?"

"Sure. Reckon I ain't no different from most folk," she said with an injured air.

"Miss Muldoon, are you a close friend of the accused?" Edgerton asked in that soft, coaxing, understanding voice he used with women.

"Whatcher mean?"

"Was he courting you, for instance?"

"I reckon you could say that."

"For how long?"

"Six months maybe."

"And during that time, did he see any other young ladies?"

"He'd not have come near me again if he had!"

"Quite so. But on the night in question, was he not rather free with his affections? Did you not, in fact, have something of a lover's tiff -- if I may use that expression -- and tell him, and I quote, to 'Sod off you fucking bastard. Don't you ever touch me again.'?"

There was a stunned silence in the court. Hearing this dignified man utter those obscenities shocked all, yet Edgerton had lost none of his dignity in the process. The words were so obviously not his own.

"Well, Miss Muldoon?"

"I... I might have said that, or something like. I was that annoyed!"

"So annoyed, in fact, that you got into a physical fight with Mary Darcy in the street, is that not so?"

"She was trying to steal him from me! What do you think..?"

"Thank you, Miss Muldoon. No further questions."

Even though she admired Edgerton's skill at discrediting the witnesses, Jillian felt no hope. More than once she had had to restrain herself from jumping up and confessing. Surely this farce had gone on long enough. She could not bear to look at the prisoner, who stood in the dock with no chance to speak in his own defence. As though he were already guilty, and the worst aspects of his life were being paraded before all to ridicule.

Well, she wouldn't have to endure this much longer. The trial could be over today, or tomorrow at the latest. Justice was swift, if not always just. In the meantime, she would have to keep her wits about her. For Sandy's sake.

More witnesses for the prosecution testified to Gavin's disreputable character, but Jillian found her attention wandering. Her eyes were drawn in fascination to the incredible *trompe l'oeil* painting on the wall behind the judge's dais. It was simply a rendering of classical pilasters and decorated panelling and the Royal Coat of Arms, but painted to look so real that they seemed truly three dimensional. It was illusion. *Trompe l'oeil*, "deceives the eye". How appropriate. Nothing was truly as it seemed, even here, in this courtroom where truth was to be ferreted out at all costs for the sake of justice. Had that painting been a little joke on the part of the architect?

By the time the court recessed for dinner, Jillian felt drained. Keir noted her resigned look with alarm. He wanted to help her, but she was leaving with Richard and Rebecca, and his own family awaited him -- Rowena, and Conn, and Moira, and several of his cousins. Megan was teaching, or she, too, would have been there. Keir wished she were, and wished he could tell her Jillian's secret. Megan was so practical and logical and understanding about most things; she would have known what to do.

Keir feared that Jillian was losing control. She had been living with guilt and fear for so long now that it would be a relief for her to confess. How could he stop her?

When the court reconvened that afternoon, Keir managed to encounter Jillian.

"Richard. Rebecca," he said, acknowledging them. Turning to Jillian he said, "This must be a great ordeal for you, Jilly. We'd all understand if you chose to forego the rest of this trial."

"Thank you for your concern, Keir," she said, "but I am to be called as a witness."

Not trusting herself to meet his gaze, lest her fear blazon forth for all to see, she quickly turned away from him and seated herself. She already felt as though she were tainted by some stigmata, identifying her as a murderer, that some discerning eye could detect. But to meet knowing eyes was too much to bear. If Marcus Edgerton looked at her like that, she would be lost.

Keir cursed himself. He hadn't wanted to arouse Edgerton's suspicions, but he should have told the lawyer not to distress the grieving widow unduly, or used some such excuse to keep him away from her. He certainly hadn't thought that Edgerton would call Jillian to the witness box. God only knew what Edgerton could make her say, once he got her under oath! And what if Edgerton suspected her, and tried to wrangle a confession from her? Damn! Perhaps he'd been stupid to hire such a clever bastard.

The Crown had finished its case, and it was now up to the defence to call witnesses. Richard Launston was the first to be summoned.

Marcus Edgerton took his time framing his questions, trying to unnerve an extremely self-controlled man.

"Mr. Launston, did you know that Mr. Kayne had been such an unpopular manager at the mills?"

"I've never concerned myself with the opinions of my employees in areas which do not concern them. Geoffrey was an excellent manager. Often the most efficient workers are the least popular."

"Why were you planning to send Mr. Kayne to England for six months?"

"There was business for him to do there."

"Is that the only reason, Mr. Launston? I needn't remind you that you are under oath," Edgerton said off-handedly.

Richard was annoyed at the implication that he was withholding information. "Since the aborted strike there had been threats made against Mr. Kayne. Things were rather unsettled at the mills. The men blamed Geoffrey for their problems, so I thought it best to send him away until the air cleared a bit."

"What sort of threats had been made against Mr. Kayne -- verbal, written?"

"Both. Some men blamed him for an incident that had occurred to one of our former employees."

"You mean Timothy Ryan, who had been savagely beaten?"

"Yes. It was all nonsense, of course. Geoffrey couldn't have had anything to do with that."

"Indeed? Mr. Launston, can you enlighten us as to what Mr. Kayne was doing on the Peterborough Road so late on such an inclement night?"

"I'm afraid not."

"You had not sent him on some errand?"

"No."

"Did he have a mistress?"

Once again, Edgerton had stunned the audience. There was a buzz of conversation.

"Order in the court!" the judge intoned as he pounded his gavel. But it took a moment for conjecture to be silenced.

Richard had visibly paled. He wondered if someone had discovered the truth, and if the entire sordid mess was about to be revealed. Carefully he said, "My brother-in-law never confided in me with regard to his private life. I can only tell you that my sister has never given me any indication that Geoffrey was anything but a devoted husband."

"Why did Mr. Kayne fire Gavin O'Shaughnessy? Was that at your instigation?"

"No. Geoffrey had complete control over the hiring and firing of men. I know that members of Mr. O'Shaughnessy's family were setting up a sawmill of their own, and perhaps Geoffrey thought that Mr. O'Shaughnessy would prefer to work for his own people."

"So his dismissal had nothing to do with the quality of his work?"

"I couldn't say for certain. It is merely speculation on my part."

"And if your speculation is correct, would you think ***that*** a valid reason for depriving a man of his livelihood?"

"Objection, m'lord. That is a hypothetical question, and irrelevant to this case," the Crown attorney said.

"Sustained. Please confine yourself to the facts, Mr. Edgerton," the judge said.

Marcus Edgerton nodded to the judge as if acknowledging his superior wisdom. "Aside from many of his employees, can you think of anyone else who had a score to settle with Mr. Kayne?" Edgerton asked Richard.

"No."

"Mr. Launston, did not Geoffrey Kayne inherit a substantial share in the family business upon the death of your father?"

"My nephew, Alexander, inherited a share, and as trustee, his father was administering the boy's estate."

"So Mr. Kayne had a say in the business."

"On the boy's behalf, yes."

"Did you resent that?"

Richard had begun to relax when he had realized that no scandalous revelations were forthcoming. But now he was once again on guard. "Not particularly. We always had an amicable business relationship."

"But not a personal one?"

"I didn't say that."

"Thank you, Mr. Launston."

Edgerton invariably left the witnesses itching to say more, to somehow defend themselves against implied aspersions upon their characters.

Jillian wondered if she could maintain her deception under his verbal scrutiny. Her mind worked feverishly, anticipating his questions, forming truthful but noncommittal replies. Her hands felt icy cold despite the kidskin gloves she wore. As though the blood had frozen in her veins. And surely it had, that moment that she had shot Geoffrey. Something within her had died then, and could never be resurrected. Nor would she ever again feel the freedom of a clear conscience. It was almost preferable to be punished by the law for one's misdeeds. Paying for one's sins freed one from the burden of them.

She was relieved and disappointed not to be the next one called to the stand. How she wished just to get it all over with -- whatever was to happen!

It was the Widow Moore who was summoned. She was a petite woman in her early thirties, who had retained some of her once-notable looks. She strode to the witness box as if with a vengeance, and faced Edgerton and the crowd defiantly.

"Mrs. Moore, is it correct that the accused, Gavin O'Shaughnessy, visited your farm on the day in question?"

"That's right."

There were many oohs and aahs from the audience, as people were quick to assess the situation and pass judgement.

"Why was he there?"

"He did odd jobs for me. There's always work to be done on a farm. Never enough hands." She spoke as if in self defence to the spectators, drawing her dignity about her like an invisible suit of armour.

"Did he work for you often?"

"Fairly often. He's good with his hands. I mean, he's a skilled carpenter," she added, blushing at the titters that her remark had elicited.

"And you paid him well for these jobs?"

"Oh yes."

"What time did he leave your place on the day in question?"

"Maybe an hour shy of dusk. It's a long walk back to town, and I remember thinking he'd be walking partway in the gloaming, and it being Halloween and all."

"So he left your farm rather late in the day, with money in his pockets?"

"That's correct."

"Thank you, Mrs. Moore."

The Crown attorney asked only one question that was particularly revealing: had Mrs. Moore paid Gavin with a five dollar bill? "Certainly not," was her reply.

There were several character witnesses to testify to Gavin's sober work habits. Edgerton's queries were precise and brief. There were few people in town who had anything favourable to say about Gavin.

Finally Jillian was called to take the stand. She felt absurdly calm, now that she was facing the man who might be her executioner.

"Mrs. Kayne, you were the last person to see your husband alive -- aside from the murderer, of course. Could you tell this court about your husband's actions that evening."

"Certainly. Geoffrey arrived home rather late. I had already dined, and had allowed the staff to leave for the Halloween ball, seeing no point in delaying them, since I had no idea what time Geoffrey might be expected home. Geoffrey's supper had been laid out in the dining room. I did not join him for the meal, since I had to put my son to bed. I heard Geoffrey go out not long afterwards, but he didn't speak to me before he left."

"So you have no idea where he was going?"

"No." Jillian decided it prudent to reveal as much of the truth as she could. "I can only tell you that he was in a foul temper when he arrived home, and was not pleased with me for dismissing the servants so early. He gave me the distinct impression that he did not care for my company that evening. So perhaps he merely wanted a ride to blow off some steam."

"Your husband did not tell you the reason for his anger when he arrived home?"

"No."

"Was your husband accustomed to carrying large sums of money on his person?"

"Yes, as a matter of fact, he was. He often carried ten or even twenty dollars about, which was ridiculous really, since we have accounts with all the merchants in town. His argument was that a gentleman was never completely attired without his billfold suitably padded."

"Did you know that your husband had a mistress?"

There was a gasp from the spectators, who were surprised by the certainty of Edgerton's assertion. He was evidently about to reveal some new and startling information.

Jillian, too, was momentarily off guard, although she had anticipated such a question. She smiled wryly at her interrogator. "A woman never likes to think that her husband prefers another woman to herself, Mr. Edgerton. But most of us are realistic enough to allow for the possibility."

"Then it will surprise you to know that your husband was seen in the company of a lady, by the accused, on his way home from the Moore farm on the evening in question."

Edgerton paused amid the uproar. It took the judge several minutes to restore order.

Richard Launston was as rigid and pale as a statue. His entire life was about to be exploded.

Jillian suddenly realized that she was responsible for all this. It was because of her actions and her reluctance to admit her guilt that Gavin O'Shaughnessy now sat in the prisoner's dock, that Widow Moore would undoubtedly be ridiculed or spurned by her neighbours, that Mr. Shier, the clerk, feared the loss of his job, that Rebecca's infidelity was about to be revealed, and that Richard's, and probably his son's life, would be irrevocably changed. But there was nothing she could do to stop it now.

"And you did not know, Mrs. Kayne, that Gavin O'Shaughnessy had threatened to expose your husband's illicit liaison? Or that your husband had given the accused two five dollar bills, and sworn him to secrecy?"

"No, I did not."

"Who was this woman, Mr. Edgerton?" the judge inquired.

"That's the irony of the situation, m'lord. My client didn't get a good look at the lady, since it was getting dark. But Mr. Kayne didn't know that."

Richard tried not to relax visibly, although he felt as if his limbs had turned to porridge. He knew that any physical sign of relief, no matter how slight, could incriminate -- at least in the eyes of the townspeople -- and was glad to see that Rebecca had not lost her composure. But that shouldn't have surprised him. After all, deception was her forte. No doubt she had experienced quite a thrill at the threat of discovery, he thought bitterly.

Jillian felt faint. She had felt the colour drain from her face, but people would attribute that to the shock of learning that her husband had betrayed her. The Crown attorney, it seemed, had not the heart to cross-examine her. She was relieved to be dismissed, and hobbled back to her seat more awkwardly and unsteadily than usual.

Then there was only the summing up to do. Marcus Edgerton spoke eloquently. He held the entire court in thrall for over half an hour as he retraced for them the steps of both victim and accused on that fateful day. He concluded by saying, "Gentlemen of the jury, remember that we in this civilized country of ours do not hang a man on circumstantial evidence. Think of how your own actions could be construed, or misconstrued, in a given situation." He gave them a moment to think.

Edgerton shook his head sadly. "I tell you gentlemen, none of our lives bears too close a scrutiny. We all have guilty secrets; we've all done things we're ashamed of. We wouldn't be human if we didn't. Certainly some of us have more to repent than others.

"Gavin O'Shaughnessy hasn't exactly been a model citizen in this community. But that doesn't mean he's guilty of murder. Geoffrey Kayne wasn't a model citizen either.

"The Crown's case is built upon three facts. The fact that Gavin O'Shaughnessy arrived late at the dance. Well..." He shrugged. "... how many others were late for the dance? We ***know*** where Gavin was -- on a long walk back from the Moore farm, five miles out of town. The wonder is that he had the energy to go to the dance at all." He paused to allow for the chuckles, but took no credit for them. He seemed utterly absorbed in what he had yet to say. "And after such a long walk, what would Gavin O'Shaughnessy have been doing a mile out of town on the Peterborough Road, which is in the opposite direction from the Moore farm? Lying in wait for Geoffrey Kayne on the off-chance that he might appear? Not even a fool would have done that. Geoffrey Kayne had had no known plans to be in that vicinity that night. Even his wife had not known where he was going."

"The fact that Gavin O'Shaughnessy had money. Well, we've heard that he did indeed get it from Geoffrey Kayne, but not from a dead man's pocket! Did not Gavin tell Katie Muldoon that there was "more where that came from"? Does that sound like a man who had murdered the golden goose or discovered it?

"The fact that Gavin O'Shaughnessy had threatened Geoffrey Kayne does not prove his guilt either. We've heard various people testify to Mr. Kayne's unpopularity with most of the millworkers. We've heard that more than one person bore him a grudge. Remember that Richard Launston was planning to send the victim away for six months while hostilities subsided. Geoffrey Kayne must indeed have been unpopular.

"We've heard that Gavin O'Shaughnessy's manner is belligerent, and that he's quick to use his fists. But a gun, gentlemen? Where did he get it from? And more importantly, why would he shoot Geoffrey Kayne? My client might be a blackmailer -- not a pretty thought, I grant you, gentlemen -- but we are not trying him on that charge. Gavin O'Shaughnessy, a murderer? I think you'll find that impossible to comprehend.

"Think of those who had motives for killing Geoffrey Kayne -- a jealous husband, even the adulterous woman, supposing that Geoffrey had threatened to reveal their affair? Any number of employees or former employees who had a grudge against a boss who we've heard was unfair. Perhaps and most probably it was nothing more than robbery by an itinerant traveller -- remember that Geoffrey Kayne carried large sums of money on his person. He had already been deprived of ten dollars that afternoon, so perhaps the thought of losing yet more money had prompted him to fight his assailant, thus resulting in his death.

"But we are not here to determine how and why Geoffrey Kayne died, merely to determine whether that man, Gavin O'Shaughnessy, did willfully and maliciously cause his death.

"I submit to you, gentlemen of the jury, that there is not one solid fact linking Gavin O'Shaughnessy to Geoffrey Kayne's death. If you have even the slightest doubt as to his innocence, then you cannot, in all conscience, find him guilty of murder."

The jury was out for nearly two hours -- an unnervingly long time. If the verdict was "guilty", Jillian decided she would stand up then and there and announce her own guilt. She played the scene over and over in her mind. So convinced was she that the delay could only mean the worst, that when the jury finally returned, she was practically on the edge of her seat, ready to rise.

"M'lord, we find the defendant, Gavin O'Shaughnessy, not guilty of the murder of Geoffrey Kayne."

Chapter 57

Keir was ecstatic that evening. He, Rowena, and Megan celebrated "their" victory with champagne, although the two women were somewhat bemused by the intensity of Keir's joy. Certainly they were glad that Gavin had been found innocent, but Keir's euphoria seemed excessive for a cousin he hardly knew or had cared much about in the past. They both felt that he was hiding something from them.

When Megan was helping Rowena in the kitchen, she asked, "Do you think Keir is protecting someone? I mean, do you think he knows who really killed Geoffrey Kayne, and so he hired that renowned barrister to ensure that an innocent man didn't hang?"

"That thought had occurred to me, too," Rowena admitted. And it frightened her. At best it made Keir an accessory to murder. At worst....

"He didn't do it himself," Megan said quickly, noticing Rowena's frown. "You need have no fear of that!"

She was so adamant that Rowena smiled. Sure, if only Keir would come to his senses and marry Megan, she would have fewer worries about his future. Megan would be a devoted and companionable wife, who'd keep Keir in line -- of that, Rowena had no doubt. She already felt a motherly warmth for the girl, and admired her strength and determination.

Now she noticed an uncharacteristic crinkle of worry on the girl's brow. "And what is that you're afraid of?" Rowena asked her.

"That Keir is protecting Rebecca Launston. I think Rebecca was Geoffrey's mistress. Maybe she killed him because she was tired of him but he wouldn't let her go. She seems to have that kind of effect on people," Megan said drily.

"But Keir has no interest in Rebecca now," Rowena said, hoping her words were true.

"She had a powerful hold on him once. Can you see Keir resisting her plea for help? I'm sure she can play the woman in distress very admirably! If she entreated him, would he not do the chivalrous thing and save her from the gallows?"

Put like that, Rowena could not help but agree. "But if Rebecca ***was*** Geoffrey's mistress, then perhaps Richard is the murderer. Maybe Keir was hoping this fancy lawyer could ferret out the truth. Though, despite their differences, I doubt that Keir would relish seeing his cousin hang." Thank God that Jeremy had been spared all this. To think that his trusted manager and son-in-law had been murdered....

And then Rowena had a flash of insight. She couldn't say why, but she was suddenly convinced it was Jillian that Keir had been protecting. Hadn't he been consoling the bereaved widow quite often these past months? Was Jillian capable of murdering her unfaithful husband? Perhaps, given the right provocation, any one of them was capable of pulling a trigger. But if it had been an accident, Keir would do what he could to prevent Jillian's life from being completely destroyed, of that she was certain.

With relief she said, "I have a mother's instinct that we're wrong. You yourself know that Keir would never cover up a murder simply because of past... alliances. ***If*** he did such a thing, it would be for a just reason. Don't you think that?"

Megan brightened. "Of course! You're right!" She was such an emotional mess that she couldn't even think straight anymore, she realized.

It was crazy what Keir had done to her. She had come to Launston Mills a happy, self-assured young woman who had known what she'd wanted and had set out to achieve her goals. Now she was filled with self-doubt and even despair.

Rowena, remembering herself when she was young and tender with love, said, "You run along and keep Keir company while I finish up here."

Megan smiled gratefully at Rowena, but wondered if there was any point to her matchmaking.

When she looked at Keir -- that handsome, laughing, vital man she had loved the first moment she had met him -- she felt a most unladylike urge to be crushed in his arms, with his mouth on hers, demanding, exploring. She blushed at the thoughts that whirled through her head and set her pulses racing.

Restlessly she walked over to the french windows to look out at the frosty night. The deep snow was glazed with a thin coating of ice that glistened and sparkled in the moonlight. Perhaps it was the austere beauty of the night that made her feel so emotionally volatile.

When Keir came up behind her and said, "You seem strangely moody tonight," Megan swung around to confront him.

"I can't stand this any longer, Keir! You might hate me for saying this, but I feel compelled to tell you. Please hear me out," she said, forestalling his interruption. She couldn't look at him as she said, "You know that I love you, and always have. Molly always told me it was an infatuation that I'd be relieved of one day, like one is of indigestion. But she was wrong.

"God knows, I don't have any illusions about you anymore. I'm too old to believe in infallible heroes, nor would I want one. I like you as you are.

"And it's because I love you that I can't go on like this, pretending that we're just friends. I can't stay with you, alone in this room, craving your touch, yet being kept at bay. What do you want from me? Why do you torment me like this?"

As she looked at him, her gaze intense, anguished, Keir realized that she had matured from a feisty, bedraggled waif into a beautiful and desirable -- and still feisty -- woman.

She turned away from him, afraid of the answer she was forcing him to give, and cursed herself for a fool. She should have kept silent. Surely even a platonic relationship with him was better than none. Wasn't it? But she found no answer in the darkness of the garden.

She quivered as his hands bracketed her shoulders.

"You never have been a conventional girl, have you? Perhaps that is why I love you. Don't you know you're supposed to let the man do the asking," he said with a grin.

She turned to him, her face alight with surprise. She managed to say, in the same teasing vein, "You've been taking your own sweet time about it."

"And I'm lucky I didn't lose you."

"I'm very loyal."

"Too good for me, I think."

"Ha! Try me."

"I intend to do just that."

Epilogue - 1875

The joyful laughter that trickled in through the french windows caught Keir's attention. Megan was out in the garden, playing with the children. Keir grinned as he watched their antics, wondering how dishevelled they would be by the time the guests arrived, hoping that Megan would never lose that endearing vivaciousness.

She was dressed in a green-accented cream silk gown that swept into a modest bustle. She looked as young and beautiful as the day he had married her. Not for the first time Keir thought how fortunate he was to have Megan share his life. They had had their disagreements over the years, and she had proved every bit as stubborn as he had expected. Yet he had never known such happiness as she had given him.

And the children -- Rena, Adrian, Alan, Tessa -- were a delight. Megan wanted a houseful of children, which pleased 'Gran' only too well.

They had survived one tragedy which had darkened their lives. Several years ago, two year old Kate had succumbed to diphtheria. Of course, it was common for children to die from the various diseases and epidemics for which doctors had no cure. And they were fortunate that none of the other children had been stricken. But that had been an anguished, difficult time. And though they would never forget their rambunctious little Kate, the other children filled their lives with love and laughter. And now Megan was expecting again, and was radiant with health and vitality.

Life had been good to him in other ways, these past eleven years. His newspaper was now a daily, and doing well. The printing business had been so successful that Keir had founded a printing and book binding manufactory.

This year, at the age of thirty-seven, Keir had been elected mayor of Launston Mills -- now a town of over six thousand inhabitants. The gods had a fine sense of irony.

He sometimes wondered what he had done to deserve such good fortune.

These thoughts made his task all the harder. He was writing Rebecca Launston's obituary.

Rebecca had become more capricious over the years, flitting in and out of affairs, dashing off to Toronto or New York or even the continent for months at a time. Since Richard had built that fanciful summerhouse on Sturgeon Lake eight years ago, Rebecca had lived there during those summer months she was home. She'd developed a passion for sailing, but couldn't swim. The previous day, she and her male companion had drowned when their boat had capsized.

Keir pitied Richard, who had had little happiness in his life.

And with the current economic depression, which promised to be a long one, the Launston empire was beginning to crumble.

Most of those farmers who had not abandonned their exhausted lands to head out to the fertile west, had converted to mixed or dairy farming. Some farms stood empty and neglected because the sons had been drawn to the cities, and not one had remained behind to work the land. All this was destroying Richard's milling interests.

The best stands of timber in the area had long ago fallen to the axe, and lumbering was forced farther north each year. Smaller operations were being absorbed by consortiums, and Richard was finding it increasingly difficult to compete with these. Local businesses, like the "Ryan Lumber Company" which utilized the abundant but less noble woods, were unaffected by this, and prospering

The railways in which Jeremy and Richard had so heavily invested were constantly in debt and in danger of bankruptcy. Richard had not even been successful in his bid for the mayoralty - as Megan had once predicted -- to say nothing of his failure to secure a seat in either the provincial or federal legislatures.

Richard had become something of a recluse these last few years, and now that his son was at Oxford, he really had no one. Even Jillian did not often see her brother. He scorned the causes she had embraced -- Temperance, women's rights -- so they did little but argue when they did meet.

Keir let his thoughts dwell on Jillian for a moment. Although she needed reassurance from time to time, she coped well with her guilt. Yet that tragedy had left its mark upon her. She looked older than her years -- her hair streaked with grey, her face lined, her eyes infinitely sad. If one caught her at a pensive moment, she seemed to be carrying the burden of the world upon her frail shoulders.

It was Alexander who gave her strength. The boy was sixteen now, and a student at the same college that Keir and

Richard had attended long ago. When he was home with her, that burden seemed to be lifted.

It was during his long absences that Jillian travelled about, attending meetings, giving speeches. She even made twice yearly treks to the States, where she met with the most active members of the women's movement. She had founded the Women's Fortnightly Club, which met to discuss such topics as factory conditions, child labour, health care, sanitation, and most importantly, how women could attain the power necessary to politically enact reforms in these areas.

Megan was a faithful member of that club, while Rowena was active with the Temperance movement. Keir smiled to think how liberal-minded he had become, living with two such strong and dedicated women.

Keir's thoughts were interrupted by three-year-old Tessa, who ran into the study calling, "Papa! Papa! Guests are here!"

Keir pushed his work aside, and scooped the impish child into his arms. Megan watched them affectionately from the doorway. "Have you finished your work?" she asked.

"It can wait."

He straightened Tessa's bow, and took her hand. He embraced Megan with his other arm, and the three of them strolled into the garden.

Beneath the pure, blue, sun-washed sky the guests gathered for this annual celebration. It was Adrian's, and Canada's, eighth birthday.

Rowena marvelled at the size of the gathering, all family and friends. There were a few she missed this year -- dear Margaret Worthing had died, but Simon was here with his family -- yet how many beloved faces there were! Even Brigid (Sister Immaculata) had come up from the convent in Toronto for her annual visit.

Rowena noticed the stranger before anyone else. She knew who he was instantly. How like his father he looked! She walked up to him and said, "You must be Donald."

He smiled broadly, and with an American twang said, "And you must be Aunt Rowena."

Donal's son was heartily welcomed by all. Donal had died last year from an old war injury, a rebel to the end. But his son was determined not to lose touch with his family. He regaled them with stories of his family's escapades -- their years in California during the gold rush, their move back east so that Donal could

Watch for the new novel by Gabriele Wills:

Moon Hall

Two women who live a century apart. Two stories that interweave to form a rich tapestry of intriguing characters, evocative places, and compelling events.

Escaping from a disintegrating relationship in the city, writer Kit Spencer stumbles upon the quintessential "Norman Rockwell" village in the Ottawa Valley, where she buys an old stone mansion, "Moon Hall". But her illusions about idyllic country life are soon challenged by reality.

Beneath the seemingly calm backwater run powerful currents, dramas already close to breaking the surface. In her rural community of farmers, Hippies, and Yuppies, Kit unwittingly precipitates events that will change them all forever.

Violet McAllister, the "ghost" that reputedly haunts Moon Hall, comes vividly to life through her long-forgotten diary. From the gritty shantytown of the newly-minted capital of Canada to the extravagant balls given by the popular and flamboyant Governor General and his wife, Lord and Lady Dufferin, Violet's tragic tale unfolds. Kit feels a bond with this strong and passionate woman, and realizes she must grasp her own happiness while she can.

Moon Hall is a haunting tale of relationships in crisis, and touches on the full spectrum of human emotions - from raw violence and dark passions to compassion and love.

Afterword

As a former history and English teacher, I've long been fascinated by the rich, but neglected, social history of our country.

Particularly interesting to me is the history of my own home town, Lindsay, Ontario. Riots at the mill, the devastating ague epidemic, the invasion of Orangemen from Omemee, Peterborough Militia searching Lindsay for William Lyon Mackenzie, and the "great fire" of 1861 are just some of the real events of Lindsay's intriguing past that are portrayed in this novel. Other incidents were typical of any pioneer community and some, like the Rebellion of Upper Canada, incorporate a few real historical characters with the fictional.

This book was carefully and thoroughly researched to provide a realistic portrayal of what life was like for those indomitable pioneers. My bibliography of 150 books includes first person accounts, such as letters and diaries, biographies, sociological analyses, and scholarly tomes. I learned about all aspects of 19th century life, from food and clothes to transportation and architecture. I had access to the Lindsay Public Library's archives, where material such as maps, directories, drawings, and photographs added another dimension to the background information that helped my story come to life.

In order to allow myself artistic licence, I called Lindsay "Launston Mills" in the novel. However, anyone who knows Lindsay will recognize streets and areas.

If you have any comments to make about this novel, please contact me via email at books@mindshadows.com.

Gabriele Wills,
Lindsay, Ontario,
April, 2003

fight in the Civil War, and then his affiliation with the Fenians, who had made hostile forays into Canada a few years ago.

Rowena's heart was full as she watched her nephew, so like his father in looks and charm. She wished that Donal were here now to see what had become of the town he had once so readily envisioned, but then abandonned. It was she who had hated Launston Mills, and she who had found her destiny here.

Into her mind sprang a memory, whole and sharp as if it had happened yesterday instead of forty-three years ago. She and Donal and Moira seated on a warm granite rock gazing out at the promised land. Before them stretched the mighty St. Lawrence River, which funnelled all the hopeful newcomers into the wild and waiting heart of a raw, new country. What dreams and expectations they had had then! How young and innocent they had been!

Rowena lovingly stroked the carved loon that Donald had brought her -- a present from Donal who had made it for her after realizing that her original one had perished in the Great Fire. He had always wanted to give it to her himself, but had never found the time to return for a visit.

Touching it, she could almost feel Donal's own sensitive hands shaping it, and remembered watching him carve the other as they'd sat on the misty riverbank under the willows. So many memories! Perhaps that was why Donal had never come back.

But now she really must stop dwelling on these poignant thoughts before she became truly maudlin.

What a gay afternoon it was! Long tables were laden with food - turkeys, hams, roasted suckling pig, a variety of salads, dozens of pies, enormous bowls of strawberries with pots of cream nearby, and, of course, a gigantic birthday cake. Children gamboled about the lawns; there was endless chatter and laughter. From Main Street could be heard the marching bands that played in the holiday parade.

There was much applause when Keir planted a maple tree along the street in front of the house, in accordance with his first policy as mayor to beautify the leafless town. One day Launston Mills would become renowned for it tree-lined streets.

The photographer arrived, and, after much scouting about for wayward children, and organizing the enormous group, pictures were snapped and the moment preserved.

In the drawing room of The Brambles, a photographic portrait of Rowena was taken that day. She wore her favourite blue dress with a delicate lace collar, and the cameo brooch that Keir had once given her. Her silver-streaked hair was mostly hidden by her muslin cap, though she'd spent a great deal of time that morning knotting the heavy mass neatly at the nape of her neck.

The photographer froze an insignificant instant of her life, but one of the few that would survive intact for posterity. This was how future generations would see her -- through the deceptive, impersonal, two-dimensional eye of the camera.

An aging woman in stiff Victorian posture, her lips pressed into a stern line, her fine bone structure obscured by sagging flesh.

Who would imagine her as a sprightly girl, a beauty in her day, a woman who loved and had been loved, a woman whose courage and faith had sustained her and given comfort to others?

Perhaps an observant descendant might glimpse something of that indomitable Irish spirit in those clear eyes that stared so keenly from the photograph.